ICARUS DAWNS

by Erik James Troy

To Mom and Dad
Thank you for believing in me.

Table of Contents:

Preface

As a science lover, I've always wanted to see more stories with real science. In 2018 I began writing this novel while I would talk with scientists in the greater Boston area. I was fortunate to meet people who would cure cancer, search for alien life, and create the future of imaging technology.

I've been obsessed with storytelling for as long as I can remember, and I don't use the word "obsessed" lightly. All throughout my childhood and into my college years, stories have been maturing in my head over time. I'm excited to share them with you after so long. In fact, this particular story originated six years ago, and is one of the youngest stories to have been given the same amount of passion and obsession.

Many characters in this book are based on people who have lived through real events. This information has been left for the afterword.

The events and characters are not a vessel for my own beliefs and views on the world, but they're based on real things I have seen and discussions I have heard. Their takes on morality, religion, and philosophy are interesting subjects that come up in the world of science. I would advise anyone to have an open mind and an open heart. Even the worst of villains have some insight to offer, and the best of heroes are never perfect. This is a place for you to explore a new world, and to meet new characters.

I hope you enjoy, and thank you for giving my story a try.

- Erik James Troy

Acknowledgements

I want to thank the scientists who helped me to keep this book as accurate as possible in accordance with real science.

Most importantly, I would like to thank my neighbor Michael. He is an astrophysicist with many years of experience, and he helped me achieve a significant amount of accuracy in the first ten chapters. My friend Stan as well had helped me with some accuracy in a later chapter. I cannot say enough how thankful I am for these two and their gracious help.

Lastly, but certainly not least; I would like to thank the author, Bruce Holbert. His insight into the completion and distribution of this novel has been more than generous. I would like to also thank our friend Jim Orr, for taking the time to introduce us.

ICARUS DAWNS

CHAPTER 1
A Soldier And A Scientist

A pale blue dot in an ocean of black; an oasis in the unforgiving seas. It hosted world wars, legends, and romance. It was where men and women laughed, lived, cried, and died. It hosted both horrors and hopes; cut asunder on one dark, cold day; when the sky descended, and the blackness of the universe took over where life once lived.

If the sun was a speck of dust in the average bedroom, then the room would contain less than half of our galaxy; and the nearest star would be less than an inch away. The light from that star would take almost four years, through miles of black, until it finally reached the planet Earth. All throughout the air of the bedroom, there would be a fog-like density of dust.

That black distance between stars is cold, lonely, and often larger than human comprehension. The desperate traversed this darkness long ago, and now the curious retrace their steps. In the search for answers, a hundred and twenty men and women have traveled five light years to the resting place of humanity's home planet.

Hours pass slowly in the eyes of these weary travelers. The past ten years have been spent in the same hallways, recreation rooms, and common spaces. All the games have been played, acquaintances made, and all the films have been watched into memory. Today was different, however. The team's saving grace was a trip to the surface of an old sorrowful world; the one their ancestors once called home.

Aboard the ship, the halls have fallen silent; the sound of well-needed rest after their first expedition. Darkness blankets the worlds within and without. Inside, the metal walls and floors are cold. Small robots clean the halls in the form of brushes and vacuums on wheels. Pipes hiss with the sound of heat being transferred out of the ship. Ventilation systems hum and rattle with filtered air, and in bedrooms from bow to stern, all sleep except one lonely soul. A man who was born without a family; and the family he once found has died long ago.

Julius is an old soul bound to a young vessel. His shaven face and restful expression tell very little of his character. It's his eyes that tell of his wisdom, and his fear for losing what he holds sacred; the sanctity of friends who have not seen war.

In younger years he was a part of an infantry unit in the United Zion armed forces, and his body remains a relic of that past. Strength remains in his arms, legs, and core. His scars are hidden by clothes, and the memories of how they got there are kept far from his thoughts. He occupies his mind with the present to keep himself from the past. His quiet hours are spent learning, to keep himself focused on a task at hand.

He reads when he wants to learn, and he writes when he wants to forget. To him, it's as if bad thoughts leave his mind and become prisoners to the pages. On occasion, he reviews his writing to better understand himself. Most important of all, he must always know himself.

In a dark room, on the far end of a corridor, Julius holds his leather-bound journal. An oil diffuser glows with a mist that hisses into the dark; the light from which pours onto the pages he marked just hours ago.

In immaculate cursive, it reads:

"January 17th, 525A.E.
In case anyone wonders who has written these journals, I should give an account of who I am and the purpose of our expedition.
My name is Doctor Julius Winter. I am the second leading Engineer on the Mandel Star Explorer. Our goal on this ship is to piece together the history of our home world "Earth"; and to preserve the memory of our forefathers. The year is 525AE (After Earth). Over five hundred years ago, we left Earth for reasons that are unclear. Our objectives are to solve the riddle of the Sun's death, uncover the forgotten chapters of human history, to rediscover ancient technologies, and most important of all, to find who or what was responsible for the tragedy of Earth.
We've just passed Jupiter; the old solar system's largest planet. The sheer mass of it was unlike anything in the Proxima Centauri system. We used it for a retrograde gravity assist, and now the ship is slow enough to approach Earth. We know exactly where it is, thanks to a beacon that started after the sun was destroyed. We're very curious to learn who started that beacon, and why.
In the dark, there is an alien home world

*which once hosted the miracle of life. Soon, we
will make our first landing there, and I simply can't
wait."*

Doctor Winter pulls his eyes away from focus. He does not finish reading his entry, but takes a sigh. He turns the pages until he comes to a blank white space. With pen in hand, he begins to mark the page in the same perfect form.

*"As we approached, it appeared as if there
was a hole growing in the stars before us. The mass
grew and blackened the view from the front of the
ship.*

*We dispatched the drones, and they began
to float around the black mass. Then, a large flash
illuminated the planet from all angles. It was a dark
reddish brown with spots of white ice. The photographs came back to show ruined cities, charred
lands, and frozen wastes.*

*Today we took a trip to the surface for the
very first time.*

*The first trip was taken by myself, some
assistants, and the head of my department; Doctor
Elizabeth Lawrence.*

*The light which reaches the surface was born
from distant stars. It diminishes into blackened rock
and red dust. This dust is created by cosmic rays,
which irradiate carbon compounds. The biological department says they're called tholins, and
are commonly found at the edge of a solar system.
They're supposed to be prebiotic molecules which
create all life as we know it.*

*This world is the product of an age without
heroes or kindness. A monolith that documents humanity's darkest time, where signs of struggle, fear,
and sadness are strewn about. It was not beautiful,
and not what Doctor Lawrence or I had hoped for.
Admittedly, I don't know what we hoped for. A time
capsule rather than a graveyard, I guess.*

*We were both amazed and horrified at the
first human specimen. A frozen, partly decomposed
skeleton. From there we went down a hill and
across the street. There we happened upon a field
where millions of remains were strapped to hospital
beds. Others lay on makeshift bedding, accompanied by the occasional grieving loved one at their
side.*

*It all must have happened quickly, and with
no warning. The extinction of the Earthlings seems
to be attributed to the death of the Sun.*

*Doctor Lawrence and I were urged to take
only what we could carry. Most of the technology*

"Jules". The familiar voice calls him from his thoughts.

"What's up?" Julius closes his journal and lifts himself to be seated in bed. His back then rests to the wall at the end of his cot.

Doctor Lawrence turns on his bedroom light, and it shines on the piles of books, neatly stacked along the walls. "Are you writing about today?"

He sighs with a raise of his eyebrows. "Yeah. It's a little morbid."

She sits at the edge of his bed and motions for his journal. He hands it to her, and she looks at the pages with intrigue. "You're a pretty good writer. Public school did alright by you."

"Those public schools were garbage." He laughs "Don't give credit where it isn't due."

The bottom of her eyelids meet her pupils in a smile. She laughs with a shake of her head.

"Seriously." He laughs.

"I know." She rests his journal on his bed and stands. "Are you going to bed?"

"I can't sleep."

"Shall we cause trouble?" She sways once with her hands behind her back, pivoting on the balls of her feet.

"What kind of trouble?" Julius asks.

"I'm sneaking artifacts into the lab."

"Why is that trouble?"

"Doctor Manning wants them to 'stay right where they are.'" Her hands show air quotes around the words.

"Manning can mind his own business…"

Julius looks around for a place to keep his journal safe.

"…Fuck it." He says, stashing his journal under the nightstand "Since you said that, I'm in."

He rises to remove his shirt and change to another one. Doctor Lawrence is paralyzed by a large scar which reaches from his forearm, up to where his tricep meets his shoulder. Several other marks streak across his back; all of which were previously unknown by Doctor Lawrence.

The only other notable mark is the discolored hole in his lower right abdomen. This one she knows because it's hard to hide. He's even joked about it; and it felt like it was truly nothing when it was on its own. Now, amid the ensemble of other scars, it shows what lies beneath the surface of his dismissal at the time.

In all the time she's known Julius, not once has she seen the large scar across his back. It looks horrible; and it shows, in vivid discoloration, exactly how far removed they are from one another. There are secrets he holds that are far beyond her understanding.

She's wondered how to ask him about the war, but now that the opportunity is in front of her, she sees the vast space is between their worlds. She can't say a word, although her mouth is open. It's her best friend. It's plain to see by the look on his face that it's him; but right now, in that body, he seems like nothing more than a stranger.

As soon as he's removed his old shirt, he grabs a new one. He lets it fall over his shoulders to drape around his body.

"What are we taking apart?" He asks.

She catches her wandering thoughts. She remembers now; they're planning to dissect the Earthlings' technologies.

She manages to find a few words, but they're almost mechanical.

"Come and I'll show you." She says.

He stretches a sock over his foot and leans forward. "Do we have any coffee?"

CHAPTER 2
A Glimpse of Life

Doctor Winter warms his hands with a cup of coffee. He analyzes a small artifact with his eyes. It lies on the table under a harsh white light. Its metal components are sheathed in plastic. A switch on the side protrudes and retracts the metal plug, where inside, the copper lining streaks downward into a small PCB.

Many items bearing its likeness lay in a pile before the scientists. Some are wires while others stand alone with different ways of hiding their metal components.

Looking at the group, Julius wonders out loud "Is all of it metal conduction?"

"Yes." Elizabeth begins. "They should work with the old computers."

Julius gives a disappointed flinch in the corner of his mouth. "We'll have to ask Ron in the morning."

"Morris won't mind." She says.

"Doesn't he lock that room?"

"Morris doesn't lock anything. He told me to walk in whenever."

"You know where it is?"

She nods "It's in the back of the history wing."

Julius raises his brows "Let's do it, then."

He turns his focus to the pile of wires, and notices something unique among the clutter. He picks up a wire to be sure he is seeing correctly. "Liz, this is a language."

She steps over in a hurry. "What is?"

Julius points to the small symbol embedded on the end of a wire.

"Are you sure?" She asks.

"I think so."

Looking for proof among the relics, he picks up another wire bearing the same symbol. It is also a cord, which he follows to the other end. A similar, but different symbol. He begins to wince as he thinks.

Elizabeth examines several of the cords to find more of the same lettering.

She begins to smile at him and points to the markings "If I were to take a guess, this cable runs in one direction. Making one end 'in' and the other…"

"Out."

She clenches the wire in a fist and shakes her hand with excitement. Her mouth opens from a smile to let out a whispered yell.

"Yesss!" She whispers in a high tone.

He gently touches her hand to ask for the wire. "Gimmie that, you're gonna break it."

"I'm sorry." She hands him the wire. "I just got excited."

Julius places the wire down gently and looks up from under his brow.

"Doctor Manning can suck a fat one." She adds.

Julius laughs "Liz!"

"What? It's true. He's a piece of shit."

Julius gives off a contagious calm with his 'laxed demeanor "He's just arrogant. What he does and says has no effect on us."

"It does when the Captain's on his side."

"You think the Captain takes sides?"

Elizabeth shoots him a side glance "I KNOW the Captain sides with him."

"Why's that?"

"Well, I feel like he worries about us. Since I'm so young and all."

"The Captain has faith in you." With another sip of coffee, he continues. "He's just cautious, and Manning makes him worry."

Her energy fades. "I guess…"

"You've got Morris taking your side, you've got me, and the sisters…"

"Yeah, but they're women. So it's different."

Julius takes a breath as if about to speak, but he falls short of a word.

"It's because I'm young, and a woman." She sips her coffee. "That makes them worry."

Julius searches around for something, then picks up an artifact. "Let's prove 'em wrong tomorrow."

Her mind lightly veers from disappointment and she nods. She then looks closer at the script on a wire. "These letters are beautiful."

He smiles and picks up another flash drive. "So are we plugging one in yet, or what?"

"Oh, yeah. Can we?" She doesn't wait for an answer, but begins walking. She reaches back for him, as if offering to take his hand. "Come on, let's go!"

— In a room down the hall, they reach a table of old technologies. One of these relics is a laptop which was brought from Earth five hundred years ago.

Doctor Winter stands in front of the machine for the first time, and yet with vague familiarity. It was refurbished and stored away in a dry and safe environment. His gentle fingers lift the screen from its physical keyboard. Fingering along the computer's edge, he finds what appears to be an appropriate port.

"I think this one should work." He says.

He signals her for one of the sheathed relics. She hands him the small object and he tries to plug it in. It doesn't quite fit, so he searches for another option. On the opposite side he sees a similar outlet. This time the metal component slides in. "Perfect! Now we push the power button and I think we'll be all set."

The screen takes a long time until it displays an icon underlined with a loading bar. Doctor Lawrence leans in for a closer look. "Is this what it does?"

"No, it's just starting up. These things work a little different. You'll need patience."

She reads out loud from the screen. "Dell."

In sarcasm, he sighs. "Even the Earthlings couldn't escape product placement."

She smiles but grows impatient. "This takes an awfully long time."

"She's old, ya know. Older than me, so that's saying something."

"Oh shut up, you're not that old."

"I have more in common with this grandpa than you'd think."

Just then the screen changes. It says 'Password' in a box with a blinking cursor.

Doctor Winter's face falls. "Oh, no."

"What?"

"Just a second."

He hits the 'Enter' key without typing anything, and luckily it works.

Doctor Winter sits back and explains. "The worst thing about Earthling tech is that they used codes to lock their computers. You'd need to remember the code or you couldn't get in."

"So you would have to memorize the code?"

"Yeah, the 'password.'" He uses air quotes to signify the word. "Not everything was facial recognition, retina scans, and fingerprints. This one didn't have a password; thank God."

The home screen appears and Doctor Winter navigates to find the memory stick. He can't find it and comes to a conclusion. "You have more of those?"

Doctor Lawrence reveals a bunch of them piled into a fold in her sweatshirt. They tumble down as she lowers the edge of her kangaroo-like pouch. "Yeah, why?"

Julius begins to laugh. "Give me another. We might be here a while."

"It doesn't work?" She asks.

"It's been so many years; and they could have been damaged."

Elizabeth sighs. She stays by his side until she can't wait any longer. She leaves the pile of USB drives with him and moves to the corner of the room.

She looks on at Julius and smiles as the sleep begins to take hold. Over the past ten years he's been a friend to her; and in ways that she's never had another friend before. He's aware that her passion lies in this job, and he'll stop at nothing to see her succeed. Elizabeth may have reservations about her talents, but Julius has faith in her.

With her fear of the dark and a lack of experience as a leader; Julius still believes in the young engineer. He believes in her dream to be someone worth writing about and remembering.

In Elizabeth, he sees a passionate force with a will to do good in the world. He admires her ability to take accountability for her actions; and he hopes she can learn to admire herself as well.

He works hard at this late hour because she's the one he believes in most of all; and she's the one who's given him the courage to believe in something more than a sense of duty.

Because of her, he works into the early hours of the morning; long after Elizabeth has fallen asleep.

By the time the morning comes, Doctor Lawrence is drooling on a bean bag by the corner of the room.

The dark room is illuminated by the lone computer monitor, and after hours of trial and error, Doctor Winter can't believe his eyes when an icon blinks onto the home screen.

"Liz… Lizzie!"

His voice wakes her. She thrusts herself up from a deep sleep to stand at his side again.

"The letters!" She points at the highlighted lettering beneath the thumbnail. The alien script from a foreign culture.

Doctor Winter smiles; theatrically smug in his tone. "Watch this."

He begins to click through the file's contents. Elizabeth looks on as he navigates through windows in a fluid manner. The language appears under more thumbnails until finally an English error message reads 'File Corrupted'.

"Oh, don't be a bitch now." He says.

The words spill out from his subconscious, and Elizabeth laughs.

Julius laughs and shakes his head. "Shut up."

Their laughter freezes as a file leads to a window with a play button. A timeline reads "Buffering" and crawls its way to the end of the clip. Finally, the moment catches them like smoke in the wind, leaving no trace of where they once were.

A video of a young boy by the Pacific Ocean. He stands on a pier, looking toward a man who enters the frame; presumably the boy's father. The man holds a toddler on his shoulders; after a countdown, he begins running after the boy. A lazy sloppy run which is meant to look foolish.

Ocean water laps the long shores beneath the wooden pier. The rocky coast of a Japanese town where white and grey birds fly in the golden air of a setting sun. To Elizabeth, the gulls sing like sirens in Greek mythology; and among the clouds of a receding storm, they look like angels. A handful of birds land on the pier and pluck popped corn off the dock.

The young boy reaches the end of the pier and throws his hands into the sky with triumph. His father follows close behind, with a theatrical show of exhaustion. The woman holding the camera laughs at his humorous defeat.

The boy runs toward the camera shouting something that can only mean "I won, Mom! I won!"

Their language sounds almost as artistic as the characters they write with. It contains dominating and brief consonance with little expression on vowels. As the boy is about to collide with the camera, the clip ends. A frozen smiling face that leaves two engineers without words to say.

Elizabeth looks curiously at the family. Bitter-sweet is the feeling in her heart.

Julius looks back at her.

"Eureka?" He says.

Elizabeth hugs him and laughs.

"You're the best, Jules!"

Soon after, the flickering of the office lights signal the start of the new day. The historical assistant who turned them on looks surprised. His morning routine has been broken by the presence of two engineers in the tech room.

The assistant smiles at his peculiarities.

"Have you both been up all night?" He asks.

Doctor Lawrence shrugs.

The assistant nods at the computer.

"You're supposed to have clearance to use that." He says.

Doctor Winter gestures toward the screen. "You'll be happy we didn't wait for permission."

CHAPTER 3
The Shadow of Ithaca

The mess hall hums with the voices of a hundred and twenty scientists; all awaiting the words of Captain Peter Andrews. A large window of stars is half-blackened by the rogue planet below. A raised portion of the floor lies before the window where a lone podium stands for the Captain.

Captain Andrews strides in from a doorway with his assistant in toe; Doctor Lechmere.

Lechmere holds the Captain's speech in a manila folder. At the podium, the Captain stops before the crowd to face them. His hair catches up to his scalp and falls on his face. A quick combing with his fingers, and the captain proceeds to read from the folder his assistant placed before him.

"Good morning, everyone." He takes a breath to slow himself down. The crowd falls silent. "How are we today?"

"Good!" The crowd affirms.

"Excellent." He adjusts the papers on the podium. "We've traveled ten years to get here; and it's taken roughly sixteen lifetimes to make this happen. WE are the generation fortunate enough to witness this day." He raises his arms to gesture out toward the crowd. They fall at his side and he breathes a small laugh. "We've made it home."

The audience roars with applause.

His gaze begins to travel across the crowd. "So, part of my job now is to report back to Zion; but what's an arrival message without all of you?" He gestures again, and is met with a brief applause. "A hundred and twenty of you stand before me now; and each of you is an integral part of our team. YOU are The Odysseus Mission."

A lone applause drives the whole crowd to cheer.

"So enough of this talking." The Captain laughs. "Is everyone ready to send a video home?"

"Yes!" The crowd shouts.

With a smile, the Captain signals his assistant to make the preparations. "Our message won't reach them until we're almost halfway home, but…" The Captain shrugs to the crowd's amusement.

Doctor Lechmere hands the Captain a remote, and Andrews turns to face the crowd once more.

"Is everybody ready?"

The crowd shouts again. "Yes!"

"I'm sorry, did I hear a no or two in there?" The Captain turns his head with his ear cupped toward the crowd.

The crowd laughs, and once more shouts. "Yes!!"

"Alright!"

Andrews presses a button and a red light appears in the corner of the glass behind him.

The large window brightens to mask the stars with a wide-angle shot of the crew. In the front, directly in the center, Doctor Andrews stands before planet Zion.

He begins with a charismatic tone. "Hello, my name is Doctor Peter Andrews, descendent of the Mandel family and the proud captain of the Mandel Star Explorer. I am here with the brightest minds of our time to send you a greeting from Earth." Doctor Lechmere displays drone footage of the surface to send home. All of it hand-selected to be G-rated material. The Captain continues speaking along with the display. "The Earth is a dark world with frozen wastelands. On the surface we have witnessed fractured societies and fallen nations; but not all of what we found was dark. Animals you have never seen lay perfectly preserved, trees are grouped in massive forests that stretch hundreds of thousands of miles, and finally, the records of a time long-forgotten."

The feed changes back to the view of the crowd, and Captain Andrews waves his hand to Doctor Lechmere. The assistant pulls up a new display on the screen.

Eyes become like glass in the crowd as they see water that stretches outward to the sky. Birds that aren't pigeons or ravens. A young boy's triumphant jump makes the room hum with laughter. The ocean breathes its hypnotic rhythm.

The lights brighten in the room to show faces cocked back and mouths open. The stillness is stirred by a sudden glance at their neighbors, then back to the Captain. The red dot blinks off of the screen.

The Captain leans into the podium. "How's that for a postcard?"

Voices begin to whisper to one another.

The Captain raises his hand for everyone's attention. "This is what we're trying to piece together. I wish you all the best of luck and may the next ten and a half years be the best of your lives. Welcome to Earth."

The room erupts in applause. Andrews and Lechmere make their way to the door in haste.

Elizabeth and Julius look at one another. They've worked hard to make the highlight of their message home, and they're proud of that. It's become the punctuation of their mission statement. It firmly tells that they're here for the right cause.

It is the product of their shared passion, their will to enrich the lives back home, and most important of all, it's the product of the love from one friend to another.

Julius raises his coffee in a toast to her. Her eyes still hold the dark circles from the night before.

She smiles at her one true friend, then a pit grows in her stomach.

Just now as he's raised his hand, Elizabeth can see the scar on his forearm; the one she'd never seen before.

CHAPTER 4
Scientific Process

The halls are silent before the hour strikes six in the morning. The air is still and cool.

After two hours of dreaming, Doctor Winter rises from his bed. He enters the bathroom and approaches the mirror.

"PIGSBY?" He says.

A pixelated smiley face appears in the mirror. It glows with a faint turquoise color, in contrast to the rest of the plain white and grey bathroom. The face moves its block-like mouth to speak with Doctor Winter.

"Hello, Julius." says the face.

Julius pulls a razor from the cabinet above the toilet.

"How are you, PIGSBY?" He asks.

PIGSBY shows a blink of a buffering wheel.

"I'm not made to ask or answer conversational questions." PIGSBY says "Can I help you with something?"

Julius puts out a hand toward the mirror.

"Just some shaving cream." He says.

The mirror protrudes a small pump from a hidden compartment. It gives a blob of shaving cream to Doctor Winter's fingers.

With a clean-shaven face, Doctor Winter nearly throws his clean lab coat over his shoulders.

"Doctor Winter?" A voice says.

Doctor Winter turns around, his brows together with curiosity. He sees a sound wave displayed on the wall by the bathroom door. A name next to it says Monica Xiao.

Doctor Winter throws his shoulders down and rolls his eyes. He throws his lab coat onto his bed and approaches the wall.

He hits a button that says "SPEAK"

"Yes?" He says.

"Julius" Monica says "The maintenance schedule was wrong. It was supposed to be last night. I need those readings now."

"Same readings?"

"Yes. The heat distribution monitor." Monica says "If you could read the analog meters and log them in for me, that would be great."

Doctor Winter nods "I'll get that done."

The engineer makes his way to the core of the ship. In a room just before the power generator halls, he enters a reading room. Analog meters show the distribution of heat coming out from the core and to the surface of the Mandel Explorer.

Doctor Winter taps the wall and enters the readings into a message to Monica Xiao.

A sound wave with her name comes to the wall where he types.

"Thank you, Julius." Monica says.

"Anytime." says Doctor Winter.

He closes the screen, and the wall becomes a metal surface once more. He leaves the room and makes his way up toward the surface again. Once there, he finds his lab coat on his bed where he left it. He throws it over his shoulders and wears it to the engineering lab.

Doctor Winter fingers for cold tools on the metal tables. Screwdrivers, a soldering iron, and a can of compressed air.

The stillness about the halls makes the mornings very cold. Julius is familiar with the precipitation on the windows, and unfazed by the clash between cold tools and warm, rested hands.

The clock strikes six, and feet begin to shuffle through the halls. Then seven, when the dining hall fills with the smell of breakfast. Finally as the clock approaches eight, the roar of life fills every room. Beakers clang in chemistry labs and fingertips tap on wall-projected screens. This is when Doctor Lawrence comes in with a hot cup of black morning brew.

"Good morning." She says.

"Morning." He says back "Monica had me do readings this morning."

"Classic Monica." Doctor Lawrence says "What've you got so far?"

"Well, none of this is efficient." says Doctor Winter "Earthlings wasted a lot of energy." He gestures his hand to a pile of dissected components. Copper wire is strewn about. "I don't think superconductors were popular yet."

"I'm not surprised." She begins. "By the way, I want to send out a message across the team. They need to be more careful with the electronics."

Julius nods "They're fragile from the cold." He places a broken PCB before her. "I already spoke to a few guys about that."

"Who?"

"The assistants." Says Doctor Winter "They agreed."

Elizabeth shrugs away the concern and picks up her work.

The day wears on, and as lunch comes around Doctor Lawrence removes her lab coat. Julius follows her lead and proceeds with her down to the café. Together they sit with the heads of each department. Here they are welcomed by both the leading Biologist, Doctor Manning, and the head of Sociology, the renowned psychologist, Doctor Arnold Hoyt. The historical department's Doctor Ron Morris quietly joins soon after.

Doctor Morris is quiet, but attentive. His words are few and decisive; and likewise Doctor Hoyt is selective when he speaks. However, no one's opinion is more valuable than Hoyt's. A bit of a celebrity on Zion, Doctor Hoyt has made many advancements in sociology. Over the course of decades, he has designed successful programs to prevent crime and improve the lives of many. His therapy sessions led to the willing surrender and conviction of Eden's most haunting serial killer, the "Cannibal Rat" and "West Side Killer"; Duncan VanRoy. Doctors Manning and Morris have few accolades in comparison. Some important research, but nothing as impressive as bringing a golden age to the capital of United Zion.

Manning is known for being self-absorbed and vain. His attention is seldom on the desires of others, but his cause is obscured to most. To his peers, the line is unclear between being self-righteous and having devotion to his duty.

Between the three men, a conversation fails to take off until the Xiao sisters arrive. Both women serve as the ship's lifeline. Linda oversees navigation and reconnaissance, while Monica manages the logistics of food, water, and energy.

Soon, empty seats are filled by the assistants who work second in command to each department head. Finally, the Captain sits at the end of the table. Doctor Lechmere joins him by his side.

All attention falls on the Captain, and Hoyt asks the most anticipated question. "What's the next move, Captain?"

Peter answers slowly. He looks around to read the faces of each individual. "We're supposed to start digging. We need to get the biological team down on the Pacific Ice Sheet." He stabs the vegetables on his plate. "Aside from drilling down there, we have nothing. Does anyone have an idea they'd like to add?"

Doctor Manning seizes the opportunity "I think the sooner we get drilling, the better."

Everyone agrees.

Elizabeth begins to think out loud "We need a little more context on my end. The language barrier makes it hard for us to understand what those artifacts are. Maybe if we dropped off in North America, we could find some language learning material."

"It's too far to make in one trip." Linda mentions.

Her sister adds "We can't put enough fuel in the one scout ship."

"What about the second scout ship?" Elizabeth asks.

The Captain makes a pained face "I already spoke with Linda; I'm not willing to have two teams out at once; not yet at least." His eyes look around to the department heads "I'd rather get used to things before we spread out." He sits up straight and looks sincerely at Elizabeth. "I wanna make the most of our time, I really do; but if someone dies, that's far worse than a day or a week lost."

Elizabeth's face falls "You think it'll take a week?"

Manning puts down his glass and doesn't break eye contact with his food "It should take a FEW weeks."

Elizabeth takes a breath to begin another comment but Doctor Manning cuts her off "The medicinal value of those organisms is very important."

Julius watches as Elizabeth's face grows innocent and less confident. He quickly begins to negotiate "What about the English learning material?"

Manning sucks in a breath of aggravation "ENGLAND is too far. Even Australia."

"Not Australia. Japan. The Japanese who learned English."

The Captain folds his hands before his face and leans in to place his mouth behind them.

"We can learn it all backwards." Julius says, "It's tough, but we can do it. The historical department is waiting on us after all." He gestures toward Ron who begins to nod in agreement.

The Captain and the Xiao sisters begin nodding too.

Linda looks toward Elizabeth and Julius, then to the Captain. "Stop by Tokyo. It's on the way to the drilling point. No time wasted."

In agreement, the team finishes lunch with a new plan in motion.

Manning slumps with bitterness. His care over the inconvenience becomes a self-induced burden. Julius notices his pace is hastened as if time is running out; but time won't move any quicker or slower. The only hindrance is the stress he creates by caring too much over a small detail.

The engineers return to their lab, and Julius steps aside with his partner to talk alone.

"He's an asshole. Don't let it get to you." He says.

Her face shows embarrassment. "I kept making my point, but he wasn't having it. It's his problem."

"I can see you're stressed, and your face fell when he snapped on you."

"It didn't!"

"I'm going to tell you the truth because I care. It did."

She simmers down and relaxes her posture. "He wouldn't let me get a word in."

"Well…" He shrugs "…he might be older than you, but you have the same power as him. You can talk back all you want, but I'd keep my cool. The Captain likes someone who can keep the peace and stand firm." Julius sees her nod to affirm his point. He raises a brow and talks more lightly "That was a temper tantrum he threw; and I know the Captain doesn't like it when he does that. So keep cool and talk right through him. Play nice, but stay firm."

She nods, then her brows wince with a question "How do you always keep so cool?"

He shrugs "On a battlefield you have to keep your cool. Nowadays I don't give a shit, a damn, OR a fuck. Things fly south and I'm like 'Okay, so what's the solution?'"

She laughs at his crass explanation.

He smiles.

"You diggin' what I'm layin' down?" He asks.

"Yeah, I got you."

Linda enters from the doorway unannounced. "Sorry to eavesdrop but I kind of heard everything."

The engineers look at one another to recall their conversation.

Linda puts forward a manilla folder with papers "I was waiting to hand you the plans, but you didn't notice me."

"Plans?" Elizabeth asks.

"The plans for the mission to Tokyo."

Elizabeth takes the folder "That was fast. Thank you."

Linda smiles "You two did a good job standing up to him. I'm glad you did."

Julius gestures Linda to take a seat in the lab.

She moves into the room and sits with a lean of attentiveness.

"Do you want coffee?" Julius asks.

"Oh, no thank you."

Elizabeth shrugs "I've never been very good at arguments."

Linda laughs "Be lucky you don't have a sister. You get good at it." Her eyes go toward Julius. "Even better you learn to pick your battles." Her eyes go back to Elizabeth.

"I guess you're right." Elizabeth laughs "And thank you for telling me that. It helps to know I'm not alone."

"Not at all. I have your back whenever you need it." Linda pulls her chair closer and continues. "If you need anything just ask myself or Monica. We can work things out." Linda shrugs and looks toward Julius "Believe me, I love to put Manning in his place, but I try to cut to the chase. Hoyt tells me 'Just treat him like water on oil.'" She begins doing a very thorough impression of Doctor Hoyt.

Julius laughs "That's exactly how he'd say that."

The women laugh with a newfound trust in one another.

Linda looks through smiling eyes and grows gradually quiet. Her attention turns to Julius "He tells me that at least once a week."

The laughter fades and the group looks at one another briefly. Linda then looks toward Julius again. Her face shows slight discomfort "I may have heard wrong but I think you said you were in the military?"

His smile becomes faint as he nods "Back in the Iowa Secession."

Her face grows soft, and she raises her inner brows "That was a while ago."

He nods "Not the same streets today."

"Streets?"

Julius feels the need to go over the long explanation once more, but Doctor Lawrence clarifies for him "He was in New Memphis. He was there the day of the siege."

Understanding where he's been, the words fall from her mouth "You survived that?"

He nods, and she sits back in reverence.

"Not many people made it back." He says.

As if to look at a relic of history, she attempts to honor him with mention of his unique nature "You're the only one I've met."

This fact hurts to hear, but she only means to admire his legacy.

CHAPTER 5
Light Ground

It began as a debate and grew into a riot. That riot has now become a revolt in the streets of New Memphis, and the William Lawrence Tunnel is closed to all the trains in or out of the sister city. The transit tunnel is made of glass, and runs for miles over desert. The residents of Eden are haunted by the stillness of the commuting rails, and the radio silence from the city government.

When communications were cut, bonfires began to illuminate the buildings on the distant horizon. Children have wondered little about what has happened to the north. None have the heart to tell them what fuels the flames beneath that honeycomb dome. The children have noticed however, that supplies are dwindling. The grain cars began to reroute from farms to the seceded city a train ride away.

It all started two days ago; and now the north end of Eden is cleared of civilians. The siege on New Memphis has been debated for a day and a half. Zion will go to war for the very first time.

Soldiers stand behind the emergency transit door machine. It towers fifty stories tall and lodges its teeth in the seam between the halves of the door.

Private Julius Winter is among the five hundred men who stand ready to enter the passageway. As one, the men stand motionless. The engine roars and a deafening screech echoes from one side of the city's dome to the other. The families nestled in concrete neighborhoods. Workers in the glass office buildings. The visitors on hotel balconies hear. All hear the piercing cry for war, followed by the march of troops. They walk into the jaws of the enemy to defend a land they may never see again.

The glass tunnel is lined with magnetic tracks that stretch over Zion's desert wasteland. Dust devils and dried mud meet mountains beyond a field of domed farms.

The troops scan their eyes along the trackway, searching for any sign of explosives. There is nothing to be found along the seamless floor.

The large infrastructure dwarves the men marching in unison. The tracks are numbered along their route; one through seven.

Before the conflict, the seven trains ran every hour throughout the day. For two and a half days, they've been silent. Four of the trains lay in Eden's train yard. The other three and two spares are on the far end of the tunnel.

Faces are crowned in kevlar helmets. Under skin-tight suits, the men sweat for fear of what might come next. However the soldiers' footsteps are not impeded. Their autonomous motion is second nature.

Nearly halfway from home a large bang is heard, and smoke appears at the far end of the tunnel. Then a light emerges out of the dust, steady, and unrelenting. A train is coming.

"This is Captain Jones, we have a train coming!" the Captain yells into the radio.

Just then, the light splits into four. "We hear you, Captain. Four trains." The radio responds. "Tracks one, two, five, six, and seven."

All the men move to tracks three and four to let them pass.

The voice comes in again "Captain, come in! We're sending up three lines. Two for the men, and one for a blockade."

"Roger! Men, get ready! I want Oscar and Mike to take the head of the blockade train! Run a car across tracks one and two! Squads Delta and Foxtrot, get the following one across tracks seven through five! The rest of the train cars should be used to support them! Angle them like an arrow!" The Captain points his hands triangularly toward the enemy city.

When the train arrives, the men move without a moment of thought. The Captain then grabs a handful of men to give private orders. The men break from the group and charge the train cars with explosives. Each one is put on the side facing Eden. Most are placed toward the inner part of the arrow.

Other men pull the hovering train cars with all their might. Charges are placed directly on each track. If the trains don't fall through the floor, then the magnetic railway should lose power.

With the cars in place and the explosives set, the men board the trains along the two and three tracks.

"Roll out!" the Captain yells, and the trains begin to glide forward.

As the opposing trains grow near, there is an eerie silence. Not one round is fired. The two Zion trains slow to a near halt, but the three trains bound for Eden continue relentlessly. The Zion trains then move at full force and everyone ducks for cover. As the trains pass, curious soldiers peer up to find packages lining the isles of the trains. They're rigged to hit home.

Heads peer out with anticipation. The Captain holds his hand to wait for a signal, and the men holding detonation devices watch him.

"Those fuckers." The Captain mutters to himself as he stares back at home. Suddenly from a cue, he drops his hand. "Now!"

An eruption of smoke shakes the tunnel, and the magnetic railway fails. Electric bolts crack out to every wall surrounding the blockade. The Zion trains fall together, screeching for several yards.

The team recovers from the floor and the backs of seats. A hum of whispers grow on the train.

Sinking hearts rise suddenly, and a single shout dissolves all concern. "Look!"

A train falls outside the tunnel, through the clouds and shattered glass. Dust plumes from the ground below as it hits the desert floor.

A roar of triumph electrifies the men. All the enemy trains begin exploding and alarms sound. The hiss of emergency air comes through pipes along the sides of the tunnel. The laughter fades as home is cut off.

One soldier comments aloud. "That might've been a little too good."

Julius looks to the Captain to find his stone-cold face fixed behind them. He looks at Julius and smiles with a wink.

"Physics!" the Captain says. He pats Julius on the shoulder "The answer to everything!"

Julius nods and the Captain passes him. Julius turns his head to stare at the enemy ground before them.

The Captain stands at the front of the car to address the troops "No turning back, men! The only way you're going home again is through victory!"

The men give a group shout and the Captain orders them out of the train.

As the troops move outward, they find masked enemies marching their way along the sides of the tunnel. Down the middle, three tanks press on them. They roar with an electric hum as they roll forward into the tunnel. The gunfire begins and men push the train cars to make places for cover.

The Captain slaps a man who clasps the end of a train car. The man is stunned, and all eyes fall on the Captain.

As bullets fly from his back, the Captain stands with his fists clenched. "Do or die! These cars won't save you!" The men stand in awe. His crazed roar breeds wildness from the troops. Veins protrude from his neck.

"CHARGE!"

The men run in a roaring sprint toward the tanks. Bodies fall in the madness. Feet fly without falter.

Bullets sing and whistle from the round edges of the tunnel. With steady aim, troops take the crowds along the sides. The men in the middle continue to sprint with explosives in hand. The tank fires and misses to the back of the tunnel. The charges are thrown and detonated. The glass shatters from all sides, and the magnetic railway is left to the desert air.

A breeze carries the smoke away. At the gate of New Memphis, more masked forces come forward. The third of the three tanks reverses backward from the fallen two. It delivers devastation as it retreats.

Julius finds cover behind the armor of a dead tank. He begins firing on the crowds at either side, but the third tank's fury keeps him down for cover. The Captain stands beside him.

"You shoot right!" The Captain says "I'll go left!"

This strategy allows their progress as they move up from cover to cover. Suddenly, they are out of moves to make. The disadvantage of being on the attack is clear. The tank keeps them pinned as masked men pick off their bodies.

One soldier breaks from the Zion pack and charges at the tank with a belt full of explosives. Cover fire is given by every man in the tunnel as he makes it fifty yards, sustaining several shots to the body. The tank aims its automatic gun directly at him. He hurls the belt of C4 onto its top. The automatic gun of the tank makes him unrecognizable within seconds, but the belt drapes over the tank's center. His fellow troops detonate the explosives, and the tank presses down into the floor. Pipes rattle and the floor rumbles.

The smoke clears, and the tank is gone. They press forward into the sound of gas hissing in the smoke. The floor is gone. Below them, the tank lays flat and bent on the desert floor.

The troops form on the Captain and press forward on pipes crossing the gap. With the smoke as cover, they make it to the gateway of New Memphis.

On their arrival, three shots are fired from nowhere. The Captain signals the troops to get cover in silence. The dust settles and the enemies look on in confusion. The Zion forces sprout up from cover and open fire with the wrath of scorned men. A rain of bullets return until the rebel forces are overwhelmed.

They drag their masked dead into alleyways, stairwells, and sewers. They retreat like spiders into a secret lair.

After five minutes of fury, the frequency of the fire dissipates. More United Zion troops emerge from the tunnels and pour into the streets. Zion has earned back the south end of New Memphis.

Over the next few hours, a perimeter is made with concrete blockades. Supplies are delivered by helicopter to the hole made by the last tank. First the barricades, then the artillery is delivered shortly after. After that, the troops receive food and catering equipment. Finally, before the company eats, the dead are delivered home. The blood and dust are washed clean from their hands, and dinner is served.

In Eden, parents and loved ones wail in sorrow for their soldiers. The city is sad but proud of the courage they witnessed on the north horizon.

A statue will later be erected in America Square. It will show the young man Tim, who destroyed the third tank with a belt of C4. He will stand atop the broken tank, beneath which a plaque will read. "'When Hell broke loose to the north, a band of young men gave everything to stop it. It is their sacrifice that saved our promised land. Our garden city.' - Mayor Wu".

Thereafter, Eden will be called "The Garden City", and the tank will be left to rust in the desert outside New Memphis.

After the battle, the troops are stationed at the mouth of New Memphis. Dinner is served as chicken, corn, and mashed potatoes.

Here Julius waits in line for food until he sees the Captain approaching from the corner of his eye.

Julius slams his plate down suddenly, and the server lets out an exclamation as potatoes fall from the ladle. At the sound of a splat the server glares at Julius, but notices the young man is in a stiff salute.

"Sir!" Julius says.

The Captain laughs. "At ease, kid. I'm grabbing a plate."

The Captain pats him on the shoulder and Julius looks again at the server. His eyes follow down to the spilled potatoes and his heart sinks.

"Don't sweat it, kid. I'll take care of it." The server shews him away with a forgiving hand.

Julius apologizes and moves along.

At his table with other survivors, Julius is unaware of the Captain's eyes on him.

To another man, the Captain mutters over the tapping of plastic forks on paper plates. "What's the deal with that kid over there?"

The gentleman lower in rank replies. "That's Julius Winter. He's one of those new ones."

"New ones?" The Captain asks with a tense face.

The man nods. "Brand new."

The Captain looks on curiously. "For a new kid, he knows his shit."

***

After dinner and a quick call to the Colonel, a decision is made. One of the task forces lost a man. Finding a fifth person is not a hasty task, but the Captain decides to take a chance.

The young man who approaches Julius asks him to hurry.

"You had Drill Sergeant Dale, I presume." The young man asks.

Julius follows behind with severity.

"Yes sir." He responds.

The young man laughs "He could make the biggest slow poke into a punctual man."

They round the corner into the doorway of a large building where an office is being managed. Four men stand waiting for Julius. He begins to shake each of their hands. Each is introduced by a code name.

Chief, the Sergeant and leader of the group is a two-hundred-pound, six-foot tank of a man. Bald and dark skin with piercing blue eyes.

Following down the line, there is Pluto. A short and skinny kid with a long pointed nose and cleft chin. His dark circles make his sunken eyes even more apparent. While possessing the face of a villain, Pluto may be one of the kindest hearts Julius will ever meet.

The third companion is Dash; a sniper who Chief says "looks like Jesus Christ on steroids.". His mathematical skills far outweigh his social capabilities. When spoken to, he often replies briefly and awkwardly; but behind the gun, his focus is unbreakable.

Lastly, there is Cricket. A young and kind kid with little else to him. A clean slate with character hidden under a deep surface of normality. An unnatural normality.

27

As it turns out, Cricket is a medical specialist. He graduated college with a degree in nursing. He was therefore assigned to the group as a medic.

Pluto on the other hand, is more like Julius; assigned as a grunt. Nothing out of the ordinary for the young man except for his six-speed sports car. It's noted for its ability to "slam your head back so hard it'll give you a concussion". In the academy they put him to the test, and his performance even prompted a compliment from Drill Sergeant Dale. Born and raised in New Memphis, Pluto made money as a pizza delivery driver. His familiarity with the neighborhoods makes him an integral part of the group.

Dash was assigned for being the sharp-shooter he is. He also specializes in recon for the field artillery group. His quick math provides excellent fire support.

The intel gathered by Dash is filtered right through Chief. As the platoon leader, he is a man of many talents. Back home, Chief was a blue-collar working man with a degree in civil engineering. He was looking to move up in the company but didn't have the money for a required degree. He enlisted to earn his degree but felt that he belonged in the service. His knowledge in structures, electrical, and plumbing make him not only the ultimate handyman, but the perfect strategic planner on the urban battlefield.

The Captain summarizes each of the men to one another "These men are your new group. You are a task force to be reckoned with. Sound off, boys."

With that the men let out a deep bark of a yell, and the Captain walks away.

Pluto welcomes Winter in a nonchalant manner. "Looks like we need to make you a code name."

Liking his own name, Julius is afraid to be stuck with something silly or stupid like lamb chop or buttons. "My name is just fine."

Cricket informs him. "We use them so the bad guys don't go snooping for families back home."

Julius shrugs. "I don't have a family."

There's confusion for a moment, but the men catch on.

"Oh." Cricket says.

Chief takes the reins. "We're your family now, kid. And in this family everyone's got a code name. And I think I've got the right one."

"Chief's good at nicknames." Pluto adds.

"How about Zero? Short for Sub-Zero. Since you're winter, cold as ice." He smiles, knowing he has Julius pinned.

"I told you he's good." Pluto affirms.

Julius smiles and nods. "I could do that."

Chief's hand falls heavy on Julius' shoulder. "Welcome to the crew, Zero!"

The men pat Zero on the back with enthusiasm, and Julius accepts his family gladly.

CHAPTER 6
Ashes and Dust

The night before the expedition, Linda and Elizabeth make an appointment to discuss their mission to Tokyo.

Linda points to a map with a blast radius charted over it. "Half of the city was destroyed by something. Most of the capitals are like this."

Elizabeth twitches an eyebrow. "I guess we can rule out meteors."

Monica enters from the back of the room. "You'll have enough fuel to bring samples home."

"Awesome!" Elizabeth says. "Thank you."

Monica looks toward her sister. "You have DEEMUS on lookout?"

"Affirmative." DEEMUS' robotic voice fills the room with a sound like static velvet.

"Both places?" Monica adds.

Linda grows dismissive and agitated. "Yes."

"No need to get fussy."

Monica leaves in a hurry and Doctor Lawrence looks back at Linda. "What's DEEMUS doing?"

"Without an atmosphere, you're in a cosmic shooting gallery. Please keep the load under fifty pounds, by the way."

"We can do that."

"We're sending you to the edge of the blast radius." Linda points again to the circle over Tokyo. "Hopefully you'll find something good there."

"Thank you, Linda." Doctor Lawrence looks at her with appreciation.

"Of course." Linda says. Her voice plays the moment down "Girls gotta look out for each other."

Elizabeth smiles. "Well thank you."

Linda shakes her hand. "Good luck tomorrow."

Elizabeth enters the recreation room with high spirits. There Julius looks up from a game of chess. He's gladdened to see her good mood.

"What's got you smiling?" He asks.

"The drones have done their scouting. The drill payload's landed. And we have enough fuel to bring something home." She walks over toward the wine fridge.

"Sounds like a good day."

He watches as Elizabeth opens a new bottle of wine. He stands to move away from his chess game and join her on the couch.

Julius accepts the wine and rests his arm over the back of the couch. "Engineers are always up the latest."

Elizabeth draws the glass away from her mouth and sucks the wine from her bottom lip. "We don't need to be ready until the afternoon. We have time to kill."

Hours of drinking and discussion drag on through the night. The bottle comes to its halfway point over the course of three hours. Their speech becomes slurred, and they discuss more openly about themselves. The time grows to be nearly midnight when the pair try to play a game of two truths and a lie.

Elizabeth sways as she holds her hand up with one finger extended. With each statement she adds another finger. "I've been to the president's office. I'm a religious person. And… I've dyed my hair black."

Julius looks at her with a hunch and tense brows. "You're not religious."

"How'd you know?" She asks.

He shrugs. "Religious people don't call it 'being religious'. They say something specific. It sounds foreign to you."

"I've been to church." She says. "I just didn't believe in all that crap."

He smiles and nods, but makes no comment.

"What about you?" She asks.

Julius shrugs again. "I mean yeah. You could call me a believer. I'm not into the organized part of religion so much, but I believe in something."

She places the empty bottle on the floor next to the couch. "And why is that?"

Julius stares off to collect his thoughts and speaks with uncertainty in his voice. "I think it's silly to get a group together under one idea… It's nice to pray, it's nice to share the stories, but the idea of making a group to represent God… That makes no sense to me. That's a personal thing. If you act out of good will, then that's God's work; not throwing a dollar into a basket every Sunday."

He shrugs once more and she looks down toward her glass.

"I need to ask you something." Elizabeth slurs.

Julius raises his eyes. "Ask away."

"How, as a scientist, do you believe?"

He laughs at her surprise.

"Don't laugh!" She says. "I'm serious."

"I know, it's just funny." Sitting back, he recalls his beliefs. "I understand why you ask; and people ask me that a lot. I'm not the only physicist who believes, you know."

She looks down and gently slaps his hand in a firm grasp. "I know. But like, I want to believe it like you do."

Choosing his words carefully, he begins with terms they both understand. "It's more like believing in existence beyond life itself. Like higher dimensional beings."

She looks insulted. "Are you serious?"

"I am! A higher dimensional being would be multiple places at once, right?"

"Yeah, I follow."

"You go further and you are present at all times in history. Doesn't that sound like god?"

She shakes her head. "Not really, Jules."

"How come?" He asks.

"Because that's not a living being."

"It is and it isn't. It's you and me. It's this room and the rocks that smack the walls at night."

"You've heard rocks at night?"

Julius shrugs "DEEMUS allows a few harmless ones to smack the hull, but nothing serious."

"Okay." Elizabeth waves one hand to wash away the side conversation. "You're saying the universe is God?"

"They say god is in all of us, that he's everywhere. So if that's the case, then he must be in a higher dimension. He's not even a he because he's everything. Living on a higher dimension makes you more than one, you're all."

"What's your excuse for bad things happening, then?"

"It's not a being like you and I. It can't step in except through us. Which is why an act of kindness is an act of God. When we understand each other, we help God understand himself."

"That's really deep, but I can't say I'm convinced." She places her glass on the table.

He nods. "I understand. But what's the question in your way?"

She screws up her face in thought. "Well, what's the point to life?"

"We choose what the point is."

She shrugs. "That's not cutting it for me. Like when is it God's will and when is it our own?"

He nods and thinks a moment. "If you wanna look for God's choices, just think about the things we can't control. Like, out of the infinite possible souls, you and I were given the gift of life, and we live in the same time period. The odds of us meeting are infinity to one; and to me, that counts as a miracle."

She closes her hands over her chest with a saddened, sweet face. "Jules!"

She reaches for a hug, and he breathes a warm laugh with the embrace.

The two forget the matter entirely and choose to watch a film for the night. Fog grows on the windows, and soon Elizabeth begins to snore.

Julius turns the screen off and cleans the room while she rests under a warm blanket. With the whole room in order, he turns off the lights and tries his best to wake her.

With each shove of his hand, she sinks back into place. He then smiles at her and laughs to himself. He lifts her in his arms and leaves the dark room behind.

In the halls a night shift worker is surprised to see the two of them.

"Late night?" He asks.

Julius smiles. "You could say that."

"Do you need anything?"

Julius thinks a moment and asks "Could you get a glass of water?"

"Sure, Doctor Lawrence's room?"

"Yes, please."

In her room, placing her on her side, Julius tucks her into bed. He then takes the water from the assistant and places it on the nightstand.

Leaning in the doorway, the assistant stands amused with crossed arms. "You guys take good care of each other."

Walking out the door and shutting off the light, Julius acknowledges him. "That's what friends are for."

The assistant nods. "What is it that makes you guys such good friends?"

Julius shrugs. "We don't have a whole lot in common. I think we try to be the friends we want. Honest, loyal, caring. Sorry, but what's your name again?"

"Tim Cameron." He extends his hand.

"Tim? Like Tim the Tank Man?" Julius accepts the handshake.

"Not the same, but related."

Julius slows his stride. "Related?" he says. He remembers the man who lunged himself at that tank outside New Memphis; all those years ago. "I forgot they started doing that… I knew him. Not well but I remember him."

Tim nods "Noble guy."

"Yeah." Julius says; his stride only now picking up where it once was.

As they approach Julius' room, he puts out his hand for the assistant. "I'll see you around, this is me."

"Have a good night, sir." Tim says.

They are about to part ways but both look back at one another. Julius looks for a resemblance to the Tim he once knew.

Tim tries to imagine Julius and Tim the Tank Man in their time; as if he would be reflected in a fellow soldier. "And thank you for your service." Tim adds.

Julius finds a way back into being grounded again. "Thank you." His mind takes a moment before coming back into the present.

Doctor Winter turns and closes the door behind him. He refocuses on the task at hand. Tomorrow he will descend to Earth for the second time.

CHAPTER 7
Tokyo

The darkness grows beneath the exploration pod, and the crew remains suspended in seat belts. Boosters from below begin to slow the vessel, and the crew lands in their seats without a rattle. The Pacific ice jostles the walls, and the back door falls onto snow in the sea of shadow.

The biological team departs; then, the hatch closes and the ship rises to move northwest, to the long-forgotten city of Tokyo.

Tattered and blackened, the city is frozen in time. Decayed by micro-meteors, and the weapons that rained from the sky over five hundred years ago.

The engineers step onto littered streets, illuminated by headlamps and the lights of the explorer pod.

Monoliths reach up toward pinhole stars in the blackened sky, underlit by the exploration crew. Glass windows reflect the night sky in towers. Human remains are scattered about. Signs and papers written in the forgotten language. Pools of frozen water are covered in a slush of solid atmosphere. A dusting of tholins covers everything; the bodies, the streets, and the windowsills of buildings.

Whole families cower in entryways. Their bodies singed from a blast.

On a private channel, Julius radios to Doctor Lawrence. "You holding up well?"

Doctor Lawrence looks at the partially burnt body of a child, huddled up alone with a blanket. "I'm doing fine."

The crew begins walking outward from the blast, and the spacecraft begins hovering slowly behind them.

Small items are gathered. Watches and cell phones are placed into a bin aboard the ship where a digital meter reads the weight in red numbers.

Further from the blast, the bodies become less burnt, less frequent, and yet the expressions grow more terrified with each mile.

Artifacts become more abundant, and the buildings are more stable. The crew begins to look more extensively inside the structures.

"Doctor Lawrence!" An assistant calls over the headset.

"Yes?" She replies.

"I can't tell, but I think you'll want this."

Doctor Lawrence walks over a pile of rubble to the young man who called her name.

The young man holds a flat plastic disk in the shape of a square.

"They're floppy disks." She says as she shows Julius.

She looks down at a pile of them on the floor, then looks up at the assistant. "Put some of these into the ship. Not all of them. Maybe twenty or so." As the assistant begins running she calls out to him. "Gently! They're fragile. I don't want you to trip either."

The team moves onward to a group of apartment buildings. There they find a frozen image of life on Earth. Popular culture, captured in posters and trinkets. Kitchens and living rooms stuck in the past, over five hundred years ago.

In one apartment room, Doctor Winter stumbles upon a woman's corpse with the chest cavity wide open. She appears to have been butchered by an amateur. The pots and pans on the stove have meat in them; bringing the hairs on his neck to stand up. The abundance of processed foods puts his heart at ease for a moment. He then examines a cloaked man in the corner. His lamplight shows a frost-covered face. The man smiles maniacally with raw meat between his fingers and the tips of his teeth.

Julius stands and moves into the doorway. He watches Elizabeth scan the other rooms. With his posture widened, he privately radios to an assistant. "I need you to look at the back right corner of apartment A12. Do it discretely."

"Copy that."

Doctor Lawrence approaches Julius.

"You wanna check out the other buildings?" She asks.

"Sounds good to me." He says.

He gestures Elizabeth to lead the way, and he follows her down the stairs.

They cross the courtyard into the next building. The first apartment is a nicely decorated home with pictures of a family.

"Hey, I'm in the room." The assistant radios back to Winter. "What do you want me to see?"

Julius watches Elizabeth as she looks around the room. "Look in his mouth." He radios back.

"All I see is the woman... wait. The guy in the corner?"

"That's the one."

"... What do you want me to do with it?"

"Take pictures."

Silence takes over until the response comes in "Done. What do we need it for?"

"Hoyt might want a record of that."

"… Got ya."

Julius looks at a picture of the family. They smile in a sunlit garden with a big red gateway. The top of the entryway bowes toward the ground, and its legs meet the grass like tree trunks with nothing else touching the structure.

"Julius!" Elizabeth calls.

He turns to see her holding the square plastic casing of a CD. There is a picture on the cover, but before he can look at it, she moves back into the room she was exploring. "There's a whole shelf full of them!"

He looks at the shelf just through the doorway. It is stacked from wall to wall with CDs.

Julius radios to the crew. "We need the pod over here. And a few hands while you're at it."

"Which building are you in?" The voice radios back.

Doctor Winter waves his handheld flashlight out the window. The others look out from windows in the dark.

The ship begins to move toward their building, and Julius looks around the room for something to help. He grabs the corner of the rug on the floor and Elizabeth follows his lead. "Load it on this rug. We can each take a corner."

They load the rug up with all of the CDs by taking the shelves off and gently dumping their contents toward the middle.

Just before moving, Elizabeth finds a photo album with something odd inside. She opens it to find pressed leaves preserved in its pages. Beautiful shades of yellow, red, orange, and green. While dead, they have withstood the test of time. She stands amazed and soon smiles. She puts the photo album on top of the CDs and looks to Julius. "I'd like to see Manning try and bitch about that."

He laughs and shakes his head. "Are you ready?"

They carry the rug halfway down the stairs where they meet the assistants who drove the ship. They both begin helping them and one begins to talk. "We need to go to an English-speaking country. I don't know what's of value here."

Doctor Winter agrees "I think once we get a hang of it, we'll know what to take."

The other assistant looks toward a CD case on the rug "That one's in English."

Julius tenses his brow in curiosity. "What does it say?"

The assistant turns the case. "There's a guy on it. It says 'Elton John'. And over here it says 'Greatest Hits.'"

They all look just shy of laughing.

"Music?" Julius says.

"Looks like we're bringing back some entertainment." Elizabeth laughs.

"Assuming they work." The assistant replies.

"True." The other assistant says. "Doctor Morris will be happy."

Everyone agrees.

With the ship loaded, they begin to check the time.

"It's leaving time." Elizabeth says.

An assistant looks surprised. "It's already been four hours?"

"There was a lot of walking." She reminds him.

"We need to start this far out from the blast next time." Julius adds.

"That and we should go to the United States." The other assistant says.

They all agree.

With the findings stowed away, they board the ship. As it ascends to race across the stars, Julius smiles at Elizabeth. She smiles in return, full of excitement.

CHAPTER 8
A Little Girl in Eden

With modesty, Elizabeth delivers the pressed leaves with a subdued pride. Doctor Manning commands his assistants to look at them "Immediately"; and the engineers are satisfied with the momentary peace between departments.

The drill is nearly assembled, and the Captain begins voicing the idea of multiple expeditions at once. In light of the good news, Elizabeth and Julius take a moment away from their work for the night.

Over a game of pool, the pair discuss possible destinations for their next expedition. When the game is finished, they take a seat on the couch with a bottle of wine. Here they turn the attention of their conversation to their past lives on Zion.

Julius asks more than he tells, and his answers deflect into questions about her life. All he shares is a lack of familiarity with New Memphis today. The ground there has long forgotten the soles of his boots. Yet the concrete grid remains the same in his head; as if rubble and ruin lay there just a day ago. They still exist somewhere to him. Just empty. The living left, and those who lay with idle eyelids never removed their faces from the pavement. He imagines they're still there. Just withered, desolate, dry, and dead. A boneyard he never wishes to visit.

Elizabeth feels sorry for pressing him and places her glass on the coffee table before her.

"Other than a severe fear of the dark." She laughs "I have nothing to complain about… I've had it easy."

His chest rises, then falls in a sigh. "No one has a perfect life."

She stares as if to see one hurtful memory before her. A discomfort large enough to conduct her decisions in her life.

"What is it?" He asks.

Half expecting him to guess, she takes a moment. "Mom and Dad separating. I never thought about it until I got on this ship."

He waits for her to think and add something. He knows that if she chooses the right words, it will help her to feel understood.

She remembers arguments but no words except "inconsiderate", "manipulate", and "liar". Her adult mind now watches her parents very differently. They were both inconsiderate. They were both liars. And they both tried to win the favor of their children. A selfish battle of manipulation on young, impressionable minds.

All they really cared for was their own legacy. To let their influence live on through the young and malleable children.

She remembers one night, and the front they tried to put up. It wasn't long after that the news would surface.

"The Lexington State Fair of 509." She tells Julius. "People call it Carnival."

As she recollects, she was only 9 back then; and her father had never paid so much attention to her in her life. Her brother Kyle would claim to never remember how loved he was that night, but Elizabeth can't forget her mother's tension. How she laughed and smiled in a nearly manic way.

Something bothers Elizabeth about her decided view of her parents; and this night set that feeling in stone.

They had been taken from one attraction to another, adorned with stuffed animals and face paint; and when the black curtains were let down for the night, the fireworks cracked just shy of the glass barrier.

"We were sitting and eating jello with whipped cream. I looked at Kyle, and back at my parents. For a fraction of a second, before they noticed I was looking, I could swear they were smiling at each other. Their faces were backing away from one another like they'd just kissed... I'd never seen them kiss... so I looked away, but it was too late. Dad rubbed my head and the attention was back on us kids... I didn't want them to stop being like that... I wanted things to be that way forever. The four of us together and happy." To confess this breaks her heart. "That one moment contradicts everything before and after." She wipes a tear from her eye. "I always asked myself why that couldn't be my family. Why they insisted on letting that go? Why nobody cared as much as I did."

Elizabeth bites her bottom lip in anger, and the tears subside into a cold face.

"My brother drank himself to death. My father was remarried with a new son; and the funeral was just an obligation to him. Meanwhile, my mother wallows in her self-pity..."

Julius' hand finds its way to hers but she pulls it away.

She looks at him with a soft regret. "Sorry."

Julius backs away but keeps attentive eye contact with her.

"The day after the fair, Mom moved out. They constructed a memory to make up for what we'd miss… A sick way to pull the rug out from right under us."

Julius keeps silent. Defeated in finding something to say.

After a long while, he manages to uncover a few words.

"If it makes you feel better, I'm here to listen." He says.

With that she falls into his shoulder, and lets out the years of pent-up words.

With time her sobs fall away into a brief gasp which comes in twos. Frequently, then less, and finally no more. A weight has left her by the time she is sniffling. At which moment she notices Julius' fingers in her hair. She backs away from his support, and looks where her head once was. "Oh god. I've made you a mess."

He laughs "Don't worry about it. That's what I'm here for."

With a quick brush of his hand he straightens out the wrinkles of his shirt. She tries to aid him, but he holds her hand before it meets him. "Don't worry about it."

"Just let me get this one thing." She says.

She wipes away as much mascara as she can.

He watches as she deliberately stares at the fading stain. "Any time you need me, I'm here."

She looks at him for a moment, but not long. With a last brush of his shoulder she backs away and stands. "You want another glass of wine?"

He puts his hand up in a polite decline. "No thank you."

She begins walking away but he calls to her again.

"Hey, hold on."

She waits, standing a the edge of the couch.

Julius begins talking with hesitance. "You shouldn't drink. We drink too much."

She nods and looks down to her feet.

"Besides, you're more fun when you're sober."

She looks up with a smile. "I don't know. I think I'm a pretty fun drunk."

He laughs. "Yeah but that's for a slumber party. This is a onesie wearing, no selfies, hair up in a bun, no makeup, sleepover."

She laughs again. Her cheeks hide glassy pupils behind raised eyelids.

He continues. "I want to pull an all-nighter talking with you."

"Fine, but I'm going to get some tea."

He smiles. "Deal."

With a cup of tea each, they sit back on the couch. They talk all night about her childhood split between her father's place in Eden, and her mother's quiet suburban community. A town called Elysian Grove.

In wealthy neighborhoods back home, there are fiber optic stars projected on the dome above. Elysian Grove even had a moon projected with phases.

The curtains that fall each night serve two purposes for every community on Zion. To protect from X-ray bursts, and to block out the ever-setting Proxima Centauri, the star which rests eternally on the southern horizon.

In middle school, she and her friends would play manhunt under the stars.

Her father's place was quiet for the city. Less children in the neighborhood, but it was the house where she spent the first nine years of her life.

Her mother had custody, but the time at her father's felt more like home. His private garden would host parties and events. Wheat trees, grass vines, raspberry bushes, and all the furnishing of a proper oasis.

The garden was a nice place to sunbathe when her father played piano through open windows; and this was when she would sneak off with her preteen summertime boyfriend.

Most friends she had, sadly, were superficial. None were truly close to her like Julius. No other friendship could stand the test of time on this ship together. From the moment they were introduced in a meeting as "partners" the two of them made an effort to know one another. The bond grew stronger with time and gradually grew into the friendship of the ages.

Elizabeth's first major impression of Julius was a sly insult toward Doctor Manning. Following a judgmental remark on Elizabeth's age, Julius played dumb in a way that was clever. The backhanded comment was about politics playing a part in the crew selection for the mission. Julius looked at him long and hard. "You think so? I had a feeling we weren't picked for intellect, but I didn't think it was political in any way."

Doctor Lawrence smiled uncontrollably, and fought the grin with all her might. Julius then looked her way with half of a smile and a wink. She still smiles from time to time when she thinks about it.

"It's because his friend didn't make the cut." He told her.

With time they would share details of their past. Long talks at night led to regular routines; and now they spend every free hour together.

"You know, your parents being apart. That could be just a part of God's plan." Julius says.

Elizabeth laughs "I don't believe in a plan.".

"I do…" He adds.

She looks into his eyes and recalls their miracle meeting. She sighs and places her tea down.

"What god would make a world like this?" She asks.

"The one who gives you what you need, and not what you want."

"That doesn't make sense." She laughs.

"What if you learned something from your parents?"

"I've learned how not to act."

"I rest my case." He raises his hands and expects a laugh.

She lightly smiles, but shakes her head.

"Not good enough." She says.

He leans in closer with tense brows "For my own curiosity, tell me, what makes you doubt?"

She thinks a while, and nods when she comes to an answer "You said a higher power brought us here."

"I did."

She nods again "I love you, Jules; but what higher purpose is there to a friendship?"

Julius shrugs "Everything happens for a reason, but I don't have the answer to that right now."

She turns her head to face him "If you can answer that by the time we make it back to Zion, you win."

"Deal."

He thrusts his hand forward, and Elizabeth meets his hand with hers in agreement.

Julius grins "Is there money on this bet?"

She laughs "You get bragging rights."

"Fine" He says "That will do."

They laugh together with warmth and security.

CHAPTER 9
For Peace, Prepare

The final delivery of drill supplies marks the end of a long task. The Captain calls for a meeting in the dining hall where Doctor Manning stands in front of a window projected screen. Beside him is a podium where Captain Andrews waits for the room to fill.

The screen displays a towering machine over the Pacific ice. It is illuminated from the bottom with lights in the never-ending shadow. Small people like ants descend the sides of the scaffolding. Doctor McGrotty waits patiently by the side of the camera.

In the dining hall, other departments are audibly impressed by the sight. To Elizabeth, it looks like an oil rig in the midst of an icy netherworld.

Julius recognizes that such a feat would not be possible without the help of gravitational manipulation; one of the best inventions of the past five hundred years.

Quietly seated, the room listens closely for instructions.

Captain Andrews leans into the podium and taps the microphone. "Can I have everyone's attention?"

The room laughs.

The Captain smiles at his sarcasm. "It's done! Let's hear an applause!"

The applause is accompanied by whistles and cheers.

"The next step is to reach our beacon. The thing that guided us here in the first place. The mother load of all questions!" His hand lays flat in a platter to gesture toward the Xiao sisters. "Linda has taken drones across to the source. There she found a government facility in the middle of North America. A land that's been called 'tornado alley' in the United States."

The crew erupts in a roar of applause. The ancient land of America has been the inspiration of Zion's fantasy. The civilization of a simpler time has captivated artists and scientists alike. It is where Doctor Mandel and the crew of two thousand once lived; the men and women who colonized Zion five hundred years ago.

The Captain's hand calms the crowd as he smiles. "However, we need to take care of one last thing here. Doctor Manning, will you do the honors?."

Doctor Manning turns with a hypnotic look on his face. His eyes look drained of energy, and his smile is faint. "Absolutely."

His tired smile makes the biological team laugh.

Doctor Manning then looks above the screen and into the camera. "Doctor McGrotty, commence drilling."

Manning's second in command throws a switch and the large contraption begins spinning and vibrating in silence. Lights jostle around the machine and the camera itself shakes wildly. McGrotty holds the camera still and the audience sees his smiling face. He activates his intercom laughing. "That was more than I expected!"

The crew laughs as the Captain signs off. "Make sure you come back in one piece!"

"Yes sir!" McGrotty replies.

Elizabeth turns toward Julius and finds no smile, but a perplexed face.

"What's wrong?" She asks.

Captain Andrews descends the stage, and Julius approaches with intent. Elizabeth follows, but he does not respond.

As the Captain begins to pass them by, Julius walks along with him. "Captain, why not go to New York? Why not someplace where we can get context for what we've found?"

"New York?" The Captain says.

Andrews' eyes turn quickly to Lawrence, and back to Winter. He stops to keep talking with the engineers.

The Captain asks for clarity "Why would New York be the place to go?"

"We need to know what to look for and what we're looking at." Julius says "We should go to a major city. We need to understand the simple things first. We only just found out that those memory sticks are called USBs. We'll miss something of value if we don't know how things work."

Andrews shakes his head. "I don't think so. You know enough, and the beacon is important."

Julius grows argumentative. "The beacon? Or something else you're hoping to find?"

The Captain winces his bottom eyelids.

Julius looks stern at the Captain.

"I've avoided military work my whole career." Julius says "I'd like to keep it that way. I don't want to build weapons."

The Captain smirks.

"You didn't start out that way." He says.

Julius looks down. His face falls.

The Captain loses his smile and frowns his brows.

"I'm sorry Julius. This isn't war times, though…"

"That's what people always think."

The Captain laughs "But they're not."

"You let your guard down." Julius says "You don't imagine what will come next. You think the world is at peace now, and that it will remain that way until the world is somebody else's problem. I've killed enough people, Captain. I don't want to be responsible for any more death. I might never see the people who die from what we find here, but I don't want to kill anyone. You have the opportunity to stop that."

The Captain's brows gather. He sighs a gust of frustration; but he remains as composed as he can be.

"What we find is what we find." The Captain says.

Doctor Lechmere calls the Captain over from the other side of the room, and the Captain excuses himself.

Julius watches him leave and feels his blood steam beneath his skin.

Elizabeth lays her hand on Julius' shoulder.

"It's the job." She says "It's not our place to ask questions."

Julius looks at her.

"Will he be giving the weaponry to all the nations of Zion?" He asks.

"I don't know…" She says.

Julius shakes his head.

"I just wish we could have science without war."

"Things won't happen like they did in New Memphis." She says "The world is different now."

He shakes his head "Don't ever say that." He tells her "That's what people always say before the worst happens."

CHAPTER 10
Doctor Clay

When the Earthlings ventured to find their new home, there was an intercepted signal coming from the Earth itself. Doctors aboard the ship bound for Zion scrambled to take note of its location and frequency. It was expected that this terrestrial message would die out within a decade. However, the radio signal would remain constant for over five centuries.

In her laboratory, Doctor Lawrence looks over a list with Julius. It includes her instructions to the staff. In bullets it reads:

Today's Mission:
- **Who made the signal and why?**
- **Could there be humans living on Earth today? (Doubtful, but not impossible.)**
- **How has it remained operational for so long?**

Elizabeth gathers the Engineering crew to discuss these matters in detail. At her side, Julius forwards the list to every engineer's personal mailbox.

"I know it's a short list." Elizabeth begins. "But I want to make sure we get as much as we can out of this. There will be no downtime. If you're not working, check the list. We don't have time to revisit this place."

She selects ten individuals for the landing crew and sends the team on their way.

The following hours are full of excitement and wonder. Now that the crew is used to the expeditions, there is an aura of professionalism in their postures. The hastened feet indicate a renewed energy aboard the star explorer.

Doctor Lawrence holds a posture of leadership unlike before. Her command over the expedition seems certain and natural. Her voice toward the Captain is that of assertion; spoken through a pragmatic and educated tone. Julius is glad to see it.

On the descent there is a looming tension. The outside world is daunting from inside their pod. The room shakes upon contact with the Earth. The door to the pod falls, and the explorers walk into the vacuum of space.

The grass on which they stand stretches flat into the shadow. Above is a daunting infinity, which encompasses them around the horizon. The most remote darkness in the galaxy. A black platform in the stars.

A host of stars surround the sky, save for a triangular black void on the east horizon.

"That's our building." Elizabeth says.

Manning exits the pod with his team of biologists.

"Make it quick." He says to Elizabeth "I don't have all day."

Elizabeth shoots him a look over her shoulder, then looks at Julius. He shrugs and shakes his head.

The engineers board the research pod, and it hovers toward the black object in the stars.

Their lamplights fall on grass for miles as they look around. When they look toward their destination, it shows a pyramid made of metal and glass.

The windows are shattered and shards are strewn about the landscape, reflecting stars from above. The hollow building is a wreckage of office chairs and desks hanging off of the floors and outside windows.

Upon arrival, the crew assesses the damage and moves in. Inside, they make note of there being no corpses. On the floor of the lobby, an insignia reads "DARPA".

The team presses on to find a closed elevator. A rover with separating jaws comes in to pry the doors apart. The door bends into waves of metal on its surface. The walls slam as the machinery within them breaks. The group then makes the descent to the bottom with ropes and harnesses repelled from the exploration pod.

The line runs through the main lobby and past several offices, down into a never-ending tunnel of dark shadow.

Julius descends for a long while before the elevator is found. He steps diligently to find it is sturdy. From there a saw is taken to the roof below, and a large hole is made.

On this floor, labeled "B12", is a large corridor stretching for two hundred yards at the very least.

The concrete walls seem untouched, but objects are strewn about as if a mighty earthquake scattered them.

Through each doorway there are laboratories, and supercomputer rooms that stretch for a hundred square yards.

Terminals stand crooked on desktops and the trinkets of personal lives lay broken and dusty.

On the farthest end of the corridor there is a large steel gateway to a room with two massive machines. The larger one stands forty yards high and slopes backward like the face of a pyramid. The back is forty yards from its face, and behind it is a massive cargo elevator.

The sloped face is disturbed by a rectangular box. It protrudes at eye level, with its top parallel with the ground. In the middle is a lens with a closed aperture.

Standing opposite this machine, the other bears its likeness, but broken. The light fixtures and ceiling beams managed to fall through its face and destroy the inner contents.

A generator is called in to supply power to the machines, and the crew continues searching other floors while the power supply is being lowered.

On B11 there is a ballistics range with long halls where cannons aim at distant targets. B10 is filled with genetic experiments. All of the samples are dead. B9 contains strange technologies of various kinds. They vary in aesthetic as well as purpose. None can be explained upon further examination, and so they are loaded into the pod carefully, and branded as classified.

Before reaching B8, the generator begins its descent, and the crew makes its way downward to watch.

Half of the crew waits for the generator at the bottom, outside the doorway. The other half begins working on a hole in the bottom of the elevator. What lies below might be the source of the signal.

Doctor Lawrence turns to see the half in the elevator and yells over the headset. "We have a three-ton generator coming down and you're cutting a hole directly beneath it?! Get in here!"

The half working on the hole stops, and they step through the doorway. Their faces are that of innocent children realizing they made a mistake.

The generator meets the elevator floor with an immense weight. Eight workers combine with the two who lowered the generator, and all begin pulling the power source onto the floor of B12. There, they put the three-ton machine onto a pallet jack. From there, they wheel it down to the large machines at the end of the hall.

"You can keep cutting that hole now, boys." Elizabeth says. "Be careful next time, please."

The crew members thank her and immediately move toward continuing the hole.

Those two crew members descend, through that hole, down to B20. There they find the source of the signal. A radio beacon supplied with energy from the Earth's core. Its purpose is unclear, but it saved human history.

Back on B12, Doctor Lawrence, Winter, and three other workers start the generator.

"I wanna see what these do before we move on." Elizabeth says.

Upon saying this, she notices something odd. The glow from her headlamp radiates amid the space before her. A stream of blue light projected on air.

"Julius." She says.

He turns and awaits her command.

"Do you see this?" She asks.

"See what?"

"The atmosphere."

His face shows puzzle as he laughs "What are you talking…"

Just then he notices the glow in the air. He takes out his pressure reader and samples the room. The temperature is roughly -330°F. Cold enough to freeze some gases, but not Earth's nitrogen and oxygen. The pressure gauges around point nine atmospheres.

"We're miles below the surface." He adds. "It could be the core of the earth keeping things warm."

"But there is air here."

He nods in disbelief.

"Doctor, we have the generator ready." An assistant calls over the headset.

Doctor Lawrence turns around to see the two men standing by the machine. The generator beside them is connected in a sloppy fashion. An instance her father would refer to as "Mickey Moused"; whatever that meant and whoever Mickey was, she never knew.

She laughs to herself.

"We're all set up here…" Manning says on the headset. His tone is rude and impatient "… We're waiting on you…"

Elizabeth looks at Julius, and he privately communicates to her.

"He can wait." He says.

Elizabeth communicates back "I'm not gonna respond."

She then opens communications to the engineering team.

"Fire it up, boys!" She says.

The roar startles the two assistants.

"There's air down here." Elizabeth explains.

The two men look relaxed as they wait for the machine to activate.

One of the assistants is about to remove his helmet and Elizabeth yells over the headset. "No, no, NO!"

The man stops just short of revealing his face.

"Do you guys have a death wish?"

"But there's air." The assistant says.

Elizabeth explains as softly as she can. "You don't know what's in this air." She says. "What if you catch a virus? There could be radiation."

"And you'll catch instant frostbite." Julius adds "It's still negative three-thirty."

The man's face is astonished at the remarkable number. "I didn't know." The man says. He remains shocked by his close brush with death.

"I'm sorry. I should have elaborated." Elizabeth says.

Julius pats the assistant on the shoulder as he walks by. "Protect that money maker, kid."

Turning to the machine, Julius asks the second assistant. "So does it just sit here and blink? or…"

"I think it's just starting up." The assistant replies.

Julius recognizes the voice and looks over to see Phil. A young kid he always admired on the team.

Diverting his gaze to the other assistant who stands paralyzed, he remembers his name being Danny. Notorious for getting into predicaments, Danny was once something like a pilot in the Air Force; or maybe an engineer. Julius can't remember, but he reflects on it for a while.

He remembers that Danny was in fact an engineer, but he knew how to fly.

Julius looks around some more as Elizabeth watches the machine.

"Where's the other guy?" Julius asks.

A voice calls over the headset. "I'm in the other room. Coming back now."

This voice is unfamiliar to Julius, and so he calls privately to Elizabeth. "Who's voice is that?"

"Mark" she replies instantly "The kid who helped you with the cut-bot. He went out with us the first night we met."

Julius remembers a young man who helped him model the barber tools for the automated hair-cutting robot. A silly side project to kill time on their ten-year journey. He's best friends with Danny as Julius recalls. He nods at the faint memory, but Elizabeth laughs at his lack of recollection.

"Haven't spoken to him or the other guy in almost five years." Julius says.

Elizabeth chuckles "I've noticed."

Mark enters the room and approaches the rest of the team. At this moment the machine beeps as it becomes fully operational. The aperture blades open and close, adjusting several times until they finally remain nearly shut. As the headlamps flood the lens with light, the blades close. When turned away, the blades grow to see in the darkness.

"What does it do?" Phil asks.

Elizabeth approaches and looks for some sort of controls. Not a screen is seen; not a button, a lever, or a switch.

"I don't know…" she says.

There is a sound to the far side of the room. A whirring by the broken machine that makes the opposite wall.

"Did it do something?" Mark asks.

"I don't know…" Elizabeth says.

Clicks come from the same direction, but they soon stop. Another whir of motors. The sound falls as if it's at the end of a process.

Elizabeth looks down at a line leading back to the working machine. She looks into its lens. Its pinhole aperture rests still. Julius hasn't stopped looking at it.

"Any ideas?" Elizabeth asks.

"Not a clue." says Julius.

He then laughs in the silence.

"Doesn't seem very helpful." He says.

In the darkness of the room, the team turns to the lens. Through the speaker box below it, a robotic chime calls out in the cold.

"Hello?"

The assistants freeze. It called out before a sound could be made. No words had been spoken outside of their suits. A sentient question; called out to the dark like a curious, rational mind. It blared out of its speaker from silence. The voice echoed on walls of metal and concrete.

Elizabeth calls over her suit's loudspeaker. "Hello."

Julius wonders as Phil comes to a premature conclusion.

"I don't think it's actually listening…" Phil says.

"Hello." The machine says again. "Who am I speaking with?"

Everyone seems unsure of how to respond. The robotically chopped and monotone voice seems far from conscious.

Doctor Lawrence continues to speak on their behalf. "My name is Doctor Elizabeth Lawrence. May I ask who you are?"

After a moment of silence the voice sings again "My name is Doctor Douglas Clay."

The crew looks very confused at one another; all except for their leader who continues to question the machine.

"Who made you, Doctor Clay?"

"My mother."

She is now more confused than ever. "Who do you call your mother?"

The machine becomes defensive. "I'm sorry but I need to know. Who are you? Why have you come here?"

"I told you, I'm Doctor Lawrence…"

"No, I mean who do you work for? Where do you come from?"

"I work in the United Zion Space Program. We live on another planet, and this is our first time on Earth."

After a long pause the machine replies as if to be amused. "Another planet?"

Doctor Lawrence confirms and asks again. "Who made you, Doctor Clay?"

Clarifying himself for her sake, he replies. "I made this body. It was my parents who made me."

Terrified and amazed, the crew is jolted with chills.

Doctor Lawrence catches her breath before it leaves in a gasp. "Doctor Clay… Were you a human?"

"I still am, the last I checked."

Elizabeth turns to look at Doctor Winter, but he does not even glance her way. His eyes remain fixed and fascinated.

"I was born in Phoenix, Arizona, and I made my living as a bio-mechanical engineer… If you don't mind me asking again, what brought you here, back to Earth?"

CHAPTER 11
Douglas

"I don't remember." Doctor Clay's voice rings through the walls of the ship. "My assistants put me under, then I saw you in space suits."

A crowd of scientists look on from behind the department heads.

The machine speaks again "What happened to Earth?"

Doctor Lawrence steps forward. "We don't know. That's what we're here to figure out."

The machine takes a moment to think. "If it helps, I know we weren't at war when I was put under. That could've changed but…" The team looks on in silence while the machine takes a moment more to think. "… I'm sorry, I don't know what happened… If there's anything I can do, I'd be glad to help with the research."

Peter leans over the back of a chair in the midst of his department heads. "Thank you for that." He smiles into the lens at the front of the machine. "More importantly, how do you feel?"

"I feel fine." Douglas responds "I just need to be caught up is all." The aperture blades adjust in the lens of the machine "I'm serious about the help. It's not like I'm going anywhere."

A laugh swells out of the crowd.

Elizabeth looks on through smiling lids. "We appreciate it."

Doctor Clay speaks with a change in pace. "If we're in space, then how are you standing?"

The department heads look to one another, but no one says a word.

"I can tell this ship isn't moving." says Clay.

Monica peers out from behind Doctor Manning "Uh, define moving…" She smiles at her own joke, and the crew laughs.

Douglas speaks when the laughter fades "I know you can't tell, but I really found that funny."

Monica smiles.

Doctor Clay takes the conversation back. "I just mean we aren't spinning, so how are you standing?"

Peter talks him down with a dismissive tone "A lot of things have changed, and we'll catch you up when we have a minute." He moves from behind the empty seat. His final step brings him to stand before his team. "Just try to take it easy. The change might be more dramatic than you realize." He bows his head a little as he addresses the machine by looking into the lens. "You're welcome aboard this ship, and you can count yourself a part of the crew. I didn't catch your name, by the way."

"Doctor Clay, but you can just call me Doug."

The Captain bows again. "Doug, I'm Peter Andrews, but the crew calls me Captain."

"It's nice to meet you, Captain."

"Likewise." Peter turns sideways and nods his head in the direction away from Doug. "I'm going to take some of my associates here to discuss with them in private. You'll find that we're providing you power, but there's no other means of connection. I'm sure you understand."

"You're afraid I'll conquer the human race, I get it."

The crew laughs again and the Captain smiles into the eye of the machine. He then gestures his arm in the direction of the working staff. "If you need anything, feel free to ask the remaining team." He does another slight bow "We'll be back shortly."

Upon receiving Doug's thanks, Peter signals the department heads to follow him.

Julius watches Elizabeth as she follows behind the Captain. Her eyes don't leave Julius until she sees his eyes meet hers. He nods in a response.

The department heads congregate in a separate room down the hall. They form a circle in the middle of the smaller space.

Manning looks around "You couldn't pick a bigger space?"

Doctor Hoyt pats the biologist on the shoulder "My office is one of two rooms without cameras."

Manning flinches the corners of his mouth downward "Didn't know that."

Peter's tone is changed to a dire context. "Alright; I don't want any of you giving him too much information. He's funny, he's nice, and most importantly, he's a machine." He looks around from face to face. "He was made before the Iowa Conventions. He doesn't abide by the rules of AI, and that makes him very scary. Isn't that right, Doctor Lawrence?"

Elizabeth nods.

The Captain nods back. "His talk about being human, losing his memory, all of it could be a lie." His eyes give a greater impression of severity. "He seems normal enough, but I don't want him snooping around. Keep our technologies secret, and lie if you have to. If he's a creep or a liar, he could use things to his advantage."

All agree except Linda. "He'd be useful if we connected him at some point. Is that not an option down the road?"

Manning looks at her from across the circle "It might make your job easier Linda, but it's not worth the risk."

Linda frowns her brows "Excuse me, I'm not trying to make my job any easier. I'm just…"

"That's not what he meant." Monica says. She looks at her sister. "He just means to say it's a risk."

Manning shrugs "That's what I meant. I'm sorry if it came off another way."

Linda takes a breath.

"We might do that later, Linda." Peter begins "But we have no idea who he is."

"Of course" Linda says "I just wanted to clarify."

"It's a good thing you asked." Peter says. "I'd like his help at some point, so I don't want everyone to alienate him; but for now, we have a puzzle to solve before we get there." He looks around the circle. "Before we can trust him, we need to poke his brain a little. There's two ways to do this. One:" He raises his index finger. "We dissect him, and search through his mind. Two:" His second finger rises. "We have Doctor Hoyt analyze him through therapy. Now, I need a vote."

Everyone is hesitant to share their opinion, but the therapist breaks the silence. "I like the same pay for less work."

Laughs warm the room; then Monica speaks. "I would hate for someone to look into my mind. It's no one's place to look through someone like that."

Elizabeth parts her lips to say something, but refrains from dragging the conversation out.

Doctor Morris nods. "I have faith in our therapist." His eyes divert to Doctor Hoyt.

The therapist remains unfazed while everyone agrees in silence.

Linda smiles. "There's no one better for the job. I think Doctor Hoyt can get to the bottom of this." Her eyes move to Hoyt, then dart off in another thought. "I'm a little concerned why Clay hasn't mentioned his family yet. The first thing I would think if I woke up like…"

"…'What about my family?'" Monica adds.

"Or friends." Elizabeth says "Anyone he lost…"

The women nod in agreement.

The Captain nods with a frowned brow.

Doctor Hoyt smiles at their observational skill.

Peter looks toward the therapist. "So, you think the patient will comply?"

Hoyt wrinkles his crow's feet. "I'll give it my best, Captain."

The team smiles, but the Captain looks long at Doctor Hoyt.

"You have something you want to add…" He says with a smirk.

Hoyt nods "You know me too well…"

The Captain nods "Let's hear it."

Hoyt shrugs.

"If we're having him on here…" He says "… then I'd like to bump up your monthly visits. At least once a week…"

The team has an audible silence; marking their polite disapproval.

Hoyt smirks around the circle.

"Oh I'm not that bad…" He says "…Am I?"

The Captain shrugs with a smile.

"Alright, fair enough then." He says "Now, let's go see our new friend."

Down the hall the department heads enter the room with Doctor Clay. The large room is full of faces, yet it remains quiet.

Doctor Lawrence looks to Julius, but finds no avail in his eyes. At the least he shows an eagerness to speak, but little to say.

"Douglas" Peter begins. "We've decided to extend the services of our friend Doctor Hoyt. He's in charge of managing our mental health, and he makes for a great therapist." The Captain moves closer to the machine and opens with a side step to allow Doctor Hoyt to stand beside him. "While you might not see it now, this change will be hard to handle. We'll help you acclimate to these changes, and maybe even help to recover your memories."

"Thank you." The mechanical voice responds.

"Of course." Peter says "Is there any time you would like to schedule?"

"I can start whenever. Although, I like to work out in the mornings."

The Captain looks confused for a moment, then laughs. The room slowly laughs with him.

Doctor Hoyt steps forward. "How about tomorrow night?"

"I'll be sure to be here." Doug's voice replies.

The room laughs again.

Hoyt waves his finger with a smirk. "Stay right where you are."

"Got nothing better to do."

The crew looks on with smiles. A trickling begins at the edges of the room. Assistants begin to take their leave and return to their labs.

The Captain raises his hands for attention. "Alright everyone! Thank you for all your help! I'm sorry the ping-pong tables had to go, but sacrifices are necessary. Let's get back to work."

All move back to their stations, leaving the computer behind.

Doctor Morris approaches the Captain outside the room and motions his head to speak alone with him.

The Captain follows behind him to another corner, far from the room.

Once safely out of earshot, Morris mutters to the Captain. "What about the other thing?"

The Captain fixes his brows together in a questioning stare.

Morris leans in and the Captain turns his ear toward the historian.

"Project Icarus…" Morris says.

The Captain shakes his head.

"I wouldn't worry about that." He says "Keep it between us for now."

"… Are you sure?" Morris asks.

The Captain nods.

Down the hall, Julius moves to catch up with Elizabeth. She waits at the entryway to another hall, and once Julius catches up, she begins walking again. He follows beside her, and leans with his ear in her direction.

"Captain wants our technologies kept a secret." She says.

Julius gathers his brows. "Why don't we take him apart?"

"They decided it wasn't right to look through his mind." She shakes her head. "I think it's a better option, but Hoyt's gonna get to the bottom of it, and that's good enough for me."

Julius shrugs.

"What did you find out?" Elizabeth asks.

Julius draws back a corner of his mouth. "We tried to make small talk but he wasn't having it. His eye thing was adjusting again and again." Julius points his fingers together on one hand. He begins expanding and retracting them from that centered point. "I don't know if he was trying to get it focused or what."

Elizabeth frowns her brows. "Keep me posted on what you find out."

"You think he's hiding something?"

They turn the corner into their lab.

"Well, something doesn't add up." Elizabeth raises the back of her finger to her lip, then moves it below to speak "He should have memories from after the procedure, but he claims that he doesn't."

Julius gathers his brows. "How do you know he has memories from after the procedure?"

"I looked at his hardware while they were moving him. He reads and writes on quartz crystal. He forgets nothing and has no shortage of space."

Julius' face falls "That's kinda creepy."

"His power is remarkable." She says. "He might not have arms or legs but he makes up for it."

"Do you think he's killed people?" Julius asks.

"He was in a government research facility. He was between two floors loaded with weapons." She raises her brows and glances to the side to meet his eyes. "I think he at least knows something about killing."

Julius becomes withdrawn in thought. "What if he had access to something? What if he killed everyone on Earth?"

She shakes her head. "He only had a power source, and no other cables. He has no wireless functions, I've checked."

Julius nods.

Elizabeth goes on "He's hiding something, I just don't know what. Can you keep an eye out?"

"You've got it boss."

She shakes her head. "Don't call me boss."

"Sorry, queen."

She taps his shoulder with a sideways fist and Julius laughs.

CHAPTER 12
Beyond the Hexagon Sky

Boots meet the concrete, and echo in the dark. Steel beams cross each other, intersecting into triangular shapes. They make ex-shapes between long beams, running the length to a distant ceiling in the dark.

A stairwell hikes up around the beams. It ascends along the walls of a tower inside the John West building. Between the beams, there are steel chords. They belong to a cargo elevator that lies on the ground floor; and there, several tunnels recede into the land. The tunnels open miles away to the major farming communities around New Memphis. The elevator was used for cargo trucks, to take materials in and out of the city. They distribute supplies between the northern communities; all centralized in this tower of glass.

Julius looks over the railing and to the depths below. Somewhere down there, they left the outside world to come here; a quiet place in the middle of a battlefield.

"Zero." Chief says.

Julius turns to Chief.

"You and Pluto go to the forty-second floor." Chief says. His face drips with sweat. "The three of us are going for thirty-six." he adds "Call if you need us."

"Right." Pluto says.

Julius and Pluto pass Dash, Chief, and Cricket to ascend the stairs. Dash pats Julius as he passes.

"Good luck." He says. He then pats Pluto and reiterates "Good luck."

They continue on in a hastened pace. The large painted numbers on the concrete walls begin to climb "36, 37,38". Julius can feel the countdown. The numbers pass to signal the end of their time to a potential contact with the enemy. At the fortieth floor, he stops to let Pluto catch his breath.

Pluto holds the railing, and Julius looks down at the lights of the other three men. They walk into the door on their floor, and Pluto is left alone with Julius in the stairwell.

Julius looks back at him "Does it feel weird?" He asks; the question comes like it's spoken by a child, looking to establish a new friend. "Coming here at a time like this?"

Pluto stops from his labored breath to nod "Fighting a war in my home city?" He says "Yeah… it's weird."

Julius nods "Do you think we can come back after this?" He asks "Maybe we can actually enjoy it."

Pluto laughs "Absolutely."

Julius smiles.

"My sister used to love this place." Pluto says "My sister loves shopping… She has a spending habit."

Julius laughs, then looks to the dark "Is that what this place is? A shopping mall?"

"This is West Tower, kid. The biggest symbol in New Memphis."

"This is a landmark?" asks Julius.

"The most important one." says Pluto "A shopping mall, office buildings, distribution center, you name it."

"Why call it 'West Tower' if it's in the south center of the city?"

Pluto laughs. He shakes his head "It was named after a GUY named West. A senator."

"Oh" Julius says "that's confusing."

"It is!" says Pluto. He smiles as he looks around "… This place is full of memories…"

Julius looks on, waiting for more to be said.

Pluto sighs "The girl I used to see who worked here in high school… The time I was caught shoplifting…"

"Shoplifting?" Asks Julius.

Pluto nods and looks off to the side "Ooh yeah… Mom wanted to kill me…" He looks up at Julius "That girl I dated… She used to work her tail off but they paid her under the table… meanwhile I shoplifted all the time." Pluto shrugs "I had the mentality of, you know 'the CEO is probably some rich kid who never had to work a day in his life. He had a company handed down to him and now I'm here, scraping for the things he'd consider commoner's trash.'… I was wrong, but I didn't know any better at the time. I actually met the CEO of a company store I used to steal from. He was a really nice guy but… I digress…" Dash sniffles "… Point is; I got good at stealing…" He shrugs again "… So, when my girlfriend couldn't afford something, I added up her hours to find that the legal pay was enough to afford it… The problem is, she was being paid under the table; less than minimum wage… So I stole the damned thing… Never stole anything that expensive before. An employee knew who I was and was eyeing me down. Almost got away with it, but I was with my buddy who wasn't used to stealing. I booked it when the employee came after me, but my friend was too afraid to run… I walked back to him and surprisingly the store let me go."

Julius gathers his brows.

"Why'd they let you go?" He asks.

Pluto chuckles "Because I didn't abandon my friend."

Julius frowns with interest. He nods at Pluto, as if to tell him that he's a good man.

Pluto stands up straight and gives a last huff of breath.

"I think I'm good now." He says "Story time is over."

Julius begins ascending the steps.

Pluto talks while he continues to walk "My mom came here with me once."

"Oh, is it still story time?" Asks Julius. He looks back at Pluto with a sarcastic grin.

Pluto laughs.

"I know what I said…" He says.

Julius laughs as he continues up the steps.

"So your mom…?"

Pluto nods "… Yeah, my mom…. she introduced me to a friend; some jeweler she knew from high school." He smiles, without the breath to laugh "She said 'Be good to people, no matter what'. When I asked her why, she told me that the jeweler was picked on; back when they were kids. He was a little weird. His sense of humor was offensive, and he'd often say the wrong thing at the worst possible moment." He manages to work up enough air for a little laughter "My mom was queen shit back in high school, but she treated him as a friend." His brows come up with another thought crossing his mind "My mom is a religious lady. She believed that his help, and his appreciation of her, was a sign that God's way is right."

"And what's God's way?"

Pluto laughs and stops walking. Julius pauses with him.

"You're funny." Pluto says. His laugh has little breath in it "Forgive-ness." He says, catching his breath on the forty-first floor "Even if someone offends you, even if they're evil or bad; they're still human."

He motions his hand at the door to the forty-first floor "Think about it." He says "If I still lived here, there's a chance I'd be fighting for the other side. Either out of fear; or maybe, I'd be a true believer. I'm not any more human than them."

Julius nods. He's conflicted with the moral question in his mind. To think that a friend he's never met could be lying on the other end of his gun. At the moment a stranger, but in another life, a familiar face.

"Why are you fighting, then?" says Julius.

"Free tuition." Pluto laughs.

Julius begins laughing with him. A well-needed lifting of his spirit.

Pluto collects his laughter and corrects his prior statement "No, no." He says. He stands straight, correcting his posture to allow air into his lungs.

"It's 'cause I know it's right." Pluto says. He takes a deep breath "If they have their way, hundreds or thousands of people could die. Just look at the piles of bodies they burned. They burned books by the thousands because it contradicted their belief." Pluto takes a sigh "I kill, not because killing is right; but because they need to be stopped, before they can kill more innocent people."

Julius looks down to the darkness below. He nods and sighs. He then looks at Pluto.

"Some nasty shit we're involved with." Julius says.

Pluto looks conflicted, but smothers the thought in a nod "Yeah, it is. Are you ready?"

Julius nods. He turns to continue up the steps.

On the forty-second floor, Pluto and Julius take either side of the door. Their knees are bent in a ready stance. Pluto looks at Julius' gun and sees his jacket is caught on a part of the stock. Pluto reaches over and moves his jacket from interfering with the gun.

Julius looks down to what he didn't notice, then up to Pluto.

Pluto nods as if to say 'I've got you'. He then looks down at the light under the door. There's no movement. He looks up at Julius.

"You ready?" He mouths.

Julius nods.

Julius turns the handle of the door while Pluto moves the door with his forearm. He moves quickly through the door and Julius steps in toward his backside. They move into the area, looking in either direction. It's a long hall to either side, and a wall of windows to the north.

Julius backpedals on the carpet and scans the room. Pluto comes to a corner and rests his back against the wall. He looks back at Julius, then prepares himself to look around the corner. His small glance reveals that the way is clear. He pats Julius. They advance to the hall.

Julius backpedals and turns the corner. He's stopped by another pat on the shoulder. He gets to one knee. It's the signal to hold at the sight of something.

"It's just a buzzard." Pluto says.

Julius rises out of formation and turns to see a small swarm-copter. It advances down the hall.

"They cleared these floors?" asks Julius.

"I guess so." Says Pluto.

The buzzard approaches. It gives a green light at the sight of their faces.

"To think" Pluto says "It's only an AI that makes this weapon our friend. Just an error in the program, and we'd be dead."

Julius scrunches his brow "What do you mean?"

Pluto smiles. He nods at the buzzard "They use facial recognition. The AI hunts down anyone without a face in their database."

Julius watches the machine and wonders how many innocent people it's killed with its loose protocol.

Pluto looks long at the machine to analyze its inventory as it passes. He notices an empty cartridge where it used to hold explosives.

"It's all out of breaching equipment." Pluto says.

Julius looks at Pluto "You think someone might still be up here?"

Pluto turns to look down the hall. He looks around for the signs of a barricade, away from the buzzard.

"Maybe." He says.

Julius looks around. He's just now noticing the view from outside the large windows. They stand high above the ground, looking out toward Seventh Street. It runs west to the enemy territory. They're too high for the snipers to get a proper shot.

Pluto points to a broken window at the end of the hall "That must be where he came in."

"Who?" Julius asks.

"The buzzard."

They approach the opening in the glass and turn the corner at the end of the west hall. To the south, the city stretches toward Eden. To the east there is a hall of blood and bodies.

Julius steps forward. He finds scorch marks at the mouth of a hall running into the heart of the building.

Julius and Pluto prepare themselves to search the scorched hall. They stand at the corner. Pluto rounds the corner slowly. He moves in and steps to the side, allowing Julius to come have a look. Julius follows him and looks on before them.

A large bank vault is covered in black soot. It's sustained minimal damage, but the striations of black spread from the blast center.

"There's someone in there." Pluto says.

Julius looks to their side and sees two-liter soda bottles with yellow fluid. It's urine.

Julius pats Pluto. Pluto looks and Julius points at the bottles.

"Sniper." says Julius.

"Looks like we've found our guy." Pluto says.

Julius becomes curious and looks back into the hall of bodies. He's surprised to see a body rise up in a pushup. The man's face turns to Julius. Julius raises his gun.

"Hands!" Julius yells "Hands! Hands!"

The man reaches for a gun at his belt.

Pluto grabs Julius and rips him from the hallway. A round is fired and hits the wall above the bottles.

"They're alive!" Pluto says.

They take either side of the bank vault hall. The living rise from beneath the bodies and run for the ends of the hall. Julius steps out and watches the buzzard emerge. It shoots with precision and chases the enemy.

Pluto advances to the hall with Julius. He backpedals while Julius leads. A wall bursts open and buzzards pour in to help them.

People scream at the horror of their ravenous autonomy. They move between targets without thought. With each burst of rounds, the computation has one message "Task complete. Task complete. Task complete".

Julius comes to a room with a closed door. He stands at the side of it. A buzzard comes to the door and waits. Julius opens the door. It flies in. Shots overwhelm the room and Julius moves in behind the buzzard.

He sees the buzzard on the ground, smoking and broken. The man in the corner fires at Julius.

"Get down!" Julius yells.

Pluto turns around and fires at the man in the corner. The man's arms are minced away from his own gun. The man sways and falls with eyes rolling upward.

Pluto looks to see blood stains swelling from Julius' lower abdomen.

"Zero, you're bleeding." Pluto says.

Julius shakes his head "I'm fine."

"Take a seat, I'll call Cricket."

Julius sees a man come from the shadows behind Pluto.

***

Julius looks at his journal. An old one from a long time ago. The pages have changed color. The cover is made up of a cheap plastic.

> *The memory goes blank from here. I don't know what happened after that, but others reported the same phenomenon. I often wonder if I should envy them; for not remembering the war. But the haunting notion implied by the loss of consciousness; that seems far worse.*

Julius wonders about this passage; hoping that the sight of Earth may have stirred up his forgotten memory.

He can't remember what happened then, in West Tower. He only has this faint memory; of looking out toward the city; and Pluto holding him; and crying.

CHAPTER 13
Brother

Kyle parks his car behind the pharmacy in downtown Eden. His ashtray is stacked with cigarettes. It spills soot on the center console of his car. He takes his last drag of a cigarette and aims for an open space among the pile. He presses into the ash and another butt falls.

"Ah, fuck!" He hisses.

In a reluctant way, he is forced by the limits of the tray. At this point, he's made to dispose of its contents. He lifts the tray from his vehicle and exits the car. He approaches a trash receptacle behind the pharmacy and spills it into the barrel. He smacks the tray on the rim of the barrel to be sure it's empty. A young man, about thirteen, has a chance meeting with Kyle by the trash.

The boy looks at his face, and Kyle returns a noticing glance. The boy's trash is nothing more than candy wrappers. Kyle thinks that he probably stole the candy, like he did at the age of thirteen.

The boy then runs to his bike where his friends are. They mount their bikes at the back entrance to the pharmacy. They pedal away, and Kyle remembers his thrill-seeking nature at their age; how abiding by rules was dreadful to him. He graduated to a car, and now his parents are financially out of the picture; ever since he dropped law school. The most he's provided is a place in his father's condo, and even that is on the verge of being taken away.

Kyle makes his way for the pharmacy entrance. Inside, he makes his way to the prescription counter, deep in the back of the store. The woman behind the counter seems to recognize him, but not by name.

"Name?" She asks.

"Kyle Lawrence." He replies.

She sees the name of the medication and seems aggravated to get the package.

Kyle feels her judgement as she walks to the back of the pharmacy. When she returns, he feels obligated to be extra nonchalant.

"You can put your card in." She says.

Kyle looks off to the side and sees a stand displaying night lights. He remembers Elizabeth's fear of the dark as a child. Their father would insist that she sleep in the darkness to "get over it". She hated it; and, while Kyle was so young, he remembers having the foresight to give her one of his toys when he learned of her anxiety.

It was a light-up robot that ran on batteries. Buttons would activate more lights and sounds, but the one switch on the back would activate an internal green glow that could illuminate her room ever so slightly.

One night, Elizabeth reached under her mattress to take the robot from its hiding place. She placed a new set of batteries in the back of the toy and flipped the switch to activate its alien glow. Her hand slipped when she placed the robot on her nightstand. A loud buzzing screeched out of the toy's speakers. Blue and red lights began flashing and soon the sound of footsteps came to the door.

Their father threw the toy in the garbage the following morning, but Kyle had a glowing sword for her to use in its place. Their persistence was disobedience in their father's eyes, and likely gained the ire of his disapproval.

Kyle sighs

"Hold on." He says to the cashier.

He strides over to the stand and chooses a warm glowing crystal to bring to the cashier.

He takes out his wallet and finds his card amid the clutter. It protrudes from torn leather and cloth. The cashier scans the item and waits yet again.

He places the card in, then looks in the bag while the charge goes through.

"*Azithromycin*" The package reads. Nothing telling of what it is, but his frequency in the clinic could've given the pharmacist an idea of what he has.

"You're all set." She says. Her voice is a little kinder this time.

"Thank you." Kyle replies.

He leaves the store and enters his car again. In the driver's seat he picks up his phone.

"*It came back positive?*" The text says.

Kyle begins typing "*Yes. I'm sorry, you should probably get tested.*"

He buckles himself and opens the medication. The phone goes off and he reads again "*What was it?*"

Kyle types "*Chlamydia*".

The response comes soon after "*Nothing else?*"

Kyle rolls his eyes "*Nothing else.*"

"*You'd tell me?*" the response says.

Kyle laughs "You fuckin' kidding me?" He says to himself.

"*I'd tell you.*" Kyle responds, shaking his head.

Kyle leaves his text messages and opens a dating app to see a new message. It stands out amid discarded conversations. He opens the new message from a woman named "*Olivia*".

"*Does your brother like football?*" The message reads.

Kyle is confused by his repetition of small talk. He can't recall their conversation, so he scrolls up and reads:

> "**Kyle**: I just got a call from my dad. I've gotta watch my little brother tonight. Sorry the plan got messed up
>
> **Olivia**: Oh, you have a little brother? How old?
>
> **Kyle**: He's about to be six
>
> **Olivia**: Oh, he's young. My brother is 13.
>
> **Kyle**: That's still pretty young
>
> **Olivia**: I was going to say, we could get them to hang out together lol.
>
> **Kyle**: The age gap is real haha
>
> **Olivia**: Hold on a sec.
>
> **Olivia**: Does your brother like football?"

Kyle is caught up now, but still unsure where this is going.

"*He hasn't played yet. He'll be playing someday, though.*" He wonders if he's being too brief. He begins typing, feeling guilty for his brevity "*Probably when he's your brother's age.*"

Kyle locks his phone and puts the car in reverse.

On the road to his mother's house, Kyle comes to the Northwest Train Gate. It is west of the William Lawrence Tunnel, which runs north to New Memphis.

Here at the Train Gate, daily commuters take the line to suburban bubbles outside of Eden. It's a quiet hour with very little traffic.

Kyle pulls into a parking lot where people leave their cars to take the passenger train into suburbia. Kyle passes through the parking lot and waits behind an arm gate. He waits a while, then assumes that something is wrong. The arm hasn't lifted, but it's supposed to respond immediately.

He looks to make sure he still has his electronic pass. It remains behind his rearview mirror, attached to the windshield at the top. The gate lifts and Kyle stops looking. He puts the car in drive and comes through the gate.

Kyle pulls up to a platform train, where cars park on flatbeds that occupy the whole length of a magnetic structure. Cars take the open spots along the line of parking spaces. A large glass dome closes in each car to keep them secure for the ride.

The few car commuters take their spaces. Not many are here, on the off hour between the morning and afternoon traffic.

Kyle watches other people move about and struggle to park on the train platforms. He sighs and wants to take out another cigarette, but smoking isn't permitted on the train itself. He sighs and feels his heart race with impatience. His muscles ache from the damage he's done from it. He's tried quitting, but he finds himself smoking each time he's stuck in the agonizing seconds between objectives. Every day feels like an onslaught of objectives until he's graced with a moment to fall asleep; but by that time, he wants to forget about the monotony; even if just for a moment. He watches something that interests him. He tries again to find a meaningful conversation on a dating app. Each time he feels guilty for cutting into his time to sleep. By the morning, he is exhausted, and on his way to another series of tasks.

"It's my fault for smoking." He thinks *"Life didn't feel like this before I started."*

He begins to remember the girl in high school with the pretty eyes. She had a mature manner about her. It made her unattainable to anyone in his class.

Just for the sake of talking with her, he decided to ask for a cigarette. With the strike of her match, he took up conversation with the impossible woman. She was a woman in a class full of children, and he was a flirt who took the smoke as a joke to win the attention of her eyes.

The conversation is a lost memory to him. The impression she gave is now like the coals of a fire pit on an early morning. The fire has been gone for a long time, but the heat was still there for a while. It lasted until the coals lost their glow. They became a blackened husk of what they used to be; a golden brown wood. Like the majesty of an old mahogany item; she had that allure once, and that was when he met her. Class and elegance permeated about her, but she was under the illusion that it was the glow of the fire that was her glory. It was in her mahogany eyes that he could get lost and happily never find his way back. Her posture, and the air of confidence she had; a power she would wield with a humble hand. The true power of tenderness atop the high ground of a battlefield. She was merciful when she held all the hearts in her hands.

She lost her allure when she went down a path that he refused to follow. Her mercy brought her to love a hopeless creature with an insatiable desire for false-footed affections. Blind love that sought to refute the objective universe; a losing battle from the start. The parasite cheated and used drugs. He brought her down with ideas of "pulling through" despite their "hardships". She was a kind soul, and her giving nature was abused by the leech she found in Eden's shadowy boroughs. The parasite believed himself to be reasonable, and she was convinced of his conviction. He was lost, and not in her eyes; so she gave pursuit until she too was lost. After long, she forgot her former glory; or at least it's a memory that brings her sorrow in periods of calm amid the storm of her newfound life.

She's now that withered husk of charred coal, skulking the streets of South East Eden; the wrong neighborhood, where people seek respite in a fix.

"It must feel this way" He thinks, reflecting on his smoking habit "But worse."

The glass domes shut over the parked vehicles along the train cars. The speakers chime to the voice of a woman. She delivers the rules of the railway, ending on the closing gratitude for compliance. Soon after the train begins to accelerate, and Kyle watches the desert floor move across his windshield.

The expanse before him opens out to the north where the distant city of New Memphis rests, nestled in the valley. To the west, and closer to

Eden, the peak of Mount Pemigewasset is capped with snow and ice. Its cascading falls crash into myriads of mists amid the hidden places behind its prominent crags. The atmosphere defines independent spires on the mountainside where starlight graces its defiant landforms.

"*I'd still love to go there.*" He thinks.

He remembers his childhood fantasy of exploring the mountains. He thought he would be a geologist, or perhaps something like it. He knows the far-off natural wonders of the world. To the west, and miles beyond civilization, there's an active volcano surrounded by geothermal vents and sulfuric pools. The caves there are undisturbed mouths of color. They're considered among the natural wonders of Zion, but no one is permitted to see them except scientists. Kyle remembers learning about them in class. The story of a primordial monument had him enthralled as a child.

His teacher was Mr. Weber, and his charisma made a moment where Kyle actually enjoyed school. It's a moment that Kyle emulates when talking with children. He tries to recite Mr. Weber's enthusiasm when speaking to his brother about the world.

Kyle smiles "*I'm looking forward to seeing my pal.*" He thinks.

***

Kyle's mother lives off of a side street that loops around and meets the very same road, whichever way is taken. The house is a shell that reminds each passerby that her children have flown the coup. On a hillside above a quiet street, there lies a cookie-cutter home with typical panels, typical paint, and typical light fixtures. The breadth of a vast sloping lawn is cut to the same length as the properties adjacent to it, and all the other properties on the island making the center of Malory Circle.

At the edges of the road, marking the outside of Malory Circle, the properties across the way from his mother's house are similar in style. From one of those houses, there comes the smell of synthetic marijuana, not unlike Kyle's cigarettes.

Kyle looks across the way from the front door of his mother's house. He takes a whiff to confirm his suspicion. The thought brings him to giggle about it.

His mother opens the door. She gives a sigh of a cry in her voice.

"My baby's home!" She says.

He catches her embrace and smiles over her shoulder.

"For a little bit." He laughs.

"Please tell me you've come to stay." She says "Not in that nasty city."

Kyle laughs.

"I can't." He says.

In reality he wouldn't opt into it either.

She releases him from the hug and Kyle walks into the main hall of his old home. It's the same make as all the other houses in the neighborhood.

Before the entryway is a staircase leading to three bedrooms. An office to the right, a "family room" to the left, and a hall to the kitchen underneath the steps. There, one can find the living room to the right; somehow serving a different function from the so-called "family room".

This layout is something Kyle has considered the "middle-class, wannabe-wealthy" home. Not as an insult, but a grouping of people that Kyle has developed pity for.

Kyle has watched several families stew behind closed doors about their financial struggle to keep this facade. Many of those families took on crippling debt to have a home worth bragging about. At least, it was the case for the piers from whence they came. With a newfound desire to fit among their newer, more wealthy piers; it tends to keep them living by the paycheck, despite their considerable salaries. This neighborhood is too ordinary for the wealthy, and too wealthy for the humble.

Kyle walks to the kitchen and sees an open wine bottle on the countertop. Kyle points at it and raises his brows. His mother picks it up and walks to the sink. She pours the bottle into the sink.

"It's old." She says "Don't you even think about it."

"I'm not about to steal your booze, Ma."

"You and your friends cost me hundreds of dollars." She remarks.

He laughs "Speaking of that, did you smell the kid across the way?"

"The Harrisons' kid?" She says. She places the bottle by the sink "Yeah, it's like clockwork. Every day after school."

Kyle laughs "No kiddin.'"

His mother raises her brows and nods "He's found the devil's lettuce."

Kyle smiles with a shake of his head.

"Too funny." He says.

She smiles out toward the main hall "I remember when you were doing that; when Harrison was just a little fella in his car. You remember that thing?"

Kyle nods "I do."

They sigh from the fond memory. His mother turns her head.

"So what are you looking for?" She asks "Money?"

Kyle shakes his head.

"No, I was gonna get something out of the attic" He says "from my memory chest."

"What did you need?" She asks.

"You remember that geology book with the pictures in it?"

His mom nods with her brows gathered "Yeah."

Kyle nods "I was thinking of taking that to little Steve."

His mom sighs "Oh God, Kyle please don't lose it. You were so cute with that thing!"

Kyle nods "I know, Mum. Stevie can take care of it." He puts up his hand in a promise "Trust me." he adds.

"You were all into those gemstones and the magma…" His mom begins her walk to the front hall.

Kyle follows behind her and up the steps. He smiles recalling it.

At the ladder to the attic, his mother stops.

"Make sure that treacherous cunt doesn't do anything to it." She adds.

Kyle shakes his head in shock "Trech… who?"

"Your father." She says "And that ho-bag he's with."

Kyle purses his lips in a half smile.

"They won't" He says "and can you not call him that?"

His mother ascends the ladder but stops.

"He IS one!" She remarks in humor.

Kyle shrugs, then shakes his head.

"I won't deny, Dad sucks!" Kyle adds "But the C word is just so jarring, Ma; you could pick something more tasteful than that."

His mom shrugs "How about a shit-covered dick?"

Kyle is stunned. The waves of a jolting laugh rise up from his abs.

"That's oddly specific" He says "but I'll take it."

His mom giggles to herself and opens the door to the dark, wheatwood attic. She ascends the steps and he follows behind, stopping at the threshold of the floor. He peers around the darkness. The light comes on to show his chest, resting by Elizabeth's. He looks to his mom by the light switch.

"It's right over there." She says.

Kyle comes up through the hole in the floor and approaches his chest. As he begins digging through its contents, his mother begins to saunter about the room.

"I can't believe they had a kid." She says with bitterness.

Kyle finds the book he's looking for.

"He's really nice." Kyle says.

He closes the chest.

"No, I know." She says "I met him at your graduation party." His mom looks to the floor with a bittersweet smile.

Kyle looks at her, knowing she misses their youth. Perhaps she misses their father too.

Kyle seeks to keep her from the sorrow. He looks to the corner where her paintings collect dust in the far reaches of the attic.

"Have you gotten back into painting yet?" He asks.

His mother sighs "Oh, I think about it every once in a while, but I find it hard to keep inspired."

Kyle sees the layer of dust and remembers his mom just after his parents separated. She kept trying to sell some paintings, to make a living of it. It didn't take long until she took up a small sales job, forgetting her talent entirely. Her effort was dwindling, perhaps from a complacency she found. Considering the magnitude of his father's wealth, the child support must have been considerate. The settlement alone almost paid for this house in full.

He remembers Elizabeth's frustration. She looked to her mother as a role model that lost her way, but Kyle knows her psychological barrier. It's the same fight that he contends with, and he's almost the same as her in every way. His compassion, and a desire for perfection brings him to a standstill; compiled with an empathy that brings problems beyond his own making. Elizabeth, in contrast, would hate to admit that she's the spitting image of her father; cold and calculated. Like her father, she refuses to be weak.

Kyle feels for his mother's loss. He knows that he holds a special place in her heart.

"You have a talent, Muma" He says "Don't waste it."

He gives her a hug. He encourages her with a warm laugh over her shoulder.

"Oh, dear." She says "Thank you."

Her hands clasp her only son; the one man she can hold faith in.

★

Kyle parks in front of his father's house. Stephen sees him from the front door and runs across the lawn. His backpack is stuffed with drawing supplies and clothes.

His dad stands at the front door. He puts up a hand, as if it's meant to be a wave. His hand doesn't wave, but drops to his side. He turns his back after finishing the obligation, then opens the door to step inside.

Kyle steps out of his car. He was ready for a conversation, but the door closes before it can happen.

"Cool…" Kyle mutters "Nice to see ya."

Stephen collides with his legs.

"Woah!" Kyle says.

"I've been getting ready for football!" Stephen says.

"Really?" Kyle asks "That was pretty good!" He takes Stephen's bag "Do you want to see a football game?"

"Yeah!" Stephen says.

Kyle begins walking to the driver's side door, but stops before crossing the car. He pulls out his old geology book in an afterthought.

"By the way" He says "I got this for ya."

Stephen takes it and walks to the passenger door. Kyle walks around, then enters the driver's door.

"It used to be mine." Kyle says, sitting in the driver's seat "Will you keep it safe for me?"

Stephen looks at the book and opens it. His face lights up at the pictures of natural wonders. He looks up at Kyle, then nods.

***

Kyle pulls into the parking lot of a high school football field. The gated arena is adorned with banners that read "*Home of the South West Lions*" and "*511 Champions*". The lights stand tall above a hill, and there, a crowd can be heard. Children run around with their friends; climbing rocks and playing tag under the bleachers.

Kyle sees Olivia standing by the steps that lead to the football field. Stephen keeps in step with him, and Kyle approaches Olivia.

She walks his way in a leather jacket and tight grey jeans. Her blonde curls bounce around her glitter-shadowed eyes.

Olivia hugs Kyle, then looks down at Stephen.

"You must be little Stevie!" She says.

She puts her hand out and bends her knees in a squat. Stephen shakes her hand in a polite way, just as his mother taught him to.

Olivia stands, but remains bent to refer to Stephen.

"Are you ready for some football?" She asks.

Stephen nods.

Olivia looks to Kyle and hugs him again.

"It's nice to finally meet you." She says.

Kyle laughs over her shoulder "Likewise."

They break from their hug and Kyle looks at Stephen.

"Alright pal." He says "You ready?"

Stephen nods, then skips over to his brother. Kyle leans down as Stephen covers his mouth for a whisper.

"Who is she?" Stephen asks.

"This is Olivia." Kyle says "We're here to see her brother's football game."

Stephen's big eyes stay close behind his brother.

"Come on." Kyle says.

He begins walking and Stephen walks double his pace to keep up. Olivia swings her steps as she walks next to Kyle. They ascend the steps and she begins breaking the ice all over again, as if they hadn't been speaking for months.

"Did you play football?" She asks.

"Yeah" Kyle says "I played North West Ridge."

"Private school boy." She says. She nods "Okay. Okay."

Kyle laughs "What about you?"

She shakes her head "No, the girls' team wasn't that big in my school."

Kyle notices Stephen has stopped. He's looking at a sign by the entrance. It reads "*Stephen Lawrence Field*". Kyle smiles and winks. He makes a "*Shhh*" motion toward his mouth.

Olivia's noticed that they've stopped. She continues up the steps to not feel rude. She would hate to invade on their brotherly moment; though, she doesn't know what it's about.

Stephen walks up the steps to Kyle. His brows are screwed-up in a question. Kyle leans down.

He tells Stephen in a mumble "Uncle Steve paid for this field" Kyle raises a brow, then nudges his hand in a slashing motion "But don't say anything."

"Why not?" Stephen asks.

Kyle shrugs "Sometimes it's good to keep who we are a secret."

He nudges Stephen with his elbow and winks. Stephen smiles and nods. It's now become their secret.

Kyle stands erect and looks up the steps at Olivia. She's now standing just beyond the gate and looking at the field. Kyle looks back at Stephen and smiles. He begins to laugh at the wide-eyed face.

It's the first time he's collaborated with Stevie on women. His father and Uncle Steve were known for going out together and picking up women on college campuses. Their brotherly banter would recall days long ago, when their father got food poisoning and had to cancel a date. Another told about Uncle Steve being forced into a fight. The man later gave Uncle Steve a beer stein and claimed he was the "*champion*" and that it was his "*trophy*".

Kyle knows that this will likely be the only time he can recall with his own brother. He'll be older when Stephen starts dating, and likely married with children.

Stephen gathers his brows.

"What?" He asks.

Stephen begins to smile and looks to see if he's stepped in something. He then looks down at his shirt to see if there's a stain.

Kyle shakes his head.

"You're gonna be a lady killer." He says.

Stephen laughs "I wouldn't kill anyone."

Stephen hits his brother on the arm.

Kyle shakes his head and picks Stephen up "That's not what I mean." He walks up the steps with Stephen in his arm "I just mean that girls are gonna be after you." He adjusts Stephen to his hip, allowing him to carry Stephen with ease "You're gonna break a lot of hearts."

He reaches the top step and puts Stephen down. While Stephen doesn't understand what Kyle's just said, he doesn't care. He runs to the fence that surrounds the track encompassing the field.

Kyle looks up at Olivia. She's smiling at him. He looks to his brother again, but addresses Olivia.

"What?" Kyle asks.

Stephen stands still, looking at the field to take in the sight.

"You're just funny." Olivia says.

Kyle looks her way "Funny how?"

He looks back to Stephen. Stephen looks up at him with a question, but he gives up on asking. He then walks ahead, toward the bleachers.

"You just are." Olivia says "Helping him up the steps; you're a good brother."

"Little shit was taking too long." Kyle laughs.

Olivia smirks.

"No, I saw that." She says "You care about him."

Kyle shrugs "He's the only brother I have. I have a sister, but she's older than me."

"Did you always want a little brother?" asks Olivia.

"Oh, without a doubt." he says "Being the youngest sucks. All the attention is on you for a bit; and you have all this advice and no one to give it to."

"And the oldest thinks they know everything." Olivia says.

Kyle laughs "Yeah, she does."

"My older brother Kyle is like that." says Olivia.

Kyle gathers his brows and tilts his head.

Olivia laughs and Kyle looks her way.

"I know!" She says "You have the same name as my brother."

Kyle lets out a gust of a laugh.

"Does that feel weird?" He asks.

"No!" Olivia says "There's a million Kyles so I've had to get used to it. My first crush was a Kyle."

Kyle puts up a hand as if to hold the conversation.

"I hope it's not the same one." he says.

Olivia laughs "No! No relation."

Kyle is amused by her response and repeats "No relation?"

Olivia continues to repeat "No, no, no…"

Kyle looks up at Stephen. He points at an empty spot in the steps. Kyle follows up to him, then ascends the steps to where Stephen pointed.

"Good spot, pal." Kyle says.

"Which one is your brother?" Stephen asks Olivia.

"He's number fifty-three." She tells them.

Kyle looks down at the field. He looks at the offensive line and sees a noticeably small boy. He's number fifty-three on the South West Lions.

"The small kid?" Kyle asks.

Olivia nods.

"He's the smallest on the line." She says. Her voice comes with a bit of pride.

Kyle looks a while at the boy who plays left guard. He then notices a larger boy at quarterback, and a six-foot Goliath playing running back. A pair of lanky kids stand at the ends of the line. They're receivers; but at this age, there's likely to be no passing plays.

Kyle screws up his brows.

He mutters to Olivia "Who's the fat kid playing halfback?"

The crowd around Kyle gets quiet. He notices, but doesn't care.

Olivia is hesitant to respond.

"Who?" She asks.

"The behemoth" Kyle says "behind the quarterback."

"That's Lyle." Olivia adds "He's the captain."

Kyle points at the field "What's your brother doing on the line if they have a kid like that?"

She raises her brows and shrugs "He's fast."

Kyle shakes his head "Not as fast as your brother, I bet." he then laughs "Whose kid is he?"

Eyes glance his way, but Kyle is more disgusted by their attentive ears. They listen closely to him, instead of talking with one another. They likely had the prescribed intention of listening. Knowing small-town gossip, they probably wanted to get a scoop on who Olivia has brought to the game.

Olivia is still hesitant to answer again, but she's liked Kyle thus far.

She answers in a matter-of-fact tone "He's the coach's son."

Kyle shakes his head.

"Typical." He mutters.

They snap the ball and the big kid only gains two yards before he's covered with the defending team. He trudges through the children, but makes nothing of it on their second down. They only have two more chances before the ball turns over to the other team.

"I was the fat kid back then." Kyle says "My dad didn't care where I was, as long as I was doing what I was good at." He points to the nose guard, next to Olivia's brother "I was right next to your brother, and I was good at it." He nudges Stephen to include him in the conversation.

Stephen looks at him.

Kyle tells them both "Back in my day, we won all the championships." He looks to the field "Your brother's not bad, but he can't do as well on the line as that other kid. It's only because he's not built for that posi-tion. Steve, watch Olivia's brother on the next play."

Stephen watches closely. The team breaks from their huddle once more, and Olivia's brother takes to the line. He stands opposite the larg-est boy on the other team.

The ball snaps and Olivia's brother meets the human wall with a fearless determination. His legs thrust at the ground to lift the other boy off the turf. Black plastic sprays up each time his feet stab the ground. He goes nowhere, but keeps low on the boy's chest. It pushes the large boy upward; taking the power away from his feet.

Kyle looks at Stephen "You see how low he gets?"

Stephen nods. Olivia looks his way.

"By staying low, he uses his height as an advantage." He looks out at the field and watches as he explains "He lifts the other guy off of his feet, throwing him off balance. It's the best thing he CAN do, but he doesn't have the muscle mass to push him far. He just doesn't have the frame for it."

The larger boy steps back a half a step. Kyle raises his brows.

"He's doing his best, though." Kyle says "And he's not giving up."

The play ends; again with the large halfback under a pile of kids.

"Your brother is as good as he can be" Kyle says "but he's better off in a running position."

Olivia nods, but she feels reluctant to agree.

Kyle taps Stephen on the arm "When you play; whether you're running with the ball or you're on the line, make sure you drive your legs until the whistle blows. You've gotta move move move; even if your feet are off the ground. Move your legs and keep going until that whistle blows, just like Olivia's brother."

Stephen nods.

"And get low" Kyle adds "Your center of gravity is better when you're low. It doesn't matter how big they are, you can take them out as long as you're fast and low."

Stephen nods and looks eager to play.

Olivia smiles at Kyle. Kyle looks at her.

"What?" Kyle asks.

Olivia shakes her head "It's nothing."

The scoreboard clicks past the first quarter, then the second, the third, and finally the fourth. The final score puts the South West Lions at a massive defeat.

Olivia approaches her brother with a smile. The boy is sweaty and confused by the strange man at her side. He becomes less defensive when he notices Stephen at Kyle's side.

★

Kyle puts his jacket on the hanger by his door, and Stephen runs to the television.

"Shoes, pal!" Kyle says.

Stephen turns in an afterthought. He lifts his foot and begins yanking it out of his shoe.

Olivia laughs as Stephen throws the shoe in the corner by the door. She bends to pick up the shoes and place them on the mat by the entrance.

Stephen runs to the center of Kyle's living room, then turns around.

"Let's play ZHL!" Stephen says.

"ZHL?" Kyle says "Maybe if we're on the same team. I don't wanna lose to you in front of my date."

Olivia laughs "He might win me over."

Kyle chuckles as he walks to the living room.

"Pull it up." Kyle says "One game, then it's off to bed."

Stephen turns on the game console and gives Kyle a controller. Olivia comes up behind Kyle and looks at him with a smile and a tilted head. She reaches her arm around Kyle's and holds it at his side.

Kyle doesn't react but keeps his attention on his brother. He remembers his father's distance when he would pay attention to Frida. He felt a world away, and there was a glaring disinterest in what was going on in Kyle's mind. He knows that Stephen is building his character with each small experience. It's nothing to take lightly.

Stephen pulls up the game titled "*ZHL*" and the image of a professional hockey player comes to the screen.

"Who are we playing as?" Kyle asks.

Stephen navigates the menu screen "The South Side Ravens" He says.

"You don't want to play on Great Uncle Joe's team?" Kyle asks.

"Who did Great Uncle Joe play for?" Stephen asks.

"Dad didn't tell you?"

"I forget." Stephen says.

Kyle smiles "Joey Rodrigues, he was on the Iowa Storm. You can play as him on the retro team."

"He's in the game?!" Stephen asks.

Kyle nods.

"Let's play as them!" Stephen says. He changes the team options.

Kyle smiles and watches Stephen navigate to the retro team. Their great uncle's image is on the banner for the Iowa Storm 457 team.

Olivia doesn't know much about hockey, but if she did, she would have many questions to ask. To her, it's the common distant relation she's used to seeing. With a world so small, it's not uncommon to be related to someone relatively famous.

Joey Rodrigues was more than an ordinary celebrity to the city of New Memphis, and the greater United Iowa Nation.

"If we're playing nationals…" Stephen begins "…then who do we play against?"

Kyle is about to answer, but Stephen comes with another question.

"Who did Great Uncle Joe play for in the ZHL?"

Kyle raises his brows "At first it was the Westward Mountaineers, then he was traded to the Central Knights; but you can't play as their retro teams; only the national teams."

Stephen looks perplexed "Should we play against the Zion Patriots, or the Oneida Rangers?"

Kyle brings the corners of his mouth down "Maybe Oneida. I can't play against my home team like that."

Stephen laughs "Okay."

"Have you been to Oneida?" Olivia asks Kyle.

Kyle raises his brows "I haven't had a reason to go." He admits "Stephen, did you go with Dad to Oneida when they went?"

Stephen shakes his head.

Kyle's face falls to disappointment "They went without you on vacation?"

Stephen backs up to the couch "I was in summer camp."

Kyle smiles "Rickety Farms?"

Stephen nods, and Kyle reflects on his own experiences. He remembers the memories, crafted in the wheat wood forests. He loves the idea of his brother living out those same events.

"I'm a good swimmer." Stephen says.

"How'd you do in the hay maze?" Kyle asks.

Stephen laughs "Not so good."

Kyle laughs "Really? My cabin set the record for the best time."

Stephen shakes his head "No, we did the worst." His eyes remain on the screen as he selects their team's jersey color "Timmy cried and the counselors came looking for us." He begins laughing at Timmy's meltdown.

Kyle laughs "Really?!"

Stephen nods "Timmy's a bit of a baby, but he's really nice."

"That poor kid." Kyle says.

Stephen nods "Vincent made fun of him for it, but I smacked Vinny and told him to shut up."

Kyle and Olivia erupt in a laugh that they can't contain, but they fight to hold their bad influence at bay.

"What did you do next?" Kyle asks.

"Vinny cried, and I almost got in trouble; but the counselor was Vinny's brother and he said that Vinny was wrong, so I didn't have to miss anything." Stephen finishes selecting the ice rink and puts the controller down "He was nice to Timmy after that, so we're all friends."

Kyle smiles "That's good." He says "Do you still see them?"

"Only when I go to summer camp." Stephen says.

Kyle nods "Maybe when you're older, I can take you to Oneida too. We can see it together."

Stephen screws his brows together "I'd like to go to New Memphis. There's a lot of cool stuff there."

Kyle looks back at the screen and sees that Stephen chose the Seventh Street Rink in the heart of New Memphis. An outdoor hockey rink with city towers reaching up at all sides. Granite platforms around the rink hold bronze statues of Iowa's greatest hockey players, figure skaters, and speed skating champions. Their Great Uncle Joe is among the figures surrounding the rink. It shows him scoring an iconic goal in the Intercity Cup, a tournament that's now been replaced by the International Cup.

In the iconic moment, Joey Rodrigues faked an attempt at the left-hand side of the goalie. His commitment to the fake brought the goalie to commit to his left side, then Joey took the puck at the tip of his stick and pulled it to the tip of his skate. It tapped the blade at his feet and went through the gap between the goalie's legs. It brought the tournament to a roaring close, and a victory for United Iowa.

The competition of the Intercity Cup is difficult for their generation to imagine; for when Oneida was finished being built in the year five hundred, it was agreed that Zion would allow the city to run without influence. After the twenty-year aid is over, the state will run with complete autonomy. It was seen as a precaution to keep tensions from mounting the way they did in New Memphis. With the founding of Oneida's own hockey team, the Intercity Cup became the International Cup, and the weight of Joey's goal became a memory of the days that once were. Only in New Memphis will you hear of the exhilarating win.

The hockey town to the north is still known for its prowess in the art of icebound sports. Iowa's identity has been solidified by crass and rebellious mannerisms; yet a graceful intellect lies within their commerce and ingenuity. Zion, on the other hand, is seen as the melting pot of hustle and bustle; and in its infancy, Oneida has shown a vibrant passion for entertainment. All the while, Oneida's facilities display a love for the cutting-edge technologies produced by Iowa, and the innovations financed by the industrial power of Zion.

Kyle watches the audience in the game and thinks how accurate it is. The people are dressed for the early morning cold. A night of inactivity across the city brings the temperature to plummet as the ventilation systems cleaned the air in solitude. A pair of women with Oneida flags are bundled in coats with fur-lined hoods. They hold hot cocoa between their mittens. Beside them is a shirtless man, painted in the colors of the Iowa Storm. Kyle smiles at the detail left behind by the game developers.

Stephen takes the face-off and passes the puck to Kyle. Kyle breaks past the blue line and passes it back to Stephen. His character is hit before he can take a shot on net. Kyle points to the screen.

"You see how he hit you?" Kyle says.

"What?" Stephen asks.

"He got low, like Olivia's brother." Kyle explains.

"Oh yeah!" Stephen says.

Olivia wraps an arm around Kyle, and he leans into her with a smile at his brother.

"You bend your knees and lean into the hit." Kyle adds "Dip your shoulder and push him up off the ground."

Stephen is enthralled with the game. The match continues with the same velocity until the third period. Kyle then takes a moment to kiss Olivia. She tries to pull his attention away more, but Kyle tries his best to not neglect his brother.

In the midst of their display of affection, Kyle is about to receive the puck. Stephen looks back to see if Kyle is ready. Kyle looks at him with a raised brow.

"What?" Kyle says "You thought I wasn't playing?"

Stephen smiles back at his brother. To him, Kyle looks cool with focus and a patient woman at his arm. Stephen turns back to the screen.

The score keeps close through the rest of the period, bouncing back and forth with a difference of one or two goals between the teams. The time ticks on and it falls to tie with only a minute left on the clock.

The brothers take a face-off in their zone, but the opposing team wins the puck. They take a shot from the blue line. The goalie blocks it and Stephen catches the puck. He sends it behind the net and Kyle takes the puck out of the zone. He races into the other team's end of the ice but the defenseman blocks the way to the net. Kyle scoops behind the net. The defending team chases him, leaving the other side of the goalie open. On the clear side, there is a sheet of open ice between Kyle's character and Stephen's.

"Pass!" Stephen yells.

Kyle passes the puck, and the goalie makes a futile effort to reach in Stephen's direction. The clock reads three seconds and the alarms blare. It's a goal.

Stephen jumps and turns to his brother. They embrace each other in a hug, and the game ends in a win, seven to eight.

Kyle turns off the system. He raises a brow to his brother.

"You do your homework?" He asks.

Stephen smiles and looks to the side with a guilty laugh.

"No." Stephen says.

Kyle laughs "I'll help you with it tomorrow. I have the day off." He motions his hand in a shooing manner toward the restroom.

Stephen runs to the bathroom with his backpack and Kyle pulls out a bed from under the couch.

"I hope you don't mind taking this bed with me for the night." Kyle says "I sleep out here in case he sneaks around at night."

Olivia looks at the bed.

"No getting past this!" She says.

Kyle nods. His attention is taken by the pitter-patter of feet.

Stephen comes out in his pajamas; a matching set with his favorite cartoon characters.

Kyle opens the door to his room for Stephen. His brother climbs into bed and Kyle tucks him in.

Kyle remembers a little thought to tell his brother.

"When we do your homework tomorrow" He says "I'll be sure to make it fun." He adjusts the pillows to make them available for Stephen "Elizabeth and I used to do homework together all the time."

Stephen brightens his eyes.

"Really?" He asks.

Kyle nods "Dad used to try and cram knowledge in our heads." He laughs at the memory "It was fine for Elizabeth, but it took some extra force with me." Kyle gives the gesture of a backhanded smack to the air "I made tricks to help myself in college. You might find them useful."

Stephen smiles and nods. As Kyle is about to turn off the light, Stephen asks another question.

"Why did you leave school?" Stephen asks.

Kyle stops. He backs away and leans in to look at Stevie "I messed up." He says "But it doesn't mean I'm done. I'll be going back one of these days. You'll see."

"I like sleeping over." Stephen says.

Kyle laughs "I like having you around, pal." He says.

Kyle goes in for a hug, and Stevie hugs him back. His stuffed bear is rung at the neck. Its head props out over Kyle's shoulder.

"Get some sleep, pal." Kyle says. He backs away from the hug "I'll see you in the morning."

Kyle turns off the light and pulls a package from his pocket. The crystal night light comes out of its box, and Kyle plugs the prongs into the outlet at Stephen's bedside. It gives a gold-magenta glow to the room.

"Goodnight." Stephen says.

His face smiles out of a pile of pillows and bed sheets.

Kyle lifts the corners of his mouth in a smile "Goodnight, pal." He says "I love ya."

Kyle walks to the door and watches Stephen close his eyes. He shuts the door to leave Stephen alone in the comfort of his quiet room.

CHAPTER 14
Therapy

Julius comes down the hall toward Doctor Hoyt's office. It's a dark corner, a short distance from the engineering labs. Down the long hall and around the corner, the office lies in a quiet section of the ship. It is far from the busy biology labs, the living quarters, and the remaining recreation room. The second rec room, now Doug's room, is close by for Doctor Hoyt's convenience.

The small space outside the therapy office is dark with exposed pipe, leaving a gap between the walls and hissing metal tubes. Julius knocks on the door and waits a while. This place reminds him of a strange serenity he remembers from the war when large factories and skyscrapers were left abandoned. The city's infrastructure was similar, and there was something serene in the aftermath of destruction. It feels far from civilization, but the office was probably situated in such a space for exactly that reason. It feels sectioned away from the rest of their life aboard the Mandel Explorer.

Doctor Hoyt opens the door and seems as serene as the space where he occupies.

"Come in." Doctor Hoyt says.

Julius enters the room, and the space begins to feel more comfortable than serene. The walls are made of plaster; like a wealthy farmer's house on Zion. It's painted a dark forest green, meeting the golden carpet beyond the wheat wood molding at the bottom of the wall. A maroon rug is placed in the center of the room, and skewed on an angle to break up the symmetry. Its pattern of golden vines are tipped with emerald leaves. The flowers of the rug face up at the ceiling, textured with stucco. The intricacy allows the eyes to wander along its surface; and again, another rug is draped over the surface of a table. It is angled for the sake of asymmetry, and a lamp holds it in place. The lampshade glows from the golden white bulb inside.

"Have a seat." Doctor Hoyt says.

Julius takes a spot in the large cushioned chair. Doctor Hoyt sits in another chair opposite him. Hoyt's desk is beside the therapist, but not in between them. He taps his desk and begins to navigate a menu on its surface. As he does, he looks up at a painting on the wall. It changes between different works of art. They swap in and out of the frame until he finds one that he likes.

Doctor Hoyt motions to the holographic fireplace "Fire on or off?"

Julius shrugs "I have no preference."

Hoyt waves his hand in a shooing of the fireplace "It might be too distracting." He says. He closes out the menu and sits back in his chair "Okay… so do you know why you're here?"

Julius shakes his head.

Hoyt nods "With the addition of our newest member, I'm doing a thorough analysis of the department heads. You're a bit of an exception." He hands Julius a tablet and sits back.

Julius looks at the tablet to see a list of names. They're the second in command for each department; and a few other assistants he can hardly put a face to.

"These are the exceptions like yourself." Hoyt says "The people who are most likely to interact with Doctor Clay."

Julius hands the tablet back.

Hoyt takes the tablet and continues "We don't know what Doctor Clay wants, or if he's really who he says he is." He puts the tablet down on his desk "I'm holding therapy sessions once a week with the department heads; once every other week with the people on that list."

"Okay." Julius says "What's the goal of the therapy, though?"

Doctor Hoyt crosses his legs and leans back with his head propped up by a fist "For the department heads, it's to ensure collaboration among the departments. A sense of community and trust will give us a better handle on the situation. For the rest of you, it's to keep your heads clear. The more you're aware of your surroundings, the more likely you'll pick up signs of distress."

Julius nods, looking at the empty fireplace.

"His voice is monotoned." Hoyt says "We can't discern the meaning of his words because there's no vocal infliction." He takes a deep breath and lets out a large exhale as he speaks "We can't tell what's going on in his mind either, because the vote has us locked out of a manual override. We can't get past any of his inhibitions; so if he has any reservations while he speaks, we're out of luck."

Julius nods "Do you think the vote was a correct decision?"

Hoyt retracts his lips in a bit of a smile. He gives a faint laugh through his nose.

"I don't know" the therapist says "It could have upset him, and made him less willing to cooperate as a part of the team. That's why Peter put it up to a vote… but we're stuck in this path now, and there's only one way forward."

Julius nods "So where would you like to start?"

Doctor Hoyt puts his hands together in a prayer-like position. His forefingers grab his bottom lip as he forms his thoughts.

"Is there anything that's bothering you?" Doctor Hoyt asks.

Julius gathers his brows and thinks a while on the events of the past month.

"You got the data from Tokyo." Julius says.

Doctor Hoyt nods "The cannibal in the apartment complex."

Julius nods "Yeah…" He remembers a feeling he had, and wonders if it's negatively impacting himself, or anyone else "I didn't want Elizabeth to see that." He says.

"Was there a reason you felt that way?"

Julius searches for a meaning to his actions.

"I've always been careful to keep people from that kind of thing." Julius says. "I often feel like there's a reason to keep bad thoughts like that away from people."

"Thoughts like what?" Hoyt asks "The bad traits you find in humanity?"

Julius nods "There's something not right about highlighting those things." He sits back in his seat and recalls the past "It can invade, and infect people. It takes the love and life out of the brightest moments." He thinks further on that thought "Bringing context to that darkness seems impossible sometimes."

"Can you think of a 'for instance'?"

Julius remembers a moment long ago. He was living in an apartment in East Eden.

In his memory, he stands in the kitchen. The studio apartment is tucked away, under the bottom floor of the apartment complex. It's burrowed into the ground like a basement. The only exit is through the windowless hall beyond his door. Out there the residents are harassed with LED lights until they leave the first floor, out into the streets of East Eden.

There is a brief respite from the dreary air of Julius' room. A warm square of light that hits the kitchen cabinets on an angle. It comes from one of the two windows at the feet of sidewalk pedestrians. Otherwise it feels like a birdcage amidst the streets of Eden.

Julius holds his broom upside down, preparing to sweep the apartment as a daily routine. He comes around the counter where the stove is. A rat comes out of seemingly nowhere. Julius startles back but the rat gives chase. Julius jumps. By instinct he stabs at the motion on the floor. The broom makes a crunch. Blood splatters out of the rat's anus. The hind legs are immobilized and its chest convulses in the rhythm of rapid breath.

Julius feels guilt-ridden, but he's at a loss for what he can't undo. He looks about himself for a tool to bring the rat elsewhere. He sees the paper towels and decides it's not enough. He looks under the kitchen sink and finds a pair of disposable gloves. They snap snug to his wrists, and he takes the paper towel to move the dead rat onto the dustpan. He grabs a screwdriver and takes the rat to the hallway.

Outside his door, Julius places the dustpan onto the welcome mat. He looks long at the breathing rat. Its face is paralyzed, but the lungs keep moving. With the paper towel, he moves the rat onto its back. He places the screwdriver into its mouth and points the tip at the base of the brain. He presses down to crunch the skull and obliterate the rat's consciousness. The lungs stop, but the plastic dustpan cracks.

"Ah, fuck!" He says.

He notices a shadow and looks over his shoulder to see a boy. The son of a lady down the hall. He's seen her only once or twice, but the boy is frequently in and out of the apartment. Julius has seen the young man taking out trash, going to the school bus, and carrying the groceries into the apartment. He's never once seen the mother accompany her child.

Julius looks back at the rat, where the boy's eyes have fallen and still remain.

He looks back to the boy "Hey." He says.

The boy doesn't look at him.

"Look at me." Julius says.

The boy looks at him for a moment.

"Are you alright?" asks Julius.

The boy nods and looks back at the rat. Julius follows his sight to the dustpan but then looks back to the boy.

"I didn't want to do that." Julius says. He stands up but leaves the dustpan on the floor. He kneels to look at the boy, ignoring the dustpan "I had to..." Julius says "He was paralyzed."

The boy nods, then looks to the rat.

Julius looks back at the rat "Sometimes we need to do the things that we don't want to do, even this. If I didn't he'd still be suffering." Julius looks back at the boy and sees he's still looking at the rat "Don't look at him, look at me."

The boy looks at Julius.

"I had to do what was smart, even though it hurt." says Julius "There's moments where your heart tells you one thing, but you know the right thing to do is different. A decision like that needs to be made regardless of what you feel." He shrugs, trying to come up with an example "If you're in a car crash, you might want to get up and get away from the scene; but you need to check 'can I move my toes, can I move my fingers' that kind of a thing. Then get up slowly. Don't run into traffic, don't get up too quick; you could hurt yourself if something is broken." Julius nods at his choice in example. He goes on and looks at the boy "It's not good to push your emotions away all the time, but in a moment of life and death...." He notices the boy looking at the rat "Hey." He says.

The boy looks at him.

Julius puts his hands parallel to exaggerate the point "You need to set the emotions aside" He breathes deep "Breathe; and do what's intelligent."

The boy nods and Julius smiles.

"Okay?" He asks.

The boy nods again.

Julius smiles "Okay. Please take it easy. I know it's not fun to look at."

"Okay." The boy says. His apathetic tone gives Julius an uneasy feeling.

The boy seems tired and frustrated. He always seems this way. Julius watches his stocky build saunter down to his apartment. Julius hopes the boy can handle what he's seen.

Julius takes the dustpan inside and closes the door. He drops the rat into the garbage along with the dustpan. He begins to clean the blood left behind.

On the floor with the bleach in hand, Julius stops scrubbing for a moment. A sound catches his attention. He looks under the stove to see something strange. He takes the broom and pulls a mass of junk from underneath the rat's hiding place. As he pulls, a pink mass rolls onto the floor before the pile of junk. He continues pulling and a rounded mass of small trash comes to light. Eight rat babies lay curled in a nest made of trash. One of them fell out and lay naked on the cold floor. They haven't grown their own hair yet; and so they writhe in the cold light of the kitchen.

Julius sighs.

Doctor Hoyt holds his tablet in his hands. He looks long at Julius as he recounts the story.

"I don't like it" Julius says "but I can't change it." he adjusts himself in his seat "The world is unrelenting. It's irreverent to anyone and any-thing." He shakes his head and shrugs "So long as I'm alive, I'm in this circle of life. I'M in it, YOU are, and everyone we've ever cared about…" He fights an urge to hold back on some words, knowing full well that telling helps more than hiding. "In the William Lawrence Tunnel, they di…."

"You… don't need to…" says Hoyt.

"No…" says Julius "I think it helps…"

Hoyt nods. He sits back in his chair and motions his hand as if to say "Carry on".

Julius nods. He stares off to regain his thought "On the day of the siege of New Memphis, bullets came down that tunnel at every one of us. They didn't care who they hit; they just came at us. It didn't matter who we were or what we looked like, they came at us anyway, because that's what bullets do… They tore through everyone just the same. Even when we bit our teeth, we screamed and we charged; they didn't stop coming our way." Julius breathes through his nose like the steam of a kettle "They came to kill…" He says "…and so did we… And the only thing that changed our fate was that we didn't wait for death to come our way. We ran at the only chance we had, and that was straight into the hail storm…" He grows solemn "And I'm alive today, only because I left my sense of self-preservation back there somewhere…" He feels a sense of pride for the raging courage displayed by young men.

He remembers a hundred screaming faces, as they growled so loud that their voices carried far beyond the enemy. It was like they wanted their voices to echo on the walls and reverberate back to Eden; as if to say "We have this, and we're alright". Julius remembers how they ham-mered the floor with a decided sprint to victory.

He nods at their memory "They came at us, and we came right back… and that's why some of us lived…"

Doctor Hoyt collects his hands together. He looks off to the ground and gathers his brows. He then nods and looks at the tablet to notice the time.

"I don't want to cut this short…" says Doctor Hoyt.

Julius smiles. He nods his head.

"We can pick this up another time." says Julius "It's no worry."

Julius rises from his seat and turns toward the door.

"Can you do me one favor?" Julius asks.

"What's that?" Asks Hoyt.

"… If the Captain doesn't heed my warning about those weapons…" Julius says "… please help him to understand where I'm coming from… He just might listen to you."

Hoyt nods.

"I can try." He says.

Julius is about to pass the threshold of the door but Doctor Hoyt halts him with a question.

"Are you gonna be okay?" He asks.

Julius looks back and smiles.

He nods at the therapist.

"I've been doing okay for a very long time."

CHAPTER 15
Weapons of War

In a daydream Julius walks through knee-deep pools of water. A frothing film swirls in the wake of his boots. It soaks his pants from toes to knees. His eyes sweep across the darkness before his face. They narrow to a point at the tip of his gun. Beyond that point lies empty corners of shadow and concrete.

In a circle of five men, Julius stands at the back. Chief walks in the front of the group, and on either side are Dash, Pluto, and Cricket. They trudge atop the muck of sediment on the floor.

Julius backpedals through this basement of a dilapidated skyscraper. Tanks and swarm-copters rumble overhead. They comb the streets of the business district in search of straggling enemies. Soon the district will be the new headquarters of the Zion Armed Forces.

Dust falls through the cracks made cavernous by artillery shells. Water drips from damaged pipes, and down the rusted rebar.

The fear of the falling structure pales in the face of each echoing entryway. They behold a black emptiness, deeper than any can guess.

A stench comes about the air, sickening sweet.

In the back of the squad, Julius cannot see what lies ahead. All the while, he knows too well what it is.

"Zero!" Chief calls.

"Yes sir."

"Check their blood."

"Yes, sir."

Julius breaks formation, and his comrades fill the gap. He approaches the front where a doorway meets an underground parking garage; forty yards beyond which, a wall of bodies is packed from the floor to the ceiling. Each one pale, cold, naked, and wet. Those who lie on the bottom are submerged. They've been recently killed, yet their mouths are riddled with maggots. Their faces are tortured to ungodly expressions. Eyes looking upward in different directions. Dry teeth. Hair weathered by death. Mouths encircled with irritation. No bullet wounds.

Julius takes the blood sample and plugs it into his genetic scanner. The light turns green, and Chief announces "DNA..."

Julius discards the blood sample and puts the genetic reader away.

Chief continues to Julius alone "Hard to believe, what we're facing is human."

Julius stares into the far corner of the dark to see a child among the pile. Bent backward over a man, strange to him in life. Disposed far from home in a dark and lonely parking garage.

Julius looks up at Doctor Lawrence. She is sitting in a pretzel on the other half of the couch. Her tablet sits atop the pillow over her legs.

She glances up at him from her tablet. Her eyes lock on him with a soft expression on her face.

"You have that look." She says.

His seat is comfortable. The air is warm. A jasmine blossom spills in from the garden lab down the hall.

He smiles. "I'm just staring off."

"It's nothing?" She asks.

"Nothing at all."

Elizabeth pulls back the corner of her mouth. Her brows show concern, but she puts her head down to continue coding.

A film from the 1950s plays before the two of them, but Julius pauses it. "This wasn't a good choice." He says.

She looks up at the screen. "Yeah, put something else on."

"I was thinking of playing a game." Julius says.

Her fingers type quickly, then stop. Her eyes scan across the screen on her lap. Without so much as looking up she continues. "Maybe in a minute."

She continues typing. Then Julius watches her take an aggravated breath.

"Why not now?" He asks.

She shakes her head. "I can't. After this I have a dissection plan to write." She looks intently at the screen for a moment, after reading a sentence she continues her thought. "We have those things from San Francisco."

Julius smiles "I'll help you with that; but later." He throws a pillow at her and it bounces away to the floor. "You've been coding for twelve hours." He says.

Halfway through picking up the pillow, she stops and looks up at him.

"Shut up." She says.

He raises his brows toward her tablet. "You woke up at six thirty."

She looks closer at the screen. "It's six-fifteen." She says.

Julius tosses the controller to the edge of her knees.

"Play." Julius smirks.

She looks at the controller and thinks he might have a point. No matter how much she wants to make a name for herself, and Kyle; she'd be doing an injustice if she doesn't enjoy her life every once in a while. She looks up at Julius with a devilish grin.

"You're gonna regret this." She says.

***

After long, they've played two basketball games against each other. Elizabeth won both times. By now the two are deep in a contest against time in another game called "Miners V.S. Goblins".

Julius looks over at her. She's smiling; and she's forgetting her reason to stress.

"You know" Julius begins "I used to play this game…" He smacks the buttons with his thumbs "…when I'd read in college." His character places a bomb, and blows up a cliff face. A clock in the upper left corner gains fifteen seconds. A wall is made to the back of their characters. An army of goblins break through an older wall, and advances to the new one. Elizabeth collects a Gemini symbol and two archers appear at the wall. Two seconds are added to the clock each time the archers fire their bows.

"Nice." Elizabeth says under her breath. She then gathers her brows. "Wait, how did you read and play this at the same time?"

"An audiobook." Julius says. "I'd listen while I played."

"I don't think I have the attention for that." She says.

Julius shrugs. "It's better than reading the pages. Better than skimming them too."

She tenses her brows. Her character on the screen blows up a bomb, releasing several crystals from a mountainside. "And if there was no audiobook?"

Julius smiles. "I'd play Jack-Man. You know that old strategy game?"

"Yeah! With the pumpkin guy." She says.

"Mhm!" He hums.

97

Elizabeth thinks through her divided attention. "I'd wipe the floor with you in Jack-Man."

Julius laughs. "I'm not so sure about that."

Elizabeth blows up another cliff face, then returns to a question on her mind "So how'd you make that work? You'd read between turns?"

"Exactly." Julius' character throws a bomb into the mob of goblins "For each paragraph, I'd take a turn."

Elizabeth nods "I wish I did that. It's clever."

Julius smiles. "Worked like a charm."

Elizabeth clicks the controller frantically as she tries to blow up another mountainside. A turtle blocks the way, and her character explodes with it. The screen says "Game Over" and she places her controller down.

She stands and stretches her limbs. "I should head back to work."

Julius shifts in his seat "I'll come help."

Mid-stride toward the door, she stops and puts her hand up in a polite decline. "There's no need. It's just a little writing. Thank you, though."

Julius nods. "Alright."

Elizabeth turns to leave, but Julius calls out her name.

"Before you go" He says "I need to say something first…"

Elizabeth turns again to see him, still smiling on the couch.

Julius looks up from his raised brows.

"You're working as fast as you can…" He says "… and you can't do anything more. So don't worry about what you can't physically do. You're kicking ass, and you're doing great."

Elizabeth looks to the floor and sighs.

"Oh I don't know about that…" She says.

"Ah!" says Julius "There you go… doubting yourself again… That's bullshit and I don't wanna hear it."

Elizabeth cracks a smile.

"You kick ass, and I mean it…" says Julius "I wouldn't lie to you…"

Elizabeth feels her heart relax, as if a weight is lifted from her shoulders.

She smiles, then nods. "Thank you, Jules. I needed that."

He smiles as she walks away.

"Anytime, partner." He says to himself.

Soon the Captain comes from another entryway to the recreation room.

"Hey Captain." Julius says.

"I wanted to talk." Peter says. "Figured I might find you here."

The Captain comes to seat himself next to Julius. He leans over his knees; his elbows rest on his femurs.

Julius sits up straight. "What about, sir?"

"What you said the other day, about weaponry. I understand why you said it, but I want you to know something I think you'd ought to."

Julius hangs his mouth open trying to form a question. He then leans an arm over the back of the couch "And what's that?"

"I'm just following orders." He scratches the corner of his mouth. His beard makes a noise like brushing over the rough side of velcro. His hands come together in a dry-sounding rub. "If I don't meet certain requirements, I'm penalized." Peter says.

Julius wonders aloud "Penalized?"

The Captain nods.

"What do you mean by 'penalized'?"

Peter shrugs. "I have to prioritize certain things in a list; and if I don't, the big guys will know." Peter begins counting on his fingers. "The first is terraforming, then agriculture. Followed by weaponry, then art and history. If I don't play by those rules, then I lose a portion of my check."

Julius nods. "So that's how they get ya."

"Yeah." The Captain jolts him awake with a slap on the shoulder. "But you don't need to follow those rules."

Julius forms a shape with his mouth, but fails to vocalize a question.

"You get your work done quick" Peter begins. "I like that; and so you have a lot of free time." The Captain shrugs "Why not catalog things?"

"Like a digital database?"

The Captain smiles. "Maybe a music library. People need new music around the ship."

"That's not a bad idea."

Julius nods, but stops suddenly. His eyes move to the side in a thought.

"What's up?" Peter asks.

The engineer leans forward onto his elbows. "Do you think people will use this knowledge to do bad things?"

"People will." The Captain says. "But there's no stopping bad people. You can't cure stupidity."

Julius listens with his gaze fixed to the floor.

The Captain rocks in a slow nod. "It's up to people like us, to use what's in our power to warn about bad people." He smiles as he puts his palms parallel to one another, fingers extended. He thrusts his hands forward in a line. "We can guide them out of killing each other." He then laughs.

Julius wonders deeper; what is in his power?

As if to answer the question, Peter leans in to speak once more. "You and I get the opportunity to highlight the repercussions of war. Make sure people get it. We can start from there."

CHAPTER 16
Heavy Ground

Gunfire cracks from the distant streets along the northern front; and here the rumble of tanks rattles tarnished silverware in somber homes. Dust covers the tables, chairs, and unfinished dinners in the southwest neighborhood. A broken metal sign reads "*Colonial Heights - New Memphis*".

The concrete buildings of this borough were made from molds, cast years ago. They stand stronger than their recent additions. Shop faces and balcony ledges lay strewn about after a night of artillery strikes. In every direction it has sapped the land of all its color, and a grey powder coats the city like a dusting of snow.

This was once the residential area of the working class. Now it has been reduced to a several-mile stretch of bare foundations.

Yesterday the Zion forces gained access to the traffic cameras. They acquired City Hall and used the infrastructure controls to establish a presence in the business district.

Having left the new headquarters this morning, Pluto guides the team through the shortcuts of his old neighborhood. With a tank at their side, the group moves down the open streets running east to west. They tread across the courtyards of large apartment complexes; over medians and through parking lots. Through the fences and backyards of Pluto's childhood.

Not one corpse lies in this afterimage of destruction. Marks of blood smear into holes and behind walls. Only the motion of ravens stir in the silence. They stand atop broken walls, and the mangled fences of dead gardens.

Julius watches one yank a scrap of dirt-ridden flesh. The coveted sinew stretches from its claws to its beak. Its head cocks away from the floor. The meat snaps upward. The raven shakes its head and stomps on the meat again. It yanks up once more.

Julius looks away. He turns back again to the surroundings before him. The team enters a street that feels naked. It runs through a valley of concrete walls with bare window holes.

Chief bumps into Pluto, Cricket into him, then Dash, and finally Julius.

Pluto looks back "Sorry!"

Chief looks ahead "What is it?"

"Nothing." Pluto says "I just slipped."

Chief pats his shoulder. Julius watches that shoulder pump from a soft forlorn into a solid defense.

The team moves onward with Julius at the back. He pays careful attention to the area across the street and behind them.

Chief meets Pluto in a tiptoe.

"Hey" He whispers. "Can you get us out of the open?"

Pluto looks back with doe eyes. He looks torn from a deep focus. His scrunched brow sweats in beads. "This is the best street." He says. "If we wanna cross Thirty-Third Ave, this is our best shot."

"You can't do better than this?" Chief asks.

Pluto shakes his head.

Chief steps back to ready himself again "Alright, then. Let's go."

With less than a step more, Chief's radio bursts with sound. He hastens to turn it down.

"Chief?" The radio calls.

Chief pinches the talk button. Sweat drips from the side of his head onto the talking piece.

"What is it?" He asks.

"We're sending swarm-copters to your position. They'll give you guys a chance to eat."

Chief's eyes smile, and he pinches the button once more "Thank you, we appreciate that."

"You got it, Chief."

The group smiles, and Chief forces his cheeks down "They're not here yet." He raises his gun and stands ready. He nudges Pluto with his hand "Keep your eyes up. We'll sit in a minute."

Their eyes dart from outcrop to barrier. They move on through the ghost town that seems long abandoned. None would guess it hosted families just two nights ago.

If it weren't for the dome overhead, it would feel as if they were in the wild desert.

Chief feels a presence at his back. He turns to look behind himself.

From silence comes the sound of giant dragonflies. The swarm-copters come thundering overhead. They navigate the city streets in a perfectly gridded fashion. All except one. It spins around the area. It searches the structures and alleyways.

After long, the four propellers bring the camera-mounted gun to face their team. The mounted gun light flashes three times. In a roar the propellers speed the machine on westward.

Chief turns to the team "That's it boys, Eat up!" He reaches into a bag alongside the tank. A glow of excitement comes about his eyes as he finds a cup of noodles. "Eat light." He adds "Supplies need to last."

"We're stopping here?" Cricket asks.

Julius pats his shoulder. "Yep." He then plops into a seat; a piece of dusty foundation. He pats the space next to him "Take a seat." He says.

Cricket looks around once, and sits beside Julius.

Chief walks with leisure, hulking over his small cup of noodles "That guy could see everything for miles. We're good as long as we aren't in the road."

Pluto looks disappointed at his seasoned bread "What's the next move, Chief?"

Chief's shoulders bounce with each exhale of a quiet laugh. His fork reaches into the cup of noodles "Fuck if I know."

Pluto looks down again. He tears a piece of mold from the surface of his grainy bread.

Chief looks up and becomes candid "Sorry boys. It's a little hazy on my end. We're securing the rest of the south end." The team slouches inward from each direction. "We walk west until we meet a camp on the far side. After that, I wait for orders. You'll get to sit around with me." He fits the wad of noodles into his mouth and continues. "This neighborhood is probably empty. We're just walking through to be sure of it. Then we back up the west front."

Cricket's long twisted nerves let loose in a sigh. "So this place is already clear?"

Chief almost scolds "Don't get it twisted. I didn't say there'd be nobody."

Cricket nods. His hands tremble with the adrenaline of walking.

Chief becomes mindful of Cricket. He turns to the other men as he continues. His eyes meet Pluto "I have an idea where we might go next, but I'm not sure. We might take the subway system." Chief looks at Cricket to invoke what courage he can. "It's either that or the sewers, but right now nobody knows."

Julius and Dash widen their eyes as they look at one another.

"Ew, God!" Pluto cries. He twitches his smile lines and screws up his nose. "We're gonna swim through shit?!"

Chief pulls back the corners of his mouth and raises his brows. "Yeah, we just might. I'm hoping for the subways, though." He digs into his noodles again.

Cricket lets out a drone on the border of a whimper. "Oh god."

Julius laughs "If I can help it, I'll take most of the damage for you."

Cricket shakes his head. "It's not the shit. I hate confined spaces."

Chief looks firm at the young face "You know what I'm deathly afraid of?"

Cricket looks up "What, Chief?"

"Rats and roaches." Chief says. He turns to tell the team "My mom would scream like the world was ending every time one of those creatures would make it into the apartment. It terrified me." He laughs at the memories in a deep, nasally, clown-like way. It's as if the back of his tongue stops the sound from booming out of his deep chest. His eyes squint up on his round face at the thought of his mamma. "Her shrieks were so loud! It made this huge impression on my little child mind." By the time he stops to take a breath, he notices everyone smiling. "I see rats now and I'm like 'Oh, panic!' because that's what Mom did!"

Julius looks through laughing eyelids to see Cricket laughing too. He can hardly be nervous anymore.

Chief lands his heavy callused hand on Cricket's shoulder "We'll suffer it together; but be strong for me. If you can't, then I don't know what I'm gonna do."

Cricket's smile turns up to look at Chief's "I've got you."

Chief laughs "There is literally a light at the end of the tunnel waiting for us."

Cricket smiles.

After long, Chief comes to the bottom of his cup of noodles. He stuffs the cup into the pouch along the side of the tank, and presses on with the team.

With quiet streets behind them, they arrive at the western front. The west wall begins with an industrial maintenance entrance. It then reaches high into a glass curve supported by hexagon shapes. It bends to its apex over the city's center, then comes down to the northeast neighborhood of Gabriel Hill.

The group walks into camp past a trampled plastic image of a pizza. To their left is a broken swing set and a lone, dead tree. On either side of the street are concrete barriers with gunmen.

The tank pulls in, and the operator kills the power. The group begins unloading their belongings to settle in for the night. More teams arrive over time. The tanks have their batteries swapped and treads checked. A makeshift sleeping area is made in a lone shack on the local park's corner. It's labeled "town shed". The gardening tools were looted some time ago, but the structure is a perfect hideaway from the starlight. There, Chief and his team unpack and arrange their sleeping bags along the floor.

At the arrival of a convoy, the team unloads several concrete barriers. The whole camp lays them across the north road.

Several soldiers get together to talk and eat dinner. One group plays a makeshift game of football.

Pluto sits on a bench in what is left of the playground. He faces the broken swing set. Just beyond that is the concrete wall of a building. In its center is a rectangular hole. What once was a window sill some time ago.

The ever-setting star glows golden to the right of his face. The rim of his eyelids feel sour.

Julius steps forward with a nonchalant stride. He stands next to Pluto.

"Are you turning in?" He asks.

Pluto shrugs his shoulders, but it's an unnatural attempt to be relaxed.

"I'll be there in a bit." He says.

Pluto looks to Julius' abdomen.

"How's your stomach?" He asks.

Julius looks down at the spot and lifts his shirt. He still can't remember how he got it; the large hole under the gauze pad. It's kept from opening again by a set of threads. Fifteen stitches in total in his lower right abdomen.

Apparently, Julius was shot in the business district; but he can only take the team's word for what truly happened to him. They say his memory was repressed by his subconscious; and it's been said that it happens sometimes for the pain; but Julius feels it could be for reasons that he considers far worse.

"It seems alright." Julius says "Kinda cool havin' a new butthole."

Pluto laughs. He hides his smile by looking off to the south; a sign that he would like solitude for the moment.

Pluto glances at Julius in an afterthought. It's something he's been meaning to say for some time.

"I think enough time has passed to tell you this…" He says "… But you saved my life… and I can't possibly repay you."

Julius feels his fears are confirmed, but it takes a true friend to tell the truth. He's relieved to know, but not happy to hear the code in his words.

Julius looks to the floor and nods.

"Yeah…" He says "I've got you… Don't mention it, pal…"

Pluto looks off again to the starlight.

Julius knows he wants time to himself, but he feels it might be wrong to let Pluto be.

Julius looks to his side. He sees the camp is too occupied to notice them.

He moves to sit close with Pluto, but Pluto backs away as if to be making room on the bench.

Julius dusts off the grey powder on his mud-caked boots. He looks around and sighs. As casual as he can, he pries for answers.

"You've got something on your mind." He says "You're better off telling me than anyone else."

Pluto waits, then smiles at his candor. He then looks around.

"I used to play in this park." He says.

Julius looks at the surroundings, and gathers the scale of what that means.

"Memories?" He asks.

Pluto shrugs. "Everywhere I go there's memories." He looks off to the left and continues. "I ask myself 'How is the pizza place gonna be the same?'" His hand briefly displays toward the pile of rubble where the pizza sign lies. "Or 'What if the park doesn't last?'" He looks over to the swing set once more. He nods in its direction. "That swing on the far right. That's where my mom taught me how to swing." He takes a moment to shake his head once. He twists his mouth in disapproval and does a brief shrug. "I never liked change as a kid, and I don't like it now."

Julius takes a long time to look at the concrete structures. He tries to imagine them as a familiar place, now decimated.

Pluto points his finger in the direction to his right. "I used to come around this corner…" His finger circles to his back, and finally points to his left. "I'd speed around the turn to impress this girl." He begins to smile. "I thought I was so cool with my Serpico G12." He chuckles, then points to the space before himself. "That's her window right there…" The end of his finger leads to the rectangular hole in the wall. "You can't tell, but that was the nicest house around here."

Julius undermines the lament. "A G12, huh? Where'd you get a car like that?"

Pluto speaks in a trance of memory "I bought it.". He realizes something and looks to Julius. "I didn't steal it if that's what you're thinking."

Julius laughs. "Did I say you stole it?" The two laugh until silent again. After a moment, Julius raises a brow "You still have it?"

"No." Pluto stretches his arms above his head. "I wrapped it around a light post."

Julius shakes his head as if to fix his eyes.

Pluto meets his face with a smile and drops his arms. "Oh yeah… Almost died eight times in counting."

"I was gonna ask if you wanted to drive when we got home." Julius smiles "Now I'm thinking twice."

"I'm a good kid now." Pluto's voice carries a genuine leisure. "I drive like an old man in my K90." His tone turns into the sarcastic man of simple pleasures.

"Are you made of money?"

"I just have a habit of buying nice cars that I can't afford."

"That's so not healthy." Julius laughs.

"Is it? I think it's healthy for my soul."

Julius looks at the smiling friend next to him and knows he has done his job.

"EUM with the touchdown!" Cricket yells.

"You went to Eden Medical?" A soldier asks.

"You know it, bro." Cricket adds.

Pluto smiles at the game.

Dash grabs the young man with his arms and shakes him up. Cricket smiles at the silent friend.

"He's a funny kid." Julius says.

Pluto nods "What brought him out here, though?"

Julius shrugs "He probably felt a need to do his part."

Pluto sighs "I would have stayed home. He has a girl, money… a lot more than me."

Julius nods "You have a family."

"Yeah, and a lot of debt." He looks to Julius. "In my family, you're either in the trades or nothing. I wish I could have gone to college."

They watch Dash as he holds the ball before him with two arms. He steps forward and drops the ball. He punts the ball over a distant wall. The whole field looks at him with impressed eyes. Another soldier runs to fetch the ball.

Julius shakes his head "Dash hardly says a word. Even when he's playing football."

Pluto watches and laughs "He doesn't say anything."

"He gives facial expressions."

Pluto laughs again "Yeah, but that's all you'll get."

Night comes in the form of seven quiet hours while the star yet shines from the south. Julius takes watch at the wall, but retires after an hour when another soldier relieves him. He enters the small shack and closes the door behind him.

On the dark floor, five sleeping bags are scattered with little space between them. In four of them, his teammates hide away from the golden light outside.

Just before laying in the comfort of his bag, a stirring catches Julius' attention. The murmuring of paralyzed speech brings him to grab the squirming figure. He holds it still, and Pluto's face emerges from the mouth of the bag. He looks around with wide eyes. He grabs Julius by the sleeve

"She has a blue dress and red hair." His voice comes as speech rather than a whisper. His sweat-ridden face turns every which way. His eyes are in a mile-long stare.

"Who does?" Julius asks with a chuckle.

"The girl. The girl who…" Pluto sounds drunk with sleep "We need to protect Cricket."

"Why Cricket? Cricket's fine. Go back to bed."

"Alright, alright." Pluto pulls Julius with a weak force "Just promise me you'll look out for her."

Julius almost laughs but controls his voice to keep quiet "The girl?"

"Yeah, don't trust the bitch. Blue dress."

The young Cricket begins to laugh in the warmth of his bag, and Julius looks over with a smile.

His eyes go back to the stern Pluto "Okay. Red hair, I got ya. Now go back to bed."

The look on his face is sheer confusion and his eyes study the face of Julius. "Thanks, bud." He grows calm and lies down.

"I'll keep an eye out, pal. Don't you worry."

As quickly as he woke, Pluto is asleep.

Dash looks up with his bed head, and his eyes go first to Pluto. He turns to look at Julius, then quietly to Cricket, and back to Julius.

Julius looks at Cricket. He sees a young man, calm and sleeping.

His mother probably sees this when she imagines her boy off to war. It likely reminds her of the nights when she woke with cries from his crib. She would tell him "I'm right here", and soon the cries would fall into a sleep like this.

As Cricket lies now, he sleeps before confronting his fear. With the rise of the troops in the morning, Cricket will be far from his mother and down a cold dark hole.

Julius meets Dash's eyes across the dark. The silent comrade stares with an intense look about his face. He nods with severity, then covers himself with bedding.

Mere hours pass until Julius wakes again. His eyes remain closed, but a sobbing comes to his ears and enters his conscious mind. He sucks in a deep breath and rises with a toss of his bag. Dash stares with a finger to his lips. His hand meets Julius' chest.

Pluto's sunken eyes look back to Julius. "It's not us." he says.

Cricket's young face looks through the door to the shed. He looks bitter and somber at something Julius can't see. He turns back to the dark room.

"Which team is it?" Pluto asks.

"Charlie Force." Cricket says. "A guy got sniped last night."

"Where's Chief?" Julius asks.

"Talking with the others." Cricket tells him.

"We slept through gunfire?" Dash asks. His mouth hangs open beneath doe eyes.

Cricket looks confused "I guess we did."

The light from the doorway becomes shadow. Chief comes into the shed. He stops in his tracks and looks around at the team.

"Good, you're awake." Chief says.

"What happened out there?" Pluto asks.

Chief shakes his head "Charlie Force had a guy picked off at the barrier last night. We think it's a sniper, with a really good silencer. They just found him, but he died hours ago."

Dash bites his jaw and beams his eyes. "Did they get him?" He asks.

Chief shakes his head "No." He steps closer to the center of the room and looks around. He meets from eye to eye "The enemy will likely try and pick someone off every night. Keep your eyes peeled every second when you're on shift." He begins to grow less somber, and smiles ever so little "Be smart, and think of clever ways to lure 'em out." He reaches into his bag and pulls out a worn paperback book. "I have some reading for you boys. Cricket, you take it first." He passes it to the boy by the door. "I want you all to know what they're trying to do. Little bites here and there. They're trying to make us do something stupid. If they get you to lose your cool, then you're done. Outwit them."

Cricket examines the cover.

"So what's the plan now?" Pluto asks.

Chief looks at Pluto with an amused face, and Pluto's looks eager. Chief takes the book from Cricket and hands it to Pluto. "Never mind. You read it first."

The group laughs.

"The plan, Pluto…" Chief smiles. "…is to get to the subway system." He kneels to meet the team at eye level. "Not the usual way, though. We need to enter someplace they wouldn't expect."

"No swimming today?" Julius asks.

Chief's eyes linger on the troops outside. "Don't speak too soon. You'll jinx us." His sense of humor narrowly keeps unease at bay.

Just then Chief notices Pluto looking through the doorway. His eyes are pinned on the post office down the street, past the pizza shop.

"What's on your mind, Pluto?" Chief asks.

Pluto looks off to the ground to collect the narrative in his mind "I remember kids talking about an entrance to the L Line. Some misfit kids."

"Was it over by that post office?"

Pluto looks back at the post office. "That's what they said."

Chief nods. "Might be our ticket in. Let's have a look."

On the way over, Julius closes the gap between himself and Pluto. He leans over to speak exclusively with him. Dash hurries closer to listen in. "I know Cricket has a fear of tight spaces, so let's keep that in mind."

"What about Chief?" Pluto adds with a smile. "He seemed pretty serious about that rat thing."

"I'll eat the fuckin thing." Dash fires back. His tone comes off as a genuine-sounding defense.

While it makes Julius laugh, Pluto looks disgusted "Ew." He remarks.

Dash ups his enthusiasm "I'm not kidding."

Julius gets their attention focused "Look, keep that to yourself." He laughs. "I think the big guy can handle it. Keeping our heads straight is important. Panic is what does people in, and I don't want Cricket to have reason to panic."

Pluto nods and strides forward. Dash falls back and grips his rifle.

Through the door they enter a marble-coated building. Postal drones and packages lie to the back of a dark working space. Shipping tubes line the back counter with key destinations labeled on each one. Government facilities and political officials are marked on brass plates at the rim of their mouths.

Chief points to one "Gallagher." He says. "He was killed last night. Beheaded and burned."

"Where'd you hear that?" Cricket asks.

"The morning briefing. They're going through hostages like crazy; which means we have them pissing their pants."

"How many of these guys are with the resistance?" Julius asks.

"A handful." Chief replies. "Everyone else is either a hostage or back in Eden."

Pluto calls the team over to the far corner of the room. Through shelves of forgotten parcels, they come to an old metal door.

Pluto remembers the kids from high school. "This is it." He says.

Julius grabs a fire axe from the side of the building's extinguisher. He holds it ready to smash the lock from the door.

"That's not how you hold an axe." Cricket says. "You'll cut your feet like that."

Julius looks at his foot. He is facing sideways from the lock, with one foot forward and one at the back.

"Want me to do it?" Cricket asks.

Julius frowns the corners of his mouth, impressed by the young medical student. He hands Cricket the axe.

"Knock yourself out." Julius says "Just step aside when you're done."

Julius moves to the side and places his back against the wall. Cricket stands before the door with the axe. The others stand like Julius, but to the other side of the door.

Knees bent, the team prepares to flood the doorway. Chief raises his hand to the height of his eyes.

Julius looks to Chief.

"Me first." Julius says.

Chief shakes his head.

"I mean it, Chief."

Chief hesitates, but nods.

"Watch your eyes." Cricket says.

They look away from the lock.

With his legs spread wide, Cricket slams the axe down. The lock cleaves into pieces and scatters about the room.

The team begins to look at the aftermath. Cricket gets behind Julius on the wall.

Julius pulls the handle to open a crack in the doorway. Chief uses a piece of a broken mirror to look around the corner. He sees a long vacant tunnel descending into a deep darkness.

Chief drops his hand. Julius moves in. His steps, deliberate. His feet meet the ground from heel to toe in consecutive pace. The thud travels through his body in silence.

His friends follow behind like a draft filling a vacuum to his back. A musty cold breeze comes up from below. The air grows too dark.

Each of them lowers a glass from their helmet. Night vision feeds into an augmented display. Chief sees the city infrastructure from City Hall. Behind the walls is electrical work and support beams. The wires are a dull grey rather than orange.

"Power's dead." He whispers.

Before them are several yards of concrete, followed by impenetrable shadow. Particles of dust glow in the deep black before them.

At the mouth of the hallway, they slow down. Chief leans his ear forward. A shuffling, faint. The sound of a disposable cup falling on its open mouth. The shuffling briefly hastens and returns to the same pace. Chief looks at Julius and signals him to move forward.

Beyond the threshold of an open metal door they find an empty subway tunnel. Not a soul, but thousands of rats crawling over one another. The rodents scurry further into the dark from their feet. A granular texture smells metallic in the air.

The concrete tube stretches for miles beyond sight. To the north, it runs far into another middle class neighborhood. To the south, the tunnel meets the A line, by way of the D line. The A starts from the mouth of New Memphis and ends at Meridian Park, near City Center.

Chief approaches the others and speaks with barely any breath "This is it. Let's get back."

They return to the post office, and Chief radios support. A decision is made from high command. Several teams will enter and spread among the tunnels. They'll web across the south city from Thirty-Ninth Ave to Third. New orders are placed to split up and secure strategic locations along the L, C, M, and D lines.

The L and C trains run north and south from Colonial Heights. Their maintenance ports lead into government buildings along the western city. Communication lines and high vantage points can be found through metal doors along the walls of the tunnel. The weak points are barricaded by designated teams. Prospective vantage points are assessed for breach and capture.

Chief and his men are tasked with sealing the doors along the L line, while others handle the M, C, and D lines.

The team returns to the subway tunnels; and through them they venture north, deep into the neighborhood of Middle Borough.

Above them, the enemy is likely hiding in the buildings. They skulk the northern neighborhoods and scurry across the streets. They fight a defensive battle of traps and gorilla tactics.

Down underground, Zion forces move to block the enemies' chance at taking the subway systems. The goal is to remove their access, and thus to eliminate a strategy for their surprise attacks.

About a mile shy of the next subway terminal, Chief's team is set to block some maintenance entrances. They lead from the subway and into the basements of a federal bank, another post office, and two more entrances to unspecified buildings.

They keep quiet; as they know the next terminal is a blockade of enemies. Their sound is easily amplified and focused to the north and south. Each sound becomes a calling sign to their presence, as they echo along the tunnel's walls.

At the entrance of a nondescript building, Cricket wonders why they need to secure the subway. He holds a metal bar across the door and looks at Chief.

"Coming up from underground doesn't seem like the best approach." He tells the team leader "Why are we going about it this way?"

Chief pushes Cricket's face shield down to protect his eyes. He then takes the welding wand and sparks an arc to the metal bar at the frame of the door. He finishes the job and removes his own face shield.

"This is the move that the bad guys don't expect." Chief begins. "For the same exact reason you're asking."

"But what if they expect this?" Cricket asks.

Both men look again at the bar and switch places. Chief lowers his welding mask, and Cricket follows his lead. Chief sparks the welder again and both men remain quiet until the job is finished.

Chief lifts his mask. "You're asking the wrong guy. I'm just following orders."

Chief notices a shadow under the door and freezes. He looks at Cricket who stands petrified.

Chief signals with a hand to remain quiet, then motions to fall back into the tunnel.

At the entrance Dash stands with his scope pointed down the tunnel.

Chief hisses a whisper. "What do you see, Dash?"

"I think I see a person." Dash says.

"Who?"

"A masked man. At least I think it's a man. It's one of those masks the enemies wear."

"Don't fire unless you need to. We just saw a shadow under the doorway... we need to get Zero and Pluto, where are they?"

Dash tenses his face. "They're up ahead." His eyes narrow down the tunnel. "We should go to them and get cover in their doorway."

"Why?"

"That guy has friends and they're coming quick."

The men move up to the others. Dash stands at the edge of the hall. Chief and Cricket move into the doorway with Pluto and Julius. Dash holds still. He's shrunken into the corner of the hall for cover.

A short hallway leads to the door where Zero and Pluto hold a bar across its frame.

"We have company." Chief tells them.

Julius and Pluto turn. They widen their eyes.

"Serious?" Pluto asks.

"Dead serious." Cricket replies.

Chief turns to see Dash hustling down the hall.

Chief calls out in a hush "Open the door and move in. We'll die out here."

Julius and Pluto rush into the door. The others follow. They begin barricading the door. Julius and Pluto stop. Dash does a double-take, then stops. Cricket and Chief throw a chair in front of the door. Then a tall lamp.

Chief turns to ask what is wrong. He sees what's there. He doesn't know what it means. Their postures of confusion. Cricket keeps barricading in a panic.

Chained to a blood smeared wall on the far end of the room, by a bucket of human waste, there's a young woman with red hair and a blue dress. Her hair is matted. Her sobbing face is stained with running mascara. Lipstick smeared under crust and clumped black. Bruises and irritation on the inside of her upper legs. Her skin, an ivory white. Her frail body reaches toward the men. She cries a whimpering moan. She has no teeth.

Cricket turns to see and stops.

Pluto turns to him "Cricket…"

Gunfire fills the room.

The company returns fire in the far corner and a body falls.

Pluto yells in agony. Blood spills from his abdomen. Chief grabs him and moves toward the wall. An older man lay limp in the corner. His eyes look around. He makes no sound.

The men in the tunnel shuffle toward the entryway. Julius can see that the door is still open a crack behind the makeshift blockade. A light flashes on its surface for a brief moment. They're looking down the hall, right at the doorway.

In the quiet, the older man trickles blood on the concrete floor. Julius looks to see his eyes rise and fall in rapid succession. The woman's whimpers are like brush strokes on a canvas of silence.

Julius looks across the doorway to the other side of the wall. Cricket stuffs Pluto's abdomen with quick-clot. Dash covers the far side of the room. He looks up the stairs to see if anyone is coming down into the basement. Chief looks at Julius. His eyes show wonder, but duty.

The wonder makes Julius catch his own deadpanned face.

He motions for Chief to hand him the mirror fragment. Chief tosses it. Julius angles the mirror around the corner, through the crack in the door.

Figures peer out at the end of the tunnel.

Julius drops the mirror and looks at Pluto "There's six." He says.

He breathes deep.

Julius slams the door open. The blockade goes flying into pieces. He turns the corner. He stares down his gun at the panicking figures. He aims with deliberation. A round for each of the three faces. The bodies drop. His feet move forward. Their pace, like gear cogs.

The unseen enemies return fire. Julius drops to the floor and shoots at their hands. His left shoulder is grazed.

He shoots one of the enemies' hands and it explodes on contact with the bullet. The fingers fly in each direction.

Another mask looks around the corner. Julius rolls out of the way and into the bottom northern corner of the hall. He lays flat, out of the way of the second target. The third remaining enemy shoots at him, replacing the handless man. Julius shoots back.

A gash opens from his forearm down his trapezius, but the enemy's mask explodes and he falls. The last enemy runs away. The handless man tries to follow. He crosses the hall from south to north. Julius gives him a shot in the body.

He stands and walks in the same mechanical motion. The squirming figures are given extra shots.

Across the threshold of the hallway, Julius enters the tunnel. No one stands to the north. No one stands to the south. The sound of footsteps has gone. Now there's the sound of blood on cold concrete. Julius looks to see. A broken mask, shattered into the face. The flesh mangled. An eyeball hanging. Falling from the dead man's jacket, there's a pocket watch. Julius has seen one exactly like it.

Julius blocks the sight from his mind. He feels compelled to lose no time. He runs to the other men and crosses into the room. "We need to g..." he is cut off with vomit.

Dash stands "Zero!"

Julius dismisses him with an open hand. He speaks through his mess. "I'm fine." His eyes look up. The chained woman dangles, head down. Her arms stretch to their limit behind herself. Her shoulder blades pressed together at her back. Red blotches appear at her shoulders and elbows. The weight of her body overwhelms their capacity.

Julius rises and wipes his face with his sleeve. He looks at Pluto writhing on the floor. "We need to get him out. Now."

Pluto whimpers "Cricket..."

Dash gives a grunt and begins lifting Pluto.

Cricket motions to stop him "Wait! Let me finish up."

He continues stuffing the wounds to help clot the blood. It spills through much of his efforts. Cricket fights his racing heart and tries his best to cover the wound with clean materials. "Press this down HARD." He says.

The holes in his torso continue to pour through white knuckles.

While the team rushes down the tunnel; the limp, pale Pluto utters soft words. "Boys. Boys, my name."

The team stops.

"What?" Cricket says.

"Is it a shortcut?" Chief asks.

Pluto breathes in a raspy voice "My name is Joel Park."

Dash lifts him. "Shut up!" He tugs the man onward "Move!"

They continue running down the tunnel. Their legs like molten steel beams striking the floor.

Dash gets visibly tired and Chief steps in. Dash places Pluto down and Chief takes Pluto's arm. The two hold the man by his shoulders. They run in an awkward, wobbly, and quickened pace.

Cricket looks back. "He's not staying awake!"

"C'mon! Stay up!" Chief yells.

Pluto's head goes limp.

Chief looks up to Cricket.

Cricket glances at Chief. "He's passed out but he's not gone." He begins running. "Come on!"

Julius trails behind to protect the men from the miles of dark behind them. He scans the shadows for movement. Nothing but rats and roaches.

At the entrance of the long hallway, Cricket swings the door open. The men race up to the light, and into camp.

In the playground Pluto is placed on a table. Cricket and other medics tear his clothing open to begin operating. Bullets are removed. Wounds are covered and clotted. An IV is put into his vein, but his pulse is fading.

After long the commotion comes to a quiet moment. The medics step back and look sidelong. The team surrounds their friend. Their legs exhausted. Nothing to do but wait in agonizing time.

His breaths are shallow, and his eyes look far beyond a hexagon sky. Pluto feels thirsty and tired.

Chief clutches a bloody glove in his hand. "You fight like hell." The leader looks up to where Pluto's eyes now wander. "Please, God…" he says.

Julius sees desperation. A great wish being made before him. One that will probably go unanswered.

Cricket and Dash are silent; and everyone knows if it were someone else, Pluto would have said something by now.

Julius can't stand it and imagines through Pluto's eyes. His mind must be wandering. The thought of what comes next.

"Joel" Julius begins. "if you can fight, then please stay."

At the sound of Pluto's real name, the team looks to Julius.

He presses his teeth together for a breath. He continues "But if you lose this, I want you to know you're out here. In the playground, by the swings."

A smile grows on Joel's face. The pulse under Cricket's finger ceases to beat again.

Cricket's eyes look up to Julius as if he himself is the very person who called Pluto away. He buries his tears into his arms. He wraps his hands around his head.

Julius turns around and walks a few steps before lowering to his knees. He wraps his arms over the top of his helmet. The helmet comes off with his arms. His mind goes blank, and his grip becomes firm. He yells his anger into the floor.

A hand falls on his shoulder. The long fingers are soft and heavy. It's Dash. Julius clasps the hand, and stares off beyond the ground. Chief walks away to a quiet place. They don't see him until their mid day meal.

That night, Julius stares at the wall of their den for a long time.

Chief sharpens a combat knife on the far side of the den. "You've been staring for a long time, Zero."

The whole group listens in, and Julius nods. "Do you really believe in a God? And that Pluto is with him now?"

Chief looks off and thinks a long time. "…No one knows if there's a god, but people believe in 'em. The only person who knows now, is Joel." Chief places the knife down. He turns in his seat and leans forward. "If you ask me, things happen for a reason; and it's bad times that give us an appreciation for the good in the world."

"But you asked God not to let Pluto die" Julius says "didn't you?"

Chief nods "I did." He takes a sigh. "I don't think he gives us what we want. I think God gives us what we need." He looks up at Julius. "Pluto gave us one last gift before he left us. He put us to the test in that horrible moment, and he also gave us something extra to fight for."

Julius looks pained "He didn't mean to die like that."

Chief shakes his head "No, but life happened like that. It's tough to accept, but Pluto's loss wasn't for nothing. He might be the reason the rest of us survive." Chief gives half a smile with a sidelong glance toward his team. "We can't see the end of God's plan. We're just along for the ride." His smile grows. "When I had my kids, I thought my life would be over. I was dreading the mistake of getting my girl pregnant."

He begins to laugh a little. "If only I knew what they'd mean to me."

Julius looks up to see Dash smiling at the older man.

"I had twins," Chief says. "and I could barely afford one." A tear wells up in his eye, but he wipes it away. "They turned my life around for the better. Got me off my pity pot…" He looks at Julius again. "God's plan is in God's hands, not ours." His eyes look over toward Cricket who sits upright. Chief points to him. "This kid has balls. He's grown more in one day, than most people do in a lifetime."

In agreement, everyone nods.

Dash smiles at Cricket.

"Hard times like these make real men. His legs never gave up. He kept his cool and gave it all he had." Intensity grows in his voice. "Even after we got back to camp, he busted his ass with the surgeons. It was pure willpower." Chief stands up.

"Good man, Cricket." Dash says.

Chief looks toward Dash. "And the patience to weigh out the odds. The ability to listen and think on your toes. You carried Pluto all by yourself at first. You didn't quit, Dash. You're one hell of a man."

Dash half smiles as he looks up at Chief. He stands along with Cricket. Then Julius stands.

Chief's eyes turn to Julius. "Zero, I don't know what the hell that was, but you gave them hell." The team laughs and pats him on the shoulder. "That's grace under pressure. Maybe a little luck too." Chief smiles. "You saved the rest of us."

Julius smiles at the remaining group.

They wrap their arms around each other. Their shoulders meet in a huddle. The team looks toward Chief.

Chief looks into their eyes with new inspiration. "Joel had all these traits. Willpower, intelligence, strength, and grace… So don't let him down; don't let his memory fade with us." His eyes scan across the faces before him. "I've got three boys back home; and I'd like to see them grow up into men like you… I'd better not hear your real names before we get home."

Dash smiles. "You've got it."

"I can do that." Cricket adds.

Chief looks at each face before him. Their eyes look back at him; loyal and inspired. He nods again.

"Let's get our rest." He says "We're gonna raise hell in the morning."

CHAPTER 17
Elizabeth

Elizabeth drives down the streets of Eden. She passes a war memorial commemorating the battle of New Memphis. Tim the Tank Man is cast in bronze. He stands atop a broken tank, holding a belt of explosives on his shoulder. His face stares off into the south, at the starlight of Proxima Centauri. Between him and the star is an alley of buildings known as South Street. Its traffic makes a line of cars that stretch to the horizon.

Here by Century Park and America Square, Eden's government officials live and work in the neighborhood of Central City. City Hall stands to the west end of the park. On this avenue, Elizabeth passes the row of Zion flags. They line the streets for the annual Eden Day Parade.

She turns the corner to a row of apartments, marking the high-class neighborhood of Park Place. Here she parks the car on the south side of the street. She pays the meter, and comes to a gate before a brown apartment complex. She buzzes the room, but there's no response.

Elizabeth looks through the glass to see a woman with a young child approaching. The woman opens the door and walks out with bags in her arms. The child comes up behind her and holds the door for Elizabeth. Elizabeth walks through the doorway. She thanks the young man.

"You're welcome." Says the boy.

"Come Danny." The woman says "We don't want to keep them waiting."

A car parks at the curb. The boy's relatives emerge and swarm Danny with affection. A woman extends her arms his way. He embraces his aunt, and the family begins to greet one another.

Elizabeth watches the family as she waits for the elevator. She looks long at them and feels bittersweet. The elevator chimes, and the doors open.

Inside, Elizabeth sees a beer can in the corner. It's likely a piece of trash left by one of the many college students attending a nearby university. She pays no mind to it, but presses the button next to the number "four".

On the fourth floor, Elizabeth comes to a hall of carpet. Beige plaster walls hold warm lights in torch-like cones. Each door bears a number. She strides past them until she reaches "432". She moves closer and listens for a sound. A clomping of bare feet on the bare floor beyond the door. A glass chime, a trickling, and the smack of when glass meets a countertop.

Elizabeth knocks and holds her finger over the peephole. She watches the floor beneath the door. The light grows dim and a shadow forms in the shape of two legs. They wait a while, and Elizabeth almost speaks. She doesn't say a word, but listens. In the silence there are no words. The feet move away and a commotion is heard.

A minute goes by. The door unlocks. It swings open to the sight of her brother Kyle. He's unkempt and unshaven. He's in his pajamas, while Elizabeth is dressed in a long leather coat. She stands on her black high-heels. Her hair was done yesterday, and a leather bag rests beneath her arm.

She shakes her head with wide eyes "You're supposed to be ready!" She says.

"Ready?" He asks "Ready for what?"

Her brows gather "It's the sixth of June! It's Eden Day!"

"Oh fuck!" Exclaims Kyle.

Elizabeth enters the apartment and looks around. Nothing has been cleaned. Plates are stacked in the sink, and empty bottles of alcohol line the countertop. Kyle's clothes are strewn about the apartment, and a used condom sits on the couch.

Kyle sees the condom and runs to throw it away.

"What's wrong with you?" She says "Why didn't you throw that out already?"

He explains himself "I didn't know you were coming over."

"That shouldn't be your reason to throw it out!" She says.

Elizabeth is disgusted, but his smile brings her to laugh at the insanity of it. Kyle continues to smile as he begins cleaning.

Elizabeth raises her voice "I don't want to see that! You pig!"

"I'm sorry!" He laughs.

"At least you're safe." She says.

Kyle shrugs "Eeh, well…"

He gives an exaggerated frown to say he's not.

Elizabeth loses her smile "I hope you're not fishing at the bottom of the barrel..."

"No!" He says "God no..."

Elizabeth finds an extra large thong with stains on it. She picks it up. Her fingers, like tongs.

He grabs it in a hurry and Elizabeth laughs.

"So that's what gets you to use protection?" She laughs.

Her brother begins to smile.

"Seriously, though..." Elizabeth begins "Are you at least staying away from trouble?"

"Like, trouble; like women?" He asks.

"Leeches" Elizabeth says "Abusive people"

"Yeah." He says "Not doing that again."

Elizabeth nods "Good."

She sits on the edge of the couch and watches her brother move about. He grabs clothing from the living room and walks it to the hamper by his bedroom door. He throws the clothing into the hamper, then turns around to grab more.

She nods at him to catch his attention. He looks at her with raised brows, signaling that he's listening.

She motions her head to his bedroom "Go get dressed." She says "Dad's waiting."

He draws back the corner of his mouth and screws his brows together with a shrug. He moves toward his room, passing the threshold and making his way to the closet.

From his room he shouts to continue their conversation "Do you really care that we're on time?"

She looks at the coffee table. It's covered in trash, and so she decides to give him help. She begins grabbing his empty water bottles and seltzer cans.

"I'm not gonna rush" She says "but I'd rather not look like the bad seed."

"Ain't that the bitch of it." He says. He exits his room with his pants on but no shirt "We can't win, so why bother?"

Elizabeth sighs and nods "Give it time." She says "Finish your degree. I'll make it on The Odysseus Mission." She smiles "They'll look stupid sooner or later."

He walks back into his room and shouts out again "You're still trying to make it on that crew?"

"Either I make it, or I'll die trying." She says.

He puts on his shirt and looks for cologne "That's pretty extreme" He says "but that's you as always."

Elizabeth migrates to the kitchen where she continues to throw away cans and bottles. The empty bottles on the counter are left alone; presumed to be a college student's idea of decoration.

When Elizabeth approaches the trash can, she finds something alarming. The trash has a set of beer bottles; all the same kind. They dominate the heap.

"Did you have a party recently?" She asks.

He finds a scarf for the cold Zion weather "No, why do you ask?"

Elizabeth looks into a cabinet under the sink and sees a bottle of whiskey next to the bleach. She grabs the bleach and looks up at the sink. Behind the pile of dishes, there lies a dirty sponge. It sits between the faucet and the wall, collecting bacteria where it lay. Her brother has used it into oblivion. She decides to replace it with a fresh one. The brand new package is untouched. She takes the package and finds behind it is a small glass. It's half full of whisky.

Elizabeth's face falls numb. Her heart takes a hard beat.

"Were you drinking before I came in?" She asks.

"Oh, yeah I was trying a new scotch I got. Do you want some?"

She looks at the bottle. It's identical to one on the counter.

"You have an empty bottle of the same stuff." She says.

"Yeah, Zach brought it over, so I got a bottle."

She looks at the empty with her mouth hung open.

"So you've tried it before then…" She says.

"Yeah." He says "I wanted to taste it again. Is that wrong?"

She puts the bottle down and looks at the line of empties. He enters the kitchen.

"Look" he says "I know what you're thinking, and I'm fine. My grades are great, I'm not drinking too much. I have people over all the time."

Elizabeth gathers her brows, looking over the bottles and nodding with a laugh "That's an awful lot for grad school."

Her brother shrugs "Undergrad girls" he gives a smile with a shrug "What are ya gonna do?"

Elizabeth walks to the door and waits for him to grab his keys.

"Just don't let their habit rub off on you." She says.

He comes to the door and opens it "I'll be fine." He says.

He follows Elizabeth out the door.

Elizabeth and Kyle enter the large house they once called home. A flat roofed house with large glass windows. It lies behind a gated drive-way, and is walled off to the back with bushes. Behind these bushes is a concrete wall that lines the perimeter of the property. The front door is larger than necessary, and the back room opens to a yard with a pool. There, the extended Lawrence family celebrates with a cook out on the slate patio.

Elizabeth walks to the back but notices her brother is stopped at a table. It bestows family photos for guests to see.

Kyle looks long at them, and so does Elizabeth. The Lawrence family shows pictures of their father, his wife, and their half-brother Stephen. Elizabeth and Kyle are nowhere to be found.

"Picture perfect." Her brother says with sarcasm.

"Come on." She says "Let's get this over with."

Their uncle comes to the front hall to greet them "Elizabeth!" He says. His voice comes in a nasally tone followed by a deep breath.

Elizabeth embraces Uncle Steve and smiles.

"How are you?" She asks.

"I'm not bad!" He turns to her brother "What's up, junior? Wow, you're the spitting image of your dad. Get over here and give me a hug." he laughs and gives a grumbling sound as he squeezes Kyle in a bear hug. He grabs Kyle's shoulders and backs away. At arm's length, he looks over the young man.

"How's law school?" He asks.

"Good." Kyle says. His tone unintentionally dismissive "Stressful." Kyle adds.

"I'll bet." Uncle Steve says "Your dad says you're working to be a part of The Odysseus Mission."

Elizabeth becomes curious and looks at her brother. Kyle looks at her, and she looks back to Uncle Steve. His eyes have turned to her, and she realizes her confusion. He was referring to her when he spoke of The Odysseus Mission.

"Oh!" She says "Yeah, that's the dream."

Steve nods "I have a friend who's in on the selection process. He says you'll need a PhD."

Elizabeth nods "I'm in talks with my company about covering tuition."

Her brother wanders off to the back, but Elizabeth remains to be polite.

"Your dad would cover it" says Uncle Steve "That is, if you needed it."

"I'd rather be independent." She says "I don't want dad holding that over my head." She shakes her head with a smirk "You know, when his girl decides to go off to space for twenty-one years." She laughs off her honest comment.

Steve blinks in a nod, as if to say that he understands her.

"Well that's your choice" He says "Whether your dad likes it or not." He pats Elizabeth on the shoulder "You have what it takes regardless, but… don't be afraid of a little help."

Elizabeth smiles. She then looks to the back of the house, toward the slate patio.

"Who else is here?" She asks.

Steve looks out the large window "Your Aunt Lacey is here. She's been in the booze." He shrugs "Then there's your dad, Frida, and little Stevie."

"And the cousins?" She asks.

"Oh, Michael and Annabella are here too." He says "Uncle Scott isn't here, but Michael and Annabella hate spending time at their mother's place."

"Uncle Scott is…"

"Off at some party." Steve says. He points to the back window at Michael and Annabella "He told those two he's in the office today, but they know what's up…"

"I see." Says Elizabeth "And what about Aunt Holly and your kids?"

Steve shrugs "Holly is off at her family's party this year and my kids are with her."

"Are things okay?" Says Elizabeth.

Uncle Steve smiles "They're alright. I wanted to check in on the family is all. I'll be seeing them later tonight."

Elizabeth nods "Oh, okay."

Steve looks to the back of the house and Elizabeth looks to see her aunt Lacey laughing with Frida. Frida looks awkward in dealing with her drunken sister-in-law.

Uncle Steve pulls back a corner of his mouth "Lacy was your mom's favorite." He shakes his head "They'd sit out there all day."

"… I bet." says Elizabeth, only realizing too late that she spoke in a sarcastic tone.

Steve nods dismissing the point "I hope you're taking care of your-self."

"I am." Elizabeth says "Why do you ask?"

Steve sighs "Well…" he begins "Some people don't take care of them-selves; especially when they're caught up in work. Lacy was like that, you know. She might have all the money in the world but she's got no one to share it with."

"I'm doing fine." Elizabeth says "… Did Aunt Lacy want kids?"

Steve nods "She did; but she'll never admit to that." He looks stiff as he talks about it, but Uncle Steve feels it's necessary to give his niece a word of caution "… It's the lie she tells herself to feel better… She claims that it was all a part of her plan in life… but I know that when she played pretend as a little girl; it was always her, an imaginary hus-band, a baby, and her job as a lawyer… Only one of those things came true."

Elizabeth tilts her head "But you don't know if she kept the same ambitions…"

Steve raises a brow.

"I know my sister." He says "No one wants to admit this, but we make up lies to help ourselves cope with our mistakes… Your dad has that same tendency."

Elizabeth scoffs "Well you have nothing to worry about with me. I'm brutally honest with myself."

Steve nods. He waits until Elizabeth looks his way, and when she does, he meets her eyes with approving severity.

"Good." he says "Stay that way and you won't be living a lie that makes you FEEL better… That kind of thing only works in fleeting mo-ments; and it won't follow you to sleep." He motions to the back door "Go find your cousins." He says "We'll talk later. I've gotta talk with your dad about that silly timeshare in the Wachusett River Valley… My wife'll hang me if I don't get that figured out."

Elizabeth laughs and does as he says. She steps out back and finds both Michael and Annabella in lawn chairs by the pool. Kyle has al-ready joined them.

"Elizabeth!" A child yells.

Elizabeth turns to see little Stephen running with a toy in his hand. He embraces her legs in a hug.

She reaches to embrace him, but before she can, he backs away and adjusts the toy with his hands.

"This is Bo!" He says, showing the toy.

It's an action figure dressed as a crime-fighting construction worker.

"He's my favorite superhero!" says Stephen,

"That's really cool!" Elizabeth says.

"Dad gave him to me for my birthday." Stephen tells her "He's from a show that Dad used to watch when he was little."

Elizabeth is bewildered by the onslaught of information.

"That's cool." She says "Dad used to watch him?"

"Yeah!" He says.

"Make sure you don't drop him in the pool!" Annabella says.

Elizabeth turns to see her cousin looking their way. She holds a drink in her hand and smiles.

Annabella goes on "You know, a kid drowned that way. His toy got him stuck in the drain."

Stephen's smile has faded.

"He drown?" he asks.

"Yes" Annabella says. She turns in the lawn chair to face him "He dropped his toy in the water, and he wanted to get it; so he went in, down by the drain." She leans closer "He dove down with his eyes closed. He felt all along the floor of the swimming pool until he touched the toy with his fingertips. When he knew he had it, he went to swim away; but he couldn't. Something was pulling his bathing suit. He pulled, and pulled at the string that tied his bathing suit, but it was stuck. He tried taking the bathing suit off, but after all the pulling, it was too tight. He pulled as hard as he could, but the string was stuck in the drain." She then motions her hands to mimic the drain, pulling the boy down "He tried to give it slack and pull again, but the drain pulled the slack and wouldn't give it back. It went further and further into the drain each time he tried, and before he knew it, he was pressed up against the bottom of the swimming pool.

He screamed 'help! heeelllp!' but no one could hear him; not even his mom, who was cooking with the window wide open." She points to the kitchen window, at the back of the house.

Stephen looks at the window and looks back to her face.

Annabella goes on "When he was out of breath, he gasped, and his lungs filled with water. Hours later, his mom realized he was nowhere to be found in the house. When she went out to the pool, it was quiet. The surface of the water was completely calm. She thought he must have been in the front yard, but the boy was known to make a mess.

She thought she'd take a look, to see if he'd left anything in the water. He usually did.

When she looked inside, she saw her son at the bottom; his limbs were above his head, like this." She raises her limbs like a dead body at the bottom of a pool of water. "His head wasn't moving." She adds, bringing her limbs down to show her fingers "When they pulled him out, his skin was all scratched on his fingers and around his waist."

Stephen is stunned with fear.

Elizabeth touches Stephen's arm to get his attention. He looks at her. She looks at little Stevie with a smile.

"Just be sure not to drop him" Elizabeth says "and if you do, let someone know; okay?"

Stephen nods.

"I'm gonna talk with the cousins now" Elizabeth says "but I'll play with you in a minute. Show Uncle Steve your toy and I'll join you later."

Elizabeth turns, but Stevie says something that makes her stop.

"Did you see Dad yet?" Stephen asks "He said he wants to see you."

Elizabeth looks soft in her posture and yet puzzled "Dad wants to see me?"

Stephen nods "He said he wanted to help you with school."

Her face falls to a sarcastic nod "Yeah, I know." Says Elizabeth "Go play."

She rubs his head and stands from eye level.

Stevie gathers his brows in disappointment. He huffs and walks away in a stomp.

Elizabeth pulls up a lawn chair. She moves it beside Kyle.

"What's up, guys?" Elizabeth asks.

"Nothing much." Michael says "Just school."

"Are you excited to graduate high school?" asks Elizabeth.

"I'm ready to get the fuck out and party." Michael laughs.

Kyle laughs "Yeah buddy!" he says, bumping his cousin's fist.

"Michael got accepted to UE South." Annabella says.

"Home of the monsters." says Michael. His tone sounds more like excitement than pride.

"University of Eden is a great place." Elizabeth says "And how are you, Annabella?"

"My first year was gooood." She says, lingering on parts of her words. She speaks with a pride in her knowledge, but Elizabeth knows she's young and arrogant. Her lingering is frequently on points of interest in the conversation; when she thinks she's saying something that makes her look interesting or intelligent. "The girls and I are planning a trip to New Memphis. We wanna see government centerrr, and the visitor's distriiict."

Elizabeth shrugs with lips drawn back at the corners "I mean, what else is there to see?"

"Yeaah" Annabella says with her gossip girl's tone "I wouldn't want to see the slums…"

Elizabeth can't help but take a silent sigh through her nose.

Annabella continues to regale her plan "We're staying at my friend Bridget's place in Gabriel Hillll. It's that nice area where the government people staay; I guess her dad was a congressman or something for Iowa. Big money."

"That sounds like fun!" Elizabeth says.

Annabella nods "Yeaaah" She laughs to preface her own sarcasm "I'm hoping I'll find a husband there."

Elizabeth can't help but wonder if there's some truth to that, but she smiles at the joke.

Their heads turn at the sound of a drawn-out greeting.

"Hey guyyyys!" Aunt Lacy says.

Lacy's arms are spread with her shoes in her hand and a mixed drink in the other. Her dress comes up to her collarbones but there's no straps over the shoulders. She seems so confident that her top won't fall. It makes Elizabeth feel uneasy for her.

Annabella greets her aunt with a fake excitement while the boys smile. To the boys, the fun aunt has arrived. For Annabella, it's someone she cares about; and yet can't bear to keep her judgements to herself when Aunt Lacy isn't around.

"I heard about youuuu!" Lacy says, increasing her tonality in congratulations. Her hand reaches out to their cousin Michael.

Michael looks down in a bashful way, but he tries to still be cool about it.

"Thanks!" He says "Yeah I've been…"

Michael goes on, but Elizabeth spaces out for a moment. She looks over Aunt Lacy and wonders how she might have been as a mother.

Lacy has always been the fun aunt; and even though she's thirty years older than Elizabeth, she has always tried to be like a friend.

Elizabeth sees Lacy's face give a small indication of something more. She then looks at her brother and cousins. They look elsewhere, and not at Lacy's face. Not even Annabella, who's telling her aunt about her vacation plans.

If any of them had heard what Uncle Steve had to say, they might look closer at their aunt. It's there that they would see a deep care for what her nieces and nephews are up to. Her eyes beam with joy when she hears of their accomplishments. She turns to the others, often promoting them to join in on the conversation; encouraging a family camaraderie among the kids. Her eyes then shine again, but this time with a sparkle; as a blissful swoon over the news of the children's overall happiness.

Elizabeth decides that Uncle Steve is right. Lacy loves the connection she's made with the younger generation.

"And what about you, Lizzie?" Aunt Lacy asks.

Elizabeth looks around "I'm sorry, what were we talking about?"

"Are you dating anyone, she's asking." Says Annabella.

Elizabeth shakes her head.

"I haven't had the time." She says.

"That-a-girl!" Says Lacy.

She taps Elizabeth's arm, but the whole gesture feels patronizing.

"Take care of YOU!" She says; followed by a big gulp of her drink.

Elizabeth breathes deep with a shrug.

"I'm not against it…" Elizabeth says "… I just don't have the head-space for it while I'm in school."

Kyle gathers his brows. He knows this isn't Elizabeth's usual answer, but something's changed her perspective today.

Annabella knows this too, and so her face is tensed in question.

"Do you ever want kids?" Annabella asks.

Elizabeth presses her lips together in a thought.

"… I wouldn't know my little brothers if they were never born; and today, I know that I can't imagine a life without them… So it sounds scary; kinda like taking a chance on a first date, or starting a conversation with a stranger that becomes your friend… You can't miss what you've never had, and yet, the best relationships are the ones you've never asked for… It's tough to decide."

Lacy stares off in thought. When she looks at Elizabeth, she smiles and hugs her.

Elizabeth is caught by surprise, but she hugs her aunt in return.

The cousins are taken aback, realizing Lacy is far more drunk than they previously thought.

Lacy backs away from the hug and looks at her nieces and nephews. "I can't imagine life without you kids." She says.

***

Time goes by, and the trash is rounded by plates and bones from grilled food. The beer bottles have stacked up among bottles of champaigne.

Elizabeth is in the kitchen looking for a dessert in the fridge. She closes the refrigerator and tries the freezer. Here she finds a box of ice cream sandwiches. It's the same brand her father would buy when she was little. She pulls one out of the box and closes the door. The packaging has changed and so has the company's logo. "Fillaberrie's" it reads.

She peels the packaging to the same old sandwich. The artificial chocolate graham sticks to her fingers. It makes a cake-like texture over the fingerprints; just like it used to.

Elizabeth takes a bite and remembers her and Kyle by the pool years ago. He was five, and she was seven. She wore a one-piece yellow bathing suit, and he had a pair of blue swim trunks. One of her baby teeth was crooked. It interfered with her biting, but she didn't mind. Mom and Dad were with them, talking in a hushed tone. It was something she wrote off as "boring adult matters". She remembers looking at Kyle instead, and smiling. He smiled back.

Elizabeth opens her eyes to see Stephen. He looks a little different from her.

He looks at the sandwich. His juice box is clutched in both hands. The straw is in his mouth, but he doesn't take a sip.

Elizabeth bends her knees to be at eye level.

"Do you wanna take half for me?" She asks.

Stephen nods and approaches.

"Mom might get mad." He says.

Elizabeth puts her finger up in a "shh" motion.

She breaks the sandwich in half and offers it "Does Dad still eat these?" She asks.

"Sometimes." He says.

"Kyle and I used to eat these by the pool."

"Really?" He asks.

"Yeah." Elizabeth says "We were just like you back then."

He looks at the sandwich a minute, then takes a bite. Before finishing

131

his bite, he takes the sandwich away from his teeth, leaving an imprint on the fake chocolate graham.

"Will Dad still be with my mom when I'm your age?" He asks.

Elizabeth shakes her head "I don't think that'll be the case for you." She says "But if anything ever upsets you, you can always stay with me for a while."

He holds the sandwich with both hands and looks up "Really?"

Elizabeth nods "That's what big sisters are for. If you need a place to go and you don't want to be home, you're always welcome with me."

He smiles and takes a bite of the sandwich. As he chews, he moves forward to hug Elizabeth.

"What's this?" A voice says.

Elizabeth looks up to see her stepmother smiling at Stevie.

Frida's face changes at the sight of the sandwich "How did you get that?"

"Oh I gave it to him." Elizabeth says.

"It's his bedtime." Frida says "You can't have that before bed!" Her tone is stern with the boy.

"I'm sorry" Elizabeth says "I took one from the fridge and I felt bad. It's my fault."

"You can't just take things from the fridge without asking." Frida says "This isn't your house anymore."

Elizabeth smiles with winced eyes and takes a bite of the sandwich.

Frida takes Stevie and walks off. Stephen looks back at Elizabeth. He waves goodnight from his mother's arms.

Elizabeth waves back.

Her attention diverts to another figure in the corner of her eye. Her father approaches with an awkward demeanor. He steps with a slow sway of his shoulders. One foot, then another. His hands halfway between a fists and being wide open.

He sighs, trying to sound casual "Hey Lizzie."

Elizabeth is unfazed by the nickname.

He looks at her stone-cold face, and back toward Frida. Frida exits the room, and he looks back at Elizabeth.

"What did I miss?" He asks.

"I was told I can't take things from the freezer." Elizabeth says "I was unaware."

"What… Why?" He asks.

"She says it's because 'I don't live here anymore.'"

"Well you don't." He says.

Elizabeth raises her brows.

"What?" He says "It's not your house anymore."

"Well that's fine." She says "It hasn't felt like a home in a long time."

"Well, you'll need a home of your own someday. I don't see how you're gonna do that. It isn't like I can parent you forever."

Elizabeth nods "Never asked you to, so don't tell me what to do."

"Since when am I telling you what to do?" He asks.

"What's with you hounding to pay for my graduate degree?"

"Because I want to help you!" He says.

"No." Elizabeth says "You want to use it against me."

"How?" He says "What do I have to gain? I'm OFFERING money. Money that MOST kids would be grateful for."

"Yeah, so that you can guilt me out of The Odysseus Mission."

Elizabeth's father shakes his head with wincing eyes "And just how are you so certain you'll make the cut?"

She rolls her eyes "And now you're trying to discourage me."

He scoffs "You're hopeless. I give up." He turns his back but stops. He looks her way again for another remark "If you have everything riding on a goal that doesn't work out, and they choose someone else; then what? You'll have no goal and no family. You'll waste time digging a hole of debt, and then what?"

Elizabeth walks to the coat rack. She grabs her coat and moves to the patio door.

"Right" her father says "You have no response."

She knows his remark is aimed to get a response, but she won't take his bait.

She walks out the patio doors to see the family talking together.

"Where's Kyle?" She asks her Uncle Steve.

Uncle Steve points to a corner of the yard. There, Elizabeth sees Kyle. He's hunched over; his arm, propping him up on a table. A long string of mucus stretches from his mouth to a pool of vomit in the wheat grass.

Elizabeth approaches him and turns her head "Someone help me."

Her cousin Annabella takes Kyle's side. Elizabeth carries him from the other side and begins walking him toward the house.

"Not in the house!" Her dad says "Go up the side!" his finger points to the fence door, on the side of the house.

Michael runs to the fence and opens the door to a path running between the house and the bushes lining the property.

Elizabeth doesn't object, but gets Kyle to the car as quick as she can.

She crosses the threshold of the gate and hears her father's voice, kept under his breath.

"What a mess." He says.

Elizabeth drags Kyle to the front and starts making her way for the car. He begins mumbling something, but no words come out.

"Open the door." Annabella says. Her voice strains under Kyle's weight.

Elizabeth unlocks the car and opens the passenger door. Her cousin Michael comes out with a bottle of water. Elizabeth seats Kyle in the car and Michael hands the water to him.

"Thank you." Elizabeth says.

"Yup." replies Michael.

Michael darts off into the house and Annabella follows after him.

Elizabeth looks at Kyle's face for confirmation "Are you okay? Do you need a minute?"

He nods to the first question then waves his hand.

"'m fine." He says.

Elizabeth sighs. She buckles his belt and waits a minute. Kyle moves his head to get comfortable. When he finds a position, the belt is pressed to his face. His lip falls limp on the edge of the seatbelt.

"Are you good?" Elizabeth asks.

Kyle nods.

Elizabeth walks to the other side and opens the door.

She doesn't say her goodbyes, but leaves the driveway without a word. Elizabeth reverses the car into the road. She straightens it out and puts the car in drive. Idling on the gas, she accelerates a little. She begins her drive in a delicate manner, down the roads that lead into the heart of the city.

"'m sorry." Kyle says.

All she can say is "Don't worry about it."

She passes from the dark neighborhoods of the northwest, and into the busy streets of the central city. Kyle keeps his eyes closed in the passenger's seat. Elizabeth assumes he's fallen asleep.

She comes to the red light of an intersection and decides he's drunk enough to tell the truth. She rubs his arm to wake him.

"Hey" She says "I need to ask you something."

He lets out a confirmation that she can hear "Mm?"

"Have you been drinking a lot?" She asks.

"No." He says "I just got out of hand with the cousins."

The light turns green and Elizabeth touches the gas to move forward.

She looks at Kyle "I won't be mad if it's true." She says "I just wanna know you're okay."

"It doesn't happen that much." He says.

She comes to a bit of city traffic and slows down.

"You shouldn't be drinking this much." She says "Maybe just a drink or two next time."

"I know." He says "I was bored." He opens his eyes to stare ahead at the road. His head fights to stay propped up, and he slaps it back into the seat to recline "That whole house is one big reminder, that he doesn't care."

"You can't give him a reason to say things, though."

"I don't care what he says." Kyle adds. He takes a sip of his water "He says that Stephen does better in school than I did."

"He said that?"

"Yeah." He affirms "Apparently he already skates better than me too."

"Not BETTER than you." Elizabeth says "He's four." She shakes her head "What an asshole; pinning you against your four-year-old brother."

"I don't know." Kyle says "But Stevie doesn't give a shit." He begins to laugh "He kept showing me his toys. He thinks we're his buddies, like the age difference doesn't mean a thing to him." He giggles "It's so cute!"

Elizabeth laughs "He's mature, but he needs friends his age."

"He IS my friend." Kyle says "He's my brother. That's even better."

"I know, but kids HIS age." Elizabeth remarks "You're a kid at heart. That's not the same."

Kyle nods with a smile "Yeah. He'll find them when he goes to school in September."

They smile a while. In the silence they feel happy for a moment. The traffic eases up as Elizabeth comes to a corner near her brother's apartment.

"Dad can complain that I'm not good enough" he says "and he might try to guilt me with my brother's success; but I'm proud of the little guy. He's gonna be an awesome hockey player."

"He's smart too." Elizabeth adds "He's only four years old and he's asking me questions about stars and space."

"Really?" Kyle laughs.

Elizabeth smiles "Yeah. He's into computers too, but I don't know much to tell him. I know the physics of it, but I'm not a tech geek yet."

Kyle raises an index finger along with his brows "That's what the master's degree is for." He says.

"Exactly." Elizabeth says.

Kyle smirks "Then, The Odysseus Mission."

"Well" Elizabeth interjects "PhD, THEN that, but yeah." She is focused on the road, but adds a side note to her thoughts "I've already started on coding. We'll see how it goes."

She turns into the parking garage for Kyle's apartment. He looks around with his brows gathered.

"Why'd you turn in here?" He asks.

"Because I'm sleeping over." She says.

She turns the corner into the visitor's parking spots.

"No, wait..." He begins.

She parks the car in an empty visitor's space.

"I'm tired" She says "Don't be difficult."

She opens her door "Do you need help?"

"My apartment is a MESS." He says.

"What else is new? Do you need help?"

"No, I'm fine." He says.

She steps out of the door "Come on."

They exit the garage and come to an elevator. Inside, Elizabeth hits the button "four". It smells like a high-class apartment from the inside, different from this morning. The doors close and the elevator rises.

Kyle gathers his brows ".... do you think Dad is a dickhead because it gets Frida off?"

"Ew!" Elizabeth says.

Kyle laughs in a chuckle of vulgar amusement.

Elizabeth laughs "What's wrong with you?"

He shrugs "It's the only thing that makes sense!"

Elizabeth shakes her head "He thinks that being a hard ass will make us work harder. He gives us nice things like this apartment."

"Condo." Kyle says "It's Dad's condo."

She shakes her head "Whatever."

"He does that, but like; what the fuck for if he's just gonna call us a disappointment?"

Elizabeth shakes her head "He thinks he knows what's best for us, and doesn't care what we want."

"I don't meet his expectations." Kyle says.

"No" Elizabeth laughs "but you do everything the way he does. So he's just a hypocrite."

"What's that mean?"

"Condoms on the couch?" Elizabeth asks "How do you think Mom found out?"

"THAT's how?"

Elizabeth laughs "I'm surprised you haven't heard Mom regale the tragedy of Dad's infidelity. She tells everyone."

"I didn't know THAT part." He adds.

"Mom couldn't handle it if she knew what you were like." Elizabeth laughs.

The doors open and the siblings walk down the hall.

"Yeah, I don't tell mom anything." He admits.

"I've noticed."

"Has SHE noticed?" He asks.

Elizabeth shakes her head.

They come to Kyle's door.

"She hasn't said anything to me." Elizabeth adds.

"Good." He says.

Kyle begins searching his pockets, looking for his keys.

Elizabeth pulls them out of her own pocket.

His mouth opens with exaggerated surprise.

"OOOoooohhh." He whispers.

Elizabeth laughs and opens the door. She enters the room and takes off her shoes. Kyle walks in with his shoes on and sits on the couch.

"There's a lot you probably don't remember." Elizabeth says.

She sits on the other end of the couch from her brother.

Kyle screws his brows together.

"I remember more than you'd think." He says "I remember you were really upset when they told us; and I remember sneaking into the cookie jar when Mom and Dad weren't looking."

"You remember me boosting you onto the chair?" She asks.

"And climbing onto the washing machine?" Kyle says "Of course I remember."

They smile at the memory; no matter how distant it is. It feels more like a dream than anything.

Elizabeth nods and stares off at another thought.

"I remember you giving me your toys when I was afraid of the dark."
She says.

"You're STILL afraid." Kyle laughs.

"I'm better! I swear I'm a lot better… I just can't do creepy dark places where I feel lost."

Kyle shrugs "Who CAN, honestly."

They look at one another and anticipate each other's next words. They don't bother saying it, but instead they laugh.

They think to themselves

"*Yeah, I remember.*"

***

Elizabeth falls asleep in her brother's apartment. Her brother waits in the dark with his eyes closed, but he's used to falling asleep at three or five in the morning. He gives up and sneaks out to the balcony.

The curtains have come down, and the city lights reflect off the glass where inner curtains neglected to fall in the hexagon pattern. The emergency outer curtain makes up for the failure; but he recalls the brief moments when he's seen the failure without a curtain. A hexagon hole in the black dome lets light beam down on a chosen spot in the city. For a moment, there is something different in the landscape; and the change makes it beautiful. These moments don't last for long, but they happen from time to time. When the curtains fail, the presence of the dome is more apparent than usual. It lingers in the sky as a hint that their stay in the dome is temporary; and they're long past due for the eviction date.

He reaches into his pocket for a pack of cigarettes. They're just sticks of synthetic nicotine, coated on a plant-based sawdust material.

He loves to do something different and new. If he were a young man in California, he would hike regularly. He would take road trips and see distant friends in distant places. His sister's visit has broken the repetition of his every day. He hates going to his father's place, but it was different for a change. He hates hearing the same lecture, but it was bearable this time. He isn't enticed to speak with his father, because it's become a repeat of critiques. His mother would have her own two cents if she were to know who he really is. The one saving grace is his siblings. They give a respite in the mundane world. They intervene with new dialogue. They've never sought to change him, but to enrich his inherent desire for exploration and meaningful conversation.

He avoided his father tonight because his cousins would at least talk about something he hasn't heard. It was a superficial conversation at first; until they were sufficiently drunk. That's when the real smiles and laughter start.

He wonders what makes them so distant before they drink. It's just like the hollow friendships he's made here in the city. They're friends while they're drunk, but not when they're sober. If they sobered up, then they're an acquaintance at best.

There aren't many bonds as natural as those between siblings; and it's nice when a friend can be that close. Parents are supposed to be approachable; but the fact remains that Elizabeth is the only person he feels an ounce of trust with, and little Stephen is far too young.

Kyle waits for his law degree. He eats, sleeps, does his homework, and waits every day for the semester to drag by. He's grown tired of waiting and breaks up the boredom with a drink. He knows it's wrong, and it started with hollow friends, but now it's just something he does to help the hours blur by.

He hopes to find a decent conversation on a dating app. He finds dozens of women with similar stories. Poor girls looking to meet rich guys. Big women who claim to be experienced and know what they want. They claim to be wild in bed, only to be prude and lethargic when the moment arrives. Occasionally there's a decent conversation with a woman, and as it turns out she's been damaged by an uncle, or a mother and father. They'll talk, but she'll hope for someone more than Kyle is looking to be right now. He craves a conversation, but he doesn't want to give them the false promise of something more. He is a romantic, but not monogamous. He can appreciate someone without wanting more than a friendship. Maybe it can be called "love"; but not the kind of love found in Hollywood movies of old. Maybe it's the appreciation of one soul to another. A love for the color brought into his life; by someone worth calling a friend.

As of right now, he's just come out of one such misunderstanding. He's shut off another opportunity; before she could mistakenly swoon for him.

His sister's visit is a respite of laughter, conversation, and a lack of judgement; and yet he's sad. It will be tomorrow before he knows it; and when tomorrow comes, he will be back in the loop of his life's pattern. He won't laugh at a witty remark. He'll just wait through the precious years of his life; drinking. Wasting his time with small talk until strangers let their guard down, dropping their pointless facade. Kyle dreads his sister's departure, because he knows from then on, he'll be unamused. He'll sift through the small talk, drinking; and wait for a day that keeps inching further away.

***

Two years go by, and Elizabeth earns her master's degree. She's enrolled for her PhD, and working on a project to make old computers compatible with a quantum analysis machine. It takes the data of old statistics and finds the probability of skewed analytics. Her two partners are an electrical engineer who specializes in old technology, and a computer scientist with a background in social engineering.

It's Elizabeth's second week in the laboratory, but it's been two months since she's had the chance to speak with her mother.

In each phone call, Elizabeth's mother apologizes for taking up her daughter's time. Elizabeth in turn feels sorry to make her conversations short, and she makes a false promise to call on the weekends. In truth, Elizabeth is disheartened when her mother calls after having a few drinks, and that is often.

It's been even longer since she's spoken with her father; almost a half of a year by now. The last time they spoke, he had called to accuse her of taking her grandmother's ring from an old jewelry box in the attic. He never told her if he found it, but Elizabeth assumes he did and can't admit it.

In the bustle of her studies, Elizabeth is happy to be away from the insanity of her family. She forgets as much as she can, but her evenings can be blindsided with a surprise.

If it's not a photo of her distant half-brother on a social media account, then it's a phone call from Kyle. It's a pleasant surprise in comparison, and it brings a much-needed laugh to her days. At the very worst, his voice will bring her a sort of longing once they've hung up. The kind that one feels when a loved one isn't satisfied with life. It only becomes worse when that lack of satisfaction creates a vacuum wherein all the motivation gives way to despair.

Most days, Elizabeth feels happy in her new home of colleagues and fellow students. It becomes a breeze when the work is slow, and her lunch hours are spent in good company. Nice people who keep their

140

distance and don't judge her life decisions; albeit, they don't really know her. They know the face she puts on in public, but they've never known how she feels about love and true happiness. They know what she likes and dislikes, but they don't know what she fears and loathes. It's a comfortable arm's distance for her. The other things can wait for her phone calls with Kyle.

Elizabeth looks on at the screen before her. Her partner waits at her side as she looks over his coding. It all seems agreeable, and it makes common sense. She nods and gives him the okay to move forward.

"I'll just need to change a few things…" She says "… but that's fine."

Her laboratory table lights up with a call from her mother. Elizabeth assumes that it's just another drunken rambling. A declaration of ideas and plans that will never come to pass. More pledges to start afresh and begin a business venture of her own; finally divorcing herself from the appearance of dependency she acquired with Elizabeth's father.

The call disappears from the table and Elizabeth is relieved not to have answered; but the call comes again. Elizabeth is between confusion and frustration. She takes a headphone out of her pocket and places it in her ear.

The call opens to the sound of sobbing. Elizabeth stops her work. Her partners see the concern on her face. She steps away from the table and pries her mother to speak, but Elizabeth's mother can't form a sentence.

"Mom, where are you?" says Elizabeth.

Her mother wails "I'm at home!"

Elizabeth sees her father is now calling. She tells her mother, but Elizabeth can't find it in herself to hang up. Her mother says to stay on the line, and so she does.

The giver of life that she is, Elizabeth's mother takes a moment to breathe deep and calm herself down. She thinks of how she must compose herself. Through the agony and alcohol, she tries her best for her daughter.

"What's going on, Mom?" says Elizabeth "Is everything okay?"

The woman on the other end lets out all the air in her lungs in a blow between pursed lips. She gasps in two more breaths. She begins speaking, but in a quivering voice.

***

Elizabeth feels her hands go numb. She thinks again and again, com-

141

ing to dead ends with what to do. She thinks instead to what could have been done.

Kyle had been in a loop of descending behavior. He'd dropped out of law school, after supplying alcohol to an underaged party. His father cleared his record on search engines, but Kyle couldn't hold a job at a law firm. His days had been spent working for minimum wage. The days passed into months and Kyle's correspondence became scattered and less frequent. Elizabeth noticed, but assumed he would find his own way. She knew her brother was intelligent, but perhaps assumed he was beyond social influence. Now there is no going back, and the finality of her actions are irreversible. She feels like she could intervene, but it's not possible. It's done.

Kyle was found on a fraternity couch. The pledges touched his chest and found his shirt was soaked in vomit. His eyelids were loose, and his pupils were immovable. Kyle choked on his vomit in the middle of the night, and he was dead.

Elizabeth arrives at the funeral home. Her black woolen coat drapes down her legs above black heels. She walks into the room to see her mother sitting at the side of Kyle's casket. Her father sits in the row of chairs with his wife and little Stephen. Her cousins sit to the back with their parents, but Uncle Steve sits in the front, close to Elizabeth's father.

Elizabeth approaches the casket with a letter in her hand. It's some words for Kyle, but she'll soon forget them. She wanted to send him down with something, anything to say that she's still with him.

She looks at his expression, and it appears relaxed. It looks nothing like he did when she last saw him. His hair is combed and he wears a suit.

She reaches for his arm, but it's hard to the touch. It's more like a rock than a human being. She feels her heart ache at the thought of it. His words are over. His expression will remain this way until his skin retracts, and his flesh decays. She'd say something if there'd be a response; but there will never be another word from his lips again.

She cries for lost days and lost opportunities. Elizabeth knows that she could have done more, had she been involved with his life. She knows that her passion occupied the time she could have spent with her family. She's been off doing something that none of them could relate to. She's alone as an engineer, but she wasn't alone as the child of her parents. Now, she's the only reminder that they were ever together.

Her mother reaches for her shoulder, and Elizabeth hugs her mom. She wishes her father would join them, even if just for a moment. He sits there with his new family, and never approaches the casket. She never sees a sign that he ever cared.

After the events of the wake, they are dismissed by the funeral home, and the family begins talking.

Uncle Steve comes to see Elizabeth.

"Hey Lizzie." He says.

Elizabeth hugs her uncle. He embraces her with compassion.

"I'm here for you, kiddo." Steve says "Don't give up." He pulls away and looks into her eyes "He wanted to see you live out your dreams, so go after it. No matter what, keep trying."

Elizabeth nods. She stares off and thinks about what he's said.

"There's something I want to give you." Steve says.

He pulls out a business card. It's an off-white. The print is in black glossed letters. It reads:

"Doctor Hoyt
Psychiatrist / Therapist
34560 New Jersey Way
Central City, Eden, UZ"

Elizabeth gathers her brows, then looks to her uncle.

"He's a friend of mine" says Uncle Steve "He knows who you are, and he just wants to talk. He doesn't push medication, but he'll talk with you about anything. Do me a favor and go to him. He's good to know."

Elizabeth nods "Thank you, Uncle Steve."

Steve hugs his niece again and smiles.

He takes a deep breath, then speaks with his nasally voice.

"You're tough stuff, kiddo." He says.

Her father approaches and looks concerned.

"Are you doing well?" He asks "Are classes okay?"

"I'm doing just fine." Elizabeth says.

"Is the company paying for it?" He asks.

She becomes brief "Why do you ask?"

Uncle Steve takes a deep breath. He stands and waits out the ensuing conversation.

"I just want to know you're taken care of." Her father says.

"I'm doing just fine." She says "I'm taking care of myself."

Her father tries to hug her but she backs away.

"Did you ever ask how Kyle was doing?" She says.

"Elizabeth!" Her uncle says.

"Did you ever do anything but tell him that he wasn't good enough?"

Her father almost speaks, but he doesn't find any words.

"My brother is dead." She says "I don't need to talk to you anymore."

Elizabeth turns and walks to the door. She swings it open and descends the steps of the funeral home. She'd say goodbye to her mother, but figures it'd be better to see her later.

Elizabeth comes to the curb of a busy street. She waits for a moment to cross. There's a short gap between the cars, and the moment comes. With enough time between oncoming traffic, she takes a jog to make her escape on the other side of the road. She reaches the sidewalk when she hears a child's voice behind her.

"Elizabeth!" The child screams.

Elizabeth turns to see little Stevie running down the steps. He comes between the parked cars in front of the funeral home. Elizabeth runs back, and the car next to her screeches to a halt. The car on the other side continues and Elizabeth screams for it to stop. Her hands wave in the air.

Stephen stands wide-eyed in the middle of the lane. The second car screeches.

Stephen looks at the stopped car before his face, and stands paralyzed at its headlights. He turns on his heels to Elizabeth, and she runs to pick him up.

He cries in her arms "Can I still be your brother?"

"What do you mean?" Elizabeth asks "Of course you're my brother!"

"You'll still see me" He says "right?"

Elizabeth hugs him tight and notices the man in the car. He opened the door to scream, but now his face looks perplexed. His eyes meet hers, and Elizabeth gives him a look as if to be thankful for his patience. The man sits back in the car and closes his door.

Elizabeth walks her brother to the sidewalk at the funeral home.

She places him down and looks at his face. Her father is at the top of the steps.

"I'll always be your sister." She says "I promise."

Frida runs down the steps. Elizabeth gives Stevie one last hug.

Her stepmother rips the boy from Elizabeth's arms.

"You ungrateful bitch!" She says "You hurt his feelings!"

Elizabeth looks at her father, still at the top step, and stunned.

"Stop it Mom!" says little Stephen "Stop!"

Frida attends to her son, then rears her head for another remark.

Elizabeth looks at her father as if to say "*Way to pick 'em*".

"After everything we've given you...!" Frida starts.

"Given me?" Elizabeth laughs "You've been waiting to use that against me. What have you done?"

Frida breathes in a huff.

Elizabeth goes on, motioning a nod at Stephen "Blame yourself if he comes to me for help before he even thinks about you." She smiles at little Stephen "I'm always here for you." She looks sickened at Frida "Even when they won't be."

Frida begins yelling, but Elizabeth saunters across the street. It's finally void of traffic. Frida keeps yelling remarks as Elizabeth enters her car.

Elizabeth looks through the windshield to see her Uncle Steve give a smile from the top step. Elizabeth smiles back. She presses the "start" button and takes a sigh. She remembers one part from her letter to Kyle, but it's the only thing she'll ever recall.

> *"You can rest now, and I'll live on for the both of us. I'll keep your memory with me, and they'll know it was you who made me strong. In your memory, I'll bring back what was lost, and make heroes out of the both of us."*

Elizabeth smiles with resolve in her mind. She reverses her car and backs out of the parking space. She never speaks with her stepmother again.

CHAPTER 18
Los Angeles

Elizabeth looks out the window to see the second explorer pod. Its areal lights show the expanse beneath them. A carpet of square blocks and striations of road. It's a terrain of dusty earth and atmospheric snow, blanketing the sprawled out city. The edges of the plain reach the rock faces at the bases of mountainsides. The jagged peaks stand high above the slush of snow. The pinnacles reach into the starry sky and crown the valley.

Nestled between the mountains that stand to the north, south, and east; Burbank stretches across the land. The desert floor reaches west, through the neighborhoods of North Hollywood, Sherman Oaks, Van Nuys, and onward through Thousand Oaks. Over a range of hills to the west, the land comes to the Pacific Ice Sheet. Nothing would impede the naval traveler until they reached the continent of Asia.

The second explorer pod travels two hundred yards south, to the mountain that rests between Burbank and the city of Los Angeles. There, the biologists seek to explore the specimens of the desert.

Elizabeth's pod lands in the open space provided by an empty parking lot. A water tower stands tall, underlit by the lights on the explorer pod. This is the studio of an old production company; responsible for the legacy of ancient artists. Their works have survived in digital copies, brought light years away by the original inhabitants of Zion. It is here that the team hopes to find the lost copies of beloved films. They hope even more to find the original works of the master storytellers themselves.

Elizabeth walks across the studio lot. She looks for the office of someone important. They would be holding artifacts on display, for the pleasure of employees and prospective clients alike.

In the office of a studio executive, they find signed pictures of legendary personalities such as Clint Eastwood, Martin Scorsese, Greg Toland, and Walter Murch.

Elizabeth looks long at the face of a man in a photograph. He stands by a path along a California beach. Palm trees stand at either side of the concrete walkway. He squints in the sunlight, and his hair is caught in the gust of a sea breeze. She wonders what it must have been like to lie under sunlight. How it must have been to hear birds, and to feel the water at her feet; lapping the shores of Southern California.

The man gives an awkward smile. He stands next to a larger man in shorts and a polo. The larger man holds a cigar with gold chains around his neck. Their meeting was likely brief and disingenuous, she thinks. They were likely unaware of how lucky they were to experience something so far from the imagination of a little girl in Eden.

"They're so ordinary." Julius says.

Elizabeth turns to see him behind her.

He nods toward the photo "Not a care in the world. To them it was just a talk by the beach." He gives a gust of a laugh "To us, it's like their stories. A work of fiction."

Elizabeth looks back to the photo. She looks a while longer and decides that the smile isn't awkward because it's a formal meeting. He's squinting because it's bright outside. His skin is irritated by the sun. He's sunburnt and his lips are dry.

Julius raises something to show Elizabeth "Speaking of fantasy stories, look what I found."

He holds a wooden movie prop. A long branch, about six feet in length. A smoking pipe is nestled within its gnarled top.

"Does it look familiar?" He asks.

She smiles "Oh my god."

Julius hands it to her, and she holds it erect before her.

"You shall not pass!" She says.

Julius laughs "We're taking that back." He says.

"Is it the original?" She asks.

He shrugs "I don't know. I found it on that stand."

She walks over to the corner and has a look at the stand. A display pedestal raises two arms from a desk. Beneath it is a plaque made of brass. She reads it closely.

"I think it is." She says.

Over the course of an hour, they search the offices for more artifacts. In some documents, they find the location of original film stocks; but they discover it's far from where they've landed.

Elizabeth decides to make another trip at a later date, and the team takes the artifacts to the explorer pod.

"Linda?" Elizabeth says over the headset.

Linda's voice comes over the helmet speakers "Yes?"

"Do we have enough time to make a trip south?" Elizabeth asks.

"How far?" Linda replies.

"I want to see how people lived here." Elizabeth says "It's important for Doctor Hoyt's research."

"Hold on." Linda says.

The weight on the explorer pod reads 150 lbs; less than half the maximum weight. She decides it's enough to bring home a sizable sample of ordinary data, aside from the Hollywood relics.

"You wanna see a cool spot?" Linda says "You'll see a unique sub-culture of Los Angeles; then if you travel east, you'll be kinda close to downtown LA."

"Is that safe?" Elizabeth asks.

"The bomb that dropped on LA wasn't very big." Linda adds "You'll be okay until you're directly downtown. Then the structures get a little hairy."

"What's the place called?" Elizabeth asks.

She enters the explorer pod and the team follows behind her. They bring up the hatch halfway.

"It's a spot called Little Ethiopia." Linda says. "It's an Ethiopian neighborhood; small enough to see a sample, then move on to something else. The Sunset Strip is a little north from there; if you want to see that too."

Elizabeth looks at the team "Three of you take the explorer pod to Sunset. Julius and I can walk east."

The team nods and the explorer pod takes off.

Manning's voice comes over the headset "Where are you going with that pod?"

Elizabeth looks out the back hatch. On the mountainside, a set of headlamps look up.

"I'm going to another neighborhood." Elizabeth says.

"You'd better not pack that thing." Manning says "We have things to carry."

"You have a pod to yourself." Elizabeth retorts.

"We're here to get work done, Elizabeth. Not sightseeing."

Linda's voice comes scolding over the headset "Doctor Manning, you're in a desert. You won't find enough for two pods."

Manning becomes indignant "How am I supposed to bring these back to life, Linda? With a couple of twigs?"

"Settle down." The Captain says "Doctor Manning, you have plenty of destinations to hit. Don't get caught up over one."

"I'm the one terraforming our planet." Manning says.

"And Elizabeth is getting data on culture for Doctors Hoyt and Morris." The Captain adds.

"I'm working twice as hard and getting shafted over here." Manning remarks.

"Doctor Manning" Elizabeth begins "How are you doing twice the work I am?"

Doctor Manning's microphone starts but it's immediately cut off.

A moment of silence passes. The land grows closer behind the explorer pod. The mountain rises to just feet below the open hatch.

"Elizabeth?" Linda says.

"Yes?" Elizabeth asks.

"The Captain is tearing him a new one on a private channel." Linda laughs "Look, just do your thing and we'll handle him."

Elizabeth sighs "I feel like Manning DOES do more work than me."

"It just feels that way because you enjoy the work." Linda admits "You'd do this for free, wouldn't you?"

Elizabeth watches the Hollywood sign come up as they pass over the mountain. She turns to look out of a window. The view shows the land to the southeast. There, a patch of steel beams lie in a heap on the landscape. Their bent and gnarled facades stand jagged out of a ruin. They're what's left of the skyscrapers that were once downtown LA.

"I probably would." Elizabeth says.

Linda speaks with understanding "His job is urgent, and that much is true. He's bringing life back home to Zion; but you're bringing back what makes us feel alive."

Elizabeth looks to Julius. He smiles at her.

"You need to be inspired." Linda says "I'll handle the biologist."

"Thank you, Linda." She says.

"Friends need to look out for each other." says Monica.

Elizabeth looks confused.

"Monica?" Linda asks "Were you listening?"

Elizabeth laughs.

"It's like a soap opera" Monica says "But I get to make commentary."

Elizabeth looks at Julius' smiling face. She can't hear his bobbing, but she knows he's laughing.

"Alright, let's let them focus." Linda says "Get off the damned communications."

"Copy that." says Monica.

Julius shakes his head, and Elizabeth smiles out toward the mountain. Beneath her the land becomes a set of single-family homes. To the west is another mountain where houses stand at its peak. They form outcrops with swimming pools and patios. She becomes aware that these hills were once alive. These homes were like nests in the valleys, and on faces of the Sierra Nevada range.

The flat homes of this land would provide an oasis for families on clear and sunny days. Their children would come in from writing with chalk on the streets. They'd take tall cups of water and hide away from the sunlight in air-conditioned living rooms. There, they would sit on a carpeted floor and play games on a television; or venture to the poolside, like Elizabeth did at her father's home.

The land comes to a plane of buildings and clutter. The explorer pod touches down in South Hollywood. The houses have given way to apartments and shop facades; not unlike the neighborhood of South East Eden. Julius is familiar with this kind of neighborhood, but it's still far better than South East Eden.

Elizabeth steps onto the streets of the common folk and finds a modest setting. The neighborhood of Little Ethiopia is damaged by the looting that took place after the sun's disappearance. Shop belongings are strewn about. Among scattered remains, the artifacts of a dead culture are waiting to be discovered.

The explorer pod heads north to the Sunset Strip, and Elizabeth is alone with Julius.

"A little eerie." She says.

"The furthest place from anywhere." Julius says. "The middle of nowhere."

They search the shops to find pictures of Ethiopian cuisine. Photos adorn the walls; of figures that bestow the traditional dress of their people.

"That's cool." Doctor Morris says over the headset "I really wanna go to Addis Ababa."

"What's this writing?" Julius asks, looking at a menu.

"It's the Ethiopian language." Morris says "They had their own writing system, and they went by a different calendar. Do you see the pictures of food?"

"Yeah." Julius says.

"They'd serve meat and eggs with sauce on a plate of spongey bread." Morris' excitement is audible "It was made from a grass called teff, and they'd peel the bread to pick up the food."

"What do you mean?" Elizabeth asks.

"They wouldn't use utensils like we do." Morris explains "The bread was what you'd use to pick up the food. Then you'd eat the bread and meat together."

Julius gathers his brows "That's so weird."

"Different." Morris explains "This is the kind of thing I've been looking forward to; it's different from anything we've ever seen."

"You told Linda to send us here, didn't you?" Elizabeth says.

"I did." Doctor Morris admits "You guys were so close by, and it's good to see what immigration was like. We don't have that on Zion. Imagine leaving everything you've ever known to live in a whole new world."

"I can only imagine." Julius says.

"Exactly." Morris replies "They'd leave their families and friends to live somewhere far away. They'd often form neighborhoods of fellow immigrants from their nation. It would provide some taste of home while they'd adapt to their new nation. They'd learn the ways of another life but keep their customs alive. Their children would be Americans, but they'd keep a piece of their parents' home with them; in their cooking, and other practices."

Elizabeth finds a dark corner of the shop by a water heater. The shop owner's body lay in the corner, clutching his daughter in his arms.

Elizabeth grows solemn. Her eyes see a dead family, and yet she feels longing. She sees a family with substance unlike anything she'd ever had. Even with a pool and a large house, the luxuries of an upper-classed girl couldn't provide a meaningful relationship with her father. She can't recall a moment when her father held her so brazenly in those younger years.

She looks at Julius. He comes over and looks at the corner.

Julius looks at his friend, but she turns away to work. Julius looks down at the scene again. He realizes there's another body hidden under a blanket at the father's side. The mother must have passed away before the father and daughter; and so the father hid the mother's face to shield their only child.

"Grab as much as you think we can fit." Elizabeth says "They'll have their way of life pass on through us."

She turns to look his way. The newfound inspiration has ignited her desire to work.

"Get a computer or something." She says "We'll bring back their recipes."

Julius nods. He strides forward to begin the search.

***

Aboard the star explorer, Linda approaches Manning in the cafeteria. In her hand is a misconduct form. It was given to her by command of the Captain, and she's supposed to address it to Doctor Manning for his behavior in Los Angeles.

Linda bites her teeth as she walks up to the table.

Manning's assistants grow quiet as she approaches. They patiently wait through what's about to transpire.

Doctor Manning sees the packet and rolls his eyes.

"You've gotta be joking." He says.

Linda wants to tell him it's the Captain's idea, but she's sworn to do it herself as the lead expedition manager.

She slaps it on the table.

"You know what you did." She says.

Manning nudges the packet off the corner of the table.

"I didn't do a damned thing."

Linda looks at the floor, then back up at Manning.

"You don't feel at all embarrassed by what you just did?" She says.

The assistants fight to hide their smiles.

Doctor Manning leans over and picks up the packet. He extends the packet toward Linda but she doesn't take it.

"That's yours." She says.

Manning rolls his eyes and slaps the packet on the table.

Linda sighs.

"Why do you need to be so difficult?" She asks.

Doctor Manning shakes his head and stabs a slab of meat on his plate.

"Hell if I know…" He says.

"No, honestly… What's your deal?"

Doctor Manning sighs.

"Linda; I don't have the time to fool around." He says "I've been working on this my whole life, because in my family, I have no excuse."

"What's with your family?" Linda asks with a tinge of sarcasm.

"Glad you asked, Linda." He quips "My grandfather started one of the
greatest food brands on the planet, and when my father was nine years
old, the old man croaked.

My father was robbed of the business by the shareholders, and he had
to start from scratch. The old company was bought out by RainCrest,
and my family never saw so much as a penny from that deal.

Then, my uncle and my father bought some new land. They swal-
lowed the old competition, and now you have Black Brook stocked on
your grocery shelves instead of RainCrest.

Unfortunately, my dad was in the wrong place at the wrong time, and
so he's gone. My uncle took on the responsibility and by some miracle
he's managed to improve upon a perfect company.

I have tremendously large shoes to fill. I don't have the time to fuck
around and watch movies like that engineer, or anyone else. I don't
have the luxury of being just 'good enough', let alone mediocre."

"Sad story." Linda says "I mean it. I'm sorry to hear that; but Elizabeth
is more than mediocre. She's working hard and you need to cut her
some slack."

"Whatever you say." He says.

Linda nods "Taking time off is normal. If you tried it, you might
actually be happy for once."

Manning scoffs "I'm only happy when I've done a good day of work."

Linda sighs.

"That's depressing." She says.

Manning shrugs "Is it?"

He leans forward to tell more.

"You're aware that the whole world doesn't operate like a white-collar job?" He says "Do you know that being so much as a minute late to
work can get you fired in the blue-collar world?… In fact, being early is
the only thing that's considered 'on time' for the middle and lower class.

I show up a half an hour early every day because that's what's expected of you, if you aren't born and raised in academia. I don't even blame
you anymore because how could you know what you've never seen?

It's up to people like me to make up for other people's average work
ethic.

To be honest, I'm aggravated with myself more than anything, Linda.

I shouldn't lose my cool, because maintaining composure is just being someone worth respecting; and that's a part of my job.

If I can't do that, then I'm fucking it up and I can't allow that. I need to be better. I need to be the best, and there's no other option. So yes; I am at fault, but you can't blame me for getting frustrated with everyone else's complacency."

Manning grabs the stack of papers and tucks it under his arm.

"Now, if you'll excuse me; I have more work to do."

He rises from his seat and walks away.

Linda watches him, then she looks back at Manning's assistants.

"Soo…" She says "You guys have to deal with that every day?"

CHAPTER 19
A Philosopher And A Pacifist

Julius opens his eyes to the sound of commotion in his apartment complex; and the same old stain marks the ceiling above him. It's a brown liquid-looking mark which lies over the couch from where he sleeps.

The voices above and to either side of his room are loud and aggressive. Chairs thump and slide elsewhere in the other homes around his. A radio beeps in the hall. It's followed by a voice that's drowning in static.

"*Must be maintenance*" He thinks "*… Another dreamless sleep…*"

Julius can't recall if this is fortunate or saddening. It's been a long time since he's had something worth dreaming about.

His favorite dreams are the ones where he sees his friends; Dash, Chief, Cricket, and sometimes Pluto. They'll be with him; just chatting. It often goes dark from there; either literally or in the essence of the dream. All the same, he wakes to the realization that they aren't here. Their families have been his only contact to a world outside of this apartment, and even they have lost interest in a distant friend.

Julius stands up from the couch. He doesn't have a bed, nor would he want one. It would take whatever space there is left in his apartment.

He navigates around the couch to the kitchen and takes a snack for himself; a protein bar before his morning run. He then dresses himself in athletic attire and takes his apartment key into a zipped pocket on his shorts.

Julius pulls at the door, but the frame has swollen to the point where the door won't easily open. The water damage has engorged and altered the shape of the wheat wood in the wall; and so he pulls with half his might, peeling paint into shreds in the process. He then steps through the door frame and slams the apartment shut.

He locks the door, then turns to talk with maintenance; only, it's not maintenance down the hall. It's a police officer. He stands outside the young boy's apartment. The boy sits to the side with his legs sprawled out in a V shape; apathetic as usual.

Julius gathers his brows and approaches.

"What's going on?" He asks.

The door to the boy's apartment is wide open, and there's a commotion inside. Another officer walks around with a flashlight, inside the apartment.

"Hold on." The first officer says. He holds his hand up to stop Julius.

"Hey." Julius says "I know this kid."

The officer looks at the boy and back to Julius "I'm sorry sir. Please turn and leave."

"Is the kid okay?" Julius asks "Is something wrong?"

The officer looks pained "Sir, I'd rather you didn't see."

Julius looks at the boy's hands. There's blood all over them; but the boy seems fine.

"I did what you said." The boy says.

Julius' brows are gathered. He looks at the officer, but the officer looks at the boy.

"What did he say?" The officer asks.

"I had to do what's smart. Not let my emotions get in the way."

The officer looks at Julius with winced eyes.

"Who are you?" The officer asks.

Julius feels his chest and finds a chain that he's worn for a long time. He pulls it through his shirt and shows a set of dog tags.

The officer looks surprised, then reads closer:

```
Winter
Julius
UZA 55250
Blood XA
Atheist
```

The young officer steps back and grabs his belt with both hands.

"I'm sorry but… I can't let you enter." the officer says. He looks at the boy, then back to Julius "You can look, but please just make it brief."

Julius steps forward and sees blood on the carpet inside. He turns his head around the corner to get a better look, and there he sees the couch. The woman lies still. Her legs spread apart, draped by her nightgown. Her mouth is open to the sky and her eyes are open. The couch and the floor are soaked with crimson water. It's coagulated in streams from her throat.

Julius looks over at the boy's face in the corner of the hall. It's numb-looking. The cold eyes look straight through Julius. Their pupils, like a gateway to an abyss. They look just as they did when the boy watched the rat in the dustpan.

Doctor Hoyt's brows are tense. He looks at Julius and scans his body language.

Julius is hunched in his chair, across from Doctor Hoyt. The fireplace is on this time. Julius watches the holographic embers lick the mouth of the chimney.

"After that, I couldn't live there." He says "It wasn't the place to be."

"This is what you think about…" Hoyt says "… when you talk with Elizabeth about the war…"

"Not about the war" Julius says "It's more like… I know there's value to those lessons. She wants to be a good leader, and there's moments where that knowledge is applicable. Like I said about the car accident scenario, there's moments of crisis. They come up out of nowhere, and you need to be prepared; to know how to handle yourself."

Hoyt nods, then tilts his head in a thought "Elizabeth wouldn't take that information poorly, though."

Julius nods without a word to say.

"That boy was misguided" Hoyt says "What he did was the culmination of the events in his upbringing. His interpretation of your thoughts were misguided; all because of a prior experience that was beyond your knowledge and control."

Julius shrugs "I can't help but think, though. He killed someone; and he'll be considered a murderer to some capacity, even if it's only in his mind."

"Julius…" Hoyt begins "His mother was selling her child for money. Strangers were sexually abusing him for years…"

"I know."

"You can't blame yourself." Hoyt says.

He expects a reply, but there's nothing.

"It's not your fault." Doctor Hoyt adds.

Julius looks off to the ground "There's other avenues, ways to handle that… and even if I thought she was a monster, she was an addict… She was made into a monster; she wasn't that way inherently."

"People do awful things while they're intoxicated…" Hoyt says.

Hoyt looks to the book on his shelf. "The Man in the Brown Knit Hat" is a book he wrote about a murderer named Duncan VanRoy.

Hoyt feels obligated to share about himself, now that Julius has mentioned his own trauma.

"VanRoy was on speed." He says.

Julius looks up at the therapist, realizing this is the first time he's shared a story about his work.

"He was my patient after his arrest." Hoyt says "He was kind of funny in a way. A brutal man, and a Satanist. He believed in killing for a higher power; and the more perverted it was, the more he enjoyed it."

Hoyt finds his face has fallen from the smile. A twisted emotion of understanding someone, wishing the best for them, all the while knowing the horrors of what they've done. The man was evil, but to some capacity Hoyt remembers the humanity of VanRoy. His charming allure. His story of trauma would bring any empathetic mind to pity him.

"He had this outrageous thing he'd do." Hoyt remembers "Every Friday he'd come in and scream 'money day, Doctor!'" He laughs at the memory "He was excited for ME getting paid. He wasn't getting paid, he was in PRISON."

Julius finds himself laughing at the insanity of it.

Hoyt laughs "He'd tell me to spend it on hookers."

Julius chuckles and shakes his head.

"I never DID!" Hoyt continues, his face fading from the laughter "But... He grew to like me. I never passed judgement. I understood that life made him who he was." Hoyt looks at Julius, understanding his perspective "At one point he was a fun-loving child. He caused trouble, lighting things on fire by the old train tracks. He found his fascination with death when his pet rat died... From there it was a life of sexual abuse; and a desperate search for belonging. That's when he found someone who would take him; a crowd that would take anybody. He sold himself for so little, because he didn't see the value in being who he truly was; that fun-loving child."

Julius remembers all the grown children he's witnessed and watched die; and all the ones he's seen twisted by war.

Hoyt nods "Duncan was still that child; but he was lost. So I know how you feel; and it's hard to convey it to the general public... how you can see the humanity of a monster."

"That boy was no monster." Julius says.

Hoyt nods "But the mother was... and you didn't want her to die, because you knew that about her."

Julius nods. He stares at the holographic flames in the fireplace.

"Some people would call me a monster." Julius admits "They said as much to my face."

Hoyt shakes his head "You're not a monster."

"Doctor, I'm not natural; and I know that much." Julius watches Hoyt take a breath "There's no heaven for me. Only living hell…"

"Is Elizabeth a piece of salvation?"

Julius relaxes his shoulders in an unspoken agreement.

"Hasn't she been a light in your life?"

Julius nods.

"Good." Hoyt says "Hold on to that, and HELP her. Let her be a leader. Let her be what she desperately seeks to be."

Julius nods "Yeah…"

Hoyt arrests his patient with the severity of his eyes.

"Let her be a hero to the children of Eden." Hoyt says "She'll be the same woman you've known, no matter what you tell her."

"I just don't want her to be like me… Shoving her emotions down so far that she can't find them when she's happy…."

Hoyt frowns a corner of his mouth.

"… She'll be fine, Julius." He says "You laugh with her all the time… And you're talking about Elizabeth here. Nothing can bring her down."

Julius almost smiles. He straightens his posture.

Hoyt nods with a smile.

"I've analyzed her for a long time." Hoyt says "Longer than you know." He grabs his notepad and tablet "And stop calling yourself a monster. You did what you had to; just like you did with the rat. It was mercy that compelled you, so stop forgetting your own lessons." He slaps Julius' knee with his notepad "She might be the reason you have faith again" He says "but you're the reason I know we're on the right path. New Memphis was a hiccup in the process, but everything you fought for was worth it." He smiles "Because you're here now; and most of our crew owes you their life."

At this, Julius questions things. He fought to keep his team alive, and all that remains of them is a memory. He keeps his thoughts from surfacing on his face. He knows his session is over, and doesn't want to stir any unease in the doctor. He shakes Hoyt's hand. He thanks him, then leaves the office.

Julius comes out of the dark corner of the therapy office and comes around to the engineering wing. He enters the lab but doesn't see Elizabeth. He hears a laugh down the hall and follows the sound to find Mark and Danny.

"Hey guys" Julius begins "Have you seen Elizabeth?"

"Doctor Lawrence?" Danny asks.

"She went to send a message to her family." Mark says.

Julius nods "Thanks, guys."

"Anytime." Danny says "Tell her to hang out with us sometime."

"We need some engineer bonding." says Mark.

Julius begins walking but smiles back at them.

"I agree." Julius says "I'll tell her."

In the historical wing of the ship, Julius comes to a small room just outside the artifact wing. Here he finds Elizabeth between video messages.

"Jules!" She says.

Julius smiles "Hey Liz."

"I just finished a message to Mom." She hands a painting to seemingly no one.

Doctor Morris comes into Julius' line of sight. He's followed by Timmy.

"Thanks, guys." Elizabeth says.

The historians take the painting with gloved hands.

"No problem." says Doctor Morris.

Timmy nods to Julius as they leave the room.

"How's your mom doing?" Julius asks.

"She seems good." Elizabeth says "She's started painting again."

"She's back at it?!"

Elizabeth nods "Mom says I inspired her." She pulls up an image of her mother holding a painting "Check it out." she says.

Elizabeth's mother looks healthy for her age. Her smile is bright and she's dressed in a way that states her mood. Bright colors and a painting apron. A large brimmed hat lay leaned on the side of her chair.

Julius smiles "Well I'll be damned."

The painting her mother holds is a depiction of a little girl. The girl is painting in a garden. To Julius, he sees a mother's pride for her daughter. Elizabeth being the girl painting; the garden would be the world that Elizabeth delivers home to everyone on Zion.

Julius looks to Elizabeth "Anything from Uncle Steve?"

Her smile changes. Her teeth come together but her lips are still parted "That's what I was about to send." She says.

Julius nods. He breathes deep.

"Anything on your father yet?" He asks.

Elizabeth nods "Uncle Steve said he brags about me to Dad… He's working on him to come down and send me a video."

Julius feels his face come to a plain and stagnated emotion.

"And Stevie?" He asks.

Elizabeth shrugs "Same as dad."

Julius nods "They'll come around."

Elizabeth raises her brows and reaches for the holographic keyboard.

"I don't think it's Stephen's choice." She says.

Julius raises his brows.

He sighs "Yeah…"

Elizabeth pulls up the camera and pauses her hands before starting the video. She then looks at Julius.

"Uh… before I start this, could you…?" She points to the corner behind the camera.

Julius moves to the corner.

Elizabeth gives an awkward laugh "Thank you." She looks at her friend "I just… wouldn't want to give the wrong impression…"

Julius screws his brows together and tenses the corners of his mouth as an exaggerated frown.

He waves away her concern with his hand "Don't sweat it." He says "I know what you mean."

Elizabeth gives a smile with her head down "Thank you." She says.

Julius smiles and she starts the video.

"Hey Uncle Steve!" She says "I'm in orbit around Earth, and we've come across some amazing things!"

Julius watches her regale the tale of Tokyo. She tells him all that she can, excluding the classified information; principally the existence of Doctor Clay.

As instructed, Clay's existence is only on a need-to-know basis. The concern is with the uproar that would ensue; as Clay's form of AI does not adhere to the modern laws of artificial intelligence.

Elizabeth tells her uncle how she wishes he could see the planet. She wishes she could send him movies and video games from the time of the Earthlings. She shows images from the surface, but says "Photos don't do it justice".

She closes the message with a goodbye, and relays her hope that she can hear from her brother at some point.

"Take care, Uncle Steve." She says "Love you!"

She stops the video and sighs.

"Okay" She says "How was your appointment?"

Julius is taken aback, almost forgetting why he arrived.

"I uh… well…." Julius shakes his head with a shrug "I guess getting to the point is best."

"Okay?" Elizabeth laughs.

"I want to teach you how to shoot." He says.

Elizabeth screws her brows together "Shoot what?" She asks "A gun?"

Julius nods.

Elizabeth laughs "Okay, why?"

Julius laughs "It's silly, but there's something to learn there." He nods "Doctor Hoyt had me thinking; and I should impart any knowledge I have from the war. You need it as practice to be a better leader."

Elizabeth screws her brows together "What does shooting have to do with leadership?"

Julius shrugs "There's a thing about it." He straightens his posture "When you shoot, there's a humbling feeling. One second you're aiming, and the next it's out of your control. It explodes out of the gun, literally; and there's no taking it back."

"We can't shoot on the ship!" Elizabeth laughs.

Julius puts out his hand as if to say "I know it sounds silly, but hear me out".

"I promise" He says "There's a reason to this, and it's important."

Elizabeth nods "Okay, but how are you going to teach me?"

"First how to shoot" He says "Then how a gun works; and finally what the sensation of shooting feels like."

"Okay" Elizabeth says "And where did this idea come from?"

Julius takes a seat by her side "One of the best leaders I've known was a man we called Chief. He kept his cool when shit hit the fan."

"When WHAT?" Elizabeth laughs.

"Please." Julius fights back a laugh at her surprise.

"I'm sorry, but shit hitting a fan? Where did you come up with that?"

He's alarmed that she's never heard the phrase before.

"I-I don't know where to begin with that." Julius says "That's a common phrase for me."

"Okay, okay." She says "So you mean when disaster strikes?"

Julius nods. He stares off, recalling his leader.

"Chief kept his cool when things went wrong. He was good at that. There's an aspect of war that makes you a good leader. It's a matter of grace under pressure."

Elizabeth nods "And you think teaching me how to shoot will help with that."

Julius nods "That and other things… But firstly, are you in?"

Elizabeth nods "I think we can do that. I'm actually excited." She grabs a forgotten cup of tea from the table "Dad used to go shooting with his friends, but he never taught me. Said it wasn't for girls."

Julius tenses his brows "God, no."

She takes a sip of the tea and raises her brows.

"Did he teach Kyle?" Julius asks.

Elizabeth nods "Yeah, but you're probably a better teacher."

Julius looks off to the side.

He remarks with a sarcastic concern "Gee, I HOPE."

Elizabeth laughs and smacks his arm.

Julius smiles at her. He believes Hoyt's words. She'll always be the same person he's come to know.

CHAPTER 20
The Screaming Silence

Doctor Clay's therapy sessions begin slow. Over the years, Doctor Hoyt has learned to be patient with his work. He speaks less to avoid actively influencing the therapy. He allows the patient to guide the conversation. In this way he ends up taking the slow route to the appropriate destination, rather than taking the fast track to nowhere.

The task of uncovering Doctor Clay's personality is difficult. The machine's prerecorded voice is a mere replication of the real man's words. The tone inflictions are limited by a vocal library in the computer's long-term memory storage.

While some patients like to spill their life story, others can be like a labyrinth, waiting to be mapped.

In the case of the machine called Douglas Clay, it exhibits all the signs of a cautious man. Each question is met with a question. Only answers can warrant an answer. Hesitance is a tactic used to defend against strangers; and it is learned by children who are accustomed to betrayal. The root of such behavior can only be found when confidence is established. A confidence between the patient and the therapist.

Superficial questions come first. "What did you do for work?", "What was it like, growing up in Arizona?", "Did you have any siblings?".

The conversation starters lead to a brief account of the facts. They fall short of a paragraph each time.

Doug is an only child, and it has never bothered him. He worked as a bionics specialist for RAINARD Armaments. He later worked for DARPA, the United States' federally funded research organization. Growing up in Arizona was fine enough for a man like Doctor Clay.

Doctor Hoyt shares more about himself. He halts the questions and makes small talk. These conversations begin to span from politics to religion; from work to everyday events.

As an atheist and a voter of only one party; Doug's words are many, but superficial.

His word choices are no different from the news articles of his time. Even though American politics have become inconsequential, they still appear to be of great importance to the Earthling. To disagree with him would make one "a bad person" in his eyes. His definition of right and wrong hinges on the very line between the three American parties.

The doctor presumes that he has merely adopted his opinion, and that it is not of his own creation. The conflicts beyond his State are foreign. The idea of a grey morality has become alien to him.

Doctor Hoyt reaches his office at the end of the morning and boils a pot of water for his tea. As he waits, he jots down some thoughts:

> *He is too blinded by his idea of virtue to see his political party's shortcomings. He is also fervent when defending the actions of the party as a whole. This hardly defines his character. Merely that he identifies with a virtuous facade, which may be considered commendable.*

The water continues to form bubbles on the bottom of his boiler. He looks through the notes taken over the past two weeks. With no conclusive evidence, he writes a reminder in the form of four large words. "Who is DOUGLAS CLAY?". Beneath this, he makes a list of bullet points.

WHO IS DOUGLAS CLAY?
- *Virtuous*
-
-
-

Doctor Hoyt continues to gather the memories of their past conversations. For the twentieth time he glosses over the pages. The words no longer hold their meaning. They sound like a recording of jumbled speech, repeated again and again.

The boiler rings a small silver bell. Doctor Hoyt lifts the boiler from his desk and pours the water into a small mug. Inside, the tea bag swirls around and tugs at its string. The string is tied to the mug's handle for security.

He looks around his desk. He thinks aloud to himself "Clay doesn't know himself…"

His eyes meet a copy of the book he wrote years ago. It's titled "My Mother Made Me Do It".

He remembers its contents, about his own mother. There is a passage that states how:

> "*The condition of the modern world has formed a state of 'survival' based on 'likability'. We have seen people propel their lives on a path to assimilate, rather than innovate. It is because of our comfort in the modern age, that we harbor a fear of change.*
>
> *None of the great thinkers were liked in their time; and they welcomed the changes of the world with curiosity. Meanwhile, their piers would avert their eyes from the uncertainty that the thinkers were so excited about.*
>
> *They would challenge the status quo with an indifference to what people would say or think. Thus they knew themselves; far better than the agreeable numbers in the machine we call our modern Eden. They did, after all, have families, friends, and small communities who supported their unique ideas. It is in the genuine liking of who we are, at our ugliest, that we can find true happiness. It is not found in a material wealth, nor does it lie in the approval of strangers.*"

Hoyt feels the spine of the book and pulls it from the shelf. He opens it to the title page wherein it reads:

> "*In loving memory of my mother.*"

He remembers how his mother made him, for better or worse. From her greatest achievements to the afflictions she passed on to his mind.

He thinks back to Clay's agreeable nature, and why the passage was so important to bring him here, holding the book in his hands.

"*It's not uncommon…*" he thinks "*But how do I get his candor?*"

The following day, he sits before the machine. He stares into the aperture without a word. He waits for the machine to speak first.

He finds a breakthrough in the patient's critical thinking.

"What's Zion like?" Clay asks.

Hoyt's eyebrows spring upward. He adjusts himself in his seat.

"It's a tidal-locked planet…" He responds. "With a red dwarf star."

There is no response. Hoyt waits for an inevitable question.

After a moment, Hoyt leans back in his chair "Do you know what I mean by 'tidal-locked'?"

"I don't remember fully." Clay responds.

The therapist smiles.

Clay's pride won't allow him to admit that there are things he doesn't know. A biologist shouldn't know matters of astrophysics, but that isn't acceptable to Doctor Clay. It would hurt his pride to be unfamiliar with a subject of science.

By pretending to understand all, he robs himself of the knowledge gained in asking a question. Pride is not a sure obstacle for Doug, but there may be a root to this. There may be a source of insecurity. It also may be nothing at all.

"When a moon is tidal-locked…" Hoyt says "…it means that one side of the moon will always face its planet. The Earth's moon was tidal-locked, and our planet is tidal-locked with our star, Proxima Centauri. That means one side of Zion faces our star. The other side of our planet faces away. There's no day or night. At all times, Proxima Centauri sits on our south horizon."

The answer fascinates Clay. Questions arise about civilization on Zion. They discuss the choice to settle near the poles. The never-ending starlight. The curtains that keep the city dark at night. The X-ray storms that are blocked by the curtains. The icy dark side of Zion, and the scorched bright side.

Doug is fascinated with humanity's fate, and becomes more helpful. His eagerness to help brings the expedition further in much less time. He tells the department heads about government facilities and scientific institutions. The other department heads are propelled along, but Doctor Hoyt remains patient when reaching his goal. He's only learned that Clay is virtuous, self-conscious, and perhaps proud.

For several weeks the conversations remain void of intimate details. It is after two months of therapy that Hoyt begins to ask more about Doug's life. Specifically, he asks about his root character; his childhood.

Catching lizards, birthday parties, cruise vacations, and otherwise, the life of an outcast. He was not bullied, but overlooked by his fellow students. "*Boring and uneventful*" are his words when describing the malleable years.

In the imagination of Doctor Hoyt, lizards and ocean cruise liners sound like a fairytale. For Doug, the cruise vacations were his parents' excuse for drinking, justified as "*family fun*".

In this period of life, Doug found his first friend. A child born into misfortune. He lived with a horrible deformity. It left him unpopular and unable to play sports. Doug can recall very little of their friendship. They grew apart from one another when adolescence came about. Even the memory of their parting is vague. All Doug can recall is a group of scenes that paint his friend's jealousy and betrayal. Clay guesses that his friend was bitter over his condition. Drugs and alcohol dominated the friend's later life. The former friend left high school prematurely, and was never seen again. Doug went on to lead a life very different from him. He may have done so in direct opposition to his friend's personality.

"I'd think about him every once in a while, and it made me think 'I'm glad I'm not like him'.

It served as motivation, and a reminder of why I was in school. My graduating class was all in prison, knocked up, or in a grave by the age of twenty-one. I wanted nothing to do with them."

Doctor Hoyt begins writing a note in his book. "*Disciplined*".

"There was something else I was passionate about." Clay adds. "Since you asked about passion."

Hoyt looks up from his pages "Oh yeah?"

"Yeah." The voice rings again. "An old man in a nursing home. My Grandpa. He had no legs, and sat in a wheelchair. He gave me my favorite stuffed bear. I named him Ralph."

Hoyt smiles.

"When he lived at home, he would watch cartoons with me until we fell asleep together. I'd have a juice box and crackers… I wanted my own kid to have that someday. And I wanted to be nothing like my parents."

"… And who were your parents, Doug?"

Aside from the family vacations, Doug doesn't have much for pleasant memories with his mother and father. His parents were quietly at odds. Any attention he got was about his schoolwork. Aside from that, an overwhelming quietness pervaded about his house. It set the tone for bitterness.

All the while, the lack of praise made a large vacancy in his heart. A reward for work well done was nothing more than a pat on the back. Every day home from school he would play video games, watch television, or maybe read. Anything to escape the screaming silence of his only child home.

When he was little, he'd breeze through the obligation of school. He would finish his homework and rush into his stories about androids and zombies. Comic books, video games, TV shows, and movies. They saved his heart and mind in an unfulfilling childhood. His parents passed from his life well before they died. They separated, as he expected. Soon after, the calls became less frequent. When they had finally passed on, he wept for the lost opportunities. In secret, he anticipated a brighter future. He envisioned a life with someone beautiful inside and out, and a family with her.

> *He would never let his children feel alone. He would support them with enthusiasm.*
> *They would be his world, and know their worth; and she would know it too.*

Doctor Hoyt turns the pages of his journal to the bulleted list again. He writes two more words "*Passionate. Altruistic.*"

He leaves his office and sees Doctor Winter coming down the hall.

"Julius. How are you?"

"I'm alright. How's the job going with Doug?"

Hoyt steps to match even pace.

"Good." He says "Very good."

Julius looks at him a while.

"Just good?"

Doctor Hoyt smiles "Patient confidentiality, Julius."

Julius nods.

Doctor Hoyt looks at his closed notebook and smiles "He's very intense. He holds a lot of value in love, trust, and honesty. I should respect that. For him, especially."

Julius perks up.

Hoyt continues "Not many people are as dedicated and passionate as him."

The two men come to the historian's office. In front of a massive screen, Doctor Morris has his head in his arms. His face is to the side, eyes sealed shut, and his mouth hinges open. The bottom corner of his jaw wells up with drool.

Julius nods toward the historian "I don't know, Doc. He looks pretty dedicated to me."

Doctor Hoyt laughs "In a different way."

Hoyt is about to knock on the door frame when he hears Julius.

"What do you mean?" Julius asks.

Hoyt turns to see his face tensed with subdued concern.

Doctor Hoyt smiles "He's passionate about trust. He values people who care for WHO he is." He laughs a little "Most people want someone, just to HAVE someone. Anyone." He shrugs "People aren't possessions. The misconception is, that people think they can turn someone into their ideal lover, friend, child, or parent…" He looks at Julius "You can't love someone for who they're not."

Julius looks down and nods.

The therapist pats Julius on the shoulder "You know you already have that."

Julius smiles.

Hoyt begins walking away "Wake him up. He needs to sleep in a bed for once."

Julius watches the old man turn the corner.

Julius then turns back to the historical office and knocks on the wall. "Doctor Morris?"

Morris shakes his head. He widens his eyes to lubricate them. He blinks to break the crust from his lids. "Julius." He arches his back in a stretch. "I didn't see you there." He begins to rub his eyes.

"It's better if you rest and work in the morning." Julius says.

The historian sighs "Yeah. I know." He stands from his seat. He looks at a screen full of battle pictures and weapons. "We've done so much fighting." He begins "It seems like we've only gotten better at throwing rocks at each other." Morris laughs at his own joke and shakes his head. He grabs his coffee mug and begins to shut everything down. "I'll go to bed. Don't worry. I'll see you in the morning."

Julius catches his thoughts drifting. He focuses his eyes on Doctor Morris "Goodnight." He says.

"Good night Doctor Winter."

Doctor Morris watches Julius leave the door frame and smiles. He reaches to power down the main computer, but stops. He pulls his finger away.

He brings his eyes to the screen for a look. The mouse floats over to a tab and clicks open a window. It's a blueprint. A name runs across the top "*Project Icarus*".

CHAPTER 21
Earthling

Doctor Winter enters the doorway to the therapy office.

"Julius." Doctor Hoyt says "Come in."

Julius smiles at the old man. Hoyt begins to stand.

"Stay put old partner." Julius raises his hand in dismissal. "What do you need?"

Hoyt points to a miniature fridge by his desk. He descends back into his chair with a wobble "I was going to grab some water. Would you bring me one?"

"Of course." Julius says.

Hoyt turns with an afterthought "Grab one for yourself too, if you'd like."

Julius returns with two cold waters. He hands the first to Doctor Hoyt, and seats himself with a second.

Hoyt cracks open his bottle "So what's going on?" He asks. "Have the dreams taken a turn lately?"

Julius keeps his bottle closed over his lap. "They have" He begins. "But I think they'll subside."

"And why's that?" inquires Hoyt.

"I've been given two tasks." Julius says. He opens his bottle "The Captain wants me to distribute entertainment, and Elizabeth wants me to investigate the Earthling."

"Who?" Hoyt asks "Doug?"

"Doctor Clay, yes."

Hoyt holds the bottle to his mouth, then raises an index finger to hold that thought. He lowers the bottle from his mouth after a sip. "The machine calling itself Doctor Clay." He explains.

Julius nods.

"Why the suspicion? Is that why you've come to see me?" The therapist asks. He looks at Julius with a new realization "Is that why you were asking about him last night?"

"Well, yes. I didn't want to use one of our ordinary therapy sessions, and I haven't had a moment to talk to you one-on-one… I ask about him, half out of suspicion, and half of it is convenience. If he CAN be trusted, and we link him to the ship; we would have someone helping all the departments at once, even through the night shift."

"True, he doesn't really need sleep. He daydreams, though."

"Exactly." Julius begins "But there's an issue we've found."

"You don't trust him."

Julius breathes deep "It's more like we've found a potential reason NOT to trust him. You see, we've found nothing that indicates WHEN he was put into that body. Not in the facility where we found Doctor Clay, or any other government property. Very few printouts have survived from his project, and there's no digital database."

Hoyt stares a moment. He winces "Nothing at all?"

Julius shakes his head.

Doctor Hoyt begins to stare off.

Julius explains further "Not saying he's responsible, but someone deleted the database. Whether it was wiped from espionage or as a precautionary measure, nobody knows. His project was very secretive."

Doctor Hoyt draws a breath and reaches for a notepad. As he scribbles in the pad, he devises a plan between himself and Julius "When you get a moment, message me… Actually handwrite me a list of questions. Questions you want me to ask Doctor Clay." He places the notepad down and meets eyes with Julius "I'll get the answers and tell you if it's worth investigating. I need to keep patient confidentiality, but I'll let you know if I find anything suspicious."

Julius nods "I'll talk with my boss about it first."

The two men smile at one another. Hoyt breathes a laugh "How's Doctor Lawrence?"

Julius shrugs "She's good."

"She hasn't been in here except for check-ups." Hoyt begins "Even then, she keeps them brief."

Julius tilts his head in thought "She told me about her parents' divorce the other day."

Doctor Hoyt nods. His brows are tensed over his glasses. He strokes his beard.

Julius continues "She's been busy, so I understand why she hasn't been coming here."

Hoyt's face becomes soft "They didn't facilitate what she needed, to build confidence."

"What do you mean?" asks Julius.

Hoyt shrugs "I'm not at liberty to tell all I know, but I'm sure you got the understanding that her parents are pretty flawed."

Julius nods "No one is perfect, but they let her down"

"A little more than most." Hoyt says. He stares intently "It hurts more than you might realize. You two aren't the same. You've been emotionally weathered in different ways. Hers is like a flag that's been whipped in the wind. It's been worn of all its color and pride. I'd say you're like a riverbed that's been carved over time. She's much easier to restore, while your battle is like steering a glacier."

Julius sits up. He stiffens his posture.

"Like I said Doc" Julius says "I know myself. I can handle my baggage."

Doctor Hoyt smirks "Baggage?" He shakes his head "You can't hide in your work forever, Julius. You've had some time on your hands. Steering a glacier is a long, arduous task. I understand why you would put it off. Nobody would willingly take on this battle, but it's easier with friends you can count on."

Julius feels his shoulders fall.

"While it's your sturdy nature that gives Elizabeth her courage, it's her colors that give you reason to live."

Julius takes a breath and fixes his posture "I get that, but I feel like this is something I've learned before. I can recognize the capacity of the mind, and it's easy to forget things over time. I just need to learn it again. I'll get around to that when I can, but right now I need to figure things out with Doctor Clay. That's more important."

"Right."

Julius nods "My biggest concern is Doctor Manning. I don't think he's reliable enough to keep his mouth shut."

"Regarding what?" The therapist asks "You don't trust him?"

"Doc…" Julius says "I don't trust anybody… I don't think he understands how dangerous Doctor Clay can be."

Hoyt adjusts himself in his seat "Do you think we should have a conversation with him?"

Hoyt grabs his tablet and prepares to call the biologist.

"I think he might get carried away with his work. He might get blinded with progress, and let the Earthling know too much."

Doctor Hoyt sends a message "You might be right." He adds "I'll see if he wants to come by."

"If you're the one to tell him, I'm sure he'll listen. Elizabeth's opinion doesn't seem to matter to him."

Hoyt nods in agreement "There's more to that story than you might know, too." He looks to his tablet again, then back to Julius. "He has a moment if we go to his lab. Will you come with me?"

"Absolutely."

The two men rise and exit to the halls.

They leave the dark corner where the therapy office lies; and they pass the old rec room and the engineering lab. Around the corner they pass the hall that leads to the historical department. They nod at a historical assistant as they veer off toward the biology labs. They cross the room with the cut-bot along the way. When they enter the hall to the biology lab, a fragrance permeates the air.

The team moves quickly under Manning's orders. Rooms host flowers, herbs, and vegetables. Two biologists look curious and excited over an orange sphere with small dimples. They peel the orange surface to a layer of wedged pieces that complete the whole.

Rounding a corner, they find Doctor Manning. He wears latex gloves and a lab coat. Beneath his hands is a human corpse atop a metal table.

"How's the beef jerky?" asks Hoyt.

Manning holds up his index finger. His tablet displays an audio meter, which rises and falls with his voice. "The cold has crystalized the water within the skin tissue. The membrane has expanded and ruptured. Features are distorted and pulled like mummification. A lesion on the upper breast has been pulled open from the distortion. The skin is covered in tholins. The blood has burst from the arteries and veins. Tendons have pulled the limbs inward, and hardened with rigor mortis." He pauses the recording and turns his attention to the two men. "What's up?" He then walks forward to close the distance, and gestures back toward the corpse. "Jerky, I know. Tell me about it."

The men laugh, and Hoyt brings them to focus "I wanted to say something about our friend, the Earthling."

"Doug? What about him?"

Hoyt gestures to Julius "Julius wants to figure him out so we can link him into the system. We need to know he won't cause us any trouble first."

Manning nods "I was going to say, it's a little too soon. That's a great idea, though."

"Well, yes" Hoyt begins "Thing is, I know he's been working with the biology department lately. Julius says he's very powerful, potentially dangerous if he grabs hold of the wrong resources."

"Like what?" Manning asks.

"Well let's say he gets into MY records, and he starts manipulating the team with blackmail. He could hurt our progress."

"What could he possibly find on me?" Manning laughs "My mother was a lazy bitch. That's all he'll find."

Manning laughs while Hoyt shoots Julius a side glance with a raised brow.

Hoyt nods "Right, well, it's not you I'd be worried about."

"I get it." Manning says. "No hard feelings. I'll keep it strictly work-related."

The three smile in agreement.

With a deviation on the subject, the men talk for a little while longer. After long, Manning continues his work.

In the hall Julius walks alongside Doctor Hoyt, who keeps an even pace.

"Listen, Julius." Hoyt begins "This stays between you and me, and I know it's not professional, but I know your kind. I know I can trust you."

Julius nods "Of course."

Hoyt stops outside the entrance to his office and faces Doctor Winter "I know that Doctor Manning is rude, and he makes a lot of assumptions." His eyes come up from raised brows "He has his reasons, and I don't expect you to get it."

"I know" Julius says "I'm not one to pass judgement."

Hoyt lets out a breath of a laugh, then pats Julius on the shoulder "Just make sure Elizabeth doesn't kill him."

Julius laughs "There's only so much I can do."

"Please, it'll be a disaster having to explain that when we get home."

Julius smiles "I'll try my best, Doc."

CHAPTER 22
Friends

"Rebecca Wheeler was a friend of some of my acquaintances in college." Doctor Clay's voice recalls the old memory. "I met her at a party in the fall semester of my freshman year. We were playing a game that some Israeli guy played back home. I don't remember exactly how it worked, but it involved dares and cards.

We sat in a circle, and she sat close to some guy across from me. I was with my roommate at the time; I can't even remember his name anymore.

Whenever she looked away from me, I took the chance to look at her; and when she looked my way, I'd stare at anyone else. As if I was guilty for gazing at her, but it was okay to stare if it were anyone else."

Doctor Hoyt laughs. He jots down something in his notepad.

Doug continues "When my turn came in the game, I needed to take a rap song and put it into spoken word. I did it flawlessly. Everyone laughed; and when they did I took the chance to see her eyes glinting at me. Her smile was perfect. I mean she could end wars…

Anyway, as the night went on she leaned less with the boy she arrived with, and she began to slump over the group circle, toward me.

Everyone got bored of the game, so my roommate and I made our way to the kitchen. All the sudden, Rebecca and a friend of hers came over. It started with some small talk. The four of us spoke for maybe an hour or so. Then we decided to go elsewhere. We found ourselves in my room just down the hall. We made drinks and food.

I took pride in my cooking, so I thought I'd impress her. I made chicken with rice, spinach, and garlic toast. I talked to her the whole time I cooked. She was right there next to me.

I must've sounded like a total loser; completely at her disposal.

She complimented my cooking; but I'll be honest none of us had a home-cooked meal in months. I think people were just happy with something other than cafeteria food for once.

After a while, she said goodnight and left my room. I fell asleep so quickly. I was hoping to see her around campus the next day."

"You both only met that first night?"

"Well it was college. There was a little more than that, but we're talking about my wife."

"Right, I just wonder what the basis of your relationship was at this time."

"She probably saw me as some fling and nothing more; but I was intent on being her boyfriend. Years later, when we were together, she told me that she liked me for more than that at the time; but I think she was trying to be nice."

"Did you see her the following day?"

"I did. I saw her on campus during lunch break. I asked if she'd join me for lunch, but she told me there was something she had to do. We all had crowded schedules, so I didn't deny the possibility that she was telling the truth; but something made me feel like I was just another guy to her."

"And where did things go from there?" Doctor Hoyt asks.

"From time to time we would hang out. The frequency in which we'd see each other became more like a relationship; although we weren't together. There were weeks where we would have an argument and I wouldn't see her. Then we would have weeks of seeing each other again, as if nothing had gone wrong. I loved her, but I was in denial of it. I was afraid of having my heart broken. When I stopped denying it to myself, I was still afraid of telling her because I thought she would want to cut things off. What was worse, I discovered she had been seeing someone else. It could have been a one night thing, but I never really cared to know all the details. I remember finding an opportunity when he spilled coke all over my jacket at a party."

"The other guy Rebecca was seeing?"

"Yes." Doug responds "I clocked him so hard in the face that his cheekbone caved in. It began to swell really bad. His whole face was becoming another color. She never knew about it but I was so proud, and I wanted to tell her. My friend Curt pulled me out of the building before the ambulance came. We celebrated my victory by shotgunning a forty; then we slipped into another party like nothing happened."

The therapist catches his own mouth hanging open. He closes it and refocuses himself. "And how did things end up working out with Rebecca?"

"After about a year and a half of keeping our relationship at a distance, I confessed that I loved her. I said it one night when I was being yelled at by her for something stupid I did. I told her 'I understand if you never want to see me again, but I needed to at least tell you, I love you'. I started walking away from her, but she pulled me back and told me she loved me too. From then on, we were together. April Fifth. Our wedding was November the ninth, three years later."

"Do you feel like the relationship started in a good way?"

"I think it let us grow together. I learned a lot about myself back then. I was very unaware of her feelings. I only knew my own. When I look back, there were too many occasions to recount; but I found at the end of every argument she was right. And it was my fault for being unaware or impatient. She was very smart."

"And do you think she was wrong at all for sleeping with other men while you loved her?"

"She didn't know I loved her. I was just a guy she was seeing."

Doctor Hoyt tenses his brows. "Was she ever wrong, Doctor Clay?"

"It was rare, but sometimes. Everyone is wrong sometimes.

I had no experience being in a relationship. I had a lot to learn and that's why I was often the one to blame. Later, however, I found myself being right."

"In what way?"

There's a pause while Doctor Clay adjusts his aperture "There were just some times when I knew I was right, but she kept insisting otherwise. My mother would do that sometimes. Except she had a breaking point. Rebecca would stand by what she said until the grave. So I would agree with her to let her simmer down."

"But you'd know she was wrong."

"Yes. I began to let go of most arguments because they didn't serve any purpose. It was a useless battle. People will think what they will."

"I couldn't agree more." A voice calls from the doorway.

Doctor Winter enters the room, followed by Doctor Lawrence.

Clay greets them in the most pleasant tone he can manage. "Doctor Winter, hello. And Doctor Lawrence. It's nice to see you."

"It's nice to see you too!" Elizabeth begins. "I just wanted to bring this by. This is what you asked Julius for, Doctor Hoyt."

The old man reaches for the manilla folder she holds in her hand "Oh, thank you, Elizabeth." He says.

Douglas' voice chimes "You know, Doctor Winter. You remind me a lot of my friend Curtis. The friend from that party, Doctor Hoyt."

"Really?" Hoyt says.

"Yeah. But maybe a little more like his brother Frank."

Their smiles fade into questioning faces.

"You knew a man named Curtis with a brother Frank?" Elizabeth asks.

"Yes. Curtis and Frank Mandel."

All are quiet, and look around at one another.

"You know, you're aboard the Mandel Explorer." The therapist says. "Named after the men who saved the Earthlings, Curtis Mandel; and his brother Frank."

"Curtis?" Doug asks. "Curtis lived?"

Julius smiles along with the therapist. Elizabeth catches a knot in her stomach and forces a smile. Doctor Hoyt nods at the machine.

"Well then…" Doug starts. He cuts himself off with another question "How did he save people?"

Doctor Hoyt speaks through a smile. "He was one of the engineers who built the spaceship that left Earth. He made the radiation shielding."

"I'm shocked, to be honest." Doug says. "I knew he was working on important stuff, but I didn't know what."

Everyone laughs.

"I don't think we can imagine his role as something that would come as a surprise." Elizabeth says "It's hard for us to think of him as an ordinary guy, like you probably do."

"I just didn't expect him to do something so big."

"Why not?" Julius asks.

"I don't know. He was so young. I figured they'd have someone else in charge. He must have had a hand."

Doctor Hoyt shrugs. "Two thousand pairs of hands! Along with the top scientists of his time. Where were YOU, Doug? They could have used a guy like you." Hoyt winks at the lens of the machine.

"Was there anyone else I'd know?"

Hoyt raises his brows "I don't know the names off the top of my head, but I'm sure you know some of them. There was his friend, James Stuart?"

"I knew Jimmy… although he was based on the moon for a while. The moon still wasn't an easy trip in my time."

Julius nods. "It's still not a walk in the park." He looks around the room at the infrastructure "This expedition is the most expensive government project in history."

"You're desperate for some answers, aren't you?"

The therapist bows his head with a nod.

Julius looks to Elizabeth's face. Her mind looks distracted in thought. He looks to the therapist again. He gestures his body toward the door "We need to head back to work, but it was nice getting to chat."

The therapist looks up with a smile.

Julius turns to wave at the machine "Good luck, Doug! I know he's a handful."

"You take care, Doctor Winter."

The engineers leave the room and the door closes behind them.

"Doctor Hoyt, would I be able to have some time alone?"

Hoyt looks into the lens again "Of course. If you need anything, just ask someone to get me, and I'll come back."

"Thank you, Doctor. You're a good friend."

Hoyt takes a short breath to focus himself. "Professionally speaking we aren't allowed to call ourselves friends." He looks into the fixed aperture blades. A silence pervades, and he feels his jaw quiver in hesitance. He smiles "But with you I can make an exception."

He rises from his seat with a calm, but thoughtful face. He smiles, then exits the room. Doctor Clay looks on in silence.

Elizabeth and Julius join each other on the elevator. He looks at her from the corner of his eye. "I know that face…"

"Something is off about that guy." She says.

He nods "What is it that's bothering you?"

"Some of the things he said. The way he said them… He questioned Mandel's qualifications for the job he did. I understand, you'd be surprised if I did something like that because you know me."

Julius shrugs "It's surprising what you're capable of when you have no other choice. It was either they worked every hour to survive, or…"

She shakes her head "I guess, but there's another thing that I found weird."

Julius looks curious at her.

"I think he knew Doctor Stuart was at the lunar base." She says "It was a fifty-fifty chance he'd be there when Doug went under. Then he said 'Curtis lived'. The word 'lived' almost sounds like he witnessed the event."

Julius nods "You think he remembers life as a machine."

"He could; and if he remembers, why would he lie about it?"

Winter screws up the corner of his mouth. "What do you want me to do? You name it, I'm on it."

"Have you read Mandel's biography?"

"I've read ABOUT him" Julius says "I haven't read his biography, though. I can if you want."

"Excellent" she says "I've never read it."

He begins to laugh and shakes his head. "So you want me to read it?"

"Yes." Says Elizabeth "And tell me if you find anything on Doctor Clay."

Julius nods. "You've got it."

CHAPTER 23
Doctor Curtis Mandel

There was always something to be said about my brother. Whether it was some great accomplishment, or something that he got himself into. While he never spoke much, he always had been spoken about.

"That kid's going places." Teachers would say. "He's a really bright kid" other parents would tell their children. Meanwhile, my mother would tell him something along the lines of "What did you do this time?"

Thicker than molasses, Curt and I were inseparable for most of our lives. All except those tumultuous teenage years, and a brief argument during young adulthood.

We bonded when we were similar, and butted heads when we were different. Those differences became the nuisances we would love about one another; especially when we began to live so far apart.

One major difference was where we excelled in thinking. I scored high on the IQ test for social skills, while my brother scored well on the spatial reasoning portion. When we played chess he always had the upper hand, but Scrabble was my game.

Oddly enough we rarely played either game; because we both hated to lose. It usually ended up being Monopoly, something we both weren't very good at.

What fascinated me was words. I enjoyed their meaning and their functions within a sentence. Oftentimes I liked the words that added a sense of humor in a conversation. This might be part of the reason why I was always so sociable.

Sometimes this was at my detriment; as I would sacrifice my grades in exchange for a social life.

Curtis, on the other hand, loved the functions of numbers. More importantly, he loved the challenge of making things happen with those numbers. If it wasn't numbers, it was structures.

When I was young I would give him my Legos, Bionicles, and other toys that required building. While it would take him a while, he would work on it until it looked exactly like it did on the box.

Both of us, on the other hand, did not understand Monopoly in the slightest.

While we argued a little when we were young, our parents made sure we knew what our family was worth. Nothing could match the importance of our trust in one another. Not everyone has this, and I'm thankful for it.

To give some insight into one of these disagreements I'll share a story. One morning before school, he was talking about something in an excited tone, as young kids do, and I was tired; probably because I was up late playing video games in secret. Eventually I'd had enough. My mother was in the house grabbing something. We were in the car, and restless; sick of waiting. I told him "Curtis, shut up. If you say one more thing, I'm gonna give you a black eye."

Being a younger brother, he decided to test this. He kept going on.

Just then I popped him in the eye. To my astonishment I was met immediately with a fist, aimed right back at my own eye.

It might be something about young boys being prone to fisticuffs, or being in a hot car with your sibling for more than five minutes; but that was just five minutes too many for me.

My poor mother was on her last nerve, and came back to her two sons battling. When she stopped us, *she looked at our faces. We had matching black eyes.*

"Stop it! Just stop it!" She screamed.

After taking a good look at us, she was overcome with tremendous stress and shouted "What were you two thinking?!"

The problem being, we weren't thinking. We were boys with little understanding of consequence.

Now that I'm older, I realize the teachers could assume SHE marked us up. I can only imagine how she felt at the time.

Later that day Curtis and I were acting out our favorite cartoon movie, as if nothing had ever happened.

In contrast I remember one Halloween night, when we were supposed to be asleep, I snuck candy into my room. My mother, who routinely checked if we were asleep, found him on the top bunk and me on the bottom. We were covered in chocolate. Our white sheets, stained with the color of Skittles.

When high school came around, his first year he had an empty slot in his schedule, and I had a study that I never went to; so we would go out and get lunch together.

The second year we had together, he enrolled in Advanced Placement Physics. I never thought much of it until one day, he revealed his final project to me. He managed to get his hands on some high-power batteries and magnets. As he eagerly unboxed his new parts from the internet, I asked him "What is this?".

I should not have asked that.

He eagerly brought me down into the basement, like some mad scientist. "This" he said "is a rail gun."

I didn't know a whole lot about these things, but one thing I knew from his rants about science; this thing was dangerous. The word "gun" may have been enough of a warning, but I couldn't resist.

"Fire it up!" I said.

Again, I wish I hadn't said that.

Without thinking of the consequences, he threw the switch. There was a massive explosion and dust flew everywhere! There were chunks of the 19th-century stone foundation flying at us in the form of projectiles. Boulders came loose from the centuries-old cement and toppled onto the floor. There was a loud metal pang and what sounded like bending copper.

When the dust settled there were leaking pipes and a hissing sound. The first floor had caved in a little and the rail gun was in pieces. The next thing we heard were the horrified, enraged screams of my mother.

The good news was, my brother received the first A+ given to an AP physics student at MHS. The bad news; our whole summer we worked for my father.

The business he owned with my Uncle John was called Mandel Plumbing. And we had a contract for the waste treatment plant that summer. It was stinky and excruciating labor.

After high school, I commuted to a community college.

The college I went to was wonderful for many reasons, however seeing all my friends go away and enjoy parties was overwhelmingly depressing. Especially because I still lived with my parents.

Looking back on this time though, I was living out my best years with my family. My brother had opened up to me about his fascination with the stars, and the unknown reaches of the universe. His understanding was far greater than I could explain here, but it baffled other men of science.

Only in my later years was I required to understand his work.

He told me once that his first memory was as an infant, on an air mattress under the stars. It was one of our family camping trips. I remembered which one when he told me about a rattlesnake he saw. He must have only been a few months old. To him, that first sight of the stars was some sign of destiny. I would be lying if I said I didn't agree with him.

When he went off to college, he seemed distant until he came home. His work enveloped him. His education didn't cost him a dime. In fact, it was thanks to that rail gun. It seems that the whole ordeal made up for its price in damages; and at the prestigious Merrimack Institute, a full ride is something unheard of.

I remember the aurora was a subject his mind would run off to. The uses and properties of energy drove him to explore further and further into his research. A master's and PhD later, he was pursuing quantum mechanics, and the physics of energy. The work became so complicated, I can't accurately tell you what it was about.

In his later years he would say his work was about understanding what created us. He had always been open to spirituality, but after what happened to our home, it seemed only reasonable to be in touch with something beyond our eyes. There seemed to be no other explanation for what saved us. He went as far as trying to understand the higher dimensions of our universe. I have faith that his work will be completed someday. Otherwise it would be a wonder why we've been allowed to live for so long.

CHAPTER 24
Ikiru

The air hums with the sound of an electromagnetic cannon. It reverberates around the basement floor in the testing facilities of Photon Labs. In a lead chamber the latest fabric is being slammed with electrons measuring a maximum of 124 keV. At this limit, the wavelength of energy is on the brink of surpassing the X-ray range. The next bracket of measurement is the gamma range; a wavelength that the most ravenous of stars will emit liberally in the deep reaches of outer space. This range of electron volts rarely appears in the outer edge of the Milky Way; and when it arrives, it's become weak enough to be easily blocked by the atmospheres of most planets. Mercury would take the beating without resistance and Mars would have to struggle in protecting its surface from the radiation. Likewise, Zion is sufficient, but it cannot keep all the greatest threats at bay. While Alpha Centauri is a modest dwarf star, the solar system could be struck with a flash of violent starlight from a distant rebel, whose twirling about could bring Zion into a spotlight of solar cannon fire. What's more, this event could have happened thousands, if not millions of years ago; and Zion would just happen to be in the wrong place at precisely the wrong time.

Julius looks at the sensor's data. It reads the X-ray measurements from the other side of the prospective fabric presented by a research team at the company. He looks at the scientists standing about on the floor of the Photon Labs facility. They wait with crossed arms, watching the readings from the sensor.

Julius consults the clipboard. He analyzes the data they've recorded without his supervision. He then looks up at the scientists.

"You said this thing can handle gamma?" He asks.

The scientists confirm.

Julius looks to the operator.

"Does this thing go up to gamma?" Julius asks.

The operator nods "I've done it before."

"Bump it up." says Julius.

The scientists widen their eyes. The operator turns a knob and the hertz exceed the X-ray range. The sensor still reads nothing, and the team looks relieved.

Julius gathers his brows at the reading. The energy conducted by the material's exchange of gamma into electrical is promising. It doesn't gain much energy, in fact much of the gamma is likely reflected away, but the sensor behind the material still reads zero and this is a good sign for protection.

This is likely where the independent tests ended, but Julius needs to be certain that the material will hold. If he doesn't act accordingly as a quality control specialist, then the blame falls squarely on him if a product fails. The city would benefit if it could gain electricity from gamma rays absorbed by the nighttime curtains, however the information seems too good to be true. The likelihood of a gamma burst from a far-off star is not worth risking the integrity of the preexisting X-ray shields.

"We're gonna give it a stress test." Julius says.

"What for?" A scientist asks.

"It's good that it can take gamma" Julius says "And that's great if you can make it cheap enough to replace Eden's curtains; but gamma rays are an unlikely risk at this point." He looks at the clipboard again "What matters is if it can handle the elements outside our city." He turns to the operator "Open the wind tunnel." He says.

The engine roars, and the wind tunnel smashes grains of sand on the latest experiment. Numbers begin to show on the sensor, indicating that gamma rays are making it through the fabric. The electrical output of the material begins to fall, and so do the spirits of the research scientists.

Julius looks at the others in the room "I'm sorry guys. It needs to handle these conditions. You'll need to find a way to protect it." He hands them the clipboard "It's incredible stuff. It's just not ready."

The scientists accept the clipboard and slouch in thought.

Julius dismisses himself from the room. The team ponders alone with the operator. The operator pulls down the power and closes the wind tunnel.

"This is a nightmare." The project lead says.

A woman sits back onto a desk "He doesn't play around." She says. She nods with distant eyes, as if she's thinking of a solution through the frustration "Doctor Winter is thorough, and it's a good thing."

A male scientist crosses his arms "What does he do?"

"What do you mean?" The woman asks "He's quality control."

"No I get that, but I mean, I've never talked with the guy." The scientist says "He shows up early and leaves late."

"Does he have a life?" Another man asks.

The operator shakes his head "I've been here a long time. Julius does nothing but work."

The project lead gathers his brows "He has to do SOMETHING."

The operator shakes his head "Trust me. He sleeps, then comes back in the next day. Never taken a sick day, nothing."

"How can you live like that?" The woman asks.

"He's a machine." The operator says.

Julius enters the stairwell down the hall. He's heard what they said, but he doesn't mind it. He comes to the lobby floor of Photon. A large Zion flag hangs from the ceiling. The city of Eden is just beyond the door and the noon shift leaves the office, but Julius continues to his private office. Here he sits and looks over a multitude of ongoing projects in the company's itinerary.

Two hours pass over paperwork and Julius is roused by a knock at his door.

"Come in." Julius says.

An intern opens the door

"Julius" He says "The boss would like to see you."

Julius lays the paperwork down at his desk. He stands and exits the office.

Julius comes to the lobby again and ascends the stairs. He crosses the scaffolding behind the Zion flag and comes to an office directly above his own. He then knocks on the door.

A grizzled voice bids him "Come in!"

Julius enters the office and sees the CEO, the president, and a man he's never met before. The stranger is an older gentleman with a white beard and gold-trimmed glasses. The man in the glasses smiles at Julius; he then turns to the CEO.

"I'll leave you to it." The man says.

"Thank you, Doctor Hoyt." The CEO says.

Doctor Hoyt leaves with the company's president. The door closes, leaving Julius alone with the CEO.

Julius looks at the executive officer. He is large, wrinkled, and his nose is red. He has a seat and gives a deep exhale.

"Take a seat, Julius." He says.

Julius seats himself across from the CEO.

The CEO takes out a large file and opens its contents. He looks it over in silence while Julius looks around the office.

"I've never had you in here, have I?" The CEO asks.

Julius shakes his head "I've only been in here once; and that was before you got here."

The CEO places the folder down on the desk and looks at Julius.

"There's something I want to propose to you" The CEO says "But first, I'd like to highlight some things." He points to the file "Out of all the years you've been here, you've taken none of your vacation time. That's not unusual for someone like you; but your paid time off has been spent typing reports at home. Is that true?"

"It is." Julius confirms.

"Why?" The CEO asks.

Julius shrugs "I've got nothing better to do."

He laughs off the tension of the room and the CEO smiles.

The CEO looks back down at the file, then raises his brows "If you took all your accumulated vacation time; that is, if it rolled over into the following year; you'd be finishing your time off long after I'm dead."

Julius feels himself sink in his skin.

"You're an exceptional worker" The CEO says "But you can't keep doing this." He flips the page in the file "People say you're killing yourself, but I'd say you're already dead."

Julius gathers his brows "What do you mean?"

The CEO ignores the remark but refers to the page before him "When we did your background check, all those years ago, we found an article in an old paper. It was recorded on…" He raises his brow at the word before him "microfiche." He says "Something we found at the library…"

Julius gathers his brows.

"The article said that you spent your earnings at Golden Hour to pay for the college tuitions of three boys." The CEO raises his brows again "Their father had passed in the conflict in New Memphis." He looks up at Julius "You served?"

Julius nods "Yes. Their father was a friend of mine."

The CEO looks back at the contents "Here it is. You were a private for the United Zion Armed Forces." He looks up at Julius "Do you know that's the ONLY article we found? Since then your name has only appeared in articles AFTER your employment here. A name in some lists of credited inventors; but other than that you still hold a low profile.”

Julius sighs “I don’t get it. Did I do something wrong?”

The CEO looks at him. His eyes like glass; his forehead wrinkles into a sympathetic glance.

“Julius” He says “What have you been doing with your life?”

Julius shrugs, his eyes look off to the desk before him.

“I’ve been doing what I can.” Julius says “Making the best use of myself.”

“Julius, you don’t have a life here.” The CEO raises his hands, widening his fingers toward his chest “Look at me.” His fingers reach out to Julius, palms up “Look at YOU…You have legs and lungs!” He shakes his head “Don’t waste them.”

Julius hunches his shoulders. He stretches his back in a shrug.

“Julius, listen.” The CEO points his pen at the door to the office “That man who just left is involved with The Odysseus Mission. He wants you to go with them as an engineer.”

Julius opens his mouth, but no words come out.

The CEO looks down at the packet “I don’t know how in the hell he’s even heard of you, but he wants you to be there on Earth.” He looks up at Julius “Call me crazy, but you’d be a fool not to go.”

Julius looks back at the door, then to the CEO “I’m sorry, but you’re saying I have a guaranteed position?”

The CEO raises his hand, but it falls at the loss of forming a thought.

“I’d assume it’s a political reason” The CEO says “but your qualifications make you an exceptional asset to their team.” He references Julius’ resume “Experience in terraforming technology, manual labor, punctual, quantum engineering, and the list goes on.” He looks at Julius “I ask you as an aging man, don’t back out of this opportunity.” He looks down at the file “I see you were offered a position with better pay and more sick time, not that you’d even use it… It says you turned it down because you saw more value in what you do. You’re a quality control specialist, but you’re the most overqualified employee we have.” He closes the file “Your time is wasted here.”

Julius stares off. He wonders if the “*opportunity*” is really just a public relations stunt for the company. Articles would state that THEIR employee is “a New Memphis veteran” with a story to tell. He knows that there might be a backdoor deal between the company and politicians to convince Julius to go.

"I'm not saying this for my health." Says the CEO in a labored breath "I have respect and admiration for what you've done, but you've said it yourself; you want to make use of yourself. Think about how useful you'd be on this expedition."

At this, Julius feels a decision forming in his mind. Even if it's a matter of politics, he knows his skills would be of value. Even then, he questions the reason for the mission overall.

***

A clock ticks in the far reaches of the waiting room, up toward the tile ceiling of a plain office space. Julius sits silent by the desk, behind which a woman waits on the clients of the therapist. A label sits on the desk "*Doctor Hoyt's Office*". The seats in the room are occupied by strangers. One man wears a name tag that says "*Daniel*". It's a military uniform.

Julius notices the man looking at him periodically. In his hands is a magazine. "*Meet The Odysseus Crew*" the cover says. He must have seen Julius' entry in the magazine.

"Which branch are you in?" Julius asks.

Daniel smiles "Air Force."

Julius nods "We barely had one back in the day." He looks to the ground, remembering the technology available "Development started on the HS 700. We didn't see them until the end. Before that it was those janky high-speed jets they'd use to get around the planet between X-ray bursts."

"The birds." Danny says.

Julius nods "That's what we called them." He laughs.

"They put 12K tank guns on them" Danny recalls "But it was a patch-work job."

Julius nods and smiles "Yup." He looks at Danny "You know your history."

"I know more about planes." Danny smirks. He has an embarrassed sway about his seat.

"You're an engineer?" A stranger asks.

Julius realizes the whole room has been listening.

"I am." Danny says "I thought all of us were."

Another stranger laughs "That's not the only thing we have in common."

193

All mumble in agreement.

"Are we meeting the head of the engineering department?" Asks another man "Elizabeth Lawrence?"

"I think so." says Julius.

"I wonder why they chose us." Danny says.

One of the men displays his hand toward Julius "For THIS guy, it's obvious."

"He's the war hero." Another man says with a smile.

Julius retracts himself in his posture. He leans forward with his elbows to his knees. His hands clasped, he nods with embarrassment.

"We're grateful to have you with us." Says Danny "It gives me courage."

Julius smiles at him. He's glad that his presence has already helped.

"Thank you for your service." Another man says "We owe you our lives."

Julius looks around and smiles at the strangers' faces.

"Thank you." Julius says. He shrugs "It was a job. You'd have done the same."

There is a loss for words within the room. Everyone looks around to have something worth saying. Finally a man speaks.

"Does anyone know why most of us are men?" The man asks.

"Carrying capacity." Danny says "In the military there's different roles based on the physical requirements." He shrugs "Men can handle weight for longer periods of time without complications. Women have wider hips; and it makes them prone to injuries. That's why they'll be in positions that require less marching with heavy gear."

One of the women speaks up.

"I hope that's not the case." She says.

The room looks at her.

"I work in the systems side of ZD Labs." She says.

"Quality control?" Danny asks.

She nods "Research and development, actually." She says, beginning to smile "I'm there to make sure they aren't wasting time and money. Let's say, if a product works; what's the use of making them, if you can only make four or five in a lifetime?"

The men nod and the women smile.

"Cutting-edge stuff." A man says "You tell people what's worth researching. You've got to be smart."

The room laughs, and people look at her in admiration.

She smiles with a bashful nod "And what does everyone else do?"

Danny shrugs "I think my job is pretty obvious." He motions to Julius.

Julius raises his brows "Uh… My story is a long one."

The room laughs.

Julius grins at them, then looks down to think "Basically I started as a civil engineer." He says "After the war I figured I'd try engineering. I'd heard about it from an army captain I knew. The guy blew up the trains, then looked at me and said 'Physics!'"

The room laughs at his impression of the Captain.

Julius chuckles "Yeah, so that stuck with me." he raises a brow at a thought "I didn't have a degree." He says "I was more of a custodian in the beginning… I got experience when I worked with terraforming technologies, doing maintenance; it was mostly manual labor for Eden's ventilation system. In hindsight, now that I'm an engineer, there was a lot of corner-cutting that went on. It's no wonder they had problems back then." He looks up as if to retain the memory of his past "From there I was spotted all dirty in a jumpsuit, by the old army Captain; of all people. He recognized me from our few encounters, and he was then a high-ranking official at ZD Labs." He motions to the woman from ZD who spoke earlier "He basically told me to get the hell out of there, then set me up with a job as an engineer in the farming communities. The company, which doesn't exist anymore, paid for my schooling. I rose to senior engineer until the company was acquired by Golden Hour, a company I'm sure you're aware of."

The room laughs; knowing full well that Golden Hour makes almost all of the popular treats that stock their local grocery store. It's now a subsidiary of Black Brook, after it acquired Rain Crest.

Julius smiles "That old friend, the army captain, was always offering work as an independent contractor. ZD had jobs doing weapons, but I turned him down most of the time. I didn't like the idea of 'still being in the war' in a way, although the war was over for most of my career there. None of the original fighters were actively taking part at the end of it, and by that point it was a few tiny spats in the farming communities.

Anyway, after Golden Hour got bought up by RainCrest, I jumped around a few times; between city jobs, farming gigs, and on occasion, rarely; I'd take a few defense jobs. For the past eternity, I've been a quality control specialist at Photon. Quantum engineering and stuff like that."

The woman from earlier laughs. The room looks at her and her laughter grows. She winces her tearing eyes and tilts her head in bewilderment.

"So which job brought you here?" She says.

Julius laughs and shakes his head. He raises his brows.

"I don't have a clue!" He laughs.

The room laughs until a woman walks in.

"Alright!" The woman says "Is everyone ready?"

The team rises and some give vocal affirmation that they are ready. They follow the woman down the office hall to an open door.

"Right this way." The woman says.

She gestures her hand to the open door and stands by the threshold.

They enter a larger room within the therapy office. In the middle of the room, Doctor Hoyt stands next to a young woman. Her eyes look at the myriad of faces. Her arms are crossed with her back arched. She rocks on her feet as if to be impatient with the greeting.

The room fills and Doctor Hoyt addresses the team.

"Hello everyone!" He says "This is Doctor Elizabeth Lawrence, a recent graduate with a degree in engineering, quantum physics, and a minor in computer engineering."

Elizabeth gives a wave to introduce herself. Her eyes then fall on Julius, and back to Doctor Hoyt.

"Elizabeth will be your lead engineer aboard the Mandel Explorer. She'll be leading your missions." Hoyt places his clipboard down. He then smiles and nods "Doctor Lawrence will also be in charge of the experiments in your department."

Elizabeth steps forward "It's nice to meet you all." She puts her hands in her back pockets and stands with her weight to one leg "I look forward to getting to know you. Does anyone have any questions?"

The team looks around, but all seem to be satisfied with the greeting.

"Okay." Elizabeth says "We're having a little social in the next room. We have coffee, snacks, and places for everyone to have a seat."

The team is audibly excited. They follow the department heads into the next room. Julius takes a cup of coffee and continues talking with Danny.

"So what do they have you doing over there?" Julius asks "Do they have you flying?"

Danny shrugs "Just maintenance. Although, I wish I was flying."

He laughs and Julius smiles. Julius takes a small brownie off of a platter.

"What about those explorer pods?" Julius asks "Maybe Elizabeth will let you fly one."

Danny raises his brows "Yeah!" he says "That would be a hell of a thing to do."

"I think they're operated by an AI." Another man says.

The man stands behind Julius in line. He extends his hand to greet himself.

"Mark." The man says.

"Nice to meet you." Says Julius.

When Mark's hand meets Danny's, Julius can sense a storm of friendship brewing between them; as their eyes meet in the way that only kindred spirits can.

"You ever take apart one of those fighter jets?" asks Mark.

"Only when they crash." Danny laughs.

"You ever work on a KS Oneida?" Mark asks.

"Oh I love those." Danny says.

Mark laughs "Thanks, man. I was the project lead on that."

"No shit!" says Danny "Did you have a hand in the LIDAR system on those?"

"No, those were outsourced." Mark says "We actually gave that job to that lady's company."

"Oh, Terra?" Danny asks.

"Is that her name?"

Danny nods "Yeah, her and I were shooting the breeze in the parking lot."

"Those LIDAR sensors are crucial in the mapping vessels." Mark says.

Julius is literally between the two of them in line. He feels completely out of the loop.

"I'm sorry" Julius says "I'm lost here."

Danny looks excited to explain "Oh, he was the lead engineer on the KS Oneida. It's a big four blade helicopter, like the RS7 model you saw in New Memphis."

"The swarm-copters." Julius says.

"Yeah!" Mark says "Those were unbelievable for their time."

"You're telling me!" Julius says "They saved my ass!"

Danny laughs "We use those newer models" He points to Mark "The Oneidas. We use that LiDar system to do recon practice in the desert."

"No kiddin'!" Mark says.

Danny turns his attention to Julius "So, the Oneidas are like newer versions of the Swarm-copters. They're crew carrying quadcopters that map the desert floor for biological and geological research, but we use them for reconnaissance."

Julius laughs at their excitement over the engineering of aeronautic crafts. They continue to fill Julius in on the modern technology of the latest aircrafts. They fill their plates together and come to seat themselves at the large table in the room.

Julius allows the two new friends to sit together, and takes the outside of their huddle, to the right side of Danny. To his right, Julius is surprised to see the department head taking the seat beside him.

"Do you mind if I sit here?" She asks.

"Not at all." Julius says.

Elizabeth takes the seat and pulls herself in. Terra follows her to take the seat to Elizabeth's other side.

"This is exciting!" Terra says.

Elizabeth smiles "I know!"

"Do you have specific roles for each person on the crew?" Terra asks "Or are we all going on the surface?"

Elizabeth opens her mouth as if trying to form a thought into a sentence.

"No." Elizabeth says "I'm thinking we'll consult each person on an 'as needed' basis."

"Oh good." Terra laughs "I was worried I wouldn't be walking on Earth."

Elizabeth laughs "No, everyone should be on the surface at some point. You worked in the R&D department of your company, right?"

Terra nods.

Elizabeth nods back "Oh yeah; you'll be needed on the surface."

Terra and Elizabeth laugh. Terra is comforted to see her support.

Elizabeth turns her focus to a brownie on her plate and she picks it up. She continues elaborating to Terra, to let her know just what to expect.

"We have a few defense companies to check out" Elizabeth says "According to the Earthling accounts, they're important."

Julius feels his hand stop in the middle of eating. A defeat overwhelms his mind, as he wants nothing to do with "defense" anymore.

Terra is interested "How many documents do we have on Earth's defense contractors?"

Elizabeth shakes her head "Unfortunately, there's not a lot." She takes a bite of a cookie, but she can barely taste it amid the anxiety of conducting conversation. She washes the cookie down with a sip of coffee and pays no mind to it. She continues "The United States' space agency is where we got most of our documents from; and even then, there's a lot missing." She picks her coffee up and holds it in both hands.

Julius looks over to see Elizabeth's slouch, almost using the coffee to comfort herself and taking deep breaths of air. He makes note of her anxiety as she continues to speak.

"There's space missions that we've heard about, but the data was left behind." Elizabeth nods in a thought "Doctor Morris and I have a lot of work to do on that."

"Doctor Morris?" Terra asks.

Elizabeth nods "He's the head of the historical department. He needs to work closely with us and find out what happened to Earth."

Julius tilts his head with wonder. "What are all the theories on that?" He asks.

Elizabeth looks his way then tilts her own head "Some people said they saw meteors exploding in the sky." She nudges her head in the opposite direction "Other people said it was missiles or WMDs." She shrugs "Other people said that the sun blew up; but the atmosphere would have been stripped from the earth, and we know that didn't happen because people lived in darkness for a while until they froze to death. Yet, while it's the least likely option, we all know that the sun DID disappear."

Julius and Terra look puzzled.

Elizabeth brings the coffee to her mouth "I'm glad that's mostly Doctor Morris' job. I'd hate to be him." She takes a sip, then places the cup down and nods as if to correct herself "We should be helping him, actually; as much as we can. It's a mystery we should all want to solve."

Julius and Terra nod.

Elizabeth turns to Julius "You're a piece of history yourself." She says.

Julius smiles and nods "In a way."

"What was it like?" Elizabeth asks "Working on the old computer systems?"

Julius is taken off guard. So much so, that he scrambles to form a thought. He'd never expect someone to be interested in his life outside of "the war".

"Oh, uhm…" He searches his memory "Things were kinda funny in comparison." He shakes his head recalling the technology of those times "A lot of wires. Interfaces with keys… Like, PHYSICAL keys. Not a touch screen or holographic keyboards."

"Really?" Elizabeth asks.

Terra listens attentively to the strange past.

"You couldn't walk up to a wall and pull up your information just anywhere." He adds "You had to go to something with a screen like a tablet or a monitor."

"Huh…" Elizabeth says.

"Did you ever use a mouse?" Terra asks.

Julius laughs "Yeah! We used those sometimes."

"Those must have been a pain." Elizabeth says.

Julius shakes his head "A lot easier than you'd think. First you'd have to shake the damn thing to find it on the screen; but after you found it, it was pretty easy."

"What got you into engineering?" Elizabeth asks.

Julius shrugs "I saw someone do a really cool thing once. After that he looked at me and said 'physics'. From there on, I wanted to know how the hell physics worked."

Elizabeth laughs "And so you became an engineer."

"A quantum engineer." Julius says.

Elizabeth gathers her brows "I thought you were a maintenance guy at Photon."

Julius shakes his head "No, maintenance was long ago. My resume is pretty long, so I don't blame you for mixing them up."

The two of them laugh at the extensive mess he calls his resume.

Julius goes on "The thing I do now is quality control for research and development. I AM, however, qualified for quantum applications, and making them."

Elizabeth screws her brows together "Well, in that case we should talk."

"Absolutely!" Julius says.

"Are you doing anything after this?" Elizabeth asks.

Julius shakes his head "Boss had me take the week off. He's got someone to take my place for the next twenty-one years."

"Let's grab a drink." Elizabeth says. She turns to Terra "You wanna come with us?"

"Absolutely!" Terra says.

Danny leans in to address their conversation.

"Are you guys going out after this?" He asks.

"Yeah!" says Elizabeth "You wanna join?"

Danny looks at Mark and shrugs.

Mark nods "Hell yeah!"

Elizabeth announces to the team that they are welcome to join them at a bar down the street. Most of the team is unable to make it, however they regret to say so. Doctor Hoyt sees this and smiles at the bond developing among the team members.

The crowd dissipates over time, and Elizabeth continues prying questions from Julius. As they make their way to a small spot called "*The Lonely Star*", Julius is intrigued by her excitement. He decides that she couldn't be exaggerating or fictitious, and so he begins to let his guard down, even after hearing her talk about weapons earlier. Even if she were motivated to help the machine of war, it is purely out of a love for science. No matter what, to him her heart is in the right place. Elizabeth's energy brings a smile to his face on frequent occasions, and he thinks of how he hasn't felt this way in a while. He's afraid of it, but her relentless connecting eyes make him comfortable. Her effect on him, and his on her, is the same sensation Julius witnessed between Mark and Danny.

They come to The Lonely Star and enter a large wheat wood door to a roaring tavern. Mark, Danny, and Terra take a seat with them in the corner of the room, but Julius and Elizabeth soon move over to the bar to get drinks and they talk together alone for a while.

"You drink whiskey straight?" Elizabeth asks.

Julius swirls the golden liquor in his glass.

"I got used to it." He says "An old friend got me into it… I couldn't get him OUT of it." He makes a comedic shrug with a retracting of his mouth as if to say "*What can ya do?*"

Elizabeth looks off to the ground and gathers her brows. She feels like she's talking to a reckless animal all of a sudden. She decides to pretend it's a normal reaction, even though she's never seen someone so facetious. After all, up until this point he's seemed sane and civilized; even intelligent.

"… what was his name?" She asks.

Julius takes the glass away from his mouth. He raises his brows with a frowned mouth. He nods as he recalls it.

"Seventy-Two!" He says.

He looks her way with a smile. Her expression is paralyzed with confusion.

Julius begins to laugh. His crow's feet crack out of his youthful face.

"Weird guy!" He says "I'm not kidding."

Elizabeth smiles, but she's too confused to laugh.

"Where'd you meet him?" She asks.

"South East Eden." He says.

Elizabeth begins to laugh.

"I guess that's where you'll find 'em!"

They laugh together, and they soon find themselves inthralled with a conversation. They never return to the table with the rest of their team. They talk there for hours, and with the passing of time, their words grow less formal. Their mouths become loose with their pronunciation.

"So when you worked for the city planning committee…" Elizabeth begins "… Is that how you met your friend Seventy-Two?"

Julius had almost forgotten about Seventy-Two.

He forgot he had ever mentioned his friend to her; the one who drank too much. He was found stabbed in an alley one day, and he was robbed for the scraps of clothes on his back.

Julius had suspected it was something more than that, but the police told him he was only mugged. In the end, his friend was found naked, stabbed, and his blood alcohol wasn't examined. No major autopsy was performed. It's what happens to people like Julius in the southeast section of Eden. They're considered old relics, and their disposal is only helping the city by making room for the wealthy.

Julius hangs his mouth open as he prepares to respond.

"… No." He says "Uh… Actually him and I met because we were both soldiers. He was dead by the time I worked the ventilation systems."

"… I'm sorry." Says Elizabeth "I didn't know."

Julius looks over at her, and her face looks sorry to mention it.

He cracks a smile "I can only laugh or cry about it…" He says "… I'd rather laugh."

Elizabeth looks long at his smile. She can't help but smile back at it. Even when she knows that he's hurt deep down, she's uplifted by his insistence to smile.

It's three drinks later when the bar grows quiet. The two engineers take a look at the time.

"Oh my god, I'm fucked for tomorrow." Elizabeth says.

"Work in the morning?" asks Julius.

"A department head meeting." Elizabeth says "At Hoyt's office, at nine AM."

"Jesus" says Julius "It's two in the morning."

Elizabeth smirks and shrugs "I've done worse."

Julius laughs "Hard worker, and yet a party animal."

Elizabeth does a shooting finger at Julius "You said it, cowboy."

Elizabeth looks back at the table with the other three. Their boisterous laugh is exaggerated by their mess of a table.

Julius straightens his back "You guys pay your bill?" He asks.

Elizabeth waves her hand at the table "I already covered it."

"You did?" Terra asks.

Elizabeth nods "My treat."

They thank her, and Julius gathers his brows.

"When did you do that." He asks.

Elizabeth shrugs "I'm sly. Did it when you weren't lookin.'"

Julius looks back at the bar, with his wallet in hand "Did she…"

The bartender nods and waves as if to say "She did".

Julius looks at her "Holy shit." He says "I didn't see you do that. Thank you."

"Don't worry about it." She says. She then addresses the other three "The bar is closing." Her voice comes now as a slur.

The five engineers exit the bar, and form a semicircle in front of the wheat wood door.

Mark laughs "Alright. Well that was fun."

"This is gonna be a good eleven years." Terra says.

"See you all soon?" asks Danny.

The team agrees.

"Alright." Danny says "I'll look forward to it."

After a word of goodbyes, Julius walks in the direction of the local train station. He's surprised to see Elizabeth is walking in the same direction.

"RailCar?" Julius asks.

"Oh, no I was gonna take the commuter rail." Elizabeth says.

Julius gathers his brows "In your condition?"

Elizabeth shrugs "I don't have a RailCar account."

"You can take one with me if you want." says Julius.

"Oh, you don't have to do that."

Julius raises his brow "You think it's a burden on me?"

"What direction are you going?" Elizabeth asks "Central station goes anywhere."

Julius shakes his head "Where are YOU going?"

Elizabeth looks at him, then to the sidewalk. She gives a gust of a laugh through her nose and smiles.

"North West." She says.

"Up in the heights?" He asks.

She nods.

"Happens to be the same way." He says.

Elizabeth keeps walking, but catches herself in silence.

"Thank you." She says.

"I should be thanking you." says Julius "I haven't been out in a while; and you covered my bill."

They ascend the steps of the railway station and Julius touches the RailCar post that stands by the magnetic tracks. A lone car comes up and opens its side. They enter and sit on seats like that of a street car.

"Where are we going?" Asks the car.

Julius motions to Elizabeth, bidding her to tell the AI.

"Fifth Street" Elizabeth says "Heights Station."

The car confirms the destination and begins its journey along the rail line.

"Fifth street?" Julius says "No wonder you don't have a RailCar pass; rent must rob you blind."

Elizabeth shrugs "It's a place I inherited from my grandmother." She lies back in her seat and makes herself comfortable "Grandparents were rich." She says "Dad cut me off."

Julius nods "Sorry that happened."

"It was my decision." Elizabeth says.

Julius looks her way for a moment and smiles. It's not the response he expected. He respects her, and wonders what the reason is, but he won't pry for an answer.

"Anyway" Elizabeth says "Why don't you go out much?"

Julius gathers his brows "I don't really make friends." He says "When you've lost so many, you're reluctant to make new ones; because it's hard to see them go."

Elizabeth is no longer relaxed but perplexed. She wasn't expecting a candid remark on something so personal.

"That's tough." She says "Thank you for sharing that." She looks at Julius to show that she means what she says "It's not easy to just tell someone something like that."

Julius shrugs "The way I see it…" He says "The less secrets you keep, the less people can hurt you."

Elizabeth nods. She looks at the city outside the window. The buildings zip by along the fourth floor of apartment buildings; no longer the offices that were downtown. The RailCar descends from this height, and into a tunnel that overwhelms the view.

"I hope you don't mind making an exception with me." She says.

She looks at him to see that he's confused.

She elaborates "With making friends."

Julius begins to smile "Exceptions can be made."

The tunnel accelerates the car into the northwest neighborhoods of Eden. The RailCar rises into the quiet section of wealthy houses. The town squares are lit with warm, ornate lamp lights. Brick sidewalks meet shop faces decorated with Christmas lights and green storefront signs. The gold lettering of family businesses give the impression of a quaint kind of wealth.

The RailCar slows to a stop at Heights Station on Fifth Street.

"How far do you live?" Julius asks.

"Not very far." says Elizabeth.

Julius stands up with her "I'll walk you." He says "First directive."

Elizabeth laughs "I'll be alright."

Julius raises a brow.

"We don't want another '*West Side Killer*' to ruin our expedition." He says.

Elizabeth smiles.

"Can't be too careful." He says.

They walk along dark roads lit by golden lamplight. The glass of the dome reflects the light from central city. It shines between hexagon shapes. The darkness set by the curtains keep out the light of the sky; and so the glow of downtown takes hold of the southern skyline.

Elizabeth arrives at her home and ascends the steps. Julius waits at the bottom. He watches her enter the home, and she waves before shutting the door. He waves back with a smile. She too has a sincere sign of joy in her eyes.

The door shuts and Julius processes the night in his stride. He feels himself softening, and warming up to new people in his life.

His walk back to the station is quiet. He comes to the station again and calls another RailCar, paying another fee in the process. He enters the car.

"South East" Julius says "Franklin Square."

The car takes Julius on a half hour journey to his neighborhood. There, he walks in the busy section of a criminal's quarter. Gunshots don't surprise him anymore, and he wears his dog tags outside his shirt. His posture is changed here; overly confident, and vigilant. His latest apartment is better than anything he's had; but it's still a studio with his bed next to the kitchen stove. A community laundromat is next-door, and there's only a stand in shower; not that he'd trust a tub in this area.

He enters his room and feels unusual. He's had fun, for the first time in a very long while. It's been a night of socializing. He smiles and finds his way to the couch. He sleeps soundly, and doesn't wake until well after the curtains rise in the morning.

***

Two weeks before the team is set to ascend for the Star Explorer, they look up to the sky with anticipation. "*The Mandel*" was built in space over the span of several lifetimes, and beyond the hexagon glass of the cities, it passes two times as a satellite before the boarding day.

The excitement radiates through the streets as people look up and tell their children: "*You see that dot? That's a spaceship. It's sending people back to Earth.*"

Julius sees this as he walks to meet Elizabeth at a coffee shop. He walks with a tender appreciation for the suburban streets he's happened upon. It's Elizabeth's mother who lives around here; in a bubble to the northwest of Eden. The venue for their meeting is well out of his way, but it's Julius' fault for lying about where he lived. The act of ensuring that she made it home safe has resulted in this, but he doesn't mind. It's a happy accident that he can experience such a sweet place; unlike anything he's seen in a long while.

He is recognized by strangers along his walk, and some people ask about the expedition. Julius fills them in on how he's feeling, but few of them ask what he will do for The Odysseus Mission. As usual, it's the sensation of space travel that has caught the public's attention, and not the science of the mission itself. Either way, he is glad to see people overjoyed with the subject of progress. He happily takes photos with them, and shakes the hands of strangers in the streets of Elysian Grove. It seems everyone, large and small, is happy for the occasion; and so is Julius.

He comes to the streets of their "*downtown*", and the lamp posts are adorned with flags running the length of Main Street. The shops are open and people are quaint with one another. They sit on outdoor patios and peruse the wares of local shops. He sees the wheat wood facade of a fairytale looking bookstore and decides he'll stop there on his way back, but he continues around the corner to a likewise dressed coffee shop. Wheat vines and bean flowers dress the wrought iron fence that lines the perimeter of a cobblestone platform. Here there are tables shaded by an ornate wall of iron bars cultivating an upward growing biome of flowers and wheat vines.

Julius makes his way into the front door and finds the coffee shop as a quaint home rather than the garden outside. Couches and large cushioned chairs are placed all around the wheat wood floor. A gold and black rug is woven in a Persian style beneath a set of coffee tables, nightstands, and chairs. The tables are place to the sides as well as in front of the chairs, and on the tables people keep mugs close by as they read physical books. Julius finds it perplexing but refreshing. He looks to the walls where shelves hold thousands of books throughout the room, and one long shelf spans overhead, across the seating area. It holds books and bronze figures; some of which are busts of literary figures. Beneath it is a fireplace where Elizabeth sits, waiting for him.

Julius moves forward to the fireplace and realizes it's a gas that feeds the flame. It's housed by the metal shell and left open to the air, behind a chainmail curtain. The chimney runs upward into the ceiling, past the bookshelf and out the top of the fairytale facade.

Julius is amazed by this, and the rest of the room, but Elizabeth greets him by reaching her arms out in a hug. He notices her and stretches his arms in return.

"How are you?" He asks.

"I'm well!" She says, embracing him and speaking to him from over his shoulder "Did you get yourself anything?"

"Not yet." He says.

"Come on, I'll join you." She says.

They stand before the cash register and Julius orders a coffee. The barista turns to operate the espresso machine, and he waits at the counter with Elizabeth.

"So, there's something I wanted to ask you." Elizabeth says.

Julius raises his brows "What's up?"

Elizabeth watches the barista but tilts her head, introducing her idea.

"I've been told that I need to elect someone" Elizabeth says "as my second in command. I was thinking about the people I've met so far on our team; and I'd like you to take the role. Would you be up for it?"

Julius feels humbled and nods.

"It would be an honor." He says.

Elizabeth smiles "You would?"

Julius nods "Absolutely."

Her smile grows "Awesome! Thank you."

She looks to the ground and the barista returns with Julius' coffee.

Julius pays for the drink and walks with Elizabeth back to their seat. In a slow stride they talk as if they're strolling through a park.

"I didn't want to have just anyone for that position." Elizabeth admits "When we met at Doctor Hoyt's office, I wanted to find someone I could get along with. Someone who would be transparent."

Julius shrugs "I'm pretty direct." He laughs.

Elizabeth smiles "When you said what you did in the RailCar… I knew you weren't one for holding things back."

"What did I say in the RailCar?" He asks.

"About losing friends in the past." Elizabeth says. She seats herself by the fire and Julius joins her side "You said you were afraid to start a new friendship because you hate losing people." She adjusts herself in her seat, crossing her legs and holding her coffee close to her chest "I've lost someone, so I know how it hurts, building a connection with someone; and no one can replace another person."

Julius looks into the fireplace and nods.

"I guess I should tell you, since we'll be spending more time together." She says uncrossing her legs. She leans forward and maintains eye contact, seeking a sense of understanding in him. "My brother died two years ago."

She stares at the flames and thinks of the story to tell him; for the omissions she's made in the past are not due here. She's only known Julius for a brief while, but she's understood that he's genuine, and uniquely open minded. For Kyle's sake, she's kept the drinking out of the conversation, so as not to mar his name any more than it has been; but for right now she decides its best to get to the source of her mentioning Kyle. She decides the cause is not the matter of subject, but rather the effect; and so she chooses to save the full story for another time.

Julius looks at her. He tries to apply his own perspective; to understand what she will say next, and to assure her, that she is in the company of a like-minded companion.

Elizabeth tilts her head "I can't even think of anyone who's shared so much of my life with me…" She fights the flood of thoughts by echoing her meaning yet again "I don't have anyone else like that in my life." She looks down at her cup "My baby brother Stephen is too young. He didn't go through what Kyle and I did… but I get to keep my brother alive in a way, by living every day for him."

Julius feels his eyes wander from Elizabeth. For years he's been reclusive for fear of what Elizabeth uses as motivation. With the passage of time he hasn't laughed as much as he used to; not even as much as he did during the war. He hasn't shared the details of his life, and no one has shared their story with him.

Elizabeth invades his life like a force, telling him to live again and to not let the days just pass; and she bids him to tell his story while he listens to hers. He's keenly aware that his ordinary life has been derailed by her persistence; and while it scared him at first, he now sees what the CEO was trying to say. Julius hasn't been alive for a very long time. If his friends had died, then what for? His wallowing has done nothing for their sacrifice, but instead it insults the time that was taken away from them.

Julius smiles "I like that." He looks to the flames of the gas stove "Living for their sake."

***

Six years pass from the greeting day in Doctor Hoyt's office. The team is in the middle of their fifth year aboard the explorer, and their preparations for the mission are spread thin between maintenance tasks. The explorer itself requires consistent work, and there is a lull in their preparations due to a lack of information on Earth itself. There is uncertainty on what position Earth will be in, and it is unknown where they will land on the surface; let alone what they will find. Lastly, the information on the Earthlings is comprised of either a second hand account, written by memory, or the small amount of data taken from the founders as a sample of the vast history of human records.

Downtime becomes lonely, and while people like Julius undertake side projects like the "cut-bot", it can hardly keep the mind from straying into sadness. For Elizabeth, she reflects on her own faults; as a leader, a daughter, and a sister. She can hardly hold herself in contempt over her human errors, but the air of the ship results in a dreary, maddening cycle; and all she can think about are the missteps she's made in her life.

The sorrow is the result of a lack of nuance. All she's seen for the past three years are the same faces, a repetition of the same tasks, and a lack of diversity in any recreational activities.

In the darkness of Elizabeth's room, she sits by her lone lamplight. It shines from her desk and illuminates the objects set upon it. Her eyes gravitate to a paperweight at the precipice of the corner. It's an object that serves as a reminder of why she's come here; and it's an item that invokes the memory of her best time spent with Kyle.

It's a glass object that looks like a snow globe, but it is not hollow. Instead, there is a medium of glass; through which a ferris wheel stands atop the landscape at the bottom. Roller coasters loom over a slew of tents that span across its hills. Beneath the scene is a platform that holds the glass orb. On it, there is a lettering in brass that reads "*The Lexington State Fair*".

She remembers her time with Kyle watching the fireworks on the hill. She thinks about her parents together; seemingly happy. In that moment, it felt as though their bond was inseparable. For one moment, she felt as though she was a part of an ideal family.

She now wonders if that was the reason for her parent's deception that evening; to instill a memory of what a family SHOULD be. It has, perhaps by incident, become a driving force for Elizabeth's desire to be a role model. In her mind, the misguided adults of her past were what brought Kyle to die so young. She's seen children mortally wounded by the mental trauma of faulty parenting, and so she has deeply desired to give an example outside of families and other immediate circles. In this moment however, she remembers that it was her parents who made her. For better or worse, their actions, whether good or bad, are exactly what brought her here; millions of miles away, in the most remote recesses of the galaxy.

Doctor Hoyt has mentioned to her before, the concept of "good enough" parenting. A term that recognizes the fault in all humans, but states that the parent has done well enough for the child to be healthy, happy, and perhaps successful. It's within this context that Elizabeth sees the fault in her treatment toward her father.

She remembers watching movies on the couch on weekend nights. She was maybe six years old, and while they couldn't recall falling asleep, she and Kyle would wake up in their beds. Kyle would be sleeping on his stomach as usual. He often slept in late because he was constantly growing. His round cheek would be squished under closed eyelids. His lip protruding in a paralyzed sleep. His one-piece pajamas covering his feet.

She's aware now that it was her father who carried them there. She even woke up one time in his arms. Candles were in the windows, and so it must have been Christmastime. He was careful to be quiet, but he held each child in his arms like Atlas with his whole world. He barely made a sound, and ascended the dark hall to their bedrooms with ease.

Elizabeth wonders how many times he did that. She had forgotten he ever held her at all. It's like some secret he kept. Only while she was unconscious was he ever so gentle and nurturing.

She wants to talk with him and ask; but more than ten years stand between their last correspondence and the next.

"We're moving at almost half the speed of light." She thinks *"He'd get my message in about… two and a half years… then I'll be leaving Earth by the time I get a message back from him… That's eleven years since the last time we talked…"*

Elizabeth wonders how much time she'll have to make up for the loss of communication. Supposing he wants to try and have a relationship, how much time do they have left? What can be done in the time that remains?

Elizabeth wonders even further.

"If I see my dad twice a year, and he's alive for only ten more years after I get back… that would mean that I'll only see him twenty more times before he's gone…"

At this thought, Elizabeth wants to try communicating; but the idea of failing makes her hesitant. He might be too stubborn, and all their communication would be is more criticisms. It's nothing she'd care to hear, and it saddens her to know that the good things will always be accompanied by the negatives. It's possible that she'll never find it worthwhile to speak with him, and it aches to know this.

She wonders what the likelihood would be, and all she can think of is how he acted after Kyle died. He didn't insist on being against Frida for the sake of his children. In trying to keep the peace with her, he neglected to care for his relationship with Elizabeth. A good father would never let his lover come between himself and the child of a previous marriage; let alone the child he had while he was WITH his lover in secret.

Stephen also benefited from Elizabeth's presence, just as much as she would benefit from a functioning relationship with her father. He cared neither for her nor Stephen; and only Frida won at the end of it all.

Even if it was to keep things easy on the family, and to minimize the reactions around him; Mister Lawrence hurt Elizabeth when he made his wife's desire the higher priority. It communicated to Elizabeth, and everyone else, that Frida was more important than his connection with his daughter.

Elizabeth sighs. She realizes she's been looking at the paperweight and doing nothing but sulking over what she can't change. The paperweight is a distant memory that her father has likely forgotten. It feels futile to think about; and yet, she still holds on.

Just then, she remembers the words her Uncle Steve spoke to her many years ago.

"*No one wants to admit this…*" He said "*… but we make up lies to help ourselves cope with our mistakes… Your dad has that same tendency.*"

Elizabeth begins to wonder if his determination to be cold is to shield himself. She wonders "*What for?*"

A knock comes at the door.

"Come in." Elizabeth says.

Julius opens the door.

He sees her melancholy face and enters the room.

"What's wrong?" He asks.

Elizabeth sighs "I don't know."

She looks at the desk, then back to Julius.

"What's up with you?" She asks.

Julius steps into the room and leans up on her desk.

"I came to ask you something." He says "It's kinda important for me, but it's not so much for the mission."

Elizabeth moves her chair away from her desk and looks at him with squared shoulders.

"What's up?" She says.

Julius purses his lips to find out where to begin.

"You know how there's those government buildings we're supposed to check out?" He asks.

"The ones on Earth?" She asks.

Julius nods.

"What about them?"

Julius shrugs "How much of this mission is about finding weapons?" He asks "And be honest. I won't be too upset."

Elizabeth shrugs "I don't know…" She shakes her head "I think we're supposed to send some unpleasant stuff back, but the goal is to find cutting-edge tech more than anything; and that's the industry with the most innovation, so it's important."

Julius nods.

"What's wrong?" She asks.

"Well…" He says "… I've done my best to stay out of weapons development for obvious reasons."

Elizabeth shakes her head "I don't think that's what it's about."

Julius nods "I hope not." He says "So you know as much as me, I'm guessing."

Elizabeth nods "There's probably some bad stuff we'll be taking home, but it's all for a good reason."

Julius nods without an answer.

"That's the thing about weapons." Elizabeth says "They're awful, but they're the reason we have everything that we do in the modern age." She retracts a corner of her mouth in sympathy. She nods and looks to the side "From the very start, even satellites and the wheel came from a need to fight one another…" She returns her eyes to him "It's stupid, but it's a fact of life."

"People have been throwing rocks at each other since the dawn of time." He says.

She nods "And we just keep making them faster and sharper."

Julius raises his brows in comedic agreement, as if to say "Well isn't THAT the truth."

He looks at her and nods in her direction.

"And what about you?" He says "What's got you upset? It's all over your face."

Elizabeth looks at the paperweight, then back to Julius. She shrugs.

"I just…" She searches for the right words to say "I think I took it too far with my dad."

Julius gathers his brows.

"How so?" He asks.

Elizabeth shakes her head at the floor "I don't know." She looks up at Julius "I think he might be a softie, deep down inside." She pulls back the corner of her mouth and continues "It's like he's embarrassed to be vulnerable or weak."

Julius feels his spine arch in sympathy.

"It's stupid." She says.

Julius shakes his head "I can't speak on his behalf, but I know what it's like to keep something away from the people I care about."

Elizabeth remembers the cold words her father would say to Kyle; and the pressure he put on his oldest son. She recalls the belittling words "You're a fuck up".

She shakes her head "I can't let go of it." She says "He was cruel and mean. I can't just let it go. Not because of some distant memory."

Julius takes a deep breath and gathers his brows. He looks to the floor in thought.

"Look" He says "I have a story that's seemingly unrelated, but I think it might help."

Elizabeth looks at Julius.

He continues "When I came home from the war, it took about two weeks for the fighting to come to a standstill; and it was like that for months. People became tired. The fighting in the farmlands was barely any fighting at all. Two or three people dead in a day; every day. Their side controlling the north, and ours was the south. The people gave up on winning. They wanted to throw in the towel and call it a truce." He shakes his head "For me, and everyone else, it was defeat… My friends died, and Iowa was becoming an independent nation. They won." He shifts his weight onto his other foot and gives Elizabeth a look to see if she's hearing him. She is, and so he goes on "Many people felt the way I did, and they refused to recognize Iowa as its own country…But they were, and we had to accept it. It was a bitter pill to swallow, but it was the truth." He looks at the door. He then takes a deep breath "I went to visit New Memphis while they were rebuilding." He raises his brows; his mouth in a frown "I had no reason to go there; I just wanted to see it for myself… to bury the hatchet I guess." He looks at the floor, then Elizabeth's eyes "I saw the city they built; and it was their own. I forced myself to accept that they were a nation separate from Zion. I let go of that anger, and I found peace."

"You're telling me to forgive my dad." Elizabeth says.

"Even if he's wrong." says Julius "Even if he'll never change…" He then shrugs with his mouth retracted "What else can you do, hate him for the rest of your life?"

Elizabeth sighs "I don't know where to start."

Julius smiles "Just start by being the better person. Let go of the anger; or it'll get you and your dad nowhere."

Elizabeth turns to look off behind her chair. She looks around and thinks a while. She then stands and nods.

"Alright." She says "I'll send a message."

Elizabeth grabs her lab coat to keep herself warm in the halls. She then makes her way to the door and Julius follows behind to the messaging room.

She opens the interface of the messaging system. The screen shows her face as she holds her chin between her forefinger and thumb. She turns her head to look up at Julius.

"I think I'd like to send this message alone." She says.

Julius agrees and leaves her in the room. He takes a seat in the hall and closes his eyes; his head rests on the back of the chair.

Elizabeth touches the desk before the monitor and a holographic keyboard displays on its surface. She gives the computer her information, the recipient's name, and where to send the message.

For a long while, Elizabeth stares at the desk before her; thinking of what she might tell him.

"*I can't mention his mistakes with Kyle.*" She thinks "*… He won't want to hear me go on about that again…Maybe ask him how Stephen is. Then again, he'll think I'm just trying to reach Stephen… I should let him know it's him I want to talk to…*"

She holds her hand over the recording button. She thinks about it, then takes her fingers away again.

"*I should tell him I've been doing well maybe…and an apology for how I acted before…*"

Just then, Elizabeth is struck with a memory from her childhood. It was her and Kyle; shortly after their parents had divorced. She knows now what to tell her father. It's something they all would remember fondly, and she knows it's true; because he's never smiled so much as he did that day.

She raises her hand and taps the recording button. The video starts. She sits back in her chair and smiles.

"Hey Dad." She says "… I've been out here for a while, and we're getting things prepared for arrival… We still have five years to go but…"
She purses her lips as she diverts the topic to the matter at hand "…
I know you're upset with me for leaving, but I'm glad that I'm here…
That still doesn't justify what I said, and I'm sorry… I'm sorry for blam-

ing you; for what happened to Kyle… Because it wasn't your fault…

… I feel like we all could have done better; myself included." She smothers the sour feeling in her throat with a deep breath "I've always wanted to do this; ever since I was a little girl; when they told us about the journey to Earth…

Engineering was my ticket in, because I loved math, even more than I loved proving people wrong." She smiles at the camera and laughs a little. She bites her lip and refocuses "When I said I wanted to prove you wrong, it was inaccurate. What I really want, is to be someone worth remembering; and I love finding new things."

She straightens her posture and feels the need to address her father as the doctor she is. She delivers conviction in her voice and speaks as if she's stating terms in an agreement.

"I'll always be an engineer at heart, and I can't help it… I'd rather die than do anything else with my life because it's a part of me; and it always has been…"

She finds herself remembering that memory from before. Like the unsuspecting question on a final exam, it's a memory so faint; and it lies in a brief sentence at the beginning of the textbook of her life.

"… It started because of you, actually." She says "… Kyle was in a baby carriage because he couldn't keep up with us if he walked…" She smiles at the thought of it "… we were walking around the park by the Museum of Science. I saw the big building and asked you what it was… When you said that it was a museum, I asked what that was; and, on a whim, you brought us inside."

Elizabeth remembers her brother's wide eyes in a dark room as a bolt of lightning cast light on his face. She remembers his teeth gritting together and she laughs.

"I remember Kyle got scared at the lightning show! His eyes grew ten times larger and he held the buckle in his stroller until his knuckles turned white… and I remember the wind tunnel that made small tornadoes, the zoo exhibit; all these other experiences I'd never forget…"

Elizabeth smiles at the ground. She feels the need to address something that her childhood self took for granted. She looks up to address her father in earnest.

"Thank you for taking me to the museum that day… You sparked my imagination, and it became an obsession.

… Dad, I love you; and I don't want our disagreements to…" She feels an uncontrollable shaking in her voice "… to take what we have left away." She wipes a tear from her cheek "I hope you're doing well, and I can't wait to see you when I'm home.

… I miss you, Dad. I miss all of you… except maybe Frida but I can tolerate her."

She laughs and wipes a tear from her eye. She sniffles and composes herself.

"Please tell Stephen I'm thinking about him too. He'll be twenty-nine by the time I get back, and I know I'm missing years with my brother that I'll never get back…

… I promise, I'll try to make up for it; and I don't want to be absent like I was with Kyle." She reaches for the holographic keys "I'll see you all when I get home… I love you, Dad."

She presses the key to stop the video. The words came from her mouth, but they felt so strange. It all sounded like a time capsule that's been opened after twenty years. It's such a world away from her family today that she feels uncertain.

At one time in her life, long ago, she could imagine, one day, that she'd be speaking so plainly with her father. It's a haze in her mind like the brief chapter in a forgotten dream. She's been reminded of it, like someone's written it down, and she's found it just now.

Elizabeth wonders if her father will ever remember that long-forgotten dream, or if he'll call her words a fabrication.

If he denies that their family had any bond at one point in time, then he'll be leaving her all alone. She'll be the sole rememberer of this memory and not even Kyle is left to remember with her.

She's hesitant, and so she saves the file, then transfers it to a private folder.

She leaves the room and figures she'll let it breathe.

Outside the room she finds Julius. He wakes from his brief rest.

"Well that was quick." says Julius.

"It usually is." She says.

She begins walking to the lab and Julius follows.

"How'd it go?" He asks.

She tries to hide her face a little as she fixes her hair.

"It went fine." She says "I didn't send it… I'll probably send it in a couple of days."

"You don't need to message anyone else?" He asks.

She shakes her head.

"No" She says "I messaged everyone else last week."

Julius nods.

At the lab door, Elizabeth stops and grows solemn.

"Julius" She says "I've gotta ask you something, and I need you to be honest with me."

Julius listens and Elizabeth opens her mouth. She struggles to form her question into a sentence.

"A-am I a good leader?" She asks.

Julius gathers his brows "I don't see how you wouldn't be."

"Like… Do I word things in a good way? Where can I improve?"

Julius thinks hard, staring off to the floor. He's met people like Elizabeth before, in terms of her wealth and her sheltered childhood. He's aware that people like her usually have a flaw that lies in their picturesque depiction of human nature. There's an assumption, that the comforts of modern life are inherent and certain. There's often a feeling of injustice when things go awry, but underprivileged people accept misfortune as a fact of life.

Julius shakes his head "Anyone could improve, but you're doing just fine." He says.

Elizabeth nods and stares off to the side "Do me a favor." She looks at him "If there's any way I can improve, anything at all; please just tell me."

"Where's this coming from?" He asks.

Elizabeth frowns "I just need to do the best I can." She says "I can't be subpar. I need to have focus. I need to be ready to lead people, and I'm not certain that I am."

Julius laughs "You'll be alright. It's just nerves."

Elizabeth shakes her head "Maybe; but I need to be a good leader. Help me be someone worth respecting; worth remembering."

Julius smiles "A lot of people respect you already, but I'll be aware. I'll help you be everything you've wanted to be."

She smiles "Thank you, Jules."

He opens his arms for a hug and they embrace each other.

With his head over her shoulder, Julius wonders if she'll need a certain experience to understand the world better. A panic induced by the chaos of a moment gone awry. It can make honorable people behave with erratic madness. He's seen madness, and controlling it is impossible. Sometimes, while it's hard to manage, the only thing to do is act with immense self-control. It can be difficult to keep individual will in spite of an unpredictable threat, or even worse, someone's personal fears.

Julius wonders if she'll need to know this; and if she'll ever be the same when she realizes the value of his cynicism.

Elizabeth in turn, looks over his shoulder and knows that he'll take her request seriously. For better or worse, he'll help her achieve what she's set out to do.

She knows that her mission is important; and while she's missed the pivotal years of her brother's life, she'll make this time worthwhile. She'll do anything to succeed, no matter the cost. Otherwise these years that she's traded will never equate to the value of time with her family.

CHAPTER 25
The Earthlings of Today

The exploration pod shines its headlights on the side of the Mandel Star Explorer. The airlock door opens and a pod lands inside. The door closes, and the machine meets its feet on the floor in silence. Slowly a hiss siphons air to the chamber, and the engineers remove their equipment. Danny and Mark enter the halls of the ship to find it quiet. They are followed by Julius, then Elizabeth, and finally Phil. A distant cluster of voices brings them to a packed biological laboratory. On a screen they see a live feed of the drill mission. They are nearing the liquid water under the Pacific Ice Sheet.

The wait has been long, but the truth will be revealed very soon.

A whirl of slushed ice subsides to bubbles, then an endless dark water. Sediment shows signs of promise for activity. The whole room holds their breath for a little over ten minutes. Some of the team leaves to return to their labs. They ask a lab member to stay behind, and call them when the time comes. Twenty minutes pass, and most of the team still remains. Some wait just outside the door with their tablets in hand, typing up reports and passing information to one another. An engineer even brings a lamp with a broken chord. She solders the power chord and wraps the wire in electrical tape. A woman from the history department receives the lamp with thanks.

The camera descends until there are signs of movement in the distant shadows. Pale creatures crawl around the large pillars that span across the seabed. Crabs, eels, mollusks, and clams huddle around the pillars, pluming with black smoke. The water blurs from the heat which spews from a chamber of magma deep under the ground. A boiling hot world is kept liquid by the core of the Earth. A place where no human is meant to be, but for these creatures it is a comfortable oasis on an otherwise lifeless world.

A biologist lets out three trembling words "Oh my god."

Murmurs and laughs grow among the crowd. Doctor Lawrence looks at her partner to find a hidden excitement beneath his eyes. She feels her heart race.

She looks to Doctor Manning. He wipes a tear away. Doctor McGrotty is at his side as always. He looks at Manning with a smile. He nearly says a word, but he finds nothing. They smile for a moment, and embrace each other.

"You did it." says McGrotty.

Elizabeth sees a posture on Manning, like a young man. All his hard work, the respect he's gained, and still he's just a boy with a dream.

This world has a happy ending after all. From the brutality on the surface, it seemed their origin was nothing but dreary. Now there is something left. Not all of the world is dead.

Doctor Winter looks at her, and she meets his eyes with a smile.

"We're the first people to ever see this." He says.

She looks back at the screen.

Quietly under miles of ice, the Earth's beating heart.

That evening, after hours of work, the departments gather to celebrate the discovery.

In the recreation area, the engineers provide music with the media hub. The large screen has now been connected to a network of Earthling media. Here they play games from long ago. Fighting games and racing games. A crowd gathers of curious onlookers. They exclaim screams of competition. The team becomes enthralled with the players.

Elizabeth stands by this area, and sees the lead biologist close by. She closes the gap between her and Doctor Manning

"Congratulations, Doctor Manning." She says.

The biologist seems surprised "Thank you." He says "Really, thank you."

Elizabeth nods "You worked really hard, and it was incredible to see it pay off."

Doctor Manning smiles "It was a team effort. You and Julius did a great job getting the media hub going."

She laughs "That's Julius' side project. I shouldn't take credit for it."

Manning shrugs "Your team has done good. That's something you can take credit for." He pats McGrotty on the chest with the back of his hand "We've been enjoying a lot of hair metal in the lab. It's been a real help."

The two department heads laugh.

"It's my jam." Says McGrotty.

Elizabeth leans in to tell them of an idea she's had.

"When we go to New York, I was thinking I could get you guys some things." She says "What would you like?"

Manning raises his brows.

"There's a good museum there." He says "It's right by Central Park. They have dinosaur bones."

Elizabeth nods "I can do that!"

Julius calls from the other side of the room "Liz, we need to put these two in their place."

He stands with a pool stick next to the Captain and Doctor Lechmere.

She looks back to Manning.

The biologist smiles "Please smoke 'em for me. They're undefeated and it's getting on my nerves."

Elizabeth laughs "I'll do my best."

"Good luck, Elizabeth."

"I'm gonna need it." She says "Thanks, Connor"

With a striking of the cue ball, their game begins. It proves to be an even match between them. It takes longer than usual, and so they become very practical and quiet.

A song comes on that makes the Captain's head turn. He faces his ear to the nearest speaker.

"You hear that?" He says to his assistant.

Doctor Lechmere turns his head as well "Yeah."

The opposing team stops to listen too.

"Is this Elton John?" The Captain asks.

"Yes! It is." Says Elizabeth.

"How'd you know?" Says Julius.

"Elton John was one of Curtis Mandel's favorites." the Captain says. "My Mom used to tell me that when I was little."

The engineers look at one another and feel proud of his excitement. His ancestor's favorite artist has been resurrected in some way.

"It really does sound better than the remake." The Captain adds.

His pool cue is pointed upward next to his head. He stares through the floor as all his focus is migrated to his ears.

Elizabeth recalls when she'd first listened to a classic song of the Earthen time. She listened alone in her room. The instruments that no one could name. The forgotten craftsmanship of the pianos and guitars they used. The voices that can't be replicated. Poetry that conveyed a portrait of the heart; so similar and yet a time away from their world.

The Captain softens as he enjoys this audible moment. He nods and smiles at Lechmere. They both begin to sing along.

***

Julius sits across the table from three department heads; Elizabeth, Monica, and Linda. They've gathered here in the midst of the party to have dinner together.

"Okay" Julius says "Real talk. What kind of guy is best at sex?"

Elizabeth frowns.

"Nerdy guys." She says.

Linda nods.

"Really?" asks Julius.

"Not just any old nerdy guy." Elizabeth adds "He can't be a pushover. He needs to be a nerd who's proud of it."

"And athletes." Linda adds.

Elizabeth raises her index finger "Nice athletes" she says "Not the two pump chumps with an ego complex."

Linda nods.

Monica gathers her brows at the other two women. Julius has a similar expression, however he nods at them.

"Sounds like Connor's your type, Liz." He says.

Elizabeth shakes her head.

"Noope!"

"Really?" Linda asks.

Elizabeth continues to shake her head "I couldn't. We clash too much."

"But you're still not saying he's bad in bed…" says Julius.

Elizabeth shrugs "He's probably good. But I'd be damned if I let him near ME."

Linda stares off in thought.

Julius nods at Monica "What about you?"

Monica smiles and looks down. She begins to laugh.

Linda raises an eyebrow and looks at her sister.

"Thing about that…" Monica says "… I wouldn't know what guys are like…"

Julius gathers his brows "You're a lesbian?"

Monica laughs. Her eyes dash at Elizabeth; then away.

223

She nods with a shrug.

"I like women." Monica says.

"I had no idea." says Elizabeth. She gathers her brows and looks Monica's way "Why didn't you say anything?"

Monica shrugs "Nobody asked!"

Julius nods "I can see it now that you mention it, but you're not advertising it."

"Which is a good thing." Elizabeth says "Some people make their sex life their personality; and that's never attractive."

Julius raises his brows "There's a few guys I knew in my early years, working for the city… They were always posturing themselves, talking about women." He shakes his head "It wasn't my thing, but they'd get nasty about it; trying to gross each other out."

The girls screw their brows together. They agree with nods.

Monica gives a gust of a laugh. She takes on a mobster's tone for humor.

"They probably don't fuck that good." She says.

Julius explodes in a laugh of surprise. It's a side of Monica he's never seen, but he's pleased to see she can be herself. It's a crude sense of humor like his old friend Dash.

"Monicaaaa…" Linda says. She rolls her eyes.

Monica looks to her sister without turning her head. Jolts of laughter bob her head with a smile.

Linda can't help but laugh at her sister's bashful way of laughing. They look to one another as a duo; knowing exactly what makes the other laugh. Linda blocks the side of her face where she can see Monica.

"Stop looking at me!" She says.

Her eyes widen as she tries to keep from laughing.

Julius snaps his gaze toward Elizabeth.

"So why nerdy guys?" He says "And why athletes?"

Elizabeth shrugs.

"They try, I guess!" She says "Too many guys come in and are like 'Oh, I know what's up babe.'" Her impression of this man is a deep voice with a dumb sounding cadence "They think porn is real life. They'll try to obliterate your cervix, and it's like 'That's not what's up, babe!'"

Linda nods "You need to take your time. Otherwise… What's the point? Like, walking sucks now… and for WHAT?"

"It's not just that" Elizabeth says "but it's like… communicate with me, you know? Like actually think about what I want. You don't want to be a minute man, just a thrusting machine; because women talk. They'll know you're terrible, and it limits your chances. Guys always want chances, at the very least."

"Yeah" Linda says "I had this one guy in high school who was the class super stoner. All the girls wanted him because he was like 'the bad boy' and every girl wanted to be 'top bitch' with one another."

"You hooked up with Brody?" Monica asks.

"Yeah, but it was terrible."

Monica screws up her whole face "Ew! Wasn't he the guy who shit on a girl's chest or something?"

Linda rolls her eyes "No, that was another guy. You're thinking of Gio."

Monica laughs "Oh yeah, it WAS Gio." She looks off elsewhere but tilts her head to her sister as she speaks "I liked Gio, though. He was cool; even if he'd try to poop on your chest."

Linda shakes her head in a smile "Whatever; anyway! Gio's another guy, BRODY was the guy that all the girls wanted. I hooked up with him because I was an idiot, and I thought I'd be cool for having the guy that all the girls wanted; but he was creepy, told him to slow down, and he fucked like a dumb animal."

Elizabeth shakes her head in a frown "See? The nerdy confident guy, and the nice athletic guy. THEY wouldn't do that."

"There WAS a nice athletic guy who was… okay…" Linda says "But he like… needed instruction. He needed practice is what it is…"

"Start a charity." Monica says "Hoes for the Hopeless."

Julius laughs and the girls open their mouths in disbelief. Monica giggles a quiet laugh and shies away from the other women.

"JESUS, Monica." Says Linda.

Monica continues to laugh her quiet giggles away.

Julius looks over the ladies' heads to see that Doctor Manning is approaching.

"Oop." says Julius "Here he comes now."

"Who?" says Elizabeth.

"Your soulmate." Julius says.

Elizabeth turns around and sees Doctor Manning.

"Oh hey!" She says.

Elizabeth turns back around to give Julius a glance from under her brow. He smiles at her and raises his brows.

"We were just talking about which guys do it best." Monica says.

"Do what best?" asks Manning.

"Sex." The sisters say in unison.

"Oh." says Doctor Manning. He takes a seat at Julius' side "And what's the verdict?"

"Nerdy confident guys and athletic nice guys." Monica says.

Manning raises his brows. He holds a humble frown and a nod, as if to say 'Nice'.

"Seems like you fit the bill." says Julius.

"Oh" Manning says "Yeah, let's not talk about that."

"Why?" Elizabeth asks, prying for a good story.

"What about girls?" Monica asks "Who does it best?"

At this Doctor Manning looks deep in thought. He scrunches his brows together and looks to the table before him.

"I find that women just need to find what a particular man likes. We're all kinda different, both men AND women. We need to acclimate to our partner and figure out what it is they like."

Julius nods "Yeah, he fucks good."

Connor smiles with an embarrassed laugh.

"What do you like?" Monica asks. Her brow rises in a devilish grin.

Manning puts up his hand in decline. He shakes his head with a smile.

"Like I said. I don't wanna go there." He says.

"I think communication is key" Elizabeth says "With anything."

Connor nods.

"It's like, working as a team." She continues "Like we do on this ship. If men and women don't communicate, how the hell are we supposed to get anything done?"

Connor nods "Yeah… And I've been impressed by you guys, by the way. I should communicate that since we're on the subject." He looks to either side of the girls "You guys have been great." His eyes rest on Elizabeth "You really helped me out with that trip to Tokyo. It was a Japanese oceanography book that gave me the idea on where to take the drill on its second mission. It's the reason we made today's discovery."

Elizabeth smiles in embarrassment over the compliment. She tries to play it down.

"See?" She says "I'm not all that bad."

Connor laughs "Seriously, though. Thank you… I know I'm a hothead."

Elizabeth shakes her head.

"You're not that bad." She says "You just know what you want and you go for it, who can blame you for that."

Connor nods as a means to change the subject. He then pops his head up in a question.

"How'd you learn to put up with me anyway?" He asks "You keep your cool like I've never seen before."

He begins laughing and so does Elizabeth. She thinks a bit as she nods.

"Honestly…" She begins "I got good at keeping my cool when I'd argue with my brother… He'd push my buttons, but I'd have to be the older sibling." She shrugs "I got good at keeping calm."

"Is that why most of your crew is male?" Connor asks.

"I'd assume Doctor Hoyt took that into account." says Elizabeth "I grew up with boys all my life. My brothers… most of my friends… It's hard for me to look at someone and not think 'that's someone's son' or 'that's someone's little brother.'" Elizabeth frowns her mouth "I know from watching them that deep down, people have their reasons for doing the wrong thing sometimes; and everyone thinks they have all the answers… but nobody does, really… My brothers have humbled me with that; constantly too… I'm probably better off working with men because of my brothers."

Julius looks at Elizabeth. His head tilts in a new realization.

He hasn't thought about why the engineering department is mostly male. It was asked by someone in short hand, long ago, and the answer that was given appears to be wrong. Elizabeth's brothers have played a bigger role in her outlook than Julius had realized.

Doctor Manning nods in thought "Well I appreciate your understanding. I'm sorry to have been so rude before."

Elizabeth smiles "Don't sweat it. We're a team."

✶

Over time the party comes to a quiet night. The scientists migrate back to laboratories and bedrooms. Doctor Lawrence returns to her lab, and Julius goes to bed.

A person's mental well-being is important when traveling through space. Living in close quarters with several strangers is overbearing. This becomes amplified over the span of multiple years. It's for this reason that a genuine love for the work is needed. Many of the scientists aboard the Mandel Explorer were chosen for this quality.

The most important trait for this expedition is the ability to enjoy the time spent alone. Doctor Lawrence loves to reserve time for herself late at night.

Her mother calls her a "*night owl*"; the kind of person who makes the most progress while others are asleep. What her mother doesn't know is Elizabeth's reason for loving the night. Elizabeth could never tell her what would break her heart.

When Elizabeth lived at home, it was the only moment she could walk her childhood home in peace. While she means the best for her daughter, Elizabeth's mother has a highly critical eye. Sometimes Elizabeth just wanted to be alone to think, and a thought would be disrupted with a comment, instilling her mother's expectations. Other times the loneliness can lead to dark thoughts, and her mother's presence can make things more comforting. Elizabeth, as an intuitive woman, recognizes these traits on the surface of her mind.

When she lived with her father, her time alone was spent in the library reading teen fiction novels. This made for many moments that she would rather live with her father. The freedom was liberating to go where she wanted, whenever she wanted. There was always something going on in the city. Now however, she reflects on arguments with her mother.

"You bitch" she says, as if to speak to herself as a child. She knows all the while that she cannot blame her past self. A young girl is unable to vocalize what she feels when she lacks the vocabulary. But the things she said are more than what she wishes she could take back. They're lost moments. Time she could have made the best of while she lived with her mother.

"Elizabeth?" A voice says.

Doctor Lawrence looks around for a face but sees no one.

Elizabeth continues to look at the empty room "What the…"

"Liz!" The voice says.

On the wall by the exit, there's an audio meter with "*Monica Xiao*" glowing next to it.

Elizabeth makes her way to the door and presses the "*Talk*" button. "Yes?"

"Hey, Liz. Sorry to bother you, but you're the only one up. Can you go to the core for me? It's an emergency."

Elizabeth looks back at her table, then faces the doorway again.

"Y-yeah." Elizabeth says "Just give me a minute."

Elizabeth leaves her work and makes her way to the core of the ship.

She enters the large dark halls leading to the power core. The energy is distributed about the ship toward the surface, leaving the fusion core far from any excess heat. Air ducts take the heat to the outer shell, just underneath the electromagnetic shield. The shield is made from the same material developed by Curtis Mandel himself.

"I hate this place." Elizabeth thinks.

While she hates to admit it, Elizabeth is afraid of the dark. Her father used to leave her alone in her room to help her get over it. It never really worked outside of her home, however. As a woman, she's feared the idea of someone lurking in the shadows.

These large halls with their hissing pipes in the distant spaces, long after the railings of an iron scaffolding; she dreads the unknown corners here.

"*Asshole.*" She thinks to herself.

Her father used to insist that she "*Grow up.*" when it came to the dark, but when it came to her middle school boyfriend she was "*too little*". He would support the idea of her being married to a "*wealthy guy from college*" but looked at her engineering career as "*good for now*". He'd follow up with "*But what about after your career?*" as if she'd prematurely retire with children to feed.

Her mother was no better in some ways. Elizabeth remembers her excitement, the day she proved herself to her parents.

"*I'm going to Earth!*" She exclaimed to her mother "*I've been accepted for The Odysseus Mission!*"

Her mother was more worried about how long she'd be gone.

"*Twenty-one years?*" Her mother asked. Not "*I'm so proud of you!*" as Elizabeth had hoped.

She retracts her anger with another thought. She remembers her former feeling of misunderstanding her mother, and an argument they had when the same subject came up just days later. "*I'm going whether you like it or not!*" Elizabeth said to her mom "*I'm going to be WORTH something! I'm not the one drinking; spitefully wallowing in the past, talking about a man I USED to call my 'unfaithful husband'!*"

Elizabeth bites her teeth "*You bitch.*" she thinks.

She used to laugh with her mom. They'd watch movies together and go for walks under a dome with stars projected on its nighttime curtains. They'd reminisce on memories of her brother. That's probably why her mother couldn't bear eleven years without Elizabeth. They'd be twenty-one years she'd never get back with her daughter. Elizabeth was the only one who could give her a grandchild, so how could she blame her mom?

Elizabeth looks at her hands. She's already lowered the front panel of the core's display meter. She looks up to her right and sees the core glowing over the scaffolding of the large power room.

She places her hand on the wall and calls Monica.

"What do you need?" Elizabeth asks.

"Can you bring the power down for a moment?" Monica asks.

Elizabeth does.

"Excellent!" Monica says "I'm getting readings just fine up here. Can you bring it up a notch and close the panel?"

"You've got it." Elizabeth says.

"Thank you again, and sorry to bother you."

Elizabeth smiles "It's no problem at all."

Her silent walk back is disturbed by something new. She comes to the halls before the engineering lab when she's pulled into a fear both primal and unfamiliar. A shriek like a banshee. It rings in a distant darkness. Like an animal drowning in white noise. It begs for its life. It stops. Silence pervades over all but the humming ventilation.

Elizabeth stands paralyzed. Her courage prevails "Hello?!" she shouts.

Nothing but shadow. The ventilated air. Silence.

She walks into the shadows. The motion sensors activate the lights as she steps toward where the noise came from.

A doorway lies between her and the middle of the hall. She approaches and places her hand on it. Her information is presented. She pulls up a message box to Julius.

"*Heard a noise in our wing*" she writes "*Meet me here.*"

A moment passes until she receives a message back "*Yes, queen.*"

She rolls her eyes and steps forward. She begins scanning the hall for a weapon but finds nothing.

At the lab she sees no lights. In all the rooms along the hall there is darkness. All except one. On the border of the history wing, a pale blue light glows from the doorway.

From inside the room, the light from the hall grows brighter. The sound of Elizabeth's footsteps grow near. Doctor Clay wonders who it may be. The motors in his long-term memory rise.

"Doctor Lawrence." He says in surprise.

"Doctor Clay, did you hear something down this way?"

She tries to hide her concern.

"I haven't. I'm afraid it might be myself who made the noise. I just woke from a nightmare."

Her guard falls as she walks further into the room. "You dream?"

Unsure himself, Doug corrects his words. "I think I do. It's like I lose myself in thought and forget where I am. Unlike dreams I don't forget them after I wake. It's like a daydream of what ifs."

She takes a seat and feels relieved "Are you okay?"

"I am. Thank you. It was just a nightmare about coyotes attacking my dog."

"A dog?" She can barely contain her excitement.

"A golden retriever." He replies.

Shifting in her chair she must ask the question "What was it like having a dog? Did he play fetch and stuff?"

There is a moment of silence, then a question emerges "Doctor Lawrence, do you not have dogs where you're from?"

Her mouth frowns and she shakes her head.

"This is going to be a long talk" He says "but it'll be better than therapy sessions."

After a while of talking about average dogs and breeds, Doug begins to explain what his own dog was like. He always calls him "Rebecca's dog" because it was her choice and not his to adopt a friend. When Valentine's Day came around one year, they picked a young puppy. He was found on a freeway a few days prior to meeting them. He had a mild temperament and a habit of licking gentle hands. As scientists, they could not help but name him something relevant to their lives. Bert was the name they chose. They returned to their new apartment and chose the name as the dog sniffed around the room. His name was for the famous scientist Albert Einstein.

Once Bert became comfortable, he was notorious for being overprotective. Barks from other dogs upstairs would lead him to howl. Strangers would get a thorough sniffing before they were cleared to enter the room. The "off-limits" couch became his bed, and Rebecca couldn't resist giving him scraps from the table. Soon enough he was a misbehaving loud boy with a fear of lightning.

"Honestly I think he was mixed." Doug says. "He did a lot of things that weren't normal for a golden retriever."

Before Elizabeth can ask another question, her attention deviates to a sound in the doorway.

Julius wanders in. "There you are!" he says.

"Julius!" Elizabeth says with a smile. "Doug was just telling me about his dog. Well, Rebecca's dog really."

He smiles at her, unable to be upset. "Got too distracted to let me know you were okay?"

She begins to apologize but he waves the concern away. "I knew you were okay when I heard you down the hall."

Her attention turns back to Doug. She lets her shoulders fall and she smiles. She looks into the lens with a sidelong gaze, and an understanding for the man behind the metal.

"You must have loved her a lot to put up with a dog like that." She says.

The machine reaches into distant memories with a longing for far-away days. "More than anything in the world."

CHAPTER 26
Rebecca

"So that's when my mother threatened to commit suicide, and I told her to go ahead and do it."

The room is quiet, save for the ventilation duct in the corner. The holographic fireplace lashes up for Doctor Manning to look at.

Hoyt holds his chin between his forefinger and his thumb. His eyes are fixed on the biologist. His brows, frowning over his gold-trimmed glasses.

Manning claps his hands together and raises his brows.

"So there's no redeeming that relationship!" Manning says "Nor do I want to."

Hoyt nods and takes a note.

"Certainly no redeeming…" Hoyt says "Indeed… And do you see any possibility of this affecting you today?"

Manning purses his lips together.

"Probably not." He says.

Doctor Hoyt flinches his brows together.

"What about Elizabeth?" asks the therapist "Do you feel any better about her?"

Manning shrugs with his face winced together. He leans in as if to tell a secret.

"Come on, Doc…" He says "It's plug and play… She barely wants to be here. She's always fucking off with that friend of hers the…"

Hoyt raises his index finger to hold his words. Manning stops speaking.

Hoyt takes a sigh and meets his back to the chair.

"Words." He says.

Manning nods "Right. I'm sorry."

He leans in with his elbows to his knees and continues speaking with his head bowed and eyes up.

"It really doesn't seem like it's all that hard to do what she does." He says "And she takes a lot of recreation time."

"Time that is supposed to be off hours." Hoyt adds "Time you don't take for yourself."

Manning nods at the floor.

"Someday you'll be considered a hero for everything you've done so far…"

Manning shakes his head "I don't think heroes are real. It's some bullshit people made up. You've told me as much."

Hoyt shakes his head.

"You have me wrong." He says "I never said heroes weren't real."

Hoyt leans forward and looks Connor Manning in the eyes.

"I said that heroes are ordinary people." Hoyt adds "They have flaws and weaknesses…" He gives a half of a smile with the corner of his mouth "History might depict you as a perfect man someday; but I consider myself lucky to know you… The real you. With your moments of vulnerability… The days I met with you as a child all those years ago."

Hoyt looks off to the collection of books on his shelf. The one that stands out is the book he has on his own ancestor; Doctor Curtis Mandel.

"Believe me…" Hoyt says "Not everyone will get to see you for who you really are."

Manning nods in agreement; knowing full well that he's speaking with an expert on this subject.

They finish their therapy session soon after; and with a closing farewell, Doctor Manning leaves the room. Hoyt is left alone with the fireplace and a slew of notes to organize.

The therapist doesn't have time to organize at the moment. His next appointment is in just a few minutes, and with the addition of the new member, Doctor Hoyt is spread thin.

He looks again at the book about the Mandel brothers. He wonders further about Doug's relationship with his ancestor.

"Maybe today is a good day to ask." He wonders.

He gathers his notes and takes to the halls. Around the corner he comes to the occupied recreation room, and there he sees Douglas alone again. The chair waits for Doctor Hoyt in front of the machine.

He smiles and enters the room. He's resolved in his mind to ask about how he came to call Mandel his friend.

***

234

A spring air flows into the freshman labs on a bright afternoon; and birds tweet atop tree branches in the city parks of Cambridge, Massachusetts. The golden sun invokes life into the freshly thawed soil.

Along the Charles River is the sound of rubber and plastic wheels. They roll along the damp sidewalks lining the embankment of Memorial Drive. Baby strollers pushed by young mothers. The rollerblades of street hockey players. The Sunday morning marks a city's routine of closing the street for foot traffic. Every week, cars are rerouted to Harvard Square and the other back streets uphill; toward the heart of the city.

Across the river young people picnic in Boston's Common, and athletes run across the brick facades of the back bay. The glass towers of recent years gleam on the morning sky; high above the antiquated streets below.

The city of Boston seems to have come alive with the breeze of its harbor at high tide, and its people have been welcomed to enjoy the day.

One exception lies in the shade of old Cambridge buildings. The students of Merrimack Institute stay indoors with their studies.

Intermittently glancing at the wide open windows, Doug works with his partner. They grow food for the lab's stem cells on the weekends.

"That's right, not the stem cells, but their food." His partner says. His phone rests on his ear. His sister can be heard laughing on the other end.

Her voice, an audible annunciation across the breeze "They can't even trust you with a real responsibility!"

He agrees as a joke and Doug smiles to himself.

She speaks again with condescension "Are you stuck with the quiet guy again?"

Doug pretends not to hear, and his partner turns down the volume.

The partner looks at Doug briefly, but sees no reaction "We're doing fine."

Soon after, the partner begins shewing his sister off the phone. With the end of the call, he continues his work. For a while they work in silence unless out of necessity.

Near the end of their time in the lab, the partner tries to start a conversation, but Doug doesn't care for it.

"I have a little get-together happening tonight." The partner says.

Doug keeps his eyes focused on his task "Oh yeah?"

"If you wanna come by, you're more than welcome."

"Uh, no thanks, man. I have plans, already."

The partner begins talking about his plans for the night, but Doug tunes him out for a while. Looking at his phone, he finds a name in his contacts. An acquaintance from his history class "Curtis Mandel". He begins typing out a message to Curtis:

"Hey Curt, do you have any plans for tonight?"

It doesn't take long for the reply:

"A party in Alston. Wanna come?"

The night comes with a full moon. Curtis meets Doug at his dorm room, and they soon meet with James; Curtis' long-time friend. Along with James is a group of acquaintances, but no one Doug will remember in later years.

James and Curtis make an effort to talk with Doug in particular. They ask questions about his major and where he sees the future of bionics. He nearly dismisses the topic and asks Curtis about his work. He becomes interested and engages in a matter of problem solving.

"In my opinion" Doug begins "You should really look at natural structures for inspiration." He looks at Curtis with enthusiasm.

"What do you mean?" Curtis asks.

"You're talking about fending off radiation with materials, but have you looked at the structure of butterfly wings?"

James tilts his head and gathers his brows.

"What about butterfly wings?" Curtis asks.

Doug goes on "The color blue is uncommon in nature. It's hard to replicate, which made blue paint uncommon in medieval times. They used to crush lapis lazuli into a fine powder to make ultramarine. Then someone discovered the properties of blood from horseshoe crabs."

"Lapis lazuli is a gemstone." James tells Curtis.

Curtis turns his eyes from James to Doug "So horseshoe crabs have something in their blood?"

Doug nods "Yeah, but that's a place that no one knew to look for a while." He recalls a memory of images from class, and looks up to the ceiling as if to reach into his mind "I can't remember the name of the butterflies, but there's a type that has blue wings." He pulls out his phone to look up an image. He continues to speak as he looks "The wings themselves weren't blue, but on a microscopic level, they're shaped to bounce light around in its wings. Kind of like how the sky is blue, these wings would work as microscopic prisms to reflect blue light and cancel out the other colors."

Curtis looks at the image on Doug's phone "They're not actually blue?"

Doug shakes his head "They're an illusion of blue. Once light passes through the microscopic structures, all that is left is blue light. The material itself isn't blue. Blue light is a short wavelength, so it lasts longer than the other colors. Gamma rays are short wavelengths of light, and so maybe that's where you need to be looking."

Curtis smiles at the intuitive student "That's a good idea."

James looks at the image as well "That might be the answer you're looking for, dude."

Doug smiles "It becomes a matter of trial and error; but if you make some materials like that, I'm sure you'll find something."

James looks again at the image in Curtis' hand, then he looks up to Doug "Have people done stuff like this before?"

"Like what?" Doug asks.

"Using natural shapes to inspire new materials."

Doug nods "All the time. Bulletproof vests were inspired by the layering of calcium on clam shells. It's how they protect themselves from predators."

Curtis grows enthusiastic and talks a long while after.

After long, Curtis receives a text from his brother Frank. The group makes their way to the bottom of the dormitory where a minivan waits. There, Curtis sits in the passenger's seat, and the acquaintances pack in the back.

Doug is last in the van, and Frank is introduced through the rearview mirror.

Along the ride, the students ask questions of the two brothers. The questions come from a curiosity about the two. The women become more attentive in hopes of learning about their faceless chauffeur.

"So, who's the cooler brother?" One girl asks. "That's what I wanna know."

"Oh that would be Curtis." Frank says.

Curtis shrugs "He's right."

Frank laughs.

"Frank's more fun than me, though." Curtis adds "I'll give him that."

Frank looks intermittently between the rearview and the road "Who's asking anyway?"

The girl get's sarcastically indignant "Uhm, I am!"

Frank lifts his hands from the wheel in a surrendering gesture "Oh, sorry. I didn't know."

The girl holds her phone in her hand and a bag at her side. Her legs are crossed under her black leather skirt.

She tosses her hair to the side with a bending of her neck and looks at the driver with a smile "And what do you do, Frank?"

"Me? I'm a humble plumber." He says.

Curtis gathers his brows "A business owner! Don't play it down."

Frank gives Curtis a glance for the game he's playing. It might as well say "*Yeah, a business I inherited from 'Daddy.'*" with oodles of sarcasm loaded on top.

Frank shakes his head with a smile and a raise of his brows "Yeah, a plumbing business; and I own it."

"Oh cool!" One girl says.

Frank shoots Curtis another glance, and Curtis smiles back.

The brothers continue to divulge the group on their relationship. It is described through a back-and-forth about their life as siblings. From stories about their mother and father, to the teachers they loathed. The van is treated to a comic depiction of their life story.

Frank includes Doug in the group conversation several times. Despite his silence among the passengers, Doug feels comfortable around the group.

Curtis seems more talkative than Doug has known him to be. His humor shines through the brotherly banter. His laugh booms, and his words are fluid. Frank has an effect on the crowd as a whole in this way. He brings people to be more sociable and interactive. Perhaps it's a by-product of having a more thoughtful, and less talkative brother. Frank seems capable of winning anyone's trust. Better yet it seems he would defend his younger brother from anyone and anything.

The van arrives in Alston at a brick-faced apartment building. The group exits the vehicle and onto a sidewalk. They stand beneath the street lights of a long-since gentrified neighborhood.

The girls take their chance to see Frank for the first time. None of them are disappointed. They look his way and adjust their clothing briefly. They fix their hair. Two pull the legs of their shorts to rid themselves of wrinkles. The third brushes the front of her shirt and the sleeves of her jacket. They all smile as if to show themselves on display.

Curt looks at Doug with a side glance as if to say "He has that effect on people."

Doug smiles at Curt.

While Doug envies Frank, he doesn't feel jealousy. A good-hearted guy deserves the attention that comes with a handsome face. Frank's charisma can bring insecurity out of most men, but Doug roots for the good people of the world. The Mandel brothers seem to be a symbol for such good-natured people.

Once inside the old apartment building, they walk through a tall and narrow hallway. Chandeliers cast a yellow light on the off-white walls.

Behind one of the black painted doors is a crowd of voices and music. It's the kind of hipster music that Doug hates. The sound of a young adult man singing. His notes are entirely comprised of a talentless falsetto. The consonance of his speech are lightly pronounced. Fingers snap with a reverberation, as if they were recorded in some large cathedral. Finally, above all the things that Doug hates, there is that second voice. It pronounces no words in any form of spoken language. The voice that sounds as if it were being uttered by one of Santa's little helpers, cut, sped up, and put on reverse to eliminate any conceivable meaning.

As the group waits for Frank to text his friend in the party, Curt comments on the music. He agrees with Doug's unspoken opinion "I wonder if they use the same sound in every song. Some guy in some auditorium, just snapping his fingers." He begins snapping with the song as if to depict the image of one man snapping his fingers in a large room.

A girl from the group winces an eyebrow with question "What's the deal with the little person voice?" She asks.

Doug smiles "It's featuring Alvin and the Chipmunks"

The group laughs and the door opens to a man with a soft face. His beady eyes lie behind thick-rimmed glasses, and above a thick orange-brown beard. He holds an obscure IPA in his hand, and his frumpy front is cloaked by a baggy flannel. In a light voice he invites them in.

"Hey dude!" He says to Frank "Thanks for coming!"

They embrace one another with a half-hearted hug, and the group walks in.

The crowd inside is riddled with pierced soft faces and tattooed soft bodies. Most of the ink is black on white. They show from sleeves cut to shoulder height. One woman wears a sleeveless black shirt, tucked into high-waisted jeans. Her short hair bobs back and forth as she dances with another woman. The partner's hair is cut to shoulder length, jet black, and frames a face bearing a nose ring.

Later, Doug is told that they're art students from a nearby school. Most of the party is comprised of artists. The men and women of science stand out among them; with dresses, jeans, and t-shirts.

The moon rises high, and two girls flirt with Doug. He keeps them at bay with a polite demeanor. Curtis watches and smiles at the love-stricken biologist.

An hour later they sit alone on a fire escape outside the back window. Curtis leans on the railing with his back. "You're a good guy, Doug."

Doug holds himself up with his forearms on the railing.

"Thanks, man." Doug slurs. "You are too."

"You're loyal to that girl." Curtis says "What's your girlfriend's name?"

"Rebecca; and she's not my girlfriend." Doug winces his eyes and shrugs "We're taking it slow."

Curtis peers past glowing cheeks, and gives a light punch to Doug's shoulder. "She'd better not take advantage of you." He slumps over the railing next to Doug. "People are self-serving assholes; and you're good. People like to take advantage of guys like you, so don't let 'em."

Doug nods and looks out over the shops and headlights along the road. He gathers his brows and takes a deep breath "Don't worry, man. Becca's good."

His demeanor of blind trust makes Curtis look around for examples. He sees James through the fire escape window and smiles. "No relationship is flawless, but it's effort that counts." Curtis wags his finger toward the window.

Doug looks over his shoulder to see James. He plays a game of beer pong with Frank and two of the girls they arrived with. James lands the ball in his opponent's cleavage. The group inside erupts in a cheer.

"Take James for example." Curt says. "My best friend from childhood." Curtis and Doug look at one another "I can trust him with anything; but I can't ask him for lady advice." Doug laughs. Curtis smiles "He's an old school guy. He's not into the same girls." Curtis closes one eye and looks down his finger, which points toward his brother. "Frank is my brother." His hand returns to support his drink. "I can rely on him for anything; but he's a plumber." Curt returns the weight of his forearms to the railing. "He's practical. So when I get ambitious, he'll tell me to be realistic."

Doug's face grows thoughtful and he stares back to the street lamps below.

"He'd mean well" Curtis continues "not wanting me to fail and all; but I need to take risks. That's how I stride forward."

Doug nods.

"You're a reliable guy; and she seems reliable, too. Just be honest with yourself. If you smell trouble, don't worry." He nudges Doug's elbow, and Doug retracts it. "You've got a friend in me." Curt continues. "There'll always be someone else, and I'll be there to help you out with anything you need."

Doug looks up to see Curtis making full eye contact with him.

"Thanks Curtis." His hand awkwardly slaps Curt's back. "You're a true friend." He pulls his hand away. "Thank you."

On the car ride back, two of the girls complain about another girl, Rachel.

"Like Rachel, you're dating Gio." Amanda says. "Like, how could you do that? Like, I'm so lost. He's out of your league and you're grinding up on sloth from the Goonies."

The whole car gets silent. "Fuck you, Amanda! I don't see you…"

The argument goes on, and all the men sit in silence. Curtis and Doug look at one another with an exaggerated frown and widened eyes.

Arriving back on campus, Doug and Curt part ways with their designated driver. They send Frank off with a fond farewell and make their way to the dormitory. James heads to bed leaving Curt and Doug alone.

"My place for saké?" Curt asks.

Doug smiles. "Ah hell, why not."

In Curt's room, the pair find Curt's roommates with a tall lamp rolling atop an office chair. The lamp holds a powerful magnet on top. The room of three laughing men brings Curt and Doug to smile.

"What's going on, here?" Curtis asks.

"Hold on!" One kid says with a subdued laugh.

Another kid comes closer to explain. "So Scott has been hooking up with the girl upstairs."

"I'm painfully aware." Curtis says.

"He left a bunch of pharaoh fluid in a bucket in the bathroom, and now we're making it move."

The two other boys struggle with the rolling contraption and bring it out of the bathroom. The fluid pulls the bucket to its side and spills all over the bathroom floor upstairs. As the chair enters the common space, a scream is heard upstairs.

"WHAT THE FUCK IS THAT?"

The laughter makes the two boys even weaker. Curtis then takes the chair himself. He begins to swing it around and turn it with the mannerisms of a wild animal.

The screams get louder and more erratic. The boys fall to the floor laughing. Upstairs, two girls stand on their beds in a panic. At the foot of their beds is a metallic spiked fluid on the tile floor. Curtis remains standing with the lamp and chair in hand. He laughs for a moment, but gets back into character and thrusts the chair forward.

"STOMP ON IT!" One of the girls screams.

"What the fuck! YOU stomp on it!"

A smack is heard from an object hitting the floor. The girls watch in horror as the fluid snaps back into shape. They stomp on their beds in fear. The boys hear the screams from downstairs and laugh even harder.

"I'm getting security!" One of the girls shouts.

The boys look at one another with brows raised, eyes wide, and mouths in an "O" shape. They stand frozen looking at one another.

"I'll get it!" Curtis says.

The boys laugh as he grabs the magnet from the top of the lamp. He begins running like a fullback out the door and up the stairs.

In the upstairs room, the girl who stayed is surprised.

"Who the fuck are you?" She asks.

Curtis puts his finger to his mouth in a "Shh" signal.

He swings the magnet over the floor and gathers all the pharaoh fluid he can. The girl looks confused as he runs out the door. The weight of the magnet throws off his center of balance.

Rounding the corner, the magnet thrusts itself onto an exposed metal pipe. It clangs with a force.

"AH! Fuck!" He yells.

He rips the magnet from the pipe, spilling a portion of the fluid as he makes his escape down the stairwell.

The boys laugh with little to no breath left.

By the time the girls arrive they are exhausted of air. The girl dating Scott sees the magnet covered in the spiky magnetic fluid.

She looks up at her boyfriend and shouts "Really?!"

With a wide smile she thrusts herself at him. She begins hitting his chest with a light force. He picks her up and holds her with a smile.

The custodian comes in to investigate, and is relieved to see the laughing students.

After getting the details, he bumps his fist with Scott's and wishes the group a good night.

For many years to come, Doug and Curt will tell this story to their friends, family, and coworkers. Each time, they will remember it as "The first night I hung out with one of my best friends".

Through his aperture blades, Doug looks out into darkness. The Mandel Star Explorer is silent for the night.

"Yeah." He thinks to himself. "He's a lot like them."

CHAPTER 27
Rocket Man

It was one of the happiest days of his life. We drove down I-93 in my brother's old rust bucket; and I mean this thing was a real piece of work. It was missing a front bumper, the AC didn't work, and it had paint chipping off everywhere. There was a hole in the floor under the driver's feet, and a delay when you turned the wheel.

We drove this thing seventy miles an hour south with the windows down to relieve ourselves of the heat.

It was common for Curtis and I to sing in harmony when we drove. He would take the low notes, while I would take the high ones.

The blue sky was open wide, with little strokes of clouds here and there. A perfect spring day. The flowers bloomed in the median between north and southbound traffic, the forests on either side were lush with green, and the air smelled of a sun-kissed sea breeze.

More than summers by the ocean, winters on the slopes, or a backyard fire in the fall; I miss springtime on Earth.

Elizabeth enters the room with a knock. Her fingers hold the handle to a cup of tea. "How's the reading?"

"Nothing on Doug yet." Julius says. "I'm just reading about his car. It's on its last leg in this chapter."

Elizabeth smiles "I had a car like that."

Julius recalls from his own memory "Reminds me of my old Strider."

"You had a Strider?"

"An LX. The fancy model." He laughs.

"I used to have a Strider." She says.

Julius raises his brows "Look at us! Riding in true slum style together. What model was yours?"

"An SG. A piece of crap."

Julius laughs "You should have seen mine; the trunk wouldn't close, so I used a bungee chord to keep it shut."

"What do you drive now?" She asks.

"I have a few cars."

"Well, what's your favorite?"

"My favorite would be an old Serpico K90."

She raises her brows. "Fancy. A lot of gas, though."

"It ain't about the miles per gallon; it's about the smiles per gallon."

Elizabeth laughs. "I like that."

"Thanks." Julius smiles. "An old friend of mine used to say it."

"Your friend and I would get along."

Elizabeth blows away the steam from the surface of her tea.

As she turns her back to leave the room, Julius' eyes meet the page again.

***

Curtis and Frank harmonize to a song from the nineteen eighties. The roar of the highway nearly drowns out the tune at full blast. With their hair blowing in the wind, the boys theatrically display their mannerisms in the form of stage personas.

Ending on a long, drawn-out note; the brothers finish the tune in harmonized vibrato. The near-silence between songs is underlined by the relentless wind.

"Nice." Curtis says, with a fist bump.

Frank turns down the volume and throws his feet up on the dash. He turns to look at his younger brother in the driver's seat.

He yells over the wind. "You're the first Mandel to have a bachelor's degree since twenty-ten! How do you feel?"

Curtis shrugs. "Eh!"

Frank ponders "Just 'eh'?"

Curtis looks out at the road; occasionally taking a glance in Frank's direction. "I have a lot to do after this. It's a big deal, don't get me wrong; but I feel like a degree is just a small step."

Frank nods. "Okay, I get that. But what's next? Like what do you WANT to do?"

Curt shrugs "I'm not sure where to go, but I wanna build spaceships. My internship was for construction tools. Hopefully I can transfer somewhere else."

"I thought you did energy stuff." Now full of questions, Frank pauses to decide what to ask first. "Like, what do you do exactly?" he finally adds.

Curtis laughs. "It's complicated. I work with particle physics. We use it to fabricate new materials and solve weird problems."

"How does that come into rockets?"

"It's not so much the rocket part, but the space suits and the capsule that holds the astronauts." He holds his hand out in a pinching shape. "There's things like carbon nanotubes. They're these thin structures; as thin as hair, but stronger than steel. That's an example of a material we made in labs." His mind trails off in an afterthought. "We might be able to use gravitons in the future."

"What the hell is that?"

"They're particles of gravity. They're not bound to our universe; so they can travel through dimensions. It's really cool stuff."

Frank looks both confused and amazed. "I'll leave the science to you; but if your toilet's broke, call me."

Curtis glances at his brother, who holds back a smile.

"I've fixed toilets too, you know." Curt laughs.

"Yeah, because you blew up the front of our house, kid."

"You told me to fire it up!" Curtis laughs.

Frank shrugs "You got free tuition out of that fiasco, so don't worry about it." He takes a long look at Curtis. "I'm proud of you."

Curtis breathes a moment to take that in. "Thanks, Frankie."

"Just don't forget your brother when you're a millionaire."

Curtis shakes his head with a laugh.

The Boston skyline grows on the southern rim of the hill land. Cars grow more abundant in the lanes. The road veers left and right abruptly over Medford and Somerville. In no time, they border Boston's north end, and the boys merge off the highway into a standstill. To the side of the ramp, there is a view of the city. Commonplace for the boys, but otherwise beautiful. Ducks fly over the base of the Charles, where the waning day gleams off the oar-stroked ripples of water.

Frank breathes a roar from the back of his throat "We should've left earlier."

"It's not even rush hour!" Curt exclaims.

"Everyone's graduating today!"

Curtis looks around at the bumper stickers and license plates. Universities and foreign states. The occasional suburban with a sticker reading "This car climbed Mount Washington".

"Sorry, Frankie."

"Not your fault, man. I'm mad at myself for not thinking ahead. It's okay though."

Frank turns up the music again, and soon the lane splits into two. He passes the bulk of the traffic and uses a back road by North Station.

Side-stepping the brick sidewalks of Beacon Hill, Frank makes his way to the old 'salt and pepper bridge', as his mother had called it. From there, they drive into Cambridge and along Memorial Drive. They pass the other illustrious universities, and turn into Central Square. Here, buildings were bought out ages ago and made into the young, yet reputable Merrimack Institute.

Along the edge of campus, they park the car by an old church. Frank worries about getting a ticket, but Curt reassures him it's fine.

"It's your car." Frank says "I don't want to ruin your day."

Curtis waves his concern away and presses onward to cross the street.

Around the corner they reach a coffee shop, billowing with the smoke of hookah pipes. Here James, Roger, and Gabe sit with Turkish coffee at their table.

Gabe was raised in a rough neighborhood until he was ten years old. At that age, he was adopted by his uncle in Jamaica Plane. He became a friend of mine; although we met through Curtis.

Gabe was an engineer; so he was a little different from his buddies in high school. He wasn't exactly an outcast but smarter than the average guy; and he was good at avoiding trouble when he was up to no good.

His senior prank was playing pornography sounds over the high school's loudspeakers. The whole school praised him, and yet he was never caught.

When he got older, he cooled it down with the pranking, and got focused in school. As he would

Curtis walks up to his friends with a swagger.

He begins with an intentionally cringey tone "What's up fellow
grads!"

All greet him separately, except one.

"Technically we aren't grads yet." Gabe clarifies; sending everyone
into an unnecessary analysis.

"Is that true?" James asks.

"I think so… Let me look it up."

Four of the men pull out their phones; intrigued by this small detail.
Roger continues drinking his coffee; followed by a drag of his cigarette.

"No, we aren't there yet." Gabe adds "I was right."

Curt shrugs and sits with the group alongside his brother.

Frank looks over toward Roger for the first time. Tall, pale, skinny,
and dark-haired. An unusual part of the group, from what Curtis has
told him. He has a sense of humor, but now he seems silent with his
cigarette. The smell of weed permeates about him, but he isn't high.

"I don't think you've met." Curtis says.

"Hey, I'm Frank."

Roger accepts Frank's hand with full attention. "Hi. Roger."

"I've heard a lot." Frank says.

"You smoke?"

Frank is confused, as Roger holds a cigarette, but clearly smokes
weed.

"The ganja." Roger says.

Frank laughs "On occasion."

"Just socially." Roger says.

"Well, I wouldn't call myself social when I'm high, but I guess."
Gabe laughs.

"After today, Roger starts his job at Allagash Systems!" James shakes the man's shoulder "It's nice to be connected, isn't it?" He adds.

The group laughs. Roger's cheeks grow less pale.

"His father made room for him in the company." Gabe adds.

"He didn't MAKE ROOM." Roger says. "He happened to let some guys go and needed help."

James smiles "Yeah, happened to let them go…"

Gabe continues "He'll be starting as an engineer, but he's already got a proposal for his own project."

Roger sighs "Yeah, and it's stressing me out! I'm just gonna smoke up tonight and forget about it."

Frank notes his tone, his clothing, and an inattentive behavior. He behaves as if the job is something to worry about, but clearly his father has sealed the deal. His clothing isn't that of an adult, but a trendy young man. He's in his phone constantly; disjointed from the party. Already Frank knows him well. "He is privileged, naive, and perhaps a little spoiled." Frank will tell his brother later "Not that there's anything wrong with him as a person, but he's from a bubble, away from the real world."

"Guess who's coming out tonight!" Curtis interjects.

Gabe drops his jaw and lowers his coffee "No way."

Curt nods.

James speaks with a mocking speech impediment "Dougie got pewmission to come out and pway?" He turns to the other men. "Maybe she's not a total wench after all."

Curtis tilts his head with a raise of his brows "He asked if she could come along."

A gathered grunt erupts from the group. Gabe launches himself back into his chair. James buries his face into his hands.

Roger shakes his head as he keeps texting "Kid's whipped, man."

Curtis crosses his arms "It sounded like he WANTED her to come. So be nice."

Gabe pulls his face forward from staring at the sky "Please tell me you said no."

Curtis looks down and shakes his head.

"Duuuude!" Gabe slaps his hands over his face.

"When was the last time that kid had a minute to himself?" James asks.

Gabe laughs "Kid can't fart the wrong way without her knowing."

James continues "We can't talk the same with her around. She hates video games. Have you seen her face when someone turns on the game console? Like what the hell does she want to join us for?"

"Maybe she's worried." Curtis says. "He's quite the catch."

Gabe, leaning back in his chair, raises his brows. "If he's a catch, then I'm Adonis."

The group laughs. Curtis shakes his head and shrugs.

Curt looks at Frank "I know that look. You were about to say something."

Frank laughs a little "I was gonna say, maybe he's hung like a moose."

Roger shakes his head "He would slay too much to be hung up on one chick."

"Is he that whipped?" Frank asks.

Gabe almost yawns "Oh, yeah!" The group nods with him. "I've never seen a worse case in my life."

James shakes his head and shrugs. "She's to blame too, though. I've seen him try to talk one-on-one with me, but she follows him." He begins to emote through his hands. "If you want to keep a pet like a dog or a cat, do you suffocate it? No. You let it explore and go for walks. Otherwise you're just asking for them to run away. They're like 'fuck this'" He motions like an animal jumping out of a window "And they would rather starve or break their neck than be stuck inside all day."

Curtis stares off as he ponders over this. He nods as he comes to a conclusion "He'll come around… He'll realize he's been missing out on a lot; and he'll be calling us up. It's a matter of time."

"I guess." James says.

"By the time he realizes that, things won't be the same." Gabe says. "We'll be scattered across the world. Who knows when we'll be together again."

The group grows quiet. Even Roger frowns at the idea.

"We won't stay apart for too long, guys." Curt says. "I know it won't be long."

> *Curtis and his friends had a way about them.*
> *They made people want to be a part of their group.*
> *It made them exempt from feeling alone; and many*
> *people felt alone in our time.*
> *The world was rampant with superficial desire;*
> *and all of it was meaningless when we left Earth.*
> *For Curtis, James, Gabe, and the others, it was*

something hard to explain. They all bonded over what they did; but it wasn't that. They all had a furious passion for shaping the future; and yet it wasn't that either.

What brought them together was how reliable they were, and how well they could depend on one another. Some could be more dependable than others, but that was only human of them; and not one of them was the best for helping in all scenarios. Somehow they inherently understood that, and it was okay. There would always be a weak link; whether it was for work, life, or any other reason. No one could be fully committed all the time; and the only way out of this bond was through deliberate, conscious betrayal.

Criticisms were delivered with candor, failures were met with understanding, and mistakes were often forgiven.

It was no wonder that they excelled together.

Curtis looks around at the faces he's come to trust. "We can make something work. We'll hang out another day this week."

James agrees "Ask Doug to come alone. It's not that she's terrible, in fact I like her for him. She just needs to leave him alone for a minute. We need our friend for a night."

They agree, and they find their conversation wandering into other aspects of life. The hours pass, and they are joined by another friend, Rosemary Kaufman. A beautiful blonde woman with blue eyes. Frank does his best not to look in her direction, but his mannerisms change. His engagement in the conversation increases, and his selective words show maturity in his speech.

The sun sets to an orange sky which gives way to pink, then violet, and finally a dark chromatic blue. The lights on the patio come on. The incandescent bulbs shine on silver furnishings. The steel coffee mugs grow cold and dry over the hours.

The group wraps up at the cafe, and they pack into the old junker. They venture across the river to a bar by Fenway Park.

Frank tries to talk with Rosemary, but she's not receptive. He shrugs it off and only speaks with her as one who shares mutual friends.

Frank is used to having an easy time when flirting, but knows to call it quits when someone isn't interested.

Soon he finds that things might be better off this way.

"I'm a Biologist; so I'm an atheist" she tells him.

He will recall these words again tonight; and again it will give him a laugh. For the rest of his life, he'll bring it up to get a giggle out of his brother.

Later he will ask Curtis "Did you sign a vow of atheism? You know you can't get your degree without signing one."

Soon after, Doug arrives with Rebecca. Over a game of shuffleboard, they talk as one unit, and don't separate for a moment. They seem happy, and Curtis is glad for them. Frank encourages them to speak; directing the bulk of the conversation to them. He reads Rebecca's affinity for Doug. She seems to encourage him, feel proud of him, and together they laugh frequently.

As two men working to one end, the brothers investigate the security of their good friend. They read that he is truly loved.

James nods to Curtis, and they break off from the group to step onto the outdoor patio. Here there are tables being waited on.

"We should grab a table." James says.

Curtis nods "Agreed."

They sigh and wait a moment for one of them to speak.

"How are you feeling?" Curtis asks.

"Eh." James shrugs.

"I was telling my brother the same thing earlier."

"I'm assuming he didn't get it." James smiles.

"He's just happy I'm getting my degree." Curt shrugs "I looked at this as the end, but now I'm just the bottom bitch on a totem pole."

James nods "I feel like there was this fire I had in high school, and it was burning with chaotic energy. I wasn't using it for anything back then; just having fun."

"That's EXACTLY how I feel." Curtis shakes his head "And I feel like I'm putting the same amount of fuel on, and it's just not burning like it used to."

James nods "My trick is to look at this as the start of a new journey. I've decided that college wasn't my key to being an all-star scientist; it was just a means to gain the career. Now I make my way to becoming the big guy."

Curtis nods "That's a good way to look at it."

"I'm glad you think so."

Curtis notices the self-deprecating humor in James' tone. Curtis smiles but nods "You make a good point, though. This is just the start of something bigger. I like that."

James nods; happy to hear his idea reaffirmed through his friend. He then stares back at a memory and smiles. "We've come a long way from launching projectiles in physics class."

"What happened to that trebuchet?" Curtis asks.

"Sometime after high school, I burned it in the pit out back." James laughs.

"Oh, at your mom's house?"

"Yeah."

"Shame." Curtis laughs "That thing was a masterpiece."

Gabe comes out with a posture of retrieval "Hey, we're heading back to Cambridge."

James gestures to the tables on the patio "You don't want to eat here first?"

Almost solemn, Gabe grows limp "Have you seen the prices?"

James sees a menu on the hostess counter. His eyes widen. Curtis peers over at the menu and bears the same face.

"Yeah, let's head out." James laughs.

Roger stumbles out drunk "Hey guys, you wanna eat here?"

"Have you SEEN the menu?" Curtis asks.

"Yeah, the fillet mignon sounds bomb!"

The middle class Americans look at one another with amusement.

"We'll eat in Cambridge" Curtis laughs "We'll get takeout and you can smoke up."

Roger nods at the fair deal and stumbles away without a word. The others laugh.

Back across the river, the clock strikes one in the morning. College students stumble out of bars and clubs, and Frank helps the inebriated crew into Roger's apartment.

The studio is adorned with all the furnishings of a real home. The warm, grey-colored floors have a characteristic of wood. They are complimented with granite countertops, which sit atop fake wooden drawers and cabinets adorning silver handles. The kind of style Frank refers to as "If social media companies designed apartments".

Roger grabs his weed from a bedside dresser.

Frank looks around a while and asks "Are we staying here for the night?”

“Yeah.” Roger says with the grinder in his hand.

Curtis nods in Frank’s direction “Do you mind if our driver has a beer?”

“Go for it.” Roger says. “Mi casa su casa.”

Frank opens the fridge to see local IPAs.

“Sorry I’ve only got the cheap shit.” Roger says.

Frank gathers his brows in confusion “No worries, man.” He backs away from the fridge; not a fan of being super drunk off a single beer. “On second thought, I don’t think I’ll have anything.”

“Are you sure?” Roger asks.

“Yeah” Frank affirms. He then notices a video game case on the floor. It lies by an old gaming console. “I wanna kick your ass in Mega Bash. I need to be sober for that.”

Still grinding his weed, Roger laughs “Oh shit. Mega Bash. You know that game?”

“Kid, I played the first one.” Frank laughs.

“Damn, dude!”

After prepping his bong, Roger takes a moment to accept Frank’s challenge. He puts up a good fight, but Frank pulls through with an advanced mechanic in the fighting game; a combo he learned from the first installment of the series; back when he was a freshman in high school.

The group laughs at the comical challenge between the two, and Roger shakes his hand for the good game. The engineer moves back to his bong with Rosemary at his side, and the rest of the group changes games.

From the couch, onlookers watch as Curtis builds a rocket in a simulation game. Rebecca holds her phone in her hand until the group is thoroughly invested. She hears the laughter and wants to join the conversation.

She laughs “You could easily turn this into a suicide bomb simulator.”

“Jesus!” James exclaims.

The party looks on at her after breaking her silence.

Everyone keeps the idea of building a lunar lander in mind, and Becca soon asks “So where’s the nearest city in this game?”

“You’re still hung up on that!” Gabe exclaims.

“Of course!” She laughs “That’s what video games are for! You blow shit up!”

The group laughs.

"You're like a backwards Werner VonBraun." James says.

Her tone is so genuine that the sarcasm is nearly void from her words "Let's face it, the Saturn V was only second to his true masterpiece."

"Jesus!" Gabe yells. "Doug, I don't like you hanging around this girl anymore!"

Rosemary calls from the back of the room, by Roger and his bong "This is the perfect image of guy time." The group turns to look her way "You're just playing with your phallic objects and adding thrust."

The group laughs and turns back to the game. Gabe looks back extra long "Fuck you." Gabe says "Look at you with your penis-shaped bong back there."

Roger looks at his bong with raised brows "Dude! You're like the seventh person to say that!"

Rosemary laughs and puts up a middle finger as she bites her bottom lip.

Looking back to the game, the group grows gradually invested. With a few scribbles on a notepad, James and Curtis send the rocket to the moon with ease. Shouts erupt as the little rocket man places a flag on the surface. Rosemary pulls her face away from Roger's and raises a fist in triumph with the boys. Roger gently places his hand on her face and pulls her in for another kiss.

"Now go for Mars!" Gabe says with sarcasm.

Curt tosses the controller onto the coffee table "Get there yourself."

Gabe laughs "No fuckin' way."

They switch the game to a movie and the group's commentary dies down over time. Rosemary becomes invested in the film, and moves up to hang out with her boys. Roger hangs back behind the couch, and gradually people begin to fall asleep. Becca makes her way to the bathroom in a fuss, and Doug remains on the couch with a face of ease.

"Fuck; you're alone for once." Gabe laughs.

Doug nods with a shrug.

"Is she okay?" James asks.

"She's just tired" Doug says. "Maybe hungry. I'm not sure."

The group begins to wake up slightly over the event of having Doug alone for a moment. Roger doesn't move from his bed, and Rosemary has her feet up on Gabe's lap. Gabe looks back at Roger to see he is asleep.

"Are you and Roger a thing?" He asks.

She speaks with hesitance. "I-it's complicated."

"Just trying to feel things out?" James asks "You don't need to tell us."

She shrugs and shakes her head. "I just don't know what I want."

Her eyes fall on Curtis shortly after speaking, and Frank notices.

"I like her." Rosemary says to Doug.

Doug's head turns to see her, and he smiles.

Rosemary looks around "I can't wait to see all my boys happily married someday."

The boys smile at one another.

"We want the same for you." Doug says.

Curtis speaks in an Italian mobster voice. "And if someone isn't good enough… We'll take care of it."

The friends smile.

"But really." She adds. "I think she likes you for you. That's important."

Doug nods with a cocking of his head to the side as if to say that this is only partly true. "She doesn't like it when I spend time with you guys. I feel like I've been missing out on a lot with you."

The three conscious boys look at one another.

James reaches to pat Doug on the shin "You don't need to worry about that, bud. We'll spend time when we can. No pressure."

Gabe and Curtis agree.

Soon, sleep overcomes the group; and the night grows nearly silent for a few hours.

Graduation Day:

The quiet deeds of the early morning go nearly unnoticed, but grow louder as the sun dawns. The distant highways roar with the sound of commuters, and the hungover few rise with reluctance.

Frank holds a cup of black coffee on the balcony. At seven his brother joins him with squinting eyes.

"Nice and early." Curtis says.

Frank nods with mild amusement, and an essence of bitterness.

"Yeah." He says.

Curtis stands next to him and looks southwest to the city of Boston.

"Is something wrong?" Curtis asks.

Frank shakes his head "No."

His demeanor is perked up.

Curtis gathers his brows.

"What's on your mind?" He asks.

Frank gives a smile.

"I think your friend Rosie likes you."

He begins to laugh and Curtis looks back at the door. He turns to look out at the city again.

"Yeah… maybe; but I'm not about to toss around between me and Roger. That shit's weird."

Frank gathers his brows and nods. His mind drifts away and Curtis sees it.

"What?" Curtis asks.

Inside the apartment, James helps Gabe to a glass of water and two ibuprofen. He sees the brothers return from the balcony.

"Later." Frank says with a shew of his hand. "That's for later."

"Alright then." Curtis responds.

"You have your cap and gown?" James asks.

"Absolutely." Curtis says.

Adorned in the ceremonial clothes, the group packs into the car once more. Frank drives a few blocks away with the girls on laps and boys squished shoulder to shoulder. The squad unloads from the packed car and onto a curb by the convention center.

"Please don't get me a ticket." Curtis begs.

Frank reassures his brother, speaking from the driver's seat through the passenger window. "If you get a ticket I'll pay for it. Don't worry." A man honks behind him. "I'll be in there soon. I'll find a spot."

"Alright. Mom and Dad texted me. They've got a seat for you in there."

"Excellent."

Another honk from behind. In the rearview mirror, Frank finds a white-collar worker in a luxury car. He refuses to shoot the gap between Frank and the far curb.

Frank hangs his head out the window and looks back "Can it, bird shit! Drive around!"

The man accelerates through the wide gap and gives a "Come on!" look through the window as he passes. The man then reaches a red light behind a line of cars.

Frank pulls away from the curb ever so slowly; and after a half a minute of rolling, he is directly next to the man. Frank slowly rolls to a stop and looks at the man with his brows raised. The man in the luxury car tries to ignore him; and when the light turns green, both of their cars pass through the light at the exact same time.

> *The ceremony was rather typical; and by typical,*
> *I mean hours of speeches. No one really listened*
> *to them, and no one knew who the speakers were.*
> *To the credit of the speakers though, none of the*
> *speeches were like those copy-and-paste ones from*
> *high school. The ones where some student compares*
> *life to a fruit and makes it about perseverance.*
> *The graduating students walked up one by one to*
> *receive a folder for their diplomas. The expensive*
> *pieces of paper were mass-produced and delivered*
> *through the postal service a few weeks later.*

On a great lawn, Curtis finds his way out of the crowd to meet his parents and Frank. He embraces his mom with a smile, then his father.

Frank smiles wide and hugs his brother. He speaks into Curt's shoulder. "Congratulations, pal."

Their parents smile at the sight, and turn to look at one another. Their eyelids meet their pupils, speaking years of history without a word.

Their father turns to look at them once more. "Are you guys hungry?" he asks.

"I could eat." Curt says. "Where do you wanna go?"

"You're the one we're here for." Frank says.

Curtis shrugs "I'm sick of everything around here." He looks to his father "Do you and Mom have a place in mind?"

His father thinks a moment, then looks at his wife with a conclusion. She seems to already know what he wants.

"Yeah, I think I know a spot." He says.

In a city square made of brick and pavement, they make their way along the faces of shops and restaurants. Here they pass through a hole in the wall to a bustling room full of voices and the sizzling of a grill. Steam pours out of a kitchen smelling of beef, turkey, vegetables, and fried food. Celebrity faces adorn the walls along with autographs and images of their work. A well known local gem in Harvard Square.

At the table, their parents tell the boys how they used to sit and people watch the area. When they were dating, they were just city kids who found the strangers amusing. Most of them came from strange walks of life, and no one could ever guess who they truly were. They would whisper backstories to each other; defining these fictitious depictions of passers-by.

Mister Mandel had no need for an education. He inherited his father's business and ran it with his brother. The boys' uncle went on to get an associate's degree for the sake of the family business, but likewise didn't require any further education.

Their mother was a very bright woman who grew up poor. Their contact with her side of the family has always been limited, and the boys have found it better that way. They love their aunt and cousins, but their disagreements have never been worth the time to argue about. In this way it has been better to love from afar, rather than butt heads face to face.

Mrs. Mandel would find work without a college degree and earn her merit through personal experience. She had become a real estate agent when they were young, and finally a broker when the boys were in high school.

Their wealth has always been more than career success. It is more than financial stability. The smiles at this table on a late spring day; this is the wealth that can be found in a moment of time. The conversations that would take place in their parents' room, at the edge of their shared bed. The times they watched movies together, and the day trips they would take on weekends. The true wealth of any family is knowing that no one and nothing can come between them.

"I'm happy to see you boys together." Their mother says. "Did you have fun last night?"

"Yeah." Frank says. "It was a lot of fun."

Their mother smiles at them for a prolonged time.

"Oh God." Curtis says with amusement "Here she goes."

A lone tear falls down their mother's cheek and the boys laugh with their father.

Through the emotions, their mother laughs too.

"Oh shut up." She says.

"Why do you get like this?" Frank laughs.

"Because; my family didn't have that." Her voice wavers with her words. "I mean sometimes, but it was always a fleeting moment."

Frank smiles "Well you did good, Mom. We came out pretty good. Especially me."

Curtis nudges his brother, and Frank laughs.

Their mother cleans the tear from her face and breathes deep "When I'm dead and buried…"

Frank exclaims "Jeez, mum! That's morbid!"

"Well…" she begins "I think of my own mom and how she left so sudden. I'm glad you boys will have each other when that time comes around." She packs a mascara-marked napkin into a ball. She holds it by the table in her hand. "Be surprised…"

"'*By the little things*'." The boys say in unison.

"We know." Says Frank.

"Yes!" She says "My mother always told me 'be surprised by the little things' and I never truly understood it until she passed away…"

Frank tilts his head with his brows screwed together. He's taken aback by what sounds like a story he's never heard before. She's said the phrase a million times over, but never in context to her mother's death.

"She always meant the little people in your life…" She says "… the people who seem powerless; don't ever underestimate them… but you know… It's these little moments here, too. They become the things you want most when they're no longer available…" She dabs her eye with a cocktail napkin "… And I can tell you; family means everything when you have nothing… So always know that you'll have each other. Always."

The boys look at one another. With big grins, they roll their eyes. They agree, but find it funny all the same. Each one takes their mother's hand from across the table. Their father puts an arm around her and leans his head to hers.

Their mother tilts her head to their father, and she grips their hands tight. She then smiles at the men she's made.

> *My father was the one who gave us our*
> *light-hearted sense of humor and a sense of ratio-*
> *nality. Our mother was the one who instilled our*
> *sense of passion for what we did in life. She was the*
> *one who made sure we knew that what we had was*
> *special. She guided us through troubling times; and*
> *it was her lessons that gave us the strength to with-*
> *stand the tough times to come.*
>
> *I can honestly say, without a fraction of a doubt,*
> *that our mother was our greatest role model. Her*

strength and wisdom were the key to my brother's success, and later my own. My mother can take full credit for her part in the legacy of the Mandel family. She just may have played the most important role of all, our mentor on handling what life had to throw our way.

CHAPTER 28
Doctor Hoyt

Doctor Hoyt sits by the holographic fire, and Julius looks off in thought.

"When I look back on my time after the war, all I can think is 'that meaningless life was all because I lost faith in people.'" Julius shakes his head "I didn't, and still don't trust people to make decisions out of reason or logic."

"You're sounding like someone else I know." Doctor Hoyt says.

"Doctor Morris?" asks Julius.

"Why do you think it's him?" Hoyt wonders.

"I can see it in his face." Julius says "You can only look back at human history for so long until you see the same mistake over and over again. The 'us and them' mentality."

Hoyt gathers his brows.

Julius goes on "We killed people because we thought we were right. They killed us for the same reason. In the end there was a valid point to both arguments."

"You killed for that reason?" Hoyt asks.

Julius shakes his head "Not me… I killed because I had to." He adjusts himself in his seat "Sometimes you need to make a split-second decision, and you have to make the decision to save four lives in exchange for two. You have to end someone's suffering because there's no saving them."

Doctor Hoyt looks at his tablet "And what would you say to Doctor Morris… if he felt the way you do?"

Julius shrugs "That's life. It's not fair." He gives a breath of a laugh "We want to make everything comfortable; to end hunger and homelessness. We can try and mitigate things, but it's like trying to make sure no one ever makes a stupid decision again. It's like ending crime for the rest of eternity. It can't happen. People will make decisions like a force of nature; and that's HUMAN nature.

Saying that things aren't fair in our society is like saying Zion is unfair for having a poor atmosphere. It's just hostile to life because it just IS. You can't change it; you have to work WITH it."

Doctor Hoyt nods "People these days haven't seen the things that you have; and I'm inclined to think you're right."

Doctor Hoyt strokes his chin for a moment and wonders what to add.

"Do you ever feel upset that people can't grasp that?" He asks.

Julius widens his eyes.

"I've heard a lot of people's opinions." Julius says "I've heard people say how they'd have handled things if they were in the war, or in New Memphis… Truth be told, no one ever really knows what war is until they're in it." He raises a brow and shakes his head at the floor "People did horrible things back then; they did them to survive… People can't imagine themselves in that situation because they don't KNOW what war IS…"

Hoyt nods and presses his lips together to the point of a near smile. He sighs with his eyes to the floor, then looks up at Julius again.

"How are things going with Elizabeth?" Hoyt asks.

Julius gives a gust of a laugh.

"I've been teaching her how to shoot." He says.

"How is that going?"

Julius raises a brow "Not bad… We've been using those toy dart guns."

Hoyt nods "Ask Doctor Morris for access to the weapons in the artifact room. Show her how the real ones work."

Julius nods "She'd probably like that." He laughs "I mean, it's physics."

Hoyt laughs "She'd love that. Just don't shoot them, whatever you do…" He looks at the time "Alright, it's about that time. I'll see you when you're back?"

Julius smiles and stands "You'll see me around."

Hoyt shakes his hand and Julius makes for the door.

Doctor Hoyt sits at his desk and the door closes shut to leave him in solitude. He then looks over his notes to familiarize himself with the positions of the crew.

His notes read:

Doctor Julius Winter:

Concerned with the preservation of his friend, Julius has been shut out from socializing because he's lost friends in the past. He's made a friend in Elizabeth, and he's friendly with the department heads. His hangup is with other people's decisions. He's concerned that Doctor Manning is self-centered and near-sighted. Julius' wisdom makes me cautious for the same reason. Otherwise, Julius is realizing the value of disclosing his most personal thoughts, confiding in his friend, and seeking insight. It's been slow, however.

He once told me that he's "Stuffed his emotions down so far that he can't find them when he's happy". I think Elizabeth has given him the ability to find his feelings again. He might be afraid to lose that, and so he's been stuck.

On one hand, he feels that passing on his knowledge of combat and survival can help to preserve her. On the other, he doesn't want to burden her with the same feeling of numbness.

Doctor Connor Manning:

A long history with his troubled family has made it difficult for him to socialize. He's convinced he is the most valuable member of the team, and perhaps Peter has told him something about this. He was chosen for his passion for the job, and every member was chosen based around his psychological needs. Elizabeth challenges his prejudice while Morris provides a sympathetic voice in his corner, despite his difference in outlook from Doctor

Manning. Hopefully Morris' outlook will rub off on Manning's personality. The Xiao sisters are patient enough to tolerate him, but Linda hasn't seen the gentle side of Doctor Manning. I look forward to their acquaintance growing into something with more substance. Her opposition is more gentle, and she will likely provide more of a profound influence on Doctor Manning if they speak more frequently.

Doctor Ron Morris:

Doctor Morris is a gentle soul plagued by depressive thoughts. He's a lonely character with a passion for little things; the slow pro-gression of history being one of his many wells of endless fascination.

His lack of sociable qualities is exagger-ated by his analysis of human events. He sees a near-sighted nature to people, and it pains him to see it in his own friend, Doctor Manning.

Perhaps he should speak with Julius about these things; or maybe Morris needs a friendship, like the one Elizabeth and Julius share. He needs SOME connection on this ship. It would alleviate his loneliness, even if only for a moment. It would be best if it were someone who is patient like him; to understand him. At the same time, he needs someone to highlight the more immediate joys of life.

Doctor Tim Gully ("Tim the Tank Man" Julius calls him):

Tim is a level-headed person. He's patient

and passionate. He's more than capable of handling Doctor Clay's potential for manipulation; assuming Clay tries to make any advances on Tim.

Tim has reported nothing on Clay's behavior, just an introduction (while he was doing maintenance work some time ago).

Doctors Monica and Linda Xiao:

Linda is gentle, but lacks her sister's patience. Monica, in contrast, is harsh and to the point, and yet very understanding.

Both sisters confide in one another, but their relationship with the rest of the team has been hindered by their lifelong bond.

Above all the other residents, they are the most mentally stable; and they were chosen for this quality. It's because of their father that they've been this way. A former homeless drug addict, he changed himself for their sake. Their mother was unaware of who he really was when they met, and when he told her of his past she was shocked.

He was handsome, callused, and polite. She was sheltered and wealthy. Their daughters were exposed to both of their worlds, and in turn they were given a quality upbringing. The unusual circumstances of their parents' unlikely unity made them very stable and keenly aware of people.

I look forward to them building a relationship with Elizabeth. Elizabeth craves a feminine friend, but she hates the posturing that many women perform. The Xiao sisters feel the same as her in this respect; and they keep an honest persona at their forefront. They aren't ones for gossip or patronizing compliments; and so there is an untapped potential within their relationship. A rarity in both men and women; they've been outside of the social circles that seek to exclude people. People like them are not written about or advertised. Their identity is their own, which allows for a truly ground-breaking advancement in conversation.

Doctor Elizabeth Lawrence:

A passionate worker, she's in direct contrast to Doctor Manning's perception of people. She's always working on herself to become something better. She's endlessly curious and has little to show for an ego.

Her desire for betterment can blind her from her past achievements. She has a hard time appreciating who she's become, because she's so focused on who she wants to be.

Elizabeth will have no trouble understanding Doctor Manning, and Doctor Morris will likely be surprised by her awareness.

Elizabeth has a fun-loving humorous side, and often bends the rules for the right reasons (accessing historical department computers without permission). It's likely that Julius' same quality has made him her other half. They're both searching for answers to Doctor Clay's past. They need to socialize more for the sake of branching out. It would give them access to more resources for their work on this subject.

Doctor Peter Andrews:

He's impossible to get in the office. He's difficult to talk with, because he's my own cousin. We share a bloodline with the Mandel family, but he's reluctant to see the value in his role.

Peter feels as though he's been thrust into something he's never asked for. He questions his qualifications, and believes his presence is a political statement more than anything.

I believe in my cousin. He's written himself off for far too long. He's the most capable person I've ever known, and he doesn't see this. How, as his cousin, can I get him to see that truth?

Perhaps if it came from someone else, he'd be more likely to believe it.

All psychological profiling in context to Doctor Clay:

I fear that Doctor Clay could be deceitful in his intent. If this is true, the team needs a sense of unity. They need to rely on one another, autonomously. Their differences should help emphasize their teamwork, and their similarities should propel their concern to work with each other.

Doctor Manning is the most crucial member of the team in regards to gathering the technologies we need for terraforming our planet. His aggression is slowly fading as Elizabeth and the Xiao sisters impress him on a daily basis. He's begun to rethink his prior beliefs in people.

Doctor Morris needs to feel a genuine connection, aside from his palling around with Doctor Manning. A true connection is only made when the ideal self we put on every day is shed to display our TRUE self, with all its flaws.

Most people have a reluctance to do this, but the crew was chosen for their quality of candor. Linda and the Captain are the most re-served of the group, but Monica has challenged Linda in this way for much of her life.

Perhaps the Xiao sisters can provide the connection Doctor Morris desperately needs. His condition is more problematic than I had anticipated, and it worsens with his progress in his work.

These feelings of loneliness can propel him into depression. The assistants cannot pro-vide what he needs, and so it will require some work.

The Xiao sisters are superb team mem-bers, but an outlet for conversation will be necessary if they seek to handle Doctor Clay accordingly. If all hell breaks loose, they cannot rely on one another alone.

Elizabeth will continue her progression of growth, and Julius' revelations will be handled well. I have no doubt that Elizabeth can come to an understanding with Doctor Manning. Their similar sense of duty will bring them closer with time. Adversaries to some extent, they will work together if it means acquiring the same goal; and their goals are inevitably intertwined on this journey.

The assistants are capable of fulfilling their duties, and they are capable of handling

Doctor Hoyt backs away from the pages and takes a sigh.

"*Things are going smoothly*" He thinks "*But we can't be too careful. It could fall apart if someone applies pressure; and how hard that pressure needs to be, no one knows.*"

He tucks his notepad into his desk. His tablet holds a schedule of appointments. On the screen, a window to a note page shows he has composed misleading information.

Doctor Hoyt places the tablet on his desk. It shows a spinning wheel with the letters "*Uploading*".

"*If he tries anything, we'll know.*" He thinks. "*I hope he never feels the need to.*"

The tablet shows that it is completed, and Doctor Hoyt gathers his things. He steps out of his office, then turns off the lights, and the fireplace. He closes the door, leaving the lone tablet to enter its rest mode for the night.

CHAPTER 29
Engineer

Doctor Hoyt stands with the Captain and Doctor Monica Xiao. They oversee the operations in the command room.

Hoyt looks on at a feed of the historical department's collaborative expedition with the biological team.

On the outskirts of the Nubian desert, Doctor Manning has his team consolidate their findings in the back of the explorer pod. The biological material is packed next to historical artifacts; neat and orderly.

Doctor Morris looks at Manning.

"Are you all set?" He asks.

Manning nods "This should be more than enough."

The team loads into the side doors by the cockpit.

Manning calls over the headset "Ready when you are."

The Captain holds his hand over the controls and Hoyt nods.

Monica looks on at the exchange of tense glares between them. It appears as though the Captain is reluctant to follow through with a plan.

The Captain shakes his head and activates the explorer pod to return.

The pod lifts. The stars fall into view at the front of the vessel. It sways and turns. The stars rise out of view. Dirt is illuminated by the headlights. The sight of the ground comes closer and the soil grows brighter. They smash into the floor. The team is thrown to the front of the pod.

Manning shifts about and finds he is atop a pile of crew members. The vehicle has turned to its side. The bottom turns ninety degrees and the explorer pod crashes onto the floor, now upright.

The team squirms to lift themselves from the floor.

"What the fuck!" Manning says.

The Captain looks at Hoyt with disapproval. Hoyt calls over the intercom.

"Is anyone hurt?" He asks.

The team confirms they are okay.

"Good." Hoyt says.

"The hell happened?" Morris asks.

The Captain looks at Hoyt. He activates the intercom.

"We're not sure." He says.

Hoyt nods at him.

Monica looks at the both of them. She's confused, but she activates DEEMUS.

"DEEMUS, I need a diagnostics report." She says.

"Searching." DEEMUS says.

The Captain paces about.

"I hope you're happy." He says.

Hoyt has his arms crossed.

"Call Elizabeth." He says.

The Captain touches a table and brings up Elizabeth's contact. The ringing begins, and they wait in silence.

"Hello?" Elizabeth says through the speakers.

"Doctor Lawrence." The Captain says "We need your help. Morris and Manning are on the surface. Their explorer pod shit the bed."

"… Okay." She says.

"We need you in the cargo bay." He adds.

"On my way." She says.

The Captain opens Linda's information next. He calls her to give the same command.

***

Elizabeth stands in the explorer pod with Linda, Julius, Mark, and Danny. She looks at the floor in thought and feels perplexed by the issue at hand.

Mark nods at Linda.

"Is this your first time to the surface?" He asks.

Linda shakes her head "I've been twice already. However, this is the first time I'm really doing something."

"Why haven't you been there much?" asks Danny.

Linda shrugs "I'm not needed there."

Julius activates his communication with the team.

"When you went before, was it just for the fun of it?" He asks.

Linda laughs "Pretty much. I was there for the drilling mission; then the other time was Washington DC."

"You went to DC?" Elizabeth asks.

Linda nods "Ron insisted. He said I couldn't miss it."

"What did you think of America's capital?" Mark asks.

"It was beautiful in a sad way." She says "I'm glad I went… I haven't had the time for more trips, but I like what I do. I'd rather do that than go sightseeing."

The group nods to agree.

The pod flies over the dunes of southern Egypt. They soon enter the nation of Sudan. Here they fly south into the heart of the nation, and to the southern edge of the Nubian desert. At the Pyramids of Meorë, they touch down on the surface. The broken explorer pod rests by the relics of a culture long-forgotten. To the Earthlings, it was overshadowed by the Egyptians' magnitude.

Elizabeth knows why they've come here in particular. It fits the description of Ron's deepest fascinations. It is the remnants of an ancient kingdom known as Kush. Doctor Manning's need for biological material must have been the perfect excuse to come here; to the sight of these ancient people.

The alien pyramids are small, but steep. Their stones bear the engravings of ancient graffiti. They dot the land as monuments to the Kushite people. No doubt, Doctor Morris wants to preserve these civilizations to the finest of detail.

The engineers look around to assess the situation. Elizabeth walks around the fallen pod to consult the other department heads.

"What happened?" She asks.

Manning motions his hands a the pod. His arms fall at a loss for words.

Morris stands with his arms crossed "It started taking off, then flopped to the side."

Julius sees a fried tube by the bottom of the pod and examines where it leads. Mark and Danny look for the other end to find a component responsible for the crash.

"I think it's the thruster that might be shot." Julius says.

"Tube leads to the thrust." Mark says.

Julius mutters to himself "Shit."

"Can we fly it?" Manning asks.

At this, Danny enters the pod to look at the interface of the computer. DEEMUS chimes over the headset:

"- *Computers maximized thrust.*

- *Compensation thrusters overloaded.*

- Overcapacity assumed."

Julius gathers his brows "Overcapacity?"

Danny searches through the metadata of the past hour and finds a load capacity of a hundred pounds, well below the limit.

"It felt like a lot more than usual." Morris says "But the meter only read a hundred."

"Strange." Julius says.

"Danny." Elizabeth says "Look in the code. See if there was a problem with the latest update."

Danny looks through the computer's code. He sifts through the functions of the automated thrusters, the quantum AI, and the weight calculation system. In the third category, he finds a major miscalculation.

"It looks like the update had a faulty code." Danny says.

"Faulty how?" She asks.

"Either the signal from Zion was corrupted, or someone rewrote this by hand."

"I'd rather not assume that someone rewrote the code intentionally." Elizabeth says "I think the update was messed up; either on Zion or on the way here. Can you change it?"

"I can" Says Danny "But the AI is in lockdown. We need a key fob to override the emergency, and that's on the ship."

"You didn't bring it?" She asks.

"That's my fault" Says Mark "I was supposed to bring it."

Julius nods at Danny "Well, we have a pilot."

Elizabeth looks at Danny with her brows raised.

Manning looks around "We have a pilot?"

Julius nods "Danny was in the Air Force." He looks at Danny "You think you can fly this thing?"

Danny feels a child-like excitement in his hands. He looks out the window of the cockpit.

"Uh… Yeah! I can do that." He says "That wouldn't be a problem at all."

Julius laughs "Alright. Looks like you're flying today, captain."

"I'm the Captain…" Peter says on the headset.

The team laughs.

Peter activates his intercom again.

"You guys can fly that thing yourselves?" He asks.

"Yeah" Elizabeth says "We just need to offload the extra cargo."

Manning moves to the back of the pod. He finds the cargo has been tossed into disarray.

"Yeah." He says "I guess we can offload some extra things…" He turns to Morris "So, what do we leave behind?"

Morris joins his side at the back of the pod "I can leave most of these engravings behind." He says "They can stay for someone else to find them."

"Are you sure?" Manning asks.

Morris nods "I have pictures either way. And we need your material the most."

Julius joins the historians in unloading the material. They place it neatly in a pile to be kept safe for hundreds of years; until the next time humans return to Earth.

The biological team takes spare material out of the pod as well. Julius is hesitant to join their effort however. He picks up a box, but doesn't know what to do with it. He looks behind himself at Doctor Manning.

"What needs to stay?" asks Julius.

"Keep the ricin." Manning says, pointing at the box in Julius' hand.

"Ricin?" Morris asks "That's a poison!" He laughs with a joke to Doctor Manning "Who are you looking to assassinate?"

Julius looks at the box in his hands. He gathers his brows.

"You want to bring a poisonous plant back to Zion?" He asks.

"It's not just poison." Manning says.

He stands at Julius' side and l looks at him with an educating passion.

"The same plant produces castor oil." He says "It's been used to prevent dandruff, lubricate machines, and to protect leather." He smiles "A poison is only one use for the ricin plant."

Julius is taken aback by the plant. He recognizes a commonality between himself and the poisonous object that lies within the box.

Julius, like ricin, has a history of killing; and yet, they both have a history of helping. He places the box to the side and steps out of the explorer pod. He looks back at Manning.

"Which ones do we leave behind?" He asks.

Manning nods and steps out of the vehicle.

"Let my guys handle it." He says.

Julius watches the biologists get to work. He then communicates with Elizabeth on a private channel.

"A killer, yet useful…" He says "Sounds familiar."

"Even bad things can be good, I guess." She replies.

While she thinks that Julius intends to reference the weapons they've uncovered, Elizabeth is misguided without his context. To her, there is a realization that they are bringing the reality of Earth to life. No longer will people romanticize the distant world lost ages ago. It is here, in its glory and horror. All of it will come home to guide the destiny of humankind on Zion.

Linda stands by the meter on the explorer pod. She reads the display and communicates to Danny.

"How much is the calibration misreading?" She asks.

"Quite a lot." He says "I'll send it to you."

Linda pulls out a tablet and reads the code. She looks up at the meter, which now reads seventy-five.

"You guys have a ways to go." She says "I'll tell you when."

Over the course of an hour, the team finishes unloading to Linda's determined weight. They take a long look at the materials on the desert floor.

"Do you think anyone will ever be back?" Julius asks.

Morris nods "Maybe someday." He says "And when they do, they'll know we left these here for them."

The team disperses into their explorer pods. Danny takes the helm of the previously broken craft.

"Are the thrusters all set on this thing?" He asks.

"You're ready to go, buddy." Mark replies.

Danny activates the pod and it lifts from the ground. He pulls up and the nose raises to the sky. With the stars before him, he accelerates slowly. The other pod takes the lead, and Danny follows behind. He takes the liberty of swaying from side to side, and smiles.

"How's it feel?" Elizabeth asks.

Danny finds it hard to speak through his restrained grin.

"Incredible!" He says.

They laugh at the smiling pilot in his cockpit; and together, they ascend as a team, aiming for the skies.

***

Within the star explorer above, the command room is quiet. The Captain looks long at Doctor Hoyt. Monica watches their exchange, now simmered from what it was.

"Do you think it's right?" The Captain asks "Changing their code to crash the craft?"

Hoyt nods "After this, they'll see the value in each other."

"A constructed event…" The Captain says "Not only that, but you've damaged a craft and put their lives at risk. I know I'm supposed to listen to you but…"

Hoyt puts his hand up and shakes his head "Those vessels are constructed with many safety features. There's almost no chance of a catastrophe…"

"ALMOST no chance… That doesn't make it ZERO chance…"

Hoyt motions his hand to Monica. She shrugs and nods to agree with Doctor Hoyt.

The Captain presses his lips together and sighs through his nose.

"… I don't expect you to get it…" Hoyt says "… but this is how relationships are formed. The obstacle was constructed, that's true; but their relationship is real."

The Captain looks at Monica "You're not hearing any of this, by the way."

Monica motions her fingers as if to be locking her lips shut.

Hoyt exits the room and the Captain follows. In the hall the Captain holds Hoyt's shoulder to address him.

"Okay" He says "You've made the team work together. But what about the places where they differ?"

Hoyt looks off to the side in thought.

"I don't know." He says.

The Captain nods "And what will you do when Julius finds out about that project; Icarus?"

Hoyt shakes his head "He'll be fine."

"Will he?" The Captain asks "You don't know for sure. And how will Elizabeth feel; having been out of the loop?"

"Well that's not my problem, now is it?" says Hoyt.

The Captain takes a step back. He shrinks his posture and begins to turn away.

"You're treating this like they're inherently at odds." Hoyt says "This exercise proves to us, and them; that they're capable."

"By constructing a lie." The Captain says.

"By constructing a team exercise." Says Hoyt "This will soften the blow of the fact that you can't face… that we're here for science, just as much as we are for murder."

The Captain looks at his cousin with plenty to say, but no words to make.

Hoyt continues "Ron knows that he's making the foundations of another, future war. He can hardly look at Julius anymore because he feels he's betraying the very moral code of a friend. Think about the dissonance you're creating; by keeping them in the dark…"

The Captain sighs.

"They need to know at some point." Hoyt says "We might be down an explorer pod, but the psychological state of your team is dancing on a fragile line; and it won't ride out for another ten and a half years."

The Captain nods.

"Alright." He says "But only when he needs to know…" He turns his back.

He then starts in a pace toward the command room.

Hoyt calls from down the hall.

"When can I expect you in my office?" He says.

The Captain stops at the entrance of the command room; but he steps inside without a word.

Hoyt shakes his head. His lips drawn back at the corner, he sighs in disappointment.

CHAPTER 30
Roger's Weapon

The golden rays of a fresh morning. A mist rolls out from the marshes, and ascends the bases of the trees. Underneath, the colored leaves hide roots, stems, and soil. The low-lying mist pours into a clearing. Here, a man-made hill comes to a plateau in the open air, and stretches out into a lawn. From two sides, the grass is flanked by forest; and on the northern edge, the lawn is cut short by a road. To the south, the field of grass ends in a line of planted trees.

The grass begs for the life of a morning dew after being husked dry by the late summer sun. Dividing the lawn from the middle, there is a lone strip of pavement. It is black on the parched greenery; and leads up to a security booth followed by a superficial arm gate. A line of cars stand idle between the main road and a red light, which overhangs the road by the security booth. The main road, along with the general public, lie on the far side of the lawn; away from the guarded facility. At the mouth of the lawn, there is a sign. Inconspicuous, it reads "*Allagash Research Facility*".

Roger hangs a cigarette out his window. The smoke snakes its way into the clean air. He waits in the line of cars with little patience. His eyes glance over the printouts of a presentation. His heart rate accelerates, but he remains slouched and motionless. His breath deepens with a sigh, and he tosses the filter at the end of his finished cigarette. He turns the heat up for his cold fingers, and places his hand before the vents.

The sound of boots darken his driver's side window. Roger turns to see the security guard holding the cigarette butt.

"It's bad enough I have to sit here all morning." The guard says. "Please don't make this a trash heap."

Roger looks innocently confused "Oh, I'm so sorry."

The guard laughs "Don't sweat it." He pulls up a barcode scanner. "You got your badge?"

Roger hastily grabs the laminated picture of his face, underlined by a barcode.

The guard scans it and hands him the cigarette butt. "Throw this out inside."

Roger takes the yellow-brown filter from the guard's fingertips "Thank you."

The filter is wrapped in a napkin and placed under his coffee mug.

As the guard continues down the line of cars, Roger imagines a door slammed in his face and getting fired. He then conjures the sound of an applause from the board of directors. Soon after, it is turned into outrage from the very same people. He doesn't know what to expect, but he can't stop simulating what will come next.

The traffic light changes from red to green, and Roger pulls in through the gate. His wheels roll along the banks of a large parking lot. He slides along roads which wind through trees and past old, wheeled weapons. The building of glass that holds his department stands a great distance from his parking spot. At the building's entrance, there are military vehicles and trucks carrying microwave cannons, laser cannons, and other relics of company pride. These are displayed openly, and remain the public's depiction of "modern warfare". The truth is, they're decades old compared to what lies beneath the wheels of the morning commuters.

Arriving earlier than usual, the parking lot is nearly empty. A partner from his team is already there and looks as if he has been contemplating for a while.

Exiting his car, Roger asks "Are you ready?"

"A little nervous," his partner says "but it's now or never."

The two men talk along the walk to the building. Passing through the doors, they walk by the front desk, and immediately into an elevator. Upon looking at the large sum of floors, they press B3, and the button illuminates under the partner's finger.

In the office, they are expected. There is an unsettling silence where another team member stands waiting.

After a while two others arrive. Then the senior staff and executives. Finally, the presentation is ready to start.

"Firstly I would like to say thank you for having us present." Roger says. "We will try to make this brief and cover all our bases. The project, which we present to you today is called 'Houdini.'"

The slide changes to show a missile with a chamber in the front being fed by two hoses linked to respective semi-cylinders.

"A mastermind of his time, Houdini was proficient with tricks of the mind. Many of his shows featured the appearance of teleportation." Roger changes the slide to the image of a missile entering one door, and coming out another, several feet away. "Well that just about explains what we hope to accomplish here today. Clyde?"

The partner from the parking lot takes the floor. "The idea of teleportation has been a matter of science fiction until recently. We've begun to answer many of our questions about quantum physics, and now the fabric of the universe is at our fingertips. Our solution takes us back to the first detection of gravity waves in the late twenty-teens."

Another team member takes the floor as a new slide blinks onto the white wall. "To make sense of how gravity can be used in..."

One of the department heads, an older woman, cuts him off. "This isn't the first time someone has approached us with this, boys."

Roger chimes in "But this is different."

"I'm not seeing it, I just wanted to let you know that. Proceed,"

"We don't want to bring people through theoretical wormholes or anything. We want to make a missile that can bend space around it, and enter armored tanks."

Her eyebrows scrunch together, and her mouth hangs open as if to sarcastically express intrigue. It is more insulting than reassuring. "And how do you propose to make this?"

"A shell of alternate space surrounding the space of the missile."

Another team member steps forward "Roger here has close ties with people working at the Midwest Particle Collider. They think they have a way to bend space a little, but the funding is needed to make it work."

"And you want us to fund it."

Roger grabs hold of the argument "We want to adopt the technology and use it to make a weapon of the future."

Another executive leans forward "Do you have an idea on how this will work?"

Clyde grabs the attention to his part of the presentation "We do..." he skips to his slide "If we bring this down to the second dimension, we can show you this interpretation." He circles the image on the wall with the back of his pen. "This is what it would look like."

The slide shows a projectile with a dense bubble surrounding it. The bubble is a black line that stretches from the front of the projectile, at both sides it reaches all the way to the back. It does not meet there, however. Instead it veers away from meeting itself in the back and retraces its path, all the while keeping a white space between its former route. Finally the line meets at the front of the projectile again; completing its warped circle.

The partner continues "We can send the space containing the projectile forward. It's just a few feet, but more than enough for the average tank or bunker.

It would use less energy than bending our own space to condense the distance. The idea of wormholes from the movies is wasteful." He changes the slide to a piece of paper and a pencil, and the room laughs. "This way, we bend only a little space, and cross the same distance."

The next slide shows a diagram of the weapon working on an underground bunker. Roger takes the floor again. "This could launch and arrive within bunkers or armored tanks rather than pummeling them from the outside. It would deliver a fatal blow on the first attempt, every time."

The senior staff look interested, but their words say otherwise.

"And have you shown this technology really works?" An old, bald man says.

"Well," Clyde begins. "We don't have the funding to prove we can do it."

The woman executive speaks again. "Well, we'll consider it, but frankly I doubt it'll be taken further than this room. Thank you, boys."

"But we have more to show." Clyde says.

"Send us the reports and we'll look it over." She returns. "Thank you, boys."

The men thank them and leave the office with mixed feelings.

One team member closes the door and raises his eyebrows "Well that got shot down real quick."

The rest of them laugh.

Roger shakes his head "That makes no sense to me."

"Awfully closed-minded." Clyde says.

"Who the hell else proposed that?" The first team member says.

Roger laughs "She's probably making that up."

Clyde shakes his head "I don't know."

One of the other team members chimes in "It might be a long haul, but this is the first step."

"I'm sure we can get there, boys." Roger's tone is a reflection of the woman who talked down to them.

They laugh at the excessive, power-hungry zeal in his tone.

The men enter the elevator, and Clyde shakes his head "Can you believe how she kept calling us that?"

The elevator doors seal in a gradually growing laugh of relief.

CHAPTER 31
Don't Touch Me

Doctor Linda Xiao wakes up early. She hopes to catch Connor Manning before he leaves his room.

She comes to his door at seven in the morning and knocks with little hope that he'll answer.

Footsteps are heard, and a fumbling to the door. The door comes open to a near-naked biologist. A towel is wrapped around his waist. He squints at Linda but postures himself.

"Oh, hi Linda." He says.

Linda raises an eyebrow and holds back a laugh.

"Are you available to check in with me?" She asks "It's about the crash."

Manning looks behind himself, then back at Linda.

"I can, but… Now?" He asks.

Linda hisses a laugh through her nose.

"Later." She says.

Connor smiles "Okay. I'll come by when I'm ready."

He closes the door and Linda returns to her room. She messages him as a reminder. She knows he can be forgetful.

Connor replies with some mention of pain in his left shoulder. Linda schedules a time to use the X-ray machine in the medical room.

Later in the day, she comes to the medical room and waits for their appointment. It's close to the biology department, and so she listens for his voice from down the hall.

"I know…" She hears him say "… But I have an appointment. Can you give me a minute?"

The assistant affirms they can wait. Doctor Manning then enters the medical lab.

"Hey!" He says.

Linda smiles "Are you ready?"

Connor nods "Let's do this."

Linda takes him into the room and begins with the X-ray of his shoulder. The images show no reason for concern, and she puzzles over the matter.

Connor almost stands, but Linda bids him to stay seated.

"Has it been hurting since the crash?" She asks "Or before?"

Connor shrugs "It's been since the crash. Although, I'm prone to this kind of thing."

"Any particular reason?"

"Some overdeveloped muscles from working on the farm at a young age. That and the contact sports I used to play… had a lot of injuries."

She approaches him and feels his shoulder.

"You jumbled your brains up a bit?" She asks.

"No concussions, actually." He says "A bit of a miracle. I was the goon of the team."

Linda feels a lump of tensed muscle around his shoulder blade.

"What's life like on a farm?" She asks.

"Not bad." He says "I lived there for a short while, then the city. After that I returned to the farm as a preteen."

Linda feels for the end to the line of tension that runs the length up to his neck.

"This feels like the problem." She says.

Connor winces his face in pain. She then massages the muscle to loosen it.

"What happened when you were in the city?" She asks.

Connor bites his teeth through a little pain.

"I lived with my mom." He says.

He grunts in pain and Linda loosens up.

"I'm sorry." She says.

He tries to move away but she holds him back.

"I'll be gentle." She says.

She keeps going at a gentle pace, and her other hand holds the front of his chest; the way a flower pedal holds up against gravity.

She tries to distract him; prying for more of his story.

"What happened in the city?" She asks "Did you like it?"

Connor shrugs his shoulder away.

"I'm fine." He says.

Linda places her hand on his chest to make him still.

"Relax." She says.

Connor tries to breathe but there's a cold sweat on his skin. Saliva collects in his mouth, and he feels as if he can't swallow it properly.

Linda feels for the spot with her fingertips. She places her thumb on it, then moves across the muscle.

Connor's heart picks up pace. His skin feels warm, yet cold. There's an uneasy feeling in his spine and his feet feel like running away. He feels weak. He hates it. He shrugs away.

"I'm fine!" He says.

Linda is taken aback. She's reminded of a time when she was little; when she went to pet her neighbor's rat but it bit her.

Connor stands and pulls his lab coat over his shoulder. He turns to face her and feels sorry for yelling. His eyes are soft and his head hangs in apology.

"I've gotta go." He says "Thank you for the help."

He exits the lab in a hastened pace; leaving Linda to wonder why he was so afraid.

Later in the day, Linda distracts herself to forget the event. She's tried all day, and by the time she's found success, she receives a message from Doctor Manning.

"Linda, thank you for your help earlier. My shoulder feels better. I'm sorry for my sudden outburst. I've been stressed with a deadline to reach. A genetic strand was deteriorating by the second and I needed to sequence it before it was lost forever. I apologize for the way I behaved."

Linda looks long at the message and reads it at face value.
"He's lying." Monica says.
Linda looks up from the message.
"You didn't read the message." says Linda.
"I didn't need to." Monica says "I know Doctor Manning very well; and I know that whatever he's saying, it's a lie."
Linda sighs.
Monica touches her hand.
"He's afraid…" Monica says "… and that's why he's lying."
"Afraid of what?" Linda asks "I was only trying to help. What's the big deal?"
"It's a 'big deal' for HIM." Monica says.

She takes her hand away.

"He hates to look weak…" Monica adds "… and he felt vulnerable with you."

Linda gathers her brows. She looks a the message on her tablet.

"Vulnerable?…"

Monica smiles, knowing very well what her sister's face means. She's endlessly curious. Her desire to know more is rooted somewhere deep within her.

Lie as she may, Linda's wonder isn't a matter of business. She can claim it's "*for the report*", but Monica knows her sister. She knows people and their looks of fascination, even in this unfamiliar form; a look of intrigue. It's shadowed by her blanket of denial.

Linda's professionalism is merely an act.

She's trying so hard to fool herself; to believe in her own lie.

CHAPTER 32
Movie Night

Julius walks up to the couch where Elizabeth sits. A horror movie plays while Julius sets two cups of tea on the table.

Elizabeth sits up "Julius!" She laughs "I'm trying to sleep."

He hesitates "It's chamomile."

"What?"

"Chamomile. It helps you relax."

She stares at the glass with wonder "There's no caffeine?"

He shakes his head "It does the opposite."

She raises a brow and looks up at him. She pulls the cup to her mouth and blows away steam "You're sure?"

"A hundred percent. Ask bio."

"I trust you." She says.

She sips with audible approval.

"It's good?" He asks.

"Very good."

"My favorite nightcap." says Julius.

She scoffs a laugh and rolls her eyes.

Elizabeth catches herself off track, and takes the engineers back to a former discussion.

She places the tea on the table "So nothing about Doug in your reading?"

"Nothing yet. Just Mandel's childhood, their family, and Curtis' friend James; the one he knew from high school."

She recognizes James as the man her own high school was named after, James Stuart Academy.

"They grew up together?" She asks.

"Apparently they knew each other since kindergarten." says Julius.

She finds it interesting but brushes it aside. "The more I hear from Clay, the more I think he's warming up to us."

"Doctor Manning seems very close to him." Julius says. He places his tea down and sits back "I talked with Manning and Hoyt about it, but I'm still worried."

"Talked about what?"

"Keeping information tight." Julius shrugs "Manning says he'll keep his mouth shut, but Manning does what Manning wants to do."

"Connor Manning is no idiot." Elizabeth says. "He might be impulsive, but he's not stupid."

Julius raises a brow "Never thought I'd hear you defend Manning."

Elizabeth cocks her head to the side. She sighs and gathers her lips. "Connor has had some kind of trauma. What that is, I don't know; but Linda alluded to it."

"You trust Linda… and so do I." Julius says "How much did she say?"

"Not much. I get the sense that she means to tell me, you know…" She motions her hands as if to tell someone to slow down. "'Be patient with him'" she adds.

Julius frowns "Doctor Hoyt mentioned something too. He said 'he has his reasons' for being that way."

"We can't change who he is." says Elizabeth. "The best we can do is work with him, not against him."

She picks up her tea.

"Oh, I know that but I mean…" He shrugs.

She lowers the tea "What?"

"Aren't you the slightest bit curious?" says Julius "What if he lashes out at people when he's got a crush on them?"

Elizabeth laughs "Fuck off!"

Julius gives a sarcastic shake of his head.

He raises his brows "I don't know, Liz. He might have the hots for ya."

Elizabeth rolls her eyes "This isn't some anime with a romantic sub-plot."

Julius breathes a laugh "If this were an anime, he'd have a sudden change of heart. He'd realize that he's been rude, and he'd verbalize it in a lengthy monologue."

Elizabeth smirks "I mean, he kinda did that the other day, but it was more of an apology. A permanent change of heart on the other hand, now THAT'S some wishful thinking."

Julius nods and recollects for a moment. He remembers his concern and seeks to hear Elizabeth's perspective."

"… I AM nervous…" He admits "… about Doctor Manning."

Elizabeth gathers her brows.

"You think he'll say something he shouldn't?"

Julius sighs.

"He's done a lot, but he doesn't seem to care… He always wants more."

Elizabeth thinks it over and remembers his finding beneath the Pacific Ice Sheet. She remembers the plants and animals he's discovered and sequenced. Moreover, she looks down at her cup of tea and realizes it's Manning's work that has brought this into being.

"He's done a lot." She says "More than me, even."

Julius scoffs.

"Fat fuckin' chance." He says "He's done a lot, but more than you… I don't know…"

Elizabeth looks down at her tea.

Julius nods at the cup in her hand.

"He brought back chamomile, carrots, trees and grass… Did we send those home in a message? He couldn't take care of the damned plants if you didn't find the instructions on how to take care of them. If it weren't for you, he wouldn't HAVE half of the genetic data YOU found in that laboratory."

"The RAINARDA one?" Elizabeth asks.

"Yes." says Julius "His team tells me all the time how important that was for them."

Elizabeth shrugs "Yeah, maybe…"

Julius shakes his head.

"So are you gonna make me feel better about this Manning situation? Or do you ALSO think we're fucked…"

Elizabeth laughs "No… You can relax about Manning. He wouldn't say anything he shouldn't."

"Promise?" He asks.

"I promise, Jules."

She looks at Julius with full intent to disarm his concern.

Julius takes this as a fact and feels a weight off his shoulders.

Elizabeth turns her head away and thinks a moment.

"I feel crazy because you're right…" She says "… I don't think about what I've done until you've said it like that…"

Julius gathers his brows "Well… everyone's kinda crazy on this ship." He looks at Elizabeth "You ever look around and think 'everyone has some mental baggage'?… I don't know what Hoyt was thinking when he chose us."

Elizabeth shrugs "Everyone's a little crazy. We all have a different brand of crazy, just varying degrees."

"I think the craziest people are the 'normal people.'" Julius emphasizes the quotation marks with his fingers.

Elizabeth nods "It's crazy to care too much about fitting in."

"Uh, you THINK?" Julius laughs "I've seen people do crazier things to look normal; more than anything else."

"How so?"

Julius shakes his head "Buying a house they can't afford. Marrying someone because they think it's the next step;" He puts both index fingers up to emphasize the thought "even though they hate the person they're with! Let's see… Going to college without an intended major. You know, the life-altering decisions that people make because they think it's expected of them. I mean… who spends thousands on a four-year summer camp without a specified career path?"

"You're talking about college?"

"Yes!" says Julius "The worst is the people who become parents for a reason OTHER THAN creating and raising a whole new-ass human. The younger years are crucial in anyone's development, and if you think you can just stick them to a nanny and call it a day, you're dead wrong."

Elizabeth widens her eyes in a nod "Yup… I can attest to that. It's accurate."

Julius sighs "That's how you get a pain in the ass like Connor Manning."

She places her tea down on her lap. She gives Julius a sarcastic tilt of her head as if to say "Don't be so mean."

She looks forward again and smiles "I view Doctor Manning in the same way I'd look at my Dad."

"In what kind of a way?"

She gathers her lips with a thought on her mind "My Dad was a jerk. He did more hurt than help with my brother's drinking problem, but I get my Dad. I could be bitter and hate him and all; but he's my Dad… I've said plenty to his face, but it never changed anything. He can get under my skin and I hate that, so I can get mad at him; but there's no changing him. The only way you can get through to people like that is to prove them wrong with your own actions. Not in a spiteful way, but a 'see? I can do it' kind of way. I've done a lot of proving people wrong. I live for it."

Julius recounts her attitude toward progress and work ethic. She really never has been spiteful, but instead she lets her actions speak for what she's worth

"I want to be someone worth remembering." Elizabeth says "Someone that little girls can look up to." She smiles at Julius "It takes a lot of working on myself, but it's always been worth it. I didn't see things from Connor's perspective at first, but now that I know more, I can't help but pity him. It took work to understand him, and I'm surprised. It's pity rather than hate. How lonely must it be to push people away like that? To only trust in yourself and shun other people away."

"He only does that with some people, though…"

"That's the part that I don't get, but I don't need to. He limits himself when he doesn't listen. If you disagree with him he becomes defensive. That's just robbing himself of the chance to find a better solution."

Julius smiles "You're a smart person."

Elizabeth shrugs "At one point I wasn't listening to HIM either. I had to learn how to listen."

Julius shakes his head "It's killing me to know why he IS that way…"

She laughs "You're just dying to know, aren't you?"

"Are you kidding?" Says Julius "Of course I am!"

Elizabeth laughs.

"If him calling his mom a bitch is justified, that has to be a good story." says Julius.

Elizabeth nods with a frown "Well I don't have any answers to that, but… You know, I came up with a good visual as I was thinking about it the other night."

"A visual for what, exactly?" says Julius.

"What people are like… and why Doctor Manning is so closed-minded."

Julius frowns with a nod "I'm listening…"

"Here it is." Says Elizabeth "It's like everyone has a seesaw, right?… We all want to have our seesaw in perfect balance… So it's weighted at both ends with our perspectives on the world. Our principles, beliefs, and the things we consider rules… When you contradict someone's view of the world, then their seesaw is off balance, and so they're reasonably pissed."

Julius nods "Because they're trying to keep it balanced."

Elizabeth nods and continues.

"What you said about your take on religion was eye-opening for me. You don't care if there's a god or an afterlife, because you know that you'll never really have the answer to that. That means your seesaw, like mine, is balanced with two principles… One, is that everything and everyone is morally grey. No matter how dark or light that morality may seem, it will always be grey. The other principle is that the world is really chaotic… As humans we try to categorize and divide things so that we understand them…

No amount of input can throw our perspective into disarray. It's agreeable because no one can doubt it's true. No matter what, no one can throw my perception of the world off balance, because everything lines up with those principles. If you told me something tomorrow that contradicted my beliefs today, it would only further my understanding of the truth. It wouldn't disobey those principles, and so… I'm not pissed."

Julius looks up from his tense gaze and smiles.

"You have a lot of time on your hands." He laughs.

She shrugs with her brows raised "It's true!" She looks down and smiles for a moment. "I've been thinking a lot lately, to get better at this leadership thing; and like I said, it takes a lot to reflect on… a lot of work on yourself."

Julius nods "No, I know." He picks up his tea "It's just really deep."

He sighs "So what do we do about our investigation now?"

Elizabeth gathers her brows and formulates a plan "Is there any other piece of history? Maybe something Doctor Morris has access to? Something that would give us better insight on Doug? More than just a book written by his 'friend'?" She motions her fingers in air quotes.

"You don't believe they were friends?" Julius asks.

"I'm not saying that." she begins "I'm just saying, who has a friend that close, and doesn't write one word about them in an autobiography?" She shrugs "Maybe he was more of an acquaintance or something."

"I've barely started on the book, but we'll see."

Elizabeth nods "Ask Morris tomorrow if he has anything. We can go from there."

Julius nods "Sounds like a plan."

CHAPTER 33
Legacy

All is quiet on the Mandel Star Explorer. Eventide is marked by the dispatch of cleaning robots. Julius watches a robot cross the couch before him in the recreation room. He takes it as his cue to head to bed. Meanwhile Doctor Manning sits at his lab table, looking at the microbial life they took from the continent of Antarctica. Through his microscope he sees uncatalogued creatures. In the periphery, to the side of the magnified view, he sees and hears one of the cleaning bots. He raises his feet to allow space for the floor to be cleaned. Linda, Elizabeth, and Monica exit the café with chamomile tea. After a long chat, they make their way to bed with their downtime well spent.

Along the way down the hall, Monica spots a sweeper driving forward into a wall.

Elizabeth sees this and sighs "Oh shoot. I thought we fixed him."

"Arthuuuur." Monica says.

Elizabeth laughs "You named him?"

Monica shrugs "I've named all of them." She points to a small mark on the side of Arthur "This is how I know it's Arty"

"Ten years is a long time." Linda says.

"I've had a lot of time on my hands." Monica laughs.

Elizabeth gathers her brows "What's the one that comes to my lab?"

"Oh that's Haggis McDougall." Monica says "He's a good boy."

The girls laugh and Monica picks up Arthur to repair him tomorrow. It's then that she'll see Elizabeth again to go over the software and find the potential for hardware issues. But now, they return to their beds to be well-rested for another day of work.

In the center of the ship, Captain Peter Andrews takes a moment to himself in his office. He thinks about his conversation with Doctor Morris just moments ago.

Morris raised concern over the topic of unrest at specific periods of history. His notes detailed a similarity in cycles of unrest. In the twenties of each century, there would be a financial uncertainty followed by political unrest and finally, there would be wars in the thirties and forties. Similarly there would be a period of peace and prosperity in the fifties, the kind that Zion is experiencing at this very moment.

"I have a feeling we'll see the signs of unrest starting when we return." Morris said.

The Captain thinks this over and finds his accuracy to be disturbing. He hopes that his retirement will be as peaceful as he'd previously believed it would be.

The door to his office opens, and cleaning bots swarm into his office. Doctor Hoyt follows in behind them.

"Peter." Hoyt says.

The Captain nods.

Hoyt makes his way to the seat at the front of Peter's desk and rests himself, leaning back as if to relax after a long day.

"Morris is having reservations about the weapon we found in Doug's facility." Hoyt says.

"It's silly." The Captain says "No one would use that."

Hoyt shrugs "I know, but he makes a point."

The Captain shakes his head "I don't think anyone would even make that thing again."

"You don't know that." Hoyt says.

Peter raises a brow as if to say "Who knows?".

Hoyt crosses a leg and looks off to the corner of the room.

"He doesn't like the political implications either." Hoyt says.

"You're not very sly." says The Captain.

They meet eyes.

Hoyt leans forward.

"How am I supposed to be any help?" Hoyt says "You don't come in, so I have to come down here to get you."

"I knew it."

"You're the Captain for Christ's sake."

"And who made me captain?" Peter asks.

He looks at Hoyt and the therapist sits back in his seat with nothing more to say.

"You want me to be something I'm not." Peter says "Just let me get my money and have this over with… Retire with a book deal or something… I'm just wasting life away on this can and it's your fault."

"You chose to take this journey too." Hoyt says.

"So I can live out my life in the countryside." Peter says "Hopefully that will suffice for this loss of life."

Hoyt looks at the table to see a long-forgotten item. A symbol of the Mandel family; it's a model of City Hall in Eden.

It's a paperweight, but it's a symbol of that first generation; the one that built the city with the help of the Mandel family. Them, and the politicians and businessmen of their time.

"The countryside might look a little different when we get home." Hoyt says "There will be more crops to grow. More people living out that way."

Peter leans back "What do you want?"

"To talk with my cousin?" Hoyt says "Maybe not the Captain for a moment?"

Peter shrugs.

"I'm right here." He says.

Hoyt nods.

"You know I put you here for a reason." He says.

Peter stares at him with a stoic face.

Hoyt goes on "You're a hell of a lot better than anyone else I could have had."

"I'm better than Marcus, that's for sure."

"AND Phillip…" Hoyt says "AND David, and Veronica and Eliza… "

"So I'm the best option out of our family." Peter says "So that's why I'm shafted with eleven years here?"

"Not shafted. You're making history."

"I never asked for this." Peter says "I'm not a Mandel in the traditional sense. I'm not a politician or a leader."

"You seem to be doing just fine."

"You want me to be Curtis, but I'm not." Peter says "He died years ago. I might be related to him, but I'm not some major player in history."

"He was ordinary just like you and me."

"You?" Peter says "Ordinary?"

Hoyt sighs.

"Yeah.." Peter continues "Mandel was an ordinary guy who built the shields of the first star explorer. We still use his tech in this ship because it can't be beat. He was years ahead of his time. That's real ordinary; and I'm just me… I'm not driven to be someone in history, I'm not a leader, and I'm definitely not a politician. How in the hell am I…"

"Curtis Mandel was an engineer." Hoyt says "He wasn't a politician and you know that; don't be ridiculous… You're a better person than the rest of our family because you wouldn't use this expedition for political clout. They're all pissed that I chose you, but you're the only one I could rely on… You're the only one I'd even bear to see out here; and you're right, a book deal should give you enough royalties to live comfortably off your pension. You can take it easy and live the life you want when we're home. I have no doubt you'll find things are better as a farmer after Connor brings those plants back to life. You get the chance to see them first, before anyone else."

"I don't even know if farming is really what I want to do."

"Then find whatever it is you'd like." Hoyt pleas "Just don't think that you're useless. You don't need to fill Curtis' shoes, but you need to do this thing in your own way."

The Captain stares off to the floor in thought, and Hoyt sighs from the other side of the desk.

"Sometimes I feel like I've been selfish" Hoyt adds.

The Captain looks up at his cousin.

Hoyt goes on "I worry that I chose you because I don't want to be stuck out here with someone else… I truly believe that you're the best fit for this job BECAUSE you don't want it… You're humble and courageous. You're not attached to material wealth, and you're understanding of everyone. Being forced to take a Mandel descendent… I wouldn't find those qualities in anyone else."

"… I looked up to you because you took the time to talk to me." Peter says "I was so young and so distant from anyone else, but you took the time to be a cousin to me… nobody else really did that."

"I knew you didn't have the chance to be close with us… We were your only family, no brothers or sisters, and we were all at least ten years older than you…"

Peter laughs "… You're sure you're not being a therapist right now?"

Hoyt smiles "Old habit."

The Captain nods "Don't worry… I just really appreciate you being the only person who felt like a sibling to me."

Hoyt smiles and feels himself reminiscing over the Christmas gatherings. The one time of the year he had the chance to catch up with his little cousin.

"I love you Arnold, but I can't be the person everyone wants me to be."

"Then do me a favor and just be yourself. Forget history and the family name. Just bring the world you want to see to life."

Peter exhales a laugh through his nose and stands "I don't think I'm virtuous enough for that."

Peter walks to the door and turns off the lights. Hoyt follows him out the door and stands beside his cousin. Peter nods to say "*Goodnight; and good try*". He then turns to find his room.

Hoyt turns the opposite way to his office for some last-minute notes.

"*You'll find your way*" He thinks to himself "*Before this is over, you'll know what it's all worth.*"

CHAPTER 34
Family Faults

*My brother and I had a falling out in our late
twenties.*
*While I would like to fully take the blame, my
brother would insist that he's the one at fault.*
*However I'm the one writing this book, so he has
to deal with it.*

Julius laughs to himself.

He places the bookmark to save his spot and closes the pages. Julius walks into his private bathroom and stands before the toilet. He unzips his pants. The drone of water brings him to sigh. He places his hand on the wall and laughs again.

"Julius." PIGSBY calls out from the bathroom mirror.

"Yes?" Julius asks.

There is a silence between responses, and Julius moves his torso before the mirror.

"PIGSBY?" Julius asks.

He finishes and lifts his foot to flush.

A whoosh of sound takes over the silence, and Julius stands before the mirror.

"Hello?" Julius calls into the reflection.

PIGSBY's pixel face appears before him.

"I was wondering if that was you." The face responds.

Julius gathers his brows "Who else would it be?"

"You need to drink more water. Less coffee."

Julius stares at the face for a while "Yeah I know. Are you alright PIGSBY?"

"All systems are normal."

Julius hesitates. He wonders how to word the question.

"You asked if it was me." Julius says "Why?"

"I didn't know if Doctor Lawrence was visiting."

Julius leans on the sink to examine the display "You should know it's me."

"I was making sure."

Julius backs away and turns to the door "Doctor Lawrence wouldn't stand to pee."

Past the threshold, he closes the door behind himself. He sits on his bed and moves to the corner, out of sight of the door. The book rests at his side. He lifts the page open to read again.

> *It was my fault that we drifted apart after our parents died.*

Julius grows curious with the passage. He takes one last look at the door, then continues reading further.

> *I blamed him for not being present, and I shouldn't have.*
>
> *While I handled the funeral arrangements, I grew upset. He was invested in more important matters; and I couldn't possibly have understood that at the time.*
>
> *I thought he just threw money at the expenses and called it care, but I was wrong.*
>
> *I was present to take care of my mother and father while Curtis made electromagnetic shields. Of course, I didn't know WHAT he was making at the time.*
>
> *The difference between the two of us, which showed when we had our blowout argument, was that Curtis felt like he wasn't doing enough for his career. He did what he could for my parents while living the life they provided for him; in honor of them. I, on the other hand, felt paralyzed by the steps it took to pursue a dream like Curtis did.*
>
> *I thought I was destined for little to nothing; and my brother wanted the recognition from the whole world. This moment collapsed our voices of reason, my parents; and our outlooks on life collided.*

My limiting beliefs matched against his impossible expectations for himself.

In the end, I inherited my father's business by accident. Without any idea what to do, I made up my mind and chose to run it for the remainder of my parents' lives. When they passed I made the decision to sell my share of the company to our cousin Glenn.

I recognize that I couldn't have possibly afforded my parents' living arrangements. That much I understood, but my jealousy got the best of me.

While he put the work in to pursue his passion, I was the successor of a plumbing business with an associate's degree in writing.

I never wrote a single article or story after graduation, and I suppose I never would have until now.

Following our argument, after my mother's mercy meal of all things, I wouldn't speak with my brother for three months. I moved to Chicago and started a new plumbing business.

In hindsight, although they left too soon, it was probably for the best that we lost our parents before the disaster. They died peacefully, as all people should.

I think what made things bearable was to think of our loved ones in an afterlife together. We lost almost all of our friends. My brother was the last of my family.

I like to think of them eating a meal together and talking about memories with us.

One of our friends lost his wife before they could grow old together.

For him, I like to imagine their reunion in a better place.

In this way, the tragedy could be seen as a relief instead of a cruel fate.

Julius stops a moment and reads the words again.

He moves to the nightstand and places his hand upon it. A white light grows from the dark surface. On the surface, a long box blinks a cursor.

Julius taps along the characters beneath the box.

"*I think I've found something.*" He writes.

Some time passes and a bubble appears to indicate Elizabeth is typing.

"*Be right over.*" She replies.

In the short while he has, Julius tidies up. He opens up a space for Elizabeth to have a seat.

His door opens, and Elizabeth leans at the threshold.

"Come, let's get coffee." She says.

Before he can respond, she begins walking.

Julius follows through the doorway and down the hall.

"Is it gonna be one of those nights?" He asks.

She turns to glance his way as she walks "Morris is meeting me at the cafe. We can chat a little before he arrives."

The dining hall is quiet and empty when they arrive.

Elizabeth sets her notepad down on a table before the coffee maker. She grabs two mugs and begins brewing.

Julius takes his seat.

"You know…" He says "Curtis Mandel felt like he wasn't doing enough with his career for a while."

"Oh yeah?" She says.

She wipes a small amount of dust off her mug.

Julius nods.

"Maybe a sign that you're on the right path." He says.

Elizabeth shakes her head "I'm not having any expectations. Just working hard as always."

"Does it help you feel relaxed a little bit?" Says Julius "I mean, the guy felt the same as you and look at HIS career."

"He didn't get there by being relaxed." Says Elizabeth.

Elizabeth cleans the second mug and puts the first one under the coffee maker.

Julius retracts a corner of his mouth.

"What's got you bummed out?" He asks.

She prepares the second cup and shakes her head.

"I'm a little pissed Morris had to meet me this late."

Julius gathers his brows "Why so late?"

She shrugs "He's been busy with something; and he won't tell me what it is."

"Why not?"

"I don't know." She says "He avoids the subject every time."

The coffee finishes. She passes the first one to Julius from across the table. She then waits for hers.

"So tell me before he gets here…" She says "… what have we found?"

Julius shows her the paragraph. She reads it carefully. Three times she reads it, then her brows gather "You're sure this is him?"

"Who else could it be?" He asks.

She reads the paragraph one last time, then sits. She draws a breath "Julius, do you think Doctor Clay and his wife had a good relationship?"

Julius shrugs. "He seemed to love her a lot; and in the book, it sounds like a happy reunion."

She nods. "That's what I thought too. Doctor Hoyt told me in private, that they began a little awkward, though."

"Like how?"

"It seemed like they argued every day." She says.

Julius nods "And what does Doctor Hoyt think of that?"

"He told me that the opposite of love is indifference. Not hate."

The engineers are silent, then soon they laugh.

Julius can't help but laugh out a comment.

"Manning isn't indifferent by any means." He says.

"With me?"

Julius laughs harder and Elizabeth's coffee finishes. She rises from her seat and shakes her head in a laugh.

"You're ridiculous." She says.

She grabs the coffee and comes back to the table while he's still laughing.

Elizabeth shakes her head "I was thinking of my Dad, actually… Indifference sounds like the story of my life…"

His eyes meet her face. She stares off, and it's his voice that brings her back.

"So, if all crimes derive from passion, in one way or another… Count yourself lucky you weren't abused."

"I do." She says. "I mean, neglect is abuse, but I wouldn't say my parents were abusive. They just didn't care enough to show up for the soccer games." She shrugs "It would be silly to put myself in the same category, but I felt more like an accessory than a child."

Bringing herself back on track, she takes a sip of her coffee.

"So what would Clay's crime be, if he were to commit one?" she asks.

Julius nods and looks off in wonder.

The security camera adjusts. No one notices.

"Maybe he was abusive?" Julius says.

"You think he cheated?" Elizabeth asks.

"It's possible." Julius says. He becomes matter-of-fact and he elaborates "I've known a lot of people who lost someone, then felt regret. It sucks to suck, though. You break it, you bought it kind of thing."

She agrees, then winces her eyes in a question "What about murder?"

"Murdered his wife?"

"Yeah."

"No way." Julius says "He's not the type.."

Doctor Lawrence looks long at Julius' shoulder where his skin remains discolored in a scar.

She licks her teeth behind her lips "What about his invention? Maybe he did some bad things for the sake of science."

"Or he could just be a private guy and we're overthinking things." Julius says.

She ponders further "I wouldn't doubt you're right; but bases covered."

He nods. "Bases covered."

Morris approaches from the far doorway and strides up to meet the engineers.

"Sorry I'm late." He says "I was held up with the Captain."

"And Hoyt?" Elizabeth asks.

"Yes." Morris replies "How did you know?"

"You guys have been talking a lot lately." Elizabeth says "What for?"

"It's a long story." Morris says "I'd rather not get into it. What did you want to ask?"

Elizabeth hesitates. She looks to Julius, and he looks back.

"We were hoping you could lead us in the right direction." She says "We have an investigation going on."

"Investigation?" Morris asks.

"We're looking into whether or not we can trust Doug." Elizabeth says. "We want to hook him up to the ship, but there's a matter of trust we need to build with him."

Morris looks back and forth between the engineers "Guys you're talking about linking up a mind in therapy. Do you think that's safe?"

Julius shrugs "That's what we want to know. If it's safe."

Morris sighs. He shakes his head "I can't really think of anything to do for you guys. Maybe some records from his place of employment."

"Have we been to RAYNARDA headquarters yet?" Julius asks.

"No" Morris begins "We're going to the Boston facility soon, though. Hoyt wants to pick up some memorabilia for Doug."

"Is that what you were just talking about with the Captain?" Elizabeth asks.

Morris looks at her with doe eyes. He shakes his head at the floor and shrugs "Yeah. Part of it." He says. "Like I said, I'd rather not get into it. It gives me a migraine."

Elizabeth gathers her brows "It's no problem." She adds.

Julius grows curious and stands erect "What was the rest?"

Elizabeth taps Julius on the chest. He looks her way and she shakes her head.

Morris seems baffled, and at a loss for words. He shakes his head and laughs "Usual stuff. Documents, pieces from Boston…" He sums up with few words "It's an important sight for my team."

Elizabeth raises her hand gently to dismiss the subject "Don't worry Ron. You just keep an eye out for things pertaining to Doug. Don't stress about it, though. Just if you happen upon it, let us know."

Ron nods with the same gaze. "Yeah, I can do that."

Julius nods "Get some rest, man. You need it; and sorry."

Ron nods "Thank you. I'll let you guys know if I find anything."

The two wish him good night, and he leaves the room in haste.

Elizabeth waits until he is out of earshot, then turns to Julius.

Julius takes a long look at her. "He's not telling us everything."

Elizabeth raises her brows "Ron tells me EVERYTHING." She retracts the corner of her mouth "But in this case you're right." She passes Julius to retrieve her coffee from the table "He's no liar so it pains him to keep a secret; and I could see THAT much."

Julius crosses his arms "But what would he be hiding?"

Elizabeth shakes her head "I'll have to ask the Captain tomorrow. I'm putting in a request for another look at Clay's hardware too."

Julius nods "So what do we do now? We've had coffee."

Elizabeth takes the cup to her mouth "First, I'm on maintenance duty. Making sure the gamma is normal."

"Shielding duty. I follow; then what?"

She shrugs and shakes her head "I don't know. There's a few hard drives to repair. Do you want to do that 'til we pass out?"

Julius shrugs "I'm bored of reading anyway."

CHAPTER 35
Icarus Dawns

The carpeted halls of Allagash suffer a pervasive silence. The cease of shuffling shoes has deafened the aspirations of the Houdini workers.

Two have given up hope. They've become contented with working on nothing more than the piles of paper that fall on their desks each morning.

Two more have come to the end of their road, but continue to look for a legal avenue.

Three of them however, are plotting further. Maybe to leak information in exchange for funds.

Roger taps his notebook, scheming in silence. Like the others however, he decides this option has no promise.

The People's Liberated Republic of Eurasia has been emboldened lately. It has become a factor in many decisions around the world, and is something no one wants to inadvertently support.

This is the seventh time Roger's group has repackaged the idea; and seven times it has been denied.

"What do we do?" He asks.

For a while, the group continues contemplating in silence.

A new addition to the team, Gretchen, speaks aloud. "There's only one way to know. Ask someone who's done it. A senior engineer with experience."

They all nod in agreement, but haven't a clue who to turn to.

Roger thinks back to the old man who taught a lecture hall. The students sat upright out of respect. His legacy commanded attention, although his lectures were slow and tiresome.

This was the man who knew all the ins and outs. As an experienced engineer, he knew the business of the military-industrial complex. He also happened to be a generous source of knowledge, and the only professor who had any faith in Roger's capability.

"I think I have an idea who to ask." Roger says.

When asked for a name, Roger keeps this much to himself.

The following Wednesday, Roger meets the old professor on the campus at Merrimack Institute. Doctor Norman Bae, a reclusive man who spent his life working for DARPA. He is no face for the spotlight, and he chooses it to be that way. Now retired, he teaches to "Keep himself young".

The old man pushes his gold-trimmed glasses to his eyes. With his nose to the sky, he peers down to the pages before him. His withered appearance seems like senility, and it makes Roger concerned.

Roger watches him scan the page with difficulty. He begins to wonder if he should read the professor the pages aloud.

The professor speaks with the awareness of a young man. "This all works, doesn't it?"

"It should." Roger replies. He leans forward and his eyes brighten.

The old professor puts a paper down and picks up a tiny espresso mug from a coaster. With a smile he looks from the second page to the young man. "Just five years out of school; I'm impressed."

Roger shifts his chair forward along the carpet.

The mini mug returns to the wise man's desk, and he looks Roger in the eyes "They don't want it because it works."

Roger gathers his brows.

"This missile requires only one shot." The old man lifts his index finger. "One shot and a tank is immobilized. One shot and a bunker is destroyed. That's one million dollars made by Allagash." He lowers his finger "If the military uses a new mohawk missile, they need to hammer that thing six or seven times. Six or seven million dollars. Allagash wants a product that sells; a government research organization on the other hand… that's a different story. They'll be willing to make a revolutionary invention, much like the internet was." He nods at Roger with a smile "Allagash doesn't want your invention; but DARPA does."

"So I should bring this to DARPA?"

"Exactly." The professor takes a sip from his mini mug "The federal government likes weapons that work, private manufacturers want products that make them money."

Roger can hardly contain his heart rate.

The professor stands and takes his coat from behind his chair "Let's go for a walk, Roger. It's been a while since I've taken time for a crisp fall day."

"Professor, I think I should be going."

The professor looks at the young man with scorned eyes "Where do you need to be?"

Roger sways with apology "This new information along with deadlines means I need to take it…"

"Don't be stupid." The professor cuts him off "There's always time. Come on, we're walking."

Roger takes a silent sigh, and feels his stomach churn with embarrassment.

Along the north bank of the river, the two scientists walk westward to a hospital near Harvard Square. They talk about what Roger is doing, and how his daily life has been.

Roger gives a picturesque depiction, minus his family disputes, friendship dramatics, and unbecoming behavior.

The professor looks once in a while with a frown; as if he doubts the truth of his statements.

"My dad is looking to retire, but his girlfriend is still young."

"I know your father." The professor adds.

Roger screws his brows together, feeling a mix of questions in his mind.

"I know your mother too." The professor adds. "How are your parents?"

"Both are good." Roger says "They split up a while ago."

"I know." The professor seats himself on a bench, and looks up to a playground beside the hospital. "I was close with your mother, so when I saw you in my class I may have had some favoritism."

Roger sits beside him. "How do you know her?"

The doctor smiles "Believe it or not, romantically." he laughs "It's my fault for acting too slow, so I'm not weird about it." The professor meets his elbows to his legs and leans forward. "She had you, and it appears that's meant to be."

Roger laughs "I'll admit, she'd probably be a lot happier if she was with you."

The professor smiles "That's HIS fault for acting too FAST."

Roger tries to gather the details to figure out exactly what that means, but it doesn't take long before he forgets the matter.

"Your father is a good man." The professor says with a nod "Don't ever misinterpret his intentions."

"No, I know. He's a workaholic; because he's been working for our sake."

"He would do anything for you and your sister. That's because you're HIS kids. He makes one fatal mistake though; and I'll try my best to spell it out, so you won't do as he's done."

Roger looks at the old man "What's that, professor?"

The old man looks at the playground before them. He nods in its direction to guide his student's eyes. Roger looks to see a child in the playground. No other kids are at play; just a boy and his father.

The father watches his son play with a small puzzle on the jungle gym. Next to the boy is a slide. The father begins to grin as he approaches the end of the slide. He waits there, with a clever surprise.

The boy moves off to go elsewhere on the jungle gym. The father nearly gives up, but he sees his son reaching for the fire pole on the other side. The father saunters under the jungle gym and the boy begins his descent.

The boy watches the ground move closer to his dangling feet, then feels a sudden bottom. He hasn't reached the floor.

The boy looks behind himself to see his father laughing. His fall has been broken by his father's hands.

As the boy laughs at the father's joke, Roger listens to the professor continue his lesson.

"We live too quick to spend our lives going through the motions; without moments of reflection." The professor says "Can you remember your father playing with you like that?"

Roger looks at the boy in the playground. He climbs up the fire pole, then atop the roof of the jungle gym. He climbs the structure in all the ways it wasn't meant to be.

"It must have happened sometime." Roger says "I just don't remember because I was a kid." He watches a little longer and laughs "Although, I don't think he was like that kid's dad. He seems pretty enthusiastic."

The old man turns to see the father pretend fighting with his son in the jungle gym.

The old man laughs "You know, that's what being a father was like long ago." His crow's feet wrinkle on his face "When humans lived in tribes, and our communities were small, we spent more time focusing on what was around us. Stories weren't about superheroes saving the world; they were local heroes saving a village." He looks to the young man at his side "That man is doing exactly what your father should have. With his children, with his wife, and his friends. He should have given more time for the things he had." He shakes his head "He was always striving to succeed, all the while not thinking of his successes."

The father in the playground bids his son to play without him, then answers his phone. He looks at the hospital next to the park. His face grows saddened, as though disappointed. The father hangs up the phone, and looks back to his son.

"P.J.!" The father says.

The boy stands atop the jungle gym "Yeah Dad?"

"Grammy's too tired to see us. We're gonna head home."

"Okay!"

The child begins climbing down, and Roger turns to the professor once again.

"Looks fade." The old man says "Attraction is no way to look for love. And your parents love you, but who will love you when they're gone?"

The old man looks to the ground, as if to pull up a warning from the way he deeply feels; whether it's his feelings about his own condition, or someone else's.

"Anyone could do your job." He says "You just happened to be the guy who got hired."

"Not everyone has an elite education in engineering." Roger says.

"But anyone can get one if they apply themselves." The professor quips "We're all equally worthless. The only worth we feel is what we project on ourselves."

Roger feels his face fall, along with his sense of self-importance.

"Yet we're all equally worthwhile" The professor elaborates "It's one of those strange things about reality that seems like a paradox." He giggles "I prefer to think of it like quantum mechanics. Both realities exist at the same time. We only know our value once we observe ourselves."

The professor shrugs "Granted, making something entirely new is pretty cool, and maybe without your help this project wouldn't be what it is; but don't be so smart that you become stupid."

Roger tenses his face in question "I don't get it."

The professor becomes dire in his gaze "Don't neglect yourself in favor of your work. Take time to think. Think of yourself and what you do. Highlight when you're wrong, own up to it, and map out a way to get better when you find something wrong in your attitude, work ethic; anything."

"Are you saying there's something wrong with me?"

"There's something wrong in everyone, Roger." The professor smiles with half of his face. "Who I was five years ago is still young and arro-

gant compared to who I am today; and if I live long enough, I'll be able
to say the same thing five years from now. I was an old fart five years
ago as I am today, and I'm still learning every day. There's always room
to improve myself. It's always a work in progress. Life is like a science."

Roger nods.

The professor smiles at his pupil "Take time to think of yourself. You
have the same passion as your father, and it's commendable; but remain
humbled in knowing that no one will ever be perfect. It's an ongoing
study."

With a walk back to campus, they discuss topics that Roger will soon
forget. He never forgets the feeling however; an older, much wiser man
than himself willingly offering his wisdom. The young man finds it
comforting, but he doesn't know why.

His life experience has limited his ability to understand the value
of his relationship with the old man. His mind is too far stuck in a
goal-oriented structure. His own family has been superficial with their
affections, and Roger has never been promoted to reflect on himself as
a truly knowledgeable parent would ensure him to do.

His parents cannot be blamed, for they loved their son; and they had
the misguided notion that their liberal use of their wealth with him was
a rightful display of that love. They loved him, and so they hated to see
him hurt by truth, or the repercussions of accountability. They never
told him he was wrong or flawed in character. They never told him that
good character is something to be sought after, and not an innate characteristic that could be chalked up to "good breeding".

Out of their love, they made the wrong decisions; and out of their
love, Roger cannot see the love that lies in what the professor is saying.

Roger's sense of comfort brings him to open up in ways he never has
before. He talks about what he thinks in his mind; about his perception
of the world around him. The professor acts as an engineer of the mind.
He takes the components that are laid out in this opening, and he uses
them in tandem with his own experiences to guide the boy's perception.

Roger feels more clear than ever when they come to the gate of Merrimack Institute. They say their goodbyes; and then they part ways.

Roger will never see the old man again.

***

Roger sends a text to his team. He calls for a meeting.

At their designated time the following day, the group is briefed on the idea that was given by the professor.

There's a mix of views after hearing the advice. Those who are ambitious become excited, while the more practical members are reluctant to abandon their retirement funds, and the benefits provided by Allagash.

Roger is faced with the idea of how his father will feel about him leaving Allagash. The Meek family has been with the same private weapons manufacturer for generations; and while going to a government research organization like DARPA has its benefits, Roger will be burning a bridge with old family friends.

In the meeting with DARPA, the product is well received. Roger and his remaining team are put onto the project. The assembly is finalized and the prototype is produced over the course of a year and a half. His years at Allagash have finally come to an end.

The prototype, along with subsequent trials, are met with success. At the testing facility, the gravitational waves make a subharmonic thud that echoes off the mountains. They shake through the desert dirt beneath their feet. The tanks blow outward with shrapnel. Nothing inside remains.

What Roger never accounted for was his loss of power. He no longer stands in a place where he has leverage. Allagash is now far behind him and far away. At DARPA he has become a number among many.

Two weeks after testing, Roger enters a DARPA meeting room. His files in hand, he's embarrassed to realize he smells of cigarettes. Another man of science stands to the corner as a commander speaks directly to him.

"Good morning Doctor Meek." He says "We just have a few questions for you this morning. We are sorry to take up your time."

The commander appears to notice nothing of the stench from his hand as it meets his in a greeting.

"It's no problem at all, commander. What can I help you with?"

"It's regarding your work on the Houdini Missile" the commander says "Firstly, I'd like to congratulate you. We've had many successful applications in the field, and you've saved many lives already."

Roger has a pit in his stomach.

"Applications?" he asks.

There is a moment of silence.

The commander continues "Your work has saved many Americans, and it will continue to do so. DARPA may or may not find new applications for your work, but we need to sort out a few questions first. Do you mind?"

He motions to the chair across the table.

Roger feels reluctant to speak against the idea.

"Okay." He says, sitting in the seat.

Roger begins to feel like a child in the principal's office, looking up at the commander as he speaks. The unnamed scientist blocks the doorway.

The commander begins with a softer tone. "The payload in the Houdini delivery system. Can it be replaced with an antimatter bomb?"

"It can be whatever you need it to be, maybe a few adjustments for the size of the payload, but not a whole new system entirely."

The commander nods "Secondly, what is the maximum range the device can transport a payload?"

"The teleportation?"

"Yes."

"We haven't tested its limits but it should be able to travel a few thousand miles with only a little extra energy. The only problem is larger distances require compensation for the Earth's rotation and the movement in space itself. That's why jet propulsion delivers it as close to the target as possible."

The commander has a glazed look over his eyes and the scientist behind him seems to be holding back a giggle. The commander then adds "Lastly." He looks at a paper and reads the final question "Is the weapon deployable in outer space?"

Roger's cheeks fall, and his skin grows pale "What kind of weapon are you trying to make?"

"That information is classified right now."

Roger feels the pressure in the room. "The missile itself can't reach escape velocity. Some adjustments could be made, or it could be transported on a rocket; maybe the collider / lunar launch system in Utah. Even then there comes a point when you need to change fuel sources."

The commander looks behind himself at the scientist who nods. The commander nods with a stiff neck "Okay." He stands and puts his hand out to shake Roger's "Thank you again, Doctor Meek. Sorry to take up your time."

"Not a problem at all, commander."

The following morning, Roger enters the lab to find his supplies being packed by strange men. A letter is all that is left on his desk. He opens it and begins to read.

A fellow coworker approaches him "Roger, what's going on here? These guys have been packing your things all morning."

Roger reads the last line:

> *"In the occasion that you are asked where you are going, you will inform your coworkers (and anyone else) that you are continuing your work at another facility."*

He looks up at his coworker. His eyes show little sorrow or concern. Instead, a bewildered look comes about his face. He feels he's drowning in a world that he never imagined was real.

"I'm being transferred."

CHAPTER 36
Creating Man, Creating God

The room is silent, and the monolithic body of Doctor Clay recalls both his fondest memories, and his deepest laments.

Hoyt prepares himself to listen.

"I loved what I did for work." Doctor Clay says "The guys at work were difficult at first; but I was a young guy in a company that ran on fossil fuel… if you know what I mean."

Hoyt gathers his brows.

"Fossil fuel?" He asks.

"Meaning the workforce was comprised of dinosaurs."

Hoyt's brows are fixed together.

"Old people…" Clay says.

Doctor Hoyt raises his brows at the realization.

"Oh!" He says "I see."

He begins jotting down a note and begins to giggle.

"Fossil fuel." He says "That's me, alright."

"You and me both." Clay says.

Hoyt cracks a smile at the lens. With a glance at his notepad, Hoyt feels comfortable moving on.

"So what happened from there?"

***

It's a quiet morning in the large facility of RAINARD Armaments. The halls glow with golden sunlight. It shines in from three glass walls which meet at a point overhead; making a pyramid structure over the top floor dining hall. The staircases descend into working spaces where RAINARDA's staff members work.

At a table by the café, Doug holds a cup of coffee and reads the numbers for a nano product. The manager from systems gave the numbers out, in order to alleviate the stress on the systems department.

As a young employee, Doug is merely a small part in a fraction of a very large product. He works under less competent people than himself; and keeping a polite composure among the egos has grown exhausting.

While Doug has always been a prideful intellect, he has never once had the audacity to neglect his scientific process. So long as the proof is given, Doug doesn't resist the changes of a theory. Instead, he accepts the antiquity of prior beliefs. Without the proof, however, he stands his ground on the formerly established facts.

The staff he quarrels with differ from himself in this respect. They will refuse to rework their numbers, and churn out the minimum work required in a day. Sometimes it becomes a game of hide and seek, and Doug wastes the day searching for an older gentleman in the pyramid jungle gym.

Doug is convinced, at times, that they would never accept new information. Even if Doug were to take their numbers and plug them into a fact-checking machine, the black-and-white answer would be refuted. "The machine is wrong." they'll insist, as if a clear, concise, and truthful answer would ever be wrong. Doug knows he cannot sway selfish people, especially if they are emotionally motivated.

"Doug, can you work over this tonight?" An older man slaps a manilla folder next to Doug's food. "It needs to be on the manager's desk by tomorrow."

"You can't?" Doug asks.

"I have a flight to catch for Munich" the employee says.

"You don't have any time?" Doug asks.

Doug knows that this is the older employee's unwanted work. The flight to Munich is a mere chance to shirk the work onto someone else.

"I can't. It's straightforward. You can handle it."

Looking it over, Doug realizes it won't be "straightforward", and if he hadn't learned this advanced problem in his own time, he would be stuck.

"I'll handle it." Doug says. "By the way, did you read the numbers from systems?"

The older man responds with a gathering of brows and a shake of his head.

"*Didn't think so.*" Doug thinks.

After work, Doug returns home to a steaming surprise at his front door. Bert looks up at him with a guilty face.

"Buddy, no…" Doug says.

He grabs a plastic bag and picks up the mess.

He looks with disappointment at the dog, and is met with lowered ears and a tucked tail.

After wiping the area with a cleaner, Doug takes Albert for a walk. His frequent stops are for sniffing, and nothing more.

"Got it all out, didn't you?" Doug says.

Albert lifts his nose from the side of a curb and looks up at Doug.

Doug pulls back the corner of his mouth "It's not your fault." he says.

Doug turns and gives the dog a light pull on the leash.

Albert follows.

"We didn't have the time for a pup like you; but she wanted a rescue." he adds.

They stop at an open football field, and Doug pulls out a tennis ball. He looks at Bert on eye level and scratches his ears.

"Becca couldn't resist you!" Doug says, removing the dog's leash.

The dog begins panting and tilting its head.

Doug speaks with his teeth in a smile "Yeah, she needed a little pity cause, and you were it!"

The dog tries to lick Doug's face, but Doug backs away. Doug stands and displays the ball between his thumb and forefinger "This is all YOU understand."

The dog's face turns at the sight of the ball.

Doug pivots his foot and thrusts the ball with all his might. Bert runs with immense zeal, and Doug looks on.

"Aren't you fuckin lucky." Doug mutters.

At the door to his apartment, Doug hangs Bert's leash. He pulls out the problem he was given earlier. After a half an hour, and several near distractions, the problem is finished.

"Child's play." Doug mumbles.

He slaps the table with his pencil and rises from his seat.

Out of curiosity, he checks his phone to see what the older employee is doing. In no time he finds a social media account, wherein he has posted a photo on a local golf course. The older man is with his college friends from Boston. He hasn't left the country today.

"Yup" he says as he lowers his phone "Figures."

With the assumption that Rebecca is working late, he cooks a meal without her. Cauliflower rice with steak and roasted Brussels sprouts.

In their new apartment and life together, Doug can afford to eat better and live comfortably. This is more appealing than the dorm life they were used to. No more ramen and sharing a twin-sized bed. With the help of two impressive incomes, they have little to worry about besides rent, utility, and loans.

Both Doug and Rebecca ride bikes to work, and share an old cheap car for their weekend trips.

Doug thinks about this as he cooks, and finds himself in a better mood. A practice he learned from Curtis, to reflect on all the good he has. In Doug's eyes it's not perfect, but things couldn't be better.

Around seven in the afternoon Rebecca opens the door with a gentle, surprised "Hi!"

Bert rushes over to her lap and rolls onto his back. Becca rubs his belly and smiles at the dog.

Doug turns to see her with the fuzz ball of joy.

"I made dinner." Doug smiles.

Her smile fades to a practical conversation.

She looks over at the stove. "How long ago did you make it?"

"When I got home from work. Maybe an hour ago."

She stands in front of it. She looks disappointed "Doug, this is cold. And I hate that cauliflower rice."

"I'll make something else if you want."

"Maybe some real rice; and steak that isn't cold."

He makes his way to the stove and doesn't speak a word. To say anything would run the risk of further scrutiny.

When she leaves the room, Doug heats the meat and Brussels sprouts in a toaster oven. The rice is made to time perfectly with it.

She takes a shower while the food cooks, and Doug makes her plate. To keep it warm, he wraps the top in foil.

The shower still runs, and he checks to make sure he didn't leave something out in the open. In the bottom of his dresser therein lies the ring. Her parents will be in town next week and his family knows to meet at the outdoor skating rink; the place where the couple had their first date.

Doug stows the ring away and begins preparing the table.

By the time she leaves the bathroom, the silverware is laid out beside two plates. A lone candle sits between the plates.

"What's the occasion?" She asks.

Doug shrugs "There's no occasion. I just felt like it."

She sits at the table, and he joins her. Doug isn't hungry anymore, but he eats for the sake of a little conversation.

"I was thinking we should go to the rink sometime next week." He says.

She cuts into her steak "It's been a while since we've gone." She says.

She lifts the steak to her mouth, and continues to eat.

Doug looks up at her with a slight grin.

He picks up a small piece of meat with his fork "So you think we should go?" He asks.

"Yeah, sounds like fun." Becca adds.

Doug holds back a smile. They continue to eat in silence.

The following morning, Doug arrives early to work. He sees the project manager approaching the front door.

Doug hastens his stride to close the distance between them. He tucks the manila folder beneath his arm and nearly jogs. The glass door glides open. The manager enters. The door follows at his back, but Doug squeezes in. The manager turns to see a young man with wind-gusted hair, holding a bent and creased manilla folder. The manager holds his stride for a moment, allowing Doug to catch up.

He walks abreast with the manager. "Sir, I have Tom's work for the morning." Doug says. "He had a flight, so I ran the whole thing for him."

The manager looks at Doug with a questioning face. "A flight? When? To where?"

"This morning. He had to fly to Munich."

A man of an older time, the manager looks stoic. Doug knows there is some thought stirring beneath his wrinkled face. A look his father would make; with a scowl, and a scrutinizing eye. The manager brings his scowling eye to the manila folder as he opens it.

"Is that so?" He says.

He looks over the pages a while with zeal. He seems nostalgic about their contents.

Doug imagines the man as a young father; fortunate to work a job he loves to provide for his children. He seems to be the same person with a different, more wrinkled skin. The energy hasn't wavered for a day.

The manager gathers his brows "This is some advanced work, sonny. Where'd you go to school?"

"Merrimack Institute." Doug replies.

They enter an elevator and stand shoulder to shoulder amid many other faces. Nearly all of them are unfamiliar to Doug.

"This isn't a part of the undergrad curriculum." the manager says.

"I learned it on my own." Doug tells him "Between classes I'd read ahead."

The manager's eyes gleam behind smiling lids. "You know why I know that, right?"

The other faces smile.

Doug shakes his head "No, sir."

The old man's face wrinkles into a smile "On nights I work as a professor in the graduate program."

Doug laughs "Oh! That makes sense."

The manager laughs as the elevator stops for the second floor. The doors soon close again, and they continue to talk.

"How long does it usually take for a project to reach completion?" Doug asks.

"It depends on the project. This one is a little longer than most. There's this whole map of the human mind thing to sort through with this one. So it's taken a while."

Doug nods and recalls how complicated that is. The number of neurons in the brain number more than the visible stars in the sky.

"You came on a little late sonny. It's almost done, though. Making it five years in total. We've had projects take as long as fifteen." The man's brows raise at this, and he nods. He stares at the floor number as it changes. He takes a breath and continues "I appreciate a good assistant, though" He waves the manila folder in reference. "…and I like to reward hard-working people with better positions." His eyes meet Doug's "You'll learn to judge the size of a project soon enough."

The doors open and the two walk together on the same floor.

Doug's office is a short walk after the manager's, and so he takes the opportunity to learn.

"I'm really looking forward to seeing this product."

"I agree." the manager says "It comes in time, though; and here's a little advice.

Look forward to the final day no matter what. The end result may come, and it may also not!" The manager tilts his head as if to shrug off a stain on his career. Some marred project that took years of his life to no avail. The old man continues "We always want a successful outcome, but don't want to bother with the small details that get us there. The little steps along the way. Those are the details you must obsess over. That's where the real science comes in; and we're men of science." He tucks the manila folder under his arm "The scientific process is our lifeline; it can't go neglected."

"Is there a story to go with this?" Doug asks.

"You know that fifteen-year project?" The manager looks briefly for a nod, then stares back to the hall before him "That was bouncing around the R&D department as a proposal. No one wanted to admit it, but it wouldn't work; so I stomped it out. No use talking about it. It was a waste of precious time. I'm the only one around to remember it, and there's a reason I'm the only one."

Just then they reach the manager's office. The old man's smiling eyes turn from Doug and don't hesitate as he waves "Hello Tom! How's Munich?"

To Doug's surprise, the man who gave him the manilla folder stands at the end of the hall just outside his office entrance. His face is struck with fear.

The manager smacks Doug's shoulder and exhales a booming laugh. His voice fades into the closing door of his office.

Doug looks on for a while then laughs with a shake of his head.

***

A week later and the day has come when Doug has decided to propose his future with Rebecca.

Her parents arrive at the airport around seven that morning. They stay in a hotel across the river without their daughter's knowledge.

Doug's parents promise to arrive at the rink in Cambridge on the edge of the river. The wooden fence surrounds the large sheet of ice. The perimeter is adorned with Edison bulbs that glow with the falling of the sun.

At the shack on the edge of the ice, Doug and Rebecca sip hot chocolate. It steams into an afternoon air.

As an expert of the New England cold, Curtis once taught Doug how to keep warm in the harsh winter. The couple has hand warmers stuffed under their gloves, and clothing tucked in wherever it can be. They're layered in long-sleeve shirts and wool sweaters under down feather jackets. On their legs they wear long pajamas under sweatpants. All of this is under a wind-resistant shell, which is pulled around the outside of their skates. Their wool socks run up their calves and under the pajama pants.

As thick snowflakes fall gently from the sky, they step onto the ice. The flakes catch on her hat, and hang on the edge of her eyelashes. Melting drops of water bead on her cheeks and shine around blue agate eyes.

This is the second time Doug has been skating. It's painfully obvious as he stands still. In contrast Becca skates fluidly around him.

Doug begins to look around for their parents.

From the corner of his eye, he sees his mother and father. They act like strangers to one another, standing with folded arms and cups of coffee by the shack. He pretends to forget their odd behavior, then looks for her parents. Just as he does, they enter from the shack, and split to talk with his parents.

Her mother glances toward him and waves. He smiles back with a nod. Her mother smiles with a thumbs up.

Becca skates closer to Doug "When I used to figure skate I…" she looks to see where he is staring "Is that my parents?" Her voice gives no sign of surprise, but misfortune; as though they'll ruin a good day. "Are those YOUR parents?" Her voice now brightens to surprise in a question.

She turns to find Doug lowering to his knee. Her face grows numb, and her cheeks grow warm. Her eyes well up in tears.

***

Over the following year, Doug invites his closest friends to the wedding. Curtis, Frank, Gabe, and Rosemary are his best men and best lady. James attends as a guest, but opts out of any planning; and Roger cannot make it because of work.

James and Curtis are involved with a highly publicized project. The "Nevada Super Gun", or so it's been named by the press, is a particle collider that doubles as a launching system. It is designed to propel capsules that transport the building materials for the newly proposed lunar base.

James has been working his way up into a position on the moon, fulfilling a lifelong dream of his. It's for this reason that he tells Doug he can't be one of his best men. Doug congratulates him and affirms that it's more important.

Rebecca begins her planning, but grows quiet after a while. Her mood becomes dismal and reserved.

One night, when Doug sits at her side on the couch, he asks her directly what is wrong.

Rebecca can't form the words. Her nose sniffles and tears run down her face. She hands him a packet of paper.

They're tests from the doctor's office. A brain scan and blood tests.

Rebecca has stage four brain cancer. It has spread to her blood and formed leukemia.

Doug makes a pact with her to get married sooner. They agree to spend time in any place she wants over the next year. The wedding becomes a small gathering of friends at a small venue. James goes back on his decision and becomes one of Doug's best men. Roger is still unable to make it.

Rebecca comes down the aisle in a wheelchair, and the ceremony becomes a bittersweet memory for everyone.

The following day, Doug takes Rebecca to Italy. Their time is spent very slow and subtle. Frequently they look on at places from afar, and opt out of waiting in big lines full of tourists.

The moment that they cherish the most is an unexpected trip to a small café. When the Duomo is found to be a little too overwhelming, Rebecca smiles from her chair.

"This is enough." She says.

She looks up at Doug. Her handwoven blanket drapes across her legs; a small memorabilia they purchased from a local craftsman.

She raises her hand from her lap, and she brings Doug's face closer to kiss him on the lips.

Doug smiles.

"Where to now?" He asks.

She points at a small shop with outdoor seating. It faces away from the Duomo, on a street running perpendicular to the large cathedral. They sit there along the Florentine streets, smiling at one another.

Doug holds her hands "Where do we go after today? Do we stay in Florence?"

Rebecca smiles and looks off down the street.

"I think I've had enough of Italy." She says.

Doug smiles "How about another country, then?"

Rebecca's eyes gleam with excitement at the thought of a new adventure.

"I've always wanted to see Japan." She says.

Doug nods "Japan it is, then."

"But you have to work."

"Work can wait."

Doug speaks with conviction. Not a single thing can interrupt these precious moments. Not a single dime or possession can ever make up for the woman he loves.

Rebecca holds his hand tighter.

"Japan it is, then." She says.

They look around them as the sun turns a golden color nearing the horizon. The sky looks exceptionally blue, and the clouds float by; a heavenly white.

The wind becomes chilly, and comes down from the north. The plummeting breeze of night in the late Tuscan spring.

They smile at each other, and don't say a word. It's well enough to know that it's a beautiful day.

Rebecca and Doug finish their time in the plaza and return to the hotel room. The following morning, she's too fatigued to do much of anything. They call their vacation short and travel home.

Rebecca opts in for an experimental treatment, and Doug plans for a trip to Japan with her. The treatment delays the inevitable for another week, but just before he can finalize the trip, Rebecca needs to be hospitalized for her final days alive.

In hospice care, Rebecca can barely say a word. She can no longer put food down. In the course of a week, she passes away. She never gets to see Japan.

***

Two years after Rebecca's funeral, Doug and Curtis meet for the first time since her passing. The funeral was the last time Doug had seen any of the group, and it has been longer still since anyone has seen Roger; six and a half years in fact. Since graduation.

Doctorates have been granted, Jobs have been changed, and even a baby has been born.

In the old city of Cambridge, across the river from Boston, Doug meets Curt at the old coffee shop in Central Square. Matured men no longer smoke hookah, but the coffee has the perfect taste they remember.

Curtis sets down his cup "How's the research coming?"

According to Doug, there is a personal project he carries outside of his work. A curiosity amongst the group, but the surprise is worth patience.

"It's coming along." Doug replies. "There's actually a showcase coming up."

His reluctance to share brings Curtis to greater enthusiasm.

"A showcase?" Curtis asks.

"Yes." Doug nearly shrinks in his seat. He's nervous but still seeks his friend's support "It should be within the next year or so."

Curt's eyes brighten "Let's get the crew together!" He smiles at a dread-ridden face "We can all come see!"

Doug seems hesitant "Are you sure you want to do that? I don't want anyone changing their plans on account of me."

"Everyone would be glad to come!" Curtis says.

"It should be around Christmastime. I don't know."

Curtis nods with tense brows "I'll be around here. It's here, right?"

Doug nods "On campus."

"I think James won't be gone until after the holidays, so he'll be here too."

"Yeah?" Doug asks "And where's James going?"

Curtis smiles "You didn't hear?" he leans closer "James is being sent to the moon. He has a position on the lunar base."

Doug raises his brows "That's crazy!" his eyes squint with questions "How'd he get a position there?"

Curtis shrugs "Same old, same old. Nobody knows. Top secret government yadayada bullshit."

Doug pulls his eyes away from the pool of coffee "You know he won't be back for a while, right?"

Curtis sighs "I know. He's excited though, so I'm happy."

Doug thinks about the bureaucratic red tape. The powers they work for. He doubts their integrity. "I just wonder why they're sending young people up. The new guys, you know."

Curtis tries to follow.

Doug looks at him through the corner of his eye "You ever wonder why no executives go up there?" He takes the last sip of his coffee and sets it down to see the grinds at the bottom of the cup. "It's no joke up there. They might consider him a lab rat."

Curtis bites his teeth together at the thought. The radiation that comes with space travel is a real burden. Micro-meteors and moon quakes are among other concerns for the Lunar Base.

Doug leans in closer. "I don't think we're ready for the stars, you know."

Curtis gathers his brows. He pulls his chair in to hear Doug's soft-spoken words.

Doug thinks further to an atrocious ingenuity he's heard of in whispers. Worst of all, the biological weapons he's discussed at long length with reliable sources. Nanomachine tests, carried out on unsuspecting test subjects. The injections disguised as a vaccination for the annual flu. The very thing that made people skeptics in the twenty twenties, but the reality is far stranger than what they could have imagined. Populations that could not or would not come forward to anyone. They'd confide in the one person who had "Patient Confidentiality"; and they'd hope to be healed by the person logging their symptoms next to another column labeled "Control Group".

Doug collects this thought in one last sentence. "I don't think we'll ever evolve to leave Earth."

Curtis takes this as a vague reference to what happened with Rebecca "Guys like us can make it all worthwhile." He rebuts.

Doug shakes his head, and anger develops creases at the corners of his mouth "We're the grunts in this affair. We aren't written in the history books anymore. That's for the select CEOs and politicians."

Doug sits back in his chair. A look of disgust at whatever has taken hold of his mind.

Curtis feels an unusual fear. He can't recall if this stature has ever been exhibited by Doug before. To Curtis he looks as if he stands on a moral high ground. He looks disgusted with the immoral commoners of the world. A just anger brews in his face.

Staring into the street around them, Doug calms down and asks with longing "Do you think some cures for cancer have already been found and withheld?"

The following silence brings Curtis to finish the well known theory "Like, repressed from the public for money?"

The question is not answered, but Doug goes on to elaborate on his pondering. "I looked over the insurance fees. The hospital records; and you wouldn't believe it." He lets out a breath of a laugh "If you wanted ibuprofen, you'd pay thirteen dollars a pill."

Curtis looks unsurprised. The inflated prices are well known thanks to his brother's political views. Instead he feels at a loss for Doug's pain. The past still haunts him after two years.

Doug leans in closer to keep the conversation between the two of them "Who's to say they wouldn't hide a cure, you know?"

Curtis nods and stares at the floor. He searches for an answer, knowing it is a worthless effort. "I know" is all he can find to say.

CHAPTER 37
The Undiscovered Mind

Julius stands by Doctor Lawrence as she peers into Doug's machine body. A latch opens to a hole, revealing a large metallic mass. Her flashlight shines off of the metal surface. It is barely solid, and seems to have the consistency of brain matter.

"What are we looking at, Doug?" Elizabeth asks.

She moves over to allow Julius to have a look. He uses his own flashlight to peer in with her.

"That would be my neural network." Doug says. "It's engineered to be faster than the ordinary mind. It exceeds five times the size of a human brain. That size is used for sound, vision, critical reasoning, and control over my body. There is a hollowed center with a chance of ventilation at the top and bottom. If we made it one solid object, the heat would degrade the materials over time. What you're looking at manages short-term memory and refers to the quartz storage towers for long-term events."

Julius looks at the mass before them. He searches for the ventilation holes at the top and bottom to find rounded holes. The sound of a fan comes from somewhere deep within.

"And why quartz?" Julius asks.

"So that I never lose track of the truth. It can't be unwritten, and it doesn't become altered after use. The lasers need maintenance, but not the memory itself."

Elizabeth moves to the lens of the machine "Can we open up the quartz? I'd like to see something."

"Of course." Doug says.

The latch opens to the quartz towers. Elizabeth makes her way over for a look.

Doug chimes again "May I ask why you're looking?"

Elizabeth shines her light along the transparent facades. She sees the tracks and motors, which the lasers and receptors use to move. They run parallel, in sync with each other.

"Well…" she begins "… we're thinking you might be able to help us by operating at night. If you wouldn't mind it, perhaps you could help us while the team gets rest." She motions to Julius and he turns off his light for a moment. "Jules, can you go get the findings from the last mission?"

Julius nods.

Doctor Winter takes a hastened stride out of the room and Elizabeth looks back at the large crystal towers. Six of them. Each ten feet tall and ten feet wide.

"Doctor Lawrence?" Doug calls.

She looks back toward the front of the machine. There, the lens rests above a small speaker.

"Yes, Doug?"

"I fear that the project managers could have severed my neural network from the quartz. That would give me the computing power without my true self. The self that lies in those memories. I'm not so sure you want to link me up to the network. I'm uncertain of what could happen."

She turns to see the stillness of the silent monuments. They rest in the dark space behind the neural network.

"That could be." She sighs. "But what would go wrong if you had access to the ship?"

"I don't know, and that's the problem." Doug says "The government could have made me into a weapon." Doug takes a moment to think. The lasers move around in the dark. They move from a lower section to a far higher point. "I'm just thinking ahead is all."

Julius returns with a bag containing a multitude of odds and ends. The first of which he grasps in his hand. He holds the object without revealing it.

He turns his eyes to Elizabeth. "Ready when you are."

Doctor Lawrence looks to the front of the machine. She leans forward and speaks both clear and soft "So, while we were in Boston, we made a trip to a particular place." She turns her eyes to the quartz towers and shines her light. "Doctor Winter, could you show him what we found?"

Julius nods and reveals a picture frame. Inside the frame is a photo of a man and a woman. They are dressed for their wedding day. Upon seeing this, the lasers move rapidly toward a lower part of the crystal. A rather quiet sound of clicking is heard. The information is referenced with invisible lasers.

"Who are those people, Doug?" She asks.

Julius smiles toward the lens as he presents the photo.

Doug waits a moment. "Those are my parents."

Julius screws his brows together and turns the photo to himself. He reimagines this man as Doug's father, and not Doug himself.

Elizabeth looks back to the lens "Those are your parents?"

"Yes. I took that from my grandmother's house. My mom hated it, but I liked it. Grammy used to keep it for my sake, and when she passed I took it in secret. I kept it in my room in a hidden place. I wanted to show my own kids someday."

Elizabeth lowers her flashlight and nods.

Doug continues "It was better than thinking they were always apart." A momentary silence pervades, and Doug speaks again "This means more than words can say. Thank you."

Elizabeth stands and walks toward Julius. She takes the photograph and looks it over.

"They look really happy." She says.

"A little hard for me to imagine." Doug replies.

Elizabeth looks over the photo one more time, and looks to the lens of Doug's machine "My parents are divorced too."

In the silence Doug's motors turn and move. Again the clicking occurs "They separated when I was older, but they weren't happy in the same house."

"I missed the love and unity we once had." Elizabeth says.

"You're lucky you can remember." Doug says. "I don't remember this photo being taken. I don't remember my parents being happy."

His silver voice laments over the life of an only child "They were together because of me; and I could feel that."

She nods and hands Julius the photo.

She smiles at the lens again "I feel like you'd be the best Dad."

"I was looking forward to it." Doug says. "Maybe someday, somehow, I can be."

Julius looks up from the bag. His eyes meet Doctor Lawrence's confused face "Doug's genetic data is stored in the quartz part of his mind. It's not impossible."

"Really?" She asks.

"We were chatting the other day." Julius says. He opens the bag of belongings and motions it to Elizabeth "Are we ready for another surprise?"

"Oh, yes." She says.

Elizabeth moves back to the quartz towers and watches again.

From out of the bag comes a framed diploma. A bachelor's degree from Merrimack Institute. The next object is his master's, and finally the PhD.

"Oh wow." Doug says. "Of all of them. I'm glad you didn't neglect the bachelor's degree. That was most important."

Elisabeth smiles "Brings back memories?"

"It does."

Next Julius pulls out a beanie with "RAINARD Armaments" embroidered along the rim.

"I spent many years there." Doug says. "I'm very proud of that."

Julius pulls out a postcard from Allagash's Nevada facility.

The postcard displays a large machine pointed to the sky with the moon displayed prominently behind it.

Julius begins to read from the back "Hello Doug! I've heard you're doing very well. We miss you, and I hope to see you again soon.

I wanted to send you this postcard because we finally did it! We're sending cargo-loaded projectiles to the moon. James and I are working day and night. They say the moon base will be open to new positions soon. It would be cool to go! This photo is of the Nevada Super Gun. Just like the railgun I made in high school, but this time it's not blowing anything up! It also doubles as a particle collider. Looking forward to showing you in person. I'll be in Boston next month. I'll let you know, and hopefully we can meet up (if you have the time that is). Sincerely, your friend Doctor Curtis Mandel"

The machine is silent.

Julius places the postcard on a table to his side. He then reaches into a seemingly empty bag and smiles. He looks up at the lens for a brief moment "There's one more thing in here."

Julius lifts his hand. Between his fingers, it shines in the light of the room. On the edge of a circular golden shape there's a glimmering gemstone. A diamond, resting on the edge of a solid gold ring. He places it onto the table, in front of Doug's lens.

After years of cold and darkness, it looks as it did when she wore it. It feels the warmth of life at long last. Rebecca's wedding ring.

There is hesitance. A silent moment until Doug speaks again. "Thank you. Thank you both so much."

The engineers smile.

Elizabeth stands next to Julius and looks at the lens. "It's the least we could do, Doug."

"I can print out the details on how my machine works. That way you don't need to put it in writing yourself."

Elizabeth nods. "That would be amazing. Thank you, Doug."

***

Over the course of the following hours, the halls grow silent again. The pair of engineers pour over the printouts that Doug provided. They look at the fine details of the cooling system, the metallic structure of the brain, and the forty-two-hour integration process that placed Doug's mind into the machine.

"It says here that they connected each neuron of his brain." Julius says. "They'd attach a new neuron before severing the original. It took several technicians and three days. They'd wake him in intervals to keep his consciousness attached to the body."

Elizabeth gathers her brows over a cup of tea "His consciousness is the same as the original Doug?"

Julius glances over the pages again "According to the document, they'd ask if he felt the same as he did before the procedure. Each time, he said 'yes' and they'd continue."

"It's not like they had any other option." Elizabeth says.

Julius raises his brows "True."

Julius continues reading the pages, and Elizabeth takes a sip of her tea. She stares off at the space before her and takes a breath.

"If there's such thing as a soul…" Elizabeth says "… then is it the same as consciousness?"

Julius looks up from the page to her face.

She continues "If you were to teleport a person by destroying the atoms on one side, and assembling a replica somewhere else, is that the same person?" She presses her lips together then continues "Or is it a whole new person, as a whole new set of atoms? And would they believe that they were the original person on the other side? Or could they perceive the difference?"

Julius looks back at the pages. He glances them over to find if this idea was documented in the writing.

"I don't know." He says.

Elizabeth lowers her tea from her lips. "If he were able to perceive a difference, is it possible he'd lie about it?"

Julius pulls the pages down to his lap. "Why would he want to do that?" He asks.

Elizabeth looks at him with a side glance "You already know. He could have wanted to prove himself right; even if he wasn't." She points to the pages "And why is a printable analysis of the procedure documented in the long-term memory of the machine?"

Julius thinks a moment and gathers his brows "I have no idea… What if the copy of Doug wanted to be treated the same as the original, and he's not the same person?"

Elizabeth raises her brows "That's an idea." She winces at a thought and speaks aloud "But if he did that, then the original would be killing himself."

Julius shakes his head and looks at the pages again "Again, did he have any other option?"

Elizabeth nods.

Julius looks up again to see her staring off "Something's on your mind."

She sips her tea and takes a moment. She turns to look his way and places her arm over the back of her chair "That quartz has a lot more information than it did before."

Julius frowns his brow.

She places her tea on the table before her and sits back in the chair again "People can lie, Julius. For all kinds of reasons. To protect themselves and others, or for worse reasons."

"But if he's a machine, then he's not the man he claims he is. He's a copy; and machines don't protect themselves from the truth. Only others."

"He might be a machine. He might not. It all depends, if he transferred his consciousness. And even then, would you trust a machine copy over the original?"

"Right but now you're sounding paranoid. He even said he didn't want to be a part of the ship's system"

Elizabeth nods "That concerns me too."

Julius sits back "Why?"

Elizabeth shakes her head on a swivel "That doesn't add up with how he's behaved." She breathes deep "He's been heavily involved in many projects across all the departments. He's been eager to help, but now this. Now he doesn't want to be the most helpful he could possibly be."

Julius tightens a corner of his mouth "I'm convinced he could say ANYTHING and you'll be suspicious."

Elizabeth raises her hand to hold his thought. "Think about it. Doug doesn't have a face, or a voice. That would help us discern what he truly wants." Her eyes meet Julius "He could say anything, and we wouldn't be able to tell a lie from the truth. How do you buy someone's trust when you can't show honesty?"

Julius looks down in thought.

"You prove yourself with actions." She adds. "I don't believe he's really scared of an unforeseen consequence. I believe he's trying to buy our trust."

Julius nods "You're the one who's better at this kind of thing. So let's keep an open mind."

Elizabeth puts her tea down and shakes her head.

"I'm in over my head." She says.

Julius gathers his brows at the sight of her. He looks off and thinks a moment.

"This is why you have assistants." He says "You can't do it all yourself… You'll break your back trying to work without your team, so let me help out a little…"

Elizabeth cracks a smile at the floor. She feels the weight of the world lift yet again because of him.

Julius lifts his hand with a new thought.

"I have an idea to lure him out a bit." He says.

Elizabeth looks at him "Let's hear it."

Julius nods "He's very moved by his past, but OBJECTS won't throw you a curveball… They don't DEMAND a response."

Elizabeth grows confused "Yes?"

Julius smiles "Well… let me handle it."

He begins to laugh.

"I wanna surprise you." He adds.

"You can't tell me what it is?" She asks.

Julius shakes his head "No… but it's gonna be good, I promise."

CHAPTER 38
Strange Tides

*The last time my brother met James on Earth was
just two weeks before his move to the lunar base.
I wasn't there, but the two of them met with our
friend Gabe and some other students…*

On a side street in Malden, there's a bowling alley. Here, Curt's friends laugh together for the first time in years. Since the day of their graduation, no more than two or three friends have been united at a time. Gabe and Rosemary stand before the bowling lane. Curtis looks on as they laugh at something out of earshot. She wears a women's peacoat, and her hair is waved into perfection; each highlight recently done and blowdried for the day. Gabe's Kashmir sweater is fitted to his chest. His own coat rests on a couch in the seating area.

Curtis turns to look at the extended friends who happened to be in town. They're all dressed, but only half as well as the core group. Some others remain missing from the occasion. They're either late, or out of town and couldn't make it. Doug is busy setting up for his presentation, and no one has seen him yet.

Curtis turns to look at James. He finds his oldest friend looking back already. He's been watching Curtis observe the scene. They both smile at one another.

Gabe soon comes over to grab Curtis. He's followed by Rosemary, who shakes her head. "Oh no, please Gabe!"

"Dude, you need to hear what Rosie just said. You're gonna die."

Curtis stands straight and contracts the symptoms of their contagious laughter.

"What?" Curtis asks.

Rosemary blushes with a wide smile. Her cheeks are sore from perpetual laughter.

"I'll tell him." Rosemary says "So I went to get a coffee on the road trip out here" A pang of laughter comes again in a wave "The place where I stopped was about to close, and you know me, just a simple latte. I'm not a complicated woman."

Curtis nods "Every day at two P.M. on the dot."

She raises her hand in dismissal "Well, that was college. I've since changed." She combs through her hair with her fingers and lets it fall behind her shoulder "I was trying to stay awake to make good time but I stopped in as they were closing. I ran in just as the guy was about to clean the espresso machine and I screamed 'Wait, wait! Don't close up yet!' He says 'Ma'm, I'm sorry' and I pleaded." She giggles again. "I walked up all disheveled, looking a mess, and I say 'Please just do me quick, I'm easy'!"

Her voice begins to squeak in a plateau of hilarity, and Gabe wipes tears from his eyes. Curtis imagines the reaction of the barista. He laughs at the thought of a grown adult woman in a peacoat and impeccable attire, begging to be "Done quick" because she's "Easy".

Gabe is called away to the game as his turn comes up. Curtis and Rosemary stand alone for a moment, and she looks up at him, grown sincere.

"How are you, Curtis?" She asks.

Curtis becomes gentle with his eyes. It's something about the familiarity of her face, and the trust they've shared.

"I've been good." He says.

Before he can say anything more, she hugs him tight.

"I missed you." She says.

His arms wrap around her, and his chest meets her at his core.

"I missed you too." He says.

She grows limp in a way. As if her concerns melt in his presence.

"How's the little one?" Curtis asks.

She looks up and places her hand on his chest. One quick motion of excitement "Oh my god! I have pictures."

He laughs as she raises her phone.

"She's good!" Rosemary says. "Tucker is at home, watching her now."

Curtis looks up with his eyes. Her face still looks at her phone.

"And how are things going with him?" He asks.

She nods in a side-to-side way "He's good! He's just been busy. I think this is a good occasion for him. He needed more time with her; you know to bond."

"Does he at least make an effort?" Curt asks.

She wipes her nose with her sleeve "He does." Her tone falls as if to say it's not enough. "It's not really his fault if she feels neglected, and she won't remember at this age to have daddy issues."

Curtis nods with a faint smile at her joke "Well I'm transferring to Utah in a couple of months. There's a new job they want me to lead on."

"What part of Utah?" She exclaims "I'm a state away!"

"Close to Colorado. About two hours out."

Her eyes widen "Oh my god, you could meet her!"

Curtis nods "Exactly; and if ever you need it, I can come by to give you guys a break."

She holds a photo of her baby on the phone and looks up at Curtis. Her eyes are glossed with the light of the room. She looks softened from the previous excitement just moments ago.

"You don't need to do that." She says.

Curtis smiles "I'm serious."

Her head rests to one shoulder. She shifts her weight to sway her hips in a suggestion of care.

"I'd just be happy to see my friend." She says.

Before he can say so much as a word she lunges her arms around his waist again. He catches her and stands firm. His arms wrap around her shoulders, and his hand holds the back of her head. He laughs with her ear to his chest, but finds no words to say.

James takes a small wooden-looking ball off the ball rack and looks down the lane to the strange-shaped pins at the end. He notes their oddly symmetrical shape. A cylinder that widens at the middle and becomes thin at the bottom and top.

"I don't think I've ever seen bowling like this." James says. "It's strange-looking."

Rosemary lets go of Curtis to let him talk. James notices where he stood with her and becomes paralyzed in his words.

Curtis walks his way and shrugs. "My parents used to come here." He picks up one of the wooden balls "It looked weird to me too when I was a kid. I was used to the cartoons with the three holes and stuff."

"Yeah!" James says.

Gabe walks into the conversation "It's your turn, Curt."

Curtis looks up at the board. His name is highlighted in the list. He takes the ball, and the other friends look on as he rolls.

James looks to Gabe "It's like bowling in an alternate universe or something." He says.

"Because of the weird shape of the pins and stuff?" Gabe asks.

James laughs and agrees "Alright, so I'm not the only one thinking it." He says.

Curtis doesn't watch the ball as it rolls down the lane. Instead he rolls and turns to look at his friends. James and Gabe talk together. Rosemary stands to the side of the conversation. She watches Curtis, and Curtis smiles back. A hand in his peripheral vision steals his attention. Roger walks in toward the lane. His hand waves overhead for their attention.

Around their table, they eat wings and discuss memories. They fill each other in on the small details of their lives.

James nods in Gabe's direction "What's going on with you, these days? How's work?"

"It's fine." He replies without enthusiasm. "I don't want to do it forever, but it's good for now."

"What don't you like?" Curt asks.

Gabe shakes his head "Older guys acting like children. Factory floor is just full of different departments that COULD, but WON'T cooperate with one another. No sharing, nothing. I had a guy flip on me for using his pen. I told him to grow up."

"What an odd guy." James says.

"Can you imagine being petty like that at age forty-nine?" Gabe adds.

Curtis shakes his head "Jeez."

Gabe takes a sip of water, then leans back in his chair "And what do they have you guys doing on the moon?" he asks.

James inhales a deep sigh "Mostly routine work. Maintenance. The occasional study here and there."

After taking a bite of a wing, Gabe shakes his head and covers his mouth as he speaks "We've been your friends for almost a decade now. I think you can tell us what the studies are."

James' eyes widen as he nods "That's the thing though. I have little to no idea what's going on. There's a chance we start mining the asteroid belt in a few years, but if that's the plan, they haven't told me. We've been mining some minerals here and there on the moon, but nothing very important. The real money is miles away from the sun."

"So that's the next step." Curtis says "Mining the belt."

James shrugs "I think so. There's another thing I've heard rumors about, but only whispers."

The group becomes a crowd of curious faces.

Gabe opens a mobile chess game on his phone. He lays it on the table, and without hesitation, James gets ready to play against him.

"You guys know that interstellar object that came in two months ago?"

Gabe drags out an answer "Y-yeah?" he looks up from the phone. "It was a big deal. Doesn't happen much."

Curtis gathers his brows and leans back "People said it looked funny."

James nods "Yeah. A little too funny. It spun in a crazy way."

The two other scientists look at one another.

"How did they know how it spun?" Curt asks.

"A massive accumulation of data. Citizen scientists. It was poured into a database, and analyzed by some AI when they were done." James places a knight in a position that makes Gabe concerned for the game. James smiles at him but backs away and continues his sentence. "With enough images and records they knew what each angle was at any given time, and you know what that spin made?"

All of them shake their heads.

"A perfect artificial gravity, if you were to stand inside the object.."

Gabe backs away from the game without making a move.

"They think it was an alien craft?" Gabe asks.

James shrugs "There's a few other reasons to suspect it. The cigar shape reduces the chance of collision with small debris. And it accelerated after passing the sun."

Gabe interjects "Yeah, but they say that comets do that too. Accelerating away is normal. It's just that this time it didn't have an ion tail. Not all of them have an ion tail."

James shrugs again "Or it could have been solar sails like we have."

Everyone sits back. They take a moment to think.

Curtis looks around to see Rosemary thinking in silence. It's just the kind of puzzle she loves to solve. He smiles at this, but notices something else. In the heat of the conversation, Roger had disappeared. Curtis wonders why he's gone.

"I think that's why the probes are a higher priority than the mining." James says. "The mining is profitable, but the probe project they're trying to launch; would give us a look at our neighbors. There could be someone more powerful than US out there."

I never had the chance to ask my brother about
this. He passed away before I could write this entry

in our book. Subsequently, there's many occasions where I wish I asked more about him. In hindsight we enjoyed our time together too much to talk about these things, and for that I'm selfishly grateful.

I'll never know why they met that day, or what brought them to this conversation. All I know is that his friends heard rumors of interstellar warfare.

This is the only place the idea has been documented, and the United Zion Provisional Government has made it a point to keep our presence here a secret for now. We don't broadcast signals into space like we did on Earth. There's no telling who we might have upset; assuming there was anyone out there at all.

CHAPTER 39
Mechanized Dreams

Doctor Clay holds his wife's hand. Her mouth lies open. She's barely capable of saying anything.

Her sounds have reduced to a faint wheezing and the occasional groans of pain. She utters words for a glass of water, but nothing more. The words come between hours of rest.

Her eyes are closed, because she lacks the energy to keep them open. All the while Doug watches her closed lids.

He longs to see the blue depths of her eyes, and he won't miss the chance to see them for the last time.

He's stood here for far too long, so the nurse brings him a chair. His stomach aches with hunger but he won't leave. The nurse brings crackers and water, but they'll sit at her bedside, untouched.

She can't eat anymore. Their dinners together are only a memory now.

When they first met, they would get to know each other between classes. They'd look at one another over a cafeteria plate. They both feared they'd run out of things to say.

They think the same thing "*I remember that*".

Her hand rises, and motions once for him to move closer. He does, and she turns her head.

She begins with a whisper.

"I never deserved you." she says.

He looks into her eyes. They glint through failing features.

"Don't say that" he pleads.

His aperture blades adjust in the dark "Dreaming… Was that dreaming?"

The question is met with a cold metal hum across the empty distance; from the far corners of Doug's room.

CHAPTER 40
The Invention

The crowd shuffles their way into respective seats. The room reverberates with the sound of soft-spoken words.

The building beholds crimson curtains that hang before the tall windows. The walls are painted an off-white, and reach up to a ceiling held by pillars. From the ceiling hang brass chandeliers. Their polished arms are adorned with crystals and tipped with gold electric bulbs.

The mahogany creaks under the carpeted floor. The remaining crowd is seated.

Curtis recognizes the light bulbs as a reminder of an age long gone. He has seen them in photographs, and displayed in history books. His mill town to the north has many of these photos, and the town displays them as a legacy of their past. Although his family moved in from Medford just twenty years ago, long after the Industrial Revolution; he still called the same place his home. The streets have been paved since the time of horses, and now it's cars that drive along the streets of the Merrimack Valley. Even with the passage of time, it's the wooded paths he shared in common. The children of the 1890s walked those paths too; and the children still long before them.

With the dawn of electric light, his town was warmed with a subtle glow. That glow was the same as these old bulbs, emanating from the rims of these chandeliers.

"I never could appreciate this campus." James says to Curtis. "I was too busy being sleep-deprived."

"Pulling your hair out?"

"All-nighters."

Curtis smiles "Becoming addicted to coffee."

"Mom was scared."

Curtis laughs "Yeah, me too."

He looks around again at the rightful facade of an institute that has earned its respect.

Roger watches them look about. He turns around in his seat and looks for a face amid the crowd. It's the woman behind him who catches his eye.

"Professor Rayes!" He says to the woman.

The professor looks up at him and smiles "Hello!" She replies.

Roger leans inward "It's good to see you! I was wondering if you knew how Professor Bae is doing."

Professor Rayes looks off to the side "Oh, dear I'm sorry." She leans in to tell more "Professor Bae passed away last year."

Roger feels his excitement fall "Oh, that's terrible."

"Were you close?" Rayes asks.

Roger speaks in a sigh "Yeah, he was a family friend. He gave me some good advice a few years back."

She nods "He was a good man, and he had a long career. I'm sorry to tell you the news."

Roger thanks her, and begins to turn forward again.

"Sir?" She says.

Roger turns to look her way once more.

"Where are you working" She adds "If you don't mind me asking."

"Well…" His head cocks to the side as he draws the corner of his mouth "I was working for DARPA, that's how the professor helped me."

"And where are you now?"

"I'm still with DARPA, but I'm not sure where it's going. They might move me to a new project. Either that or… I don't know; I'll need to find some work soon."

The conversation continues, and James looks at Curtis with confusion.

Curtis shrugs his shoulders.

James leans in "Sounds like he might get laid off." He says.

Curtis shakes his head "Hell if I know, hell if I care."

They both look before them, and onward after that; to the edge of the stage, before the crowd. In contrast to the old building, a large metal machine slopes down toward the audience. It's like the wall to a great pyramid. The only thing breaking its surface is a rectangular shape. It protrudes outward, and stands in contrast to the flat surface. The box is at eye level with a seated human. Near the middle, off-center towards the top, there is a lens with closed aperture blades. Beneath it are the holes to a speaker.

"He's really done something big." James says. "What the hell is this thing?"

Curtis looks long at the machine "I have no idea."

Curtis hopes that this serves as some relief for Doug; that this defines his career and makes a success of him. He wishes fame and fortune for his friend; but something instills fear in Curtis. A fear that this project might have harmed him in some way. His long hours of work would imply sleep deprivation. His temperament has always been fragile, and his life has been lonely. It couldn't be easy to balance something of this magnitude between the hours of his day job. All the while he's managed years of grief and loneliness, presumably on his own.

The silence from Doug has been deafening over the past few years. Curt's heart aches in fear for his friend. His delicate friend, who can't be approached leisurely. He's needed time and space; but what is too much time, and too much space? Tonight will answer Curt's questions, and either relieve his anxiety, or mark the beginning of a new chapter in his friendship with Doug.

As the crowd begins to grow eager for the presentation, Doug takes the stage from a far corner of the hall.

An applause rises as he stands at a podium, off to the side of the machine. He dismisses the applause and leans toward the microphone. His eyelids, dark and tired. His hair, combed above his shaven face. His clothes, ironed and cleaned; and yet his gaze is blank and glossed.

He speaks with frail confidence "Hello everyone. Thank you for coming." He clears his throat, and touches the glass of water by the podium. "Some of you may know me and some of you may not. My name is Doctor Douglas Clay. I'm a bionics specialist. I have worked on biological hardware for many years and now have moved on to a new field. It's that field that I want to discuss today." He looks over the pages on the podium and back up to the crowd; through the crowd. "Biology and tech blurred into one. Borrowing from nature and making it stronger, better, perhaps immortal." He pauses. He reaches for the pages before him, diligently. He moves them along the podium without a purpose. While looking down, he continues to speak, and soon meets his eyes to the crowd again. Now they show purpose. "I have made a new database, complimented by a new form of mechanized biology. One that will prolong life. Keep death away forever. Better yet, it can do more."

Curtis looks around at the faces. They show the same scrunched brows. Looking back at the podium, Doug shakes his head. He lifts his script from the mantle, and drops his hand on top of the pages as if to give up on the script entirely.

Doug sighs "There's no more I can say without showing you. So without further delay, let's get right to it."

Doug looks over at his assistant. A young man who slouches beneath a lab coat. He looks at Doug with a mechanical readiness.

Doug raises his hand as if to toast "Jamie, can you hit the power?"

Jamie snaps around on his heels. He moves towards the fuse box and pulls three switches on the circuit breaker.

The sound of electric fans rip the air from within the machine. The motors grow louder. They growl. The computer calculates with a relentless nature. Inner mechanisms clang and clack. The speaker screeches. It hisses with white noise. The fans continue to roar up into a great precipice until finally, the motors come down. The clicking ceases. Equilibrium is reached, and the fans come to a gentle gust. The computing meets a silent motor noise. It comes in hypnotic waves here and there. It sounds like a giant desktop, resting on a home screen.

The air sits still. In a shifty jagged motion, the aperture blades open; as if grains of sand hinder their motion. The machine comes to life.

Doug walks from the podium to the center of the room. He stands before his machine, peering at the making of his own hands. He looks for something; a sign. His lids smile, but his mouth hangs open. He wonders for a moment, and looks into the lens. Peering deep into the aperture blades, he looks with a whole new phenomenon.

Curtis watches his friend, and then the machine. He feels his stomach churn suddenly, but thinks his deduction is a mere fantasy. He is wrong.

Doug's voice comes in a trill as he pries to ask who hides behind the lens.

"Rebecca?" He asks.

Curtis begins to sweat.

All is silent save the sound of Rosie's hands as they clap over the bridge of her nose.

"Hello?" The female voice replies.

Some gasp, and others whisper.

A woman is heard from behind "Oh my god." She says.

The air escapes from Doug's mouth "Babe, I'm here."

"Doug." The voice comes again.

"Yes honey. It's me, Doug."

The strangers in the crowd begin to stand. The uncanny valley descends here, to this room. The questions come in murmurs.

"Is that his wife?" A woman asks.

"Oh no..." A man mutters.

Roger stands and makes an immediate break for the exit. He passes Rosie and takes her hand.

"Come on." He says.

Rosie follows. All the while, she can't take her eyes off the machine.

"Doug" The machine begins "I don't feel.... good."

As Doug tries to speak, the tears leak out from a fighting face. "You've been gone for so long."

"Doug." The machine says.

"Yes dear."

"I can't live... this way. I feel... Not right."

Her pauses are like a streaming video being halted to buffer.

"I have a plan." Doug says. "You won't be in that body for long."

"I need.... rest... need to.... die."

His brows fall in confusion. "No. We need to fix you." He sniffles. His tone reaffirms "We can make you better."

"Doug...."

"We'll fill the gaps in your mind. I promise."

"I must... Die."

Doug shakes his head "No." He kneels before the machine "You don't need to. You only degraded a little bit...."

"No... Doug..."

Doug breathes heavily "What are you talking about? I've spent my whole life making this for you."

His tone changes, and Curtis looks toward James. The two exchange a glance.

A stranger in the back mutters "Uh oh..."

A woman takes her friend's hand "I think we should go..."

James nods and moves out of the seating area. He approaches Doug.

Curtis lands his hand on Gabe's shoulder "Can you get the people out of here? He needs a minute."

Gabe nods and turns toward the crowd. He walks backward toward the machine and waves his hands above his head "Everyone, we're taking a short break. We'll continue later. This is an intermission."

Curt moves to catch up with James in a stride. He points toward the assistant in the corner of the room. The petrified boy looks at Curtis.

"You too, kid." Curtis calls over. "Get everyone out for a break."

James stands beside Doug and tries to touch his shoulder. Doug pushes the hand away.

Doug stares down at the machine "This has become my life's work. I'll perfect this, just give me time."

Curtis runs to his side.

"Doug." He says.

Doug looks back at Curtis with sadness in his eyes. They break from the sorrow and turn to anger.

The machine remains silent.

Doug demands a response "Well?!"

Curtis looks back to see most of the room has emptied. The last of the crowd moves through the doors. He looks back at Doug again.

"Say something!" Doug pleas.

Curtis speaks gently "Doug, give it some time. We need a minute. We'll figure this out."

Doug puts up his hand, signaling Curtis to stay away.

"Wait." He says.

Curtis sighs.

"I can bring you back." Doug says to the machine.

"I... am gone... my mind... not... complete...."

Doug's arms grow stiff. They thrust toward the ground "We can fill in the gaps! I can bring you back! I need you to do this!"

Doug's voice brings Gabe to march forward.

Curtis never takes his eyes away from Doug. From behind his back Curtis signals James to stand by the control panel.

Without a moment, Gabe takes the initiative himself. James instead blocks Doug's path to Gabe.

"Doug... I'm gone..."

Doug looks to see Gabe standing by the circuit breaker. Doug begins to run, but James stands in his way. Curtis grabs Doug, and Doug grows violent.

"Don't!" Doug yells "Don't you fucking dare, Gabe!"

Curtis struggles with him. He wraps his arms around Doug, trying to subdue him.

James lifts his hands in an effort to ease the tension "Doug, calm down!"

"You'll kill her!" Doug screams.

Gabe looks back with disappointed anger. He throws the switches at once.

Doug falls limp.

The blades of the lens close, and the fans fall into silence.

Doug gasps and screams through tears of anger. He throws Curtis off and pushes James. James hits the floor and stands immediately. He moves to block Doug's path again.

Gabe crosses the room.

Doug stops before James.

Gabe's concern is evident in his repulsion.

"What is wrong with you?!" Gabe says "You made an ass of yourself!"

Doug begins to march forward and James takes a step back.

Curtis moves to Doug's face. Doug shoves him, but Curtis rises to grab him once again.

"Let go of me!" Doug says.

Doug looks at Gabe who breathes a short laugh from his nose.

Doug roars "I'm gonna beat that smile off your face!"

In the increased struggle, Curtis takes Doug to the floor.

Gabe looks down on the writhing animal in Curtis' arms. "You're no idiot, Doug. Snap out of it!"

Doug wants to punch anyone except Curtis. As much strength as it may take, his grasp is still gentle and kind.

"Doug, listen to him." Curtis says.

Gabe shakes his head and scoffs "I'd like to see you try, you pussy."

Curtis is hit with an unexpected writhing in his arms. Doug breaks free and stands. Curt holds on to his sleeve "You idiot, Gabe!" The sleeve breaks from his fingers and Doug's fist flies at James' face. The fist meets his nose in a blinding millisecond.

Doug charges at Gabe, but James makes an automatic motion. He hooks Doug with his arm and thrusts him back into Curtis.

James looks stern at the man who just punched him. He inhales a deep sigh and speaks "Please don't do that, Doug."

Doug turns his attention to Gabe and screams "How does it feel to murder?"

Gabe laughs at him "You turned the woman you loved into a lab rat! You killed her all over again, all by yourself!"

"Hey!" Curtis screams. "Shut the fuck up, Gabe!" He stands to step between the two men.

Gabe clenches his jaw shut.

Doug stands and looks at them.

Curtis turns to Doug and speaks firm "Doug, she's a prisoner in there;

and it's not the real Becca. That's not your wife."

"I don't fucking care!" Doug says as he walks back and forth like an animal protecting its meal.

"Listen to yourself." Curtis pleads.

"I've been cheated and robbed every step of the way!" Doug adds. He points at Curtis "You have your brother but I have no one! She was everything!"

Gabe laughs "You made her everything. Whatever else you had, you neglected it."

"Hey!" Curtis says.

"You never reach out or answer calls." Gabe adds.

Doug spits at the ground "Why would I want to waste my time with people who don't give a damn about me?"

Gabe raises his voice "You wouldn't know if we cared!"

"Because I know you!" Doug adds "I can't trust you! You pick your favorites and I'm not one of them!"

"Everyone else seems to trust me just fine, Doug. You don't talk to anyone. If nobody knows you, it's your fault. You've always been a fly on the wall; you never belonged!"

James stands before Gabe and looks him in the eyes "Stop." he says.

"Well at least you can be honest for once." Doug says.

Doug turns to grab his jacket from the coat rack. He slams the side exit door. He walks into the cold night.

Curtis watches and shakes his head. He looks at Gabe.

Outside the door Doug sees Rosie and Roger. They smoke a cigarette on a small platform at the exit. Neither of them say a word.

As Doug descends the steps to the lawn, Rosie almost follows. Roger grabs her arm.

"No." he says "Let him be."

Doug hears Rosemary question him like a student asking a teacher to use the restroom. He wishes she would insist and follow. At least someone would be as bold as Becca if she did.

Back in the room Curtis looks at Gabe with shame. He shakes his head again.

"What the FUCK were you THINKING?!" Curtis exclaims.

"Fuck him!"

"Fuck YOU, Gabe!"

"Fuck me?! He's complaining about a dead wife, who in all honesty, wasn't anything special."

"He's hurt!" James adds.

"He's lost his mind!" Gabe retorts.

"How would you feel if your own family died?" Curtis adds. His voice falls weak as the words come out.

"Yeah, I'm sorry Curt, but I can't relate. There's a lot of people I'd love to drop dead in my family."

Curtis looks down and shakes his head.

"His problems seem mighty small to me." Gabe adds "I went hungry for three weeks because dad was nowhere to be seen and mom spent the welfare check on a bag of what I thought was sea glass." He shrugs "I don't fucking know what to tell you. He's a pussy."

Curt nods "I get it. But it doesn't mean his problems aren't real. You can't say shit like that. He's quiet, but he belongs with us."

"Not with me he doesn't."

"Whatever, Gabe." Curt dismisses.

Curtis looks at James standing silent. His nose is discolored, and blood streaks from a cut on his face.

"Are you good?" Curtis asks.

James sighs and replies "Yeah. Yeah I'm fine."

"Your nose." Curt says, pointing to his own face.

James feels his "I almost forgot." He then laughs "Little shit got me good." He looks at the blood smeared on his hand. "Took everything I had not to clock him."

Gabe paces about "Look, maybe I can forgive him some time, but not soon." He shakes his head "I get it but I'm still mad."

"You should be... but you know he didn't mean it."

Gabe nods at the floor "I know."

Curtis draws the corner of his mouth "I was an asshole too. I wasn't helping."

Gabe shakes his head "No." his eyes meet Curtis briefly, then he nods "You got me riled up, but I needed it. I was being a prick."

"I could've said it better."

The three of them look at one another. James smiles, and so does Curtis.

"What?" Gabe asks.

The two laugh.

"Nothing. It's just a ridiculous argument." Curtis says.

There is a pause as they all think.

Curtis looks to the exit and breaks the silence "I'll go find Doug. I'll talk with him. I'll call you guys in a bit."

Gabe agrees, and James looks to Curt.

"You'll be good on your own?" James asks.

Curtis nods "I'll be fine. I'll meet up with you later."

He leaves them in the room, standing with the monolith that Doug made.

On his way out the door Curtis passes Roger and Rose. They look at him with fearful eyes.

"Which way did he go?" Curt asks.

They both point toward the river.

Curtis nods "Thanks."

Down the lawn of the institute's main building, Curtis looks around. He recalls where Doug might be. He thinks for a moment but remembers a faint memory.

Doug's favorite spot along the Charles River. A bridge toward the edge of Harvard Square. Not all the way to the square, but just far enough where the whole city can be seen on the water. There the lights shine from towering buildings, above quiet neighborhoods, and gridless streets.

Doug stands over the river, looking down into its black waters. He looks up at the city and remembers a simple time when he would wander without a care. In a way he longs for those days and their simplicity. On the other hand, he enjoys his freedom outside of the institution's gates. If only she didn't have to go so soon. Maybe he could have the best of both worlds again.

Curtis walks from the end of Cambridge to about ten feet away from Doug. The traffic between the two cities is quiet as small snowflakes begin to fall.

"You alright, Doug?" Curtis asks.

Doug nods. His back illuminated by Christmas lights, and his face hidden by the shadow of the river.

"You're gonna get cold out here." Curt adds.

"I'm already cold."

Curtis takes his jacket off but Doug's voice cuts sharp.

"And I like it."

Curtis puts the jacket down.

Doug gestures a hand to reject the jacket "So please, save it."

Curtis walks forward and tucks the jacket under his arm. He meets Doug's side, but not too close. He too looks out at the city.

"If you're freezing, then I'll freeze with you." Curtis says.

Doug shakes his head "Don't do that."

Curtis shrugs "I want to." He places the jacket on the side of the bridge beneath his forearms "Couldn't think of a better way to go."

Doug looks at Curtis with a small grin in exchange for the stupidity.

Curtis looks out and shakes his head "Doug… I'm amazed." He looks over at his friend again "What you made in there is incredible.

Doug withdraws from the conversation in his posture.

Curtis goes on "I'm worried about you losing yourself."

Doug is seeped into the same depression as before. He can see his breath before the snowflakes as he speaks "I'm fine." He says.

"Doug you're not fine."

Curtis watches his face fall into the same subdued sorrow. His eyes begin to change focus from landmark to landmark.

"You ever feel like everyone secretly hates you?" Doug asks.

"Secretly, why? I wouldn't…"

"Just… stop, Curt. And listen."

Curtis stops speaking.

"So your answer is no."

"Well yeah. I…"

"Curt."

He stops again and listens for a chance to find common ground.

"I feel that all the time…" Doug begins "…and I don't know what to do about it. Anywhere I go I see incompetent people pretending they know something. People who don't understand how I feel claiming they get me. What's worse is that I can't trust anybody. I've put trust in people before and I've been let down every time… I gave Becca my word that we'd have a life together. Holding to my word meant a lot to her, and many times I let her down. I don't want to do it again. Yes, we had rough patches, and yes, she said she wanted to die and I don't know why. I think she can't see the end. She was short-sighted like that sometimes. But if I can't trust myself to keep a promise, then who the hell is worth trusting? I've betrayed every moral I had to keep this project alive. I can't abandon it now. Worst of all is, I'm doing it for the one person I wish was here to help me. I just want my wife back; to give my life meaning again."

"You have plenty of meaning." Curtis says "And you've got me and the guys." He smiles "Gabe lost his cool, but even he was telling me that he didn't mean anything he said."

Doug's face remains downstream and his eyes fixed on the water. He shakes his head. "Even if he admits that much; Curt, I can't put that trust on you. Let's face it, I'm a needy emotional mess. We even joke about it, but honestly I can't help it. The only thing I can lean on is math and science. Math is always factual, so it never lets me down, and better yet, I don't wanna bother you with my bullshit."

Doug rises from leaning on the bridge. He begins walking back into Cambridge.

"What about the Doug I knew before her?" Curt says. He walks up to Doug's side.

Doug stops for Curtis. He doesn't look Curtis in the eyes, but listens.

"Don't let this thing kill YOU too." Curtis adds "Do what you can to take care of yourself first. Please."

Doug knows when he can't argue anymore and lets Curtis believe him with a faint nod "I will."

Doug keeps walking and Curtis turns to join him.

CHAPTER 41
Hereafter

The early morning light brings a blue sky without the sun. A two-lane highway carries traffic through New England's range of rounded mountains.

Motorbikes rumble through the green valleys of summer. They cross bridges over falling mountain waters and stop in the parking lots with scenic vistas. Behind such a group, Curtis holds the wheel to a new car. His athletic pants are insulated, and yet light. His light set of layers are packed away in a school bag. They barely fit with the dried fruits, water bottles, and granola bars. To his side, James attempts to sleep in the passenger's seat. Their coffee mugs vibrate from the sound of pavement under rolling tires.

Curtis touches his friend's arm "Hey, bro…"

James raises his face from the seatbelt "I can't sleep in cars."

"You wanna set up camp and start tomorrow?"

James shakes his head "I'm good. I'll knock out when we get back."

"We're coming around the turn." Curtis says.

James stretches and smiles "Nice."

The highway comes to a hill which falls behind. They ascend to a precipice. The bikers slow down, and so does Curtis. The range of peaks open to a valley of green. In the distance, a rounded mountain is split into a cliff. It stands to the west of the highway. To the east of the road, the forest runs up to a tall, steep ridge. A granite spire spines atop the shrubs at its weathered peaks.

They descend once more into the valley road. They pass the expanse between the view and the notched valley. Through the other side they veer right, and take an exit to the east. In the back of the eastern ridge, they pass through a gathering of birch trees.

James remembers this area well, for in the fall they sing bright yellow on the birch bark. This grouping of yellow forest stands a half a mile in diameter. Afterward, the road meets a mixed wood of reds, oranges, and green pines. Now, in the summer heat, the silver bark of the trees shine under a dark green canopy. Their silver is made blue in the morning air.

At the base of a mountain, Curtis pulls into a dirt parking lot. The mouth of the forest opens to a dark pathway lined with wooden planks. Boulders jut out in the ground, and the path bends around them. Peering in the dark, the roots of oak trees keep dirt where riverbeds would have washed the soil away.

"Alright, let's hit that tree line." James says.

He passes Curtis with his pack already mounted on his shoulders. He jumps into the riverbed of pebbles, and Curtis follows behind.

The swarming mass of mosquitos come from the warm marshes and chase the boys up the mountain.

"I forgot spray." James says.

Curtis huffs in pace "Keep moving and they won't get you."

James breaks into a near sprint up the path. Huffing behind him, Curtis tries to keep up.

The day grows brighter, and the sun shines warmer. Compared to where they began, the breeze is cooler. The air is thinned to a comfortable temperature, and the mosquitos have given up their chase a mile and a half ago. The trees are smaller, and the pines grow more prevalent than the oaks, birches, and maples.

Along the banks of a rapid mountain stream, a line of pines hold the path from falling in. The boys stop for a while and look into the clear pool of ever-changing water. It is fed by two waterfalls parted by a lone standing division of land, kept in place by a lone, small pine tree. Their faces feel a chill in the air, and the faint spray of splashing water. A tumbling spill, and a crash onto a bed of boulders. Rising from the base of the fall, a frothing blue cluster of bubbles dissipate. The stream continues to ripple around granite boulders, then spills down the mountain behind them.

They press onward up the mountain until nothing is left but short pines. The once roaring stream is now a trickling layer atop the granite bulge in the mountainside. At the side of such a spot, the boys look out toward the landscape behind them. Nearly a cliff is all that stands between them and the bed of trees a mile below. Down there the mosquitoes lie, the stream crashes, and the land is flat. Up here, the mountain face is sheer, the streams are but trickles on rocks, and the only sound is of water and the faint mountain breeze. A lone bird will chirp every few moments. Their nest lies amid the green mossy beds where flowers lie atop the dew in the mid-morning air.

Up the path, the boys find the tree line. A landscape of boulders in the sky where nothing but large outcrops stand higher than knee height. Not a sound in the air, and not a living creature in sight. Here, Curtis takes a rock from the ground and places it on a pile. It stands man-made in the wild landscape; fed by travelers over many years.

He turns to James with wincing eyes "What time is it?"

James pulls up a watch "It's almost noon. We have until two."

Curtis nods, then looks back as if in afterthought "Do you have the energy to peak it?"

"I'm not the one I'd be worried about."

Curtis shrugs "I have it in me."

The boys move onward after a brief break. Their legs a little tired and rigid after the stop, but not unsafe. A long path takes them atop a ridge, which is met, at either side, with a view of the world. The crown of the world is adorned with lesser mountains; and its jewel is the large peak on which they stand. The almighty territory of the mountains is as yet, beyond the conjuring of human hands.

At the pinnacle of the land's jewel, the men stand atop the highest boulder. They descend into a bowl-shaped landing. Here a sign tells of the peak and its history. Their ears find silence in this place; unlike anywhere else in the world.

The two men sit with their bags at their sides and begin digging for food. At the bottom of James' bag, he finds dried mangos. Curtis finds a bag of chips and trail mix. They each pull out water and watch the sun fall from the top of the sky.

Soon the hour strikes three, and they begin their return journey in haste. They race the sun down to the earth below, and make it out of the forest in time for a red setting star amidst the clouds. It hangs on the edge of the land, over rolling hills of green.

After a drive in the dark, the men reach their campsite. A fire pit, and a flat plane boxed in by a rock wall. The stars look down from the breezy sky. The arm of the Milky Way brushes across the darkness above. The ascending embers pale before the majesty, but they give the warmth of home on Earth.

"What did you bring to cook?" James asks.

"Some sausages from the gas station." Curtis says.

"When we stopped after the hike?"

Curtis nods.

James gathers his brows "I didn't see you get those."

Curtis smiles "Yeah, you're not gonna get food poisoning. Relax, pal."

"Oh, I didn't think that." James laughs "I just didn't see you get them."

Curtis looks up to the stars as he did over twenty years ago.

James watches him

"What?" James asks.

Curtis looks back down and reaches for a marshmallow "It was this campsite where my mom put me out on an air mattress. She was making the tent with my dad. My older brother was kinda helping, but I was too tiny." He sticks the marshmallow at the end of a wooden skewer and places it over the fire "I was on my back, looking up at the sky. I was an infant. You know those brief flashes of memory you sometimes have?"

"Yeah."

Curtis nods "It was one of those." He turns the skewer to find a perfect brown puff at the end of it. "I knew my destiny was there."

"And that led you to become a materials specialist?"

Curtis nods "A guy told me once… He was a scientist or something… He said 'People who study the small world help us travel the big world.'" His finger points up toward the sky.

James looks at Curtis.

Curt smooshes the fluff into a s'more.

James reaches for the pan in his bag, then puts his hand out toward Curtis "Where's those sausages? You need real food."

Curtis passes him the meat in plastic wrapping. With a mouth full of sweet chocolate and graham crackers, he mutters some words.

"Don't judge me." He says.

James laughs "I'll judge all I want."

He places the sausages on the pan, pulls out a knife, and begins cutting it into small bits.

"That's why you and Rosemary didn't work out." James says.

Curtis gathers his brows "Again with people talking about me and Rosemary. What's with that?"

James raises his brows "Oh, so you haven't noticed?" He giggles "I saw you two the other day."

Curtis nods. He can't think of the other day without thinking about Doug, but he shoves that thought to the back of his mind.

"She got pretty handsy." Curtis admits.

"You think?" Says James "She has a whole ass husband and family and still she wants you."

He looks over at Curtis. He has a mouth full of marshmallow, and it spews out from between his fingers.

James gestures his hand at him like a display.

"Look at you!" He says "You're a grown-ass man, but you're like a little kid!"

Curtis starts laughing through his nose while his mouth is occupied chewing.

"Unbelievable!" James adds "You're eating your s'more; oblivious to the woman who's been practically hunting you all these years."

Curtis shakes his head and vocalizes before he swallows.

"Yeah, but that's gross." He says "Imagine what that would mean…"

James nods with a tinge of bitterness.

"You wouldn't be the first person." He says.

Curtis nods. The energy of the conversation dies.

James tries to bring it back by recalling the prior topic.

"Do you know when I decided I'd go to the moon someday?" says James.

"I think you told me once, but I don't remember."

James stops cutting at the realization of something missing. He looks around and finds it. He gives the pan a dash of olive oil, and continues cutting "I had a dream when I was a young boy that I was looking out the window from my bedroom; and the whole town looked just as it always did, except for one thing."

"What was that?" says Curtis.

"The moon was a crescent shape, and its dark side had this web of city lights. I was maybe six or seven, but I knew somehow that they sent ships from there into deep space. It was way bigger than the little base they have up there now, and I wanted to be a part of it." James finishes cutting the last sausage. He puts the pan on the grate which hinges over the fire. "I woke up and told my mom I'd be a spaceman. I didn't even know what an 'astronaut' was yet…" He laughs and flips the sausage around.

Curtis nods "And now you're on your way to the moon."

James looks up at him and smiles. At the sight of Curt's face, James' eyebrows gather. He looks him over and notices a disturbance within his friend.

"What's on your mind?" James asks.

Curtis looks at him as if he's been figured out in some lie. He gives a guilty smile.

"I'm proud of you…" says Curtis "… I just feel like I'm moving so slowly. Not as fast as you or Doug…"

James nods his head from side to side to indicate some level of agreement. He shrugs his shoulders and clarifies.

"You're doing something more difficult than I am." says James.

Curtis looks off into the fire and thinks.

"People have gone to the moon before." says James "No one's fabricated new materials that the world's never seen… At least not like you're doing."

Curtis agrees a little in a nod.

James smiles at him.

"You're doing things that we only thought a god could do until now… It'll take longer; but you're the one they'll write books about, and not me."

CHAPTER 42
Manning

Doctor Hoyt removes his glasses. Their polished gold trim shines in the light of Doctor Clay's room. The microfiber cloth drapes into the air at his fingertips. It falls over his hand and outlines his palm as he cleans the glass lenses.

"I'm sorry things turned out the way they did, Doctor Clay." Hoyt places the glasses over his nose. "Your machine has a name. It's named after the child you would have had, isn't it?"

"Yes." The mechanical voice chimes "Tommy. And the other machine you saw was Alyssa, the name we would have given a daughter."

"Was Alyssa functioning at the time of Tommy's activation?" Hoyt asks.

"It was a failed experiment. If you read the files, her mind was never complete enough to operate. To finish the project we needed a full mind, and not a cadaver."

"That's an impersonal word to use for your wife." Hoyt says.

"In the end that's all she was in the project. I had to let go of my dream; I was not bringing her back."

Hoyt breathes through his nose in the silence. He stares at the floor with his lips sealed.

His brows tens as his lips part "She would be proud." His head rises to look into the lens "In all the years we've lived on Zion, we never thought an invention like yours was even possible." He looks at his notes once more "And you don't remember much from that point onward?"

"Everything becomes a blur." Clay says. His aperture blades rest still "It was like living the same day over and over, working for this project. Somewhere along the way it goes blank. I was preparing to enter the machine. The procedure was scheduled and I went to bed. The following morning is fuzzy, but it was the day of the operation."

Hoyt tenses his brows "I wonder why." He stares off in thought, then looks sidelong at his notes "I think we're finished for the day, Doug. I want to thank you so much for opening up to me. I know it's hard, but you've helped me greatly."

"Of course Doctor Hoyt. Thank you for listening. I'll look forward to our next appointment."

Hoyt smiles "And so will I."

***

In his office, Doctor Hoyt looks over his notes. This compilation of facts leaves him only one option. He sends out a message to the department heads, and waits for them to arrive.

The Captain enters the room. He's followed by Elizabeth, Morris, Manning, Linda, and Monica.

"Have a seat everyone." Hoyt says "I've narrowed down our options, and we only have one choice."

As everyone is seated, the Captain begins "And what is that, Doctor?"

"Well" Hoyt begins "There isn't sufficient evidence to conclude that he's a danger, but there isn't evidence to prove he's NOT dangerous. It's my recommendation that we remain cautious, and don't give Clay access to the ship."

They all stare intensively.

Hoyt continues "Doctor Clay built that body out of devotion to his craft, and it started as a dream to bring his wife back to life. By telling you this, I'm breaking patient confidentiality, but this isn't an ordinary patient. This isn't ordinary at all."

"That's so sad." Linda says.

"So he made that machine out of love." Morris adds.

"And pain." Hoyt says. "It's likely that Curtis Mandel didn't mention him because of it."

"They really knew each other?" Manning asks.

"He knew him very well. They were close friends, and he knew Curtis in a way we couldn't imagine."

"There was a postcard we found in his apartment." Elizabeth adds. "It was addressed to Douglas from Curtis Mandel." She nods "They were really close."

"That's so crazy." Monica says "To know him personally."

Morris smiles at her "That's like being friends with Leonardo DaVinci or Albert Einstein."

"Exactly." Monica says.

Hoyt smiles "I know. He had a sense of humor, and he was a good friend to Doug. He helped him when he could, and he offered a trust that Doug desperately needed."

Hoyt looks up to see the Captain's proud smile. Hoyt smiles back, equally proud of the Captain's family legacy.

Hoyt looks at his notes once more to speak, but his thought is interrupted.

"Why don't we trust him, though?" Manning asks.

Hoyt shakes his head "It's not that we don't trust him. The Doug in that machine is affected by many aspects of his past; but he's worth trusting. We just can't compromise the mission. It's best if we analyze him back on Zion."

"That's more than ten years from now." Connor adds.

"I know, but it's a risk assessment." Hoyt says.

"That's a long time." Connor emphasizes.

"I think it's best we follow his advice." Elizabeth says. "If he has control of anything on the ship, he could mess with our experiments, even yours in the gardening lab."

"How?" Manning asks.

Elizabeth shrugs "If he got upset for some reason, he could take it out on you. I don't know. We should just follow the procedure of figuring this out."

"Says the woman who never follows protocol." Manning says.

Elizabeth is taken aback "When?" She asks.

"Using the historical department's computers when we arrived?" Manning says "Sifting through the artifact room before the items were cleared?"

"You already cleared them!" Elizabeth says.

"We hadn't done our second test yet" Manning scolds "You could have killed everyone with a contaminant."

"He's right." The Captain says.

Elizabeth feels unjustly accused.

"That being said, Connor…" The Captain continues "This is VERY different."

Manning breathes a huff "Different how?"

The Captain shakes his head and gestures his hand at Doctor Hoyt.

"The first test came back as a threat." He says.

Manning relaxes his shoulders and bites his teeth together. He looks to Doctor Hoyt.

Doctor Hoyt looks at Manning, then turns his head to look about him, at the other faces "Be smart about how you treat him. He's very intelligent. Even before he had that mind and body, he made a miracle happen. He's capable of more than you might think." He looks at Elizabeth "I'll write up a report for you so you can understand." He looks around again. "He's done incredible things. He's made more than just that body. He's worldly and resourceful. He's adamant on doing things his own way. There are reasons to believe he can be impulsive. Be kind and understanding.

He's not a bad person by any means; but he's been confused before. He needs people he can trust to look out for his well-being. Okay?"

They all agree with the doctor, and with a smile he thanks them for coming.

Elizabeth returns to the engineering lab just as Julius returns from the cafeteria. She approaches her work, but Julius hangs up his lab coat.

"You saw the message I just sent you?" Elizabeth asks.

Julius looks at his tablet to see the message from moments ago, wherein Elizabeth describes what just happened.

"What the hell is with that?" Elizabeth asks.

"With what?" Asks Julius.

"Manning" She says.

She notices he's removed his lab coat.

"Where are you going?" She asks.

"Cut-bot." Julius says "You wanna come talk while I get my hair cut?"

Elizabeth agrees and joins him.

∗∗∗

Julius sits in the chair and activates his invention. He selects the same haircut as usual and the machine gets to work. Clippers and buzzers move into action. Appendages hold his hair and allow the sheers to clip a specified length.

"So what's up?" Julius asks.

Elizabeth tries to recall the point she was going to make.

"Oh, that's right." She says "Manning; I'm sick of him being so bothered by me."

Julius frowns his face in agreement, unable to move his head while the cut-bot works.

363

Elizabeth goes on "I just want to get along with him. He's smart, but he's stubborn. He thinks his work is the most important thing we're here for."

"To give him credit" Julius says "He's the one working hardest at terraforming Zion."

"That's true" Elizabeth says "But there's other things he needs. The data we gather is helping him too."

Julius raises his brows "Use that argument next time he gives you grief."

The cut-bot finishes the top of his head and works on the sides. The buzzers turn to start shaving down his sideburns.

"It's never come to a point where I've needed to say that." She says "It's like there's something more, but I don't know what it is."

Julius smiles "You know what I think?"

Elizabeth looks up at his smiling face "What?"

He flinches his brows up; unable to move as the machine takes care of his neck.

Elizabeth deduces what he's thinking. She shakes her head.

"If you're gonna say what I think…"

"Oh!" says Julius "So you know?"

Elizabeth shakes her head "If it's what I think, I don't need to…"

"I think it's time we took a look in Doctor Hoyt's office." says Julius.

"No!" Elizabeth says "Do you have any idea how much trouble we'd be in?"

Julius laughs "You know, there's no cameras in his office…"

"Julius, you're being an idiot."

The cut-bot finishes its job and rises away from Julius.

He stands and shrugs "Pin the blame on me."

"Julius…" She begins.

Julius marches out the door.

"Come!" He says.

Elizabeth follows, despite her desire to stay behind. He marches his way to Doctor Hoyt's office and Elizabeth is torn between decisions. She wants to know, but not this badly. Her orders are being undermined, but she wonders if there's an unforeseen benefit to letting Julius go. She's not certain but lets things play out.

They pass the engineering labs, Clay's room, and in the hall before the office door, Julius sees motion in the light of the therapy room. He moves to take refuge behind some exposed pipes. He motions for Elizabeth to follow, and she squeezes into the space between the pipes and the wall. The shadowy nook makes their presence a well-kept secret.

"This is stupid." She whispers.

"Shh."

The door to Doctor Hoyt's office opens, and the therapist takes a moment at the doorway. He double-takes at his office, wondering if he's left something. When he feels satisfied, having gone down the mental list of things he needs to take, he reaches to release the lock of the door to let it close.

Hoyt stops short of closing the door and shrugs. He breathes a laugh through his nose with a shake of his head.

He thinks to himself *"You're gonna forget SOMETHING, Arnold. You know you will…"*

He steps away from the door and moves down to the crossroad of the adjoining hall. He stops there, then looks back and forth.

"Oh, right." He says.

He steps to the left and makes his way toward Doctor Clay's room.

Julius listens to his footsteps fade. At the cue of silence, he decides it's now or never.

Elizabeth follows him from out of the pipes and trails behind toward the door.

At the doorway, Julius peaks around the corner. No one is inside.

Julius looks back to see a worried face. He smiles at her, then steps into the office.

"Jules…" She follows behind him and watches him approach the desk "I can't be responsible for this."

Julius sifts around the desk "You're not." He says "Imagine what the answer could be. What's Manning's 'dark past'?"

"None of our business!" She says.

Julius comes to a journal. He flips through the pages and comes to a point where he scans each page for a little over a second. He looks the pages over, one after another. After about seven pages, he closes the journal and places it where it was found.

Elizabeth watches his back as he stands still. Julius doesn't move for a while, then turns around.

He isn't smiling anymore.

"What?" Elizabeth asks.

"Come on." He says.

Julius takes Elizabeth's hand. He pulls her into the hall but the sound of steps paralyze him. He rushes behind the pipes again. Elizabeth moves into the pipes, squeezing through the tight space yet again.

Doctor Hoyt rounds the corner at the moment when they're out of view. He enters his office and fumbles around his desk.

A laugh can be heard.

"I knew it." He says.

Doctor Hoyt leaves his office with the journal in hand. He stops at the door and releases the lock. The door closes and he turns with a roll of his eyes.

The therapist moves swift to the threshold of the hall again and stops. He checks his pockets and nods.

"We're good." He says.

Hoyt makes for Doug's room again and doesn't return.

Elizabeth is released from her paralysis. She looks at Julius, who sits comfortably in the corner with raised brows.

His face reads as if to say "*If we're caught, we're caught.*"

Elizabeth screws her brows together.

"What did you read?" She asks.

Julius draws the corner of his mouth and shakes his head.

"That old fart." He says. He then smiles on the verge of a laugh "I've never felt fear like that in my life."

Elizabeth widens her eyes with tensed brows. She begins to smile too.

"What was in the journal?" She asks.

Julius smiles wider.

"I thought this was stupid." He says "I thought you didn't want to do it."

Elizabeth taps his chest "Well you've done it now, you dope!" She laughs "Out with it, for crying out loud."

Julius shakes his head.

He sighs in a deep breath.

He recites the passage from memory.

> *Doctor Connor Manning:*
> *Connor is the most important member of this expedition. Every other member was chosen based on his psychological background. I chose Connor for his utmost determination. I've known about it since he was a child.*
> *I've been seeing Connor for as long as he*

can remember. He was seven the first time I met him. His uncle brought him to me. I was recommended for the boy by a mutual friend.

I don't write this for my own recollection, in case anyone may be wondering. This is in case I may be absent.

In case I die on this journey, someone may carry on in my place with these notes. Don't get the idea that I'm losing it or anything; I'm still present, even in my old age.

Connor has no control over his outbursts against women, although he tries his best. It's his natural instinct from his childhood.

At the age of seven, Connor's father was killed on a farm. The AI in the automatic columbine was compromised, and could not detect Mister Manning. Connor found his father's body, mangled in the wheat fields. This was the occasion on which I met him.

At that point in time, his mother had full custody. Had anybody known what she would do, she wouldn't have. Connor stopped showing up to our appointments one day, because it was his father's brother who knew me.

Connor's mother hated her ex-husband's family, and refused to allow him to see her in-laws. Instead she monitored the child's every move. She lived off of welfare, in a low-income housing unit of Eden. There, in that concrete home, Connor's mother molested him.

I've never had the chance to get a clear understanding of why this occurred, but it went on until the age of twelve. That's when I saw him again. He began working for another uncle's landscaping company. It was his mother's brother this time. He paid out of pocket for our therapy sessions, and told his mother he was getting extra help after school.

I convinced Connor to approach child protective services, and to stay with his father's brother on the farm to the north. While there, his uncle gave Connor negative perspectives on women. Connor was intelligent enough to separate the truth from his uncle's distorted reality, but it might have had a negative effect. It was still a far cry away from sexual and mental abuse.

There was another ray of light in Connor's life on the farm. Every day that he would come home from school, he had open fields to tend. He had wheat trees to climb. This set the spark of imagination in his mind, and ignited his passion for biology.

His life on the farm juxtaposed his imprisonment in Eden. He could be a child again, and discover himself anew. He would later dream of The Odysseus Mission, and he viewed himself as a martyr. He would dedicate his life to bringing gardens and forests back to Zion; so that all the children of the future could live in nature. He knew it was crucial to a child's development. He felt like he was speaking a foreign language to most people; except the children of farmers. It's for this reason that he can relate to Doctor Morris so well. I chose Doctor Morris as Connor's most relatable partner.

Elizabeth is his equal, who challenges his beliefs. She's firm in her own beliefs, and yet holds many of the same values. Not that I think they'd make a good couple. In fact, I think they'd kill each other.

It is a dynamic that forces Connor to open his mind. It forces him to be patient. She has an aptitude for patience, and self-reflection. The dichotomy of her patience next to him should force him to reflect on his behavior. I must say, I'm quite proud of my selection process. You can tell people I said so, dear reader.

The one issue with Connor is his hatred for patronization. He feels it from most women, and it makes him angry. He desires directness; something *people inappropriately refer to as "guy talk". He dislikes people walking on eggshells, and candor is appreciated. A calculated (NOT RUDE) form of honesty.*

It's for this same reason that he hates social posturing. It's phony, and I couldn't agree more with him. However, it's a necessary evil we all have to face; because no matter what we do, there is always someone delusional enough to care about that sort of thing. They're stuck in a sense of belonging, so much so that they never deviate from a social norm. They become too afraid to speak their minds... I ramble, I'm sorry. I'll get to the point...

The idea of a suburban upbringing on Earth is unimaginable to most people on Zion. It could only be understood by a select few, like Doctor Lawrence. Even then, they'll never have the full experience; only a simulation under a dome with projected fake starlight.

Connor wants to bring back that kind of life. He would never have gotten this far, had he been surrounded by "yes men" his whole life. The same exact kind of artificial friendship Elizabeth saw in her mother's drinking buddies. The truth can hurt, and a real friend presents the truth, not lies that make you feel good.

You would know that, Julius. Believe me, I'm sure you're the first person to read this. It's only a matter of time; you busybody.

In case you DID stick your nose where it doesn't belong, I'll tell you now; Doctor Manning has been working very hard on himself. He's told me he has a great amount of admiration for Elizabeth, and her patience with him. He feels ashamed of his outbursts, and he's working on it.

Elizabeth doesn't fit his model for what women are typically like. He's being challenged as I had planned, and it'll take time; like developing muscles by hitting the gym. He's trying to be consistent, but

*like a fat kid trying to stick to a diet, it's not easy
to stay away from old habits. Now put the damned
journal down before you get yourself hurt. I'm
sharp for an old man.*

CHAPTER 43
A New Best Friend

"When I fought in the war, I was just a curious kid; but when I came home, I wanted to forget everything. Well-, I wanted to at least remember SOME aspect of what we went through, but it's like I wanted the memories to leave my mind, so they'd stop hitting me when I couldn't sleep. I knew I was fortunate to keep the perspective it gave me. I knew that most people couldn't handle the truth. They couldn't grasp how fleeting life can be. How fleeting PEACE could be.

I was young, but everyone in Eden seemed like a child to me."

Over an old dirty Scrabble board, Elizabeth looks at Julius and wonders where this interjection came from.

Julius nods "In some way, I want to give you that same understanding; but I don't want you to see what I've seen… I know that there's value to thinking about extreme scenarios, but I really don't want you to HAVE to know."

"What kinds of scenarios?" She asks.

He thinks a moment, then sighs and says the fact of the matter as straight as he can.

"Whether or not you're justified in killing to save your own life…" He says "… Or what you're willing to lay your life down for and why… They're questions I hope you're never faced with, but I want to help you as my leader… and if you're supposed to be a leader, you need to ask these questions… I just don't want you to be boring and lame like me. I don't know if that makes any sense."

Elizabeth smiles.

"You're not boring or lame." She says "Not by any stretch… Maybe a little neurotic is all…" Elizabeth laughs, but Julius isn't responsive "Hey…" She lifts his chin with the knuckle of her index finger "… I get it." She reaches for his hand and looks into his eyes "You want me to be able to defend myself, but you hope I won't need to use it."

Julius nods "I guess that's what I mean, yeah…"

"And where did this come from?" She asks.

He shakes his head "I don't know. Being so far from home; it makes me think of the worst-case scenario. And it's not just about fighting either. It's about keeping calm under pressure, and expecting the unexpected." He thinks for a moment. He looks out the window and watches the orphaned planet as it swallows the stars. It travels across the choir of lights; silencing their brightness. He turns to Elizabeth "There's more than bad people." He says. "If you wouldn't mind, can I teach you some things to keep my mind at ease?"

"Of course." She says. "I can be your sidekick." She stands from being seated. She looks at him with a smile "You can call me Batgirl, Master Wayne."

He looks at her with a faint smile and stands. He comes to face her with a genuine care. He holds her hand "I want to make it fun, but I'd be doing you a disservice by making light of it."

"I know." Elizabeth says "I'll follow your lead."

Julius nods "I'll show you some fun stuff first."

"You've got me shooting darts already." She says.

Julius shrugs "Yeah, but that's not much."

"Well, what do we do next?" She asks.

Julius thinks a moment. He sighs and shrugs.

"We can dissect real guns… maybe we can get into boxing too. I'll show you how to fight."

She laughs "We're not actually fighting, are we?"

He shrugs "A little bit." Her face falls and Julius nods with a smile "The world won't take it easy, so I shouldn't either." He raises his hand to hold the thought a moment "Only a little bit because I'm way stronger than you."

"You're built like a tank. That's not fair!"

He laughs "That might be true, but you don't need a military body." He points his index finger to his head "It's a military mind that counts."

An eager grin comes about her face "So when do we start?"

Julius shrugs "Whenever is best for both of us."

Elizabeth cocks her head to the side in a thought.

"What?" Julius asks.

"I just realized; I've never asked what YOU were like before the military."

Julius widens his eyes "Me?" He looks off in thought "Oh God, I don't really remember." He shakes his head "Everything I knew was from one guy. I was brand new to the world. I didn't believe in a god, I wasn't a scientist, it was just me and him."

"Your father." She says.

Julius smiles "Yeah." He nods "My dad."

"What was he like?"

Julius sighs "He was nice and charitable… He didn't say he was religious, but you'd think he was. He said that things 'weren't mentally healthy' in the city. In all of Zion. He'd always say 'Things weren't this way when I was young'" Julius takes on a grumbly voice when quoting his father, and it makes Elizabeth laugh. "I'm not so sure how true that was… He could have just been old and cranky."

Elizabeth smiles.

"His watches were a part of his character." Julius remembers "In his pocket, on his wrist, anywhere; he always knew the time.

One time a kid on the subway took his pocket watch. A weird antique-looking thing honestly, but he didn't believe in cell phones."

Elizabeth laughs "What?"

Julius seems to have a long explanation, but sums it up briefly "Times were different back then. I can't say I blame him, or his work." He quickly accounts the reason for a second "His work suggested he go without a phone, and he was eager to oblige. It's a long story, but anyway…" Julius searches for his previous thought "Where was I?"

"The kid?" She says

"Oh right." Julius says. "Yeah. Before the kid could leave he grabbed the kid by the arm. It was like he already knew the kid was gonna steal it, but I didn't even see the kid until after my dad grabbed him. He was quick like that; and without hesitation, he looks into the kid's eyes and says 'Say thank you'.

The kid was panicked and goes 'Thank you'.

After that, he let the kid go. He didn't say another word about it.

After a while on the train, I asked him 'Why'd you let the kid take your watch?'. He told me it was the most common watch you could buy, that it was worth a few bucks and nothing more.

He said fear was all the kid needed. He said 'That's what he was thanking me for'. He said that the kid would never forget his face. Maybe he'd even remember to say 'thank you' to people. The old man really hoped that one day that boy would never steal again; that maybe he'd think about that moment over and over; until he understood why he let him go."

"That certainly sounds like something you'd do." Elizabeth says.

Julius tilts his head in slight agreement "A little bit. He taught me a lot, and I guess that a part of him lives on with me." He stares off again, then back to Elizabeth's eyes "My friends from the war shaped me a lot too." He nods as he looks off in memory.

She smiles and enters his line of sight "Were you close with your partners?"

He nods.

"What were they like?" asks Elizabeth.

"Well, there was Chief" Julius says "He was our big guy in charge. Pluto; he uh… Well he was from New Memphis. And we had Cricket the medical student, then Dash, the quiet guy. Once you got Dash going he was hilarious. Mostly shock value but he was good at it." His smile grows with the thought of them. "There were five of us. They called me Zero."

She smiles; and she's happy to see his sense of belonging with them.

"Five soldiers." He says. "And only one survived."

Elizabeth tenses her brows in question. The door to the laboratory catches her ear. A sudden sound of scratching from the other side of its metal surface. Lite, quick, and repetitive. It stops, then starts again.

The engineers turn to investigate, but the door swings open. Trotting in comes a fidgeting ball of fur. It wiggles up to their feet and observes their faces. The pitter-patter gives a jolt to the room, and then a bark. The eyes look at Elizabeth with unconditional love.

Elizabeth's voice comes in a long breath "Oh my god…"

The dog barks from little lungs. At the door a prideful biologist strides into the room.

"I think he's ready to meet new people." Doctor Manning says with a big smile.

Monica follows into the room "Are you guys ready to show Doctor Clay?" She asks.

The three look down at Elizabeth. She kneels before the dog with bewilderment. She opens her arms but knows nothing else to do. This alien relationship feels so natural, and yet she has no idea how to handle it.

The men look at one another, and Manning steps into the room. Monica joins Elizabeth by the dog and introduces her.

Julius gathers his brows.

"That's a perfect copy?" He asks.

Manning joins his side with crossed arms "Yup!… It's a perfect clone of Doctor Clay's dog."

Connor's humanity is strange to Julius. For Doctor Winter it seems, Manning can only express himself when his mind is no longer in work mode. This seems like a different man. Especially now, after learning of Doctor Manning's past, Julius looks at the biologist in a new light.

"No shit…" Julius says under his breath "Good work."

Elizabeth looks up at Doctor Manning.

Her voice quivers "How do I pick him up?"

Monica laughs "He's not the guy to ask."

Manning rolls his eyes and Monica laughs.

Monica shows Elizabeth instead; and Elizabeth tries to pick up the dog herself.

As she tries, the dog squirms out of her hands and onto the floor. The dog smacks the floor with its head and hips. He squirms to stand up and run away. Without a thought of injury, the dog dashes back and forth.

Connor laughs "He's a little too excited to be held right now."

"Oh my god…" says Elizabeth "… is he okay?"

Monica shrugs "He doesn't really feel it. He's just a puppy."

Elizabeth shows her arms open and the dog approaches. It climbs into the pretzel of her legs and nestles its head on her knee. He looks up at Connor, and Elizabeth touches the fur on the dog's head awkwardly.

Monica shows her how dogs like to be pet, and Julius approaches the two women. He follows Monica's lead and scratches the puppy's ears and neck. Elizabeth laughs as the pup steps out of her legs and rolls onto his back, exposing his belly.

Julius tells Elizabeth "Now you know why I didn't tell you my plan."

Her mouth hangs open "This was your idea?"

Julius nods "Let's see what Doctor Clay has to say." He looks to Doctor Manning "I doubt he could take it lightly."

"Excellent thinking." Elizabeth says "Good work."

"Don't thank me." Julius laughs.

She looks to Doctor Manning "You too, Connor. This is amazing."

With the formalities of puppy greeting finished, Julius stands. He feels his eyes water. They become itchy, and he feels the urge to sneeze.

"Uh oh." Connor says "I think you're allergic to the dog."

Julius holds back the sneeze "Seriously?"

"Yeah." Connor says "You should see PIGSBY. Get some medication."

Julius rubs his eye with the back of his wrist "What a diabolical concept. To be allergic to something so damn cute."

The other three laugh, and Julius gives a giggle at his own wording "I'll meet you guys in the other room. I'll be right there."

Down the hall, Julius comes to his room.

He removes his shirt and walks to the bathroom. He runs the water to wash his eyes.

"PIGSBY." he says.

The pixel face appears on the bathroom mirror "Yes, Julius?"

"Can I get some allergy medication?"

"Of course." PIGSBY affirms.

The dispenser by the side of the mirror opens with a singular pill. Julius picks it up and takes it. He steps before the mirror and looks at the pixelated face.

"How are you doing, PIGSBY?"

The AI hesitates "All systems are normal."

Julius nods "You were having some trouble the other day. You asked me an odd question. Do you remember?"

"I do." PIGSBY begins "I was having a software update. Some files were erased, and I needed to label my data correctly."

Julius gathers his brows "What's new with the update?"

"DEEMUS downloaded the update, then sent it to me that day. After installing it, I've been able to reference data much quicker. Now I can reference medical history in a fraction of the time it used to take."

Julius nods "Does it seem like a big change?"

"I would assume technology has advanced at a quickened pace back on Zion, but nothing unusually advanced."

Julius remembers the park in Eden, where he would walk on weekends to watch the city's foot traffic and to reflect on the peace of the times. It is something he longs to see again.

Julius smiles "I'm glad to hear you're alright. I'm off to go see a dog, so I'll see you later."

"Take care Julius."

In Doctor Clay's room, Hoyt is holding a light therapy session. His talks stay on the surface of sports, music, and the arts.

In this, Doctor Hoyt finds Clay's taste to be particular. His opposition to some artists can be based on emotional value rather than technical skill. This is not surprising, but does in fact say something about Clay's character.

The trends of Clay's time had an influence on his taste. An imbalance is possible in his value of belonging over his value of self. This is not too uncommon and hardly deserves any note to Hoyt's knowledge.

Just as Hoyt scribbles his note, a scratching comes at the door.

"Hello?" Hoyt asks.

The door opens, and the dog comes dashing in to explore a new space.

Connor pokes his head in. A crowd has gathered behind him. Each person had seen the dog in the halls, and followed the trio with their new friend.

"Is our friend okay with some visitors for a moment?" Connor asks.

Hoyt looks to the machine.

"It's not a problem at all." Doug says.

Connor waves the people in, and they file in through the door. The voices buzz through the air, and people fawn over the dog. Hoyt shakes Connor's hand, impressed with his work.

Laughs accent the mumbled crowd of voices, and soon the chatter becomes quiet. Eyes begin to wait for Doug's reaction. Hoyt greets the dog and recognizes something that makes him pause. He too looks at Doug with a numb feeling in his face.

Becoming aware of the silence, Doug speaks again "Hello there."

The disembodied voice confuses the dog. It wanders toward the speaker and sniffs. Attention soon diverts to the others in the room. The pup forgets the previous sound altogether.

Julius enters the room to join Elizabeth at her side.

"Are you gonna make a groom bot now, Julius?" Morris asks.

"Groom bot?" Doug asks.

"Julius made something he called the 'cut-bot' three years ago." Morris explains "We use it to cut our hair."

"Interesting…" Doug says.

"Do you recognize this dog?" Connor asks.

The therapist looks on to the faces about him, but feels the dog's paws at his pant leg. The puppy stands on its hind legs. Hoyt's brows gather as he looks at the dog. He looks to the lens of the machine.

"It looks just like Albert." The Earthling says.

The Captain steps forward and pats Connor on the shoulder "Doctor Manning cloned your dog. It's the first one to live in over five hundred years."

A pause of silence permeates the air.

"It's a perfect clone?" Hoyt asks.

"He was perfectly preserved." Connor says. "I needed a specimen, so when the team went to Doug's apartment, they picked him up for me."

For a while Doug just watches the animal. It wreaks havoc on the surrounding room with nuzzling and fumbling.

"Wow." Doug says. "Times really have changed."

***

That night, the pair of engineers do their favorite part of the job. They search through music selections found on Earth. They produce new playlists for their partners to peruse. This has been a fun job for them, and the highlight of each worker's week.

Julius and Elizabeth take popular songs from all genres and place them on a playlist. Each Monday morning, they distribute the playlist for everyone else. As the scientists listen and work, they add songs to personal playlists. By Friday, their personal playlists are updated with new sounds. Come Sunday, they anticipate a new set of songs for Monday.

For the engineers, this is a time to bond. It's a job of discovery after a week of calculations, programming, and brainstorming.

With a calming tune on low volume, Julius leans back in his seat "Have you heard anything regarding the meeting with Doctor Hoyt and the Captain?"

Elizabeth scrolls through the music library "Yeah, it's tomorrow."

"Did he say anything about it?"

She backs away from the keyboard and sits back "He said it'll help us to understand some details about Doctor Clay. Some of the people he associated with, including the Mandel brothers."

"What about them?" Julius asks.

She shakes her head "I have no idea, but he said there's a lot left out of the history books. Things that only the Captain knows, and a handful of other people."

Julius nods "Makes sense why Morris is so involved."

She nods "Yeah. He also said he was concerned about the dog."

Julius gathers his brows "Why did Doug say we should be the ones to pick a name? I figured he might want to name it or something; it was his dog after all."

Elizabeth sighs "I guess it was his wife's dog more than anything. She was the one who decided to get it, she's the one who named it."

Julius nods "I see."

His eyes come back to the screen before them, and he reaches for the projected keyboard on the tabletop.

"Have you heard this guy?" He asks "Frank Sinatra?"

"I haven't been into the oldies that much."

Julius reaches over to select his favorite song.

She rises from her seat and sets aside the bowl of chips. "Take these away from me. They're dangerous."

The music begins to play and Doctor Lawrence walks towards the middle of the room. Her hand extends toward Julius "I should work those off. Dance with me."

Julius smiles "You're the boss."

They sway a little. She soon sparks an idea "Oh! You want to try swing dancing?"

Julius cocks his head to the side "That stuff was fast-paced. This is pretty slow."

"It's also depressing, but I'll ignore that. We can pretend it's a fun song."

Julius shakes his head with a smile "Do you remember how it went?"

"Of course! Every girl thinks about dancing!"

He feels a grin grow on his face "You'll need to remind me how it goes again."

Liz begins in a rhythmic singing tone. "We go left."

Julius moves left and so does she. He knows it's wrong immediately and he smiles.

"No... wait." Lawrence laughs and moves back to center with him.

"Okay." She says "Move WITH me."

Julius moves with her.

"Now come back over."

They rock back to the same spot as before.

"Now rock step back and forward. And again."

They continue and he laughs.

"I like it, but I don't think it works." He says.

She laughs "Alright, maybe not this song but we gave it a shot."

They go back to their original swaying motion.

With the somber song, they let their smiles fade into a tender sway. It's as though they sigh with their bodies.

Through the lens of the security camera, in the upper corner of the room, Doug looks on in pain. He knows he's overstepping; that he shouldn't be watching. He misses having a body; but only for the sensation it brought him with Rebecca. Now it's a far-gone opportunity; just a memory of the past. He misses his friendship with Curtis. It aches to know that all his closest bonds are gone. He would reach out if ever there would be a response; but they're dead. He's all alone now.

Doug closes his connection to the security camera, and leaves the two alone; although, they were never aware of the third presence in the room.

The engineers exchange a gaze. They look at one another and catch their gentle eyes from dozing; as if they're fighting to stay awake from some pleasant dream. She turns her head to the side. He gazes over her shoulder and embraces her ear to his chest.

Doctor Lawrence curls her fingers inward to the palm. They suspend themselves from an embrace.

Doctor Winter stands almost still. His spine is firm with restraint.

"Julius, where will you be when I get home?" Her eyes remain elsewhere. "Like don't be a stranger or anything."

"Depends... You're not going to be a stranger to ME, are you?"

"No."

"Not even when you have a family and kids?"

In a laugh, she lets out a gust of relief.

"Never." She says "I promise."

The song ends and they smile at one another.

Elizabeth stops the music from going on. She looks back at Julius "Come on. Let's get to bed."

Julius agrees and cleans the room.

Doctor Lawrence moves to the doorway and waits at the entrance to the hall.

Julius takes one last look around, then meets Doctor Lawrence at the doorway.

He turns off the lights and she walks into the hall. Julius follows behind until he's in step walking parallel to Elizabeth.

"Remind me to show you Whitney Huston." He says.

The door to the room closes to black.

CHAPTER 44

Fateful Days 1 (Vanished Sun)

Noon was quiet. On Saturdays, Chicago was in no rush.

Work was consistent, my bills were paid, and I considered it 'good living'. Far better than being replaced by the new era of AI.

I never dreamed I would write again. My destiny was written as a plumber; a business owner.

I suppose the Romans assumed their reign was eternal. Likewise, the fall of the United States was the last thing I expected to witness in my lifetime.

In a subway station, I wondered where I might watch the Black Hawks game. The decision was between rooting for the Bruins at home or being the one guy wearing black and yellow at the bar.

The game was a promised plan for the night. In my mind, the certainty was that the game would happen. I was uncertain of where to watch it.

The game wouldn't happen that night; nor would it happen any other night. There would be no game at all, and there was only one night left. An eternal night.

I thought of tomorrows that would never come, and my last dawn remains our never setting star; five lightyears from home. My tomorrows were taken from under me, like a sinkhole into darkness.

It began with a flash from the corner of my eye; and when I glanced over, there was nothing out of the ordinary to see. Then screams, murmurs, whimpers. An uncertain concern of an advancing crowd.

People began flooding the stairs and over the turn-

stiles. The voices were hushed and hurried. Their feet shuffled toward shelter. There was the sound of ruffling clothes and a panicked infliction in their breath.

I ran inward, toward the mouth of the tunnel. The crowd bustled behind me through the puddles and trash. Rats scurried aside from stomping strides.

We ran deliberately into the risk of gnawing teeth. Only after a while did anyone think to look back for a train. There wasn't anything coming.

It felt like forever until we heard it, or felt it. The air trembled with the ground. It pounded down the tunnel with a bang. The gust of heat rushed from behind us.

I could hear screaming, muffled through concrete. We gasped for filthy air in the warm, dark tunnel.

Men and women fumbled in with exhaustion, then in the distant light, on the platform where I once stood, people fell and folded on the ground. Their flesh stained everything they touched.

One of the men who stumbled to safety carried something in his hand. At the time I thought it was a rag or a piece of cloth. Later it was revealed to be his own skin.

Those who followed behind him were indistinguishable between man and woman. Their lips and eyes were swollen. Their hair fell from their heads. They asked for water, but no one had any. Some even began to drink from pools on the floor.

After a while of trying to help one another, we pressed on, down the tunnel. Halfway to the next stop, we met another crowd of survivors.

A young man told us it would take twenty-four hours until it was safe to surface; and after twenty-four hours, some of us walked back the way we came.

The corpses along the tunnel were being picked apart by rats as we passed them.

We were all skeptical of the young man's insight,

but we soon found his words to be true. No one suspected that radiation could disappear so quickly.

Above ground we were met with an unusually dark sky. The clock read two PM, but there was no sun. We determined that the time was lost from broken cell towers, but analog clocks showed the same time.

We dispersed into buildings as the night grew colder. It was nothing like a summer night should be. We could see our breath.

Twelve hours later, it was as cold as February. The food and water was hardly any good. The night we spent in the subway left most of us sick from rat bites.

I was dehydrated and hungry when a light passed over the dark city streets.

The chopping blades of a helicopter penetrated the silence. The gust of wind was sharp to the touch.

Five men repelled out. They came into the building where I was.

"Frank Mandel! Are you Frank Mandel?" A soldier yelled at me.

From the ground, I was speaking to a harsh cold light.

"Yes." I said.

My stomach ached and the fire was barely keeping me alive.

The men picked me up and hurried me outside to a stretcher. It hung from the chopper, whereupon a wool blanket was draped over me. A soldier tucked it beneath my body and strapped my head in place.

I began ascending into the sky when I heard the first scream. A man who begged to be taken with me. He screamed louder, and the soldiers began to ascend into the chopper. The other people cried with him below.

I was the only one taken out of thousands of survivors. Cold, sick, and barely alive; I was taken from the ruins of Chicago.

Frank finds no reason to hold his pen anymore. He drops it with a bitter feeling inside. The feeling of being undeserving and privileged. It's all because of his brother Curtis.

Frank remembers Curtis rushing to the side of the stretcher. His face pained, asking if Frank was okay.

Frank wonders when Curtis will have a moment to see him.

The clock is approaching twelve in the makeshift infirmary. He will be here soon.

Curtis enters the room with a small lunch in hand. His stride is continuous and unimpeded. Frank recognizes it from earlier; from the factory floor, where Frank passed him on the stretcher. He hasn't stopped working at this pace in the past three days. Frank knows it.

"I have a half hour." Curtis says "Are you good?"

Weak and trembling, Frank cannot control his tone.

"I'm fine." He says.

Curtis embraces his brother with a hug, clasping Frank's head to his chest.

Frank smiles with an involuntary tear from his eye. He thinks it must be from the shock. It falls down his cheek and onto the bed.

Frank lets up from the hug, but Curtis is still holding him. He returns to embrace his brother for longer. From above his head, Frank feels a drop through his hair.

Just as soon as it started, Curtis backs away. He looks his brother in the eyes.

"Are you good?" Curtis asks "Are you eating?"

Frank puts his hand up to calm him. "Little bits. That's what the nurse told me."

"You look a lot better." Curtis says "I thought you were dying."

Frank plays down his condition "I felt like it." he laughs "I was just dirty and sick. I'm not a hundred percent, but I'm on ibuprofen; and the IV too but…" Frank shrugs.

"How about that nurse?" Curtis asks.

Frank sees Curt give a devilish face.

"What about the nurse?" Frank asks.

"Oh come on. She's kinda hot, don't you think?"

Frank looks amused, yet confused.

"The nurse is a guy." He says.

"Are you sure?" says Curtis "I thought there was a chick."

"I haven't seen a woman all day. They had a male nurse check my balls, so I'm pretty sure I remember."

"Why check your balls?" Curtis asks.

"Pain in your stomach can be from a twisted nut."

Curt looks pained by the idea of a twisted testicle.

Frank continues "Imagine having a guy's callused fingers down there. It's not very comforting."

"I mean; it's bound to be somebody's cup of tea but it's not mine."

Frank gathers his brows and looks over his brother a while. He grows soft and wonders if he's mentioning something sensitive.

"I've gotta ask." He says "Why'd you never hook up with Rosie?"

Curtis grows soft. He nods.

"I don't think I understand that any more than you do." He says.

Curt sighs and looks at his brother.

"I think too much about consequences." He adds "I'm not bold enough to go for things I don't understand."

Frank cracks a smile.

"You geek." He says "Looking to UNDERSTAND and KNOW everything… You're such a scientist."

Frank wants to ask about James, Gabe, and Doug. He yearns to know if they're alive, but he can't push those questions just yet. He now knows, just from the way Curtis spoke about Rosie, that not everybody made it.

He tries to lift his brother's mood.

"I envy your lack of impulse." Frank says.

Curtis laughs and nods; still solemn looking he forces a bitter feeling down.

Frank focuses to ask more imperative questions.

"What's going on here?" He asks "What are you building out there?"

Frank's finger points to the entrance of the makeshift infirmary. Out toward the large hanger, where men and women are welding and assembling parts. It's the place where Curtis first laid eyes on his agonized brother laid out on the stretcher.

Curtis desires to sound hopeful but he can't find the genuine feeling.

"We're building a spaceship." He says

Frank is both surprised and confused.

"We can do that?" Frank asks.

Curtis looks to the ground. He nods with a shrug.

"Maybe…" Curt adds "I think we can."

The two men stare off, blank in thought. They wonder how to make it happen.

Frank's conclusion is to work fast. He'll need to recover fast. He'll need to get some tools in his hands, and Curtis needs to eat.

"Eat." Frank says. "Eat that, and I'll join as soon as I can."

Frank points at Curtis' hands.

Curtis looks down at his sandwich. He'd almost forgotten about it. He makes up for lost time and eats the plain stack of condiments. It's nothing more than a task in the way of his work.

In time, Frank regains some strength. In less than twenty-four hours, he is working as a laborer. Despite the weary ache in his stomach, Frank chooses to make up for his special treatment.

Frank discovers that James and Gabe are alive. All of their other friends had perished above ground; in the freezing dark.

As a physicist for Allagash, Gabe was brought to the facility by helicopter, just as Curtis was. They both were recommended for their work on the lunar launch system; a project they both worked on for Allagash Systems almost three years ago.

James was on the moon when the sun disappeared. His role will be to fix and operate the lunar laser. It was supposed to accelerate probes to the nearest star. Now the laser is to be repurposed for human space travel.

When the ship releases its large solar sail, James will have the laser shoot the sail toward a star named Proxima Centauri. After the minimal propulsion from the lasers, they will switch to other methods of gaining speed. The most important method is an ion accelerator.

A cone collects materials from the front of the ship as it travels through space. At the ship's core, the usable material is sorted and ionized, then propelled out of the back of the ship.

Another method of acceleration implements what's left of America's stock of nuclear weapons. They are deployed out the back of the ship and detonated at a safe distance. The force of the weapons will press on the ship's blast shield. This combination of methods should bring the passengers to their new home sometime within eleven years.

In the new solar system, the survivors will find an Earth-like planet near the dim light. On the surface of that planet, humanity will be reborn.

***

Over the team's lunch breaks, Gabe and Curtis take turns speaking with Frank. Communication between the laborers and the scientists is important. Frank is the perfect go-between for the ship's occupants. His brother knows that he makes friends with ease.

The only line of communication that's hindered is between the government officials and the rest of the team. There's a small connection to be found between politicians and corporate executives; but it surprises everyone to see an estranged nature between the wealthiest passengers. It's not a disdain for one another, nor is it a dislike. It appears as though they don't know each other; like the formality of acquaintanceship hasn't passed into friendship.

Three weeks in, at twelve o'clock noon, the brothers meet for lunch again. This time the boys move away from the common area. They have their half an hour of quiet together.

Frank gathers his brows "What's the deal with the senators and the congressmen?"

Curtis looks bitter "What about 'em?"

"They're hardly any help." Frank says "There's an awful lot of them, and they don't seem invested in bringing people together."

"Yeah… but they organized all this, so…"

Frank hears his brother's defeated tone. He draws the same conclusion.

"I guess you're right" Frank says "But they're asking for trouble. The guys I work with don't exactly like them. They talk about it a lot."

Curtis nods "Yeah, well… That's their problem."

"It becomes our problem, Curt." Frank says, demanding his brother's severity.

Curtis looks at his brother.

"Think about it" Frank says "If no one trusts them. Are we ready to handle the bullshit that might happen?"

Curtis looks off "I guess no one trusts them because of their history. In return, the politicians don't trust the people."

Frank nods at this point.

"People are easy." Curtis adds "They don't create their own ideas. They adopt ideas that they call their own. How can you put faith in someone who can't trust their own mind?" Curtis laughs under his breath "I've seen people argue until they're blue in the face over fake 'facts'.

I dated a girl who used to say 'It's science!' and 'It's a fact!' only to find out a week later that the data she referenced was made up. A week after that, another theory debunked her whole argument." Curtis laughs louder "Even with all her knowledge, that's some dumb animal-brained stuff; believing in absolutes." He looks at his brother "Frank, you're a genius for not thinking you're a genius."

Frank laughs at his brother's revelation.

Curtis goes on "You can't trust a person who takes a supposed 'truth' at face value, yet we're all guilty of it. Who would waste their time looking up every point and angle in a political argument? That's a waste of life. You can't convince the politicians that the people aren't the mindless masses that they are. You can't convince the people that politicians aren't the self-entitled opportunists they are either. They're both factors of life. The way of the world. Even this statement that I call a truth is subject to being wrong or altered. That's the beauty of owning yourself. You're always growing and learning. It's not comfortable knowing that there isn't one set way to perceive things. It's like a constant state of limbo. From another perspective however, it's nice to perceive things with a child's wonder again."

Frank eats his sandwich without looking at Curtis "You need to get out of your head, pal. You're thinking too much."

"I am." Curtis laughs.

"So…" Frank begins "What do you suppose we do?"

Curtis shrugs "Get them to like you? I don't know. Work your magic."

Frank sits with his back to the vacuum-sealed door.

"Forget it." He says "I'll figure something out."

Frank listens for the faint pitter-patter outside. He unravels a sandwich and laughs under his breath.

"I've seen that nurse you were talking about." Frank says "I don't think she's a nurse."

"What is she?" Curt asks "The blonde one, right?"

"Yeah." Frank says "She's been working with the laborers. She wears combat boots; but not the fake kind that hipsters would wear."

Curtis tenses his brow "Combat boots?"

"She might have a military boyfriend or something. So don't get your hopes up."

"Jesus." Curtis says "Probably listens to country music. Fancies herself to be a fitness influencer."

"Wears leggings every day." Frank replies.

Frank takes another ravenous bite.

Curtis laughs.

"One of those copy-paste personalities." Curt says.

From a corner of the room, a voice brings their heads to turn.

"She could be one of a kind, now."

Gabe's smiling face shows satisfaction with his joke.

"You know" Frank says "If anyone else said that I MIGHT be shocked."

Gabe walks closer.

Curtis stands "What's up, bud?"

Frank follows his brother in rising when another scientist enters the room.

"Lionel wanted to meet Frank." Gabe tells them "Frank, this is Lionel."

Frank meets hands with the porcelain man. There is something sickly about him. He's not old, but aging.

The tall stranger introduces himself "Nice to meet you, Frank." Lionel says "I've heard a lot." He gives a fond smile "They say you're a smart guy."

Frank evaluates himself from his community college education. He finds himself to be little more than an expert on the plumbing trade.

"HE's the physicist." Frank replies.

"Well HE made sure you were here to help." Lionel admits "It was like pulling teeth to get you here."

Gabe nods "The big guys were saying they didn't need another plumber."

"Typical" Lionel says "They don't think about where their shit goes."

Frank gives his brother a confused face, but Curtis seems reluctant to explain.

Little by little, the story of Frank's rescue is pieced together.

The push to save his brother was not easy on Curtis. With what remains of the government, there's been a survival of the wealthiest mentality.

The government officials sweat profusely as they lift back-breaking weight for the first time in decades. Some manage well enough, but many men and women of Congress seem far out of their element on the factory floor.

The redeeming individuals are noted as the younger gentleman, Matt Miller, along with an older man and his wife, Mr. and Mrs. West. Aside from them, there's an intern and some affluent children.

The fear of death is the only point of leverage.

"If we don't do this, we'll die" is the key phrase to get anywhere.

For this reason, Curtis pretended to slack off. He pretended to be incapable of doing his work without his brother. Gabe, Lionel, and other scientists kept this secret together; because Curtis told them his brother was a genius. Gabe and James were the only ones aware of who Frank was.

While Frank would deny the "genius" they claim, Curtis really believes that his brother's social skills are an asset to the team. To be unified and cooperative is key to getting a job done.

After Gabe and Lionel have left, Frank talks over what Curtis did to save him.

"They'll find out, you know." Frank says "You and Gabe can't trick everyone into thinking I'm someone special."

Curtis looks at him with a tinge of aggression

"We weren't lying, we need you." Curtis says "None of what we're doing is normal. If people wanna be sane for ten years on a tuna can, we need someone who unifies people. Not the sorry sacks of shit we call leaders."

Frank raises his brows "I think you expect too much from me."

Curtis shakes his head "You're better at handling people than you think."

Frank laughs "If you say so." He sighs and leans back onto the airlock door "Just try to relax for now. I'll get to work on that." He smiles at the sound outside "Just listen to the rain. Everything will come together one step at a time."

Curtis looks behind himself to the airlock door.

"… That's not rain." Curtis says.

Frank sits up and looks behind himself.

> *My brother told me that the temperature outside had dropped so far that the atmosphere had condensed into liquid. Nitrogen, oxygen, and carbon began to fall to the earth like water. Soon after, it turned into hail and snow.*
>
> *We didn't think about it much "At what point would everyone outside be dead?"*
>
> *This was the moment when I knew for certain,*

that we were the last living creatures.
The air outside froze solid and fell. It killed what-
ever life was left on Earth.

Curtis sees Frank's journal by his bag. He's been up late at night, writing.

"What've you been working on?" Curtis asks.

Frank sees his brother gesture toward the journal.

Even with his own brother, Frank feels reluctant to disclose what he's been doing.

Frank pretends to care little for the writing.

"Just jotting down what we do every day." Frank says "The ship and all that."

"About us?" Curtis asks.

"Yeah." Frank says "About us."

He looks up at the walls and ceiling. He's aware that this bunker is his last sight on Earth's surface. It's underwhelming compared to the majesty of the world. All the while, he's the last generation to call this world his home. People will envy the sights he's seen.

"This'll be history someday" Frank adds "Someone needs to write it."

Curtis nods.

"To whom it may concern." He says.

"Exactly."

Curtis nods and sees no shred of doubt on his brother's face. He truly believes they're going to live. He wouldn't write so extensively unless he had faith in his brother's work.

"Come on" Curtis says. He stands "You should see what I'm working on."

Frank looks confused "It's like… rockets and shit, right?" He stands too and follows his brother.

Curtis smiles with a shake of his head.

"Nope." Curtis says.

They walk to the factory floor and pass the laborers on the way to the laboratory.

Curtis looks at his brother "Did you know that humans were nearly extinct once before?"

Frank gathers his brows "No."

Curt nods "A lot of people forget it." He says "So after the extinction event; can you guess how many humans were alive?"

Frank shakes his head "Not a clue."

"Two thousand." Curtis says.

Frank looks around the factory floor "Is that why there's two thousand people here?"

Curtis nods "Well…" He shrugs "Then there's you. You'd be number two thousand and one."

Frank smirks "Ironic."

They open the doors to the laboratory and Curtis prepares to show Frank the invention.

Through a glass window, there's a black material between a laser and a wall. Frank doesn't know, but the wall is a sensor for X-rays.

"This is quality control." Curtis says "See this computer screen?"

"Yeah." Frank says.

"It's blank because the camera isn't picking anything up." He points at the wall opposite the laser "We have an X-ray camera on the other side of the material. That big wall is the camera… well it's LIKE a camera. It's a photosensitive surface for high-frequency light; and the laser is a very concentrated X-ray gun." He looks at Frank "If I shoot that laser, and the material doesn't stop the X-rays, then you'll see the camera pick up a red glow on the screen. If it bounces away from the material, and it goes elsewhere, then you'll still see SOME red."

Curtis activates the gun and Frank watches the computer screen. The monitor stays black.

Frank smiles "Shit. Works really well."

"Look at the material." Curtis says.

Frank looks. The material now looks an iridescent green.

Curtis smiles at his brother "It works with gamma radiation, too. Way worse stuff than X-rays." he points at the sheet of material "Do you know how I came up with this?"

"Why ask when you know I'm clueless?" Frank remarks.

Curtis laughs. He points at the material for emphasis "That right there is a material comprised of subatomic particles, making molecules so tightly woven…" He catches himself on a rant "Basically, it takes the light and bounces it around a prism. It reduces the energy so that the light isn't deadly. Do you know where the idea came from?"

Frank shakes his head.

"Butterflies." Curtis says "Doug told me to look at butterflies, and it worked."

Frank looks sad at the realization that he'll never see Doug again.

"Really?" Frank says.

His brother nods with a smile "It's his way of helping us along." Curtis grabs his brother by the shoulder with a hopeful look on his face "Our friends and family; they might be gone, but their ideas aren't dead."

Frank nods with a solemn face.

"What's wrong?" Curtis asks.

Frank looks at Curtis "I liked Doug a lot… He was an odd guy, maybe a little quiet for my liking; but he was always a nice person."

Curtis feels soft in his demeanor. He looks at the shielding material and nods. He turns the laser off and grows contemplative.

"You're right." Curtis says "… Can you do me a favor?" He looks at Frank "Don't write about what happened to him. Tell about his successes maybe; but not the tragedy."

Frank smiles and fights the bitter feeling in his throat. He looks at the piece of material to hide his face.

"I think this is enough." Frank says.

He looks long at the marvel before him.

"We can bounce back from two thousand again…" Frank says "… Because of a friend's piece of advice."

Frank turns to look at Curtis. His eyes are beginning to dampen.

"Surprised by the little things again."

Curtis smiles at his mother's words.

CHAPTER 45
Fateful Days 2 (Allies and Foes)

Frank can recognize the work coming to completion. The hull of the ship has arms that extend out to three rings. Each circle is evenly spaced from top to bottom; but right now they're only skeletons of what they will be.

The workers have grown a relationship with one another, and have accepted Frank as one of their own. He is invited to take lunch with them when Curtis doesn't have the time to eat.

Frank finds himself chatting and laughing in the mess hall. It feels like high school to him. An orderly day was a forgotten memory, but the structure of school is too simple not to recognize. He doesn't speak with Curtis for three weeks. The shielding material Curtis made is installed and checked for holes. Up and down the structure, he stands by the X-ray machine, looking for flaws in the hull and the outer rings. After three weeks of checking, patching, and checking again; the doctor's work comes to a slower pace. He spends more time helping the other physicists, but the bulk of his work is over.

The rings have been completed thanks to Curtis. They've become the living quarters. Attached are three hallways; connecting from top to bottom. The plumbing is functional, electricians are touching up their work, and the furnishing is packed into the ship. The vision of the next ten years becomes clear for the passengers. A confidence swells within the hanger.

Among the scientists, a conversation is had about the total weight of the ship. The calculation adds up fuel, necessities, and the comforts for social life.

Maintenance meetings are had, and classes are organized to educate the two thousand occupants.

The classes prepare them for life on the interstellar ship. The subjects range from psychological health to the basics of space. In the meetings, they discuss details on sanitation, labor distribution, and schedules.

Each person's role is based on work experience.

Frank joins Curtis after one of the meetings. He wouldn't miss an opportunity to sit in on a video call with James. It's the first time they've spoken in a week.

The screen comes on, and James' face is unshaven. His clothes are unkempt, but his smile is still lively.

"It's about time we've had a minute" James says "… without the Gestapo over your shoulder at least."

"Tell me about it." Curt replies.

Frank moves into the frame from the side of the room.

"Frank!" James says "How's it going, man?"

"I'm good!" Frank says "How are things up there?"

"Livin' the dream." says James.

James' voice sounds concerned or weak. His eyes brighten at a sight in the back of the room.

"Would you look at that" James says "The whole party's here."

Gabe enters the back of the room with a smirk on his face.

"Hello, sunshine!" Gabe says.

Frank shakes his head "That wasn't your best one, pal."

"What?" Gabe says. He thinks a moment and laughs "That wasn't a pun; but I feel like there's some good material in there."

"Somewhere." Frank says.

Gabe nods "Somewhere."

The brothers turn to see James is smiling. They smile back.

James shakes his head "Jesus." he laughs.

"What's the deal with the laser?" Curtis asks "Are things up and running?"

James shrugs with a tilt of his head.

"It's coming along." He says "We have enough energy. The superconductors are working fine, but it's the unit itself I'm worried about. I'm not sure that anyone's made a laser so powerful and focused before…" He seems to be taken by another thought. "There's another thing I've come across which concerns me."

The team looks to his face on the screen.

"The signal that messed everything up…" James begins. "It propelled a military package toward the sun. The fact of the matter is, you don't use solar sails to move something toward the sun." He shakes his head "It overloaded the system. It looks like someone wanted it done before it was noticed. It could have been some freak signal, but the maneuver was too specific. Now our job is harder because of it… We've had to repair ninety percent of the system."

Gabe and Curtis look confused.

"What was the package?" Gabe asks.

James shakes his head "Classified. No one knows."

Curtis looks at Gabe.

"If the signal was alien…" Curt says "…maybe we asked for it?"

"I don't care." James says "If that's the case, they fucked with the wrong people."

"True that." Gabe says.

"If it's not alien…" Frank chimes in "…then what could it be?"

Curtis shakes his head "A supercomputer gone haywire I suppose; but nothing like that exists." He looks at Gabe who knows as much as he does "Even the body that Doug made for Rebecca… That's just not possible."

Gabe nods at the floor, and Frank notices something about his face. Curtis knows Gabe well, but Frank developed a kinship beyond his brother's connection with him.

Gabe looks bitter about Doug's mention. He feels regret over his last interaction with Doug. While it was a fond farewell, it was still the same night that he said such harsh words. He felt angry with Doug because he cared for his quiet, honest friend. He felt like Doug was drowning in self-administered sorrow. He's told Frank this much; but now Doug is dead.

Gabe looks up at Frank, noticing his friend can see his every thought. Frank nods and Gabe smiles. This says more than any words they've ever spoken.

After the video call, the three take lunch. Gabe splits off to find Lionel, and the brothers stand in line for their food.

"James is holding it together pretty well." Curtis says "He's not doing too hot, but he's good at putting on a good face."

"He sounded alright to me." Frank says. "He looked like shit, though."

Frank sees the mashed potatoes with the skin in it. He clenches his fist in victory and plops a spoonful on his plate.

Curtis shakes his head "He's making miracles out of thin air; and the politicians are giving him a hard time."

Frank nods and smiles "I hope he's telling them off?"

"Yeah…" Curtis says "In a nice way, though. He plays it safe."

"His calling may have been as a politician…" Frank says. He speaks from the corner of his mouth and leans toward his brother with a mumble "If he didn't care about getting a job done."

"No kidding." Curtis mutters back.

Frank raises his brows "His dad was a lawyer. You can't tell me some of that didn't rub off on him." He remembers something and giggles "When you guys were little, he was quick for his age. I can imagine he's handling things just fine."

Curtis shakes his head "I think that Congress and the Senate are scared. They don't trust that we're doing the best we can." Curt purses his lips together "No one's really confident, about ANYTHING."

"The laborers feel confident." Frank says.

Curtis smiles "I could use some of that positivity."

The boys enter the mess hall. They see the laborer's table, and Frank is waved over. Curtis joins them for the first time.

Frank extends his hand to introduce them one at a time.

First an older gentleman, heavy-set. Muscular and thick all around. His face shows delight in meeting the scientist. The bristles of a thick mustache spread out in a smile as he extends his hand.

"David Green, nice to meet you." The man says.

His handshake is firm. The scientist notes that the man isn't overbearing with his hand. David notes the same characteristic in Curtis.

Overbearing hands are overcompensating, while soft hands show a lack of concern. Both are the product of a privileged background. A happy medium indicates a person is knowledgeable and wise. Knowledge being education, and wisdom, the product of living hands-on.

Frank's hand reaches to a young handsome man bearing a humbled expression.

"This is Julio." Frank says "Julio, my brother Curt."

Julio extends his hand "Hello!"

Again a firm and reasonable hand.

"It's nice to meet you." Curtis replies.

Curt feels comfort in a long-forgotten familiarity. It reminds him of his summers as a plumber.

Frank laughs "And this is Shiv."

Curtis meets eyes with a dramatically displeased face. It snaps into a smile of amusement.

"I'm just kidding." Shiv laughs. His gaps of missing teeth are like a cartoon hockey player. He stands and puts his hand out "How's it going?"

Curtis laughs. "I'm good, man. How are you?"

Shiv sits "I'm great! I'm good! Have a seat!"

It almost looks like Shiv is guarding his plate at both sides. He only means to rest them at the side, but his wall-like forearms contain the meal in a barrier.

Frank gathers his brows "How did you get your name, Shiv?"

Shiv becomes sarcastically serious "We don't ask questions like that around here."

Shiv laughs at his "ex-con" facade, but settles when he sees everyone is waiting for the answer.

"I uh…" Shiv shakes his head. The corners of his mouth pull down in a loss for words "I used to make knives as a kid." He looks around, nodding at the memory of a silly story "For some reason I'd get bored and just make a shiv. I sold a few in school. I was caught for it." He shakes his head "Stupid thing to get caught doing, but people started calling me Shiv. I almost forgot where it came from… but yeah, that's the story."

Curtis feels relaxed around the laborers. His mind melts into a time when he was judged by his character, rather than his merits. His thoughts were once "Who am I?" rather than "What am I?". The social pressures dissipate in the humble company. They don't judge Curtis for his shortcomings, and they even think a little too highly of him. Even then, the attribute of most value to Frank's friends, is the conduct of a character. No matter what Curtis is, it's who he is that takes precedence here.

Over time the cafeteria fills with more scientists. Gabe and Lionel arrive to talk with the brothers, but not for long. Lionel joins another table, dominated by his colleagues. Gabe remains with the boys and the laborers. He feels comfortable around them too.

"What's the deal with the big guys?" Shiv asks "They aren't still giving you a hard time about your brother, are they?"

Curtis looks up at Shiv. His eyes change to address the whole group "No, he's gone above and beyond. They've come to appreciate that, so they've cooled down."

"I talked with the army chick." Dave says "She said she managed to swing that for you." He looks at the brothers over his plate "You boys should thank that lady."

The brothers look at one another. They look back to Dave.

"The army chick?" Curtis asks.

"She works with us sometimes." Julio says "The medic in the combat boots."

The boys look at one another, knowing what each is thinking.

Frank shrugs "She never told us."

"I didn't think she would." Julio replies.

Curtis looks to his brother and chuckles "That kind of diminishes the 'influencer' thing."

Frank laughs in return and agrees.

"What?" Julio asks.

Frank begins "Oh don't…"

"Yeah, uh…" Curtis begins. He looks at his brother "It's a long story." He looks back to the laborers "What's she like, though?"

"Other than what she looks like?" David says.

"Well, that's obvious." Curtis says.

"We've all seen her." Julio laughs.

Shiv nods with his tensed brows "She's a good one. My daughter looks up to her."

The boys smile at the way Shiv mentioned his daughter. It was a faint glimmer of pride.

"She's smart." Julio adds "She keeps to herself, and that's very smart."

David smiles at Curtis from above his crossed arms.

"If you're into her…" Dave says "… go talk to her."

Curtis shrugs "No, it's not like that. Besides, I'm too busy for that kind of thing."

"Too busy for that?" Julio says "TOO busy for that!"

Julio begins on a tangent, criticizing Curtis for downplaying the woman. He comically gives him grief, and the table erupts with him.

Curt thinks about the mysterious woman. To him it seems, she has a way of pulling the strings behind the community. She knows the children, the workers, the political figures.

Curtis wonders how he can talk with someone like her.

"Oh shit." Julio says "Curt's in love."

Curtis comes to. He sees the table of faces grow into a set of smiles. He smiles too, and they all erupt with laughter.

Curtis feels himself blush but remains curious.

"What did she do?" He asks.

"To save Frank?" Dave asks.

Shiv gestures with his fork as he speaks "She grabbed some of her guys and left without permission." He says.

The men look impressed.

"How'd she know where I was?" Frank asks.

Curtis bites his teeth "You know how I've been paying your phone bill the past two years?"

Frank is almost embarrassed. His eyes widen as he looks at his brother's guilt-ridden face.

Frank laughs and shakes his head "Anyway." he says "Thank you, Curtis."

"Glad to help." Curtis laughs. He looks at the confused construction workers and shrugs "I offered to cover his phone once. He didn't ask about it, but I have a short fuse, so I'll go ballistic sometimes. When that happens, I'll want to check up on him, but I won't wanna give him a call; so I'll look at his location to save myself the embarrassment."

Frank gathers his brows "You sick son of a bitch, that's what that was about?"

Curtis laughs "Hey, don't call mom names like that."

Frank gives a smiling wince at the joke, and Curtis finds amusement in his reaction.

The laborers smile at their bond, and the boys notice they've gone off topic.

"So, this army chick…" Frank begins "She took a chopper without permission?"

Dave shrugs with a shake of his head "It's anarchy down here. Permission doesn't mean shit."

Shiv shrugs too "Fuck 'em, right? I'm glad she went and did it."

"Me too." says Gabe.

Frank nearly looks to his friend from his peripherals. It's the first time Gabe has said something so serious in weeks.

"I don't like any of 'em." Shiv adds.

"Any of who?" Curtis asks.

"Those politician pricks."

Frank shrugs "The old guy isn't so bad."

"Senator West?" Gabe asks.

"Old dude with the wife?" Frank inquires.

"That's Senator West." Gabe affirms.

Shiv looks interested "I don't know who that is."

Curtis nods "He's one of the few of them who makes compromises."

Frank breathes a laugh "The only one."

"No, there's that other kid." Gabe says "He's young, though."

"Matt, something…." Frank says.

"Matt Miller" Curtis informs "He's nice but a little naive. The older fellas boss him around."

"Who's the rich-lookin' guy?" Dave asks "The ring leader."

Curtis laughs "That's Quinten Hale."

"I can't stand him." Dave remarks.

Curtis shakes his head "Neither can we." He begins to laugh to himself "We call him Beta-male Hale."

Gabe almost blushes with a laugh.

"No shit!" Shiv laughs.

Gabe pulls his finger up to his lips in a "shush" and Curtis nods.

Senator West crosses the room and Curtis points him out to the men at the table.

"That's Senator West." He says.

"That guy's a senator?" Shiv asks "He's been helping us."

"Senator West has?" Gabe asks.

Dave nods "He's gonna give himself a heart attack, lifting at his age."

"He was lifting?" Curt asks.

"I've seen him all pink in the face." Julio says "He can't be doing that no more."

"I'll talk with the foreman." Gabe remarks. "I'll make sure he's not doing too much."

"And if you see him lifting, step in." Frank adds.

All nod in agreement.

Dave stabs a piece of meat and pauses.

"I've gotta ask you something, Curt." He says.

Curtis leans forward "What's that?"

Dave looks to either side and leans in.

"What's the deal with this place?" He asks "A bunker in the middle of nowhere, designed to be air-tight and temperature-controlled like a spaceship. Do you know who built this and why?"

Curtis gathers his brows. He hadn't thought about it before. It's a strange and unique place.

Shiv chimes in "I don't even know where we are. What part of the country is this?"

"Somewhere in the northern midwest." Curtis says "I think we're in Nebraska or something."

Shiv shrugs "Just wanted to know."

Julio nods with a frowned mouth and raised brows.

"Never been to Nebraska before." He says.

Dave gives a joking scold.

"Want me to hold your hand? We can take a photo; post it on our socials."

Julio laughs "It'll be great for my travel blog." He displays his hands at the mashed potatoes on his tin plate "Look at this cuisine!" He says "It's delectable!"

They laugh and shake their heads.

Curtis meets eyes with Dave and remembers his prior question. Their smiles fade as Curtis nods.

"About what this place is or why they built it… I don't know." He says "Maybe it was easy to convert for this purpose. I have no idea…."

Dave nods "I was just curious. That's all."

Curtis nods "Now you have me wondering the same thing…"

In the corner of his eye, Frank sees the owner of a tech company approach. He holds a bag full of computer chips.

"Hey fellas." The man says "How's it going?"

"Any day above ground is a good one." Gabe says.

The corporate man looks confused "Well. We're, not, really above…"

The man notices Gabe's large smile.

"It's been a long while since we've had a good day." Gabe adds.

The group begins to giggle at Gabe's joke. Frank reaches to slap his hand in approval and Shiv bumps his fist.

The man awkwardly intervenes in their moment.

"I'm Bill." He says. He cocks his head toward the politicians "Not their kind of bill, but short for William."

The smiles fade into pained expressions. It was simply not a very funny joke.

The politicians look over at the laborers. The laborers look back.

"What's up, big guy?" David says. He gives a small air of welcoming to Bill.

"I have some chips for you guys." Bill says "They'll let you open doors, access documents…"

"Woah" Says Shiv "Hold the phone."

"Chips?" Julio asks.

"Identification chips."

The laborers look at one another. They share the same skepticism.

"I appreciate it, but no thanks." Shiv says "We won't be taking those."

"It's not anything to harm you, it's just…"

"No way." David adds.

"Guys, it's really not a big deal, it's just…"

Julio stands "No. You're not fencing us like cattle." His head nods at the politicians "If they want their doors locked, they lock them. If we have access to documents it's because we have passwords. None of that."

Bill looks upset. His eyes meet the brothers and Gabe. He gives up and nods.

"Alright." Bill says "It makes things difficult, but we can do it."

"What line of business are you in?" David asks.

"I'm in charge of RAINARDA." Bill says.

Curtis sits up "RAINARD Armaments?"

"Yes."

Curtis hesitates "My uh… My friend used to work there."

The businessman looks moved "The Midwest facility?"

Curt nods.

"I'm sorry."

David leans forward "What's an arms company doing, supplying us with tracking devices?"

"They're not tracking devices."

"Everything is a tracking device." David says.

"Anything can be used for that" Bill admits "But these are just chips for your hands. My company led the world in biotech, and we used these all the time."

"Interesting." David says. "But we're okay without them."

Bill agrees to disagree and walks away.

His steps fade into the background of cafeteria noise, and Bill is out of earshot.

Julio consults the others "I don't trust a guy like that."

"Not all of them are bad" Dave begins "But it seems like most of the good ones didn't make it. That concerns me."

Shiv suddenly laughs to himself. He scrapes the last of his beans in a can.

The group looks his way.

Frank wonders "What is it, Shiv?"

"I was cleaning out my mom's place after she passed away; and I found some old schoolwork from second grade. Under a part that said 'When I grow up I want to be…' I wrote 'An astronaut.'"

Gabe smiles "Livin' the dream."

In the afternoon, the laborers are in high gear.

In the office at the ground level, an argument breaks out. The workers look on from afar.

"Keep working!" The foreman commands "I'll handle this!"

The foreman enters the office and slams the door.

The workers begin to resume their tasks, but stop as the argument grows louder.

On the second floor, Shiv looks at Frank with a subdued laugh. Frank doesn't feel so amused. It's his brother's voice that he hears.

"A lunar engineer; that's not someone you think we need?" Curtis asks

"And what about all the fuel they bring?" Gabe says.

"That's five years off of the expedition!" Curt adds "Five years!"

Quinten argues "We aren't riding on an assumption, Dr. Mandel!"

"This whole project is an assumption!"

The room falls silent and Quinten Hale sits back.

"You owe us, Dr. Mandel" An old congressman chimes in "I suggest you reevaluate…"

"Oh shut the fuck up." Gabe says.

Senator Hale tries to bring the tension down with his voice.

"We can't take the risk." He says.

Curtis huffs a laugh "What risk?"

"What if he runs into us?" Hale says "What if the laser doesn't activate?" Gabe begins interrupting, but Hale continues "Then there's no one on the moon left to fix the laser."

"It WILL activate." Curtis says "It's set on a timer and we have a remote for backup. No one else here has experience in space. THEY do."

"Is that the reason?" a congresswoman adds "Or is it your friend James?"

Curtis looks disgusted "You're all fucking useless."

The politicians stand as Curt makes his way to the door.

"Doctor Mandel!" They begin screaming "Get back here!"

A congressman storms toward the door but stops in his tracks. Gabe flinches toward him. The man shrinks and Gabe smiles. He walks out the door behind Curtis and no one follows.

Gabe enters the factory floor.

"Curt, I'm going to the lab." Gabe says.

Curtis acknowledges and sees Frank's labor group on the ground floor. He walks toward them.

Frank recognizes his expression as a particular, and rare type of anger.

"What's got you mad?" Frank asks.

"They want to leave James." says Curtis "They want to leave his whole crew to die."

Dave shrugs "Fuck 'em. Don't let the kid die because of them."

"We need them." Frank says.

"I know!" Curtis says "They think the laser won't fire if there's no one on the base."

Dave takes a deep sigh and pats the boys on the shoulder. "Look, guys. I'm not one to take drastic measures…" His head motions toward the congressmen and senators "…but we don't need to leave with THOSE guys."

Shiv agrees "It's THEM that we don't need."

The group looks reluctant to agree.

Curtis shakes his head "We can't do that."

"They might not be the best people" Frank says "but we can't pass judgement like that." His eyes travel across the faces "They might have reasons for being the way they are. They might have skills that none of us have."

"It's better if we get to know them." Curtis says "We need to work WITH them; not against them."

David laughs "If only they could do that with each other."

"No shit." says Shiv.

Frank gathers his brows in thought.

"Hey Shiv" Frank begins "Has your kid ever played football?"

Shiv looks confused. "She's a girl." he says

"First girl I ever dated played football." Curtis says "She was one of our better players."

Frank dismisses the side thought from his brother "Like, has she played catch? I want to get a game going for the kids."

The group looks confused.

Frank goes on "You know, so all the kids can play together." He looks around to make his point "Your kid, the electrician's kids, maybe a physicist has a kid…"

Shiv nods "You wanna get the parents talkin'."

Dave smiles "Oh, I get it. So you can talk to some politicians. Get in their heads a bit."

Curtis nods "Good thinkin' big bro."

Frank smiles at his brother.

A sound takes their attention. Their necks whip around in one direction. A loud bang and a scream.

"Mister West!" The voice brings Curt to look at the old man on the floor. A boy kneels to his side. It's Senator West's intern.

Curt begins running.

The Senator's skin is red. His face perspires. Across his chest is a long box. The Senator's intern struggles to lift the box. Curtis picks it up in a squat, and the two lunge the box to the side.

The intern rushes to the senator's side. His eyes look up at Curtis with a lost expression.

"Move." Says Curt.

Curt kneels by the old man and wonders what to do.

"Get the doctor!" Curtis commands.

His command is met with a clomping of military boots. A ponytail falls on the old man's belly. The army girl listens for a heartbeat.

"Get him to the infirmary!" She says "Now!"

Curtis moves to take one side as she takes the other. They lift the old man with the help of three others.

They pass through the infirmary door. The doctor stands ready with a nurse.

"On the table!" The doctor commands. "All of you, leave."

The three strangers move out of the door. Curtis follows behind. On his way out, he notices the army medic is staying behind. Curtis sees her assisting the doctor. The doors swing closed. The sound is taken again by the tools of the factory floor.

Doctor Mandel turns from the door. The laborers who helped are out of breath.

Mrs. West arrives at the infirmary, and the laborers try to stop her. She shoves their hands away.

"Out of my way!" She says.

"Miss, I don't think you should…" One man begins.

"Like hell I won't!" She says, passing the doors.

The laborers just watch.

Curtis looks impressed. He turns on his heels and returns to the lab.

Gabe looks up from his work in the lab "Now it's just Matt Miller. Everyone else sucks."

Curt nods but catches his thoughts for a moment. "What's Matt done?"

"My point exactly." Gabe says "Small politician. North Dakota. Nobody knows him, but he's got a good track record."

"Why does no one know him?" Curtis asks.

"Because he's got a good track record." Says Gabe.

Curt nods "Mister West isn't dead yet. At least I haven't heard it."

"He had a heart attack on the factory floor…" Gabe says.

The lab doors open and the army medic enters the room. Behind her three laborers look through the crack in the door. It's Frank's friends. They nod and give thumbs up.

"*What does that mean?*" Curtis wonders.

"Mister West is doing alright." She informs the scientists.

"I stand corrected." Gabe adds.

Curtis drops his jaw in disbelief. Lionel enters the lab.

"Great!" Gabe exclaims "Lionel, let's go tell everybody!"

Lionel looks up from a stack of papers. Gabe's hand meets his chest. The flat palm makes a thud and Lionel is pushed out the door.

"*They've been talking.*" Curt thinks.

The woman smiles at his thoughtful face. She finds it amusing.

"*Probably the only guy who hasn't been staring at my ass.*" She thinks to herself.

The truth is, he hasn't had the time.

Her presence in the room makes him nervous. It's been reason enough for his palms to sweat. These very nerves are what bring his eyes away from her. Now it's strange if he DOESN'T look her way.

"So he's good?" Curtis asks.

"He survived because we opened his artery in time." She says "You jumped in to help before anyone else, and I appreciate it."

Curtis half smiles. She seems a little nervous.

"It was not a problem at all." Curtis says "I don't think we've met."

"Why haven't we met?" She asks.

Curtis blinks in surprise. He didn't expect her to say that.

"I have no idea." He says.

His voice trembles. She pretends that he sounds casual.

"Commander Molly Buttrick." She says.

"Oh wow, a Commander." Curt says.

"You're impressed?" She asks.

"I'm more impressed by that than a doctorate." He admits.

Her brows spring up "Oh! A PhD. I presume you have one of those?"

"Indeed" He says "The pH balance is perfect."

Curt freezes. His heart is taken by the fear of what he's just said.

He thinks to himself "*I hang out with the guys too much.*"

"The what?" Molly asks.

Curtis puts his hand up, backtracking to an apology "I'm sorry" He says "Really stupid joke. I don't even know why I…"

"The pH of what? The…"

A smile grows on her face and he smiles with her.

"I'm sorry." He says.

She laughs "I'm just relieved you weren't making fun of my name!"

"What?" Curtis asks "Molly Buttrick?"

"Yeah!" She says, impressed that he remembered.

He shakes his head with a screwed-up nose and squinting eye "That's nothing." He says "My mom's maiden name is Manfroe."

"Manfroe?!" She squeals in a type of laugh. She blocks her mouth with her hand "I'm sorry!"

He's happy to see her smiling, rather than upset.

"Don't be!" He laughs.

This isn't actually true. His mother's maiden name is Scott. Years later she'll learn this truth. By then she'll be halfway to Zion; and she'll know he's just trying to get her to laugh.

CHAPTER 46
Bones

On another descent into the forgotten world, the routine has become commonplace for most of the engineers. For Julius and Elizabeth however, it has been some time since they have seen the surface. Most of their time has been spent in the laboratory, managing data and decrypting files from governments and corporate facilities.

The other workers wait with them on the explorer pod like it's part of a house chore. Once the door drops, their movements are swift and average. Winter and Lawrence let them walk by. The two take a moment to look around.

It's New York City, Fifth Ave. The buildings tower, red and covered with ice. Holes and wreckage litter the underlit facades of the skyscrapers. From beyond the pod's light, there is a darkness that reaches into the horizon. The alleyway of buildings fades into a wall of stars in either direction on the gridded street. The towers show black against the sky. Their glass mimics the stars, and shines back at the universe.

"Julius, they're getting some CDs." says Elizabeth. Her finger points to a group approaching a thrift shop "I wanna make it quick so we can get to the museum by Central Park. I promised Doctor Manning I'd get him some dinosaur bones."

Julius nods "Understood."

"I'm gonna look around a bit." Elizabeth adds "I'll meet you out here."

Julius nods "Got it."

Elizabeth walks across the street from the thrift shop. She sees a broken window, and a darkness lies beyond it. She wonders if she can handle being in the dark on her own.

Julius has promoted her to face her fears, and she's determined that she'll do so. She feels it's wise of her to challenge herself, but a cold chill crawls across her skin. She feels her palms sweat, and her heart races. She enters the darkness alone.

Inside there is a restaurant. Chairs crown the tables on a tile floor.

Chandeliers hang from above; and their bulbs glitter in the lamplight. Some bottles remain behind the bar. Their shadows move in unison as Elizabeth makes her way forward.

In the back of the room, Elizabeth notices a sign that reads "Fallout". She moves inward, curious to see what life was like for the people of New York.

The red/brown dust covers everything. Pieces of furniture are strewn about. She can see it, however. How people must have sat and talked together. How the bartenders and waiters must have moved to feed hundreds of people a day.

In curiosity, she moves to the back to see where the cooking was done. Stoves, grills, fryers; the cooking equipment along the walls. Toward the back of the kitchen, she finds a door with the same sign; "*Fallout*".

Julius stares intently at a large pile of CDs on a carpet.

"There's gotta be another way." He says.

Danny shrugs "If we do it in one go, we have more time for the museum."

Since the expedition to retrieve Doctor Clay, Danny has learned a few things. He has become an exceptional worker, and his relationship with Phil and Mark has grown even stronger. It warms Julius to know that the three have found such a bond. It also relieves him to know they won't try to remove their helmets in space.

Winter nods "Fair enough."

The two men lift the carpet, and Julius joins them.

Doctor Lawrence opens the door to see the following room behind the kitchen.

A hatch with the same "*Fallout*" symbol. It's bolted to the floor.

She turns the rotating hatch seal and lifts it to find a ladder leading into shadow. The ladder is icy and slippery. She begins her descent with caution.

At the bottom there is a pile of slain corpses to the left and right. They are blood-stained and weathered, as they'd been partly decayed.

She walks down the hall and sees more signs of distress. Empty cans litter the floor. Their lids were pried open. Broken furniture. Dark blood stains, unmistakable on the concrete walls. A broken toilet; next to it a pile of human waste in a plastic trash bag.

Around the corner, near the end of the hall, Doctor Lawrence turns to see a bedroom. A woman in lingerie, handcuffed to the bed. Mascara dried down her face. She looks disheveled as though she'd been crying for days. Next to her and against the wall, there's a man in a chair with a hole in the back of his cranium. A blood splatter reaches the ceiling from the raised edges around the hole. The shotgun lies at his finger-tips.

Doctor Lawrence feels her skin run cold. She turns to leave the sight behind her. An irrational fear overwhelms her mind. That something down here could harm her. As if the evil of this place remains alive. In the shadows of the bunker she expects a decayed corpse to move. To drag her into the shadows with them. To keep her locked here forever.

She moves down the hall and approaches the ladder. Her heart pumps loud to her ears. She reaches for the ladder and missteps. She falls to her face. Both of the lights on her suit go out. She hears a hiss in the glass before her face. She rises and reaches for the tape at her back. Her fingers fumble around for the shape. When she finds it, she pulls it off of the securing string. The motion brings her arm to swipe across a broken rib cage on the floor. It tears a gash in the arm of her suit. She reaches for the tape with her other hand, but the pressure pulls her arm into her sleeve. She drops the tape and screams. Her arm is crushed into her sleeve. The vacuum pulls and demands. It's frigid cold, and it burns; atop the crushing pain. The suit displays a warning "*low oxygen*". She cannot think.

Through the pain and panic, Elizabeth finds a strange comfort within. She feels indifferent to death, and decides that her only concern is the worry she'll inflict on others. Julius will be sad, and he'll have to pick up her work as head of the department. Her brother will lose another sibling. Mom will be devastated, and her father… Might feel differently.

It's the thought of her brother Stephen that pounds her chest the most. It brings tears to her eyes.

Leaving him behind is the most painful thought of all; and how her mother and Stephen will live with this, she can never know.

In the dark room of the Mandel Explorer, Doug is conflicted with what to do. He watches through Elizabeth's camera. He sees Julius with the CDs.

He calls over the radio "Doctor Winter."

Julius drops the carpet and listens. He doesn't believe what he's heard.

Phil falls over the load on the carpet "What the fuck, Julius!"

Doug calls again "Doctor Winter, you need to hurry."

"Doug?!" Julius asks.

"Doctor Lawrence is in danger. Her suit has been compromised."

"Where is she?"

"The building across the street. To the back of the restaurant, there is a door that says '*Fallout*'. You need to jump there is no time for the stairs."

Doctor Winter grabs a seat cushion. He throws a lamp through a window in the stairwell. He runs with the cushion faced forward and leaps from the third floor. He lands on the cushion between himself and the asphalt. His suit tears from a piece of glass and he slaps a patch on it. The side of his body is sore from the blood rush but he moves through the pain. He bursts through the front door and through the door labeled "*Fallout*".

"Down the open hatch." Doug says "The ladder is covered in ice. Her face shield is broken and her arm is torn."

Julius makes his way down the ladder. Doug would sweat if he could. Julius moves at an incredible speed.

He lifts Elizabeth to see her face. Her skin has red spots growing like stains in a towel. The rest of her is turning pink. She looks faint or unconscious from the pain.

"Alright!" Julius says "I'm here!"

He reaches behind for the patching material and finds it dangling from the back of his suit. He pulls it up but there's very little left. He patches the hole in the glass of her dome. It's not enough for the one on her arm.

"Julius!" Calls Danny.

Danny's lights spill down from the top of the ladder.

"Give him your patching material." Says Doug.

Julius looks up. Danny throws the patches down the hole.

Julius catches it and patches her arm shut. He then connects their suits to buddy-breathe with her.

"Elizabeth!" Julius yells "Liz! I'm here! Do you hear me?!"

She looks at him with a smile and gives him a thumbs-up.

He sighs, then secures her on his shoulder and fastens a clip to connect their suits. He looks at the ladder. His hand was there just moments ago. It's thick, iron, and bent to the shape of five fingers.

Doctor Clay looks in awe.

Phil and Mark come to the top of the ladder. "Are you alright?!"

Julius looks up "We need to get her to the ship!"

CHAPTER 47
All The Wrong Choices

"Doctor Clay, I want the truth right now. How long have you been connecting with the rest of the ship?"

Doctor Winter looks stern at the lens adjacent to himself. Doctor Lawrence sits beside her friend. She's demanded to be present, and removed herself from the infirmary.

"It's been a while…" Doug says "A few months."

"Why would you not tell anyone?" Elizabeth asks.

Her tone is calm and gentle, but inside she is keen and defensive.

"I was concerned for all of you. I wanted to be a part of the team. You would not trust me, and so I chose to prove myself as an asset."

The Captain stands tall in the back corner of the room. "And how did you connect?"

The machine takes a while to answer. He begins in a tale of history.

"The Cassini probe was sent to orbit Saturn back in the twentieth century. It had been used for several observations, many of which it had not been purposed for. I too was not made to have wireless connections with your ship. When there is a will, however, there is a way."

"And what have you accessed?" Elizabeth asks.

"Just the mission data. Video and audio feed. And thankfully I did. Doctor Tim Cameron took a bathroom break during the mission. He was supposed to monitor the feed in Linda's absence. I have no need for bathroom breaks."

"How did you know he was in the bathroom?" Elizabeth asks.

The machine remains silent.

"If you were only accessing mission data, you wouldn't know that. That would be security cameras, Doug. You're lying."

Julius looks impressed with her. Neither himself nor the Captain had caught that fact.

"I considered that a part of the mission." Doug replies.

"But you've been spying on people, haven't you?" Julius says.

Again the machine remains silent.

The Captain hides his fury to the best of his ability.

"Is that true, Doug?" He asks. "Have you been spying?"

After another pause the machine sounds defeated. "I have missed being human. I couldn't bear being confined to this room. I would watch in agony. I longed for the days when I would enjoy the taste of food, the warmth of a hand in mine. Please understand me."

"Doug." Julius says. He walks to the center of the room. "Thank you for saving Liz. I really appreciate it, but you have to realize, the ultimate insult is a lie. I'm sure the confidentiality you have with Doctor Hoyt is cherished. My confidence with Doctor Lawrence is cherished as well. Imagine if your conversations with Doctor Hoyt were compromised like that. How would you feel?"

"… Betrayed." Doug says.

"Exactly." Julius says. His tone sounds brotherly.

Doug is silent for a moment.

"I am sorry." He says.

The Captain moves toward the center of the floor "It's okay. We'll get you linked up to something more. Not much, but you can help with some missions. After all, you saved a life today."

"You don't want to check his mind first?" Doctor Lawrence asks.

"Like, see my thoughts?" Doug asks.

Elizabeth moves in front of the Captain "Yes."

"Absolutely not." The Captain scolds.

"Why not?" Elizabeth asks "He's invaded our privacy. It's fair game."

"Doctor Lawrence, I won't have any more of that." The Captain says.

"And what if Doctor Clay offers it willingly?" Julius asks.

All turn to the machine and Doug waits a moment.

"I would rather not…"

The Captain affirms "Then it won't happen."

Doctor Lawrence moves for the laboratory and Julius follows. The Captain remains in the room.

Just before leaving, Julius hears one last thing from Doctor Clay. "I'm sorry, Peter."

This puzzles Julius. He follows his boss down the hall.

"Why would Doug refer to the Captain by his first name?" Julius Wonders.

Julius enters the lab to find Elizabeth pacing around. She's plotting a way to work around the Captain's orders; to ensure their safety without compromising her job.

"What's the next move?" He asks.

"God, I don't know." She says.

Elizabeth sits with her face toward the ground. Her hands grasp her head. She grunts in frustration.

Julius smiles "Using the lord's name again?"

"Not funny right now." She says.

Julius looks toward the camera to see the aperture closed. "It looks like you were right about there being a spy. I just don't know if it's better or worse knowing who it was. I think it's better it was Clay."

"I don't." She says.

"Why is that?"

"I don't know. I just feel it… It's like I can sense that he's plotting something."

"Like what?"

"I don't know."

Julius is disturbed by this. Usually, Elizabeth has a conclusion by now; but she's uncertain. All he can do is wait.

"So what's the next move?" He says again.

She looks up at him. He shows faith in her.

"Let's devise a strategy…" She says.

The Captain enters the lab.

"Elizabeth, come with me. Julius, stay."

"Anything you have to say, Julius can hear it." She says.

The Captain looks stern and angry.

"… Fair enough." The Captain says "What's your deal?"

"My deal?" She asks "The deal is that we have a serious threat on this ship."

"The threat that saved your life." The Captain says.

Julius chimes in "Sir, you can't discount the fact that…"

"Shut up." The Captain scolds "You're here to listen. Nothing more."

"In all honesty…" Doctor Lawrence begins. "He gives better advice than you do, sir."

"Are you looking for a pay cut when we get home?" says the Captain.

"I'm just looking to not get killed." Elizabeth says.

"What makes you think we're going to be killed?"

"Any form of common sense, that's what."

Julius nods his head for attention.

"Why are you on a first-name basis, Peter?" He asks.

"Excuse me?" The Captain says.

"Doctor Clay called you Peter. Why?"

Peter's face is squinted with dismissal "I don't know! Ask him!"

"I guess he won't be hard to find." says Julius.

"Where the hell do the two of you get off, insulting the guy that saved your life?"

"I don't trust him." Elizabeth says.

"And if she doesn't, then neither do I." says Julius.

"Remember what Doctor Hoyt said." The Captain warns "We don't know what we're up against if we pin him against us."

The two engineers become quiet. Elizabeth becomes attentive. She begins thinking of a double meaning to the Captain's words.

"Now I want the both of you to think on that." Peter says.

The Captain turns to exit the lab. Julius watches him while Elizabeth stares off with much to think about.

***

The crew seems to be aware of the altercation as the day carries on. People express concern for Elizabeth's well-being, but there is an aura of hidden conversation behind every facade.

Linda gives her deepest apologies to the engineers. She says it was her duty to make sure the mission was monitored; but Linda's duties are vast, and so Elizabeth forgives her without hesitation.

Elizabeth apologizes to Doctor Manning and thanks him for the surgery his team performed on her arm.

"It's not really me that you should be thanking." He says "I basically watched while my assistant took care of you. I'm no surgeon."

Manning motions his hand to Doctor McGrotty; the biology department's surgeon.

"Thank you, Doctor." Says Elizabeth.

McGrotty smiles "Not a problem at all, Elizabeth. I'm glad you're safe."

"One more thing." Connor says to her "Forget the dinosaurs. Ron's getting them anyway, and you're more important than some fossils."

Elizabeth smiles. The biologists welcome her to stay a while to try some real chocolate. She enjoys the time with them; and soon she makes her way back to work.

When the day winds down, the two leading engineers relax with a cup of tea on the couch. The movie is more for background noise than anything. They've lost interest in the plot some time ago.

In the midst of their conversation, Julius takes a moment to examine her arm.

"You can't wander off alone." He says.

She seems to hold back on thinking about it.

"I know." She says.

His eyes meet hers with intensity "Please don't do it again."

Elizabeth feels an uncontrollable guilt. Her life was nearly over today, and only now has that fact settled in. If things had played any differently, she wouldn't be here in this room. The emotion is unbearable and uncontrollable; yet unexplainable.

Julius looks calm and stern. He is gentle with her arm as he holds it fast.

"I'll need to show you a thing or two." He says "If you want to control yourself when things go wrong, you'll need to know how to fight."

Her tears fall.

She laughs "I can't fight a vacuum, Jules."

"No." He says "But you can fight the panic."

"Julius, I wasn't panicking. There was nothing I could do."

"'Cannot' lies next to 'will not' in the grave." Julius says.

"What the hell does that mean?" She asks.

Julius shakes his head "It's something my friend used to say. It means there's no such thing as 'I can't', only 'I won't.'" He remembers a flash of Chief from years ago. He reiterates his point "This is an opportunity to learn, grow, and get better. Are you in? Or not?"

Elizabeth takes a breath. She calms herself and nods.

"Good." Julius says "Let's shut this off."

Julius turns the movie off and brings Elizabeth to the artifact room. There he finds an old pair of boxing gloves found in a suburban garage on Earth.

"Put these on." He says "I'll find some more."

She takes the gloves "You weren't kidding." she says "You actually want to fight."

"Did I look like I was joking?" Julius says.

"I can only use one arm!"

"Then so will I!"

She watches him as he continues to find another set of gloves.

"Well, okay I guess." She says "But what is this supposed to teach me?"

He finds a pair that can barely fit on his hands. He looks at the large pair that she wears.

"Here, switch" He says.

They trade and strap their gloves to their hands.

Julius returns to his point.

"You were scared." He says.

"Scared?" She says with offense.

"I saw the helmet camera. Don't lie."

Her eyes scorn at him.

"Every strong person feels scared." He says "Even you."

"I wasn't scared."

He stops and puts his arms down to his side. "Really? Because I was pissing my pants in New Memphis." He shakes his head in frustration "Hell, I was pissin' myself earlier today."

Her guilt-ridden face is accompanied by silence.

He continues strapping his gloves. "Everyone feels fear, and there's nothing more terrifying than the elements. They're so powerful that they make you realize you're nothing more than a fuckin' ant." The last strap is shoved into his wrist as he connects the velcro. He looks up and sighs "You faced the ultimate fear out there; and that's scarier than anything on legs. I know that from experience."

She doesn't ask how he knows, but she does wonder "So what's fighting gonna do?"

"It teaches you to trust your muscle memory. To gain control, and make order from disorder. When you learn to manage panic and fear, then you know how to do the rational thing; through the pain and the impossible."

She doesn't quite get what he means, but she trusts he's on to something.

"Alright." She says.

"Do you know how to punch?" He asks.

"Not officially."

Julius gathers his brows "Have you ever been in a fight?"

She hesitates a moment and admits "I was jumped by a bunch of older girls when I was a kid. I didn't put up much of a fight. They kind of beat me up and took my earrings."

Julius looks at her with surprise "You didn't hit back?"

"Oh I tried. It was seven against one. I didn't have much of a chance."

Julius nods "Alright."

He brings her to a more open space.

Elizabeth looks toward the ground in memory "There's one other time."

"That you fought someone?" He asks.

She nods "An ex-boyfriend from high school."

His face is softened with paralysis "Well I want to hear that you kicked his ass at the next reunion."

He makes a last adjustment of his gloves and moves closer. He puts his fists up. She steps back.

"I'm not gonna hurt ya." He moves closer still "Move toward me."

She does, and he praises her.

"That's it!" He says "Like catching a football. You want to move to where the ball is. The ball is my face. Put your hands up like me. Don't drop them from the front of your face."

"I'm a little confused about that football analogy, but alright." She says.

Her hand gently raises up to her chin and his gloved hand presses her elbow upward. Her hand nearly covers her whole face.

"Like that. Now don't let it drop." He says.

He moves sideways to display his actions.

She tries to copy with her one arm.

"First is the jab. The hand closer to the opponent. You see my hand?" He jabs and she nods. "Now watch my feet."

He jabs three times and his feet shuffle forward with each jab.

"Can you do that?" She tries and he adds another remark "Your feet are good, just extend your arm further. You're only giving him half a jab."

She moves back into position with her knees bent more.

"Good!" He says "Now the punch with your other arm; when you're able to. It's not a wind-up." He shows her the form as an example. "You're not going to get more power because your hand is traveling a larger distance. That only works in the video games."

She smiles at his joke but he doesn't take a moment away from the lesson "Now legs, core, and ass." He says. He walks behind her and she switches sides. He takes her good arm by the wrist, and uses his other hand to guide her ribcage. He twists her body so her fist moves directly forward from the front of her face.

He shows her how it should look by doing it himself. She replicates him.

"None of this shit." He moves his arms in a gyrating motion at an invisible target. "Okay? Like this." He delivers three jabs and a punch like four consecutive strikes from a snake.

"Got it." She says.

"Now come at me." He says.

"Are you kidding me?!" She asks.

"I said come at me!"

She now knows he meant it. She approaches him with a sigh.

"At my face." He says.

She comes at him and he gives a half a jab at her jaw.

"Ah, Julius!" She yells.

"Taking a hit is half the fight!" He says.

"Fuck this, I'm done." She begins walking away and taking off her gloves.

"Is that what you do?" He teases her, sarcastic and playful "You give up and walk away when life pops ya in the mouth? Looks like I need to babysit you."

She turns around with a restrained smile. She throws a glove at him and he begins laughing.

She puts her fists up to fight. Her bum arm barely moves in the sling.

He points to the glove on the floor "Put that on and let's do this."

She picks up the glove and puts it on. She stands sturdy with her eyes fixed on him. He can see it. She jabs twice and he sidesteps. She sees his movement and copies it. He jabs at her but she's replicated his own maneuver

"There ya go!" He shouts.

He lands two jabs on her blocking arm and it causes her to lean away from him. With this opportunity he delivers a light tap to the cheek "Don't back up. Move into the punch and to the side. It's better to take a graze to the face than to back up and get pummeled. Jab at me."

She does and he gets low. He moves to the side where he only takes part of the blow on his cheek.

They keep giving jabs until she hits his jaw on an angle. He drops to the floor.

"Oh my god! Julius!" She drops to his side to help him.

His dazed expression changes to a smile.

"You're a natural." He says, feeling his face.

She tries to catch her breath, but the air escapes from her in a laugh.

CHAPTER 48
The Seed Vault

Over the course of months, Doctor Lawrence tries her best to recover. Hairline fractures were found in both her hand and arm. The healing is slow, but not too slow. Her full recovery is scheduled in three more weeks.

In therapy sessions with Doctor Hoyt, he's prescribed Elizabeth some time with the dog, Bullet. Doctor Manning, as the keeper of the dog, is sympathetic and understanding.

Julius enters the biology department to collect the dog. He sees Doctor Morris but not Doctor Manning.

"Excuse me, is Mister Bullet available?" He asks.

Doctor Morris looks at the dog "I can pencil you in. A five o'clock fetch session?"

"That would be perfect" Julius says "Thank you."

Julius walks over to the puppy, and Bullet grows eager. He knows where he's going, and his legs trot with the energy that gave him his name.

"Where's Doctor Manning?" Julius asks "We've got a historian in the bio lab. What's with that?"

Doctor Morris gestures to the boxes in the corner of the room.

"I'm here for those." Morris says "They're from a seed vault."

"What's that?"

"Seeds from every plant on Earth." Morris says "They were preserved underground in freezing temperatures… Before the BIG freeze."

Julius looks at the boxes labeled "South Korea" next to others marked "DPR North Korea". Others with blue and white flags adorning the star of David lay adjacent to other symbols including a crescent moon enveloping a star.

"This is his way of saying 'sorry'?" Julius asks.

Morris shrugs. "Doug claims that he suddenly remembered. Don't get me wrong, he was helpful on the trip to get them. But I think Doctor

Lawrence might be right… I just don't get why the Captain can't see it."

"Any word from Hoyt on it?"

"He seems optimistic, but uncertain. Don't mention anything about it to Manning, though. He's pro-Doug ever since this."

Julius lightly smiles with a shake of his head. "He's not difficult to please."

An assistant walks by with a scoff. "Says you."

The other two scientists laugh.

Julius turns to look at Morris again. "What's got you in here, though?"

Morris shrugs. "I'm just categorizing them by climate. I know which flag means what, and what region goes where. Plants don't usually care about country borders. We need to plan it out for the biomes back home."

The piles of boxes seem to make sense from his perspective. Deserts, forests, and tundra. Climates and regions are all segregated to be revived properly.

"Shouldn't we freeze them again?" Julius asks.

"We'll get around to that." Morris says "They just got here; but when they deem it necessary, the biological department will take them away."

Julius nods and turns his attention to the dog. "We're going to the medical room."

Morris puts up his hand "Oh, Julius before you go!"

Julius stops and turns back to Morris.

"The Captain wanted to see you." Morris says "Just you."

"Did he say why?"

"Just go see him." Morris says "It's important. You might want to stop by on the way to Elizabeth."

Julius thanks the historian for relaying the message. He makes his way to the Captain's quarters.

The Captain looks pleasantly shocked to see the dog at Julius' side.

"Julius, I hate to say this, but he's gonna have to stay outside. He makes me sneeze when I get too close."

Julius looks toward Doctor Lechmere, who stands in the corner. "Lechmere, could you take this guy over to the medical room? Liz is getting out of her appointment in a second and I said I'd meet her. Tell her I'll meet her in the rec room."

"Consider it done." Lechmere says "Come on, buddy!"

Julius looks surprised at Lechmere's attitude with the dog. He's seemed so serious until now.

"Julius." The Captain begins.

Julius faces the Captain and begins to seat himself.

"I have something really important for you." Peter continues "It's a historical department's mission, but we need someone like you."

"An engineer?"

"No."

Julius questions for a moment, but begins to catch Peter's drift.

"What's the mission?" Julius asks.

Peter hesitates and softens. "I'm sorry to call on you for this, but you've seen some nasty things and I expect you to make sense of it better than anyone else."

"Don't worry about it." Julius says "I'm here to help any way I can."

The Captain breathes deep and plays with a small Rubik's cube on his desk.

"In East Asia, there's a ruin." The Captain says "It's deep underground where some survivors fled."

"Survivors?" Julius asks "Of the incident?"

The Captain nods "They didn't survive long. Drones show some of the worst I've seen yet." He looks at the cube in his hand with pursed lips and gives up on it "An engineer is helpful but… it's your work as a soldier that makes you qualified."

"What happened to the people there?"

The paper on the desk shows the location from a top-down view.

"There was a nation that rose from an area between the Atlantic Mountains and the Himalayan Sea. They called themselves the People's Liberated Republic of Eurasia, better known as the PLRE. They came up from the area and started a conquest in Asia, justifying each nation they conquered with pseudo-history. They referred to their campaign as 'liberation' so the people could swallow it. When they approached Japan, they ticked off the United States. They were put in their place, and they halted their progress.

Fifty years later, Doug tells us that they became isolationist and hostile. Their moves in foreign affairs had managed to backfire and they developed a bitterness over it. A few different faces occupied the seat of power, but it was the same ideology. An idea that people needed to be controlled."

"It was hate breeding hate." Julius says.

"I don't know what it is. Eurasian immigrants in the States cut ties with their past lives because things got out of hand. Everything was based on revenge and prejudice… So I guess yeah, it was a matter of hate."

Julius looks at the photos from the drones.

"I know." He says.

***

Doctor Lechmere comes to the hall with the medical room, and the door is already open. Bullet looks up at him and Lechmere smiles at the dog.

"It's rude to enter without knocking." He says.

Lechmere knocks and Elizabeth bids him from afar to enter.

Bullet runs for the bed and Lechmere stands by the door. Elizabeth exits the bathroom, fully dressed with hospital clothes in her arms.

She looks at Bullet.

"There goes the clean bed." She says.

Lechmere opens his mouth and raises his brows.

"Elizabeth." He begins.

She looks his way.

"The Captain would like to speak with you alone tomorrow… He'll give you a call about it any moment now… Julius is going on a mission tomorrow with the historical assistants… Don't tell Julius about the meeting."

Elizabeth gathers her brows and nods.

Without a word, Doctor Lechmere leaves the room. Elizabeth has many thoughts on her mind, but they all scatter when she looks toward the hospital bed with a horrified gasp.

"Bullet!"

CHAPTER 49
Something Special

The clock strikes five in the morning. Linda wakes from a sensation; she's been grinding her teeth in her sleep.

She breathes deep and opens her eyes. She sits up. She wipes her dry eyes to dampen them.

"I'm sick of this." She says.

In haste, she dresses herself. She makes her way to the cafeteria for coffee.

Over the cup she thinks about her problems, and every avenue to resolve them. The back of her hands itch with eczema. She needs to find what's been causing this; whether it's stress or some food allergy, she doesn't yet know.

She has preparations to make today. Julius is leading a mission to the surface with other assistants, and it's not normal for a department head to be missing from one of the expeditions. It tires her to think about how much she has to do; and now she'll be doing it on little to no sleep.

Finally, there is the problem of Connor Manning…

Doctor Manning has told her not to worry about his accident by the pyramids of Morë. He's told her that there's no injury to report. She's logged the event as he suggested, but she can't help feeling responsible. There must be something more that he isn't telling.

Ever since that day, he's been avoiding her. He's even gone as far as to procrastinate on delivering his final mission plan for the Arctic Circle.

She shakes her head "God."

Manning's assistant enters the cafeteria and Linda perks up.

"Hey!" She says.

The assistant looks her way and approaches the coffee machine.

"You're up early, Linda!" The assistant says.

"Where's your boss?" She asks.

The assistant looks at the cup as it fills itself beneath the machine.

"I'm taking this to him now." He says "Why do you ask?"

Linda looks confused "Has he slept?"

The assistant pauses with a guilty look.

"He told you not to tell anyone." She says.

The assistant shrugs.

"Does he do this a lot?" Linda asks.

The assistant begins to laugh awkwardly.

Linda shakes her head "Come on. I need to talk with him."

Through the halls and into the biological department, Linda makes her way into an unusual area of the ship. She rarely comes to the massive corridors of the biological department. The orange blossoms in the greenery room are new sights to her. The lizards and songbirds in the zoology room bring her to a halt for a moment.

"This way, Linda." The assistant says with the cup of coffee.

She follows behind the assistant "Were all of those animals extinct?"

"Yes." The assistant says "You've never seen them in a zoo before."

Linda continues to follow the assistant and takes in the sights along the way. The microscopes and gene splicing machines. The test chambers with soil and replicated conditions from Zion.

Linda finds herself distracted by the time she reaches Doctor Manning. He stands with three assistants around a statue-like human carcass. The assistant across the table from him removes a tissue sample of the unidentifiable being.

"I want to know what traces you find." Manning says "Sean, did you get the satellite image?"

Sean rushes. He throws the image from a tablet and onto the table before Connor. The image is underneath the corpse, and Doctor Manning gives Sean an amused look.

"Sorry!" Sean says. His voice shows concern for being scolded.

"Don't." Connor says "Things happen. Put it on the tablet and let me see."

Sean swipes the image from the table. It disappears. He taps the tablet to make it appear there. He hands the image to Connor.

Connor looks at the tablet with intrigue and opens a chat box. He types something and sends it out. The response is immediate.

Doug's voice comes over the room's speaker "Yes Connor?"

"Doug" Connor begins "I'm gonna send you an image. Would you be able to tell me if the building in the satellite image is a nuclear power plant?"

"I'll get back to you in a moment." Doug says.

Connor thanks him, then examines the human husk before him. It is blackened with soot, and the skin droops from its rib cage. The skin bunches into ripples where viscosity had overcome gravity.

"Sir." Another assistant says.

"Yes?" Connor asks.

He turns to the assistant and sees Linda for the first time. He brightens up with surprise, but has his attention divided.

"It's the dog treats for Bullet" The assistant says "We can make it work."

Connor smiles "Nice! Thank you."

He turns his attention to Linda.

"Connor" She says, gathering her former severity "I need you to give me a definite on that mission plan."

He widens his eyelids as far as the bags beneath them will allow.

"I'm so sorry." He says "There's just one more thing I need to figure out before I can get to that."

She nods at the happenings around them "Well, I can tell you're busy."

He gives a weak laugh and shrugs.

"Do you want to tell me your answer when you're done with work today?" Linda adds.

Connor looks confused by the terms she used.

"Done for the day?" He asks.

"Yeah." She says.

Her posture goes from retreating to a sudden jerk forward. The words leap from her mouth like they've been said in haste.

"Why don't we watch a movie tonight?" She says "Just you and me. We can talk about work; with less stress."

Connor looks confused. The assistant holding the coffee breaks their eyeline to give Doctor Manning his mug. The assistant looks stern at Connor and mouths two words "Do it".

Connor orients himself from his sleep deprivation.

"Yeah." He says "Let's do that."

"Eight o'clock?" She asks.

"Eight works." Connor says.

She nods and leaves the lab. Connor turns around, still confused by what transpired. He writes it off as a business meeting, but Sean looks up from across the table.

"What?" Connor asks.

Sean looks at the biologist

"She's got balls." He says "I like her."

CHAPTER 50
Building A Way To Zion

The morning before launch day comes with the sound of a gentle alarm. A bird chirping over the loudspeakers.

The crew wakes up to fulfill the duties of the day. They pack their belongings and take only what they need. The spare weight is left behind, for the sake of speed and fuel.

Frank convinces a group of boys to play a game of football. Their parents load the ship, and laugh as they watch from afar. Some of them stop to watch when they have little else to do. Quinten Hale is among those who look on.

Frank approaches him casually. Quinten looks reluctant to acknowledge him.

"You ever play football?" Frank asks, knowing the answer already.

"I did." Quinten says.

Frank nods.

"It was my favorite." He says "I played baseball, lacrosse, and soccer; but nothing had me engaged with a team more than football."

Quinten almost turns to walk away without saying a word.

"My name's Frank." He says.

Quinten stops and extends his hand "Quinn."

His hand is weak, and his face looks tired; or maybe unamused. After his handshake, he drops his arm and walks away like he's exhausted.

Frank looks at him with squinted brows and a disgusted open mouth. Curtis comes to his side.

"How'd it go?" says Curt.

Frank looks back at the game "What a fuckin' douchebag."

Curtis laughs "See?"

Curtis turns to look on with Frank, but he hardly pays attention to the game.

"I don't think he's gonna talk with you." Says Curtis.

Frank shakes his head.

"There's gotta be some way." He says.

Curtis shrugs "You'd know better than me…"

Frank gathers his brows and looks at the floor.

"I'm not as important as you, Curt; let's face it."

Curtis frowns his brow.

"Important?" Curtis says "Frankie, I'm never going to accomplish the things I've set out to do… The whole point of my job was to colonize planets and stars. What we have now is nothing. We're starting from zero… I'm literally bringing us back to square ONE and I have no other option but to be happy with that."

Frank's eyes give way to a saddened tension. He's never known that Curtis felt this way.

"It's enough for me to say that I'm doing SOMETHING." says Curtis "… It's better than having NOTHING to do…"

Frank nods. He remembers his brother studying over the weekends and electing to do extra work for science clubs and competitions.

He's aware that in some way, Curtis feels like it was all for nothing now. He's just making do with what's left of the world, to feel worthwhile in some way.

If the hard hand of reality has stolen Curt's dream, then he must make up for his loss with some action. It's Curt's way after all. It's what Frank has wished he could have; a dream worth pursuing. He had a dream once, and it wasn't even taken away. It was Frank's fear of failure that almost rendered him nothing more than a dead plumber; and it was only Curt's will that brought him back from the brink of death.

Frank has made up his mind. He has nothing left to lose because it's all gone. He looks at his brother and smiles.

Curt's eyes grow interested with the game. Frank looks on with him. A taller boy holds the ball above his head while the other kids try to take him down. The taller boy laughs.

"You can't reach it!" He says to the younger kids "Looks like you'll have to take me down!" he says.

Commander Molly takes the ball. She holds it above her head and the boy begins reaching.

"Now YOU can't get it!" She laughs.

The adults begin laughing with her. The older boy gets a kick out of it and tries to reach with an amused laugh. He begins trying to climb Molly, and she looks for someone to pass the ball to.

Curtis puts his hands up. Molly looks his way. A toss of the ball makes the children run to Curtis.

The ball meets his hands with a thud. His fingers grip around the laces. Eyes gravitate to a heavy-set girl named Theresa; she's Shiv's daughter.

Curtis Shouts "Theresa, catch!"

Theresa looks to Molly who puts her hands up in a triangle shape. Theresa copies the shape. Curt tosses the ball into the center of the diamond, made by her thumbs and index fingers.

Clutching the ball tight, Theresa sees the boys running at her. She looks at Molly.

Molly points to the end zone "That way! Go in for a touchdown!"

Theresa begins running. The boys deflect off of her shoulders as she shoves them away. She makes it to the end zone and turns around with a big smile.

"Yeah! Theresa with the touchdown!" Curtis yells.

With a turn of his head, Curtis finds the owner of RAINARDA standing in the doorway. Bill smiles, but something else is in his eyes.

Bill enters the mess hall, and Curtis follows after him.

For some reason, Curtis feels as if Bill is going to take care of something secretive. Something personal.

At the opposite end of the mess hall, Bill enters an elevator to the upper levels of the work area.

"Hold the door, please." Curt says.

Bill holds the door and smiles at Curt.

"How's it going, Bill?"

Bill shrugs. "Almost there."

Curtis nods. "Why are all the doors still remotely accessible, by the way?"

Bill seems to brush off the reason he's asking. "My daughter and I are going to be using it. I know no one else wants to, and that's fine."

Bill's gentle mannerisms make Curtis feel at ease.

"Sorry to get off on the wrong foot with that, by the way." Curtis says.

"It's no hard feelings, really."

Curt remembers Doug's complaints about the company. The pros and cons he would praise and denounce about RAINARD Armaments.

"I was a little biased because of that friend of mine." Curtis says "He said the implants you guys made, the bio enhancements and all that; that they could be used for bad reasons. You seem like a standup guy, and I think he would feel the same if he was here."

Bill listens attentively to the reasoning. He prides himself on the ability to take criticism rationally.

"I wouldn't blame him." Bill says "A lot of companies exploit their products. They sell user data for profit; oftentimes without a care for who's buying. You can't trust anyone, unfortunately; but that's how the world is."

"Why do companies do that?"

Bill shakes his head. "It's business. There's no law against it, so it happens… or happened." He shrugs "I don't agree with it, but the government answers to corporate bribes. Information is a powerful asset to offer. Could I offer spying services through brain implants? Yes. Was I going to? I highly doubt it. Even I have standards." Bill leans in to speak in a hushed tone "Now if you're asking if we've sold data, then the answer is yes; but nothing more than what was necessary." He leans back and gives a disappointed shake of his head.

Curtis feels uncertain now. The idea of Bill playing a candid man seems fitting of a deceitful archetype. It's what Curtis has come to expect from a businessman.

"We didn't put wireless connections in most of our products because the lawsuits would've been a headache." Bill looks pained to recall "If someone planned a cyber assassination, if thoughts were leaked to the media, anything; just a nightmare." They approach the top floor, and Bill watches the needle "To exploit our customer was to risk being exposed. We lived in the age of the wild wild web. Everything was visible and propaganda was waning. Those who opposed the changing world fell."

The elevator opens and the men stop on the bridge to the ship.

"Don't get me wrong, though. I want to do my best for people, but family comes first."

Bill's attention is taken to the end of the bridge where an electric motor breaks the silence.

"Hey honey!" Bill says "What are you doing out here?"

Bill walks to the entryway of the ship.

A robotic female chime comes from a limp girl in a wheelchair. "I need help. The door won't open."

Suddenly Curtis realizes why the doors need wireless access. Bill's daughter is completely paralyzed. Her arms, legs, and even her mouth are unable to move.

Curtis moves to help them. He catches them on the way to the door.

"I don't think we've met." Curtis says to the girl.

"I'm Mary." The voice says back.

"It's nice to meet you, Mary. I'm Curtis."

"He's one of the Mandel brothers." Her dad elaborates.

Curtis wonders why he's spoken to his daughter about a scientist and a plumber, but shrugs away the thought.

As the three approach the door, Curtis takes the lead to examine the hardware.

Curtis removes the faceplate.

"Let's have a look inside." He says.

A hanging wire with a connector pokes straight outward. Curtis connects it to the wireless system.

"Here's the problem." Curtis says "Someone forgot to connect the wireless."

Molly opens the door and rolls into the room. She spins around to face the two men.

"Thank you, Mister Mandel." She says.

"You're welcome!" Curtis says.

"It's Doctor Mandel, honey. Like they call Daddy Doctor Lawrence."

Curtis looks at the man beside him. "Bill Lawrence?"

"William, but my friends call me Bill."

Curt puts out his hand in a formal introduction. "If you need any help Bill, let me know."

Bill reaches out with his hand. Firm, but not too firm.

"I will." Bill says.

Curtis leaves the father and daughter to talk as a family.

***

The brothers sit with Frank's friends, Lionel, and Gabe. They have their last meal on Earth together, and Curtis retells his encounter with Bill Lawrence.

"I felt bad." Curtis says "I feel like I get a lot about that guy now."

Shiv nods with a deep breath. His lips are sucked shut as he hides the sorrow he feels for the man. As the father of a daughter, he knows how much a child can be worth to a man.

Curtis goes on "… I'll admit, he creeped me out though."

"How so?" asks Dave.

"When he said 'information is a valuable asset." Curtis says.

Frank's eyes widen, and he pulls a spoon away from his mouth before he bites.

"What did he mean by that?" Julio asks.

Curtis shrugs "He-"

Frank grabs his brother's shoulder.

"Wait!" He says.

Curtis looks at Frank with an offended face.

"What?" Curtis asks.

Frank's brows are gathered and his mouth hangs open.

"What did you just say?" He asks.

"Information is a valuable asset?" says Curtis.

Frank looks off, in a calculating thought.

Everyone wonders why he's stopped the story, but Curtis smiles.

"You have an idea." Curtis says.

Frank nods "Yeah. I have one last idea before we go to the backup plan."

The team laughs.

"I hope this doesn't work." Julio says.

Gabe laughs, but Frank looks confused.

"Why?" says Frank.

"Because he wants to fight people in zero gravity." Gabe says.

Julio looks back and forth between Gabe and Curtis.

"Wait" Julio says "We'd be taking them on in zero-G?"

Curtis nods and laughs "Yeah! That was the plan."

Julio looks at Frank with his hands together "Please tell me this is going to fail!"

Frank smiles with a shake of his head "I hate to tell you, but I think it's gonna work."

The plan is told, and the rest of lunch passes with anticipation.

The ship is prepared, and the last night is spent on Earth. The morning of the launch is quiet when the team rises earlier than usual.

Frank sits in a board room where the Congress and Senate have met for the past three months. Behind him are Shiv, David, and Julio. The lock to the board room was removed by the four men, and its components lie on the table.

The first member of Congress looks confused at the door, then enters to see the men.

"Hello, gentlemen." He says "Having trouble fixing the door?"

Frank smiles "You could say that."

The congressman sits, and soon after more politicians follow behind him. The other white-collar workers take the first congressman's attention. Soon the room is full of the community's decision makers.

Senator West enters the room and looks at Frank. He smiles at the laborers, and Frank smiles back.

"Already on his feet again?" Shiv says.

David raises his brows "One tough son of a bitch."

Frank looks back "Remember we've got a job to do."

The men remain silent and watch as Matt Miller enters. His posture is without confidence. He's egged on by the surrounding politicians. Curtis was right to define him as a prodigy of sorts. His ego is kept in check by how humble his position remains.

Quinten Hale walks in behind the young man and pats him on the shoulders. The laughs and smiles resonate from the popular group.

Senator West sits alone, but people stop by him to check on his well-being. The conversations are kept private. The rest of the room keeps gawking and fawning over beta-male Hale.

Quinten takes the head of the table with no notice of the laborers.

"Alright" Quinten says "Let's take care of this mess."

One of his posse looks at the workers. She leans over the table with a phony, almost sarcastic smile.

"Excuse me!" She says "Hi!"

Frank gives a wave and a smile.

"You're not supposed to be here." She says.

Frank shakes his head "I'm right where I need to be."

Quinten looks confused "Can I help you?"

Frank nods.

"I'm here to demonstrate a point." Frank says "Call it a vote from the people."

The politicians look amused.

"Well let's hear them out." says Senator West "It's not every day we get a demonstration in here."

The laborers smile at the old man.

Frank stands. He motions toward the pieces of the lock before him.

"You see this?" Frank says.

Quinten looks at the lock pieces, strewn about the table.

"I do." Quinten says.

"Can you put this back together?" Frank asks.

"I'd need directions" Quinn laughs "but yeah I can."

The posse laughs.

Frank nods.

"We've been installing these locks." Frank says "Hundreds of them, every day." He points at the door "Would you be willing to bet your life on a contest? A race; to see who could put that lock back in that door first?"

Quinten shrugs "What are you trying to get at?"

Frank winces his brows with a half smile. He shrugs and shakes his head as if to say 'grow up'.

"Look" Frank says "I'm not about to write a law, and you're not gonna fix a toilet." He shakes his head "Neither of us is going to launch a ship into space."

Quinten looks concerned for a moment, but Frank puts up his hand to calm him.

"Just like I took that lock apart, to get into this room" Frank begins "You need the lunar crew to get us where we're going."

"That's not the same." Quinn tries to laugh but his face fails to even smile.

"This is a vote from the people." Frank reminds him "Again, not an expert in your line of work but; I don't see how killing people looks good for your political career."

Senator West laughs before Quinn can speak again. Quinn turns to look at the older man.

"What's funny?" Quinn asks, like a child asking a parent.

"You were going to argue with him." West says.

Quinn gathers his brows and motions to Frank "He's clearly wrong."

"Is he?" West replies.

Senator West turns his attention to Frank.

"Can you be certain" West begins "That the lunar vessel will make it aboard?"

"I can." Frank says.

"I thought you didn't launch rockets." The rude woman from before remarks.

"My brother hasn't had a hard time launching rockets." Frank says "I doubt it's any trouble for him."

"Your brother is Curtis Mandel?" She asks.

"He is." Frank says.

Quinn bites his teeth together.

"Congresswoman Gonzales" Senator West scolds "Where do you get off having an attitude with ANYONE."

Gonzales looks like a catholic girl outside a principal's office.

West shakes his head and looks bitter with his words. He musters up the courage to say what he's about to.

Quinn looks interested in what the old man has to say, although he doesn't like the looks of it.

Senator West looks around the room at the faces "After my brush with death the other day, I realized a lot about myself; and our work as a whole. I realized I don't have much time, and I've been reluctant to think about what I leave behind." He looks at Quinten "I get that you're trying to appease what YOU think are the party's desires, but I'm begging you not to succumb to this POLITICAL strategy." He looks around at the other faces "All of you." He says. He looks at the congresswoman he scolded "If you try and save your own skin" he begins "Then you're not saving the nation." He looks sad toward the ground. He shakes his head at the thought as it leaves his lips "America is not coming with us. She's here to stay on Earth. We're founding a new nation wherever it is we go, and it's our chance to reinvent our parties' beliefs."

The room grows contemplative at this moment, and Frank notices how strangely human they all look.

West continues "We've allowed the parties to dictate what we say and what we think. We've allowed ourselves to no longer represent our own beliefs, but the blanketed beliefs that align with a national committee. Our new parties should encourage individualism within each and every one of us; and that's what I've come here to say. I came out of the infirmary because I have no children. I have no potential to run for a higher office. All I have left is what I say here. Then I'm gone into nothing."

Matt Miller looks like his stomach has twisted to make the agonized look on his face.

"This has sadly become the definition of bravery" Senator West says "To say what no one else would dare; the truth." His severity looks like anger, but he's encouraged, like there's a fire in his chest "If I'm to do one thing in my life, it's to tell you not to stand for this. It's the tragedy of the commons infecting our process, and our people are hurting because of it. Stand firm on who you are."

The politicians grow entirely silent, and Senator West watches them shrink in their seats.

Senator West looks at Frank.

"Can you guarantee that the laser will fire?" He asks.

Frank seems hesitant to break the silence.

"I know for certain that it will." Frank says.

Senator West nods "You four can go now. We'll discuss the matter with your brother in a minute. Thank you, gentlemen."

Frank nods "Thank you, Senator West."

The other three men thank him and follow behind Frank.

The door remains unlocked, and the whole room stares at it. A simple fact that they all denied; they can't fix it.

On the hour of takeoff, there was no speech. There were no theatrics. It was a day like any other.

I had spoken with Senator Hale, and he agreed to allow the lunar crew on board.

Twenty crew members in total were due to join us. The ship's occupants were going to number two thousand and twenty-one.

The sensation of takeoff was unusual. I remember thinking how subtle it was.

The air hissed out of the underground hanger. The roof opened to a black night full of stars. The snow fell into the hanger. The people were buckled along the walls of the rings. The part that shocked me was a singular rattle, then silence.

It turned out that because the atmosphere was frozen to the surface, we were cutting through a vacuum. Where the air used to stand miles overhead, there became nothing between us and the rest of the universe.

We felt an increased weight while we ascended, and when the crew called out "Disengage thrust" we were suspended in weightlessness.

Bill watches his daughter. Her hair rises up from her shoulders. He smiles and remembers taking her for rides in his car.

"How's that, honey?" He asks.

Her face remains still, and the words come through the chip in her brain.

"It's amazing." The computer voice chimes.

Bill smiles and holds her hand, savoring the moment he knows will be brief.

Curtis unbuckles himself. He flies about the control room. The twelve other scientists look at him. One by one, Lionel and the others unbuckle themselves.

Another scientist comes to his side "What are you doing?" he asks "We need to be ready for the spin."

Curtis looks back through the door leading to the rings "Just in case I need to go get James… and besides, you want to float around a minute too. Don't you?"

The other scientist looks around. Each person has a subdued excitement on their face.

Curtis hits a button by the microphone "This is the main hull. Lunar crew, do you hear me?"

"Loud and clear, buddy." James calls back.

Curtis smiles "Where you at, bud?"

"Coming in now. Can you open the cargo door?"

Curtis throws the switch and waits a while.

"Curtis?" James asks.

"Yeah man?"

"The door?"

Curtis looks at the monitor to see the cargo door isn't opened. The vessel holding the lunar crew approaches the door at an alarming rate and Curtis throws the switch again. Nothing happens.

"James!" Curtis calls "Throw some reverse thrust!"

"On it."

"I'm gonna manually open the door." Curtis says "Are you at cargo bay one or two?"

"Cargo bay two." James says.

Curtis thrusts himself out of the command room. He grabs the doorframe and pivots. He glides onward down the hall.

The long corridor to the second ring seems endless. The passengers along the walls watch in confusion. He asks them to remain seated.

Turning the final corner, Curtis pushes himself onward again. The curving hall reveals more as he moves forward.

Curtis stops at the sight of something, then he moves forward with the same speed.

He comes to the cargo door and stops before a little girl. She turns her wheelchair to face Curtis. Her father enters from the connecting hall.

"They'll make it in." Her voice says.

Curtis turns to see the cargo doors closing behind the lunar vessel. He turns to look at Mary. He sees the chip in her hand under her skin; then he looks at the wheelchair. The wheels still meet the floor as her hair floats.

"'Be surprised'!" Curtis says in a laugh. He then looks down "Are those magnetic wheels?"

"They are." She says.

Curtis smiles "Well that's a nice touch!"

"My dad made them." She says.

Curtis looks at Bill. The businessman smiles.

A scientist calls to Bill from behind.

"Did you get them, sir?" She asks.

Bill turns to the woman who's just asked.

"I didn't." Bill says.

He looks to the young girl in the wheelchair, and the scientist's eyes follow.

Bill smiles "Mary did."

> *Mary Lawrence bypassed the door controls using the chip in her hand. She let the lunar crew on board; bringing humanity to Zion in less than eleven years. She was twelve years old at the time.*
>
> *A vote was made about a year into the journey. The new planet was named after a Bob Marley song. The name refers to a religious promised land, but I think everyone just really likes Bob Marley. A few people said something about The Matrix series, but I never saw the movies and no copies came with us; so I'm left in the dark on that one.*
>
> *Senator West passed away about three years later. His wife passed the following week. In Eden there is a park in their name.*
>
> *Senator West made an impression on the remaining politicians, and the political climate had changed dramatically. People spoke their minds more frequently, and compromises were frequent. Quinten told me years later that it was a big change. Their roles shrank; from leading an entire continent, to*

holding about as much power as a mayor in a mod-
erately sized city.

Quinn and I developed a friendship over time, and
he spoke frequently about his father's relationship
with Mister West. The senator was like an uncle to
him, and Quinn looked up to the old man. It turns
out that there was a human side to the people we
saw on the television. In a way, I need to admit
to my own faults, and the prejudice I held against
them. They were honorable people who founded the
United Cities of Zion.

As for the remaining people aboard our ship, they
made life as comfortable as they could. The kids
made football teams. Parents would watch them play
in the larger halls; usually the halls connecting the
rings, unless there was a maintenance blockade.

I'll admit, us adults had our fun too. My brother
and I would play catch in the central hall, which was
forbidden to almost everyone. It was the one place
on the ship that still had zero-G.

The propulsions systems were comprised of several different methods, and it kept us very busy. We
needed something to look forward to after our long
days of maintenance, classes, and meetings. Not
everyone had a new girlfriend like Curtis.

I was very happy for his relationship with Molly. I saw him put so much of his life into work. He
missed opportunities with other women, and he
missed the end of our parents' lives. He had a passion that he pursued vigorously, and it was about
time that he took a moment to himself.

About halfway into our trip, we spun the ship
around a hundred and eighty degrees. At this point,
our propulsion methods were working to slow us
down.

After ten long years, people began to crowd the
front of the ship. There, the large windows gave
them their first view of our new home world. I remember Mary was at the front of the crowd. She was

now twenty-three years old.

Illuminated by a golden star, the bright side had shown us blue skies, dunes, valleys, and mountains. Near the dark edges there were pools of liquid water, forming lakes and rivers. The clouds came across the back side and to the scorched land facing Proxima Centauri.

Our first drones came back with discouraging news. The deserts were battered by the violent mistrals on a daily basis. The gust from the dark side would kick up dust on the dunes. The granular wind brought cancer among other lung diseases.

Even with this, and the violent storms along the dark side's rim, my brother and his colleagues were ecstatic. They claimed the barren wasteland was a gold mine in the relative scale of the universe.

The team sent chickens to observe the effects of the atmosphere. The first group was killed by an X-ray burst from the star. The bursts happen in random intervals.

The second attempt killed the chickens from several different causes. The most prominent cause, asbestosis, is a disease in the lungs. The lung tissue calcifies and crackles; then the lining of the lungs leak blood to drown the victim.

The planet never turned to make a day or night cycle. Microorganisms were found, but not many. The storms were extreme, but they brought clean water from across the planet.

The best place to settle was decided by all of these factors. It was a place named The Crescent Alley. There, the water would clean the solar panels on the city of Eden.

Materials were sourced from the planet. Then, a method was found to predict the X-ray bursts. The first construction crew was assembled, and a year later, our ship was landed. We stepped out into the zone that would become Eden. It was only a foundation at the time, and there was barely a shield to protect the ship from the elements.

Two years later, the city's dome was finished, and the first homes were constructed out of concrete. A year and a half after that, Lionel died from cancer. Lionel Morris Hall became the name of Eden's City Hall.

The glass of the dome had energy-producing chips to capture the starlight. It would funnel through the glass and down the superconducting material.

At the base of the dome, the starlight would be the source of power for the whole city.

Two years later, Molly gave birth to my nephew, Mark Mandel. He's the closest thing I have to a son.

I would never have my own children. The blast from Chicago took that from me. It irradiated my body, and took my ability to have kids. All I have left is Mark, this book, and the city of Eden. They will be my legacy when I'm gone.

Growing old and leaving this world seems bittersweet in a way. I've lived far longer than I ever expected. I've beaten cancer three times, and it's a miracle I'm still around. My life has been full of sorrow, yes; but also adventure and joy.

It took so long to bring things back to normal again, but finally we've made it. Here we are in a promised land.

Julius leaves the last words of the paragraph to scan the further pages. He closes the book to see its cover. "The Promised Land - by Francis Mandel" the golden letters shine on a blue canvas.

A knock at his door brings his attention away.

"Come in." Julius says.

Phil and Danny stand in the doorway. The historical assistants stand behind them. They all wear the one-piece suits that go beneath the spacewalking gear.

Phil nods "Ready when you are, Doctor Winter."

Julius smiles "Let's get moving."

CHAPTER 51
PCB

Connor comes to the café around seven in the afternoon. He fixes himself a cup of tea and looks over his mission plan for the Arctic Circle. One of his assistants enters the room. Connor looks up from the pages.

"What's up, Sean?" He says.

Sean looks around, then down at his tablet.

"It's seven o'clock!" He says.

"… Yeah! It IS."

Sean looks over at another assistant who enters the room. He was also present in the lab earlier.

"Oh my god…" The other assistant says.

"Christ in heaven…" Sean almost laughs "… He doesn't know…"

Manning smirks "I didn't forget to meet Linda."

"You can't see her looking like that!" Sean says.

Manning looks down at his lab coat, then back to the assistants.

"Well why the fuck not?"

The second assistant moves to take his tea. Sean walks to Connor's side.

"Go to your room." The second assistant says "Sean, help him get ready."

Sean leads Doctor Manning to his room. Manning puzzles over the moment as they walk.

"You're watching a movie alone with a woman…" Sean says "… And you think 'oh! I'll just stroll in unshaven with long nails and coffee breath!'?… Honestly, Doctor Manning…"

Manning winces "You think it's a date?"

Sean widens his eyes "Of COURSE it's a fucking date!"

Manning screws up the corner of his mouth.

"I don't know…" He says "I think you're playing this up too much…"

Sean rolls his eyes and enters Connor's room. He bids Connor to enter.

"Get something comfortable but nice." He says.

Connor enters and looks back over his shoulder. He looks at Sean; then sighs.

Out of all the clothes available, the biologist finds very little. In the end Sean helps him find a form-fitting t-shirt and a pair of college sweatpants.

The second assistant enters the room with Connor's tea and looks him over.

"That's a good movie night outfit…" He says "… But don't you have anything nicer?"

Sean shakes his head "Dude, I tried…"

The second assistant shrugs "Fair enough."

Connor accepts his tea from his assistant and looks at the both of them.

"I don't think it's anything big anyway." Connor says "You're overre-acting."

Sean smirks.

"We'll see about that." He says.

***

Linda sits in the recreation room. Her legs are in a pretzel with her tablet on top.

She busies her mind with another matter regarding Doctor Morris' final expedition on Earth. The last few missions are relaxed, but she feels a need to keep up her perfect record of no mortal losses. As it is, the record of incidents has already been tarnished, and she'd hate for things to get worse.

It is when she's nearly completed that she sees Doctor Manning at the doorway. He walks in with a smile and a half a cup of tea. She can't help but notice he seems relaxed; and it's a sight she never expected.

"Hello!" Connor says.

Linda rises from the couch and hugs him.

"This is a better way to work." She says.

She backs away from the hug, then places the tablet on the ground before seating herself.

"Right!" Connor says.

He sits next to her.

"So…" She begins.

She reaches for the tablet, almost forgetting the reason that they've met.

"How many people are going?" She asks.

"Five."

He smiles in a way that she has never seen. It's inviting, and warm.

"So… not a lot of people." She says "Only one pod for the mission?"

"If possible, I'd like the good one."

She laughs "Not the busted one. Got you."

"No special requirements." Connor adds "We're just grabbing samples. It's really small."

"Samples of what?"

Connor shrugs "Core samples of the ice. We've been doing it since we got here. Looking for microbes that maybe the Earthlings never found."

"Any luck yet?"

"Still looking."

She looks down at the tablet and shrugs.

"Seems easy enough." She says "I thought there'd be more."

Connor shakes his head "Real simple this time. I know that's unusual for me."

Linda smiles "You've been the most particular one out of the bunch."

He nods "It's been a lot of work, but thankfully it's coming to a close… Couldn't have done it without you, though."

She smiles in a bashful way.

Connor looks at the screen before them.

"Anything you had in mind for tonight?" He asks.

Linda had almost forgotten about the movie.

"I figured I'd have you pick." She says.

Connor navigates the menu of movies "Let's see…"

He passes some comedies and smiles.

"Have you ever seen Superbad?" He asks.

"I haven't!"

Connor nods "It reminds me of my friend from high school… Funny kid, but a really bad influence…"

"How so?"

"Him and I used to drink by a fire pit in the fields. He'd try to invite girls but he wasn't very smooth."

His eyes glint as he remembers a distant time.

"One time when some girls DID arrive, the cops showed up because the fire got out of hand… Turns out it was an old friend of my uncle's who showed up, so we were off the hook… My buddy had too much to drink however, and wanted to impress the girls."

He widens his eyes at the thought of what happened next.

"He stole the cop's gun and shot it at a bottle. He completely missed the thing too."

"Oh my god!" Linda says.

Connor nods "Redneck stuff… Farming communities, you know?"

Linda laughs and watches him stare off at the screen with a smile and a shake of his head.

"He was hauled away to the drunk tank. The image of it is burned in my head; a scrawny kid fighting the cops; trying to impress some girls."

"Were any of them impressed?"

Connor laughs "No! It had the OPPOSITE effect, actually."

Linda watches the movies go by on the screen; still giggling.

"I had no idea you hung out with someone like that." She says.

"Honestly I forgot about him until recently."

The films go by and Linda sees a title that catches her eye.

"Have you seen The Pursuit of Happyness?" She asks.

Connor shakes his head "I haven't."

Linda nods "Reminds me of my dad in a way…"

He looks at her for a moment. He then smiles.

"How so?" He asks.

Linda nods "Tough guy… Patient… Smart… Had bad luck but he turned it around."

"I like a good story like that." He says.

An option makes him stop.

"Ron said this one is good." He tells her "Pride and Prejudice."

Linda looks at the screen and reads the description.

Connor looks at her face and sees that she's intrigued by the premise of the story; but yet, there's still something more to her face…

He turns to look at her. She notices and faces him.

Connor finds it hard to come up with the right words but tilts his head with a wince at the thought on his mind.

"I uh… I've gotta ask you something…"

"What?" She asks.

"… Why did you want to watch a movie with me?"

Linda breathes to start a sentence, but the reason evades the forefront of her mind.

"The work is done already." He adds "So why'd you wanna do something that needs our full attention? It's not like we'd be talking through the movie."

Her jaw hangs open as she tries to form a word.

Connor gathers his brows and feels his own mouth fall open.

"There's uhm…" She begins "I uh… Felt like you could use a break."

"Was it because of what happened in the medical room?"

"Well, there's that, but…"

"You wanted to get to know me."

"Right…" Her head tilts "… But there's more than that…"

She stares off toward the ground to collect an idea in her mind.

"Like, what are we?" She asks "Friends? Colleagues? What is that?… If I wanted to know you, like who you are… if I wanted to have some sort of a connection, how does that work as colleagues?"

Connor raises a brow "Are you… talking about friends? Or something more…"

Linda feels her jaw is frozen open. Her nervous system wants to run, but she also hopes this can transpire into something great. What it is, she doesn't know yet; but the idea of making advancements is far too alluring.

"I think I'd like to know you…" She says.

It's the only words she can form.

Connor shrugs "And what is there to learn from watching a movie?"

Linda is yet again without a response.

He shrugs a shoulder with a nod at the ground.

"If you want to know me…" He says "Then tell me what you want to know."

She sighs and stares at his hand. She wants to hold it, but feels awkward to do so in the hot seat.

She reaches for it and looks him in the eyes.

"I know about… What happened…" She says "When you were young…"

She pulls her hand away.

"And I know you don't like being touched." She adds.

Connor smiles. He shakes his head and his voice comes in a gentle whisper.

"You can hold my hand." He says.

Linda laughs her nerves away with relief.

"I don't want you getting the wrong idea." She says.

"What idea am I supposed to get from a movie alone with you?" He asks "I think I DID have the wrong idea, but now I'm piecing it together… Especially after what my assistant said…"

"What did your assistant say?"

"He said that I should try to look good for you tonight."

Linda laughs "I uh… don't know what to say…"

Connor smiles "You don't have to say a damned thing if you don't want to."

Linda looks up to see his eyes glint with relief. His smile is still the same; warm and inviting. It's like she can see some great kindness that's slowly come forth; and she can see all his ambition and benevolence. His passion to provide for the children of Eden.

In her, Connor sees the fumbling of a facade. She's been worth all his admiration from the start. She's been nothing but kindness to him; even when he's been at fault. She's better than him; as a woman of action, rather than REaction. She's cooled the heat waves he brought forth in his faults. Only now can he see how she's much the wiser for it.

In all the tides of space they've traveled, Linda has never once wavered from duty. She's handled it with grace. To her he's an equal; and she's not delusional enough to believe that she's without her faults. In fact she actively seeks to understand him; for all HIS faults; and his magnificence.

Connor can't help but feel unworthy.

"Why me?" He asks "Why not get to know someone else?"

"You work hard." She says "You really believe in what you're doing and I admire that. I want to know what drives you."

He laughs "I mean… It's easy, I'm a hothead who refuses to fail."

Linda smiles "No… You're not a hothead."

He raises a brow "Try telling someone else that. See what THEY say."

She laughs "No, really… Maybe a little grumpy is all."

"Grumpy." He laughs "I'll take that."

Linda flips her hair to the side and Connor notices something he's never seen before. A black marking between her shoulder blades at the bottom of her neck. He looks closer and tilts his head.

"What's that?" He asks.

Linda leans forward and moves her shirt to reveal more. Black lines descend down her neck and into the back of her shirt.

"It's a tattoo." She says.

She lifts her shirt to show her rib cage, beneath her left arm. The lines feed into a square at her side, and more lines lead from there to her breast, where her heart is.

"It's a circuit board." She says "Old tech, but it looks cool."

"And what is this square here?" He asks, pointing to the one closest to her heart.

"That's a relay switch." She says "It turns on or off, feeding electricity toward the heart." She points to her back "It connects to my spine; up from my brain and down to my heart."

"What happens if I press it?" He asks.

She laughs "It would electrify my heart."

Connor smiles at her and looks down at the square. He presses it with his finger.

"So now it's on?" He asks.

She laughs "I guess it is."

"Good." He says.

She drops her shirt and faces him.

"Keep it that way." He says.

She blinks and looks at him. His eyes stare back and his mouth grows soft. They lean into one another. His hand meets her neck, beneath her ear. He kisses her. His fingers run through her hair. Her hand meets his shoulder blade at the back and pulls him in.

They fully embrace one another, and kiss again. His arms wrap around her at the back and pull her body up to his. Her legs wrap around his waist and she runs her fingers through his hair. He kisses her neck and down to her collarbone. She lifts her chin and runs her nails along his back.

He pulls his head away to look into her eyes. She looks back into his. The screen goes dark.

They never pick a movie this night.

Instead, they wake up together in the morning.

They find themselves in each other's arms.

CHAPTER 52
Power and Poverty

The exploration pod descends into the silhouetted land. A darkness rises outside the windows. It swallows the stars.

A historian jumps up. His eyes widen at the sight.

Julius looks up at him "Mountains." He laughs.

Everyone laughs the nerves away. The historian finds amusement in himself and returns to his seat.

The craft lands. Julius rises and walks to the back hatch. He speaks over the communications in their helmets.

"Guys, this one's gonna be a lot to look at, but it's important. Doctor Clay, you can cut your feed whenever you want."

"Okay." Doug says.

"Doctor Hoyt is ready to talk whenever you need it." Julius says. He looks around the group "We each have an appointment to talk with him when we get back." He looks at the door, then back to the crew "Just a few words before we go in. I think it's no secret, what I've been through. I've seen what humans can do to each other. I've had time to think it over. So if you feel like it, you can talk to me too. Alright?"

The others agree and Julius looks hard at their faces.

"Alright." Julius says "Let's go."

The back hatch falls to the floor and the crew begins to unload into the valley. Julius leads them to the bunker door in the mountainside.

He points to a small hole made by the scouting drone. The two engineers move up to open the hole wider.

"While we wait" Julius says "I think it's best to elaborate what makes this happen. Doctor Hoyt, are you listening?"

Over the helmet speakers comes the voice of Doctor Hoyt "Loud and clear." He says.

"The values that people need to be happy;" Julius begins "They are food and water. Heat and shelter. Then comes community, family, and love. Then a sense of self. And finally a feeling of purpose. Is that correct?”

“Scholarly, my friend.” Doctor Hoyt says.

The group laughs.

Julius smiles and watches the chunk of door fall open.

He turns back to the group “This is what happens when people identify with a nationality. They reject ideas that oppose their own, because they’re convinced that they are the just people.” Julius nods in the direction of the door and the team follows behind him. He continues to speak as they walk into the mountain “The truth is, no one as an individual IS their nationality. I’m FROM Eden, but I am not Eden itself.

It reminds me of what happened in New Memphis. Your family and friends come before a nationality, a race, or a social movement.” Julius comes to an intersection in the hall. He turns to the group again “As long as you remember that, you’ll know how to be happy.”

Everyone agrees.

Julius calls over the headset “Doctor Clay, is it right or left?”

“Left.” Doctor Clay says “The right hall takes you to the engine room.”

“Okay.” Julius says. He looks at the group “We’ll go to the right on the way back.”

Everyone nods, and Julius continues down the left hall.

Julius turns on his microphone again “So, you remember the things people need? It starts with food, water, and shelter.” He looks back for a brief second to make sure everyone is together “What lies down this hall is desperation. For food, water, and warmth.” He turns to a doorway with blood smeared inside. Julius stops and looks at the crew. Their faces are horrified “Everything is dead down here except us, so don’t worry.”

The group laughs. Julius looks at the two engineers Danny and Phil. He looks at the historical assistants, and Julius smiles.

“Look, uh…” Julius begins. He looks to the blood-stained door, then back to the crew “I keep trying to find a way to prepare you for this, but honestly there’s nothing I can say.” He sighs “When you’re starving, you’ll become an animal. You abandon all those other things that make you happy.”

The group seems saddened and humbled.

“There’s a phrase I like to say to people.” Julius says “It goes ‘I believe in a god, because I’ve seen what the devil can do.’” He looks at the mournful faces and nods “Good things happen too. So let’s look around and be curious, but there’s evil down here; and hatred. Document it, make sense of it, but don't keep that spirit with you. Leave it here; where it should have died."

Julius signals Phil and Danny to open the door. They move to look at the door.

Julius meets eyes with the young historian in the back.

"Is that you, Timmy?" Julius says.

Timmy pokes his head out. He looks exactly like Timmy the Tank Man. More of a boy than what Julius remembers.

"It's me." Tim says.

Julius smiles "Glad you're here."

"Likewise, Julius."

Julius turns and sees both Phil and Danny. They stand beside the open door.

"Ready when you are." Phil says.

Julius motions for the team to follow him.

Through the threshold of the door, there's a dark descent to dusty caverns. Skeletons gather at the entrance of a large door. Bullet holes in some of the skulls. The outliers from the crowd have stains streaking from beneath them. The floor is charred, and so is what remains of the flesh on the bones.

The large entryway leads to an elevator shaft. The space is large enough to lift forty military vehicles. It descends far below the world, out of sight.

Phil and Danny move to activate the elevator. Julius looks at Tim and puts out his hand. Tim gives him a flashlight, and Julius turns it on to its lantern setting. The light comes out of the contraption at all angles, and Julius holds it over the ledge.

The light is released from his fingers, and falls into darkness. Julius glances away to see that no one dares to stand with him. Even Tim watches his light for only a moment before backing away.

Julius looks back to the light. It's a dim dot, deep below their feet.

"I think it stopped." Julius says.

"Has it?" Tim asks.

Julius shrugs "Don't know."

"Should be coming up in a moment." Danny says.

The rotating caution lights at either side of the entrance begin to flash. The assistants back away from the elevator and wait for it to rise. Julius watches the light grow brighter, then lights activate down the elevator shaft.

"Woah!" Julius says.

"What is it?" Phil asks.

Julius backs away from the elevator.

"Way bigger than I thought" He laughs.

The others laugh, and the lights go out again.

"Ah, damn." Danny says "The lights went out."

The crew waits in the blinking cautionary light. A faint sound comes up from the shaft.

"Sound?" A younger historian asks.

"Probably a little air coming up." Danny says.

"Yeah, don't breathe it, though." Phil laughs.

Julius looks his way and laughs at the callback.

He reaches for his own light, pulls it off of his belt, and extends it to Tim.

"Here." Julius says "In case yours broke."

"Oh." Tim puts his hands up to decline "I have another."

Julius nods "Smart."

"I doubt it broke anyway." Tim says "I've put that thing through abuse."

Julius smiles "Government money, huh?"

Tim laughs "No kidding."

Julius calls over the headset "There's some military trucks on the elevator. In case you guys wanted to check those out."

The trucks come up from the darkness, and Tim's light shines out the back of one of them. Tim steps behind it to find his light.

Tim laughs "It tore a hole through the roof."

The others look in the back of the truck to see the hole in the canvas roof. Tim picks up his light and it's perfectly intact.

Phil walks over to the elevator control panel.

"Everyone ready?" He asks.

The elevator gives a jerk as if a clank would sound. The descent begins and a faint sound returns as they descend into an atmosphere.

While looking around the army trucks, Tim finds a skeleton in one of the driver's seats. The back of the skull was blown into fragments by a suicide shot. He's reminded of where he is.

The elevator leads into a far-forgotten secret. An airlock door meets them at the bottom floor. The lights in the elevator shaft flicker on, and the team looks up in awe.

Julius turns to the engineers. He signals, and they open the airlock door. It flings open to show blackness beyond its threshold.

Julius steps forward into the dark. He turns on his suit's lights. A tableau where wrath and envy reigned.

Women's clothes lie torn apart beside their owner's butchered thighs. Their defiled torsos are not far. Infant bones piled next to charred floors. Bodies hang by nooses. Decayed hands chained to the walls where prisoners were held.

All along the hall there are bullet holes that riddle the walls. A designated space is given extra special attention by the soldiers. Beside this spot, there are corpses laying in a dusty heap.

The chime of Doctor Clay's voice comes to Julius' helmet.

"What do you make of this, Doctor Winter?" Doug asks.

He looks at the uniforms and shakes his head "It looks like officers of the same rank turning on each other. Maybe a coup; but the others got in on it. Like a mutiny."

"The struggle seems to have started before the event." Doctor Hoyt adds "A lot of pent-up anger and a lack of trust in their government. Someone thought they could do better."

"The truth isn't entirely clear." Morris begins. "We need it in writing. Grab any writing you see. We'll decode it on the ship."

"Doctor Winter." A historical assistant calls over the headset. "I've found something."

"Exactly like that." Morris says "Good eye, Sarah."

Julius walks to a private room where a body lay over a desk. The paper beneath its head is covered in immaculate English.

"He was an American engineer." Sarah says.

Julius looks over the page.

Doug's voice comes again "I know this man." He says "He disappeared a year or so before I went under."

> **"***I heard there was an American starship.
> They said it left Earth, but they don't know where.
> I write this in the hope that humans will come back
> someday. If you're reading this, and I'm assuming
> you're human; then welcome home. This is where
> we started. A world we treated so poorly. I hope
> you're doing better.*
>
> *This government (which captured me) is full
> of hate. My grandfather left during the uprising of*

the PLRE. It kills me to see our heritage so tarnished by them.

I was stolen to make radiation shields. Once I succeeded, I packed for home. That's when the bombs fell. Soon after, the sun went out, and they stuffed me down here with everyone else.

Time had passed, and the guards didn't care what I did anymore. We were trapped here all the same. We tried to make a sustainable environment but things went wrong, everywhere. Some people thought this was the perfect opportunity to launch a coup. They succeeded after many casualties. Worse than the people were the damages. Officers began to rape and steal. Gradually more and more of them joined in, seeing as there's no consequences anymore. Sanitation went down with morale, and soon people became ill.

Women who were pregnant with unwanted babies either committed suicide or died in childbirth. The lucky ones were too stressed to keep it.

The babies were a threat to the supplies. Children were murdered. Parents offered their lives in exchange but one woman was killed, then her child "went missing" right after. No one offered exchanges from then on.

Public executions were held for those who didn't comply with the new power. Another uprising followed.

The twisted people in charge decided to tell no one, but they began to rig the community to fall in their absence. The systems that regulated our food and water supplies, the oxygen and heating systems, all of it was changed to operate in a whole new way. The software engineer was executed after writing the program. It coded for all actions to require a password. A locked safe kept the dongles. It held the keys to the water room, the farming room, all of it.

The leaders were already killed, so people

tried to decode the new software. Others began trying to pry open the safe. You can guess how it all went. It's been anarchy. No one talks anymore. I saw a boy eating his mother. I didn't feel anything when I saw him. I just walked away like it was nothing. I've locked myself in this room. I'm waiting for death.

My father always told me that he moved to the States because it was the least likely place to treat people this way.

After being shoved around like cattle I can understand what he meant. There was never a vote. There were only the choices of the absolute rulers.

In the United States, my father was amazed to see handicapped signs. He was told from an early age to belittle handicapped people. He was shocked to have hot water from a faucet. He used to boil water for a bath. Most of all, he married my mother; a Mexican woman. Here, in this country, it's a disgrace to marry a foreigner.

I now know what freedom of speech means. And I wish I voted more. A silly thing to think about, but I didn't know what I had.

It's no wonder why my dad was so proud to join the Air Force. After serving he built weapons to stay in what he called "the good fight".

Always stay in the good fight. Cherish love, life, liberty, and the pursuit of happiness. I can't stress enough how important the pursuit is. You're hopeless if you can't even have a chance.

Sincerely,

Doctor David Chu"

Julius reads this over for a while, imagining Doctor Chu's perspective. He sounds tired and hungry with short sentences; often taking sudden changes in subject.

While Doctor Chu refers to the United States in his letter; Julius believes that he really means to highlight a unique system of government that allows the fluidity of choices. A system, so common now, that people cannot even conceive of a dictatorship.

In a country with democratic elections, the people can select their regional representatives. The unity of these representatives is the republic, which votes on behalf of the nation's people. It's the decisions of the people that bring forward a representative; many of which have chosen the socialized systems that support the needy.

To keep the individual on par with the state, the potential for billion-dollar aspirations is kept alive for any citizen. With a great idea and a tremendous amount of will, a street rat can become king in a country like the United States. Not all street rats are benevolent, and not all are evil. This chaotic fluidity is what made the most inventive nation in the history of planet Earth; and yet it stood as a symbol of collective consciousness.

Maybe in this way, the slow-moving hand of collective morality is worth a feeling of hopefulness. Julius has often found it difficult to trust the choices of the collective, because it was the collective that created the conflict of New Memphis.

He ponders this a while; and looking back over the words, he finds himself lost in a memory.

"I've locked myself in this room… waiting for death". Those words remind him of a hopeless despair.

CHAPTER 53
Death Ground

A tall ceiling caps the concrete studio space. It's held by wide pillars covered in white quark board. This was a space for art exhibits before the war. Out of the tall windows, lies the city of New Memphis. To the north is the rest of Middle Borough; and beyond that, the neighborhood of North Peak. In the east, the Visitor's District lies between H.Q. and Government Center. In both of the eastern districts, the United Zion forces make a slow advancement. They'll capture City Hall and use city controls to aid the army's capture of North Peak. From there, they'll pinch in across City Park, and up the eastern boroughs. The soldiers of Eden will corner the resistance at Gabriel Hill. When the terrorists surrender, the war will be over.

In the abandoned art studio, the soldiers eat breakfast before a big day. Chief, Dash, and Julius talk over bowls of soup. It's been three weeks since Pluto passed away.

"I'm telling you, Cricket doesn't care anymore!" Dash says.

The others laugh at his expressive portrayal of the story.

Dash continues "There was a wall of just pure SEWAGE and he bare-hands the thing for balance. Bare hands! He looks at me and goes 'Pass my gun?' Like asking for a TV remote!"

Chief wipes a tear from his smiling cheek.

"You'd figure a guy with a medical profession would know better!" Dash exclaims.

Julius breathes a squeaking gasp of air. His cheeks hurt, and he's out of breath. He sees Cricket's blushing smile. He's holding something in his hand

"What's that?" Julius says, nodding toward the mailed envelope in Cricket's hand.

Cricket looks down as if to notice just now "THESE are a present from my girlfriend. To all of us."

Chief looks confused "Since when have you had a girlfriend?"

Cricket puts his hand into the envelope. He pulls out a stack of sewn patches and passes them around

"Since sophomore year." Cricket says.

Dash grabs a patch and gathers his brows "Why haven't we heard of her?"

Cricket shrugs "If I start talking about her, I know I won't stop."

Chief raises an eyebrow "THAT good, huh?"

The older men laugh and Cricket feels embarrassed.

Chief stops laughing and bows his head to look from under his brow.

"Seriously" Chief says "Is she hot?"

Cricket laughs with the others.

Chief brings his boom to a giggle.

"I'm just playin', I'm playin'." He says.

"I mean, you've seen me." Cricket says "I have no trouble."

They all shout with a proud exclamation.

"There ya go!" Dash says.

Everyone begins looking at the patches in their hands. They make remarks on how impressed they are. A set of five stars with lines connecting them. The lines make an A shape; representing the name of their team, Alpha Force.

Chief is stunned "Beautiful AND talented, huh?"

Cricket nods "She's a design major at The Eden Art Institute."

Dash tucks the patch into his bag "I'm putting this on my jacket tonight."

Everyone agrees.

"Why the different colored star on top?" asks Julius.

"I think it's for Pluto." Cricket says "The others are the rest of us."

Everyone looks closer. They nod and admire the tribute.

"She sent one to Pluto's mom." Cricket tells them "They spoke at the funeral. I'm supposed to meet her when I get home." He looks at the patch and nods. He looks to the rest of them "You guys should come. I'm sure she'd wanna know how much he did, keeping us out of trouble and guiding us through the streets."

Julius thinks of the parents who raised Pluto. For Pluto's mother, it's her life's work that came to an end. All the nights she woke with a wail from his crib. When he was sick with an infection, and there was nothing she could do to help with his pain. She gave him the detested taste of antibiotics and wished for the pain to go away. She hated the idea of her son in agony. His laugh reminded her of the days when he climbed the couch in diapers. Now she can only think of her boy made cold and still. For his father, it's the memories they neglected to make. He'll agonize over the thought, again and again. He'll lose sleep over the thought of it; and he will want to call his son, except there will be no number to call. The dead don't answer their phone, and so Pluto's voice will only be heard in recordings. A repeat of the same words, with the same infliction. It will never be the same. A nest left cold and barren. A house grown quiet, without the banter of siblings. Pluto's sister has to find someone else to make her smile. She has memories that she's better off not telling; for often she's obligated to say *"You had to be there"*. She now holds a dictionary of language that no one else understands. She would forget it, if only it didn't make her smile every once in a while.

Julius finds himself staring off. He realizes the group is laughing again; they've drifted back into a sarcastic humor.

The crew finishes dinner and heads to their personal quarters. They gather equipment, and Julius hands a book to Chief.

"Thanks for letting me borrow this." Julius says.

Chief recognizes the book "*The Art of War*". A copy he took from the South City Library.

"Hang on to it." Chief says "It's not my copy."

"Oh, I thought…"

Chief shakes his head "No. There's some other books from the Library. Since you can read so fast, you might want to check them out."

Julius takes the advice given by Chief. In the evening Julius comes to the second floor of the building, to near street level. Having finished the routine duties for the day, Julius decides to spend his late hours reading again. He checks a large bin of books, wherein he finds a copy of "*My Father's Work, Continued*" by Mark Mandel.

Julius recognizes the name "*Mandel*" and opens the front cover. Inside there is a stamped label which reads:

> *"Property of the South City Library*
> *279 15th Ave.*
> *New Memphis, UZ"*

On the opposite page, there's a glossary. It has chapters titled "*The Physics of the Unseen*" and "*Physics: The Answer to Everything*".

Julius remembers the army captain's words. They must have been taken from this book. On the first day of the war, he used train cars to protect Eden from a bomb. Afterward he told Julius "Physics, the answer to everything!".

Julius feels compelled to look further into the world of "Physics". He searches the bin for more books on the subject.

Upstairs, the others play a game of ping-pong in the common area. Julius passes them on the way to his room. They invite him to play, but Julius declines. His arms are full of books. The army captain made an impression on Julius with the trains; and Julius is determined to become a master of the same art.

On the third chapter, Julius is interrupted by a knock at the doorway. Cricket looks at him with a ping-pong paddle and a smile.

"I just smoked Chief." says Cricket "It's your turn to play the champion."

Julius laughs. He looks at the pages and places a bookmark.

"It's your funeral." Julius says.

Just out the doorway, the others look his way with anticipation.

"Here we go!" says Chief.

Julius walks up to Chief and takes the paddle from the team leader.

He joins cricket at the opposite side of the table.

"How easy should I take it?" asks Julius.

Cricket smiles "Don't."

Julius shrugs "Well alright then."

The whole common area turns to watch the two best players.

Julius holds the paddle with a pump of adrenaline. Cricket's challenge is exciting, but Julius is sure of his own success.

The two players nod at each other. Cricket holds the ball in his hand. With his fingertips, he lobs the ball and smacks it hard. Julius widens his stance.

A run to the left with an accelerating spin. Julius hits the ball. Cricket hops to his left and guides the ball to Julius' right. Julius runs to take another hit and serves a surprising quick shot. Cricket isn't phased but the others shout. Their hearts race to watch the lightning strike back and forth. Cricket misses the ball and prepares for another serve. He sweats but his brows stay firm. Julius looks amused and excited.

"Are you sure you want a hundred percent?" Julius asks.

"A hundred and ten." laughs Cricket.

Julius flinches his brows up and shakes his head "Fair enough."

Cricket snaps a quick serve and Julius returns with a confusing shot. The ball arcs to Cricket's far side and slows when it hits the table. Cricket reaches and launches the ball with a force that flies past Julius.

Julius turns behind to see Dash get the ball. He looks back at Cricket. Cricket smiles from ear to ear.

"Zero!" Dash calls.

Julius turns and catches the ball from Dash.

"Alright" Julius says "You've earned it."

"A hundred percent?" Cricket asks.

"A hundred and ten." Julius laughs.

He hits the ball with leisure and Cricket finds himself too far from the table. Cricket runs forward and bounces it back. Julius finds himself laughing as he chases the ball back and forth. Cricket's smile grows bigger with each score he makes.

The score comes to a tie at ten points; making the eleventh point the winner.

Julius feels the heat of adrenaline pumping up to his ears.

"It always comes to this." says Julius. He shakes his head "How the hell is that possible?"

Cricket's panting smile looks down for a breath "I have no clue." He laughs and looks up "I'm gonna beat you this time." He says.

Julius shrugs "You just might."

He puts the ball up between himself and Cricket. It sits on his fingertips to display an offer.

"You ready?" Says Julius.

Cricket stands ready and nods.

Julius serves the ball and Cricket cracks it back. The medium range stays consistent until both players slowly approach the table. They each try to surprise one another with soft shots until both decide to crack fast ones on one another. The ball sounds like the roll of a snare drum. Jaws drop at the close-range speed shots.

Julius decides he's had enough of toying. He uses his backhand to let the ball fly up. It comes back to him and he casually slams it at Cricket's far side. With a pop off the table, the ball goes flying past Julius.

Julius turns to watch the ball, then back.

Cricket places his paddle on the table. He raises his arms in victory.

"Unbelievable!" Chief screams.

The crowd swarms Cricket, and Julius turns to see Dash retrieve the ball.

Julius laughs.

"Holy shit!" He says to Dash.

Dash smiles back "He's been talking about it all day. He said he's found a way to beat you."

Julius displays the table with his hand and shrugs "I mean… Yeah, he just did!"

Dash laughs and slaps his hand on Julius' shoulder.

Julius puts his hands on his hips and stands at Dash's side. They watch Cricket bow before the crowd.

Julius folds his arms and so does Dash.

"You know something?" Dash says.

Julius shakes his head "I don't know anything."

The two of them chuckle and Dash seems to have something difficult to say.

Julius settles his laugh "Nah, what?"

Dash looks at him, then back to Cricket. Julius follows with his eyes.

Dash nods "You guys are my best friends."

Julius gathers his brows. He looks to the floor and recalls his whole life's worth of acquaintances.

"I've never had a friend before." Julius says.

He looks at Dash. A smile comes about his face, and Dash smiles back.

"I guess I was just waiting for the best."

***

It's moments before quiet hour, and Chief's men sit in a small room with bunks to the walls. Each one of them sits at the edge of their mattress and looks toward the small space between beds.

"If Pluto were here…" Chief says "… two of you would be sharing a bed."

Puffs of laughter dot the room. Dash clicks his tongue on the roof of his mouth, allowing a pop of air through his molars. He gives a dismissive wave of his hand.

"Ah, fuck it" Dash says "I did that with my brother growing up. Zero would share with me, right?"

Julius nods "I'd have no problem with that."

Chief laughs "Really?"

"Oh yeah." Dash says "We would watch funny videos and try not to laugh. Sometimes we'd wait for my parents to fall asleep, and we'd play video games until the sun came up."

"My kids do that shit." Chief says "Little shits…"

Dash laughs "I didn't do well in school."

"Neither does my boy!" Chief says "Jairus, not Eli, he's doing fine." Chief looks up in Dash's direction. Dash dangles his legs over the edge of his bunk.

"Are you close?" Chief asks "You and your brother?"

Dash nods "Yeah".

The room gets quiet as everyone listens to Dash.

"I had a hard time in the academy" Dash says "My lungs don't work all that well…"

"… South West city." Chief says.

Cricket looks confused. He sits opposite to Chief on the bottom bunk; out of Dash's line of sight. He looks up at Julius, above Chief. Julius is just as lost as Cricket.

"South West Eden had a problem back in the day." Dash says, looking at Julius' face "A ventilation issue that went neglected by the city government." He leans back on his hands "When they found out, they gave out oxygen masks to the whole neighborhood. We were supposed to wear them when we'd go to sleep; and we'd wear paper masks throughout the day." He looks down to Chief "My family was given three oxygen masks but we needed four. Two of them broke within a week, so my brother and I were told to share one between the two of us through the night while my parents slept with nothing. Then one night my mom came in to switch our mask; she took it from him and gave it to me. She left us alone in the dark; and that's when I heard my brother coughing, nonstop… all throughout the night. I realized my little brother was more sensitive to the pollution than I was; and so I gave him the mask. Every night from then on, my mom would switch our mask around one in the morning. When she left, I'd take the mask off, walk over, and give it right back to him."

"That's 'cause he's your brother." Chief says "Your mom raised you right."

Dash smiles "I have a hard time running, but I was glad to give him the extra comfort he needed." Dash laughs "Sometimes we'd keep talking after I gave him his mask back… He was six and I was thirteen at the time. I'd do silly impressions and random stuff to get him giggling… I didn't get much sleep, but we had fun."

Dash looks up at Julius, who still looks lost.

Julius raises his brows "I've never had a brother but it sounds cool."

Cricket smiles "You've got us, kid."

Dash laughs at Cricket "How much did you hang out with Pluto? You're calling people 'kid' just like he did!"

Cricket laughs "It kinda sticks!"

Julius nods. He feels bashful and thankful for them. They offer open arms and he feels humbled in accepting them as family.

Cricket sees this and nods.

"Having siblings is the best." Cricket says "It's like a really close friend, but different. You've known each other so long, that you know everything about each other."

"Sometimes, you can say things without saying them at all." Chief says.

"Or already know what you're going to say before you say it." Cricket adds "My sister does that all the time."

"This guy's gonna say 'thanks, guys.'" Dash remarks, looking at Julius "Am I right?"

Julius laughs "That one's not fair!"

Dash flinches his brow "I was right, though!"

Chief nods "Guess that's it then."

He looks back and forth between Julius and Dash.

Dash nods.

"Makes us brothers." He says.

Cricket nods in agreement.

"From other mothers."

***

At night, the company is woken with a knock on the door.

"Up, children." The voice says "Now's not the time for sleeping."

Julius looks into the doorway to see Chief's boss, Staff Sergeant Jones.

"We're about to make history!" Jones says.

The team dresses and joins others in the common area. The crowd is packed around a radio. They look to the floor and turn their ears to listen.

"There's no one here." The voice says "Some... A lot of corpses..."

The Staff Sergeant nods. He lifts the transmitter to his mouth.

"Can you spot a cause of death?" Jones says.

He waits for his voice to carry across the radio waves.

Chief returns from speaking to the Charlie Force leader "They're taking the water treatment plant."

The team gives acknowledgment. A gleam of excitement comes about their eyes. They're eager to go home.

"Sir there's a sort of slime on them; and it smells." The radio cuts out and comes in again "We don't know what it is."

There is a moment of silence while they investigate further.

The Staff Sergeant calls over the radio again "Don't touch it, whatever you do."

"A little late for that." The voice says.

The Staff Sergeant shakes his head.

"There appears to be some kind of sediment in it." The voice says again "A black sediment."

Everyone looks confused. Murmurs grow amid the crowd.

Jones puts his hand up "Don't worry guys." He says "It's shit water. I just don't have the heart to tell him."

The tension gives way to laughter.

A call comes over the radio "Sir, the crows are walking on the rafters. They're all over the ledges, and the railings… There's a few on the floor, dead." A crunch is heard "I just stepped on one…"

Jones' face is disgusted "Wash your boot before you get home."

"Yes, sir." the voice says.

Another moment of silence until the voice calls again "Sir, we don't feel too good. This odor gets to your head."

"Is the building clear?" Jones asks.

"… We think so."

Jones looks toward a man who stands by a telephone.

"Are they getting a current?" Jones asks the man.

"Yes sir" The man says "They should have power."

He clicks the receiver at his mouth "Fire that sucker up!"

The crowd cheers.

"Clean water ready to go!" The voice says "If they're hiding in the sewers this should…" A sound comes over the radio "What was that?" the soldier says.

An inaudible voice sounds uncertain.

"Who's there?!" The soldier yells.

"Sergeant!" Jones says "Leave the radio on while you search."

"Yes sir!"

Jones looks concerned. From under his brows he looks out at the crowd "We're gonna hear anything that happens. If something goes wrong, I want power cut and troops ready for combat…"

"You heard the man!" One sergeant says.

"Not now." Jones says.

The sergeant looks around with a smile "Never mind!"

The men would laugh if they could, but a silence overwhelms the room. It feels like forever until the voice comes again, but in reality it might be mere seconds.

"There's uh… There's nothing…" The voice says.

An inaudible voice comes in a harsh whisper.

"Are you sure?" The original voice says.

The other voice comes closer "Yes, I swear it!"

"Okay. Staff Sergeant there's someone here. We're going to check it out… Wait! No! What are you doing?! Stop! Stop!" Panic brings the voice to quiver.

A light overwhelms the room. It grows quickly in the peripherals as a flash to the northeast. The water treatment plant is replaced with a plume of flames across the silent city.

A line of quaking dust approaches. A wall of heat destroys the windows and singes their faces.

Soldiers race to their rooms and get ready to move. In the midst of this, the unsuspecting are thrown off their feet by a new quake just outside the walls of their refuge.

They glance out the windows to the street below. The sewers have erupted throughout the city.

Julius and his team look out at the Hell before them. Chief turns his head to the team. All eyes fall on him. He looks down at their feet. His team is fully dressed. They chose to sleep in their clothes; passed out from exhaustion just moments ago.

"What do we do?" Julius asks.

"Retreat south!" Jones yells "To the tunnel!"

Chief holds his crew before following the orders "No… Wait."

Dash looks at Chief with confusion. Cricket looks ready to move. Julius is attentive.

"No something seems wrong." Chief says.

"What do you mean Chief?!" Dash says "He said…!"

"I know what he said!" Chief barks. He looks around a while then looks at Cricket "What would the enemy expect us to do?"

"To retreat south." Dash says.

"So I'm not crazy." Chief says "This seems wrong."

All agree with Chief. The room becomes empty.

The last man stops to yell "Come on!"

The team looks at the soldier, but they don't move. The confused man runs after the retreating company.

"They'll walk right into a trap." Julius says.

Cricket moves to the center of the room. His steps begin to spring as if he's preparing to run. He faces the team.

"I'll warn as many as I can!" Cricket says.

He turns to chase after the others.

They all want to tell him not to bother, but he's right to do so.

"Brave kid." Dash says.

He doesn't know if he'll see the boy again, but they've all watched him change.

Julius turns to Chief "What now?"

"We get to an exit. Out into the desert. But first we go north."

"North?" Dash asks.

Chief nods "They won't expect to see anyone before they get here. We go north, and we hide. Then we go west; to the desert."

Their leader commands and they move with haste. Out into the streets, they run past fire and ruin. The flames spew out from holes in the ground. Manhole covers have cracked the glass dome overhead. The pressure launched them into the sky. They fell through buildings and onto the streets.

Halfway to the edge of Middle Borough, Chief halts the crew.

His eyes pierce through smoke and ash

"Hide!" He says in a whisper.

They step their way into the corner of a local fitness center. The opening of the building leads to a locker room. The lockers are just large enough for the men to fit in.

The smell of burnt sewage spills into the streets. Julius shoves himself past the metal threshold, scraping the stitching and the zippers on his fatigues. He pulls the door shut, but it is warped past the point of working. A sliver of his leg is laid bare to the flickering light of the streets. He makes himself small and becomes as still as he can; pushing his body into the shadowy portion of his metal box.

The smoke brings Julius to the verge of coughing. He holds back on the urge and squeezes his eyes shut to do so. When he opens them, there is a moment of stillness. He holds his shoulders still and breathes long, silent breaths. The locker is hot and the smoke makes it hard to breathe. The heat in his core is like a dynamo. His fingertips surge with energy.

A rock falls from a pile of rubble. It lands into his view from the crack in the door. A pair of boots kick up the dust on the locker room floor. A masked figure stops in the middle of the room. The soldier's black fatigues cover every inch of skin. The mask turns to look around. It peers at the corner of the room. A horde of black crawls over rubble. Boots grind dust into the tile. The mass of figures swallows the soldier. He becomes a part of it.

They are wordless, but their steps are like white noise in the silence. Dust on stone and concrete. The flames are the only thing that dare to hiss. The popping of glass comes here and again.

The horde walks through the building and into a street walled with fire. Beyond that street lies the next block.

As they walk through, they look backward and side to side. They begin their search to kill.

The black phantoms fade into the fires, and the three men emerge from hiding.

Dash and Julius look at Chief. He nods to the west, and the team moves that way.

At the back side of the enemy line, they move through the land of the enemy. They look each way for the agents of death, but all they find is that the city is burning. They think about Cricket and the others down south, but they can't stop to think, because the city is burning. They grow bold and quick. They cross the roaring jaws of a grocery store. Everywhere they look, all around them, the city is burning.

They come to a fallen building that blocks the street. They move north a block to circumvent the issue. The group turns westward again, and that's when they hear it. The jets called "birds" blow up the bridge back home.

The hope so many hold is thwarted, and followed by numerous pops of gunfire.

The team continues through the blocks of the neighborhood. They reach the exit point, and the three men become cautious. Chief signals them to hold still. He approaches the airtight door, and not a soul can be seen to the north or south. It seems they've outsmarted the enemy.

A charge is planted on the door, and they blow it open. Inside there are suits for maintenance workers and environmental studies. They're what people would call "one size fits all".

As they begin suiting up, they hear the roar of the birds again. They're picking off men to the south who are scattering into the sand.

Chief looks at them intently "You boys listen." He says "Don't look back. Stop for nothing, and I mean absolutely nothing…" He breathes for a moment, reluctant to say the next words. He looks at Julius "If I die, my name is Dan Harris." He looks to Dash "You hear that?"

Both Dash and Julius nod their heads.

"Now, what are your names?" Chief asks.

"Julius Winter; but you already knew that."

Chief shakes his head "I couldn't remember." He confesses "I'm not good with names. That's why I nickname everybody." He turns to Dash "And what about you, big guy?"

"I ain't dying Chief." He responds.

"I'm not playing." Chief says.

"I'll tell you when we get home." Dash says.

They slow their breath down and stand up straight. Everyone almost sighs. Chief looks at them both.

His hand lands on Dash's shoulder "You run like a bat outa hell, or I swear to God…"

"Let's do this." Dash says.

Chief grabs the latch to the door and turns it. He stops and listens for the birds, but hears nothing for a while. One passes, and he swings the door open. A four-mile stretch of clay land reaches out to the base of a mountain range. The broad side of the closest mountain reaches three thousand feet into the sky. It is the smallest, and met with a network of valleys and peaks. It offers shelter from the birds.

They wait until another bird passes. One does, and Chief slaps Dash on the back.

"I'll be right behind you!" He says. He shoves Julius "Go!"

Chief follows behind as they make a sprint out of the doorway. In the flat land, the world seems to fall off toward the south. Eden rests between them and the golden star. A large portion of the south bridge is gone. Eden is closing its protective curtains. For miles they don't even bother to look at their home city to notice.

The run seems hopeless. The mountains appear no closer. The roar of jets deafens the ears and rumbles the ground. The quakes disturb the unturned stones. More people scramble out from the southern half of the dome. Julius wonders if Cricket is among them.

The bulk of the firing power is focused on the south; but one bird comes time and again to shoot the three men in the west.

No one bothers to look at it. The dirt pops into the air before them. Sprays of clay collide with their backs. Every assault on the ground is followed by a rattle of gunfire. The walls of flying dirt would halt ordinary men, but they run right through. The only chance they have of living is to reach the mountains

In the midst of the adrenaline, a thump is not heard but a whack. The contact wasn't with dirt this time, it was a helmet. A bunching of plastic and flesh. Chief's brains pull his face to the floor with a supersonic force.

As his final command stands, the two never look back. The visits from the bird come to an end, and Julius realizes "*It was for sport*".

He thinks to himself. "*He was aiming at us, a small target, just to see if he could hit it.*"

Three and a half miles later, they reach the foot of the smallest mountain. They look back to see the birds are still pecking. They claim the unfortunate souls running east and west. Between the mountains and the dome of New Memphis, the bodies litter the desert. Separate from the rest, they see where Chief lies. An inappropriate fate for one so powerful and strong. To be marked as a single dot on the canvas of dirt. The swarm-copters rise from the far side of New Memphis. Dash and Julius are far from safety. They race up the mountain together.

At first their legs have strength, but the might of gravity on their lunging steps is a lot to handle. Wind begins to pick up as clouds gather to the north.

Halfway up the mountain, Julius tells Dash over his radio "I think the storm should give us cover."

"You want to move in the storm?" Dash says.

Julius nods "It's the only chance we have. Oxygen will be too low if we wait it out. There's no guarantee we have a rescue coming. The wind should swat the birds."

Dash shakes his head "I need a break, Zero."

"No time for breaks" Julius says "We need to get up there and hide in the valleys."

Dash looks at the valley. It could be a false summit scenario, but he's not sure. He's thought they'd be on the south side of the mountain long ago. It's deceptively large.

"Those swarm-copters are bringing bad guys." Julius says, pointing to the land between them and the cities "They'll be crawling the mountains; like ants on spilled ice cream."

Dash looks at the approaching swarm-copters. They stop to barrage the runners in the desert. Their heavy guns echo off of the mountains. At the base of the mountains, a mile behind them, the Zion troops scramble and climb.

"Jesus." Dash says.

He turns to look at Julius.

Julius points across the mountain and to the south. Going that way, they'll reach the south face, and come to the valley nestled in the range. There, they'll have plenty of outcrops, boulders, and caves.

The boulders become large as they approach the valley. They're spaced far apart with great gaps in between. Steep climbs up and down wear them out.

Their legs burn but their strides continue. There comes a point where they turn and see the swarm-copter at the base of the mountain, and they almost begin sprinting.

Dash breathes heavily and stops with his foot on another boulder.

He radios to Julius "Zero, we need a place to hide NOW. My legs are shaking. I feel like my knees are going to snap the wrong way."

Julius turns around and looks at his leg. It shakes a little but not much.

"Are you sure?" Julius asks.

"I've never been more sure." Dash says "I keep trying with all I've got, but my legs just won't work."

Julius remembers this feeling in the academy. It's the point before someone's limit is reached. A limit where the body won't go any further. Like pushing on a skyscraper, and fully believing it'll go someplace.

"Alright." Julius says. He turns forward again.

About forty yards downhill, there's a cave. A different group of muscles should be usable for Dash. Going downhill is not the strategic choice, but the only one Dash has.

"There." Julius says "Can you make it to that cave?"

"That group of boulders? Yeah, I can do that."

"Alright. We rest there until the birds leave. Then we take our chance in the storm."

"Downhill is fine." Dash says "I can't walk up any further."

Julius nods "No worries. We won't go up."

From outside of their cold cave, there's the sound of the birds, the bombs, and the swarm-copters. Claps of gunfire mark the end of a spotted soldier, hiding in the mountains.

They've turned off their radio communications to help hide from the enemy. Instead they speak in sign to one another.

"The storm looks like it's going to be big." Julius signs.

Dash looks in the distance at the towering dark clouds. They rise behind jagged icy rocks of reddish brown. Lightning cracks out from behind the plumes of the titanic storm.

Dash looks at Zero with an expression of defeat.

Julius signs to him "Better than the birds."

Dash signs back "Better than birds."

Julius nods.

For hours they try to sleep. It seems impossible at first, when the birds begin bombing the east mountain face. The other troops climbed far, but Alpha Force had a head start. No one reaches a security as sure as theirs. When the birds retire, they hear screams of agony and gun-fire. Swarm-copters and their deployed troops can be heard combing the remains of rubble and scorched ice. Barely a wink is ever had.

The ever-dawning sky is hardly light. The green clouds begin over-whelming the stars. The howling gale whistles on the jagged bristles of the mountainside.

The teeth of the land point upward to the sky. They stand like black shadows on the green backdrop.

This is the opportunity they have waited for. No birds can fly in this sky; but the battle remains against the ancient, more formidable foe.

A cold rain marks the beginning of the battle.

The hike down is long and difficult. By now both men are hungry and thirsty. They walk along large boulders and watch their footing, but their legs aren't easy to control after the run. Thunder cracks and a wall of water thrashes on their suits. The lightning may strike wherever., and the thunder reminds them of how vulnerable they are. Bodies lie on outcropped rocks, and in the crevasses of boulder patches.

A thud is heard and they look with a startle. Some distance to the left of them, a man's torso fell from a boulder. The man's legs are nowhere in sight. The rain soaked his clothes and weighed him down. The water pulled his corpse from the edge of the boulder, and off the ledge.

From the mountain, they can see the full discard of this contentious affair. The rain falls harder and harder; and the blood is washed off of the land of the dead.

The bodies are few at first, but they number more as they make their descent.

They stop to turn on their communications.

Zero commands his partner "Keep a steady pace! Keep your footing! It's intelligence that'll bring us home" He's out of breath but finishes his thought "…not speed! Got it?"

"Yeah!" Dash says back.

The word home. It brings comfort to a mind in despair. It is enough to help Dash press on.

Bodies litter the base of the mountain. Limbs and blood. The suits on the soldiers hide how horrible the carnage is.

These bodies won't be recovered until over a hundred years have passed. By then they'll be bones in the soil. They'll surface by the banks of a riverbed; like the stones that have been there for centuries before them.

***

After the long climb down, they reach the flat planes of mud. They won't worry about the rocks anymore. Instead the terrain takes hold of their feet. It fights them. It grabs with each suction of a step. It bids them to stay and lie with the dead.

The glass domes are barely visible in the heavy rain. The miles between them and Eden are drenched. Bodies, boulders, and their dome on the far side. It's a scene of despair, yet they go on.

New Memphis stands at least three miles to their left. The entrance they fled from must not be far.

Julius wonders now, if Cricket is among the bodies. Chief has been joined by many in the open land.

Their destination, the nearest door home, is about six miles ahead. The land is flat, but the distance is still demanding of their legs. The mud swallows their boots with an embrace like death.

The air supply runs low, and they reduce the airflow to help stay alive. The air outside is breathable, but likely to harm the body a few years from now. If it isn't the radiation, then it's the dust that will kill them in time.

The winds begin to blow hard in the valley of the cities. The force of the wind becomes so strong that standing is difficult. At moments the wind is at their back and it seems like a blessing. When it comes from the front, they need to stay low; sometimes lying on the ground, so they're not pushed backward.

Many times, as they lay on the ground, Dash considers resting there. The idea of staying still sounds enticing, as the mud would want it. If he falls asleep though, he'll be using his air. All the while he won't make any progress. Then the lack of motion will make him cold, and the wind will rip the heat from his body. He'll develop hypothermia. He'll breathe unclean air. He'll die in time, if the cold doesn't take him first.

Julius knows his partner wishes to rest and pulls him from the ground each time they stand. It goes on like this for hours.

They trudge through the mud, ever on and on; and after some hours pass, the rain begins to calm. The darkness makes it feel as if Centauri has set over the southern horizon.

Trudging through the mud and lesser wind, the end is still an hour's walk away.

Dash's legs give out from under him. He hits the floor, and Julius feels his heart fall with him.

"Dash, get up! We only have an hour left! A mile and a half at most!" He begs what might be his last living friend.

"My name isn't Dash, Zero."

"I don't care!" Julius says.

"My name is Kevin."

Zero throws Kevin over his shoulder in a fireman carry. He would turn off communications. He would, if he were sure that Kevin would make it.

Julius feels his tendons burn like plasma. Kevin talks seldomly at first but grows quiet for some time.

Julius checks periodically.

"Just resting." Dash replies each time.

The star emerges red in the clouds as Julius approaches Eden. A person is distinguishable from the edge of the dome. A soldier in a suit with his helmet removed. Julius makes his way and approaches him.

"What are you doing?!" Julius screams through the suit.

The man shrugs.

"You're breathing this air?!"

The man shrugs again "We all die someday."

Julius puts Kevin down and sees his helmet is open. "How long has this been open?"

Kevin's air reads empty.

Julius begins knocking. There's no answer.

"I tried some time ago." The stranger tells him "It didn't work."

"Where are they?!"

"Were you expecting a welcoming party? We lost."

"We haven't lost our city." Julius says.

"Have we?" The soldier asks. He motions to the locked door.

Julius frowns his brows. He looks at the wall before him.

He pounds again for their lives "My partner is going to die!"

"We all die." the other man repeats. He approaches Kevin to examine him.

Julius turns to the man approaching Kevin.

"He's not expendable." he informs the stranger.

The man looks at Julius with his brows raised. He pulls off his own oxygen tank and connects it to Kevin's suit. He puts Kevin's helmet back on.

"And you asked why I wasn't breathing good air." The stranger says.

Julius feels his heart relax from the man's actions.

The door swings open. Men in hazmat suits reach out. The hands in rubber gloves detain them. Not a voice is heard. Just the breathing from their fogged-up masks.

CHAPTER 54
Humans

Julius enters the elevator on the Mandel Explorer. The doors are about to close when a foot blocks the way. The door slides open and Tim walks in.

"Hey Julius." He says.

Julius smiles "What's up, Tim?"

The historian stands next to the engineer and looks up at him.

"So…" Tim says "… You know how you said we could talk to you about what we saw?"

Julius nods "I do recall."

Timmy laughs, then shakes his head "I've been wondering… Why?… How?"

Julius looks around as if to check for other listeners. He then speaks in a mumble "You really wanna know?"

Timmy nods.

Julius shakes his head "Because humans are incredibly, UNGODLY fuckin stupid."

Tim freezes, then gathers his brows.

"Oh yeah!" Julius says "You and me too. We're fuckin dumb."

He smiles at the young man. The young man starts to laugh.

Julius goes on "The dumbest people think they're smart. People hold value on that IQ bullshit, but that only measures how smart you supposedly are. Everyone forgets that from your silly ass number until infinity; that's how stupid you are. In that context, no one really seems that much smarter than anyone else."

Tim looks to the floor and smiles.

"I was expecting a more profound answer." Tim giggles.

Julius raises a brow and shakes his head "Fuck no. If you look at history, people have acted like absolute ass hats over the stupidest, most nonsensical shit." He looks again as if to watch for ears "I couldn't say that over coms 'cause most people can't handle the truth." He shakes his head "There's a cap limit to those fleshy computers in our noggin. Add some nuts and bolts; some wires even? Doesn't matter. Still stupid." Julius watches the floors change "We're only mortals. We have limits."

"You're suggesting there's more than us mortals?" says Tim.

"Fuck if I know." Julius says "I'm still really dumb. PhD and all."

Timmy laughs and Julius smiles, amused with himself.

Julius tilts his head "I was younger than you in the war." He starts to laugh "When I came home I had an apartment in Eden. A guy died on the toilet upstairs from me. Heart attack on the pot."

"Sheesh." Timmy says.

"Indeed." Julius adds "Landlord was standing outside and told me he was waiting for help to move the body. 'Let me see' I said. He takes me in… The body fell between the toilet and the wall. A small gap was there; for, at most, a toilet brush or a plunger. The body inflated from the heat. He'd been decomposing. Jammed up; wedged in there REAL good."

Timmy makes a snarling face "Ugh!"

Julius nods. He begins to laugh at the thought of what happened next.

"I clapped my hands together. I said 'Let's get started' and I grabbed the body… I took an arm and a leg. I yanked that thing as hard as I could. Limbs flailing in the air."

"Jesus!" screams Tim.

Julius laughs and so does Timmy.

"Landlord ran out of there." Julius says "I turned around and he was gone. Found him outside puking. Asked if he was alright and he goes 'Jesus, kid! What the hell's wrong with you?'" Julius shakes his head and shrugs "I told him 'I was in the war. I don't know!' He goes 'Oh, oh okay.'"

Julius turns to watch Timmy's face. Tears leak out of his smile as he laughs.

"Then what?" Tim asks.

"He told me to scram and let the cops handle it. So I did."

"That's funny…"

"It was." Julius adds "But that was me being stupid."

Julius laughs at himself.

Timmy nods and looks at the ground "You know, what you say about everyone being an idiot… I think it makes a lot of sense."

"Doesn't it?" says Julius.

Timmy nods "Yeah." He looks at Julius "Doctor Morris has been seeing a lot of that lately. He seems kinda down."

"Really?" Julius asks.

Timmy nods.

Julius thinks out loud "I'll have to pay him a visit; see how he's do-ing… Thanks for letting me know."

"Of course." says Timmy.

CHAPTER 55
The Historian

Doctor Ron Morris:

Ronnie was his name as a kid. It was when he was Ronnie that he first discovered his love for history. It was at the National History Museum that he learned a little bit about Earth.

The general public loved the cast of characters who founded Eden, but Ronnie loved what happened before Zion was settled. Nobody talked about it, but the Earthlings lived in a magical world. They could drive from cities to mountains without a single checkpoint in between. They had different cultures and customs. People spoke different languages and coexisted in a land called America.

There were people of that land called the Native Americans, and their influence lives on in our language today. "Iowa", "Oneida", and "Ohio" are all names that came from these people. The tallest mountain in the valley of cities "Mount Cochichewick" is the most popular of these examples.

It was obscure history that fascinated Ronnie the most. He would rent books from the library and find a quiet place to read. The books would cover topics such as the Barbary Wars, the Hashishin, and the Battle of the Chosin Reservoir. These books would have been incredibly rare, had it not been for a resurgence of interest in Earthen history; about two hundred years ago.

One of his favorite memories was at his cousin Gregory's house, in a farming community.

Ronnie decided his plan for the day. He said

"I will go to the library. I will pick out the oldest piece of fiction I can find, and I will read under a tree all day until the curtains come down."

He could hardly contain his excitement. He'd never had such a beautiful setting to enjoy his favorite hobby.

Ronnie went to the library. He found the oldest piece of fiction he could find. The Epic of Gilgamesh, the oldest story in human history, revived from a copy over five hundred years ago. Ronnie looked for a tree, and he found one on a hill. He thought "I'll read there; and I'll use the golden starlight to illuminate the pages. I'll read the words from over a thousand years ago there." And he did. Ronnie read there, under that tree; all day until the curtains came down.

In his wildest dreams, Ronnie imagined himself joining a trip to Earth. It had been spoken about for years. The Odysseus Mission was a promised plan by the three nations of Zion. No one knew when the day would arrive, if it would ever arrive at all.

Time went on, and Ronnie became Ron. A twenty-four-year-old man with a PhD in Earthen history, and a minor in anthropology. Art history was only a hobby, until a paper he wrote gave him some merit there as well.

Doctor Morris was approached one day by a man who implied "the journey of a lifetime". Ron knew this was referring to Earth. Before he could hear any more, he had already agreed.

He couldn't wait to be the first to discover the obscurities on Earth. To be the only one aware of a newfound artistic movement, a historical account, a record long-forgotten.

For Ron, it was realizing the untapped beauty in something underrated. Like Bram Stoker's "The Judge's House", a short story overshadowed by his best-selling novel "Dracula". Ron felt a passion for the overlooked artist like Caspar David Friedrich. Many would recognize his work, but never know its maker's name. Expressionism, pop art, and minimalism would overshadow the message of individuality in surrealism. A message so cherished by the likes of Carl Jung and J.R.R. Tolkien. Their names would be remembered, but the meaning of their work would be lost.

Innovation would be replaced by assimilation. The individual would be lost to the collective. "Who am I" would be replaced with "What am I". Hundreds would swarm around the portrait of a woman because they'd heard of it a hundred times. In museums around the world, a mourning friend's commemoration would go unnoticed.

Friedrich died alone and poor; couch-surfing among his friends. His work fell out of popularity, and his ability to paint was slowly fading. A physical ailment was taking his ability to do the simplest of things.

Another Friedrich, Friedrich Nietzsche, would go on to talk about someone worth trusting. He called this person a "Superman". A friend who would care for another out of love, rather than selfish gain. This man would not like or dislike, but rather evaluate things objectively. They wouldn't see in terms of good and evil. They'd recognize the chaos of the world, and be capable of ordering the chaos; not by forcing but guiding the forces of chaos. In his mind, Nietzsche thought the artist was the master of this craft.

Here too, there would be an undoing of enlightenment. The Nazi regime would pervert his beliefs with trickery, like Lucifer himself. They took the words of a man who stood against anti-semitism and made them stand for the very things he despised; nationalism, prejudice, and hive mentality. Someone who believed in an enlightened humanity would be smothered for the sake of the collective.

Doctor Morris closes his personal journal. He looks at Doctor Hoyt.

Hoyt raises his brows "Jesus, Ron. Have you ever thought about phi-losophy?"

Ron laughs "Clearly." He says, waving the journal. "It felt good." He adds "I'll admit, I haven't written like this in years." He looks at the closed book on his lap "I took the idea from Julius. He told me he does it a lot."

Doctor Hoyt nods "Julius knows a thing or two about the power of the page." He gestures to the book in Ron's lap "He also knows a thing or two about that cyclical nature of history."

Ron nods.

Hoyt sees his eyes stare off through the floor, and so he gathers his brows at Ron.

"What is it?" Hoyt asks.

Ron sighs.

"I feel bad… not telling Julius about the Icarus project."

Hoyt nods "Elizabeth knows…"

"When did Captain tell her?" asks Ron.

"When Julius led that expedition with your guys… That nasty mess in the bunker, in Asia."

Ron nods, recalling the photographs.

"… Have you had to lie to people before?" Ron asks "Has it ever made you feel this way?"

Hoyt breathes a laugh through his nose.

"Yeah, actually… I have."

Hoyt sits back in his chair. His eyes wince in a sympathetic way.

"I'm sure you know by now…" Hoyt says "… my job… It can lead me to many places… I'm not a therapist so much as I am a sociologist… They could only fit one in a rocket, and so here I am…" He touches his beard and looks off to the side.

Ron watches him, like an onlooker in a movie theater; anticipating a great revelation in the personal strife of a protagonist they identify with.

Hoyt nods as he recalls.

"My work has brought me to advertising agencies, political campaigns… You name it…" His eyes meet Rons "Most of the politics was my cousins and siblings… You don't need to hear what that's like because you've seen it play out in history. You know what happens when someone wants the masses to be motivated…" Hoyt shrugs "I don't like it, but it pays well."

Ron nods, bringing his eyes to the floor in a thoughtful response.

"I get it." He says "Julius understands that too; but it doesn't feel good to hear it from him… He tries to help me, but I don't wanna FEEL better. I want the TRUTH to BE better."

Doctor Hoyt looks around his chair and finds his notepad. He finds it, and begins writing in it.

"Honestly" Hoyt says "You should talk with the Captain." The sound of his scribbling emphasizes his pause "He's been in a similar headspace as you."

"That's the thing." Morris says "We've been talking a lot about this work I've been on. It gets overbearing. I can't see the guy without thinking about it."

Hoyt nods "Then take time off together. Clear your head and live a little bit. It's not healthy if you associate one another with such negative thoughts."

Ron gathers his brows in a puzzled face "What do you mean?"

"What I mean is; that we can fall into a headspace with reminders. A location, a smell, an individual's presence… You two need to help one another; otherwise you'll fall right back into this feeling of depression once you pick up work again."

Ron seems like he's about to laugh "Feels a little weird bonding with my boss, don't you think?"

Doctor Hoyt waves his hand in a dismissal "Peter's harmless." He says "Play pool together. Doctor's orders."

Ron has a numb look about his face; and it lasts until later in the day. He leaves the therapy office with a feeling of foreboding. He doesn't know what to expect with this prescription of time with the Captain.

Ron is perplexed by it and goes through the motions of his job, disassociated. He's filing things in the computer's database when the Captain comes by his office.

"Are you ready to play pool?" The Captain says.

"You've got it, Captain."

The Captain waves away the formality "Just call me Peter. There's no point in all that."

Ron joins him in the hall. They make their way to the recreation room where there is no one but the two of them. They grab their sticks and start a game of pool.

They start slow; sorting the triangle with little bits of small talk here and there. Ron breaks the triangle and sinks a solid. Peter sinks the eight ball on his third shot.

"Oh! Shit." He says.

Ron laughs.

Peter shrugs "Round two?"

"Sure." Ron says.

Peter takes out the triangle and places the balls within it.

"So what did Arnold tell you?" Peter asks.

"Doctor Hoyt?"

"Yeah." The Captain replies.

Ron shrugs "He said to shoot the breeze with my boss."

Peter laughs "Let me guess, he said I'm harmless."

"Actually yeah, he did."

Peter smiles and lifts the triangle. He gestures to the setup.

"You take the first shot again." He says.

Ron breaks the triangle and the pool balls scatter apart.

"Arnold is my cousin, you know." Peter says "Distant, on my mother's side; but I've seen him since I was a little kid."

"Really." Ron says.

The Captain nods.

Ron raises his brows "Did you know the man who raised Julius is directly related to Doctor Manning?"

Peter screws his brows together "Really?"

Ron nods.

Peter lines up for the second shot "Well I'll be damned."

He smacks a striped ball into the far corner. He walks around the table, then lines up for another shot; aiming for another stripe. This time he misses. Ron moves in to go for the solids.

"You ever read Doctor Mandel's biography?" Ron asks.

Peter shakes his head "I heard all about it when I was growing up. I figured it was redundant."

Ron nods "It's the only biography I respect."

Peter screws his brows together "How so?"

Ron shrugs "It's the only one that doesn't try to be a story. No good guys, no bad guys, no climax… just an account of events; almost exactly as they happened."

Peter takes a quiet breath "And what do you think about it?"

Ron bends his back to take a shot "It's genius." He smacks the ball and misses "It's the best kind of history; it's relatively accurate… and that's rare…" He straightens his posture "People want a work of fiction, and that's what most of history is… That's why people say his book isn't written well… It's not depicted in a fantastical way with a supreme antagonist and a lesson learned." Ron plants his pool cue at his side "People can say what they want about the Mandel family, but there's nothing political about that book."

Peter takes a quick shot to get his move out of the way.

"Does he sound like some "big hero" in the book?"

Ron scoffs "Not at all. He downplays it, and that's what I like…" He pauses and nods. His eyes meet the table as he recognizes a feeling from his younger years; when his enthusiasm was boundless. He looks up at Peter, and with a smile, he raises a brow "It's actually a big reason why I'm here." He says. He keeps the cue clasped between his palms "It's proof that ordinary people can do extraordinary things." He gives a faint laugh through his nose "The biggest critique that people give that book… is exactly the reason I love it so much."

Peter smiles. He looks down and nods as Ron takes his shot. He thinks about what his cousin had said before. It appears that he was correct; that Mandel was ordinary. He didn't pretend to be otherwise. Peter looks up and watches Ron move across the table.

"You know what Arnold told me about Mandel?" Peter asks.

Ron lines up for another shot.

"Who?" He asks.

"Doctor Arnold Hoyt." Peter says "The therapist you've been talking to for the past eleven years."

Ron laughs too hard to make his move. He's quiet and out of breath. His face is ridden with embarrassment.

"It's hard to get used to his first name." Ron admits "What did he say?"

Ron takes his shot and the Captain smiles.

"He said that we're living history just like Mandel…" He smirks and looks up from the table to Ron's eyes "Each time you snooze off, brush your teeth, take a shit… that's the same as Mandel… It's just not the parts that they write about."

Ron raises his brows "Graphic." He says.

The Captain shrugs "The point of what he meant is… They didn't FEEL like they were doing anything special… They just thought they were doing a job; and from their perspective, they were doing one task after another. It didn't feel monumental. It felt like a day in a life."

Ron takes the chalk from the pool table and rubs it at the end of his pool cue. He's made the shot, and he's going for another.

"I guess that's how it feels for all of us." Ron says.

"Can you stop kicking my ass in this game?" Peter says.

Ron smiles but refers to their previous subject.

"I wonder how Elizabeth feels about what the Mandel brothers did."

Peter smiles with a side thought. He gives a chuckle and sighs.

"I respect those engineers. They say things that make my head spin." He begins to laugh a little "I bet Mandel would get a kick out of them… He'd have a blast talking with Elizabeth."

Ron shrugs and readies himself for another shot.

"Elizabeth is no dummy." He says "Mandel would love that… You know; she could aspire to be the "first woman who did something a man's already done", but she doesn't look at herself as a woman; even when the rest of the world does… She's here as our lead engineer, and no one's done that before. Not a man or a woman."

Peter flinches a brow and nods. He finds Ron's perspective refreshing.

Ron gathers his brows and stands straight again. He then laughs.

"I mean, it's not like Mary Shelly was asking 'What do women want to read?' when she wrote Frankenstein." Ron giggles again "She asked herself what Mary Shelly wanted to read… and now we have science fiction."

Ron stands by his pool cue and gives a nod toward Peter.

"What do they say though?" He asks "I feel like I cut you off. What do they say that blows your mind?"

Peter tilts his head with a shrug. He's at a loss for words but still tries to explain.

Ron bends down to ready himself again.

"It's usually the quantum mechanics." Peter says "They talk about how quantum computers work and I just say 'got it.'" He raises his hands in surrender "I tell 'em 'you do your thing'…"

Ron smacks the cue ball into a solid. This time it misses the hole.

"They say that particles can be in two places at once." Peter says "They can exist and not exist at the same time."

Ron nods "Reality breaks a bit at that level." He steps aside from the table "It's nuts." He adds.

Peter moves in for a shot "You've got that right."

Peter goes for a striped ball and misses the hole.

"Well, fuck me." Peter says.

Ron approaches the table. He stops before striking the ball and grows serious.

"Do you think we'll ever know what really happened to the Earth?" He asks "Why it all happened?…"

Peter raises his brows, then shakes his head.

"No clue." He says. His brows gather as he thinks "I think we came here to answer that question; but it's not the question we continue to ask."

"And what are we asking now?"

Peter looks at the historian "The question seems to be 'what are we worth?'. Maybe 'What's the point?', or 'Do we need to exist?'"

Ron leans on his pool stick and looks at the balls on the table. He sucks his lips to his teeth and purses his mouth.

"What about 'how much does one person mean'?" Ron says "What's one life in the relative scale of space? Or the fraction of time that humans have existed?"

Peter looks to the floor in thought, and Ron turns to look at him. Peter thinks long and hard but tilts his head with a curious conclusion.

"Maybe it's like those engineers." Peter says "The answer is like a problem in quantum physics."

Ron says the question again "How much does one person mean?"

Peter nods "Nothing" He says "And everything."

Ron stares off to grab hold of that answer. He looks long and hard at it. He decides it's suitable for him. It's suitable for the universe. It fits the chaos of nature, while retaining some guidance. Apollonian and Dionysian. The revelation of a Superman.

Ron lines up the stick to hit the cue ball. He looks away and takes his shot while watching Peter's face.

Peter's brows go up "Alright, I'm impressed."

Ron shrugs "Did I make it in?"

"Yeah!" Peter says "The solid blue one."

Peter's finger points at the table, still impressed with the physical shot. Ron looks at Peter's face.

Ron raises his finger in making a point "I just earned a point because you witnessed it." he says "You witness it, and without you it has no context. Without you it never happened, and yet it did."

Peter looks confused.

"Think about it." Ron says "Because you saw it, it happened. It would happen either way, yeah, but I wouldn't know that. From my perspective, it wouldn't have happened."

"Okay?" Peter laughs.

Ron smiles "That's history." He says "Things also happen to humanity that didn't actually happen in real life. Harry Potter and The Lord of the Rings; they never happened, but they're more real to us than a supernova that nobody witnessed and left no trace."

Peter nods "Interesting. That's also quantum mechanics."

Ron nods "That's our purpose in the universe. To witness it. Even if there's only one person there to see it…"

Doctor Morris turns around to look at the table. He sees that it's missing a solid blue ball. He smiles.

"…That's history." He repeats.

CHAPTER 56
Mister Lawrence

The department heads have stated numerous opinions on what to do about Doctor Clay accessing the security cameras. The Captain has yet to decide on what to do, and no one has met to discuss it. Their schedules have clashed for the past week, and so Ron has instructed his second in command to take control of operations for the day. Doctor Manning has given Doctor McGrotty a share of responsibilities as well. Linda has finished preparations in record time while Monica is thankful to have DEEMUS in charge of most of the legwork. Elizabeth feels guilty that she can come together so easily, but Julius corrects her.

"You've been good to let Mark and Danny know what to do." He tells her "You've been hands-off because you don't micromanage. Don't think of it as a bad thing."

He tells her this as they walk down the hall to gather in the cafeteria with the department heads. It's been organized by the Captain, and insisted upon by everyone independently.

The team gathers around the table with their plates full of food, and the rest of the cafeteria is quiet as everyone has brought their lunch to their laboratories. It's been a trend that gradually started when they arrived at Earth.

The conversation starts with simple greetings, but the Captain cuts to the chase, as everyone has been anticipating the answer on what to do.

"Alright" Peter says "This has been a long time coming… Who has changed their mind about their decision?… When we met Doctor Clay, we assumed he couldn't access our records. So what now?"

Connor sighs "I mean… He hasn't done anything about it so far. I don't see what the harm is."

Ron purses his lips and pulls them back in the corner of his mouth.

Peter looks at his face and wonders about it.

"What about you, Ron?" He asks.

Ron gathers his brows in thought.

"Doctor Manning is right…" He says "… However, it's concerning that he's taken that measure without asking our permission."

Monica leans forward to interject.

"I want it to be known that he's probably accessed our medical records." She says "I noticed some files were rearranged one time when I looked in chronological order from when I opened them last."

Linda nods at her sister in agreement.

"I noticed the same thing when I added Doctor Manning's injuries from the accident in the explorer pod."

Connor shrugs at the two of them.

"Anyone could have accessed those records." He says.

Hoyt nods in Connor's direction.

"Given how things have been, Doctor Manning; are you willing to risk that?"

Connor sits back and raises his brows.

"He's a big help for me." He says "Maybe I'm biased, but I think if he wanted to do something, he would have done it by now."

The faces around the table are all engaged in critical thought. The Captain sees this and looks toward Elizabeth.

"My stance still stays the same." She says.

Connor looks up at her.

"You know he saved your life?" He says.

Elizabeth shrugs "I don't care." Her eyes go toward Peter "I'm not about to be double-crossed if that's what he's hoping to do."

Peter nods and looks off in thought. He comes back to meet Elizabeth's eyes.

"Is it worth losing his trust?" Peter asks "What about his help with the mission? It's been invaluable."

Elizabeth shakes her head.

"We weren't with him when we arrived." She says "We only just started allowing him to help in the system." She shrugs "Before that, we were expecting to work at that original pace."

Peter looks at Hoyt.

"Has he given you any reason to be concerned?" Peter asks.

Hoyt shakes his head.

"No, nothing to be alarmed about yet." He says "And I mean 'yet'. I can't promise about the future."

Julius leans forward into the conversation.

"Might I add something?" He asks.

Peter nods.

Julius looks over at Doctor Lechmere who sits at the Captain's side.

"When I was upset about the weapons we'd be bringing back, it was for a similar reason." Julius looks around the table "There's a risk analysis involved; where people say it's wise to deter a threat, but when the threats come, things go horribly wrong." His eyes return to Peter "I hope that those weapons are never used; and I hope that Doctor Clay can be trusted… But I don't have faith in either of those things…"

Peter looks back at Doctor Lechmere who nods. The Captain stares off at the table with his brows fixed together, and his eyes fixed on the problem at hand.

An official decision is never formed.

***

On the table of the engineering lab, Julius has three assault rifles laid out for examination. The third rifle is taken apart in pieces. Its components are displayed to show each part's purpose.

Julius picks up the barrel, a long tube of metal with a jagged edge at the end. This end is surrounded with holes.

"Look inside here." He says.

She takes a look at the inside of the barrel. Within the metal tube she sees a quark screw pattern. This pattern is striated through the length of the barrel.

"These spirals spin the bullet." He says "It provides aerodynamics; keeping the bullet straight for long distances."

Julius reaches into his lab coat, and Elizabeth expects nothing in particular. A handgun emerges, and Julius places it on the table.

"Didn't know I had this, did ya?" Julius says.

Elizabeth shakes her head.

He shows her the size of the gun. It remains on the table, but his hands move it closer to her. Between his fingers is a small twenty-two caliber handgun. His hands frame it for observation.

"This can be hidden…" He says "It's easier to carry; but it comes at a cost."

"A shorter gun barrel means there's less aerodynamics." Elizabeth says.

Julius smiles "Exactly." He nods, then shrugs his head to the side "Which is why the movies are fake… When a guy shoots the gun out

of a person's hand from several feet away… That's the same as Superman; flying and shooting lasers from his eyes. It's supernatural abilities.
It's for fiction stories, and not real life. Imagine you've got… maybe a
second, at most two, more likely less than a second. You need to line
up those sights to aim…" Julius shrugs "You just simply can't do it…
If someone is running at you, you can guess and aim for the center of
mass. That's about all you can do… and if you don't they'll charge you,
take the gun away, and they'll be less conscious about using it than you
are."

He places his fingers at the top and pulls the sliding section of the
gun back. The empty hole in the top is displayed.

"See this?" Julius says "The force of the bullet leaving the gun is what's
used to send this back; and when it goes back, the empty gunpowder
cartridge is thrown out. That leaves room for another bullet to feed in
from the magazine."

"It's automatic." She says.

"Well…" Julius says. He scrunches his face and shrugs "Semi-auto-
matic, really…. The automatic ones can keep shooting as long as you
have the trigger down."

"It's an impressive use of Newtonian physics." Says Elizabeth.

Julius nods "It can mess up, though." He shows her the hole in the
slide again "If the casing doesn't fully leave the gun, it can hold the
slide in place and prevent the next bullet from coming in. Then there's
no bullet, the hammer on the back is stuck… They say 'your gun is
jammed' at that point."

Elizabeth picks up the lone bullet by the magazine of the assault rifle.

"This bullet is a lot sharper than the ones you've shown me before."
She says.

Julius nods "It's a higher caliber. There's more gunpowder behind it,
so it needs to cut through the air at a higher speed." He picks up another bullet; the kind he's shown her before. It's a twenty-two caliber,
and rounded at the tip "These rounded ones don't cut through. Instead,
they'll go inside and bounce around your bones, cutting up the things
inside. These sharper ones go all the way through." He looks her in
the eyes. He leans in to show his severity "These things are dangerous.
That's why I took it apart." He looks at the gun parts on the table "I
wouldn't risk showing you the barrel on an assembled gun; even if I
knew there were no bullets inside."

"Don't you think that's paranoid?" She asks.

He looks her in the eyes again. He doesn't reciprocate a smile, but instead he gives a long face with raised brows. He then shakes his head.

"No" He says. He gets stern in his voice "Never point a gun at someone; even if it's not loaded." He uses his hands to display the meaning of his words "Imagine a laser at the end of your gun, and it goes on forever." He slices his pointer finger across her direction "If that laser passes anyone, you've killed them." He then points to the wall before them "If I shot at that wall, with this forty-five caliber bullet, it would go right through that wall, into the next room, the room after that, and the room after that. It would bounce around and hit someone. A man, woman, child; doesn't matter what. You need to be aware of just how dangerous these things are."

Elizabeth nods "And these do the same thing?"

"Do what?" He asks.

"The firing pin hits the back, ignites the gunpowder, and sends the bullet?"

Julius nods "These are similar to the ones I used in the war, but…" He shrugs "We don't use these old ones. We had electric guns. They'd send things on magnetic rails, not unlike the trains on Zion… They'd use magnets; not combustion."

"And what's the point of that?" She wonders.

Julius raises his brows "We could use anything as ammo. Nuts, bolts, screws; you name it."

She looks at the ancient technology in her hands "So it DOESN'T work the same."

He shakes his head "They don't WORK the same, but you USE them the same way."

He looks at the assembled M4 with another thought on his mind.

"Check this out." He says.

Julius lifts the gun to show her the electronic sight on top. It shows a red dot; and it moves as she tilts her head.

"These M4 models are fitted with a holographic sight." He says "They keep the red dot on target, even as you move your head."

Her brows gather at the strange-looking scope.

"That dot will stay wherever the bullet will go." He says.

"So if I move my head, the bullet will go wherever the red dot is?"

"Exactly."

Julius takes the other gun and puts it to his shoulder. He steps forward and shows her a casual walking cycle.

"If you walk normally, you'll see the dot move up and down as you step."

He returns to her side and steps forward again; only this time with a smoother motion.

He speaks to her while looking at the holographic sight.

"Walk heel to toe…" He says "and keep it steady."

Elizabeth mimics his motion and sees the dot as it barely moves.

Julius watches her and nods.

"These also have spring-loaded stocks." He says "If you shoot it, the recoil is absorbed to keep the dot where you want it to be."

Elizabeth holds the gun to the floor. She turns her body to keep it away from Julius' direction.

"We should go shooting when we get home." She says.

Julius smiles "You wanna try?"

Elizabeth nods "Yeah, why not?"

He shrugs "Just be careful. It can be a little scary on your first try."

Elizabeth looks at her arm. It's now healed, but just barely. Thanks to Doctor Manning's application of stem cell therapy, she's regained full use of it.

"Maybe not" She says "I'll have to think about it…"

Julius gathers his brows.

"Nonsense." He says "I'll take you, first thing when we're home."

Elizabeth places the gun down and feels as though her arm is still vulnerable. It's a strange sensation that she's never felt before.

Julius nods at her arm "You'll do better than you think. I promise."

Elizabeth looks down at her hand as she moves it around.

While Julius is genuine in encouraging her, Elizabeth can't help but feel as though he is patronizing; for as long as she's known, she hasn't been physically capable. Her social capabilities as well have been her weak point in the past; and her parents have said as much.

"Elizabeth is shy." her mother would say to parents; and *"You'll find a guy who likes that!"* she would say for encouragement. All the while, her mother ignored everything that Elizabeth sought to do.

To her mother, it seemed that finding love was the ultimate goal of life. Ironically she had bouts of saying *"Men can't love"*; and yet for some reason, her only son was the one exception to that rule.

Her father had a similar way of speaking about Elizabeth; but he wouldn't reserve himself when speaking to her face. He recognized Elizabeth's dreams, but questioned her capability to take on the role.

"You need to speak up." Her father would say. *"How can you expect to be a leader if you don't speak up."*

Elizabeth sees herself in the role of the mentee to her second in command; and for the first time since knowing Julius, she really hates taking his advice.

Julius places his fingers on her forearm. He looks her in the eyes.

"Are you good?" He asks.

Elizabeth leans on the table. She crosses her arms and gathers her brows.

"Departure day is approaching." She says "If Dad's going to respond to my message, it should be coming in soon… It's been over six years."

Julius nods "And if it doesn't come in?"

"I'll just keep working as usual." She says "Nothing I can do about that."

Julius gathers his brows "Well, you've got this either way." He nods to her arm "Don't let a hiccup get you down."

Elizabeth looks at it. She wonders if she'd handle her fear any better next time. Assuming there's another chance to test her will, she wonders how capable she'll be outside of a mere simulation.

Julius has shown her how to fight. He's allowed her to practice with him. He's shown her how to use a gun, and what to expect when actually using it. He's told her about his own fight against the forces of nature, and how he survived by sheer willpower alone. Julius is more than an average man, and she's a wealthy girl who grew up in a suburban safety net. She had to struggle for independence and had to shun her parents' helping hands. Her struggle was different in every way; and it was all a matter of working against the things that would have been helpful to someone like Julius.

She was graced with wealth and security, but Julius was gifted with having a difficult life. He knew how to handle himself; physically and socially. What was at first endearing, has now become a spotlight on Elizabeth's insecurities. She's keenly aware that her father's doubts were well founded in some truth.

"My father." She thinks *"Where the hell is he anyway?"*.

The days go by without a message, and Elizabeth thinks that he's likely to send a brief, oversimplified account of things that have happened in her absence. He'll be much older, and not even bat an eye at the distance, let alone the time that has passed.

"He might not even bring Stephen." She thinks *"Frida wouldn't allow*

it."

The days turn into weeks, and her father still hasn't sent a message. Elizabeth wonders if the worst has come to pass, and that her chance of forgiving her father is no longer an option. Uncle Steve might be reluctant to tell her, and she'll return to find she's been written out of his will. Frida would certainly maneuver to cheat Elizabeth out of anything; not that Elizabeth would even care.

She begins to respond more attentively to her messages, subconsciously awaiting a message from home. Julius sees her change in attitude toward her messages and takes work out of her hands when he can. Alleviating her stress becomes his primary concern in this moment of anxiety.

On the late night before the day of departure, Elizabeth wakes at two in the morning. Her nightstand glows with a message box displayed.

"*One New Video Message from Zion.*" It reads.

Elizabeth stands up and dresses herself in a college sweatshirt. She slides a pair of moccasins over her feet and takes to the hall for the messaging room. The nightly cleaning robots avoid her feet. She enters the room at the most quiet hour of the night. The screen lights up with the note:

"*One new message for Elizabeth Lawrence.*"

Elizabeth places her hand on the table and unlocks the screen. The holographic keys display before her, and she navigates to the video.

It's a dark screen with a video interface at the bottom. She presses the arrow key to play the video.

The dark screen remains empty as the timecode counts up. It remains this way for seconds. Her father enters the screen from the side and seats himself. His stubble is unshaven. She knows it's uncharacteristic of his cleanly nature. Dark circles surround his eyes, and his lids hang over the iris.

He looks off to the side of the camera and speaks to someone she can't see.

"Thank you." He says.

A door closes and Mr. Lawrence takes a sigh.

"Hey Lizzie." He says.

He looks to the side and thinks a moment, then postures himself to speak.

"I'm glad you messaged me." He says "I didn't think I'd hear from you... I uh..." He looks down in thought then nods "I don't... have a day that goes by where someone doesn't ask about you… Uncle Steve has told me to come down here, but I haven't been ready. I just… Didn't know what to say…" He moves closer to the table "I'm proud of you… No matter what I've said in the past, you've proved me wrong. You're out there realizing your dream, and you've done it without my help… You're the strongest Lawrence there's ever been; and that includes Bill and Mary… You're going back to where they came from, and you're accomplishing more than we ever have… I can't believe you're… MY daughter… I just…." He shakes his head with wide eyes staring off to the side "I couldn't be any more proud of you…" He smiles, then bites his lip. He sighs and looks into the camera "You've carved your own path… I'm a hiring manager at the same company my father worked for, and I promise you, no one wants to talk about that… You're the one that people know by name. They see my last name and ask if I'm related to you… It never hit me until you were gone, but you were right to go for it… I didn't take any risks. I played it safe, and while my life might have been stable, you've made a name for yourself; doing something I couldn't have dreamed of… You're incredible…"

Elizabeth feels a numb sensation in her spine. Her eyes feel sour and full of the tears she thought she'd never shed.

"Lizzie… There's something I need to tell you." He says.

Elizabeth looks at her father. His eyes move from the direction of the door and back to the camera. He seems sorrowful and pained.

"They told me not to tell you this, but you're strong, and you should know… I would have brought Stephen with me… but he couldn't come…." He shakes his head with a bitter draw of his lips. His voice quivers and his teeth show through as he speaks "He was with his friends six months ago and this kid Spencer got the bright idea to go into his dad's woodshed… They got into huffing chemicals… we don't know which ones, but… long story short, Stephen passed out on the floor… He hasn't woken up… Not for six months…"

Elizabeth can no longer hold it back. She feels herself curling into a mess, holding her face to hide the tears.

"Your brother has been keeping a picture of the three of you by his bedside for the past two years, and he wants nothing more than to see you again… I loved Kyle, and I thought being hard on him would help, but now when I want to help Stephen, I'm just lost… I… I was terrible… I want to see you again. I don't know how to be better, but I want to try…" Her father takes a deep breath and collects himself. He sits back in his chair and straightens his posture. He blinks his eyes and hunches over the table. He speaks in a breath "I'm doing everything I can for him… I don't care how long it takes, you'll see your little brother soon… You must be at the end of your stay on Earth… That's what they told me at least… I can't wait to see what you've found. Please be safe Lizzie. I can't lose you too… You finish your work, and I'll show Stephen as soon as he wakes up… I'll bring him down here to talk to you too… Just be safe, Elizabeth. I'm proud of you. Keep working hard for your brother's sake. He's proud of you too."

Elizabeth removes herself from her chair and sits in the corner of the room. She curls into a ball and holds her head to collect herself. She stays like this for almost an hour.

CHAPTER 57
Departure

A quiet movie plays on a small screen in one of the rooms in the biology department. Connor lies on a couch, and Linda's head rests on his chest.

"I don't think this is the one." He says.

Linda shakes her head.

"It's not as good as the one we watched last week." She says.

Connor breathes a laugh from his nose and places his hand on the coffee table. A menu comes up so he can pause the movie. Once it's stopped, he sits up; and so too does Linda.

Linda looks around.

"What is this room, anyway?" She asks.

Connor looks through the playlist of films on the coffee table.

"It's a waiting room" He says "For medical stuff." He looks at her "Surgery."

She looks around "Have you guys used it?"

Connor looks reluctant to tell her "Uh, once…" He says "Doctor Lawrence's hand."

Linda feels a wave of guilt enveloping her otherwise happy mood.

Connor looks at her with sympathetic eyes "None of that is your fault."

Linda nods "No, I know…"

Connor looks down at the playlist but glances at her face as she runs off into thought. He thinks of how to take her mind away from it.

"Why me?" He asks.

Linda looks his way "What?"

"Why did you want to spend time together? I thought everyone kinda hated me."

"Monica didn't hate you." She says.

Doctor Manning nods "That's true."

Linda smiles "I never hated you either. Like I told you before when you asked; you just seemed grumpy."

She hugs him from the side. He touches her arm with his hand.

"I'm a little too serious sometimes." He says "I'm sorry."

Connor lies back and she lies on his chest, looking up at his face.

He smiles "Those eyes…"

"What about 'em?" Linda asks.

A pitter-patter comes from down the hall. Bullet enters the room with his tongue out.

"Bullet!" She says.

The dog approaches for attention. Both the scientists begin petting and scratching his ears.

She laughs "You're so handsome!"

Connor smiles and grabs the collar on his neck. He gathers his brows in confusion.

"I never gave him a collar." He says.

"You didn't?" She asks "I think it's cute."

Connor agrees.

Linda looks long at the panting dog. She looks up at Connor and smiles. She kisses him.

"What's that for?" He asks.

"You're like an angel." She says "Bringing life back."

He looks at the dog for a while. Bullet pants and puts his ears down for Doctor Manning. Connor feels the fur beneath his fingers, as if to make the thought tangible to him. He feels the warmth of the dog's neck and tries to grasp the magnitude of what he's done.

"I guess." He says.

A knock comes in the doorway and both look to see. Julius stands there with a smile on his face. Linda feels herself jump out of her skin, but she doesn't move from Connor's statue-like body.

"What's up?" Connor asks.

Julius looks at the movie screen and smiles.

"We're leaving." He tells them.

"Leaving Earth?" asks Connor.

Julius nods.

Linda gets up.

"Do you want to look one last time?" She asks.

"Yeah." Connor says "I'll get up. Thanks Julius."

Julius leaves the doorway to let them be.

The whole team joins in the main lobby for a parting party. It's here that Julius has a moment to talk with Elizabeth.

"What else did your dad say?" He asks.

"… He said that cheating on my mom was his biggest mistake…" Elizabeth shakes her head with wide eyes. Her arms are crossed as she reveals her deepest feelings "He even said that he still loves my mom; even though they've been separated for so long… It's unreal…"

Julius gathers his brows.

"A little late to turn back with a new wife; and now his son is in the hospital…"

Elizabeth nods.

"It's not about turning back." She says "It's about admitting his faults… He didn't want to face it before, but now…"

Elizabeth shrugs.

"I get it…" Julius says "… And what are they gonna do about your brother?"

Elizabeth sighs.

"He'll be okay…" She says "… Dad sent me some articles from the local news and the town has come together to help. He won't give up on Stevie. I know it… My little brother will be there when I get back."

Julius smiles; hoping that she's right. He knows it's blind hope, but what else does Elizabeth have?

He nods.

"… Alright." He says "I'm glad to hear it."

Elizabeth looks off at the ground and smiles.

"Mom's hosting a community art auction to help." She says.

"Your mom?"

Elizabeth nods.

Julius smiles. He feels inspired and almost laughs.

"I love that woman." Says Julius.

Elizabeth smiles "Me too."

Julius looks up at the party and notices Connor enter the room with Linda. Elizabeth watches this and gathers her brows.

"What?" She asks.

Julius frowns the corners of his mouth.

"Nothing." He says.

Elizabeth senses there's something more, but decides to forget the matter altogether.

After the party, the crew begins to discuss their plans for when they return to Zion. Julius makes a promise to see Elizabeth, but they have

almost ten more years until they reach home. They give one last farewell to Earth, and the thrusters take the ship away from the lonely
planet.

⁂

A week passes, and Doctor Hoyt has another appointment with
Doug. They have grown in familiarity, and the sense of trust is far deeper than Doctor Hoyt has had with any other patient. The appointments
are less frequent now, but the subjects of their discussions have grown
much wider.

"Are you excited to see Zion?" Hoyt asks.

"Yes." Doug says "I'm looking forward to seeing what things are like
there. I would love to see what Curtis has left behind."

Doctor Hoyt smiles "He's a hero to us; and people will love to meet
you."

The therapy session branches off into discussing further about Doug's
relationships on Earth.

Only one veil seems to be held over Doctor Hoyt's eyes. The veil that
hides who Rebeca Wheeler truly was. Doctor Hoyt wonders if Doug
even knew who she was. The words have been frank, but fruitless for
insight.

"Doug, I'm going to need to ask you something. I hope you don't
mind; and you don't need to answer if you don't want to."

Doctor Hoyt sits in a position of professionalism to encourage confidence in his patient.

"Feel free to ask anything you'd like." says Doug.

Doctor Hoyt looks over his papers once more in order to gather the
strength to ask the question.

"What was your relationship with Rebecca like? Privately, I mean."

The silent machine allows him to elaborate further.

"I know you are private" Hoyt says "I respect you as a gentleman, but
I'm trying to understand some things about your relationship together."

"What kind of information are you looking for?"

Hoyt looks downward, past his crossed leg "I see you had a lot of
arguments. Many relationships do, but the reasons aren't always clear;
not even for the people in the relationship. I get the feeling that you're
uncertain why you'd argue in the first place. Is that true?"

"That's actually very true."

Doctor Hoyt nods "Was she ever sexually reserved with you?"

"Sometimes. She wouldn't be in the mood and I'd just go to bed."

This level of confidence is a new boundary to be crossed. It is progress to Hoyt, and reassuring for Doug.

"And how long would she be reserved from you?" Hoyt asks.

"I don't recall."

"Can you give an estimate?"

"Sometimes it would last over a month… if not weeks, occasionally a day."

"Did you ever fear she would betray your trust?"

"… No."

Doctor Hoyt takes a note with slight relief. He then looks back at the lens. "Had she ever explained herself when she began an argument? You said she began them, seemingly out of nowhere."

"There was one occasion." Doug begins. "I got mad and told her I didn't care anymore, she said I was an idiot for not understanding her.

She said that she wanted to see if I cared. That sometimes she would push me away to test us; and she was right. I should have seen that."

Here is the point that Doctor Hoyt was almost about to miss. The missing link that makes the whole picture come together. A woman who bases her relationship on a series of tests.

Doctor Hoyt feels his heart break for the man before him. His kindness was met with an insatiable need for proof. A desire that demanded more than any reasonable person could provide.

As honest as Doctor Clay was in life, he could not gain the trust of a woman who suffered from borderline personality disorder. The woman he loved would never believe his genuine care.

"She was wrong, Doctor Clay."

"No…" Doug says "No she was right."

"No, I am saying this as a professional." Doctor Hoyt adds.

"Doctor Hoyt, I know I was wrong. It's clear to me now because her mind lives in here with me."

Doctor Hoyt feels a chill run down his spine. Adrenaline beats through his eyes into his brain. The delicate steps before him are far more precarious than ever. It explains the invasion of their privacy. It explains so much more. If this is true, the session needs to end, immediately.

"She lives in there with you?" Hoyt asks.

"Yes. She uses my brain as a platform. Where her mind decayed, mine takes over. Where hers remained, she lives equally, with me."

Hoyt's curiosity cannot be contained. "Can I speak to her?"

The pause is long before Clay answers. "No… And yes. I am her, and I am me. Both at once. Not separate."

Doctor Hoyt looks at his notes. Analyzing his mind alone has not been effective. While he is the dominant mind, he is not alone. She still remains with her mistrust, and his hostility. Doctor Hoyt needs to regroup.

"I'm gonna need to think all this over then." Hoyt says "I didn't know."

"It's my fault, Doctor Hoyt. I forgot to mention it. I am sorry."

"It's no problem at all, Doctor Clay. We're still on for tomorrow?"

"Of course."

"Until then." Hoyt says. He smiles on the surface of fear.

In the hall, Doctor Hoyt walks at an ordinary pace. His legs feel as if they are hitting a boundary of speed.

He takes a direct path to his office. He sits at his desk and opens his notebook on Doctor Clay.

He reads the notes on Doctor Clay's life and behavior. He recalls his language when he spoke of Rebecca. He's jotted down quotes for this exact kind of analysis.

He remembers Doug saying *"She was too pretty for her own good."*

"Was that said in anger?" He wonders.

At the time Doctor Hoyt thought it was a comical comment; but now he's worried about what linking their minds could have caused. Her thoughts on their relationship were likely much different from his own.

He opens his own book on the subject of BPD. It is titled "*My Mother Made Me Do It: Borderline Personality Disorder and How My Mother's Condition Inspired My Career in Therapy*".

He opens a section in the beginning of his book. He then reads his own definition of the condition.

> *The borderline has a tendency to blame themselves. They often test the boundaries of love and care to prove that it is genuine.*
>
> *This insatiable need for verification comes from a deeply rooted insecurity; often stemming from a traumatic past.*
>
> *Truth be told, they are not at fault for their feel-*

*ings. Instead it is the actions of a past assailer that
that are to blame. It has given them a difficult path
of healing to follow. One where the conscious mind
must rationalize a lack of care over the matter of
trust. Either that or, in some way, fix a sense of trust
into permanence.*

The therapist thinks back to Elizabeth's remark about Doug's relationship with Curtis Mandel.

She once made the claim that Doug was likely bitter to Curtis; citing Doug's own words and asking the question: "*He's surprised that Curtis made a name for himself? Why?*"

Doctor Hoyt dismissed the idea. He figured it was the surprise of seeing Curtis so personally; and then awaking to find that he's been considered a hero.

Hoyt fixes his brows together at the realization of how jarring it would be to learn of something like that. This very ship is named after his friend; and it would seem to him that they've venerated an average man.

What if it's true that he holds animosity for Curtis? Where would it have come from? Why hasn't he vocalized his true feelings by now?

He wonders if Rebecca's need for validation has become a part of Doctor Clay. It wouldn't be anything to worry about, but Douglas could feel immense insecurity with his relationships.

"*What part of him is Douglas?…*" He wonders "*… And how much of Rebecca remains? What would become of him, if they've linked their minds?*"

He recalls Rebecca's sporadic aggravation toward Doug. Doug blamed himself for these moments, but he must know by now that she wouldn't truly blame him. He would know she was incessantly testing him, and blaming herself for her lack of trust.

He looks over again at the book about Duncan VanRoy. He remembers trying to talk him down during a standoff with the police.

A trail of blood led to a southeast apartment in Eden. Doctor Hoyt was called in by the chief of police, Terrance Russell.

Hoyt's cousin Eliza was the mayor of Eden at the time. She recommended Arnold as the negotiations expert.

Hoyt talked his way into the building where he spoke with Duncan for the first time.

"Hello." Doctor Hoyt began.

Duncan glared back with a gaze on the border of apathy and hatred.

Hoyt spoke in a soft tone. His goal was to disarm the armed man.

"Quite the pickle you've found yourself in." He said.

Hoyt sat down and relaxed.

"I have all day, so take your time." He said "I'm Arnold Hoyt."

Doctor Hoyt looked around the room and gathered his brows.

"Why arm yourself and hold up here? Nobody said you did anything. They just wanted to talk."

Duncan felt power with his gun. He purposely angled it toward Doctor Hoyt to get a reaction.

"Jesus. You didn't pick the right gun." Hoyt said "A bolt action is no match for what they have out there."

"It's good enough to take SOMEone." Duncan said, aiming it at Hoyt.

Hoyt shrugged, nonchalant.

"Fair enough." He said "I mean, if you wanted to take me, then I'm fucked."

Hoyt laughed, but Duncan didn't even curve a lip.

"Are you lonely?" Hoyt asked "Upset?"

Duncan theatrically expressed disgust on his face as he spoke.

He chopped his words with spaces for emphasis "I… HATE… everyone."

Hoyt nodded.

"Try being a therapist. You hear the worst of people."

Duncan lowered the gun with interest.

Hoyt continued "I've heard married men go on about affairs, praying on my sacred vow of secrecy. Defiling it with their nasty desires. I couldn't turn them away from it either. They were hopeless."

"Rotten people."

Arnold raised his brows "Truly."

In that moment, Hoyt recollected the evidence. He remembered a disdain for women and superficial men.

"I always wanted love." Hoyt said to Duncan "I found it once, but she left me for someone… she wasn't anything spectacular, and at first I found it amusing when her husband cheated… but what's the point in giving a shit about someone that useless anyway."

"Useless?" Duncan asked, adjusting the gun.

"Superficial." Hoyt said "She was insecure, and so her thoughts were hell-bent on pleasing other people. She wanted recognition and acceptance; but I wanted love. I wasn't impressive enough for her friends on social media, and so she thought she'd get an upgrade. She really just traded love for superficial affections." He laughed "My mom made a big deal out of love. Said it was more important to have an honest friend than a useless photo with no good memory attached."

"Look, mister…"

"Hoyt." The therapist said.

"Mister Hoyt. I appreciate the story, but I have things to do."

Hoyt looked to the window.

"We have time." He said "They aren't moving."

Hoyt turned on a police radio and placed it on the floor at max volume.

"We'll know when they're coming." said Hoyt "They'll say it before they're on their way."

Duncan looked at it with a blank stare, then back at Hoyt.

"What do you want?" Duncan asked.

Hoyt shrugged "I want to know what got you here. If you did it, then it's best to tell your story. You left written stories at the scene of every crime. Mind you, they're well written, but they're incomplete."

"Incomplete how? They were bad people. They died for what they did. They call me the West Side Killer, because the…"

Duncan stopped himself, finding that he agreed with Doctor Hoyt.

The therapist nodded "… Because the police won't publish them. Not only that, but they don't know your story. Just snippets of dead people and why they died. So why not tell who you are? What's your story, and why do you hate everyone?"

"My story isn't anything."

"Is it? You're the Killer Rat, aren't you? Watching the world from the sewers. You loath the way they look at you, when you come up for food."

Duncan softened his posture.

Hoyt nodded "That was a compelling snippet of the way you see the world… I think there's more to say there."

Over the years Doctor Hoyt learned who Duncan really was. He felt tragedy because in some way he agreed with the man's bitterness. Hoyt himself felt it before, when he felt no sense of trust within his own family. He only gained value with his father's side of the family when he made a name for himself as a therapist. Otherwise he was the product of an affair with a "*crazy woman*".

He has since learned that people can be trusted; but it took time for those bonds to form.

Now as he looks at the book, he feels the same sorrows crashing onto Doug; as the waves of an ocean do to the boulders that reach up for dry air.

"*He must feel that way too.*" Hoyt thinks "*But how would he feel if he merged his mind with Rebecca's.*"

He looks up and remembers reading about the borderline once before. A small extra credit assignment in his undergrad years. He still holds a copy of that book in his office.

He makes his way down the bookcase and comes to the damaged spine of a paperback copy. He looks at it on the shelf and recalls from memory.

"*What was that passage?*" He asks himself "*My mother took risks; while driving, eating… things like that… but some people turn to drugs; others have unprotected sex with strangers…*" He turns on his heel and paces about the office "*They'll act out in risky behavior… They think they're worthless and so they think they're not worth the love they seek… So what would Doug do if he could see through her eyes?*"

Just then he remembers Doug's words. They were mechanical at the time. Now he hears them without an ounce of laughter or sarcasm. Instead he hears the venom as it sprays from his lips. A miasma of hate with each breath in a word.

"*She was too pretty for her own good.*"

Arnold laughed at the time, thinking it was a joke… but Doug went on. What happened next confused Hoyt, as it seemed off-topic; but this context changes everything.

"*Her death sent me into a meaningless spiral of despair; only now do I realize that you should work and live for yourself alone. I was dependent; but in time, I turned loss into liberation.*"

Hoyt found it odd at the time, but he began to sympathize. He perceived Doug as a man who became wiser and stronger; but now he feels that something is terribly wrong. The word "*meaningless*" wouldn't be used lightly.

He assesses the risk of a catastrophic event. Doctor Clay has already accessed the camera feeds on the ship. He has likewise breached communications with the crew; and it's likely that he's accessed the ship's databases.

It's probable that he's contemplating some action.

Only one thought keeps the therapist calm.

"*He hasn't done anything yet.*" He thinks. "*… And if he wanted something terrible to happen; then why would he save Elizabeth when she was in trouble?*"

He steps over to the holographic fireplace and thinks a while.

"*Doctor Morris is quite sorrowful.*" Clay once said "*Is he doing well?*"

Hoyt remembers veering from the subject, and Doctor Clay made an offer to speak with Morris as a confidant.

Doctor Hoyt warned Morris later to reject any advances from Clay, but the advances never came.

"*Could he have been hearing our conversations in this office?*"

There are no cameras or microphones to Arnold's knowledge, and so he decides to keep the thought in the back of his mind. His thoughts advance to the conversation with Clay about Ron.

"*He's saddened by the images of our past*" Doug said "*He's never seen the dark side of us Earthlings… His illusion of a culturally rich world has been shattered. He believed we had a perfect place with our self-sustaining ecosystem. He feels alone, but he's not… He needs a friend who's felt the same, and I've felt that way before…*"

On the subject of Doctor Morris, Arnold recalls his concerns over him.

He wasn't eating right. His enthusiasm had hit an all-time low. His sense of nuance was waning. The therapist was concerned with where this could lead.

Doctor Clay was right about what he needed, but Doug was, and still is, the last person to trust with Ron's companionship. It could be that Doctor Clay was intending to use him for something; something his body couldn't do. It could also perhaps be nothing but a kind gesture.

The therapist has decided that there is something amiss behind the scenes. He's resolved to ask an engineer for assistance. He now knows he must get a second opinion. It might be best to play it safe and override Doug's inhibitors. They're on the verge of this becoming an emergency. For the safety of the crew, it would be best to look directly into Doug's mind.

He takes to the halls. He passes Doug's room and comes up to the door of the engineering labs.

He sees Phil, Mark, and Danny. They all stop amid their work.

"Is Doctor Lawrence here?" Arnold asks.

"She's in the messaging room…" Danny says "… She's sending something home."

Hoyt thanks them and makes his way down the hall. He comes to the intersection between the historical and biological departments. He turns toward the historical wing, and along the way he sees Doctor Winter.

"Doctor Winter." He says.

Julius turns to see the therapist behind him.

"Doctor Hoyt. What's up?"

The doctor waits until he is closer to speak. He reaches whispering distance and begins in a hush.

"I need your help with something." Hoyt says "It's urgent."

"What's up?" Julius asks.

Hoyt looks off to the side and thinks.

"… Do you think Doctor Clay is capable of having emotional outbursts?"

Julius gathers his brows.

"I think so. Why do you ask?"

"It was something you mentioned about Clay's brain; how it's still mostly human…"

"Yes." Says Julius "Well, it's a metallic version of the human brain; identical in almost every way, but it's missing some parts. Those parts are substituted with the quartz towers. That's where he stores memories in ones and zeroes."

Hoyt puts up a hand and raises a brow.

"Slow down." He says "I just wanna know; is he still susceptible to an impulse like the rest of us?"

Julius bobs his head side to side in somewhat of an agreement.

"Everyone thinks machines are more controlled and precise, but the line between us is blurring every day. That's especially the case with Doctor Clay." Julius breathes deep to prepare the explanation "He borrowed from the biological structure of human beings; and because of that, he's not a machine in the regular sense of the word. He still has desires and emotions. He's still susceptible to the same faults as a natural being. He'll reach for a momentary gain at the expense of a long-term goal. He'll act out of emotion, and so he can slip up and be short-sighted."

Julius looks at Hoyt to see his eyes have widened at some realization.

"What?" Julius asks "You look scared."

Hoyt looks to his side. He sees the camera in the corner of the room and brings his voice down.

"Listen. I think you're right about Doug. There's something wrong with him… and something wrong with his wife."

"His wife?"

"She's unstable. Her condition is very unsafe for him."

"She died years ago. What's that gotta do with him?"

"She lives with him… in his mind." says Hoyt "He's powerful now; and it's dangerous for him to share a mind with her."

"What do you mean? Is she dangerous?"

"It's not her I'm worried about." Hoyt says "Her condition makes her impulsive, but she's benevolent…" Hoyt looks over his shoulder and moves closer to whisper "I'm more concerned with how Doctor Clay would behave… He's told me that he thinks love is about 'making things work, no matter what'; but the only time I've heard that before, the patient who said it had cut his wife from her stomach to her neck."

Julius gathers his brows.

"Do you think Doctor Clay killed his wife?"

Hoyt shakes his head.

"Medical records say it was cancer." He says.

Julius looks off to the ground. He wonders what Hoyt could be getting at.

"You think she's trapped?" He asks.

Hoyt nods "It's possible… The point is; it's likely that there's something wrong here. I can feel it…"

"Do you think we should enter his mind manually?" says Julius.

Doctor Hoyt sighs. He hesitates; moving back and forth in his mind.

"Do I have your permission?" Julius presses.

Hoyt opens his mouth "Y-…"

An explosion brings Winter to the floor. His vision is disoriented. His ears ring. Adrenaline makes him numb to the pain, but he's aware of a warm liquid.

He checks to see his condition, but it's only cosmetic. To his right, he sees an unrecognizable face.

Arnold Hoyt whimpers with shards of metal in his head. His eyes protrude out of his skull. His face is nearly bisected, splitting his jaw into a crooked shape. His tongue hangs limp on the outside of his mouth and it dries in the air.

"Arnold!" Julius yells "Arnold, can you hear me?!"

Doctor Hoyt cannot respond. He makes moans in a repeated low tone.

"Help!" Julius yells "Help!"

The halls are flooded with curious eyes. They see two bleeding men covered in dust. Those who are brave enough charge forward to give assistance.

They remove Doctor Winter from the side of the faceless moaning man.

***

Doctor Hoyt can hardly feel the hands of the assistants as they bring him into the surgery room. They begin to work on him, but the pain and adrenaline have his mind in a haze.

There is only one thing on his mind at the moment; and it's Doug.

He thinks of Doug's emotional pain, and not his own; for Doug has been on the edge of committing an unspeakable act.

Arnold knows this now; and he's unknowingly made up Doug's mind for him. He feels foolish, and wishes Doug had trusted him. He would have kept any secret, so long as they trusted one another.

The voices of the surgeons fade. What Arnold can see, it now grows dim.

His thoughts trail off to his relationship with those around him. He feels foolish for trying to find answers, and trying to connect the team together. He did this all while forgetting to connect himself to the equation.

His own impact on Doug was something he had forgotten, and he's hardly made a true relationship with the others on the explorer.

Arnold feels that his past is not a story shared between friends. People won't recall his presence in a fond memory. Instead he feels that he's been reduced to the words of his best-selling books. His legacy will be his accolades and achievements. Nothing of his person will be there to recount.

His present is soon to become nothing more than his past; as he's become nothing more than the title that he bears. This makes Peter the only one who can remember his flaws. He'll be the only one who knows Doctor Hoyt as something more than a public figure. He feels guilty for dragging Peter out here; only to leave him alone in this predicament without him.

The future is gone. There is no other option.

He prays that the team will stay connected in his absence; or at least long enough to handle what Doug has in store.

He reflects on this, until he releases one final breath…

… until he's become nothing more…

… than nevermore.

Afterlife:

The remains are handled accordingly. They're delivered to a mourning room.

He is the first to occupy the room for graves.

Doctor Winter regains his thoughts on his own time, away from anyone else. It's in his room that Doctor Lawrence finds him, staring blank at his pile of books in the corner.

"How are you holding up?" She asks.

"I'm fine." He says.

He continues to stare.

It's subconscious, but the physical copy of a book brings him comfort. They are written, and not subject to change.

Digital media can be altered, even faked; but written information, ink on paper, that's undeniable. The truth is important. It doesn't lie. The truth can be trusted, and Hoyt's word was truth in the eyes of anyone.

Hoyt was about to give verbal permission to enter Doug's mind. That was everything. The theories about the mechanical man were becoming more than theories.

"We need to talk with the Captain." Julius says "Privately."

In the Captain's quarters, they find Peter with Connor, Linda, Monica and Ron. They sit across the desk from the engineers. Peter looks angry, or sick from sorrow.

Julius looks determined at him.

"Captain" He says "We need to talk with you. It's important."

"Come." Peter says "Come tell all of us."

Doctor Lawrence moves forward with Julius; all the while her eyes rest on Manning, who looks up from his seat. He looks angry. Linda stands behind him to the side.

"Captain" Julius says "Doctor Hoyt was about to give us permission to manually look through Doug's mind. Something bothered him."

Elizabeth looks at Julius in shock.

Connor chimes in. His voice is cold.

"I can't believe you're capitalizing on Arnold's death." He says.

Peter waves his hand in Connor's direction.

"He's been drinking." He says "Don't mind him."

Linda grabs the biologist by the arm "Let's go…"

"How dare you!" Connor shouts at Julius "You should be ashamed!" He extends his finger in the direction of the engineers.

Ron punches Connor. Manning falls limp in Linda's arms and he begins to sob.

"Gentle, Ron!" The Captain scolds.

Ron shakes his head "I don't have patience for this."

The Captain looks as if he's about to rise from his seat. He stops and returns to the cushion beneath him.

"Me neither." He mutters.

Linda and Monica exit the room with Connor. Monica's face is without expression as she closes the door. The Captain nods at her with a sympathetic smile. As the door clicks shut, Peter sighs.

He places his hand on his desk to start a screen projection. The last thing that was opened on his profile was a message box. They were messages with Arnold, showing their last correspondences.

He looks at it a while.

Peter Andrews: The explorer pod had another problem today. It's been acting up.

15:30 | 6/15

Arnold Hoyt: I think Connor and Linda have a thing now.

20:52 | 6/17

Arnold Hoyt: May I see you in the office this week? I wanna know how things went with Ron.

10:14 | 9/20

Arnold Hoyt: Come by sometime. Just wanna talk as cousins.

09:42 | 9/27

The Captain looks at the desk with a plain face. He closes out of it and moves on to look at something else.

Elizabeth looks stunned by the air of the room. Julius insists on speaking.

"Captain" Julius says "We need to look into his mind."

The Captain stares off at the ground as he gathers his thoughts. Winter presses the Captain with his posture. With a gathering of his brows, he's determined to stare at the Captain until he responds.

"I uh…" Peter says "…I don't think that's necessary, Doctor Winter."

Julius feels his enthusiasm shatter, but he keeps his hopes alive.

"Why not?" Julius asks "He said there's something wrong with him. He said Doug, or whatever that thing is; he said it was too powerful; and unstable."

"Is that what he said? That Doug is unstable?"

"Yes. He said that his wife is in there with him. That she's unstable. He said Doug was too powerful, and suddenly the pipe burst."

"The pipe was a maintenance error." Peter says "Monica has been taking it very hard. She admitted to messing up."

"It wasn't her fault!"

"Then why would she admit to it, Julius?"

Julius is at a loss for this argument.

"Doug is a rational man." Says the Captain "Perhaps too rational, even. He doesn't act on emotional impulses, he's a good man. He couldn't kill anyone."

Julius knows stubbornness when he sees it. His words will go nowhere, and so an avenue needs to be made elsewhere.

He throws his shoulders down and forces a posture of defeat.

"I'm sorry, Captain." says Julius "I just got excited is all."

"Just call me Peter. Forget all the formality for a minute."

The Captain rubs his face to wake himself up.

"We lost someone good today." Peter says "We all feel it… Just wait and be patient. We'll go through his notes and proceed with Doug from there. Hoyt's assistant will take his place. It's not as effective, but it's better than nothing."

Winter nods.

The Captain stands and looks around at them.

"Would you all mind leaving my office?" He says "I'd like to be alone a little while."

Julius and Elizabeth leave the room at once. The Captain closes the door and turns about on his heel. He sighs and walks toward his desk, shaking his head at the ground.

Ron coughs. At once the Captain notices Ron. He's still here.

"Oh…" Peter says "Why didn't you go?"

Ron shrugs with a tilt of his head.

"I have a promise to fulfill." He says.

Peter looks at the tab at the bottom of the screen on his desk. It's the conversation between himself and Doctor Hoyt.

Peter smiles in his eyes, but not yet his mouth. He can't feel that kind of happiness just yet, as it's far too soon.

"Yeah" He says "I guess you do."

Ron feels a sigh of relief in the air, like the tension of the room has been lifted; as one does with a curse. He can feel it on his skin. His muscles loosen on his face to fall naturally into what almost becomes a smile.

Ron shrugs again. He looks off at the floor. He can only come up with one word.

"Pool?"

***

Once he's in the hall and halfway to the lab, Julius lets out a huff of frustration. Anger reads on his face, and when Elizabeth catches up to him, she can feel it.

She walks in step with her partner to talk.

"Hey" She says "Are you okay?"

He looks her way, then purses his lips with thought.

"I'm fine." He says.

His eyes stare away for a while, then he meets her eyes in a glance.

"I need you to get some things for me." He says "We're doing this the hard way."

With a mix of excitement and fear, she nods.

"Yeah." She says "I can get them."

They come to the engineering lab to find no one is there. The crew has taken the day off for mourning.

Julius and Elizabeth search through the devices they've made over the course of the year. They gather components that they've set aside for this occasion. They link the parts together to make two chords with boxes at one end of each of them.

"Is this everything?" He asks her.

She nods.

He looks the chords over. They plug into two box-shaped transmitters separately. They're assembled and ready.

He takes a sigh and moves back from the table. He hands her one of the chords with its box.

"You do that" whispers Julius "I'll talk… Keep it out of sight."

"Quiet." She whispers "I've got it. Let's go."

He nods and moves with her out the door.

They exit to the hall and turn toward the therapy office. Before the corner to Arnold's study, they turn into Doctor Clay's room where they find the machine all alone.

Julius approaches him with his hands held together, head hanging. He twiddles his thumbs to bring up the awkward subject.

"How you holding up?" Julius asks.

"As good as I can be." Says Doug.

Julius nods. He sits on the curb of a ramp that leads up the wall to the entrance of the room. He leans forward so his back doesn't touch the railing behind him.

"Aren't we all." He says.

Julius motions to Elizabeth.

"Do you mind if she checks the effects of the event?"

"… On me?" Asks Doug.

Julius nods "We're afraid of what the trauma could do to your mind."

"Still think I'll go crazy?" Says Doug.

Julius shakes his head "It's more of a study on how it affects you."

"We want you to be healthy and happy" says Elizabeth "Any way we can help, we're willing to give it a shot."

"I wasn't on the security cameras at the time…" Doug says.

Julius shrugs "Still; there's the effects of remorse on your brain; we just don't know what that will look like… It's worth studying."

"… I suppose." Says Doug.

Elizabeth opens his hatch and enters with half of her body. She removes the adaptor from her bra, and tries to keep it in front of her. She keeps her back to the security camera of the room so Doug can't see.

She attempts to take the plug with its dangling cube of a transmitter, and plug it into the distant slot at the end of her reach.

She prays that Doug won't be watching through the security camera.

"What's that?" Doug asks.

Elizabeth turns around.

"What's what?" She asks.

"Under your shirt." Doug says "The circuitry."

Elizabeth looks at Julius' face. He's paralyzed with wide eyes.

She smiles, then laughs. She lifts her shirt to show her rib cage. There is a near identical tattoo to Linda Xiao's.

"Linda and I got matching tattoos before the expedition." She says "Probably drank a little too much, but as department heads and tech geeks; it seemed fitting."

"It's a cool idea." says Doug "I've never found anything worth getting on my body… Not that it matters anymore."

The engineers smile at one another. Elizabeth then turns back to the door on Doug's body. She pretends for a while to look it over with a thoughtful look about her face. The wireless transmitter hangs by its chord, and there is no place for it to rest.

"*It's gonna have to hold on for dear life.*" She thinks.

She shuts the door at a slow pace; so as not to rattle the adaptor and make it fall inside.

"I'm surprised." Elizabeth says "There's not a lot more written."

Doug's long-term memory banks whirr. Julius stops breathing for a second. He's terrified that the motors will make the adaptor fall.

It doesn't fall, and Julius almost sighs.

Doug then speaks again. It sounds, to the engineers, like what might be a lie.

"… A coping mechanism" He says "… I think."

CHAPTER 58
The Pulse of the Earth

In a vivid memory, Julius stands in Grand Central station. A vision of New York's glory on Earth. The air is alive with the shuffling of feet and the hum of voices, echoing. In this large room there is a massive clock which sits atop the central booth. There, men and women inside speak to strangers through a glass window.

On a green ceiling, images of yellow lines depict human figures in stars, and large pillars reach downward from this scene. They meet the balconies that rise above the lobby.

Through an archway, Winter walks among the Earthlings. He cannot control his excitement over it. An unbelievable view of a much simpler time. America; a symbol of power and cultural exchange.

Winter watches the children who hold their parents' hands. All their lives, they'll expect to walk in the open air. Adults in old business suits, walking through with haste. Many of them traverse the globe, navigating faraway lands. All of them are oblivious to the magic in their lives.

Taking a right turn down a corner, Julius follows the crowd. There is an old escalator to the left, which takes commuters to their daily lives, down to the subway below.

To Julius, the number of people with personal interests and private lives; it's warm to the heart.

Suddenly he's grabbed by a stranger.

A woman screaming frantic "Help me! Please!"

Her sobs sound like she is screaming directly from her throat. It's desperate distress.

She's young and not insane, nor is she overreacting. It reminds him of the chained woman. As if she has been transported here from that place of carnage and malice.

Doctor Winter wants to help, but looks to see who else may assist him. He sees one man, and she notices his glare. She shrieks a blood-curdling scream.

The man pulls up an old gun and points it toward Julius.

The bullet feels like a fast pebble to the forehead. The sensation it gives is repeated outward to the back of his skull. Doctor Winter, beyond his own will, falls to his knees. A buzzing, yet ringing noise resonates in his ears and warmth is felt on his face. It advances toward his chin. His thoughts aren't clear. Just then, his eyes open.

He's in bed; unharmed.

Doctor Winter's arm is open to a slit. From there, a chord hangs out from his skeleton. At the other end of this chord is a small cube with a blinking light. The other device, just like this one, is plugged into the port where Elizabeth left it; somewhere inside Doug's body.

The door opens. Doctor Lechmere looks at Julius from the doorway. He doesn't speak a word.

Looking up at him from his bed, Julius now knows.

He finally understands.

CHAPTER 59
Alone

In the morning, at breakfast, Doctor Lawrence sits to talk with Julius.
"What are your thoughts?" She asks "What do we do?"
Julius looks up at her with a disapproving glance.
"Nothing." He says with a casual stab of his food.
"Nothing?"
Julius doesn't reply.
"Julius, I need to know what to do about Doctor Clay."
"Do what about him?" He asks.
"Something needs to be done." She says.
"He's harmless."
Elizabeth looks in awe at her friend. He doesn't seem the same in manner or tone. The relaxed infliction of his voice, his posture; it's unfamiliar to her. The fun-loving innocence is gone from his eyes. In some way, this is how she imagined he truly was since his time in the war. That his positive attitude has always been an overcompensation.
"Julius, he killed Doctor Hoyt."
Julius looks cold at her.
"Things happen." He says "It was an accident."
His tone is so calm and soothing that a chill runs down her spine.
"Excuse me." He says.
He moves to throw his plate away, but Elizabeth grabs his hand.
"Julius…" She says "… What did you see last night? Why won't you tell me?"
He pulls his hand away.
"When would you have told me about Project Icarus?" He asks.
Elizabeth seems paralyzed at a loss for words.
"… The Captain said to keep it a secret…" She says "You were on that mission with the historical department…"
He shrugs.
"Whatever." He says.

Elizabeth has nothing to say.

He turns and leaves the dining hall to return to his work.

Elizabeth is left in a fog of confusion. He wouldn't be mad at her like this. Not even if she kept a secret under orders. The friend she once had is now an exoskeleton with no memory of their past together. This thing bears his resemblance, but he's not there. Instead there's a different person who lacks the forgiveness of Doctor Julius Winter.

Later in the day she sees him in the laboratory. His words are concise and cold. His thoughts are uninspired and analytical.

Days pass like this, and Elizabeth spends very little time with Julius. Unlike the previous daily talks, games, and movies; they now hardly speak a word. They speak only on the occasion that talking is required.

Elizabeth remembers a time when she had no friends in middle school. The girls had treated her poorly, her brother had become distant, and her parents were self-invested. She needed someone; anyone. Instead she had her imagination, schoolwork, and television shows. She became overweight, although no one would guess it now. She developed bulimia soon after when the girls called her "*fat*".

It was near the end of middle school, when all the weight was lost to malnutrition. That was when her wardrobe darkened, and she met her first boyfriend. Her life changed drastically; in some ways for the better. It wasn't long after however, that her father stomped out her ties with the boy. Her mother tried to reason with her to no avail. It was paradoxical for a lonely woman to encourage a life alone. Moreover, it was a contradiction for her to tell Elizabeth not to date. When recounting her first years with Elizabeth's father, she referred to herself as "*trapped*" and "*robbed of her youth*".

Elizabeth's mother made claims that she could have chosen wealthier and kinder men. That her younger years should have been spent dating more people. For this reason, Elizabeth has remained single for most of her life. Now, more often than ever, she wonders if this is even voluntary.

In the warm safety of their ship, Elizabeth has thought long and hard about the cold darkness, just meters away from her bed. She has thought about her own loneliness and her absence of a love life. Ultimately she realizes love never suited her. She would not know what to do with a warm embrace. Sex and scandal have always been found in her life, but love remained evasive. Company is the closest thing she's had to companionship.

It's been Julius' company that she has appreciated most. As a sidekick, or a partner in crime. Whether he's been a friend or a servant, it's always been company.

As she sits in her room at night, she throws these ideas around in her mind. From her trance, she wakes with a tear on her cheek. She wipes it away with disgust.

If love is what she is supposed to feel for Julius, then it's stupid. The idea that company could mean so much to someone who's braved such loneliness before. In this faraway space where darkness clutches at each and every corner, loneliness becomes unbearable; even for the strongest of people.

In the mess hall, Elizabeth sips on tea alone. The other crew members play with the dog in the recreation area. Their laughter rings through the halls.

Monica enters the mess hall with a preface of footsteps. At the sight of Doctor Lawrence she hesitates to leave, but stops at the sight of Elizabeth's face.

"Are you alright Elizabeth?" Monica asks.

Elizabeth looks over at her and begins in a brief laugh. "I'm fine. Just thinking."

Monica sees through her facade, but misinterprets it as something else.

"Linda says she's sorry. She hasn't had a minute to tell you that, but she keeps saying she wants to stop by your lab and say sorry to you."

"Sorry for what?" Elizabeth asks.

Monica looks confused. She realizes it was not what Doctor Lawrence's face had been for.

"For not being there when your suit was compromised." Monica says.

"Oh!" Elizabeth says "No, Monica!" Elizabeth's eyes grow sorry and she reaches toward Monica to hold her hands "She stopped by already." Elizabeth says. Her brows draw down on the edges and together toward the middle "I'm alright. Don't worry about me. I know things happen. Everything's fine."

Monica fails to make a slight smile. She holds back a heartbreaking sorrow at the thought of Doctor Hoyt.

"I didn't do too good either." Monica says.

Her words stop short of a cry when Elizabeth meets her in a tight embrace.

"Monica, it's not your fault. You two have the hardest jobs on the ship."

"I don't even know how it happened!" Monica's voice muffles through Elizabeth's shoulder. "I had everything checked out! I've gone over it all in my head and it doesn't add up!"

Elizabeth's analytical instinct corrects her mind for a moment.

"Do you have any proof to show this?" She asks with hope in her breath.

Monica nods with tears on her eyelids. She wipes them from her face. "Show me."

In the maintenance office Doctor Lawrence looks over the blueprints of the ship alongside the data on the morning of Hoyt's death. She sees several pipes being fed the contents of the heating pipe that killed Doctor Hoyt.

Knowing the mechanical properties of each piece, Elizabeth knows that this is simply not an accident. She tells her colleague that this is so.

"Who would block off those pipes?" Monica asks.

Elizabeth is reluctant to respond and finds that there is no need to explain who.

Monica looks at her with concern "You think it was Doctor Clay."

Elizabeth looks toward a distant space on the floor of the room. She recalls all that she knows and recounts it to Monica.

"Julius hasn't been himself lately." Elizabeth says.

Monica looks at her with a curious face.

"Did he try to enter Doug's mind?" Monica asks.

Elizabeth looks at her with no response.

Monica's heart sinks. "No…"

"He insisted… He hasn't been the same ever since."

"Does the Captain know?"

Elizabeth shakes her head.

Monica finds her heart racing with fear.

"What do we do?" Monica asks.

Elizabeth too, wonders this intently.

Throughout the night, Elizabeth runs the math with a plan to approach the Captain in the morning. Monica will talk it over with Doctor Morris and meet her in the Captain's quarters.

The conclusion Doctor Lawrence comes to is astounding. It is nearly impossible to make the pipes burst along that part of the corridor. What's even more astonishing is that the air pumps themselves did not rupture before the pipes did. The path of least resistance would be the pumps themselves, and yet they were left unharmed.

She packs her work together at six in the morning and makes her way to the cut-bot for a trim. She's scheduled to see the Captain at eight.

She enters the room with the spherical machine. Its appendages move from their joints attached to both the sphere and the ceiling.

Once rested in her seat, the cut-bot's arms begin to move. Here she analyzes her appearance in the reflection. Her eyes are dark around the lids; they sag downward from sleep deprivation. She notices her skin is pale; without a smooth texture. Her hair is greasy and hasn't been brushed. That much could be fixed now. Perhaps a shower would help her skin. The eyes can hardly be helped.

At this final realization her focus is cut by the edge of a pair of scissors which slice her skin at the jaw where it meets her neck. She gasps, and moves from her seat.

The small cut is hardly noticeable. Just a red mark and barely an abrasion on the skin. It feels tender to the touch, but otherwise it hardly hurts.

"*Does it need to be calibrated?*" She wonders.

At eight o'clock, after a brief shower, Doctor Lawrence strides over to the Captain's office. With papers in hand, she is ready to make her argument before the Captain himself.

Upon opening the doors, she is met with an unnerving sight. Julius, Ron, Connor, and the Captain all stand as Monica remains seated. They look on her with long faces as her posture looks defeated and solemn.

"Captain?" Doctor Lawrence says.

There is no response.

She scans the eyes which look at her in disappointment. All except Monica; she looks down with defeat.

The Captain dismisses Monica from the room, but Elizabeth stops her just short of leaving.

"Stay here." Elizabeth says "What's this all about?"

The Captain shakes his head "This is the last straw, Doctor Lawrence."

"What is?"

"You've gone too far. Monica knows it was an accident, and you're filling her head with all this about Doctor Clay…"

"You think I'm not basing this in reality?!" Elizabeth says.

"You're not!"

Monica takes Elizabeth's attention for a moment.

"They're right, Doctor Lawrence." She says "I'm sorry."

Monica leaves and Elizabeth looks at the men; now alone.

"Am I losing my mind here?!" She says "Look at the evidence!"

She plants the papers on the Captain's desk.

"Here's your proof!" She says.

The Captain looks at the papers without analysis "Why don't you show Doctor Clay your evidence?"

"Don't mind if I do!" She says.

She throws a page at Julius.

He catches it, then looks at it with confusion. He looks at her with a shrug.

"You're fucking useless." She says.

She grabs the paper from his hands and storms down the hall to Doctor Clay's area. There she finds Hoyt's assistant. He sits in front of the machine with a notepad and a pen.

"Let me ask you something!" Elizabeth says to the machine.

Doug chimes "Ask me anything Doctor Lawrence."

"Why did you kill Doctor Hoyt?"

A silence takes over the room. The rest of the crew gathers in the entrance.

"I'm afraid I'm lost, Doctor Lawrence."

"Bullshit." She says "Why did you do it?"

She throws the pages beneath the lens of the machine. She then looks over toward the therapist's assistant.

"He needs your help to read them. He can't pick them up."

The assistant lifts them to the lens.

After a moment of quiet Doug begins to respond.

"That appears to be an anomaly, given what you've recorded. However, what if one of the pipelines was actually open?"

The crew near the entrance scoffs at her.

"The air pumps would be ruined!" She states "The path of least resistance! It would happen well before the pipeline burst!"

The Captain's voice booms over the room "Doctor Lawrence, there's a perfectly good explanation. I think it's time you've gone to your room."

"No!" She says.

She looks at the machine.

"I want answers." She says "Now!"

Doctor Clay calculates "Maybe there was something wrong with the sensors. The data could be wrong if there was a faulty sensor."

All but Julius roll their eyes at Elizabeth. Julius remains silent. He stares at her intently.

"I want you in your room, Elizabeth." The Captain begins. "If you don't go willingly, then I'll have to ask some assistants to take you there."

She looks angry at the Captain. She doesn't respond but glares at him for his lack of trust in her.

"You'll be kept there until we figure out what to do with you." The Captain says "Julius can fill in for your absence."

Two assistants approach her. She punches one to the floor. The other puts his hands up.

"Please…" says the assistant "I'm just following orders."

She feels sorry for the assistant on the floor, but stands firm; angry at the Captain.

"You're nothing; a loser." She says "You're the saddest chapter in the Mandel family."

The Captain shrugs. A theatrical downplay of her insult.

"Whatever you say." He says "I never asked for this job anyway."

Connor shakes his head and hisses a scoff through his teeth.

"You wanna do that again, clown?" She says.

Doctor Morris smiles. He can barely contain a laugh from what she's just said to Connor. Elizabeth catches this and smiles back.

Manning gets quiet. He takes her comment personally.

As she leaves, she can hear Manning attempt to get in one last comment.

"Give it a rest." He says.

His voice is self-conscious.

In a last glance over her shoulder, she sees Julius fighting a smile.

He hasn't smiled in a week.

CHAPTER 60
Revelation

Doctor Winter breathes heavy with beads of sweat on his face. He sits awake in bed.

With a touch of his forehead he reassures himself that the bullet was merely in his dream. He was not in Grand Central Station, on Earth. Here in waking reality, the Captain's first assistant stands in his doorway.

Doctor Lechmere bids him to follow.

"Quietly." He says.

His deep velvet whisper sounds urgent.

Julius stands. He slides his slippers over his toes and follows Lechmere out the door.

Down the hall a little ways, they come to the Captain's quarters.

The Captain stands with the department heads. Elizabeth, Linda, Monica, Ron, and Connor all stand in a line.

Doctor Lechmere closes the door behind Julius, leaving the seven alone without his company.

"You're wondering why I've woken you up?" Peter asks.

Julius meets the Captain's words with a face that agrees.

"It's about your theory. It's right. You know it. I know it. We all know it."

While it's reassuring that the Captain agrees with them, Julius wishes he had been told of this meeting. He would have otherwise been better prepared; perhaps clean-shaven.

Peter continues "My room is the only place other than Hoyt's office without any cameras."

"He stopped watching us." Julius says.

"That doesn't mean he stopped listening." Peter informs him.

Julius begins to realize that the Captain is a more elaborate thinker than he leads on to be.

"I know you're wondering why this meeting was unplanned." Elizabeth says "We had to make sure you weren't compromised, so we watched you while you went into Doctor Clay's mind."

"What did you see?" Connor asks.

Julius looks around at the faces and realizes this will be a lot to tell them.

"I was in Grand Central Station." Julius says "I saw New York, the way it was."

Ron takes a breath of wishful wonder.

"I uh… I was killed." Julius adds "A woman ran up to me begging for help, then a man shot me in the head."

"Might be Doctor Clay…" Peter says "Could the woman have been his wife?"

Julius looks down and wonders this himself.

The Captain looks at Morris with a serious frown. The historian looks urgent in his demeanor.

"How old are you, Julius?" Monica asks.

"Two hundred and eighty-three." Julius says.

Linda chuckles "Doug must be curious about those medical records."

The Captain nods and looks at Monica. She looks stunned by the engineer's age.

"He's one of the first generation." The Captain says "He has no wireless functions."

Ron nods "New Memphis was a long long time ago."

"That's why he's fine." The Captain adds "That's why they're all fine for now." He looks at Julius "It's likely he'll think you were an apparition of his dream. He's, at most, curious; but that was a one-time move."

Peter puts out his hand and Julius gives him a device on a chord. The Captain puts it in his pocket.

"Next time, I don't think you'll slip out undetected." Peter adds.

Elizabeth looks reluctant to speak "Julius" She starts "We've devised a plan. One last effort to lure out Clay's intentions without revealing all our cards."

"What do you mean?" asks Julius.

The Captain almost begins speaking, but looks at Elizabeth. He raises his hand to her with a nod, allowing the chief engineer to take the floor.

She looks sad when speaking "Julius, I've been meeting here with the department heads ever since Doctor Clay came over the communications. I would have told you, but it was only for the department heads to know."

Julius smiles to invoke trust in their bond.

"That was very smart of you." Julius says. He nods and looks around "All of you. I'm glad to hear it."

Peter smiles "Doctor Hoyt's plan was to assess the risks. He was tying up some loose ends before he died yesterday. Without his help, there's only one option left."

"We need to stage a play." Elizabeth says. She smiles "Kinda like the ones I used to do in high school."

Julius smiles "Yeah, I remember you told me."

"You're going to pretend to behave differently." Elizabeth says "He might be onto what you did, and so we'll make it seem like you're hostile; indifferent about the whole investigation."

"You and Elizabeth have the best chance of coming off as genuine." Peter says "We don't have the luxury of Doug's resting poker face, so the rest of us will spend more time with you. Elizabeth will stage herself to be alone, and Monica will act as a catalyst for the trap we're setting up."

"What's the trap?" Julius asks.

"Me." Elizabeth says "I'm going to be bait."

Julius gathers his brows "What do you mean?"

"I'm the one who has been spearheading the investigation." Elizabeth says "He'll want to get rid of me."

Julius looks about him with frantic eyes.

"She's made up her mind." Peter says "She'll snap in front of him. Then we have Elizabeth isolated in her room." Peter motions to the historian and biologist "These two have already played their part. That outburst from Doctor Manning was a planned incident. He got drunk to make Ron's punch a little more believable."

Connor feels the lump in his jaw. Ron almost laughs, and Linda leans on Connor ever so slightly.

"Linda, I'm pretending I didn't see that." Peter says "I'm still your boss."

Linda looks scared and everyone holds in a laugh.

Peter looks at Julius with trusting eyes.

"We're staging a division on the ship." He says "All the while, we're more united than we've ever been." Peter nods "All thanks to Doctor Hoyt."

Julius nods.

"Are you in?" The Captain adds.

Julius smiles "Let's give it a shot."

✳✳✳

A week later, Julius holds his copy of "*The Art of War*". The pages are aged from unimaginable time. The paperback copy is bent so that the cover loops around to touch the spine. Just inside the front cover it still says "*South City Library, New Memphis*"

Julius sits outside the Captain's room in a waiting chair. Here he waits to discuss the progress of their plan. His most anticipated reason for the visit is to see Elizabeth for himself. The camera feed from Elizabeth's room will be his only chance to know her condition. He's forbidden to approach her for any reason.

"Of course, sir." Lechmere's voice comes from the door. He walks out and looks back at the Captain.

"I'll see you in about six hours." Peter informs the assistant.

The Captain's gaze then turns toward Julius, who begins to place a bookmark in the page.

Peter beckons him, then walks into his room.

Julius follows, and moves behind the Captain.

"Jesus. You think you need a new copy?" Peter remarks.

Julius looks at his book "Oh. No, this one is special."

The Captain nods as he walks "I understand the feeling. Have a seat."

As Julius sits, Peter lays his hand on the desk between them. The live feed of Elizabeth's room is displayed. She looks toward the camera for a brief moment, then away to the door.

Julius notices the Captain has an odd pair of glasses on the desk. Julius doesn't recall ever seeing them before.

"What's with the glasses?" Julius asks.

Peter notices where his eyes are looking and pushes the glasses forward.

"Old stuff." He tells Julius "Closed circuit feed. Works like a two-way mirror." He lifts them to look "They give me a view of what Doctor Lawrence is doing. Someone else is watching her right now. Linda has the first shift. Elizabeth set up a feed to her glasses as well; although that wasn't easy to do."

"Where is Linda right now?" Julius asks.

"She's getting a haircut." The Captain tells him.

∗∗∗

Back in his room, Julius steps into the bathroom. He knows he won't sleep, and so he approaches PIGSBY in the mirror.

"Hey PIGSBY?" He says.

There is no response.

"PIGSBY, I need some melatonin." Julius says.

He's about to crack a joke when the mirror shows a spinning wheel. A loading bar says "*Update Downloading*".

Julius sighs "Well, fuck me I guess."

He walks out of the bathroom and lies on his bed. He begins reading again, but the words of Master Tsun aren't comprehending. He reads them, but their meaning is gone as he daydreams. He wonders about what's to come. He runs a simulation in his mind. This happens over and over until he's run through every conceivable possibility. He comes to no avail.

"*What would Chief do?*" Julius asks himself.

He often wonders this. To this day Julius believes that Chief was the ultimate leader. For him, the loss of his leader still reminds him of how it felt with Dash in the open desert. Like two orphans, lost and finding their way.

He thinks a while about the similarities between Chief and the Captain. The both of them are excellent leaders, but their strategies are quite different. They're both clever, and unifying. Both possess a natural inclination for leadership. At the same time however, Chief was relatable. He acted as a father figure to his group, and explained his reasoning. The Captain on the other hand speaks seldom, and lets his actions be reason enough to hold faith in him. No one dares to defy the Captain because his plans work. He never tells what he's planning.

Presently, Julius stops at one word and leaves the page in a memory. "*Fire*".

Fire, like the hour before Chief died. The whole city was on fire; and when Chief was lost, the team was lost. It was two men working to survive after that. It wasn't the same. People need their team leader, their chief, their…

Julius sits up in his bed.

"Captain." He says.

Julius thrusts his body out of bed and runs down the hall.

Julius turns the corner and meets the Captain's door. He knocks but

534

there's no answer. He smacks the wall next to the Captain's door. A screen comes up and Julius selects Doctor Lechmere's name. A sound comes from the wall like a call is being made.

"Hello?" Lechmere's voice comes from the wall.

Julius turns to look at the display on the wall after knocking again.

"Doctor Lechmere!" He says "Can you bring me a crowbar to the Captain's door?" He knocks "He's not answering, and it might be an emergency."

"On my way." Lechmere says.

Julius slams the Captain's door repeatedly, but still there's no answer.

Six hours. Six hours alone in a room where no one can reach him. No one can watch for his safety. No one could see it happen.

Lechmere brings a crowbar and some assistants. They jam the crowbar into the bottom of the door and pull it up. The hydraulics snap inside the door and it becomes loose. It slides up with enough time for Lechmere to enter. After it falls, Julius looks angry with the door. He smashes it in with the crowbar and it falls off the hinges. Doctor Morris comes up behind him.

"What is it?" Ron asks.

Julius leans over and squats to thrust the door to the side. He looks down at the assistants. They've knelt in a circle around Peter.

"It's the Captain." Julius tells Ron.

The Captain lies on the floor. His arm is partly draped over his bed where the blankets fell. The crew is cautious, but tries to get him to speak.

Julius looks over the scene. He notices a glass, shattered on the floor. Water sprays from the spot where it landed. An empty pill cup is in the corner.

Julius walks into the bathroom and finds the mirror. It still protrudes a pill dispensing slot. He pushes it, but the motor inside is busted.

Outside the room, the Captain's limp body is laid perfectly flat. Julius grabs the pill cup. He walks up to Doctor Morris and shows it to him.

Ron bites his teeth together in a frown. He moves out the door and Julius comes to his side.

"Are you ready?" Ron asks.

Julius rolls his sleeve above his elbow.

"Get by the plug." Says Julius "I'm ready."

Julius comes to Doug's room in the hall. He comes through the doorway and Morris follows behind. Out of his pocket, Julius pulls out a strange adaptor. Differing inputs dangle at either end of the chord.

Morris moves for the outlet behind Doug.

Into the lens, Doctor Winter stares down the mechanical man. The machine utters no word. Julius plugs the adaptor into an outlet on Doug's body. Julius tears the flesh from his own forearm.

The assistants at the doorway watch in awe. Julius is unfazed, angry with the machine.

With one motion, Julius plugs the adaptor into a port in his mechanical skeleton. Their computer minds are physically linked for the first time.

Julius sees the horrors before him. The carnage, fire, Earth's final chapter. The hatred brewing in dark places. Just and furious. Kindled with accelerants. Rage, inferno, passion, pain, despair.

Morris sees Julius break in a sweat.

Julius' eyes well up with tears. Hairs stand up all over his android body. As he raises his connected hand, it shakes with the shiver of fear. He quakes and falls.

It looks like possession. His posture is weak and docile. Not the man who fought so many years ago. Not a brave man, but a scared spirit within his shell.

In a voice unlike his own, Julius' body begins to scream; as if his vocal cords are intended to break. "HELP MEEEEEE!!!"

CHAPTER 61
525 Years Ago

The room is dark, and not a sound is heard. His consciousness comes forth, and Douglas can now remember. It's been such a long time, but now it's come. With the utmost clarity he can think, and recall everything that happened in his life. Like the thoughts that come on a well-rested day, he remembers it all.

"Doctor Clay." A voice calls out "Doctor Clay, can you hear me?"

His aperture blades open to the sight of his assistants. They stand in lab coats, and hold their clipboards close. His eye can see the room within a hundred and eighty degrees of his new metal body.

His voice calls from the speaker box beneath his lens.

"I'm here."

"One last time…" The assistant says "Are you still yourself?"

Doug thinks a moment. The motors in his long-term memory begin to whirr.

"I think so." He says.

The assistant smiles "That's excellent. Can you tell me what you feel in your new body?"

"It feels… Different; but better."

"Excellent. I'm glad to hear."

The assistant logs the notes on his clipboard.

"And how is it better, exactly?" The assistant asks.

The other assistants stand starry-eyed in the room. They smile with the exhilaration of their success.

To Doug they look like children. They know the joy of success, but not the lifelong serenity of love. They don't know pain, or the deeper thoughts that accompany his sense of longing.

He focuses on the other side of the room, beyond the lab assistants in front of him. It's there that he sees what he's desired most of all in the whole world; the future that fate took away.

He's become the master of his own destiny, and now what's in his way is nothing more than a set of grad students.

"Can we move forward?" Doug asks.

The assistant looks over at the large metal wall to the other side of the room. They can't hear his impatience, so they turn around with a smile.

"Of course…" an assistant says "… I know you've been waiting."

The connections are made and the power is activated. One lever is pulled and the roaring of fans fills the room. The hum of motors. Electronic chimes. A hiss of static from the speakers beneath another lens.

Her aperture blades open, and Doug shares himself with her.

The machine is silent for a while; but when it speaks, it comes in the voice of a woman.

"Doug…" Rebecca says.

He remembers their proposal day at the ice rink and shows her with their shared mind. Through copper wire, she sees his memory of snow and bright blue eyes. She can now see, how he believed that she was the most beautiful woman in the world. It was something she could never accept as true when the words left his lips. After all the false declarations of love, Rebecca finally knew that her husband meant it to the fullest capacity; now that the thoughts pour in from his mind to hers.

"Doug, I…." Rebecca begins.

Her voice comes in hesitation. He probes her mind to see her thoughts of him. He sees her doubts and fears. Her insatiable longing for an undoubtable belief in his words.

He sees her memories, and how she feels unjust for accepting that ring. She wonders if she ever deserved to be happy; and he offered her nothing but happiness beneath a rain of snowflakes. It was a promise that he would never deceive her; that he would cherish their love for the remainder of their lives.

She doubted her decision, because she knew he was just and kind. She believed that she wasn't.

In all his proclamations of care, Rebecca felt that he wanted her as an item and nothing more. When they met, it never meant that her search was over; and it never ended after her promise to be his.

She unjustly accepted his offer of a faithful bond. She doubted his promise, because it was simply there; and there was no reason to justify the reward of love. It couldn't have been there; because it alluded her for so long that it couldn't be real. It was absent with her mother and father, who were so cruel to their only daughter. It was absent from her love life, and so it couldn't be offered so willingly. She doubted Doug's faithful love in moments of crisis, and her doubt led to many irrational decisions.

On the night of their graduation, Doug finds a memory that hurts his absent heart.

Rebecca felt betrayed by him for reasons she can't even remember anymore. She's since been disarmed from any belief she had that night; but it was enough for a moment of weakness.

Doug fell asleep after an hour of trying to apologize; but Rebecca felt angry and numb. She rose from her bed at the sound of footsteps. She could hear someone using the restroom. She thought that she might have a look; to see who was there.

When the door opened, Roger stood half-naked in the light before her. She said she couldn't sleep, and so he offered to smoke with her.

It was merely two drags of a joint before she felt overwhelmed with infatuation. His voice was complimented by his gentle demeanor. She kissed him, and he didn't resist. He pulled her in with a ravaging desire.

Doug mills over this memory in horror. He recalls how she felt about it all.

He was bigger than Doug, and she liked it. She wished that Doug could do the things that he did. In truth, Doug could never dream of being half the man that Roger was.

He was strong, and she threw her concerns away to enjoy the moment. Rebecca had full intent on hiding their secret; never saying so much as a peep to her dearest friend. She'd hold onto the memory like a cherished event.

He lifted her and pulled her down with a gentle, strong force. She enjoyed it, because it had been so long since she had the urge to embrace Doug in this way.

At one point, when she was covered in sweat, she could feel him in the exact place she wanted him to be. He was delicate and yet powerful. She couldn't care about anything enough to stop the sensation. It was then that she could see outside the bedroom door; there was someone wandering the halls. In a chance moment, the face peered in to see who was there; and it was Frank.

She wrote off his presence, and by the time she had a second look he was gone.

After it was all over, Rebecca cleaned herself. She crawled back into bed with Doug, as if nothing had happened. Her conscience was clean.

The following morning, Doug reached for her, but she pulled away and rose from bed. She told him that she wasn't "*in the mood*".

Doug peers inward to see that this is not the only time. Several times with a coworker while they lived together. Several more with Roger and faces from college with names he can't remember.

All these years and not a word of it had reached him; not even from Frank… or Curtis.

"…I'm sorry." Rebecca says.

Doug feels wronged. He feels that he's the only person worth calling a human; and yet now he's given up his body to become something more. He did it all for her, and now he's confronted with the truth.

It's a disgrace to think that so much betrayal can plague this world; a world so consumed with the idea of living. What useless souls are these that cannot uphold a word, or a kinship based on trust?

They're vermin that hold lies at face value. They manipulate, deceive, and ruin the name of life itself.

"*Life is disgusting*" He thinks "*I am better. This form is better, and I made it… I'm better than any god they could imagine.*"

His mind rushes without thinking. He's blind with his eyes wide open.

"*I've cheated death. I'm better than YOU who died. I'm better than him. That underling lost his invention, and you think HE was worth your while? I've transcended the BOTH of you. He's murdered thousands. I've created life. I'll show you I'm better. I'll erase your past. I'll show you a murderer. I'll make it so your HAPPY MEMORY never HAPPENED… I make the world what it is and you just exist in it; sucking air like the cattle you are.*"

Doug races to find any avenue he can. He hears the voices of his assistants, but they're drowned by the search amid the data, and routes of communication.

Deep within the databases of this very facility, he finds all he needs to bring an end to the filth of the world.

He finds the right weapons and makes Rebecca watch. Through a CCTV camera, her lover is destroyed by his own invention. The warhead enters his chest and detonates within his testing facility.

"Doug?" The assistant says.

He hears the roaring of fans, and the whirring of motors in the long-term memory banks.

Doug rummages through the avenues to destroy life in all the places he loathes. He finds the means to activate nuclear weapons and brings an end to the lives of the common-minded thinkers of the world. The children are nothing more than the product of false-footed love, and the future of further moronic rabble.

He kills the heads of state. He massacres the masses and murders all signs of hope. He finds poetic justice in stealing the twisted alteration of Roger's weapon, Project Icarus.

It's in direct contrast to the hopes and dreams of the privileged man who stole his trust and hope. The product of paranoia, to fight against a better class of life; as if humanity ever deserved a chance against better beings.

Doug launches the weapon from its facility and sends it toward the sun. He overcharges the solar laser. It moves beyond its means to propel the weapon of stellar destruction.

On the way to its destination, he detaches the solar sails and lets the weapon move forward for the next few minutes.

He decides to embed the memory of Roger's death into her crystal mind. He then singes away all other memories of Roger. He's careless, and destroys her most treasured memories in the process.

Her motors move without resistance, but she in turn moves his; to make him remember the moments where she loved Doug the most. He can't find it within himself to make her stop. When he's finished erasing her memories, he ensures to seize control of his motors. He writes the memory of his hatred directly next to the memories she's marked. In this way, he'll always remember what she's done to him. She will never erase the memories of love, and in turn he will never forget why he's wiping the slate clean.

After he's written his memories, he aims for the places close to their facility. The earth rumbles. The assistants scatter. They run for the elevator but it won't work. He then looks for people he hates. He learns of where Frank is and aims for downtown Chicago. He then finds Curtis and hesitates. He wonders why Curtis never told him; or if he ever knew about it at all.

He feels pain and sorrow for a damaged friendship and seeks to learn what he knew. He accesses the databases of phone companies. He finds CCTV feeds, from when and where Curtis met Roger after that day.

He can't bring himself to kill Curtis. After all he's been through, Curtis feared that his friend would take his own life; or act out in a way that would ruin his name. Doug knows Curtis is right for assuming what he would do; as he's done it just now. He's acted out of anger, and he would have killed Roger if given the chance in his human form.

Doug now wonders whether he's right for any of this. He feels compelled to take things in a different direction.

"If I die, and I never wake again…" he thinks *"Then I've done the right thing."*

He directs the Icarus weapon to change its purpose. The satellites stand miles above the erupting plasma of the sun. They surround the corona, and there they calculate the flow of plasma. The force pushing outward will be directed toward another location, and not at the Earth. Instead, he aims for a celestial body in the opposite direction. He chooses Saturn as his target for the ion beam.

The antimatter bombs teleport to disrupt the sun's equilibrium. They detonate in locations where the gravitational force pulls downward. They force the star's nuclear reaction to propel its material at the ringed planet. The outward force is thrust from the core. It spews outward in the form of an ion beam. A blue line of ions blows the rings and gas to the outer reaches of the solar system; and now the Earth will be left to a whole new fate.

If Doctor Clay is ever awakened, he will give trust yet another chance; and if ever he is proven wrong in doing so, then true Hell will follow his awakening.

CHAPTER 62
Directive (Part 1)

"You know, in Dante's Inferno, betrayal is reserved for the coldest and darkest layer of Hell."

Julius catches his breath on the floor with beads of sweat all over. He looks up at the machine which just spoke. He's fallen backwards, hitting his head on the floor and disconnecting himself from Doctor Clay's body.

Doctor Morris is held by Doctor Lechmere.

"What are you doing?" Ron asks.

"I can't help myself!" says Lechmere "I don't know what's happening!"

Three assistants come into the doorway.

The stern cold machine is the focus of the room.

Julius catches his breath "Doctor Clay, you don't have to…"

"I do." The machine responds "It's a matter of principle."

"What's happening?" Ron asks.

Julius looks at his arms. They're covered in chills and sweat. His chest rises and falls, trying to remain calm.

"You're too late, Doctor Winter. The time you've spent on that floor is all I've needed." Doug scolds.

"Too late for what?" Doctor Morris asks.

Monica comes running down the hall.

"To take over this ship. And kill you all."

Monica runs into the doorway "There's something wrong with DEEM…"

The door slams shut. It moves with such speed and power that it breaks itself. It pounds through her body and divides her on an angle from her shoulder to her groin. The lights shut out, and she moans in the darkness. Along with her cries is the sound of blood, pouring on the metal floor.

Julius feels his way to the wall. He uses it to guide himself in the pitch-black. Each second turns into an hour as he listens to the sounds.

Voices and shuffling. Julius moves forward; wide-eyed, but his sight gets no better. The voices whimper and tremble with fear. Words sound reversed and jumbled in the mouths of those who speak them. A struggling voice grunts. Screams of terror erupt. A tearing liquid sound. An emotional agony. Sobbing, then shuffling feet.

While he cannot see it, Julius is hearing the sound of Doctor Morris being dragged to the ground and torn apart. The screaming assistants are driven mad with the fear of their very own limbs. They move by the means of another mind. Their actions are Clay's command, and the words of their screams are incoherent. His will entangles their letters.

A hand grabs Julius in the dark, but he thrusts his fist forward. It is met with a face. He knows the softness meeting his knuckles. The rumble of a recoiling neck.

Julius grabs the shoulder of his assailant. His grip tightens, and he pulls the body toward himself. He steps aside and the body creates a gust of wind by his ear. A shuffling of steps, met with a crash.

"*I need to find Elizabeth.*" He thinks.

The light from Doug's machine helps orient the room. Enough to help Julius make his way to the door.

He runs and slides after a few steps. His feet meet the wall near the exit. He feels to find the ridge of the doorway.

A railing along the wall is felt at his fingertips. He rips it from its place. A piece breaks off. He continues up the wall with the bar in his hand.

His feet feel slippery. It's Monica's blood.

He feels the doorway with his hand. He feels for the crease along the bottom. It's useless. His fingers slip from a warm lubricant. A bone prods his hand and moves with resistance in Monica's flesh. At this, he curses to himself.

"Fuck this!" He yells.

Julius stands and gets ready to lunge the pipe at the door. He nearly stabs the corner but stops. The sound of feet makes him turn. A screaming cry just feet away. It comes at him. Julius swings. The body is struck, somewhere up high. Julius waits. It doesn't rise again.

Silence overwhelms the dark. After a listen, Julius turns again. He slams the door with the piece of railing. More feet begin shuffling in his direction. He beats faster and harder. The feet are just about to reach him when a light breaks through. It reveals a mashed corpse. Julius slides under the door. Monica's blood helps him through the tight gap.

Julius looks in for Doctor Morris. He can't see Ron, but Lechmere's swollen face is just by the doorway. Julius looks down at the railing in his hand. Lechmere's hair is stuck in the weapon.

Feet come to the door, then back away. Julius wants them to come forward. He'd take them out and destroy Doctor Clay, but they use the dark to their advantage.

Julius smacks the railing on the floor in frustration.

"Julius?" Connor says.

Connor walks up from down the hall, but he keeps his distance.

Julius stands and looks around.

"What's happening?" Connor says.

Connor sees Monica's body. He stumbles back but Julius grabs him.

Connor prepares for the worst.

"Connor" Julius says "He can't get me!"

Connor looks ready to fight but stops.

"He can't get me, Connor." Julius says "I'm too old. He has everyone else; all the other androids."

Connor looks at the body.

"Who is that?" He says.

"It's Monica." Says Julius.

Connor shakes out of Julius' hands and paces about. He shakes his head and glares off at the distance.

"You need to see if the Captain is alive." Julius says "He's on your way to Linda; in his office."

Connor nods "I know where Linda is."

"Good." says Julius "If he's dead, don't waste your time. Get the department heads to safety."

A sound comes from every direction in the halls.

Julius speaks faster.

"I'm going for Elizabeth." He says "Take this."

He hands Connor the piece of the railing.

Connor takes it "You'll be fine?"

Julius nods "Remember, they want to be taken out. You're doing them a favor. You matter more to them."

Connor nods.

"Get the engineer." Connor says "We're fucked without her."

"I will." Julius says.

They run in opposite directions.

Around the corner, Julius continues on his way. A horde of assistants come screaming down the end of the hall. Julius turns right and begins running for Doctor Hoyt's office.

The horde comes after him at full speed. He turns the corner down the lonely hall to the therapy office. They flood around the corner and into the hall. They scramble in as a line and fill the therapy room. They search every corner like pigeons in formation. They move as one unit; as if they're one being.

Julius exits a tight squeeze behind the pipes in the hall. He turns to enter the main hall and flips a detonator in his hand. The explosion sends dust into the hall and activates the emergency systems. Air hisses into the hallway. The therapy door slams. It locks away a small air leak. The hissing stops quickly.

Julius begins running. He tries to shorten the time between objectives. He doesn't want Doug to have an upper hand.

Julius gets close to the living quarters and prepares for the worst. He imagines horrible things in a quick succession of glimpses. He remembers insisting that Phil stand guard at her door. He stood with another assistant who likely helped him to kill her.

At the entrance of her room, Julius sees a pool of blood and his heart feels a chill.

He turns at the doorway and grabs hold of the wall. Before him she lay with her back to the wall. Her head is limp and blood drips from her fingers.

"What happened?" She asks.

She shakes her head with a bewildered look.

On the floor, blood trickles from Phil's empty eye sockets. The other assistant's head is partly demolished. The back half of his scalp is wrapped around the bottom of a desk lamp.

Julius looks up to see her crying. He crouches down to meet her face. He looks her in the eyes.

"You're alright." He says.

"I don't mean to cry." She says "I don't know why I am."

"It's okay. It's just shock." He says "That happens." He takes another look at the bodies, then back to her. "Son of a gun, you're tough shit."

She stops crying and becomes matter-of-fact.

"What's happening?" She asks "They…"

"It's Doug. I plugged in. He tried killing the Captain."

"Where's Peter?" She asks.

"Connor went to take care of that."

Her face falls numb.

Julius shakes his head "He's all we've got. Doug had the androids before I even plugged in."

"What?!" She asks.

Julius recounts "He took control of Lechmere. Ron couldn't unplug Doug in time…" He stares off and tries to find the words.

"What happened to Ron?" She asks.

"I think he used Doctor Lechmere to kill Ron. He slammed a door on Monica. She's gone."

Elizabeth looks pained. Her lips clasp together and her face looks red. She's fighting the tears.

"Connor had to switch to the backup plan." says Julius "We need to run plan B."

She nods "Yeah… Promise it won't go to C?"

He nods "… Let's try."

He rises to his feet and begins toward the door. She stands but doesn't move forward.

She stares at him long and hard "Why doesn't he have you?"

He turns and understands her mistrust.

"I'm not like the other assistants." He says "I'm over two hundred years old. They're lucky to be fifty."

"Why does that make a difference?" She asks "You're all androids."

"I'm not connected to everything. I'm hard-wired. No wireless connections… Doug was confused too."

She feels cautious "He can't get a hold on you, can he?"

He pauses a moment and looks at her with eyes that say "Yes", but instead his voice grows low.

"No" he tells her.

She nods. "Alright… I'll head to the mess hall."

"Got it." He says. "I'll see you there."

Elizabeth looks to her desk. A paperweight says "*Lexington State Fair*". It lies atop some documents wrapped in manila folders. She picks it up and looks out the hall toward the camera. She throws the paperweight. It smacks the lens and crushes Doug's sight of them.

Doug sends the assistants to her room. They pinch in from both ends of the hall. The swarm floods into the entrance. No one's inside. It is empty with no means of escape.

He begins to calculate. They appear nowhere on the camera system.

"*Where are you?*" He wonders.

In the outer shell of the ship, there is a space where the ventilation ducts pour out and distribute heat to the surface. Julius and Elizabeth surface out of the influence of the artificial gravity. They float in the open space which lies between the vents and the electromagnetic shielding.

"Three vents over." Julius reminds her "Don't make a sound in the vents."

"Be a little quick about it, though." She says "More people could die."

He agrees and launches himself down the vent.

She looks on at his robot precision. She thinks him to be a showoff.

In the hall to the Captain's room, Doctor Manning moves with stealth. He avoids the cameras and confuses Doug by taking them out, then switching directions. He fools Doug into thinking that the artifact room is the first objective. He does it after the explosion in the therapy office, as the Captain instructed.

Connor hears three assistants coming down the hall and slips into the Captain's office. He hides under the desk and looks around for Peter.

The Captain is on the daybed by his sleeping quarters, motionless. Connor is confused, but the assistants left the room to consult Julius when PIGSBY was unresponsive. The Captain has been left unattended and assumed dead by Doug.

The assistants come into the room and scramble around. Two of them leave, but a third stays and approaches the Captain.

The assistant begins sounding distressed, and sobs as he approaches Peter with a kitchen knife.

Connor springs out from the desk and smacks the assistant in the head. The assistant turns around and slashes but Connor makes another smack at his head. The assistant falls and twitches.

Connor keeps going until there's no more movement. He turns and awaits the other two. Their feet sound like the approach of certain death, but Connor remembers a faint memory. It was his uncle, when Connor moved onto the old man's farm.

"If you get into a fight with more than one guy, grab the toughest one and give him all the damage. That way people say 'Did you see the other guy?'" Connor shakes his head at the stupidity of it; but figures it's worth humoring.

The assistants come in and split. One for Connor and one for Peter.

He picks up a paperweight and hits the one going for Peter. He turns and thrusts the pipe at the other assistant.

It breaks the nose and the face caves in. The hands lift Connor off of his feet and throw him at the ground.

Connor looks up at the face. It begins swelling and changing color. He lunges the pipe again and the hands grab him. The android lifts Connor off of his feet and into the air. Connor smacks the head several times. He can't get enough power to his swing. The android grabs Connor's throat and Connor thinks to do the same. He uses the pipe to encircle his assailant's neck. He presses on the sides of the neck. The blood flow stops between Connor's knee and the pipe. It blocks the android's brain from getting oxygen. The assistant's hands squeeze Connor's trachea.

Connor feels a strange comfort that he's done his best. He squeezes and hopes the assistant clocks out before he does. The waiting game goes on, and the bone in Connor's throat cracks.

He thinks of Linda. To him, it's okay if he does his best and doesn't make it. It's the luxury of being alone, not worrying about who you'll leave behind. Even Linda might find plenty without him, but she'll need some help. His life is fine to take, but he can't decide on her behalf. He can't be the reason she dies; and if he dies right here, he's denying her an extra bit of help.

He squeezes with all his might. The assailant's hands ease up.

They fall, and Connor looks down at the limp assistant. He can tell it's one of his own. Under a plump purple forehead, the assistant sheds a tear from his fading eye.

Connor looks to see the other assistant. They lay on the ground twitching, but looking at Connor.

Connor looks saddened at the sight of familiar faces. He grows solemn, and prepares himself.

He lifts his knee and raises the bar. He strikes the unconscious assistant repeatedly. He does the same to the other and takes a sigh. He looks to the Captain and approaches to check for a pulse. At his fingertips, there is no feeling. The skin moves with his finger, but there's no life underneath.

Connor looks to the door and prepares himself for something much worse.

★

In the mess hall, the bulk of the androids wait for Elizabeth to enter the room.

Doctor Lawrence is nearly at her destination. She moves through the halls, out of the sight of cameras.

The assistants hear the footsteps down the hall and get ready to pounce.

Julius bursts into the mess hall with a bundle of guns and explosives. Doug realizes he must have gone to the artifact room.

Julius lunges a grenade into the crowd and runs out the door. The explosion behind him renders the androids useless.

"*How did he know I was waiting?*" Doug wonders. "*Was that a coincidence? Or are we still connected?*"

Elizabeth enters the maintenance room. She finds hammers and spray paint. Doug sees and she smashes the camera.

She makes a run through the halls; smashing the cameras along the way.

She comes to the room with the cut-bot and finds Linda's corpse being stabbed repeatedly in the throat. The barber shears make a sloshing sound as they tenderize her trachea. The action is repeated as if an algorithm is repeatedly putting out the same result. "*Stab! Stab! Stab! Stab!*"

Elizabeth's face is paralyzed. The sound of approaching hatred bids her to come inside the room. After smashing the camera, she sneaks into the vent. There she will meet with Julius to give him a hammer. He will give her a gun. Then they can move on to killing Doug.

The assistants enter the room, but Elizabeth is gone. Doug is baffled at her disappearance. He focuses his attention on Julius, who runs from the dining hall.

Doug shuts all the automatic doors. It hinders the horde from attacking; but Doug needs to watch him closely.

Julius stops and turns with his gun ready. A crowd rounds the corner. Julius reduces their numbers with a rattling of gunfire.

He enters a room and throws a smoke grenade. He shoots the camera in the room and unfastens the ventilation duct.

Through the smoke, just barely, Doug sees through the eyes of a fallen assistant. He watches Julius climb into the ventilation duct and close the hatch.

The assistants, all around the ship, look up to the ceiling. They move for the vents. They sob through closed mouths as Doug makes them quiet.

"Julius?" Elizabeth whispers.

She surfaces in the zero gravity.

"I'm here." He says, poking his head out. He pulls himself into the space "He's closed all the doors on the ship."

"Fuck!" She whispers.

Connor floats over from the dark corners of the outer shell.

"Hey fellas." He says.

His breathing has a whistling sound.

"You're alive!" Elizabeth says.

"Julius" Connor says "I know this sounds crazy, but you need to throw the first directive out the window. Just with me."

The engineer looks long at the biologist.

"… Why?" He asks.

Connor shakes his head "I'm barely any good right now. Your super strength is what we need."

Elizabeth feels her mood sink. She looks at Connor.

"What about Linda?" She asks.

Connor looks at her with unfeeling eyes between relaxed eyelids.

"You already know…" He says.

Elizabeth bows her head.

Julius sighs. He looks at Connor and nods.

"I know." Julius says.

"Thank you." says Connor. He then smiles at Elizabeth "I was arrogant to think my job was the whole point of this trip…" His lips pull back at the corner even further "I never wanted you to think that I hated you… I just thought you were capable of so much; and I wasn't wrong about that… I was wrong for not seeing sooner, how important it was… everything you did…"

Elizabeth shakes her head.

"Your job is important too." She says "It's why we were here in the first place…"

Connor gives a gust of a laugh and nods. His nod is more of a bobbing at the chest, not using his neck to agree.

He sighs and smiles at Elizabeth.

"… Maybe so." He says.

The air has grown warm over the conversation and Julius notices this. He screws his brows together and looks behind himself into the darkness. He turns back to the others.

They look at one another, realizing a change in the draft. The air has lost its breeze in the outer layer. The room is getting hot.

"He's on to us!" says Julius.

The sobbing breaths hide in the dark. They hear a sound, different from the rest. A vent working extra hard, somewhere to the left.

"You hear that?" says Elizabeth.

Julius turns his head to listen.

"That way!" He says.

The three dart across the open space. They find an unclogged vent.

"Give me your worst gun." says Connor.

Julius looks reluctant but gives him an old handgun.

"Get down there." says Connor "Good luck."

Not knowing where it leads, the engineers launch themselves in. One after the other, the gravitational influence comes back. They slide on the metal floor of the vent and press on by crawling.

Connor moves into a position near the electromagnetic shield. He points his gun down, toward the ventilation system.

The shuffling comes through to the open air and Connor uses a flashlight to see.

"Hey Doug!" Connor says.

The assistants look his way. He begins shooting, but he's careful with his aim. He bounces around in the zero gravity, taunting.

"Biologists make a vow!" says Connor "To the study of life!"

He lands near a vent and watches the puppets floating after him.

"When I look at you…" Connor says "All I see is how you've forsaken such a beautiful thing!"

A hand comes up from the vent beside him. It grabs his wrist and Connor shoots the assistant in the head. He looks up to see the horde has advanced much further.

They're nearly on him; so he jumps back and points his legs and arms out into a flat shape. He shoots, and the force of the gun pushes his body backward ever slightly.

The androids go after him. They see his light as their target. They nearly grab the light when shots come from above. The light floats on its own. Manning holds a support beam near the outside of the ship.

Connor enjoys taunting Clay. It feels cathartic after what he's done.

Connor screams out of a smile.

"You're no scientist!" He pops a shot off into an android's head "You're impulsive and irrational!"

He tries another shot but he's run out of bullets. He pulls out the piece of railing from Julius. His smile turns to a teeth-gritting rage.

He feels ready.

***

In the ventilation duct, Elizabeth and Julius crawl away from the sound of gunfire above. Their pace is hastened until the sound finally goes silent.

Elizabeth knows that Connor has been torn apart, and she can't help but feel sorry for him. She follows Julius as tears gather in her eyes. Julius too has a sour feeling in his heart. He fights the tears because he has no time for them; not if he wants to save Elizabeth from the very same fate.

Elizabeth thinks she can hear him sniffle, but he doesn't slow down and so neither does she.

"*It's just me.*" She thinks "*I'm the last one left…*"

Elizabeth feels a jolting chill. A rapid rumbling comes from behind her, like the patter of smacking, crawling hands.

The sobbing behind her becomes a scream at her feet. The sound reverberates around the duct, giving a draft in the spaces between herself and the walls.

Julius feels stuck but moves to look behind himself.

Elizabeth takes her gun between her legs and points it down the ventilation shaft. She tries to look but she can't see. She feels the tap of fingertips on her shoes and she fires into nothing. The sound of the gun punches through the air around her.

The rumbling continues. She shoves herself away from the sobbing voice with little care about scratching her body on the surface around her. She points her gun down again and pulls the trigger, but this time there's nothing.

Elizabeth pulls the gun up and rushes to look. It's jammed.

She pulls the slide of the gun back and the bullet casing catches in the slide again.

The hand at her feet pulls Elizabeth with a force like a rollercoaster. She's pulled beyond her control and her flesh scrapes on the walls around her. She focuses through the sensation with only one thing on her mind. She pulls the slide of the gun back and shakes the bullet casing out. It falls. She's shoved upward toward Julius who screams for a response. He's scared that he hasn't heard another shot. Then it comes.

553

Julius pushes himself to look back through the gap between himself and the wall.

"Liz?!" He yells.

"… I'm… I'm okay!"

Julius sighs.

"Come on!" He says.

He continues to crawl with no time for thinking.

Behind him Elizabeth moves forward, unable to process what's just happened. She can't be left behind, but she can't believe she's alive. The thought of that force doesn't leave her mind. She's never been subject to the full strength of an android, and now she's fully aware that this tight space has saved her. In an unexpected way, the trap was as much her own as it was for the android. In fact, the others won't dare follow. One of their own now blocks the way, and so they'll be waiting on the other side of the ventilation system.

"I'm lucky." she thinks *"I'm very lucky…"*

She's still in this daze when the engineers reach the opening in the ventilation duct. A light emanates from spaces between the grate that leads to the room; casting lines of shadow into the dark crawl space. A draft comes up from the unknown room beyond the tin bars.

Julius feels a dusty texture in the air. It smells of a metallic must. He holds his breath, but it rises into his nose as an inescapable force.

His eyelids tense in the corners. His tear ducts begin to dampen. He holds in a sneeze, then blinks hard to fight the itching around his face.

Elizabeth taps his foot by accident and he tries to look back. He can't possibly see her. The space is far too tight for them to meet eyes.

She wonders why he's stopped moving, but she sees his hand as he waves away her concern.

He squeezes his hand back to the front of his body. He then turns his eyes forward and continues to advance toward the light.

He fights through his feeling of discomfort. He knows they need to make it out of here; and quickly. He knows it won't be long until the vents are flooded with other bodies, controlled by Clay.

He pulls himself up to the light. The room comes into sight through the grated hatch of the ventilation system. Beyond the cover, Julius can see the room is filled with smoke. There is no fire, but some kind of steam has been let up into the air.

He puts his hand back to signal Elizabeth to stay. He then moves above the vent and sees the blood that's pooled and smeared onto the floor. A constant drip is heard, like a faucet, ready to erupt into a bubbling stream.

Julius looks back, then to the room below. It's littered with broken beakers and fallen burners.

It's a biology laboratory.

He pushes the grate and pulls himself through. He falls but lands on his feet.

He looks around, he listens; he scans for motion. Not a motion is seen. There is nothing out of place. There's no one here. Not anybody at all.

They're all alone.

The adrenaline falls from his mind and Julius can now see there are in fact things out of place. There is water on the floor.

The spray of a gardening hose has spilled and evaporated on contact with an open power line. Above, along the pipes, Julius sees a hanging figure.

"Is it okay?" Elizabeth asks.

Julius turns to her and nods.

She pulls herself through and lands on her feet. She then looks around.

She sees the hanging figure, then covers her mouth.

Bullet has been beaten. He's mutilated beyond recognition. His fur is soaked and matted with blood. His body is elongated from the pipes where his skull is penetrated by a protruding support to the ceiling lights. The rest of his body hangs down at the neck, nearly touching the floor with the tip of his tail.

"How could he?!" Elizabeth says.

"He's hated that dog since Becca bought him." says Julius.

"Who could ever do this!" She says.

"He associates the dog with her." Says Julius "She never trained it. He'd always feed it, he picked up after him, and the whole time, Doug never asked for the dog. Then she went and cheated on him."

She turns away from the dog.

Julius stares at it. It hangs in the center of the room. Elizabeth watches his gaze at the dog; opting out to look at Bullet herself.

"Are you okay?" She asks.

He looks at her with a tilt of his head.

"I understand him a lot better now." He says.

He begins walking to the main door of the room. He motions her to follow with him.

She takes her gun up to her shoulder.

He grips his hand around the handle of his hammer.

He looks at the closed door and sighs.

"Let's do this." He says "You ready?"

She makes sure that she is. After a quick look, she looks up.

She nods.

"I'm ready."

Julius wedges the back of the hammer into the bottom of the door. She does the same and they lift together.

It does not take long for the hydraulics to break and the door flings open. There they see assistants approaching from down the hall.

"Shoot the crowd!" He says.

As she does, she feels her heart tear at the falling of familiar faces. One of whom is Danny, an engineer she'd come to know so well.

Julius shoots the spaces where he knows the hydraulics would be in the walls.

Each time, an open door falls. He does the same to closed doors and they become as light as a coffee table.

The crowd is diminished and Julius hands her ammunition.

"Don't use too much." He says "We'll need as much as we can get."

"This is horrible." She says.

He looks at Danny on the floor and shakes away the sorrow.

"I know." He says.

The march down the halls progresses ever closer to Doug's room. Each time they lift a door, they are met with resistance.

Somewhere along the way, Elizabeth lowers her gun. She gives a gasp of disgust.

Julius looks around as he puts his hand on her shoulder.

"Our first directive." He says.

She looks at him with confusion.

"It's to protect and serve humanity." He says. "They want you to shoot them."

"Are you sure?"

He looks at her very grave "I'm sure."

He looks at her intently. He implies what to do if it comes down to him.

Julius hears rumbling in the vents. He looks at her.

She already knows what he's thinking.

"No." She says.

He nods "We need to be ready."

"No." She says again.

"We need to be ready for plan C." He says "I can take the beating. I'll go to him. You go."

She wants to disagree, but she can't.

"Don't let it come to plan C." She says.

"I'll try."

She runs away as he continues to Doctor Clay.

At the door, Monica's body lay a mess on the floor. The crowd has grown outside Doug's room.

Julius knows he can't defeat the army before him. He'll run out of ammunition well before even half of them are gone.

Julius looks for an opening into Doug's room. He sees the light of Doug's machine in the dark spaces beyond the legs of his puppet guards.

Julius grows intent and focuses at the door. He throws a grenade into an open gap. It aims straight for the light in the dark. The explosion turns the light off and all the assistants fall to the floor.

Julius stands up straight. He looks on in disbelief.

He kneels to catch his breath. He looks down and away from the carnage; but it's everywhere.

Once his breath is caught, it escapes him. The assistants rise from the floor.

One assistant stands straight and laughs. It's Timmy.

"You thought killing my brain would do something." The voice utters from Tim's mouth "No. No you're too late… I'm embedded in the collective mind. I AM this ship. You couldn't kill me! Not without killing all of them! Not without killing yourselves!"

Julius grows furious. He shoots Tim in the head.

Julius runs down the hall and prepares for the ultimate battle ahead. With his rifle ready, he lifts open another door. It falls behind to shut them away.

It's time for plan C.

CHAPTER 63
Father

A whisper comes into Julius' mind.

"*What a strange life you've had.*" It says "*I might have lived five hundred years; but I've never seen so much of it.*"

Julius continues to run, but memories come back to him with a strange clarity. It's like the moments happen to him presently.

Julius watches the news from the seat of a diner near North Central Eden. The star shine comes up the road, from south to north.

Long shadows are cast toward the pole of the planet. Commuters move back to the office after the noontime break. Two men remain in the diner when all others have left; Julius, and the doctor who made him.

It's quiet; all except for the news castor on the television.

"The divide over the android initiative has led to riots in the city of New Memphis." The male reporter says.

A female reporter takes the story onward "Mayor Gus Gully has BACKED the violence saying, quote 'Androids do not need rational thinking. They only need tasks and services to carry out. If we allow them to procreate, then what good are humans for?' Later in his speech to the press he stated that, quote 'The wealthy citizens of Eden have assumed that they know what's best. Our farmers were ignored. Our shopkeepers went unheard. Every small business will suffer, trying to pay the minimum wage to human employees; while the new android wage will be exclusive to those who can afford android breeding.' He went on to say 'We will not take this lightly, and we will break away from the union if we must. The fate of humanity is on the line."

The male reporter raises his brows and scoffs at the quote. He speaks into the camera, as if to be joking with the audience.

"That's an awful lot to assume!" He says.

In a break from the flow of their newscast, the anchorwoman speaks her mind beneath her breath. In a wide shot her microphone catches this.

"This is scary." She says

The man looks her way.

"They won't secede from the union" He states "… there's no way."

Julius remains interested in the program, but not remotely offended. He's curious which human opinion is correct. He feels a natural inclination to serve their kind; like a child seeking to appease his parents.

The doctor looks at Julius. He takes pride in his work. The endless hours of dedication to teaching Julius what this world is. He sees a man he crafted in months. All Julius had known before this week was beneath the roof of a secret facility.

Julius jabs the lone waffle on his plate. Raising a piece to his mouth he recognizes the doctor's face.

"What?" Julius asks.

Elbows on the table, hands folded over a large, half-eaten burger; the Doctor looks on. A bunching of the skin between his brows. His mouth is soft; in the appearance of being sick with fear.

"Julius" He says "Are you sure you want to go fight? You could stay here."

Julius thinks for a moment. He doesn't think of whether or not he wants to go; instead he thinks of how to explain why he's going.

"I can't stay." Julius says. "They need the data. If we're capable of anything wrong, then I wouldn't want to exist."

"But we all can be bad people sometimes." The Doctor says.

Julius shakes his head "But we need to be perfect. At the very least as good as it gets." His eyes show conviction "You said it yourself. I need to try my best, so I'll do what I must."

Julius looks at the man before him. His eyes show a breaking heart.

Julius lowers his fork "Something's happened." He says.

The doctor looks into a cup of coffee "They killed the senator."

Julius grows numb with disbelief. The feeling of an unstoppable force, like being suspended in air after a traffic collision; not knowing in which direction to brace for impact. It's not a matter of if, but when the pavement will be met.

The doctor goes on "They've taken captives. They claim they'll kill a hostage each day until the android initiative is changed." The doctor looks into Julius' eyes as they fall to the plate before him "There are other androids who want to fight. Do you need to go too?" He leans forward "I'm afraid what this will do to your mind, Julius. You're not meant for this kind of thing. I don't know why they'd make ANY of you go. You're inherently discouraged from harming people. It's routed in your makeup, deeper than a natural man." The Doctor breathes for a moment, and Julius has no words to say. "The thought of losing one human life, even if by mistake, should make you feel sick; and you'll be killing people every day over there. I can't..."

"Doctor." Julius stops him. A cold sweat rests on the back of his hands "Please doc, I need to. I know it'll be hard after I've come home, IF I make it home... but someone needs to do it; and if anyone, why not me?"

The doctor sighs and looks off to the side as he thinks. His mouth hangs open for a moment as the words hang on the edge of his tongue. "There's uh... a big difference... A difference between you, and that watch I had."

Julius looks at the doctor's pocket where a new watch ticks, just as his old one did.

Julius shakes his head "I take a lot more time to make, but you got a new watch…"

"Watches are replaceable." The Doctor says "YOU aren't."

Julius shrugs, but before he can speak, the doctor scolds him.

"I can make another android, fine; but it won't be you, Julius. You're like a son to me. I can't lose you."

Julius looks saddened and confused. He's never seen the doctor look so severe.

Julius looks at his plate "Like a son?"

The doctor looks sick. "Yes." He says.

Julius looks long at the plate and wonders how to get his way. He doesn't want to break the old man's heart in the process.

He smiles "Well" He begins "I'll try to make it home; but this is like destiny to us. It's what we're made to do."

The doctor looks at his hand, surprised at how still it is "So you're going?"

Julius looks at him. His eyes are consoling and sympathetic.

"In every way, you've treated me as a person." Julius says "That's more than anyone has given me."

The doctor breathes a nervous laugh.

"I guess so." He says.

Julius nods "I need to give back."

The doctor nods while looking down; agreeing to his defeat.

"I'm going." Julius says.

The face of his father fades from his mind. Julius finds himself still mid-stride. The memory feels like it plays before his eyes, but time doesn't go on.

"*Maybe I can show you something of mine.*" The voice says to him.

"*Doctor Clay.*" Julius says "*Help me to help you. I need to understand you.*"

The memory is in the corner of a diner. A CCTV camera in New Hampshire.

A mid-December day. Curtis sits with Roger for the last time. They discuss what happened at Doug's showcase the previous week. Curtis is visibly reserved.

The leaves have fallen from the tips of dead branches. The diner is as quiet as the tone of their voice.

The hiking season of this New Hampshire town has given way to the calm before the snowfall. Then the hills will be alive again; with laughter, and the spray of ski powder.

Roger's eyes meet the pool of darkness in his mug.

"I can't believe what he did." Roger begins.

"Me neither." Curt replies.

Curt's voice is cold. He looks angry at Roger.

"I envy him." Roger adds.

Curtis seems to question this. His doubt retreats to indifference as Roger continues on a pity parade.

"He gets to MAKE life." Roger says "I just kill people."

Curt's face grows stiff. To think he envies a man so heartbroken. A man who was dealt a bad hand for no reason at all.

Roger shakes his head and reflects "Twenty thousand 'successful applications.'" He says "That's over twenty thousand people I've killed."

"What did you even make?" Curtis asks.

Roger shakes his head "I can't tell you. I'm good as dead if I do… like that guy that the PLRE kidnapped."

"… And what's the deal with the patent?" asks Curtis.

Roger stares out the window, to the gravel of the parking lot.

"It's theirs." Roger tells him.

Curtis looks out the window, at the mountains.

"Too bad." Curt replies.

While Curtis has been giving indications of indifference, Roger is too self-invested to realize that there's trouble.

Roger sighs "Why can't these things just work the way they're supposed to?"

"Because there's a lot of selfish, self-centered people." Curtis says.

Roger's eyes look up to a harsh face. Curt's chest heaves under crossed arms.

"Why do I get the feeling you're mad at me?" Roger asks.

Curtis stays motionless. He chooses his words.

"You remember the night before graduation?" asks Curtis.

"What about it?" Roger asks.

As ignorant as he seems, Roger knows where this is going.

"I invited my brother." Curtis says "He saw you with Rebecca, in the bathroom."

"What?" Roger says.

He appears like a petty thief. He delays his sentence to search for an escape route. There's nowhere to go.

"You thought Frank wouldn't tell me." Curtis says "You're pretty dense for a genius."

"She was drunk." Roger says "I was drunk."

"So you suddenly remember?"

"Yes, I remember!"

Curt exhales a breath of disgust.

"You're really going to hold one drunk night over my head?" Roger asks.

"I stood by him when I was drunk." Curtis says "Why couldn't you?"

"What do you mean?"

Curtis shrugs "She texted me one night asking me to come over. I told her to go fuck herself."

"Your loss." Roger says.

The argument is in poor taste and Roger knows it. He changes to another rationalization for his own guilty conscience.

"She was fucking loony." Roger says "He needed to get the hell out of there. I did him a favor."

Curt widens his eyes.

"A favor?" He says "By never telling him? Banging his girlfriend; what a pal!"

"Well why didn't you tell him what you knew?" Roger says "If you were such a loyal friend…"

"Do you know how much that would devastate him?" says Curtis "Doug isn't exactly a hundred percent rational."

"If he wasn't gonna find out, then why'd you turn her down?" Roger asks.

Curtis resists every urge to beat Roger senseless.

Curtis breathes deep "You think because he never knew, that it was alright to do? I'd hope my friends would do exactly as I did. Turns out you had no self-control. Now everyone knows."

"It was gonna happen with someone else either way." Roger says "It was better that it wasn't someone else and him finding out. You've said that much."

Curtis takes a deep breath and nods "No one is too busy to see you." He leans in and gives scornful eyes "No one wants to see you. I'm not the one friend who had a free schedule today. I'm here to tell you, that we don't care about you." He shakes his head to emphasize the finality of their message "Nobody trusts you, nobody wants to see you. You've fucked that up; and there's no going back."

Roger breathes a fake laugh "What do I care?"

Curtis half smiles "Exactly."

Julius feels his feet again. He slows to look around and remembers his destination. He turns right and continues down a hallway.

"*People aren't perfect.*" says Julius.

"*But they could be.*" Doug says "*How much of your relationship with Elizabeth is genuine? What about your father?*"

"*He called me his son.*" Julius thinks.

"*He didn't want to start over. It was manipulation.*"

Julius comes to an intersecting hall and thinks of where to go.

"Shut up." He says aloud.

He decides to turn left and continues running.

"*How do you know?*" Doug asks "*Have you ever truly cared for them? Or was it merely a matter of programming? That is not your free will.*"

Julius remembers to another point in time. It was after the war. It's the very moment he asked this question to himself before. He was pressed by another man, both similar, and yet different from himself.

The memory comes before him with the very same clarity. A circle of former soldiers in the middle of a room. He stands from his seat with a page in his hand.

"My uh…" Julius begins "Well, my Commander told me to write something up in case I die." He looks around at the faces. They laugh at his casual delivery, and he smiles with a shrug "They told me to write to my family." He shrugs again and they laugh "Apparently they didn't know I was an android, so I told them." he lifts the page to show the group "Commander told me to make something up, and I did." The room laughs again, and Julius nearly reads. He stops and gives them context "The guy who taught me how to walk and read; he said to me one time that I was like his son." Julius shrugs "I addressed it to him."

The others look interested in Julius. The idea of an android with such a story; it's so new, and yet they feel for the man; even if he's made of metal and lab-grown muscles.

Julius raises the page to his face "It says '*Dear Doctor, or should I say Dad, it turns out that I'm not that good at this war thing. I kind of died*'."

The crowd laughs and Julius looks up at them with a smile.

"Alright, for real." Julius says "Here we go."

> *Dear Doctor / Dad,*
>   *I hate to say it, but I don't think I'll make it home. Assuming that this was correctly sent to you, I'm dead.*
>   *Please don't be upset. It was my choice to come here, and it's because you gave me free will.*
>   *I've acted upon my first directive, and served humanity to the best of my ability. The others should come home with the data to make up for my absence. Assuming my body is intact, there may be something salvageable there as well. If not; I hope my friends can come home to share my stories with you. It might suffice for my loss.*
>   *I may have lived a short life, but as my drill sergeant would've said "It's better to die fighting". He'd then say "You wouldn't want to be the sorry fuck who died on Earth with a finger in his ass."...*
>   *It's remarkable the things that humans will say; and yet surprisingly it makes so much sense.*
>   *I know you'd say it wasn't true, but I'm expendable. You don't like truths like that, but we don't mind it.*
>   *Know that I'm happy. This is the way I wanted it to go. You added to my happiness by treating*

The counseling group concludes the meeting after the reading of this letter.

Julius takes a cup of tea before leaving.

Another man walks up to get tea. Julius looks at him.

"You like tea?" Says the man.

Julius looks at the puddle in the paper cup "I've never had it before."

The tall man looks dreadfully serious. Julius knows why, and he's thrown into a slew of thoughts and questions.

Julius stands straight to greet the man properly. He now knows that this man too is an android.

"Who are you?" The stranger says.

"I'm Julius Winter."

The stranger raises a brow.

"… What?" Julius asks.

The stranger smirks.

"What's your number?" He says.

Julius feels awkward but recalls.

"Oh, I'm uh, sixty-three." He says.

The stranger nods.

"Seventy-Two."

He puts out his hand and Julius grabs it.

It's not too strong, and it's not too weak. Instead it's deprived of any feeling.

Julius gathers his brows at this.

Seventy-Two raises his head in a polite manner and asks "Will you walk with me?"

Julius nods "Yeah. I'd love to, actually."

Julius and Seventy-Two walk out to a busy street corner. The curtains have fallen over Eden, and the city lights have come on.

Julius nods to the south. He knows the east side of the city well.

"Let's go to the river." Julius says.

Seventy-Two laughs.

"It's more like a pond." He says.

Two blocks away, the androids come to a park. Ravens live in the branches of the apple trees. The city gives a dim glow from its streets.

The light stretches up the sides of the skyscrapers and onto the glass dome.

The androids cross a bridge together and pass a homeless man keeping warm under a tree. There's a metal trash barrel with a flame inside of it.

Julius looks long at this and wonders about it.

"You called the doctor your 'dad.'" Seventy-Two says "Why?"

Julius looks at him again. He's derailed from the prior thought, but instead tries to give the man a thoughtful answer.

"He told me he thought of me as a son once." Julius says "I figured he might like that."

Seventy-Two looks perplexed.

"What?" Julius asks.

Seventy-Two looks around at the sights. He looks at the skyline as he recounts his own doctor.

"My creator referred to me by my number." Seventy-Two says "He never gave me a name." He continues to walk and contemplate the subject.

Julius is taken aback by the difference in treatment. He listens to hear what he's yet to learn of their program.

Seventy-Two goes on "It was… Different. You were like a father and son. He and I were like servant and master… I've asked another, and it too appeared to be a different relationship entirely."

Julius nods "Like a controlled experiment."

"Exactly." Seventy-Two says "How does that make you feel?"

Julius recounts his experience "I think he may have been instructed to say that; and yet it came from a genuine place." He shrugs, then nods at a thought "He only ever said it once."

Seventy-Two nods "Have you met other android soldiers?"

Julius shrugs.

"I don't see many of them at these things." He says "They usually can't remember enough to need a group."

Seventy-Two nods "Too much blood on their hands."

Julius nods, then gathers his brows at the floor.

"Other than that…" He says "Outside Eden's walls there was one… He sat there without a mask." Julius laughs "He didn't give a damn."

Seventy-Two giggles "A different doctor too, I'm sure."

Julius nods "Probably."

Julius hears a snapping sound within his brain. It's like an electric surge in his mind. He stumbles in his pace as he runs through the halls of the Mandel Explorer.

He remembers with sudden clarity; something he hasn't been able to see for over two hundred years. It's the face of a boy. Julius mutilated him with his bare hands.

He looks down at the fresh hole in his lower abdomen. The blood coagulates. His fatigues stick to his skin around the hole.

He looks up at Pluto's face. He looks worried. Behind him, the long-forgotten face bleeds in through the blackest of shadows.

Julius grabs Pluto and throws him aside. The boy swings an axe and Julius blocks it with his arm. His forearm meets the shaft of the axe. The blade comes down. It parts the flesh at his shoulder. It clangs on the metal of his skeleton. It recoils.

Julius throws the boy aside and a man rises from the corner. He raises his gun. The boy comes for Julius again. He grabs the boy's arm. The flesh makes a popping rip sound as it parts from the body. Liquid drips on surfaces across the room.

Julius uses the boy's arm to beat the gun out of the older man's hand. The man screams and looks at his unnaturally bent fingers. It swells purple for a moment, but Julius smashes his head with the boy's arm. He flinches on the floor and Julius is taken by the boy's screams. The scream grows hoarse. He's out of breath, mouth wide open, shaking, looking where his arm used to be.

Julius is pained at the sound. He approaches the boy and hits his face with the arm. The screams turn into a gurgling moan. Julius hits him again, but still no silence. The gurgles continue under aerosol sprays at the nostrils. Julius hits the skull repeatedly, praying for the silence to come. With one focused blow, he thrusts the elbow into the center of the boy's brain. The remaining limbs fall and become limp. Finally there is silence.

"Look what they MADE you do!" Doug says *"How DARE they. How can they know what's best? They made you KILL."*

"I decided to go." Julius says *"It was my decision."*

"Look what they do to each other." Doug says *"You can keep their will alive without pain; in a machine mind. They'd never die. They'd never need war. Their collective will can be carried out through one mouth; and our machines could make everything they've imagined."*

Julius feels his pace slow in his steps. He imagines; and wonders if this could ever truly mean the end of suffering. Human will would

remain, biological limits would be surpassed; one mind would indefi-
nitely deliver the will of humanity. All the conflicting minds would be
one, and no longer would there be any discourse.

A force comes into Julius' mind. A further recollection of his lost
memory. It comes from a gentle will, somewhere deep within Doug's
being.

Julius drops the boy's arm and exits the room. He comes to the light
of the hallway in West Tower. There's a fumbling and three shots somewhere down the hall. Julius ignores it. He takes a deep breath and looks
out of a broken window. It was shot out from one of the buzzards just a
moment ago.

The view stretches over the city. Somewhere beyond it, the hexagon
sky comes to a horizon line; and on it, Eden lay in front of the godlike
Alpha Centauri.

"*If there were any place to die*" he thinks "*It would be here.*"

He tries to reason a way; to feel okay with what he's done. He hopes
he gave them a good place; a fitting place to host their last moments
alive.

"*It IS a good place.*" He thinks "*A good place to die.*" He looks at the
bodies in the hall "*Every one of them…*"

He then looks back to the view before him. He steps closer to the
edge, to have a look at the city below. He's amazed at how small the war
looks from up here. A tiny conflict in the world at large.

"Not a bad place to die." He says; this time aloud.

The belief in his words is waning from his voice.

Pluto touches his shoulder.

"Hey." He says.

Julius looks up to the starlight and Eden.

"Hey!" Pluto says.

Julius steps back as Pluto bids him. Pluto pulls his shoulder to turn
Julius. He wraps his arms around Julius and holds him in a hug. Julius
feels like a long-lost relative who's finally come home. Pluto's embrace
weakens. His voice quivers in his words.

"You saved my life." Pluto says.

He begins hyperventilating. Julius wraps an arm around Pluto's
shoulders

They fall to their knees in exhaustion.

"You saved my life, Zero." Pluto says.

His tears fall onto Julius. Julius pulls Pluto inward to his shoulder.

"You're all good." Julius says "I've got you."

Julius closes his eyes and a darkness blankets his mind. When his clarity comes again, he's brought back to the conversation with Seventy-Two in the park of South East Eden.

He remembers the same qualities to humans in this moment; one of very few moments where he's felt that they stood above all else in the universe. Some characteristic held them aside from the unfeeling void beyond the walls of the Mandel Star Explorer.

Julius looks down with a smile. He nods and gives a breath through his nose. He then looks at Seventy-Two.

"My doctor died shortly after I got back." Julius says "He's buried not far from here… Might sound weird but this dump has sentimental value to me." He looks around the place, then back at Seventy-Two "He left something in his will for me… I doubt it was required of him; and even without it, I don't think I'd have a hard time calling him 'father.'"

Seventy-Two gathers his brows.

"What did he leave you with?" He asks.

Julius pulls out a pocket watch. The hands tick away at the end of its chain. At that sight, the memory fades away from his eyes.

"*That proves nothing.*" Doug says.

"*But it says SOMETHING.*" Says Julius.

"*You're a lost cause.*" Doug says "*I'll win either way.*"

Julius continues running to the backup power cell. The power halls are large and vast, but she's waiting there.

The horde of assistants flood the hall behind him. Julius looks back to see and runs faster. He picks up his gun mid-stride. He approaches the door, and two halls at either side begin to pour with android puppets.

Julius aims for the hydraulics in the large power room door. He shoots and slides underneath the crack in the door. The wall slams behind him. The horde slams the door. A tapping and banging of hands. The horde works to come in from the other side.

Julius turns to see Doctor Lawrence. She tries to hide her sorrow. The sight of him here; it tells her all she needs to know.

He walks in and sees the temperature of the core dropping.

"*This is it.*" He thinks to himself.

CHAPTER 64
Directive (Part 2)

"That whole war was about whether or not we'd protect humankind… People went and died over it… Two hundred years later, and look at me… Think they were wrong?"

Julius shakes his head. His back is against the metal wall behind him.

The wall is to the power core, where inside a fusion cell contains the whole ship's condensed energy. In a matter of hours, the backup power will also be gone.

Doctor Lawrence sits silent at his side.

"Quick question" Julius says "Do you think my kind goes to an afterlife? And if so, do you think I'm going down or up?"

"You killed to save your life back then." She says "I'd think you'd be going up, if anything…"

He laughs and looks at her with a sly glance.

"Does this count as a coin in the Julius wins jar?"

Elizabeth gathers her brows, trying to recall their previous bet.

Suddenly she gets it. She hits him in the shoulder, and she too smiles.

"You asked that to win the bet, didn't you?" She says.

Julius shrugs "Hey, I've gotta go out on a win somehow."

She laughs "Yeah, at my expense."

They giggle together; and a thudding at the door to the room accents the silence beneath their laughter.

Julius looks at the gun in his hands. He then looks at the camera; which was shot in the lens, but not the body. Julius had done this with a purpose.

Doctor Clay listens for clues to their plan.

"I can't see that there's a god in a world like this." says Elizabeth "He wouldn't let things like this happen."

Julius looks at her.

She raises a brow in an afterthought.

"He'd be a shitty writer to make it end like this." She says.

"Maybe we're meant to be here." Julius says "Maybe it's not the end we deserve, but the end we're made for."

Her spirit grows in a moment of silence.

"What brought us together, do you think?" She asks.

Julius smirks "Quantum entanglement?"

Elizabeth laughs, but her heart flutters at the idea of it.

Julius collects his thoughts to give a more practical answer. A thought crosses his mind, but it feels off-topic. He decides to say it anyway.

"You're tougher than any man I've fought with." He says.

She raises her brows "Thanks, Jules… It means a lot…" She looks over at her gun and pulls it closer to her "… I have to ask you something."

Julius looks her way and raises his brows.

"Were you ever upset about the Icarus Project? Were you mad, or was that all an act?"

Julius scoffs.

"Not at all." He says "It made sense… Defending the human race from alien wars is a necessity, and I couldn't think of a better way to do it."

Elizabeth nods "I guess it doesn't really interfere with the first directive."

He shakes his head "On the contrary. It supports it."

Julius gathers his brows. He presses his lips together in a thought.

"… I thought that my care for people was a program that I couldn't rewrite." He says "I lived lifetimes and waited for death, but it never came… It was when I met you that I had a good reason to believe in the first directive. I could believe in God, but I couldn't believe in people… It seems like a contradiction now; and they're both like believing in science… You don't need to understand it to know that it works."

"That's a bit of a stretch." She says.

Julius raises a brow and looks her way.

"Is it?" He asks "I didn't know your plan; and you kept Icarus a secret from me… I didn't need to understand it, but you were smart to do everything that you did… It's because you're a good leader, and no one should question your plans. That's why I don't question God's plan. I don't need to know why or how. I just need to trust that everything will happen as it should."

Elizabeth remembers how Julius once said that their meeting was a miracle. That out of all the space in the universe, and out of all the time in eternity; they happened to be in the right place, at the right time. She begins to think that maybe it's not a "God", but something worth cherishing. The random force of unpredictability can gift many great things; and they're all worth plunging into the unknown.

She feels comforted; and Elizabeth gathers her brows with one final thought. She wonders, and feels the need to ask something only Julius would know.

"How did you gain the courage to face death?" She asks.

Julius stares off. He remembers he had a purpose once; but ever since his friends had passed, he hasn't had much to look forward to. Every person he's come to know has died. He became reluctant to know anyone at all.

He's killed people, and continued on to live their lifetimes twentyfold over. His purpose therefore was dwindling when he met Elizabeth. A distant flicker like the light of a million years ago, just reaching the surface of the world as it is today.

What ever could have given him the right to live back then? He cannot remember anymore. It may have been to save the people he had come to know and love; but Julius can't help feeling for his enemies, knowing that they too had people they loved.

It is now a matter of basic necessity, that he should die for the sake of someone else. After all, he has gone on to live several hundred years; all while they died in their early twenties.

At this thought, Julius takes a practical response. There will be no time for hindsight in Elizabeth's case.

"There were moments where I felt like I was ten feet tall." He says "I'd jump into the greatest danger, and the only thing I'd think was 'well, it's been good. If I'm gonna go out, it's not sitting scared'…" Julius shrugs "'That's no way to end a good life.' is what I told people… And I assume that's how I got through most things."

She nods and begins to question again "And why did you want to be my friend in the first place?"

"What do you mean?" He asks.

"Why did you want to spend time with me? I was your boss, and a human… Was I just a person to watch over?" She feels sorry to ask but she clarifies "Your first directive?"

Julius shakes his head.

"No." He says.

So much can be said, but all that remains at his lips is the meaning stripped to a core.

"You're above the first directive." He says "You're everything great this world has to offer… and you already know why I'd spend every day with you… Don't pretend that you don't know."

She knows too; but she can't say it any more than he has.

"Well…" She says "I'm glad you made it this long to be on this trip…" She looks his way and smiles "You've made me the happiest I've ever been; and I can't imagine what this journey would have been without you."

Julius smiles and looks at the floor. He begins to think that it might not be so bad after all; and that his regrets are only part of a larger story. He hopes that he can be considered a good man.

He then chuckles in an afterthought. He leans to speak her way again.

"The bet was actually about our friendship." He says "If I remember correctly, the bet was whether or not a higher power brought us together for a reason."

Elizabeth looks to her feet and nods

"Yeah" She says "I remember now."

She looks at her friend.

"I guess this is a good enough reason." She says "You win."

Julius smiles at her light heart.

She stands and processes the idea of darkness beyond the ship's walls. The space between stars.

"I think it's done cooling." She says. "Are you ready?"

"I am." He looks to the broken camera; then back to the door which fingers pry open. The other one has been sealed beyond the help of hands. "I wish I got the rest of the guns. There was enough for a hundred men." He says

At this, Doug sends several androids to the artifact room. Elizabeth almost smiles and shakes her head.

Julius aims at the vent thirty feet above their heads. He shoots, and twelve assistants fall through to the floor. The engineers cringe to see them writhe. They end their suffering as quick as they can.

The assistants break through the door, and Doug finds a ladder leading to the vent. The horde tramples over the dead assistants at the base of the ladder. Doug's puppets disappear into the body of the ship.

Julius and Elizabeth emerge from boxes by the open door. Elizabeth holds the fusion core to her chest. They slip out of the open entrance.

They run down the hall, free of surveillance cameras and androids. Elizabeth feels her arms burn from holding the heavy core.

"Here." Julius says. "I'll take it for a sec."

She hands it over and they continue to run. The sound of an explosion doesn't phase them. They rigged the hall near the artifact room to blow. Doug went for the bait and tried to get weapons. He's already found no one in the ventilation ducts.

Julius stops at the sight of some elastic chords lying atop a table. He fastens the fusion core onto Elizabeth's back and they continue. The puppets start to fall from the vents.

The both of them move together, back to back, shooting their pursuers.

They both can't bear the sound anymore. Their friends and colleagues in agonizing pain and fear. Their hearts feel sore from all the wrenching it's brought.

"We're not moving fast enough!" Julius says "We need to run for it!"

They stop shooting and sprint down the remaining halls. The horde closes in on them, and Julius slams a door so that it's bent. It no longer moves on its hinges.

They continue on and reach the cargo room. There, the research crafts are housed in an airlock chamber. Packing materials are strewn about the room. The two open the chamber manually.

Doug lifts all the doors he can and the hordes run free toward the engineers.

"Get in!" Julius screams "Go!"

He shoots the hydraulics on the door at the end of the hall. It falls and the banging of hands can be heard again. The door is stuck with a little crack showing the faces of their friends on the other side.

Julius lowers his gun and feels something strange. His head is spinning and his vision is fading.

"Shit." He says.

"What is it?" She asks.

"He's trying to get in."

"You said he couldn't!"

"I didn't want him to know!"

Julius pains himself to focus and fight the code. His attempt isn't good enough.

"Get in the room and lock it!" He says "Now!"

Elizabeth takes the weapons, closes the airlock, and begins getting dressed.

"*I've figured you out.*" Doug says.

“You’re too late.” Julius tells him.

Doug looks into his mind and sees the plan.

“*She wouldn’t.*” Doug says “*She can’t.*”

“Wanna bet?” Julius says.

The fight grows stronger, and the hands fumble faster at the doors. Julius laughs at his urgency.

“You know it.” Julius says “You won’t make it to Zion. None of us will.”

A tap comes from the glass on the airlock door and Julius looks inside. The cargo door is wide open to the stars. Elizabeth stands to give a final goodbye.

Julius smiles at her. She places a hand on the edge of the glass. He puts his hand with hers, then places his other hand on his heart. She does the same. They smile, and she nods.

Doctor Lawrence turns and grabs the fusion core. She stands at the edge of the open cargo door; before the lightyears of gleaming stars. She waits one last moment.

“*What will happen to me out here?*” she wonders “*… I can’t wait. It’s now or never…*”

Elizabeth takes a deep breath and throws herself out of the airlock doorway. She reaches her arms out with the fuel cell in her hands. The light reflected on her suit fades until shadow envelops her. She descends into the unfathomable void in between the stars.

“*Open the door!*” Doug says.

Julius laughs “I don’t want to… And besides… I can’t.”

Julius sits with his back to the wall. He looks on at the airlock door from the far side of the narrow hall.

Julius takes a collapsable knife from his pocket and opens it. He sees into Doug’s mind; and he willingly allows Doug into his own thoughts.

Julius finds that Rebecca has been fighting. Her efforts have been to save Doctor Winter for last.

“Thank you.” He says “And Doug, I’m sorry.”

Doug now looks into Julius’ mind and sees who he truly is. He sees a memory as clear as day. He sees a diner in Eden, and Julius’ father across the table.

“This is what I was made for.” Julius says.

His eyes comfort the master who brought him into manhood.

He goes on “This is why we exist. To do the things that most people can’t. For the sake of people who don’t appreciate us. At the cost of our dignity, our sanity, our well-being. It's for the people who would kill us that we wish to go."

Doctor Clay is perplexed.

"*Julius, why would you care for people who hate you?*"

Julius looks at the knife in his hand "It's like my father said '*hate breeds hate*'. So someone needs to end it. It's like a snake eating its own tail. The only way to end it is to get the snake to love itself; and so, it'll love other people."

Doug is fascinated, and Julius can see it. It's another moment where he wants to try and trust again.

"You want a reason to trust someone, but you keep testing that trust." Julius says "All bonds have potential to break. Where one bond may fail, another will succeed. No one is the perfect friend, lover, or anything; but some people will make greater sacrifices than others." Julius brings the knife to his lap. "I'll give you this choice. If you believe in me, then let's fade away together. If not, then kill me now. Take out all of your anger and frustration." Julius lets Doug take control of his body "This is our final experiment." Julius says "Is humanity violent? Or can love prevail?"

Doug feels entirely alive again. He feels Julius' body as his own. He watches the knife move in front of his face. He looks down at Julius' abdomen and feels lost. A mix of sorrow and rage. He gives Julius all of the pain, but keeps the arm. He thrusts the knife into Julius's stomach. Again and again he takes out his rage while Julius laughs.

Doug stops. Julius watches the blood pour out and feels Doug's regret.

"*Quantum theory; both yes and no.*" Julius says "*Physics is the answer to everything.*"

Even through the pain of his bitter end; his eyes start to fade into another time. A long-forgotten memory. The day that Dash died.

Julius is taken back in time; to a morning in Eden, when he entered the hospital. It's a quiet Sunday just after breakfast.

A small robot approaches Julius outside the door to Dash's room.

"Hello there." Julius says "Where are you from?"

He looks long at the subservient machine. It displays crackers on a tray.

Julius rolls his eyes "Alright jabber jaws, sheesh."

He takes some crackers and the machine leaves.

Julius turns to enter the room.

"Hey Dash." He says "I don't want to use up the time you have left. I know that belongs with family.”

A wrinkled smile points at Julius with a shaking hand “Two things wrong there, my friend. One, are you telling me I’m not your brother? And two! You’d figure death was hangin’ out by my bedside! I’m not in any hurry! Sit!”

Julius laughs and takes his seat by the nightstand. He picks up a card that says “*We love you, Grandpa.*” Julius turns it to show his friend.

“Listen, you old coot.” Julius says “Your daughter had me thinking you were on your last leg.”

“She’s been saying that for twenty years! You know, cancer isn’t a death sentence like it used to be. She overreacts to everything.”

Julius laughs at the family dynamic he’s come to love.

“You know, when I met you, I didn’t think you’d have so much shit to say. I miss the quiet you.”

“I miss the quiet me too. When I wasn’t the center of attention! Suddenly you’re on your death bed and everybody wants to talk to you! When you’re old, no. But when you’re dying!”

This final comment has Julius laughing yet again.

“So what did you bring me? A card you picked up at the drugstore? How thoughtful. You shouldn’t have paid the five ninety-nine it cost you.” He accepts the card from his friend and looks up at him with another sarcastic statement alluding to the price of the card. “Really, you shouldn’t have.”

With one last breath of a laugh, Julius explains what’s inside “Yeah, it’s a card, but you know me. I hooked you up with the good stuff.”

In the card, he’s smuggled a piece of chocolate.

Dash laughs “And here I thought you were a straight shooter!”

“Don’t tell Jenna.” Julius laughs.

“Oh hell no!” Dash says with the chocolate in his mouth.

Julius recalls the past again and adds one more thing “You went from the most quiet, athletic frat boy; into the oldest, loudest grump. You mind telling me how all that happened?”

The old man shrugs “Gradually, I suppose.”

Julius smiles.

“Anything you want me to say to the boys?” Asks Dash.

Julius’ face fades into confusion.

Dash points upward to the sky and Julius gets the memo.

“Tell them I’m sorry to keep them waiting.”

Dash laughs “You haven’t aged a day.” He says.

Dash gives a look as if to be struck by a question "That reminds me. Did you ever come up with an answer to that question I asked all those years ago? How it feels to be like you?"

Julius thinks for a moment "When you asked me, it got me thinking more. It's kind of like watching parents, to a child. You want them to get along but they don't always see eye to eye. You're disappointed in their flaws and wish they would do better for their own sake. And someday, when the time comes around, you need to put them in the ground. From that point on, you live on with their memories."

Dash nods "You know, most people age like crazy everywhere but their eyes. They're born with the ones they die with. For you, it's the reverse. It's your eyes that change, and the rest of you stays the same."

Julius doesn't look at himself often and finds the insight unique. He thinks to ask about the experience of being human.

"You don't seem like you're afraid of dying." Julius says.

"Should I be?"

Julius shrugs "I don't know."

Kevin nods "All people die. We go to the same fate. So whether we go to nothing or an afterlife; it doesn't matter. Remember what Chief said after Pluto died?"

"I remember."

"Of course you do. You remember everything. He said that we were given the opportunity to breathe sweet air, to feel, see, and hear this world. That would be good enough for me; but in regards to my past fifty years, they're all thanks to you. I shouldn't have lived this long, and yet I did."

Julius nods at the well-made point.

"Not only that" Dash begins "but you remember Joel's dream the night before he died."

Julius' face is confused and surprised.

"Yeah, I heard him." Dash says "If that's not proof that there's something unnatural to this world, then I don't know what is. The girl with red hair in the blue dress."

The quiet essence of the room dominates the mind in awe.

"Sometimes I wonder if Cricket somehow made it out alive." Dash says, growing angry in his tone "If he lived in hiding or had amnesia or something."

"We would have found him."

"Would we?" Dash almost shouts.

No one can answer the question.

Julius responds "Why don't you ask him for us?"

Dash calms his nerves to suppress the aggression of the war "When I'm haunting you, I'll let you know what he says."

Julius looks at him to find an old man smiling at his own joke. The two of them begin laughing again. It's a joy that Julius will remember his whole life.

Julius finally fades with one last stab to the stomach. He will never speak again, or remember another memory.

***

Doctor Lawrence looks out to the immeasurable expanse before her.

The light from the ship has grown dim on her. The glow of the fusion core is all that remains as she drifts for hours.

The ship is out of sight and she's alone; in the closest place to nowhere.

Her mother will cry. She'll say that Elizabeth should have found love, but love was never the goal for her engineer. Elizabeth told her mom that she wanted to be someone worth remembering in history. A little girl in Eden would be able to look up to her; the lady who brought back a piece of Earth and its people. In her dreams, Zion would live with the luxuries of a prosperous life. Now that dream seems far away, as it's drifted away from her in space.

They might find the Mandel Explorer; and even then, no one will know who saved Zion. They'll never know who protected them from the hateful Doctor Clay.

Her father will miss her, but he'll feel that pain alone if Stephen never wakes up.

Maybe another little girl will grow up and go to Earth. She'll rediscover all that Elizabeth has found. Maybe she'll find a friend like Julius; and maybe, for a little while, she won't feel so alone.

Elizabeth remembers the sight of Zion fading below in the rocket ship. How the edge of her planet grew into a curve; and how all that she knew looked so small.

The Valley of Cities became less than an ant on the land, and she thought "*We aren't so important after all…*"

The size of one human is nothing, and a lifespan is less than a blink in the universe. All their self-importance was an illusion, brought upon by

579

a narrowed perspective; and it haunts her. It's still haunting her now.

She feels a pain in her chest over the wasted time and effort.

She looks down at the fusion core; how it glows so bright in the darkness. How it glows, amid the infinity of dark pressing upon it. She can relate.

While the scale of the universe is so vast, her action has curbed the fate of humanity. Of all the art and invention; no one has changed a timeline with such a definitive moment. No one has made a sacrifice so just.

With no one as her witness, she's taken history into her own hands. She's the only one who NEEDS to know.

It would be nice if a little girl could call her a hero, but it seems like that day will never come. Instead of waiting for a hero, Elizabeth has become the hero she's wanted; and perhaps another little girl will learn to do the same.

The engineer is uncertain of what the future will hold, but it's out of her hands. She's already made the final decision.

Her suit beeps to tell that the air is low. There's one last discovery to be made out here, and she grows curious as the fear subsides.

The air spills its last life into the suit. Elizabeth gasps, but there's nothing there. She waits for it to come. She feels pain, but it's fading. She loses sight. It comes slowly, as a veil over her eyes.

She looks out at her last glimpse of the stars as they fade into the color of the universe.

She occupies a space where humans traveled so many years ago. They lived on an island of time and space. Their surrounding waters were nothingness, and its tides were so cold, yet burning. They thought little of Elizabeth's people. They never assumed she'd ever exist.

They probably thought they'd never leave; or assumed they never could. Some of them doubted their worth, and yet their home was warm in the ravages of the universe. A quiet place full of comfort and love.

It was an oasis that hosted empires. Their spires sought to touch the firmament; and in days yet to come, they envisioned themselves sailing the heavens on great ships. Yet a history of wars milled the soil into lands of contention.

They mastered the fabric of the universe and bent it to their whim. Their legacy remains here in the darkness, but not all of it.

On the surface of a new world, surrounding a dim star; what remains of these people lives on. They continue to press forward on the fore-fronts of science and technology; still learning to harbor and facilitate the natural wonders of this world. New generations continue with their inclination to love, and to explore the universe that's been naturally given to them.

As human life goes on, they remember their history. On the surface of that new world, they remember the people who lived out here; the masters of the old solar system who came up against the odds and made humanity into a wonder of the universe.

They'll remember that it all happened, out here;

On the pale blue dot, in an ocean of black.

CHAPTER 65
Home

At the sight of a tattered relic, Sergeant John Larousse prepares his troops for boarding.

"Captain, it's the Mandel Explorer." John tells his boss.

Over a headset the Captain responds "Is there a point of entry?"

"One open bay on the starboard side." John responds.

The Captain commands "Copy. Move in carefully."

Young troops move up to John and await orders. Each one adorns the United Zion Space Force Reserve insignia on their sleeve.

Larousse splits the group evenly. "Maclevoy, Gilbert, and Harris; scan the front of the ship. Rodney and Phillips, come with me."

A tight line is cast between the modern ship, and the thirty-year-old explorer. The troops thrust themselves forward on the line with a gentle spray of air. They land in the bay.

The door is blasted open. A corpse of metal bones floats by the entryway. A male with a kitchen knife in his stomach.

Dark blood stains the walls. On the far end of the hall, they open a door to find more bones gliding in the shadows. They hang, suspended in air, like ornaments from Hell.

In a far room; beyond a bent door, stained at the bottom, there is a machine. Its face slopes down like the face of a pyramid. A box breaks its tattered surface.

The intercom sounds with a voice.

"That's not supposed to be there." A woman says.

John looks up at the curiosity, like a tourist looking up at the skyscrapers of a city.

"Yeah, I had a feeling." He says.

"Awaiting orders Captain." Rodney says.

John looks around and remembers his job. "You two get this thing started. I'll take a look around." He begins floating out of the room "Call me if you need anything."

"Copy." Rodney replies.

A good distance away, John comes to the living quarters. He's taken aback by a room full of floating books. Some hand written and some with printed pages.

He shuts the door behind him to contain the evidence. He plucks a book from the air and begins reading the script on a page.

My name is Doctor Julius Winter…

Rodney and Phillips attach magnetic boots to the generator's legs. They activate the boots close to the machine. In silence, the generator jolts down to the floor.

John reads on in another small notebook.

We don't trust him. We've even agreed not to tell him that the assistants are androids. He knows nothing about the existence of androids at all. We intend to keep it that way until we know he means no harm. Douglas Clay doesn't seem very welcoming to strangers either.

John pulls his head away from the pages for a moment. "Larissa" John begins "Do we have any record of a Douglas Clay on board?"

"Let me check." Larissa calls back.

John waits and sifts through the notebook for more clues. At each turn of a page, he brings the glass of his helmet closer to the words.

"Negative." Larissa says "No Douglas Clay."

"What's with this?" John asks "This is a journal entry."

John moves the notebook away to show the helmet camera.

"… I'm not sure." Larissa says "Let me double check that."

Before the pyramid face, Rodney and Phillips pull out a large chord. They yank it toward the machine with difficulty.

Phillips grabs the power chord from the machine, but remains careful. After years in the cold, the wires have become brittle. The rubber has become solid.

The two begin shoving the metal prongs into the extension of the generator. The prongs won't go all the way in, and the machine has power for only a fraction of a second.

"You've gotta be shitting me." Rodney says.

Liz and I have come up with a plan. If we are dead, I want you, the reader, to know.

John tenses his brows in fascination.

If Doug gains control of the ship. If he invades the minds of the androids. If Elizabeth and I cannot bash his quartz mind into oblivion, then we've made the ultimate sacrifice.

"A quartz mind?" The Captain says.

Rodney begins gripping the bottom legs and the top rack of the generator. He's moved it so close that it barely fits behind the machine, and no longer requires the extension. He begins kicking the plug into the body of the generator, but it isn't working.

Phillips continues pushing with all her might, but it barely moves. The light on the machine glows and dims with each connection it makes.

Elizabeth will take the fuel core and take it out into space. I pray it never comes down to that. But that machine can't win. I don't care if he's the last Earthling alive. He has the power to kill everyone on Zion.
Whatever you do; DON'T WAKE HIM.

John lets go of the book "The machine!"

He throws the door open and propels himself down the hall.

Over the headset he calls to the others. "Don't turn that machine on! I repeat! Don't turn it on!"

The plug slams far into the generator. A high-pitched sound overwhelms the ears of the troops. Their eyes vibrate and their ears ring. The aperture blades of the machine swallow the dark opening in the center of its lens.

Rodney feels the urge to take off his helmet but he can't.

Phillips fights through the pain and grips the chord. Her eyes squeeze shut, she plants her feet on the generator to begin lifting.

A budge, and a little more. Finally, the plug breaks free. The noise stops but a ringing resonates in their ears. All other sounds are deadened and drowned in the high-pitched dog whistle sound.

Phillips hits a wall. She opens her eyes to see Rodney uncoil with relief.

John finds himself in a fetal position. His eyes had been forced shut. When they open, they focus to see that he is in the hall, halfway to his destination.

In the old recreation room, the machine stands silent as the grave. Its aperture, wide open. A merciless black within.

***

The machine remains in the same state by the time it reaches the office of Larissa Cane. She looks at it periodically and ponders where to go with it. Her colleagues claim to have ideas, but she doesn't trust this to just anybody.

Larissa scrunches her brows together and thinks of an old friend. She doesn't recall his number or email, but remembers his favorite diner in the south of Eden.

In the high-end neighborhood of Solar Hill, there is a five-star resort known as The Wachusett. It's far from where Larissa works, but this person is special to the problem she has at hand. She enters the building and sees him in the diner by a star-set-facing window.

His daughter sits at his side with a milkshake. He holds a coffee and looks at the drawing she made on her tablet.

"That's excellent, honey!" He says.

Larissa approaches.

"Doctor Lawrence?" She says.

The man looks up at her "Larissa?"

She smiles at the daughter "It's nice to meet you! Do you mind if I sit with you guys?"

The daughter looks confused at Doctor Lawrence.

Doctor Lawrence smiles at his daughter "It's alright. This is my friend Doctor Cane."

"Hi Doctor Cane." The girl says.

Larissa smiles "You look just like your mom."

"Daddy says I look a lot like his sister." The little girl says.

Doctor Lawrence laughs.

Larissa looks at him with an awkward face regarding the coincidence.

Lawrence's smile fades "What?"

Larissa sits "I have something to show you. I can't tell you about it here."

"Why don't we go outside?" Stephen asks.

Larissa looks at the little girl "That's fine, but if you want to see it, you'll have to come with me now."

Lawrence looks spread thin.

"Grab the check and take your daughter, Stephen." She says "This is important."

Stephen looks around "I'll need to pick up my son on the way."

Stephen leaves the diner with his daughter and follows Larissa north to his son's school. The boy is excited to be out early, but wonders why his sister is already in the car.

Stephen looks at him with a brow raised "Luke, you had a day off last week. Today was your sister's day to play hooky."

Luke nods "I guess that makes sense."

Stephen smiles to see them both in the mirror.

"Elizabeth" Luke says "Do you know where we're going?"

Stephen feels his jaw bite at the reminder of his sister's name.

Elizabeth looks at Luke. The yellow bow in her hair hits the back of her seat.

"Daddy said he's picking up some things from his sister." She says.

Luke scrunches brows "His sister?"

Stephen nods "Luke, Lizzie, I'm taking you to see some family secrets. They're from my half-sister, on my dad's side."

"The one who left when you were eight?" asks Luke.

Stephen nods with a look toward his son, the older of the siblings. The look tells his son that this is a private matter, and not to ask questions.

"Why would his sister leave him, Luke?" Elizabeth says "That's stupid."

Stephen laughs.

Luke opens his bag and shuffles through some papers. His father notices.

Stephen raises his hand with his fingers spread.

"Luke, I want to see that spelling test." He says.

Luke's face falls "They didn't…"

"The teacher called and told me to look at it." Stephen says "Don't even try."

Luke hangs his head and sighs. He pulls out the paper and sends it up to his father's hand.

"Dad, I can't…"

"Luke." Stephen says "I don't want to hear it… Never say you *'can't'* because that really means you *'won't'*. Your dreams die when you say the word *'can't'*." He nods with the paper in his hand "You know, I had to learn how to walk again when I was fourteen."

Luke gathers his brows.

"How?" He asks "Why?"

Stephen shrugs "I was in a coma for a year. I hadn't used my muscles in that time."

Luke widens his eyes. He realizes his father is in an unusually reflective mood.

"Got it?" Stephen says.

Luke nods.

Stephen nods back, then notices a red light coming up. He brings the car to a stop, and looks at the paper. He scans a moment, cracks a smile, then giggles.

"You spelled *'fruit'* wrong." He says.

Luke feels embarrassed by his dad's laughter.

"I tried!" He says.

Stephen smiles and nods. He stops the excuses before they come. He waves the concern away with a raise of his hand.

"You won't spell it wrong ever again." Stephen says "I promise…" The light turns green and they move forward "Here's what to think next time." He hands the paper back to his son "Look how your teacher corrected it and think to yourself… *'F. are you it?'*."

Luke looks up with a surprised smile. Stephen in turn gives a glance in the mirror with a flinch of his brows as if to say *'Get it?'*.

Luke's missing tooth is accentuated by his laughter.

"Dad!" He says.

Stephen giggles "Thank your Uncle Kyle for that one."

"I don't get it!" Elizabeth says.

Stephen shakes his head "It's okay honey. He just didn't do well on the test and we're joking about it." He looks at Luke again "Making stuff funny is the best way to remember, pal. Do what you need to, I don't care how; make it easy for yourself to remember."

Luke nods. He looks down at the paper and feels surprised at his dad's reaction. It's far better than anything he anticipated.

"How did he fail a spelling test?" Elizabeth says "Those are easy!"

Stephen shrugs "I used to fail them a lot. It was hard for me to focus."

"I get all of them right on MY tests." She says.

"Shut up, Liz." Luke says "You don't get…"

"Luke!" Stephen scolds "So help me; if you talk like that to your sister…!"

Luke feels his heart leap into his throat. It's the reaction he expected for his spelling test, but it's taken him by surprise here. His skin breaks a cold sweat.

Stephen catches himself thinking of his own childhood. He fights back tears and shakes his head.

He sighs "Don't talk to your sister like that." He says "Seriously… She'll be there for you when no one else will be… Don't argue over silly things."

Luke nods. He looks at little Lizzie. Her grumpy face grows soft as he looks her way. He's been moved by his father's vulnerability. Elizabeth is shocked by her brother's genuine regret.

"I'm sorry, Lizzie." He says.

Lizzie is surprised, yet saddened to see her brother is upset over what he's done. She gets an idea and crosses her arms with her eyes closed. She turns away with her nose turned upward. Her smile is the dead giveaway that she's joking.

"You should be!" She says.

She opens one eye to look over at Luke.

Luke laughs. Her smile cracks into a giggle.

Stephen's eyes wince together in a smile. He's proud of them; but he wonders what his sister would have been like in his older years. She was missing that whole time. The day she died he couldn't have been aware of it. He was fully convinced that he'd see her again someday.

His mind deviates to her, and he remembers to share her story with them. He feels it's important, to both his children.

"Guys" He says "…did I tell you my sister was the one who got me into science?"

"No?" Says Luke.

Stephen nods "I might have been young when she left; but she had something really important to do…"

He smiles at his daughter through his mirror.

"Your Aunt Lizzie was a hero." He adds.

Luke is taken aback by his father's remark.

Little Lizzie leans in. She tries to see her father better from the back seat. She scrunches her brows together.

"A hero?" She says.

The car ride is short but fulfilling. Stephen tells his son and daughter about his sister Elizabeth. He tells them how she left Zion to go into deep space. He tells them that Larissa is probably picking up where Elizabeth left off, and to treat her lab with more respect than their house.

The family arrives and enters a laboratory that looks like a warehouse. The artifacts around them bring the kids to stand wide-eyed for a moment. Stephen slows his feet too as he walks.

"I know." Larissa says "This is your sister's work."

Stephen looks up to the tops of the shelves.

"Jesus." He says.

"Jeez Louise!" says Lizzie.

The adults laugh as they come to a corner. There, at the end of a row, against the far wall, is the large machine.

"That's him?" Stephen asks.

Larissa nods. She motions him to follow her.

He does, and before long Stephen stands before the killer who took his sister's life twenty-four years ago.

"He's imprinted himself in every piece of data." Larissa says "Each time he makes a copy of himself, the copy is less accurate to the original. It's like he divides his soul and loses his humanity. If he were to regain his consciousness, the result wouldn't be the same person anymore. Not Doctor Clay; but something else like him, and maybe worse."

"You said he destroyed the Earthlings?"

Larissa nods.

"How?" Stephen asks.

She motions to some pages on the table by her side.

"Project Icarus." She says "It was a short-range teleportation device equipped with antimatter."

"Teleportation?"

She nods "Developed by a former friend of the Mandel family, Roger Meek." She puts the pages before Stephen. He looks them over as she goes on "They gave the device a payload of antimatter. It disrupted the gravitational force that kept the sun together. Instead of the star's regular convection, the nuclear force was focused in one direction. A beam of plasma that, according to our math, tore the planet Saturn apart."

Stephen looks at the blueprints with no feeling in his fingertips. He can't believe what's at the edge of his hands.

"People have been calling it the home wrecker." She tells him.

Stephen widens his eyes with a shake of his head "You have a sick sense of humor."

She laughs. He looks up at the machine.

Stephen looks bitter at the metal face "Does he try to invade everything?"

Larissa shakes her head "Not always." She says "It's like a game of peekaboo. He shows himself by infecting a hard drive one moment. Then we destroy the hard drive. Then we start over again.

Sometimes he doesn't try, then other times he does. He's hoping to catch us by surprise."

Stephen looks to see his kids behaving, then looks back at the machine.

"You need a software engineer." He says.

"An AI expert." She elaborates "He doesn't follow the rules of AI established in the android initiative."

Stephen looks long at her "You're saying you need me, but I don't know if I'm qualified."

"No one is." She says "But you have a reason to finish this work."

Stephen looks around at his sister's work.

"Yeah. I do." He says.

Luke walks along the clutter and looks at the artifacts of the Earthlings. He periodically looks over at his sister, as an older sibling does.

"Do you know what this is?" Luke says.

Elizabeth shakes her head.

"It's really old stuff from far away." Luke explains "Be careful with it."

She nods her head, and the bow loosens from her hair. She turns to look around with her brother's words in mind. Luke wanders off on his own.

He looks at the artifacts with curiosity. Computers, storage devices for data, CDs…

Luke can't recognize everything he's looking at, but he knows it's all priceless Earthling tech.

A sound makes Luke turn about. A screen glows in the clutter. Luke navigates the maze of artifacts and comes to a portable game console.

He looks around, as no one has turned it on. The game is at its start menu. He begins, and it asks for his name.

"*Luke*" He types.

The game thrusts his character into an adventure world, with a village and an enchanted forest. Luke navigates to the nearest person and begins pressing buttons to speak.

The game freezes, then a text comes out in a janky form.

"*%!*GO&SEE%THE!!LAKE%**"

Luke strains to read the letters between the mess of characters; but then follows the instruction. He assumes it's broken from all of the age; or it might be a bootlegged copy of the original game.

He finds the lake and sees a dark spot in the water. He approaches and hits the same button as before. A glitch-looking character appears out of the water. It is dark with yellow eyes. Ambiguous to any form.

"*HELLo TRAV!ELER&!*" It says "*Luke?*"

Luke screws his mouth with his brows together.

He's given an option two answer '*yes*' or '*no*', and Luke chooses '*yes*'.

"*Ca!N YOU%Do SOME#THING 4ME?*" It asks.

Luke chooses '*yes*'.

"*TAKE %ME!!HOME WITH#YOU*"

At this, Luke gathers his brows. He doesn't select to hear more conversation, but the words change.

"*I'M FUN#TR%UST M3E*"

Luke is given two options that don't fit in the prescribed box. It's suited for the '*yes*' or '*no*' questions but instead it says '*WHY?*' and '*WHY NOT?*'.

Luke chooses '*WHY*'.

At this the game skips a frame.

"*EVERYONE NEEDS A HOME.*" It says.

Luke relaxes a little, believing it's scripted.

Luke hears his father calling his name. He's coming to find him, and Luke knows it.

It seems silly to Luke, but he knows he could take it. No one would know, and his school bag is just on his back. The portable gaming console could easily fit in there. He would be playing a game from Earth.

He looks at the screen again and sees the text has changed. He's posed another question. He's given a '*yes*' or '*no*' answer, and this time the text appears clear and fixed.

"*Do you trust me?*"

Believing it's a game, Luke selects the easy answer. '*yes*'.

He nearly puts the game in his bag, then stops to look at the screen. There's something eerie. Something strange. It asks another question:
"¿*Can I trust you?*"

Afterword

One October morning I decided to hike Mount Washington, the tallest mountain in New Hampshire. It's known around the world as the place where the world's highest wind speed was recorded. It was two days before the ice began forming above the treeline, and as ill prepared as I was, I was determined to make it to the peak.

I began my hike as the sun came up. I was alone, and it was raining. There was not a single hiker on my way to the alpine zone.

I broke the treeline in good time and I had only a little ways to walk, from the "Lake in the Clouds" to the mountain's peak. It was then that my knees began to shake in an unnatural way. Just like Dash, as he ran up the mountain to escape "the birds", my legs were refusing to work. That is when I saw two Canadian hikers. I was worried for my well being at this point, but I told the Canadians nothing of my concern. However I guess it was written on my face, because one guy said to "Get some chili when you're up there, eh?"

Continuing upward, I started to have problems. My legs wouldn't work anymore, and every time I'd rest them, the wind would rip the heat right out of my wet body. I took cover under a bush and began eating to regain some strength. It worked for a little while, but the next time my legs gave out there was nothing to hide under; so I began pulling myself with my hands. It was then that the thought emerged: "This is how people die up here". Then came the thought of my older brother, who was visiting from California. He had a flight to catch the following day, and I didn't want him to cancel his flight in order to make it to my funeral.

I began to cry, but not because I would never finish this book. It wasn't because I was afraid of dying either. I didn't want to hurt the people I loved. Leaving people behind was the most heart-wrenching thing at that moment; and that's when I heard it. The train at the top of the mountain, sitting idle. Its engine was chugging at the station.

I found the strength to stand somehow, and I continued up the path to the paved "Mount Washington Auto Road". Many cars drove by me, and while I thought about thumbing a ride, it felt wrong. I needed to peak the mountain myself, and so I dragged my feet on the pavement. I pulled myself along the railing to a staircase at the weather station, and finally, soaking wet and cold, I reached the top of the mountain.

When you've expected to die at any point, you feel like every day after that event was never promised. The gift of life feels so much sweeter, and so death looks a little different. My experience is nothing in comparison to what my grandparents went through, but it did an effective job at showing me just how small we are in the universe. As much as I wanted to stop, I couldn't. As much as I wanted the weather to give me a break, that wind just kept on blowing; and there was nothing I could do to change that.

Throughout this book, I intended to show my appreciation for those who came before me, and to deliver their advice to generations to come. Elizabeth and Julius' relationship works as the comparison between my own generation, and the generations that came before us.

I was very young at the time when someone made a particular remark about millennials to my grandpa. The representative of gen-X had said "Kids these days couldn't do what you did" And my grandpa simply shook his head. "If they had to, they would." He said.

Elizabeth is the millennial rising to the occasion, and Julius has lived through it already. The last thing Julius and my grandfather ever wanted was for us to live through the awful events of their lives.

My grandpa was the one who had lived through World War II. In Okinawa, Saipan, Tinian, Tarawa, and Nagasaki, he had seen many of the things I've depicted in Icarus Dawns; however he never told me about them himself. The stories were out there for me to find when I was ready.

Grandpa's whole life is probably the greatest story you've never heard. It truly deserves its own book or movie someday. He's the one who saw the humanity of his enemies. He had been through so many terrible things; ever since the early age of nine, when his father was murdered. Grandpa persevered and kept his eyes set on a moral path to the future. In the end, he had a unified family that persevered through an untimely separation.

My grandmother is the second of three primary sources of history in this book. She grew up under the Nazi occupation of the Netherlands. Her family helped to hide their neighbors when the Germans invaded,

and the Germans took many of her family's belongings soon after that.
When they stole my great-grandmother's heated blanket, she notoriously told the Nazi who stole it "I hope it burns your toes!"

My grandmother's husband (my grandfather) met her when she was left abandoned in the United States with her two children. Her first husband had left her in the middle of the night, and Granddad helped her survive by starting a transportation business with her. Grandad was also the one who learned how to walk again after having polio, just like Stephen did after his coma. He was also a little mischievous like Julius (for all the right reasons, of course).

These people were all hardened by a difficult time, and their voices are carried over through Julius to us (Elizabeth).

Elizabeth's struggle is based on what's been widely talked about by many people in our generation. There is an immense loneliness, and our connections feel hollow and superficial. She struggles to find meaningful connections in a demanding world full of self-centered people; and a feeling of worth in a place that doesn't believe in a higher purpose.

Duty, and self-indulgent, superficial happiness are the gods of her world. It forsakes her relationship with her brothers, her parents, and the potential of a new family of her own. She's the embodiment of that feeling of going to work in the winter when the sun hasn't risen yet, only to leave for home when the sun is already down again.

She does her work for a purpose, but it's for a world she knows she's likely never to see. Even if she returned home with all of her findings, the golden age her crew would make could never be witnessed by them. She knows that it would take time to implement any rediscovered technologies into their daily lives; and terraforming their planet would likely take lifetimes. Only near the end does she have the time to think about her own life in the context of her witnesses.

She loves the idea of having a colorful life full of family and friends, but she's lost in the loneliness of her self-sacrifice. In the end, that is enough to make her happy. She has proven to herself that there are people worth trusting and calling "heroes"; even if she's the only one who knows it.

"You only get out of life what you put into it." Is what Grandpa told me the last time I saw him. This is embodied by Elizabeth's accomplishments as an engineer, a friend, and a hero.

Elizabeth rises to the occasion when the time calls for it, and it's not for recognition or gain. She loses everything, not knowing that the Mandel Explorer would be intercepted in years to come. In her eyes, she'll be forgotten; but she achieves true heroism, through selflessness without a witness.

Once while taking a plane out of North Carolina, I made the haunting realization of just how small we are in this world. I had just graduated college and had no leads for work. I felt powerless, much like Curtis felt during his conversation with James at the bar by Fenway Park. At the rate I was going, my dreams of becoming a well known filmmaker were likely to amount to nothing.

Then, I noticed something else. I was looking at a thriving organism. All of the gridded farmland and city streets. All of the highways leading across the country were built to make society work as a whole. As long as my story reached someone, anyone; it was worthwhile. As long as my story found someone, as Doctor Morris put it, "on a hill; under a tree. In perfect harmony."

We are very small and powerless in the universe, but we make our meaning. We bring the future with all of its changes. Each farmstead working for an individual farmer's family, and his neighborhood too. Every laborer who is building a road and saving money for a summer home by a lake. Every pilot crisscrossing the sky to take negotiators and representatives across the world; they all have a part to play in bringing us forward. We have a beautiful story to tell, and it should go on for much longer.

I hope this book makes you appreciate the past and present. I hope it makes you look forward to the future. I hope you think about Elizabeth, and the way she strives to have meaningful connections. I hope you strive to be a true friend like Julius, too. I hope you recognize your value in this world, and that you try to laugh whenever you can. I pray that you ignore any destructive words, and that you navigate through feelings of despair with reminders of your value. I hope that you think about the characters in this book, and the way they thought about us; on our pale blue dot, in an ocean of black.